JAMES FENIMORE COOPER was born in Burlington, New Jersey in 1789; his family moved to Cooperstown, New York while he was still an infant. He attended Yale College but was expelled. Sailing before the mast, he saw Europe for the first time on a merchant vessel. In 1808 he became a midshipman in the U. S. Navy. He resigned in 1811 and married. Cooper lived, at various periods, in Westchester and New York City, but spent his later years in Cooperstown. From 1826 to 1833 he traveled extensively in Europe. The Leather-Stocking Tales were published during the period from 1823 to 1841. Arranged according to the chronology of their hero Natty Bumppo, who appears under various sobriquets in all five romances, the sequence is *The Deerslayer* (age 22-24?), *The Last of the Mohicans* (age 35-37?), *The Pathfinder* (age 37-39), *The Pioneers* (age 71-72?), *The Prairie* (age 80-83). With his story *The Pilot* (1823) Cooper set the style for a new genre of sea fiction. A caustic social critic, he wrote *The American Democrat* (1838) as a critique of American civilization at that time. His works have been translated into numerous languages and have been enthusiastically received because of their vigor and robust narration. Never able to ignore a challenge, Cooper spent much of his later life in disputes with and suits against various journals. He died in 1851 at his home in Cooperstown.

A TALE BY
James Fenimore Cooper

THE DEERSLAYER

or

The First Warpath

*"What terrors round him wait?
Amazement in his van, with Flight combined,
And Sorrow's faded form, and Solitude behind."*

With an Afterword by
ALLAN NEVINS

A SIGNET CLASSIC from
NEW AMERICAN LIBRARY
TIMES MIRROR
New York and Scarborough, Ontario
The New English Library Limited, London

AFTERWORD COPYRIGHT © 1963 BY

THE NEW AMERICAN LIBRARY OF WORLD LITERATURE, INC.

SIXTH PRINTING

Ⓒ SIGNET TRADEMARK REG. U.S. PAT. OFF. AND FOREIGN COUNTRIES
REGISTERED TRADEMARK—MARCA REGISTRADA
HECHO EN CHICAGO, U.S.A.

SIGNET, SIGNET CLASSICS, SIGNETTE, MENTOR AND PLUME BOOKS
are published in the United States by
The New American Library, Inc.,
1301 Avenue of the Americas, New York, New York 10019,
in Canada by The New American Library of Canada Limited,
81 Mack Avenue, Scarborough 704, Ontario,
in the United Kingdom by
The New English Library Limited,
Barnard's Inn, Holborn, London, E.C. 1, England

PRINTED IN THE UNITED STATES OF AMERICA

PREFACE

As HAS BEEN stated in the preface to the series of the Leather-Stocking Tales, *The Deerslayer* is properly the first in the order of reading, though the last in that of publication. In this book the hero is represented as just arriving at manhood, with the freshness of feeling that belongs to that interesting period of life and with the power to please that properly characterizes youth. As a consequence, he is loved; and, what denotes the real waywardness of humanity more than it corresponds with theories and moral propositions, perhaps, he is loved by one full of art, vanity, and weakness, and loved principally for his sincerity, his modesty, and his unerring truth and probity. The preference he gives to the high qualities named over beauty, delirious passion, and sin, it is hoped, will offer a lesson that can injure none. This portion of the book is intentionally kept down, though it is thought to be sufficiently distinct to convey its moral.

The intention has been to put the sisters in strong contrast: one admirable in person, clever, filled with the pride of beauty, erring, and fallen; the other, barely provided with sufficient capacity to know good from evil, instinct, notwithstanding, with the virtues of woman, reverencing and loving God, and yielding only to the weakness of her sex in admiring personal attractions in one too coarse and unobservant to distinguish or to understand her quiet, gentle feeling in his favor.

As for the scene of this tale, it is intended for, and believed to be, a close description of the Otsego prior to the year 1760, when the first rude settlement was commenced on its banks, at that time only an insignificant clearing near the outlet, with a small hut of squared logs for the temporary dwelling of the Deputy Superintendent of Indian affairs. The recollections of the writer carry him back distinctly to a time when nine-tenths of the shores of this lake were in the virgin forest, a peculiarity that was owing to the circumstance of the roads running through the first range of valleys removed from the waterside. The woods and the mountains have ever formed a principal source of beauty with this charming sheet of water, enough of the former remaining to this day to relieve the open grounds from monotony and tameness.

In most respects the descriptions of scenery in the tale are reasonably accurate. The rock appointed for the rendezvous between the Deerslayer and his friend the Delaware still remains, bearing the name of the Otsego Rock. The shoal on which Hutter is represented as having built his "castle" is a little misplaced, lying, in fact, nearer to the northern end of the lake, as well as to the eastern shore, than is stated in this book. Such a shoal, however, exists, surrounded on all sides by deep water. In the driest seasons a few rocks are seen above the surface of the lake, and at most periods of the year, rushes mark its locality. In a word, in all but precise position even this feature of the book is accurate. The same is true of the several points introduced, of the bay, of the river, of the mountains, and all the other accessories of the place.

The legend is purely fiction, no authority existing for any of its facts, characters, or other peculiarities beyond that which was thought necessary to secure the semblance of reality. Truth compels us to admit that the book has attracted very little notice and that if its merits are to be computed by its popularity, the care that has been bestowed on this edition might as well be spared. Such, at least, has been its fate in America; whether it has met with better success in any other country we have no means of knowing.

THE DEERSLAYER

CHAPTER I

There is a pleasure in the pathless woods,
There is a rapture on the lonely shore,
There is society where none intrudes,
By the deep sea, and music in its roar:
I love not man the less, but nature more,
From these our interviews, in which I steal,
From all I may be, or have been before,
To mingle with the universe, and feel
What I can ne'er express, yet cannot all conceal.

CHILDE HAROLD

ON THE HUMAN imagination events produce the effects of time. Thus, he who has traveled far and seen much is apt to fancy that he has lived long, and the history that most abounds in important incidents soonest assumes the aspect of antiquity. In no other way can we account for the venerable air that is already gathering around American annals. When the mind reverts to the earliest days of colonial history, the period seems remote and obscure, the thousand changes that thicken along the links of recollections throwing back the origin of the nation to a day so distant as seemingly to reach the mists of time; yet, four lives of ordinary duration would suffice to transmit, from mouth to mouth, in the form of tradition, all that civilized man has achieved within the limits of the republic. Although New York alone possesses a population materially exceeding that of either of the four smallest kingdoms of Europe, or materially exceeding that of the entire Swiss Confederation, it is little more than two centuries since the Dutch commenced their settlement, rescuing the region from the savage state. Thus, what seems venerable by an accumulation of changes is reduced to familiarity when we come seriously to consider it solely in connection with time.

This glance into the perspective of the past will prepare the reader to look at the pictures we are about to sketch with less surprise than he might otherwise feel, and a few additional explanations may carry him back in imagination to the precise condition of society that we desire to delineate. It is a matter of history that the settlements on the eastern shore of the Hudson, such as Claverack, Kinderhook, and even Poughkeepsie, were not regarded as safe from Indian incursions a century since; there is still standing on the banks of the same river, within musket shot of the wharves of Albany, a residence of a younger branch * of the Van Rensselaers that has loopholes constructed for defense against the same crafty enemy, although it dates from a period scarcely so distant. Other similar memorials of the infancy of the country are to be found scattered through what is now deemed the very center of American civilization, affording the plainest proofs that all we possess of security from invasion and hostile violence is the growth of but little more than the time that is frequently filled by a single human life.

The incidents of this tale occurred between the years 1740 and 1745, when the settled portions of the colony of New York were confined to the four Atlantic counties, a narrow belt of country on each side of the Hudson, extending from its mouth to the falls near its head, and to a few advanced "neighborhoods" on the Mohawk and the Schoharie. Broad belts of the virgin wilderness not only reached the shores of the first river, but they even crossed it, stretching away into New England, and affording forest covers to the noiseless moccasin of the native warrior as he trod the secret and bloody warpath. A bird's-eye view of the whole region east of the Mississippi must then have offered one vast expanse of woods, relieved by a comparatively narrow fringe of cultivation along the sea, dotted by the glittering surfaces of lakes, and intersected by the waving lines of rivers. In such a vast picture of solemn solitude, the district of country we design to paint sinks into insignificance, though we feel encouraged to proceed by the conviction that, with slight and immaterial

---

* It is no more than justice to say that the Greenbush Van Rensselaers claim to be the oldest branch of that ancient and respectable family.

distinctions, he who succeeds in giving an accurate idea of any portion of this wild region must necessarily convey a tolerably correct notion of the whole.

Whatever may be the changes produced by man, the eternal round of the seasons is unbroken. Summer and winter, seed-time and harvest, return in their stated order with a sublime precision, affording to man one of the noblest of all the occasions he enjoys of proving the high powers of his far-reaching mind, in compassing the laws that control their exact uniformity and in calculating their never-ending revolutions. Centuries of summer suns had warmed the tops of the same noble oaks and pines, sending their heats even to the tenacious roots, when voices were heard calling to each other, in the depths of a forest, of which the leafy surface lay bathed in the brilliant light of a cloudless day in June, while the trunks of the trees rose in gloomy grandeur in the shades beneath. The calls were in different tones, evidently proceeding from two men who had lost their way, and were searching in different directions for their path. At length a shout proclaimed success, and presently a man of gigantic mold broke out of the tangled labyrinth of a small swamp, emerging into an opening that appeared to have been formed partly by the ravages of the wind and partly by those of fire. This little area, which afforded a good view of the sky, although it was pretty well filled with dead trees, lay on the side of one of the high hills, or low mountains, into which nearly the whole surface of the adjacent country was broken.

"Here is room to breathe in!" exclaimed the liberated forester as soon as he found himself under a clear sky, shaking his huge frame like a mastiff that has just escaped from a snowbank. "Hurrah! Deerslayer, here is daylight, at last, and yonder is the lake."

These words were scarcely uttered when the second forester dashed aside the bushes of the swamp and appeared in the area. After making a hurried adjustment of his arms and disordered dress, he joined his companion, who had already begun his dispositions for a halt.

"Do you know this spot?" demanded the one called Deerslayer, "or do you shout at the sight of the sun?"

"Both, lad, both; I know the spot and am not sorry to see so useful a friend as the sun. Now we have got the p'ints of the compass in our minds once more, and 'twill be our own

faults if we let anything turn them topsy-turvy ag'in, as has
just happened. My name is not Hurry Harry if this be not
the very spot where the land hunters camped the last summer
and passed a week. See, yonder are the dead bushes of their
bower, and here is the spring. Much as I like the sun, boy,
I've no occasion for it to tell me it is noon; this stomach of
mine is as good a timepiece as is to be found in the Colony,
and it already p'ints to half-past twelve. So open the wallet
and let us wind up for another six hours' run."

At this suggestion both set themselves about making the
preparations necessary for their usual frugal but hearty meal.
We will profit by this pause in the discourse to give the
reader some idea of the appearance of the men, each of
whom is destined to enact no insignificant part in our legend.
It would not have been easy to find a more noble specimen of
vigorous manhood than was offered in the person of him
who called himself Hurry Harry. His real name was
Henry March; but the frontiersmen having caught the practice of giving sobriquets from the Indians, the appellation of
Hurry was far oftener applied to him than his proper desig-
nation, and not unfrequently he was termed Hurry-scurry, a
nickname he had obtained from a dashing, reckless, offhand
manner and a physical restlessness that kept him so constantly on the move as to cause him to be known along the
whole line of scattered habitations that lay between the
province and the Canadas. The stature of Hurry Harry exceeded six feet four, and being unusually well proportioned,
his strength fully realized the idea created by his gigantic
frame. The face did no discredit to the rest of the man, for it
was both good-humored and handsome. His air was free,
and though his manner necessarily partook of the rudeness
of a border life, the grandeur that pervaded so noble a phy-
sique prevented it from becoming altogether vulgar.

Deerslayer, as Hurry called his companion, was a very different person in appearance as well as in character. In stature,
he stood about six feet in his moccasins, but his frame was
comparatively light and slender, showing muscles, however,
that promised unusual agility, if not unusual strength. His
face would have had little to recommend it except youth,
were it not for an expression that seldom failed to win upon
those who had leisure to examine it and to yield to the
feeling of confidence it created. This expression was simply

that of guileless truth, sustained by an earnestness of purpose and a sincerity of feeling that rendered it remarkable. At times this air of integrity seemed to be so simple as to awaken the suspicion of a want of the usual means to discriminate between artifice and truth, but few came in serious contact with the man without losing this distrust in respect for his opinions and motives.

Both these frontiersmen were still young, Hurry having reached the age of six or eight and twenty, while Deerslayer was several years his junior. Their attire needs no particular description, though it may be well to add that it was composed in no small degree of dressed deerskins, and had the usual signs of belonging to those who pass their time between the skirts of civilized society and the boundless forests. There was, notwithstanding, some attention to smartness and the picturesque in the arrangements of Deerslayer's dress, more particularly in the part connected with his arms and accouterments. His rifle was in perfect condition, the handle of his hunting knife was neatly carved, his powder horn was ornamented with suitable devices lightly cut into the material, and his shot pouch was decorated with wampum. On the other hand, Hurry Harry, either from constitutional recklessness, or from a secret consciousness how little his appearance required artificial aids, wore everything in a careless, slovenly manner, as if he felt a noble scorn for the trifling accessories of dress and ornaments. Perhaps the peculiar effect of his fine form and great stature was increased, rather than lessened, by this unstudied and disdainful air of indifference.

"Come, Deerslayer, fall to and prove that you have a Delaware stomach, as you say you have had a Delaware edication," cried Hurry, setting the example by opening his mouth to receive a slice of cold venison steak that would have made an entire meal for a European peasant: "fall to, lad, and prove your manhood on this poor devil of a doe with your teeth, as you've already done with your rifle."

"Nay, nay, Hurry, there's little manhood in killing a doe, and that too out of season, though there might be some in bringing down a painter or a catamount," returned the other, disposing himself to comply. "The Delawares have given me my name, not so much on account of a bold heart, as on account of a quick eye and an actyve foot. There may not be any cowardyce in overcoming a deer, but sartain it is there's no great valor."

"The Delawares themselves are no heroes," muttered Hurry through his teeth, the mouth being too full to permit it to be fairly opened, "or they would never have allowed them loping vagabonds, the Mingos, to make them women."

"That matter is not rightly understood—has never been rightly explained," said Deerslayer earnestly, for he was as zealous a friend as his companion was dangerous as an enemy; "the Mengwe fill the woods with their lies and misconstruct words and treaties. I have now lived ten years with the Delawares and know them to be as manful as any other nation, when the proper time to strike comes."

"Harkee, Master Deerslayer, since we are on the subject, we may as well open our minds to each other in a man-to-man way. Answer me one question: you have had so much luck among the game as to have gotten a title, it would seem, but did you ever hit anything human or intelligible? Did you ever pull trigger on an inimy that was capable of pulling one upon you?"

This question produced a singular collision between mortification and correct feeling in the bosom of the youth that was easily to be traced in the workings of his ingenuous countenance. The struggle was short, however, uprightness of heart soon getting the better of false pride and frontier boastfulness.

"To own the truth, I never did," answered Deerslayer, "seeing that a fitting occasion never offered. The Delawares have been peaceable since my sojourn with 'em, and I hold it to be onlawful to take the life of man except in open and generous warfare."

"What! Did you never find a fellow thieving among your traps and skins and do the law on him with your own hands, by way of saving the magistrates trouble, in the settlements, and the rogue himself the cost of the suit?"

"I am no trapper, Hurry," returned the young man proudly. "I live by the rifle, a we'pon at which I will not turn my back on any man of my years atween the Hudson and the St. Lawrence. I never offer a skin that has not a hole in its head besides them which natur' made to see with, or to breathe through."

"Aye, aye, this is all very well, in the animal way, though

it makes but a poor figure alongside of scalps and and-bushes. Shooting an Indian from an and-bush is acting up to his own principles, and now we have what you call a lawful war on our hands, the sooner you wipe that disgrace off your character, the sounder will be your sleep—if it only come from knowing there is one inimy the less prowling in the woods. I shall not frequent your society long, friend Natty, unless you look higher than four-footed beasts to practyse your rifle on."

"Our journey is nearly ended, you say, Master March, and we can part tonight, if you see occasion. I have a fri'nd waiting for me who will think it no disgrace to consort with a fellow creatur' that has never yet slain his kind."

"I wish I knew what has brought that skulking Delaware into this part of the country so early in the season," muttered Hurry to himself in a way to show equally distrust and a recklessness of its betrayal. "Where did you say the young chief was to give you the meeting?"

"At a small, round rock near the foot of the lake, where, they tell me, the tribes are given to resorting to make their treaties and to bury their hatchets. This rock have I often heard the Delawares mention, though lake and rock are equally strangers to me. The country is claimed by both Mingos and Mohicans and is a sort of common territory to fish and hunt through in time of peace, though what it may become in wartime the Lord only knows!"

"Common territory!" exclaimed Hurry, laughing aloud. "I should like to know what Floating Tom Hutter would say to that. He claims the lake as his own property, in vartue of fifteen years' possession, and will not be likely to give it up to either Mingo or Delaware without a battle for it."

"And what will the Colony say to such a quarrel? All this country must have some owner, the gentry pushing their cravings into the wilderness, even where they never dare to ventur', in their own person, to look at the land they own."

"That may do in other quarters of the Colony, Deerslayer, but it will not do here. Not a human being, the Lord excepted, owns a foot of s'ile in this part of the country. Pen was never put to paper, consarning either hill or valley, hereaway, as I've heard old Tom say, time and ag'in, and so he claims the best right to it of any man breathing; and what Tom claims, he'll be very likely to maintain."

"By what I've heard you say, Hurry, this Floating Tom must be an oncommon mortal—neither Mingo, Delaware, nor paleface. His possession, too, has been long, by your tell, and altogether beyond frontier endurance. What's the man's history and natur'?"

"Why, as to old Tom's human natur', it is not much like other men's human natur', but more like a muskrat's human natur', seeing that he takes more to the ways of that animal than to the ways of any other fellow creatur'. Some think he was a free liver on the salt water, in his youth, and a companion of a sartain Kidd, who was hanged for piracy, long afore you and I were born or acquainted, and that he came up into these regions thinking that the king's cruisers could never cross the mountains, and that he might enjoy the plunder peaceably in the woods."

"Then he was wrong, Hurry, very wrong. A man can enjoy plunder *peaceably* nowhere."

"That's much as his turn of mind may happen to be. I've known them that never could enjoy it at all, unless it was in the midst of a jollification, and them ag'in that enjoyed it best in a corner. Some men have no peace if they don't find plunder, and some if they do. Human natur' is crooked in these matters. Old Tom seems to belong to neither set, as he enjoys his—if plunder he has really got—with his darters in a very quiet and comfortable way, and wishes for no more."

"Aye, he has darters, too; I've heard the Delawares, who've hunted thisaway, tell their histories of these young women. Is there no mother, Hurry?"

"There was *once*, as in reason, but she has now been dead and sunk these two good years."

"Anan?" said Deerslayer, looking up at his companion in a little surprise.

"Dead and sunk, I say, and I hope that's good English. The old fellow lowered his wife into the lake, by way of seeing the last of her, as I can testify, being an eyewitness of the ceremony; but whether Tom did it to save digging, which is no easy job among roots, or out of a consait that water washes away sin sooner than 'arth is more than I can say."

"Was the poor woman oncommon wicked, that her husband should take so much pains with her body?"

"Not onreasonable, though she had her faults. I consider

Judith Hutter to have been as graceful and about as likely to make a good ind as any woman who had lived so long beyond the sound of church bells; and I conclude old Tom sunk her as much by way of *saving* pains, as by way of *taking* it. There was a little steel in her temper, it's true, and, as old Hutter is pretty much flint, they struck out sparks once and a while; but on the whole they might be said to live amicable like. When they did kindle, the listeners got some such insights into their past lives as one gets into the darker parts of the woods when a stray gleam of sunshine finds its way down to the roots of the trees. But Judith I shall always esteem, as it's recommend enough to one woman to be the mother of such a creatur' as her darter, Judith Hutter!"

"Aye, Judith was the name the Delawares mentioned, though it was pronounced after a fashion of their own. From their discourse, I do not think the girl would much please my fancy."

"Thy fancy!" exclaimed March, taking fire equally at the indifference and at the presumption of his companion. "What the devil have you to do with a fancy, and that, too, consarning one like Judith? You are but a boy—a sapling that has scarce got root. Judith has had *men* among her suitors ever since she was fifteen—which is now near five years—and will not be apt even to cast a look upon a half-grown creatur' like you!"

"It is June, and there is not a cloud atween us and the sun, Hurry, so all this heat is not wanted," answered the other, altogether undisturbed; "anyone may have a fancy, and a squirrel has a right to make up his mind touching a catamount."

"Aye, but it might not be wise, always, to let the catamount know it," growled March. "But you're young and thoughtless, and I'll overlook your ignorance. Come, Deerslayer," he added, with a good-natured laugh, after pausing a moment to reflect, "come, Deerslayer, we are sworn fri'nds, and will not quarrel about a light-minded, jilting jade just because she happens to be handsome—more especially as you have never seen her. Judith is only for a man whose teeth show the full marks, and it's foolish to be afeard of a boy. What *did* the Delawares say of the hussy?—for an Indian, after all, has his notions of womankind as well as a white man."

"They said she was fair to look on and pleasant of speech, but overgiven to admirers and light-minded."

"They are devils incarnate! After all, what schoolmaster is a match for an Indian in looking into natur'? Some people think they are only good on a trail or the warpath, but I say that they are philosophers and understand a man as well as they understand a beaver, and a woman as well as they understand either. Now that's Judith's character to a ribbon! To own the truth to you, Deerslayer, I should have married the gal two years since, if it had not been for two particular things, one of which was this very light-mindedness."

"And what may have been the other?" demanded the hunter, who continued to eat like one that took very little interest in the subject.

"T'other was an insartainty about her having *me*. The hussy is handsome, and she knows it. Boy, not a tree that is growing in these hills is straighter, or waves in the wind with an easier bend, nor did you ever see the doe that bounded with a more nat'ral motion. If that was all, every tongue would sound her praises; but she has such failings that I find it hard to overlook them, and sometimes I swear I'll never visit the lake ag'in."

"Which is the reason that you always come back? Nothing is ever made more sure by swearing about it."

"Ah, Deerslayer, you are a novelty in these partic'lars, keeping as true to edication as if you had never left the settlements. With me the case is different, and I never want to clinch an idee that I do not feel a wish to swear about it. If you know'd all that I know consarning Judith, you'd find a justification for a little cussing. Now, the officers sometimes stray over to the lake from the forts on the Mohawk to fish and hunt, and then the creatur' seems beside herself! You can see it in the manner in which she wears her finery and the airs she gives herself with the gallants."

"That is unseemly in a poor man's darter," returned Deerslayer gravely. "The officers are all gentry and can only look on such as Judith with evil intentions."

"There's the unsartainty and the damper! I have my misgivings about a particular captain, and Jude has no one to blame but her own folly, if I'm wrong. On the whole, I wish to look upon her as modest and becoming, and yet the clouds that drive among these hills are not more unsartain. Not a dozen white men have ever laid eyes upon her since she was a child, and yet her airs, with two or three of these officers, are extinguishers!"

"I would think no more of such a woman but turn my mind altogether to the forest: *that* will not deceive you, being ordered and ruled by a hand that never wavers."

"If you know'd Judith, you would see how much easier it is to say this than it would be to do it. Could I bring my mind to be easy about the officers, I would carry the gal off to the Mohawk by force, make her marry me in spite of her whiffling, and leave old Tom to the care of Hetty, his other child, who, if she be not as handsome or as quick-witted as her sister, is much the most dutiful."

"Is there another bird in the same nest?" asked Deerslayer, raising his eyes with a species of half-awakened curiosity. "The Delawares spoke to me only of one."

"That's nat'ral enough, when Judith Hutter and Hetty Hutter are in question. Hetty is only comely, while her sister, I tell thee, boy, is such another as is not to be found atween this and the sea: Judith is as full of wit and talk and cunning as an old Indian orator, while poor Hetty is at the best but 'compass meant us.'"

"Anan?" inquired again the Deerslayer.

"Why, what the officers call 'compass meant us,' which I understand to signify that she means always to go in the right direction but sometimes doesn't know how. 'Compass' for the p'int, and 'meant us' for the intention. No, poor Hetty is what I call on the varge of ignorance, and sometimes she stumbles on one side of the line and sometimes on t'other."

"Them are beings that the Lord has in his special care," said Deerslayer solemnly, "for he looks carefully to all who fall short of their proper share of reason. The Redskins honor and respect them who are so gifted, knowing that the Evil Spirit delights more to dwell in an artful body than in one that has no cunning to work upon."

"I'll answer for it, then, that he will not remain long with poor Hetty—for the child is just 'compass meant us,' as I have told you. Old Tom has a feeling for the gal, and so has Judith, quick-witted and glorious as she is herself; else would I not answer for her being altogether safe among the sort of men that sometimes meet on the lake shore."

"I thought this water an onknown and little-frequented

sheet," observed the Deerslayer, evidently uneasy at the idea
of being too near the world.

"It's all that, lad, the eyes of twenty white men never having been laid on it; still, twenty true-bred frontiersmen—
hunters, and trappers, and scouts, and the like—can do a
deal of mischief if they try. 'Twould be an awful thing to
me, Deerslayer, did I find Judith married after an absence of
six months!"

"Have you the gal's faith to incourage you to hope otherwise?"

"Not at all. I know not how it is—I'm good-looking, boy;
that much I can see in any spring on which the sun shines—
and yet I could never get the hussy to a promise, or even a
cordial, willing smile, though she will laugh by the hour. If
she *has* dared to marry in my absence, she'll be like to know
the pleasures of widowhood afore she is twenty!"

"You would not harm the man she has chosen, Hurry, simply because she found him more to her liking than yourself?"

"Why not? If an inimy crosses my path, will I not beat
him out of it! Look at me—am I a man like to let any
sneaking, crawling skin trader get the better of me in a matter that touches me as near as the kindness of Judith Hutter? Besides, when we live beyond law, we must be our
own judges and executioners. And if a man *should* be found
dead in the woods, who is there to say who slew him, even
admitting that the Colony took the matter in hand and made
a stir about it?"

"If that man should be Judith Hutter's husband, after what
has passed, I might tell enough, at least, to put the Colony on
the trail."

"You half-grown, venison-hunting bantling! You dare to
think of informing against Hurry Harry in so much as a matter touching a mink or a woodchuck!"

"I would dare to speak truth, Hurry, consarning you, or
any man that ever lived."

March looked at his companion for a moment in silent
amazement; then, seizing him by the throat with both hands,
he shook his comparatively slight frame with a violence that
menaced the dislocation of some of the bones. Nor was this
done jocularly, for anger flashed from the giant's eyes, and
there were certain signs that seemed to threaten much more
earnestness than the occasion would appear to call for. What-

ever might be the real intention of March, and it is probable there was none settled in his mind, it is certain that he was unusually aroused; most men who found themselves throttled by one of a mold so gigantic, in such a mood, and in a solitude so deep and helpless, would have felt intimidated and tempted to yield even the right. Not so, however, with Deerslayer. His countenance remained unmoved, his hand did not shake, and his answer was given in a voice that did not resort to the artifice of louder tones, even by way of proving its owner's resolution.

"You may shake, Hurry, until you bring down the mountain," he said quietly, "but nothing beside truth will you shake from me. It is probable that Judith Hutter has no husband to slay, and you may never have a chance to waylay one, else would I tell her of your threat in the first conversation I held with the gal."

March released his grip and sat regarding the other in silent astonishment.

"I thought we had been friends," he at length added, "but you've got the last secret of mine that will ever enter your ears."

"I want none, if they are to be like this. I know we live in the woods, Hurry, and are thought to be beyond human laws—and perhaps we are so, in fact, whatever it may be in right—but there is a law, and a lawmaker, that rule across the whole continent. He that flies in the face of either need not call me fri'nd."

"Damme, Deerslayer, if I do not believe you are, at heart, a Moravian, and no fair-minded, plain-dealing hunter, as you've pretended to be!"

"Fair-minded or not, Hurry, you will find me as plain-dealing in deeds as I am in words. But this giving way to sudden anger is foolish and proves how little you have sojourned with the red man. Judith Hutter no doubt is still single, and you spoke but as the tongue ran and not as the heart felt. There's my hand, and we will say and think no more about it."

Hurry seemed more surprised than ever; then he burst forth in a loud, good-natured laugh, which brought tears to his eyes. After this, he accepted the offered hand, and the parties became friends.

" 'Twould have been foolish to quarrel about an idee," March cried as he resumed his meal, "and more like lawyers in the towns than like sensible men in the woods. They tell me, Deerslayer, much ill blood grows out of idees, among the people in the lower counties, and that they sometimes get to extremities upon them."

"That do they—that do they; and about other matters that might better be left to take care of themselves. I have heard the Moravians say that there are lands in which men quarrel even consarning their religion; if they can get their tempers up on such a subject, Hurry, the Lord have marcy on 'em. Howsever, there is no occasion for our following their example, and more especially about a husband that this Judith Hutter may never see, or never wish to see. For my part, I feel more cur'osity about the feeble-witted sister than about your beauty. There's something that comes close to a man's feelin's, when he meets with a fellow creatur' that has all the outward show of an accountable mortal and who fails of being what he seems only through a lack of reason. This is bad enough in a man, but when it comes to a woman, and she a young and maybe a winning creatur', it touches all the pitiful thoughts his natur' has. God knows, Hurry, that such poor things be defenseless enough with all their wits about 'em, but it's a cruel fortun' when that great protector and guide fails 'em."

"Harkee, Deerslayer—you know what the hunters, and trappers, and peltrymen in general be; their best friends will not deny that they are headstrong and given to having their own way, without much bethinking 'em of other people's rights or feelin's—and yet I don't think the man is to be found in all this region who would harm Hetty Hutter if he could; no, not even a redskin."

"Therein, fri'nd Hurry, you do the Delawares, at least, and all their allied tribes, only justice, for a redskin looks upon a being thus struck by God's power as especially under his care. I rejoice to hear what you say, howsever, I rejoice to hear it; but as the sun is beginning to turn toward the a'ter-noon's sky, had we not better strike the trail ag'in, and make forward, that we may get an opportunity of seeing these wonderful sisters?"

Harry March giving a cheerful assent, the remnants of the

meal were soon collected; then the travelers shouldered their packs, resumed their arms, and, quitting the little area of light, they again plunged into the deep shadows of the forest.

CHAPTER II

Thou'rt passing from the lake's green side,
  And the hunter's hearth away;
For the time of flowers, for the summer's pride,
  Daughter! thou canst not stay.

RECORDS OF WOMAN

OUR TWO ADVENTURERS had not far to go. Hurry knew the direction as soon as he had found the open spot and the spring, and he now led on with the confident step of a man assured of his object. The forest was dark, as a matter of course, but it was no longer obstructed by underbrush, and the footing was firm and dry. After proceeding near a mile, March stopped and began to cast about him with an inquiring look, examining the different objects with care and occasionally turning his eyes on the trunks of the fallen trees, with which the ground was well sprinkled, as is usually the case in an American wood, especially in those parts of the country where timber has not yet become valuable.

"*This* must be the place, Deerslayer," March at length observed; "here is a beech by the side of a hemlock, with three pines at hand, and yonder is a white birch with a broken top; yet I see no rock, nor any of the branches bent down, as I told you would be the case."

"Broken branches are onskillful landmarks, as the least exper'enced know that branches don't often break of themselves," returned the other. "They also lead to suspicion and discoveries. The Delawares never trust to broken branches, unless it is in friendly times and on an open trail. As for the beeches and pines and hemlocks, why, they are to be seen on all sides of us, not only by twos and threes, but by forties, and fifties, and hundreds."

24

"Very true, Deerslayer, but you never calculate on position. Here is a beech and a hemlock——"

"Yes, and there is another beech and a hemlock, as loving as two brothers, or, for that matter, more loving than some brothers; and yonder are others, for neither tree is a rarity in these woods. I fear me, Hurry, you are better at trapping beaver and shooting bears than at leading on a blindish sort of a trail. Ha! There's what you wish to find, a'ter all!"

"Now, Deerslayer, this is one of your Delaware pretensions—hang me if I see anything but these trees, which do seem to start up around us in a most onaccountable and perplexing manner."

"Look thisaway, Hurry—here, in a line with the black oak —don't you see the crooked sapling that is hooked up in the branches of the basswood, near it? Now, that sapling was once snow-ridden, and got the bend by its weight, but it never straightened itself, and fastened itself in among the basswood branches in the way you see. The hand of man did that act of kindness for it."

"That hand was mine!" exclaimed Hurry. "I found the slender young thing bent to the airth, like an unfortunate creatur' borne down by misfortune, and stuck it up where you see it. After all, Deerslayer, I must allow, you're getting to have an oncommon good eye for the woods!"

" 'Tis improving, Hurry—'tis improving, I will acknowledge; but 'tis still only a child's eye, compared to some I know. There's Tamenund, now, though a man so old that few remember when he was in his prime, Tamenund lets nothing escape his look, which is more like the scent of a hound than the sight of an eye. Then Uncas,* the father of Chingachgook and the lawful chief of the Mohicans, is another that it is almost hopeless to pass unseen. I'm improving, I will allow—I'm improving, but far from being perfect, as yet."

"And who is this Chingachgook of whom you talk so much, Deerslayer?" asked Hurry, as he moved off in the direction of the righted sapling; "a loping redskin, at the best, I make no question."

---

* Lest the similarity of the names should produce confusion, it may be well to say that the Uncas here mentioned is the grandfather of him who plays so conspicuous a part in *The Last of the Mohicans*.

"Not so, Hurry, but the best of loping redskins, as you call 'em. If he had his rights, he would be a great chief; as it is, he is only a brave and just-minded Delaware, respected and even obeyed in some things, 'tis true, but of a fallen race and belonging to a fallen people. Ah, Harry March, 'twould warm the heart within you to sit in their lodges of a winter's night and listen to the traditions of the ancient greatness and power of the Mohicans!"

"Harkee, fri'nd Nathaniel," said Hurry, stopping short to face his companion, in order that his words might carry greater weight with them, "if a man believed all that other people choose to say in their own favor, he might get an oversized opinion of them and an undersized opinion of himself. These redskins are notable boasters, and I set down more than half of their traditions as pure talk."

"There is truth in what you say, Hurry, I'll not deny it, for I've seen it, and believe it. They *do* boast, but then that is a gift from natur', and it's sinful to withstand nat'ral gifts. See, this is the spot you come to find!"

This remark cut short the discourse, and both the men now gave all their attention to the object immediately before them. Deerslayer pointed out to his companion the trunk of a huge linden, or basswood, as it is termed in the language of the country, which had filled its time and fallen by its own weight. This tree, like so many millions of its brethren, lay where it had fallen, and was moldering under the slow but certain influence of the seasons. The decay, however, had attacked its center even while it stood erect in the pride of vegetation, hollowing out its heart, as disease sometimes destroys the vitals of animal life, even while a fair exterior is presented to the observer. As the trunk lay stretched for near a hundred feet along the earth, the quick eye of the hunter detected this peculiarity, and from this and other circumstances he knew it to be the tree of which March was in search.

"Aye, here we have what we want," cried Hurry, looking in at the larger end of the linden. "Everything is as snug as if it had been left in an old woman's cupboard. Come, lend me a hand, Deerslayer, and we'll be afloat in half an hour."

At this call the hunter joined his companion, and the two went to work deliberately and regularly, like men accustomed to the sort of thing in which they were employed. In the first place, Hurry removed some pieces of bark that lay before the large opening in the tree, which the other declared to be disposed in a way that would have been more likely to attract attention than to conceal the cover, had any straggler passed that way. The two then drew out a bark canoe containing its seats, paddles, and other appliances, even to fishing lines and rods. This vessel was by no means small, but such was its comparative lightness, and so gigantic was the strength of Hurry, that the latter shouldered it with seeming ease, declining all assistance, even in the act of raising it to the awkward position in which he was obliged to hold it.

"Lead ahead, Deerslayer," said March, "and open the bushes; the rest I can do for myself."

The other obeyed, and the men left the spot, Deerslayer clearing the way for his companion, and inclining to the right or to the left as the latter directed. In about ten minutes they both broke suddenly into the brilliant light of the sun on a low, gravelly point that was washed by water on quite half its outline.

An exclamation of surprise broke from the lips of Deerslayer—an exclamation that was low and guardedly made, however, for his habits were much more thoughtful and regulated than those of the reckless Hurry—when, on reaching the margin of the lake, he beheld the view that unexpectedly met his gaze: It was, in truth, sufficiently striking to merit a brief description. On a level with the point lay a broad sheet of water, so placid and limpid that it resembled a bed of the pure mountain atmosphere compressed into a setting of hills and woods. Its length was about three leagues, while its breadth was irregular, expanding to half a league, or even more, opposite to the point, and contracting to less than half that distance more to the southward. Of course, its margin was irregular, being indented by bays and broken by many projecting, low points. At its northern, or nearest end, it was bounded by an isolated mountain, lower land falling off east and west, gracefully relieving the sweep of the outline. Still, the character of the country was mountainous, high hills, or low mountains, rising abruptly from the water on quite nine-tenths of its circuit. The exceptions, indeed, only served a little to vary the scene, and even beyond the parts of the shore that were comparatively low the background was high, though more distant.

But the most striking peculiarities of this scene were its solemn solitude and sweet repose. On all sides, wherever the eye turned, nothing met it but the mirrorlike surface of the lake, the placid view of heaven, and the dense setting of woods. So rich and fleecy were the outlines of the forest that scarce an opening could be seen, the whole visible earth, from the rounded mountaintop to the water's edge, presenting one unvaried hue of unbroken verdure. As if vegetation were not satisfied with a triumph so complete, the trees overhung the lake itself, shooting out toward the light; there were miles along its eastern shore where a boat might have pulled beneath the branches of dark, Rembrandt-looking hemlocks, "quivering aspens," and melancholy pines. In a word, the hand of man had never yet defaced or deformed any part of this native scene, which lay bathed in the sunlight, a glorious picture of affluent forest grandeur, softened by the balminess of June and relieved by the beautiful variety afforded by the presence of so broad an expanse of water.

"This is grand!—'tis solemn!—'tis an edication of itself, to look upon!" exclaimed Deerslayer, as he stood leaning on his rifle and gazing to the right and left, north and south, above and beneath, in whichever direction his eye could wander. "Not a tree disturbed even by redskin hand, as I can discover, but everything left in the ordering of the Lord, to live and die according to His own designs and laws! Hurry, your Judith ought to be a moral and well-disposed young woman, if she has passed half the time you mention in the center of a spot so favored."

"That's a naked truth, and yet the gal has the vagaries. *All* her time has not been passed here, howsever, old Tom having the custom, afore I know'd him, of going to spend the winters in the neighborhood of the settlers, or under the guns of the forts. No, no, Jude has caught more than is for her good from the settlers, and especially from the gallantifying officers."

"If she has—if she has, Hurry, this is a school to set her mind right ag'in. But what is this I see off here, abreast of us, that seems too small for an island and too large for a boat, though it stands in the midst of the water?"

"Why, that is what these gallanting gentry from the forts call Muskrat Castle; old Tom himself will grin at the name, though it bears so hard on his own natur' and character. 'Tis the stationary house, there being two—this, which never moves, and the other, that floats, being sometimes in one part of the lake and sometimes in another. The last goes by the name of the ark, though what may be the meaning of the word is more than I can tell you."

"It must come from the missionaries, Hurry, whom I have heard speak and read of such a thing. They say that the 'arth was once covered with water, and that Noah, with his children, was saved from drowning by building a vessel called an ark, in which he embarked in season. Some of the Delawares believe this tradition, and some deny it, but it behooves you and me, as white men born, to put our faith in its truth. Do you see anything of this ark?"

" 'Tis down south, no doubt, or anchored in some of the bays. But the canoe is ready, and fifteen minutes will carry two such paddles as your'n and mine to the castle."

At this suggestion, Deerslayer helped his companion to place the different articles in the canoe, which was already afloat. This was no sooner done than the two frontiersmen embarked and, by a vigorous push, sent the light bark some eight or ten rods from the shore. Hurry now took the seat in the stern, while Deerslayer placed himself forward, and by leisurely but steady strokes of the paddles, the canoe glided across the placid sheet toward the extraordinary-looking structure that the former had styled Muskrat Castle. Several times the men ceased paddling and looked about them at the scene, as new glimpses opened from behind points, enabling them to see further down the lake, or to get broader views of the wooded mountains. The only changes, however, were in the new forms of the hills, the varying curvature of the bays, and the wider reaches of the valley south; the whole earth, apparently, being clothed in a gala dress of leaves.

"This *is* a sight to warm the heart!" exclaimed Deerslayer, when they had thus stopped for the fourth or fifth time. "The lake seems made to let us get an insight into the noble forests, and land and water alike stand in the beauty of

God's Providence! Do you say, Hurry, that there is no man who calls himself lawful owner of all these glories?"

"None but the King, lad. He may pretend to some right of that natur', but he is so far away that his claim will never trouble old Tom Hutter, who has got possession, and is like to keep it as long as his life lasts. Tom is no squatter, not being on land; I call him a floater."

"I invy that man!—I know it's wrong, and I strive ag'in the feelin', but I invy that man! Don't think, Hurry, that I'm consarting any plan to put myself in his moccasins, for such a thought doesn't harbor in my mind, but I can't help a little invy! 'Tis a nat'ral feelin', and the best of us are but nat'ral, a'ter all, and give way to such feelin's at times."

"You've only to marry Hetty to inherit half the estate," cried Hurry, laughing. "The gal is comely—nay, if it wasn't for her sister's beauty, she would be even handsome; and then her wits are so small that you may easily convart her into one of your own way of thinking in all things. Do *you* take Hetty off the old fellow's hands, and *I*'ll engage he'll give you an interest in every deer you can knock over within five miles of his lake."

"Does game abound?" suddenly demanded the other, who paid but little attention to March's raillery.

"It has the country to itself. Scarce a trigger is pulled on it; and as for the trappers, this is not a region they greatly frequent. I ought not to be so much here myself, but Jude pulls one way while the beaver pulls another. More than a hundred Spanish dollars has that creatur' cost me the two last seasons, and yet I could not forego the wish to look upon her face once more."

"Do the red men often visit this lake, Hurry?" continued Deerslayer, pursuing his own train of thought.

"Why, they come and go, sometimes in parties and sometimes singly. The country seems to belong to no native tribe in particular, and so it has fallen into the hands of the Hutter tribe. The old man tells me that some sharp ones have been wheedling the Mohawks for an Indian deed, in order to get a title out of the Colony, but nothing has come of it, seeing that no one heavy enough for such a trade has yet meddled with the matter. The hunters have a good life lease, still, of this wilderness."

"So much the better—so much the better, Hurry. If I was

King of England, the man that felled one of these trees without good occasion for the timber should be banished to a desarted and forlorn region in which no four-footed animal ever trod. Right glad am I that Chingachgook app'inted our meeting on this lake, for hitherto eye of mine never looked on such a glorious spectacle."

"That's because you've kept so much among the Delawares, in whose country there are no lakes. Now, farther north and farther west, these bits of water abound; and you're young and may yet live to see 'em. But though there be other lakes, Deerslayer, there's no other Judith Hutter!"

At this remark his companion smiled, and then he dropped his paddle into the water, as if in consideration of a lover's haste. Both now pulled vigorously until they got within a hundred yards of the "castle," as Hurry familiarly called the house of Hutter, when they again ceased paddling; the admirer of Judith restraining his impatience the more readily, as he perceived that the building was untenanted at the moment. This new pause was to enable Deerslayer to survey the singular edifice, which was of a construction so novel as to merit a particular description.

Muskrat Castle, as the house had been facetiously named by some waggish officer, stood in the open lake at a distance of fully a quarter of a mile from the nearest shore. On every other side the water extended much farther, the precise position being distant about two miles from the northern end of the sheet and near, if not quite, a mile from its eastern shore. As there was not the smallest appearance of any island —the house stood on piles, with the water flowing beneath it —and Deerslayer had already discovered that the lake was of a great depth, he was fain to ask an explanation of this singular circumstance. Hurry solved the difficulty by telling him that on this spot alone a long, narrow shoal, which extended for a few hundred yards in a north and south direction, rose within six or eight feet of the surface of the lake, and that Hutter had driven piles into it and placed his habitation on them for the purpose of security.

"The old fellow was burnt out three times, atween the Indians and the hunters, and in one affray with the redskins he lost his only son, since which time he has taken to the water for safety. No one can attack him here without coming in a boat, and the plunder and scalps would scarce be worth the trouble of digging out canoes. Then it's by no means sartain which would whip in such a scrimmage, for old Tom is well supplied with arms and ammunition, and the castle, as you may see, is a tight breastwork ag'in light shot."

Deerslayer had some theoretical knowledge of frontier warfare, though he had never yet been called on to raise his hand in anger against a fellow creature. He saw that Hurry did not overrate the strength of this position from a military point of view, since it would not be easy to attack it without exposing the assailants to the fire of the besieged. A good deal of art had also been manifested in the disposition of the timber of which the building was constructed, and which afforded a protection much greater than was usual to the ordinary log cabins of the frontier. The sides and ends were composed of the trunks of large pines, cut about nine feet long and placed upright, instead of being laid horizontally, as was the practice of the country. These logs were squared on three sides, and had large tenons on each end. Massive sills were secured on the heads of the piles, with suitable grooves dug out of their upper surfaces, which had been squared for the purpose, and the lower tenons of the upright pieces were placed in these grooves, giving them a secure fastening below. Plates had been laid on the upper ends of the upright logs, and were kept in their places by a similar contrivance, the several corners of the structure being well fastened by scarfing and pinning the sills and plates. The floors were made of smaller logs, similarly squared, and the roof was composed of light poles, firmly united and well covered with bark. The effect of this ingenious arrangement was to give its owner a house that could be approached only by water, the sides of which were composed of logs closely wedged together, which were two feet thick in their thinnest parts, and which could be separated only by a deliberate and laborious use of human hands, or by the slow operation of time. The outer surface of the building was rude and uneven, the logs being of unequal sizes, but the squared surfaces within gave both the sides and floor as uniform an appearance as was desired, either for use or show. The chimney was not the least singular portion of the castle, as Hurry made his companion observe, while he explained the process by which it had been made. The material was a stiff clay, properly worked, which had been put together in a mold of sticks and suffered to harden, a foot or two at a time, commencing at the bottom. When the entire chimney had thus been raised and had been properly bound in with outward props, a brisk fire was kindled, and kept going until it was burned to something like a brick-red. This had not been an easy operation, nor had it succeeded entirely, but by dint of filling the cracks with fresh clay, a safe fireplace and chimney had been obtained in the end. This part of the work stood on the log floor, secured beneath by an extra pile. There were a few other peculiarities about this dwelling, which will better appear in the course of the narrative.

"Old Tom is full of contrivances," added Hurry, "and he set his heart on the success of his chimney, which threatened more than once to give out altogether; but parseverance will even overcome smoke, and now he has a comfortable cabin of it, though it did promise, at one time, to be a chinky sort of a flue to carry flames and fire."

"You seem to know the whole history of the castle, Hurry, chimney and sides," said Deerslayer, smiling. "Is love so overcoming that it causes a man to study the story of his sweetheart's habitation?"

"Partly that, lad, and partly eyesight," returned the good-natured giant, laughing. "There was a large gang of us in at the lake the summer the old fellow built, and we helped him along with the job. I raised no small part of the weight of them uprights with my own shoulders, and the axes flew, I can inform you, Master Natty, while we were bee-ing it among the trees ashore. The old devil is no way stingy about food, and as we had often eat at his hearth, we thought we would just house him comfortably afore we went to Albany with our skins. Yes, many is the meal I've swallowed in Tom Hutter's cabins, and Hetty, though so weak in the way of wits, has a wonderful particular way about a frying pan or a gridiron!"

While the parties were thus discoursing, the canoe had been gradually drawing nearer to the "castle," and was now so close as to require but a single stroke of a paddle to reach the landing. This was at a floored platform in front of the entrance that might have been some twenty feet square.

"Old Tom calls this sort of a wharf his dooryard," observed Hurry, as he fastened the canoe after he and his companion had left it, "and the gallants from the forts have named it the 'castle court,' though what a 'court' can have to do here is more than I can tell you, seeing that there is no law. 'Tis as I supposed—not a soul within, but the whole family is off on a v'y'ge of discovery!"

While Hurry was bustling about the "dooryard," examining the fishing spears, rods, nets, and other similar appliances of a frontier cabin, Deerslayer, whose manner was altogether more rebuked and quiet, entered the building with a curiosity that was not usually exhibited by one so long trained in Indian habits. The interior of the "castle" was as faultlessly neat as its exterior was novel. The entire space, some twenty feet by forty, was subdivided into several small sleeping rooms, the apartment into which he first entered serving equally for the ordinary uses of its inmates and for a kitchen. The furniture was of the strange mixture that it is not uncommon to find in the remotely situated log tenements of the interior. Most of it was rude and to the last degree rustic, but there was a clock, with a handsome case of dark wood, in a corner, and two or three chairs, with a table and bureau, that had evidently come from some dwelling of more than usual pretension. The clock was industriously ticking, but its leaden-looking hands did no discredit to their dull aspect, for they pointed to the hour of eleven, though the sun plainly showed it was some time past the turn of the day. There was also a dark, massive chest. The kitchen utensils were of the simplest kind and far from numerous, but every article was in its place, and showed the nicest care in its condition.

After Deerslayer had cast a look about him in the outer room, he raised a wooden latch and entered a narrow passage that divided the inner end of the house into two equal parts. Frontier usages being no way scrupulous, and his curiosity being strongly excited, the young man now opened a door, and found himself in a bedroom. A single glance sufficed to show that the apartment belonged to females. The bed was of the feathers of wild geese and filled nearly to overflowing, but it lay in a rude bunk, raised only a foot from the floor. On one side of it were arranged on pegs various dresses of a quality much superior to what one would expect to meet in such a place, with ribbons, and other similar articles to correspond. Pretty shoes, with handsome silver buckles, such as were then worn by females in easy circumstances, were not wanting, and no less than six fans, of gay colors, were placed half open in a way to catch the eye by their conceits and hues. Even the pillow, on this side of the bed, was covered with finer linen than its companion, and it was ornamented with a small ruffle. A cap, coquettishly decorated with ribbons, hung above it, and a pair of long gloves, such as were rarely used in those days by persons of the laboring classes, were pinned ostentatiously to it, as if with an intention to exhibit them there, if they could not be shown on the owner's arms.

All this Deerslayer saw and noted with a degree of minuteness that would have done credit to the habitual observation of his friends the Delawares. Nor did he fail to perceive the distinction that existed between the appearances on the different sides of the bed, the head of which stood against the wall. On that opposite to the one just described, everything was homely and uninviting, except through its perfect neatness. The few garments that were hanging from the pegs were of the coarsest materials and of the commonest forms, while nothing seemed made for show. Of ribbons there was not one, nor was there either cap or kerchief beyond those which Hutter's daughters might be fairly entitled to wear.

It was now several years since Deerslayer had been in a spot especially devoted to the uses of females of his own color and race. The sight brought back to his mind a rush of childish recollections, and he lingered in the room with a tenderness of feeling to which he had long been a stranger. He bethought him of his mother, whose homely vestments he remembered to have seen hanging on pegs like those which he felt must belong to Hetty Hutter, and he bethought himself of a sister, whose incipient and native taste for finery had exhibited itself somewhat in the manner of that of Judith, though necessarily in a less degree. These little resemblances opened a long hidden vein of sensations, and as he quitted the room, it was with a saddened mien. He looked no further but returned slowly and thoughtfully toward the "dooryard."

"Old Tom has taken to a new calling, and has been trying his hand at the traps," cried Hurry, who had been coolly examining the borderer's implements. "If that is his humor, and you're disposed to remain in these parts, we can make an oncommon comfortable season of it; for, while the old man and I outknowledge the beaver, you can fish and knock down the deer to keep body and soul together. We always give the poorest hunters half a share, but one as actyve and sartain as yourself might expect a full one."

"Thank'ee, Hurry, thank'ee with all my heart—but I do a little beavering for myself as occasions offer. 'Tis true, the Delawares call me Deerslayer, but it's not so much because I'm pretty fatal with the venison as because that while I kill so many bucks and does, I've never yet taken the life of a fellow creatur'. They say their traditions do not tell of another who had shed so much blood of animals that had not shed the blood of man."

"I hope they don't account you chicken-hearted, lad? A fainthearted man is like a no-tailed beaver."

"I don't believe, Hurry, that they account me as out-of-the-way timorsome, even though they may not account me as out-of-the-way brave. But I'm not quarrelsome, and that goes a great way toward keeping blood off the hands, among the hunters and redskins—and then, Harry March, it keeps blood off the conscience, too."

"Well, for my part I account game, a redskin, and a Frenchman as pretty much the same thing, though I'm as onquarrelsome a man, too, as there is in all the colonies. I despise a quarreler as I do a cur dog, but one has no need to be overscrupulsome when it's the right time to show the flint."

"I look upon him as the most of a man who acts nearest the right, Hurry. But this is a glorious spot, and my eyes never a-weary looking at it!"

" 'Tis your first acquaintance with a lake, and these idees come over us all at such times. Lakes have a general character, as I say, being pretty much water and land and points and bays."

As this definition by no means met the feelings that were uppermost in the mind of the young hunter, he made no immediate answer, but stood gazing at the dark hills and the glassy water in silent enjoyment.

"Have the Governor's or the King's people given this lake a name?" he suddenly asked, as if struck with a new idea. "If they've not begun to blaze their trees, and set up their compasses, and line off their maps, it's likely they've not bethought them to disturb natur' with a name."

"They've not got to that, yet; the last time I went in with skins, one of the King's surveyors was questioning me consarning all the region hereabouts. He had heard that there was a lake in this quarter and had got some general notions about it, such as that there was water and hills, but how much of either he knowed no more than you know of the Mohawk tongue. I didn't open the trap any wider than was necessary, giving him but poor encouragement in the way of farms and clearings. In short, I left on his mind some such opinion of this country as a man gets of a spring of dirty water, with a path to it that is so muddy that one mires afore he sets out. He told me they hadn't got the spot down yet on their maps, though I conclude that is a mistake, for he showed me his parchment, and there is a lake down on it where there is no lake in fact, and which is about fifty miles from the place where it ought to be, if they meant it for this. I don't think my account will encourage him to mark down another, by way of improvement."

Here Hurry laughed heartily, such tricks being particularly grateful to a set of men who dreaded the approaches of civilization as a curtailment of their own lawless empire. The egregious errors that existed in the maps of the day, all of which were made in Europe, was, moreover, a standing topic of ridicule among them; for, if they had not science enough to make any better themselves, they had sufficient local information to detect the gross blunders contained in those that existed. Anyone who will take the trouble to compare these unanswerable evidences of the topographical skill of our fathers a century since with the more accurate sketches of our own time will at once perceive that the men of the woods had a sufficient justification for all their criticism on this branch of the skill of the colonial governments, which did not at all hesitate to place a river or a lake a degree or two out of the way, even though they lay within a day's march of the inhabited parts of the country.

"I'm glad it has no name," resumed Deerslayer, "or, at least, no paleface name, for their christenings always foretell waste and destruction. No doubt, howsever, the redskins have their modes of knowing it, and the hunters and trappers, too; they are likely to call the place by something reasonable and resembling."

"As for the tribes, each has its own tongue and its own

way of calling things, and they treat this part of the world just as they treat all others. Among ourselves we've got to calling the place the 'Glimmerglass,' seeing that its whole basin is so often fringed with pines cast upward from its face, as if it would throw back the hills that hang over it."

"There is an outlet, I know, for all lakes have outlets, and the rock at which I am to meet Chingachgook stands near an outlet. Has *that* no colony name yet?"

"In that particular they've got the advantage of us, having one end, and that the biggest, in their own keeping; they've given it a name which has found its way up to its source, names nat'rally working upstream. No doubt, Deerslayer, you've seen the Susquehanna, down in the Delaware country?"

"That have I, and hunted along its banks a hundred times."

"That and this are the same, in fact, and, I suppose, the same in sound. I am glad they've been compelled to keep the red men's name, for it would be too hard to rob them of both land and name!"

Deerslayer made no answer, but he stood leaning on his rifle, gazing at the view which so much delighted him. The reader is not to suppose, however, that it was the picturesque alone which so strongly attracted his attention. The spot was very lovely, of a truth, and it was then seen in one of its most favorable moments, the surface of the lake being as smooth as glass and as limpid as pure air, throwing back the mountains, clothed in dark pines, along the whole of its eastern boundary, the points thrusting forward their trees even to nearly horizontal lines, while the bays were seen glittering through an occasional arch beneath, left by a vault fretted with branches and leaves. It was the air of deep repose—the solitudes that spoke of scenes and forests untouched by the hands of man—the reign of nature, in a word, that gave so much pure delight to one of his habits and turn of mind. Still, he felt, though it was unconsciously, like a poet also. If he found a pleasure in studying this large and, to him, unusual opening into the mysteries and forms of the woods, as one is gratified in getting broader views of any subject that has long occupied his thoughts, he was not insensible to the innate loveliness of such a landscape either, but felt a portion of that soothing of the spirit which is a common attendant of a scene so thoroughly pervaded by the holy calm of nature.

CHAPTER III

Come, shall we go and kill us venison?
And yet it irks me, the poor dappled fools,—
Being native burghers of this desert city,—
Should, in their own confines, with forked heads
Have their round haunches gored.

SHAKESPEARE

HURRY HARRY THOUGHT more of the beauties of Judith Hutter than of those of the Glimmerglass and its accompanying scenery. As soon as he had taken a sufficiently intimate survey of Floating Tom's implements, therefore, he summoned his companion to the canoe, that they might go down the lake in quest of the family. Previously to embarking, however, Hurry carefully examined the whole of the northern end of the water with an indifferent ship's glass that formed a part of Hutter's effects. In this scrutiny no part of the shore was overlooked; the bays and points, in particular, being subjected to a closer inquiry than the rest of the wooded boundary.

"'Tis as I thought," said Hurry, laying aside the glass, "the old fellow is drifting about the south end, this fine weather, and has left the castle to defend itself. Well, now we know that he is not up thisaway, 'twill be but a small matter to paddle down and hunt him up in his hiding place."

"Does Master Hutter think it necessary to burrow on this lake?" inquired Deerslayer, as he followed his companion into the canoe. "To my eye it is such a solitude as one might open his whole soul in and fear no one to disarrange his thoughts or his worship."

"You forget your friends, the Mingos, and all the French savages. Is there a spot on 'arth, Deerslayer, to which them disquiet rogues don't go? Where is the lake, or even the deer

39

lick, that the blackguards don't find out and, having found out, don't sooner or later discolor its water with blood?"

"I hear no good character of them, sartainly, friend Hurry, though I've never been called on, as yet, to meet them, or any other mortal, on the warpath. I dare to say that such a lovely spot as this would not be likely to be overlooked by such plunderers; for though I've not been in the way of quarreling with them tribes myself, the Delawares give me such an account of 'em that I've pretty much set 'em down, in my own mind, as thorough miscreants."

"You may do that with a safe conscience, or, for that matter, any other savage you may happen to meet."

Here Deerslayer protested, and as they went paddling down the lake a hot discussion was maintained concerning the respective merits of the palefaces and the redskins. Hurry had all the prejudices and antipathies of a white hunter, who generally regards the Indian as a sort of natural competitor and, not unfrequently, as a natural enemy. As a matter of course he was loud, clamorous, dogmatic, and not very argumentative. Deerslayer, on the other hand, manifested a very different temper, proving, by the moderation of his language, the fairness of his views, and the simplicity of his distinctions, that he possessed every disposition to hear reason, a strong, innate desire to do justice, and an ingenuousness that was singularly indisposed to have recourse to sophisms to maintain an argument, or to defend a prejudice. Still, he was not altogether free from the influence of the latter feeling. This tyrant of the human mind, which rushes on its prey through a thousand avenues almost as soon as men begin to think and feel, and which seldom relinquishes its iron sway until they cease to do either, had made some impression on even the just propensities of this individual, who probably offered in these particulars a fair specimen of what absence from bad example, the want of temptation to go wrong, and native good feeling can render youth.

"You will allow, Deerslayer, that a Mingo is more than half devil," cried Hurry, following up the discussion with an animation that touched closely on ferocity, "though you want to overpersuade me that the Delaware tribe is pretty much made up of angels. Now, I gainsay that proposal, consarning white men, even. All white men are not faultless, and therefore all Indians *can't* be faultless. And so your argument is out at the elbow in the start. But, this is what I call reason. Here's three colors on 'arth—white, black, and red. White is the highest color, and therefore the best man; black comes next, and is put to live in the neighborhood of the white man, as tolerable and fit to be made use of; and red comes last, which shows that those that made 'em never expected an Indian to be accounted as more than half human."

"God made all three alike, Hurry."

"Alike! Do you call a nigger like a white man, or me like an Indian?"

"You go off at half-cock and don't hear me out. God made us all—white, black, and red—and no doubt had his own wise intentions in coloring us differently. Still, he made us, in the main, much the same in feelin's, though I'll not deny that he gave each race its gifts. A white man's gifts are Christianized, while a redskin's are more for the wilderness. Thus, it would be a great offense for a white man to scalp the dead, whereas it's a signal vartue in an Indian. Then ag'in, a white man cannot amboosh women and children in war, while a redskin may. 'Tis *cruel* work, I'll allow, but for them it's *lawful* work, while for *us* it would be grievous work."

"That depends on your inimy. As for scalping, or even skinning a savage, I look upon them pretty much the same as cutting off the ears of wolves for the bounty, or stripping a bear of its hide. And then you're out significantly, as to taking the poll of a redskin in hand, seeing that the very Colony has offered a bounty for the job, all the same as it pays for wolves' ears and crows' heads."

"Aye, and a bad business it is, Hurry. Even the Indians themselves cry shame on it, seeing it's ag'in a white man's gifts. I do not pretend that all that white men do is properly Christianized and according to the lights given them, for then they would be what they *ought* to be—which we know they are not; but I will maintain that tradition, and use, and color, and laws make such a difference in races as to amount to gifts. I do not deny that there are tribes among the Indians that are nat'rally pervarse and wicked, as there are nations among the whites. Now, I account the Mingos as belonging to the first and the Frenchers, in the Canadas, to the last. In a state of lawful warfare such as we have lately got into, it is a duty to keep down all compassionate feelin's, so far as life goes, ag'in either; but when it comes to scalps, it's a very different matter."

"Just hearken to reason, if you please, Deerslayer, and tell me if the Colony can make an onlawful law? Isn't an onlawful law more ag'in natur' than scalpin' a savage? A law can no more be onlawful than truth can be a lie."

"That *sounds* reasonable, but it has a most onreasonable bearing, Hurry. Laws don't all come from the same quarter. God has given us his'n, and some come from the Colony and others come from the King and Parliament. When the Colony's laws, or even the King's laws, run ag'in the laws of God, they get to be onlawful and ought not to be obeyed. I hold to a white man's respecting white laws, so long as they do not cross the track of a law comin' from a higher authority; and for a red man to obey his own redskin usages under the same privilege. But 'tis useless talking, as each man will think for himself and have his say agreeable to his thoughts. Let us keep a good lookout for your friend Floating Tom, lest we pass him, as he lies hidden under this bushy shore."

Deerslayer had not named the borders of the lake amiss. Along their whole length, the smaller trees overhung the water, with their branches often dipping in the transparent element. The banks were steep, even from the narrow strand, and as vegetation invariably struggles toward the light, the effect was precisely that at which the lover of the picturesque would have aimed, had the ordering of this glorious setting of forest been submitted to his control. The points and bays, too, were sufficiently numerous to render the outline broken and diversified. As the canoe kept close along the western side of the lake, with a view, as Hurry had explained to his companion, of reconnoitering for enemies before he trusted himself too openly in sight, the expectations of the two adventurers were kept constantly on the stretch, as neither could foretell what the next turning of a point might reveal. Their progress was swift, the gigantic strength of Hurry enabling him to play with the light bark as if it had been a feather, while the skill of his companion almost equalized their usefulness, notwithstanding the disparity in natural means.

Each time the canoe passed a point, Hurry turned a look behind him, expecting to see the "ark" anchored, or beached in the bay. He was fated to be disappointed, however; they had got within a mile of the southern end of the lake, or a distance of quite two leagues from the "castle," which was now hidden from view by half a dozen intervening projections of the land, when he suddenly ceased paddling, as if uncertain in what direction next to steer.

"It is possible that the old chap has dropped into the river," said Hurry, after looking carefully along the whole of the eastern shore, which was about a mile distant and open to his scrutiny for more than half its length; "for he has taken to trapping considerable, of late, and barring flood wood, he might drop down it a mile or so, though he would have a most scratching time in getting back again!"

"Where is this outlet?" asked Deerslayer; "I see no opening in the banks or the trees that looks as if it would let a river like the Susquehanna run through it."

"Aye, Deerslayer, rivers are like human mortals, having small beginnings and ending with broad shoulders and wide mouths. You don't see the outlet because it passes atween high, steep banks, and the pines, and hemlocks, and basswoods hang over it as a roof hangs over a house. If old Tom is not in the 'Rat's Cove,' he must have burrowed in the river; we'll look for him first in the cove, and then we'll cross to the outlet."

As they proceeded, Hurry explained that there was a shallow bay formed by a long, low point that had got the name of the "Rat's Cove," from the circumstance of its being a favorite haunt of the muskrat, and which offered so complete a cover for the "ark" that its owner was fond of lying in it whenever he found it convenient.

"As a man never knows who may be his visitors in this part of the country," continued Hurry, "it's a great advantage to get a good look at 'em before they come too near. Now it's war, such caution is more than commonly useful, since a Canada man or a Mingo might get into his hut afore he invited 'em. But Hutter is a first-rate look-outer and can pretty much scent danger, as a hound scents the deer."

"I should think the castle so open that it would be sartain to draw inimies, if any happened to find the lake; a thing onlikely enough, I will allow, as it's off the trail of the forts and settlements."

"Why, Deerslayer, I've got to believe that a man meets

with inimies easier than he meets with fri'nds. It's skearful to think for how many causes one gets to be your inimy and for how few your fri'nd. Some take up the hatchet because you don't think just as they think; other some because you run ahead of 'em in the same idees; I once know'd a vagabond that quarreled with a fri'nd because he didn't think him handsome. Now, you're no monument in the way of beauty yourself, Deerslayer, and yet you wouldn't be so onreasonable as to become my inimy for just saying so."

"I'm as the Lord made me, and I wish to be accounted no better, nor any worse. Good looks I may not have—that is to say, to a degree that the light-minded and vain crave—but I hope I'm not altogether without some ricommend in the way of good conduct. There's few nobler looking men to be seen than yourself, Hurry, and I know that I am not to expect any to turn their eyes on me when such a one as you can be gazed on; but I do not know that a hunter is less expart with the rifle, or less to be relied on for food, because he doesn't wish to stop at every shining spring he may meet to study his own countenance in the water."

Here Hurry burst into a fit of loud laughter, for while he was too reckless to care much about his own manifest physical superiority, he was well aware of it, and like most men who derive an advantage from the accidents of birth or nature, he was apt to think complacently on the subject, whenever it happened to cross his mind.

"No, no, Deerslayer, you're no beauty, as you will own yourself, if you'll look over the side of the canoe," he cried. "Jude will say *that* to your face, if you start her, for a parter tongue isn't to be found in any gal's head, in or out of the settlements, if you provoke her to use it. My advice to you is never to aggravate Judith, though you may tell anything to Hetty, and she'll take it as meek as a lamb. No, Jude will be just as like as not to tell you her opinion consarning your looks."

"And if she does, Hurry, she will tell me no more than you have said already——"

"You're not thick'ning up about a small remark, I hope, Deerslayer, when no harm is meant. You are *not* a beauty, as you must know, and why shouldn't fri'nds tell each other these little trifles? If you *was* handsome, or ever like to be, I'd be one of the first to tell you of it; and that ought to content you. Now, if Jude was to tell me that I'm as ugly as a sinner, I'd take it as a sort of obligation and try not to believe her."

"It's easy for them that natur' has favored to jest about such matters, Hurry, though it is sometimes hard for others. I'll not deny but I've had my cravings toward good looks— yes, I have—but then I've always been able to get them down by considering how many I've known with fair outsides who have had nothing to boast of inwardly. I'll not deny, Hurry, that I often wish I'd been created more comely to the eye, more like such a one as yourself in them particulars, but then I get the feelin' under by remembering how much better off I am in a great many respects than some fellow mortals. I might have been born lame and onfit even for a squirrel hunt; or blind, which would have made me a burden on myself as well as on my fri'nds; or without hearing, which would have totally onqualified me for ever campaigning or scouting, which I look forward to as part of a man's duty in troublesome times. Yes, yes, it's not pleasant, I will allow, to see them that's more comely, and more sought a'ter, and honored than yourself, but it may all be borne, if a man looks the evil in the face, and don't mistake his gifts and his obligations."

Hurry, in the main, was a goodhearted as well as good-natured fellow, and the self-abasement of his companion completely got the better of the passing feeling of personal vanity. He regretted the allusion he had made to the other's appearance and endeavoured to express as much, though it was done in the uncouth manner that belonged to the habits and opinions of the frontier.

"I meant no harm, Deerslayer," he answered, in a depre-cating manner, "and hope you'll forget what I've said. If you're not downright handsome, you've a sartain look that says, plainer than any words, that all's right within. Then you set no valie by looks, and will the sooner forgive any little slight to your appearance. I will not say that Jude will greatly admire you, for that might raise hopes that would only breed disapp'intment; but there's Hetty, now, would be just as likely to find satisfaction in looking at *you* as in looking at any other man. Then you're altogether too grave and considerate like to care much about Judith, for though the gal *is* oncommon, she is so general in her admiration

that a man need not be exalted because she happens to smile.
I sometimes think the hussy loves herself better than she
does anything else breathin'!"

"If she did, Hurry, she'd do no more, I'm afeard, than most
queens on their thrones and ladies in the towns," answered
Deerslayer, smiling and turning back toward his companion
with every trace of feeling banished from his honest-looking
and frank countenance. "I never yet know'd even a Delaware
of whom you might not say that much. But here is the end
of the long p'int you mentioned, and the 'Rat's Cove' can't
be far off."

This point, instead of thrusting itself forward like all the
others, ran in a line with the main shore of the lake, which
here swept within it, in a deep and retired bay, circling
around south again, at the distance of a quarter of a mile,
and crossed the valley, forming the southern termination of
the water. In this bay Hurry felt almost certain of finding the
ark, since, anchored behind the trees that covered the narrow strip of the point, it might have lain concealed from
prying eyes an entire summer. So complete, indeed, was the
cover in this spot that a boat hauled close to the beach, within the point and near the bottom of the bay, could by possibility be seen from only one direction, and that was from a
densely wooded shore within the sweep of the water, where
strangers would be little apt to go.

"We shall soon see the ark," said Hurry, as the canoe
glided around the extremity of the point, where the water
was so deep as actually to appear black. "He loves to burrow
up among the rushes, and we shall be in his nest in five
minutes, although the old fellow may be off among the
traps himself."

March proved a false prophet. The canoe completely
doubled the point, so as to enable the two travelers to command a view of the whole cove or bay, for it was more properly the last, and no object, but those that nature had placed
there became visible. The placid water swept around in a
graceful curve, the rushes bent gently toward its surface,
and the trees overhung it as usual, but all lay in the soothing and sublime solitude of a wilderness. The scene was
such as a poet or an artist would have delighted in, but it
had no charm for Hurry Harry, who was burning with impatience to get a sight of his light-minded beauty.

The motion of the canoe had been attended with little or no noise, the frontiersmen habitually getting accustomed to caution in most of their movements, and it now lay on the glassy water appearing to float in air, partaking of the breathing stillness that seemed to pervade the entire scene. At this instant a dry stick was heard cracking on the narrow strip of land that concealed the bay from the open lake. Both the adventurers started, and each extended a hand toward his rifle, the weapon never being out of reach of the arm.

" 'Twas too heavy for any light creatur'," whispered Hurry, "and it sounded like the tread of a man!"

"Not so—not so," returned Deerslayer; " 'twas, as you say, too heavy for one, but it was too light for the other. Put your paddle in the water and send the canoe in to that log; I'll land and cut off the creatur's retreat up the p'int be it a Mingo, or be it only a muskrat."

As Hurry complied, Deerslayer was soon on the shore, advancing into the thicket with a moccasined foot and a caution that prevented the least noise. In a minute he was in the center of the narrow strip of land and moving slowly down toward its end, the bushes rendering extreme watchfulness necessary. Just as he reached the center of the thicket, the dried twigs cracked again, and the noise was repeated at short intervals, as if some creature having life walked slowly toward the point. Hurry heard these sounds also, and pushing the canoe off into the bay, he seized his rifle to watch the result. A breathless minute succeeded, after which a noble buck walked out of the thicket, proceeded with a stately step to the sandy extremity of the point, and began to slake his thirst from the water of the lake. Hurry hesitated an instant; then, raising his rifle hastily to his shoulder, he took sight and fired. The effect of this sudden interruption of the solemn stillness of such a scene was not its least striking peculiarity. The report of the weapon had the usual sharp, short sound of the rifle, but when a few moments of silence had succeeded the sudden crack, during which the noise was floating in air across the water, it reached the rocks of the opposite mountain, where the vibrations accumulated, and were rolled from cavity to cavity for miles along the hills, seeming to awaken the sleeping thunders of the woods. The buck merely shook his head at the report of the rifle and the whistling of the bullet, for never before had he come in contact with man, but the echoes of the hills awakened his distrust, and, leaping forward, with his four legs drawn under his body, he fell at once into deep water and began to swim toward the foot of the lake. Hurry shouted and dashed forward in chase, and for one or two minutes the water foamed around the pursuer and the pursued. The former was dashing past the point, when Deerslayer appeared on the sand and signed to him to return.

" 'Twas inconsiderate to pull a trigger afore we had re-conn'itered the shore and made sartain that no inimies harbored near it," said the latter, as his companion slowly and reluctantly complied. "This much I have l'arned from the Delawares, in the way of schooling and traditions, even though I've never yet been on a warpath. And moreover, venison can hardly be called in season now, and we do not want for food. They call me Deerslayer, I'll own; and perhaps I desarve the name, in the way of understanding the creatur's habits, as well as for sartainty in the aim; but they can't accuse me of killing an animal when there is no occasion for the meat or the skin. I may be a slayer, it's true, but I'm no slaughterer."

" 'Twas an awful mistake to miss that buck!" exclaimed Hurry, doffing his cap and running his fingers through his handsome but matted curls, as if he would loosen his tangled ideas by the process. "I've not done so onhandy a thing since I was fifteen."

"Never lament it; the creatur's death could have done neither of us any good and might have done us harm. Them echoes are more awful in my ears than your mistake, Hurry, for they sound like the voice of natur' calling out ag'in a wasteful and onthinking action."

"You'll hear plenty of such calls, if you tarry long in this quarter of the world, lad," returned the other, laughing. "The echoes repeat pretty much all that is said or done on the Glimmerglass in this calm, summer weather. If a paddle falls, you hear of it sometimes ag'in and ag'in, as if the hills were mocking your clumsiness, and a laugh or a whistle comes out of them pines, when they're in the humor to speak, in a way to make you believe they can r'ally convarse."

"So much the more reason for being prudent and silent. I do not think the inimy can have found their way into these hills yet, for I don't know what they are to gain by it; but all

the Delawares tell me that as courage is a warrior's first
vartue, so is prudence his second. One such call, from the
mountains, is enough to let a whole tribe into the secret of
our arrival."

"If it does no other good, it will warn old Tom to put the
pot over and let him know visitors are at hand. Come, lad,
get into the canoe, and we will hunt the ark up while there is
yet day."

Deerslayer complied, and the canoe left the spot. Its head
was turned diagonally across the lake, pointing toward the
southeastern curvature of the sheet. In that direction, the
distance to the shore, or to the termination of the lake, on
the course the two were now steering, was not quite a mile,
and their progress being always swift, it was fast lessening,
under the skillful but easy sweeps of the paddles. When
about halfway across, a slight noise drew the eyes of the
men toward the nearest land, and they saw that the buck
was just emerging from the lake and wading toward the
beach. In a minute the noble animal shook the water from
his flanks, gazed upward at the covering of trees, and, bounding against the bank, plunged into the forest.

"That creatur' goes off with gratitude in his heart," said
Deerslayer, "for natur' tells him he has escaped a great
danger. You ought to have some of the same feelin's, Hurry,
to think your eye wasn't truer—that your hand was onsteady—when no good could come of a shot that was intended onmeaningly, rather than in reason."

"I deny the eye and the hand," cried March, with some
heat. "You've got a little character, down among the Delawares, there, for quickness and sartainty at a deer, but I
should like to see you behind one of them pines and a full-
painted Mingo behind another, each with a cocked rifle and
a-striving for the chance! Them's the situations, Nathaniel,
to try the sight and the hand, for they begin with trying the
narves. I never look upon killing a creatur' as an explite,
but killing a savage is. The time will come to try your hand,
now we've got to blows ag'in, and we shall soon know what a
ven'son reputation can do in the field. I deny that either
hand or eye was onsteady; it was all a miscalculation of the
buck, which stood still when he ought to have kept in motion,
and so I shot ahead of him."

"Have it your own way, Hurry; all I contend for is that

it's lucky. I daresay I shall not pull upon a human mortal as steadily or with as light a heart as I pull upon a deer."

"Who's talking of mortals, or of human beings at all, Deerslayer? I put the matter to you on the supposition of an Injin. I daresay any man would have his feelin's when it got to be life or death ag'in another human mortal, but there would be no such scruples in regard to an Injin—nothing but the chance of his hitting you, or the chance of your hitting him."

"I look upon the red men to be quite as human as we are ourselves, Hurry. They have their gifts and their religion, it's true, but that makes no difference in the end, when each will be judged according to his deeds and not according to his skin."

"That's downright missionary, and will find little favor up in this part of the country, where the Moravians don't congregate. Now, skin makes the man. This is reason—else how are people to judge of each other? The skin is put on, over all, in order that when a creatur', or a mortal, is fairly seen, you may know at once what to make of him. You know a bear from a hog, by his skin, and a gray squirrel from a black."

"True, Hurry," said the other, looking back and smiling. "Nevertheless, they are both squirrels."

"Who denies it? But you'll not say that a red man and a white man are both Injins?"

"No, but I *do* say they are both men. Men of different races and colors, and having different gifts and traditions, but, in the main, with the same natur'. Both have souls, and both will be held accountable for their deeds in this life."

Hurry was one of those theorists who believed in the inferiority of all the human race who were not white. His notions on the subject were not very clear, nor were his definitions at all well settled, but his opinions were nonetheless dogmatic or fierce. His conscience accused him of sundry lawless acts against the Indians, and he had found it an exceedingly easy mode of quieting it, by putting the whole family of red men, incontinently, without the category of human rights. Nothing angered him sooner than to deny his proposition—more especially if the denial were accompanied by a show of plausible argument—and he did not listen to his companion's remarks with much composure of either manner or feeling.

"You're a boy, Deerslayer, misled and misconsaited by Delaware arts and missionary ignorance," he exclaimed, with his usual indifference to the forms of speech, when excited. "*You* may account yourself as a redskin's brother, but *I* hold 'em all to be animals, with nothing human about 'em but cunning. *That* they have, I'll allow, but so has a fox, or even a bear. I'm older than you, and have lived longer in the woods —or, for that matter, have lived always there, and am not to be told what an Injin is or what he is not. If you wish to be considered a savage, you've only to say so, and I'll name you as such to Judith and the old man, and then we'll see how you'll like your welcome."

Here Hurry's imagination did his temper some service, since, by conjuring up the reception his semiaquatic acquaintance would be likely to bestow on one thus introduced, he burst into a hearty fit of laughter. Deerslayer too well knew the uselessness of attempting to convince such a being of anything against his prejudices, to feel a desire to undertake the task, and he was not sorry that the approach of the canoe to the southeastern curve of the lake gave a new direction to his ideas. They were now, indeed, quite near the place that March had pointed out for the position of the outlet, and both began to look for it with a curiosity that was increased by the expectation of finding the ark.

It may strike the reader as a little singular that the place where a stream of any size passed through banks that had an elevation of some twenty feet should be a matter of doubt with men who could not now have been more than two hundred yards distant from the precise spot. It will be recollected, however, that the trees and bushes here as elsewhere fairly overhung the water, making such a fringe to the lake as to conceal any little variations from its general outline.

"I've not been down at this end of the lake these two summers," said Hurry, standing up in the canoe, the better to look about him. "Aye, there's the rock, showing its chin above the water, and I know that the river begins in its neighborhood."

The men now plied the paddles again, and they were presently within a few yards of the rock, floating toward it, though their efforts were suspended. This rock was not large, being merely some five or six feet high, only half of which elevation rose above the lake. The incessant washing of the water for centuries had so rounded its summit that it resembled a large beehive in shape, its form being more than usually regular and even. Hurry remarked, as they floated slowly past, that this rock was well known to all the Indians in that part of the country and that they were in the practice of using it as a mark to designate the place of meeting, when separated by their hunts and marches.

"And here is the river, Deerslayer," he continued, "though so shut in by trees and bushes as to look more like an andbush than the outlet of such a sheet as the Glimmerglass."

Hurry had not badly described the place, which did truly seem to be a stream lying in ambush. The high banks might have been a hundred feet asunder, but on the western side a small bit of low land extended so far forward as to diminish the breadth of the stream to half that width. As the bushes hung in the water beneath, and pines that had the stature of church steeples rose in tall columns above, all inclining toward the light until their branches intermingled, the eye, at a little distance, could not easily detect any opening in the shore, to mark the egress of the water. In the forest above, no traces of this outlet were to be seen from the lake, the whole presenting the same connected and seemingly interminable carpet of leaves. As the canoe slowly advanced, sucked in by the current, it entered beneath an arch of trees, through which the light from the heavens struggled by casual openings, faintly relieving the gloom beneath.

"This is a nat'ral and-bush," half-whispered Hurry, as if he felt that the place was devoted to secrecy and watchfulness. "Depend on it, old Tom has burrowed with the ark somewhere in this quarter. We will drop down with the current a short distance and ferret him out."

"This seems no place for a vessel of any size," returned the other. "It appears to me that we shall have hardly room enough for the canoe."

Hurry laughed at the suggestion, and, as it soon appeared, with reason, for the fringe of bushes immediately on the shore of the lake was no sooner passed than the adventurers found themselves in a narrow stream of a sufficient depth of limpid water, with a strong current, and a canopy of leaves, upheld by arches composed of the limbs of hoary trees. Bushes lined the shores, as usual, but they left sufficient space between them to admit the passage of anything that did not exceed twenty feet in width and to allow of a perspective ahead of eight or ten times that distance.

Neither of our two adventurers used his paddle, except to keep the light bark in the center of the current, but both watched each turning of the stream, of which there were two or three within the first hundred yards, with jealous vigilance. Turn after turn, however, was passed, and the canoe had dropped down with the current some little distance, when Hurry caught a bush and arrested its movement so suddenly and silently as to denote some unusual motive for the act. Deerslayer laid his hand on the stock of his rifle, as soon as he noted this proceeding; but it was quite as much with a hunter's habit as from any feeling of alarm.

"There the old fellow is!" whispered Hurry, pointing with a finger and laughing heartily, though he carefully avoided making a noise; "ratting it away, just as I supposed; up to his knees in the mud and water, looking to the traps and the bait. But for the life of me I can see nothing of the ark, though I'll bet every skin I take this season Jude isn't trusting her pretty little feet in the neighborhood of that black mud. The gal's more likely to be braiding her hair by the side of some spring, where she can see her own good looks and collect scornful feelings ag'in us men."

"You overjudge young women—yes, you do, Hurry—who as often bethink them of their failings as they do of their perfections. I dare to say, this Judith, now, is no such admirer of herself and no such scorner of our sex, as you seem to think, and that she is quite as likely to be sarving her father in the house, wherever that may be, as he is to be sarving her among the traps."

"It's a pleasure to hear truth from a man's tongue, if it be only once in a girl's life," cried a pleasant, rich, and yet soft female voice, so near the canoe as to make both the listeners start. "As for you, Master Hurry, fair words are so apt to choke you that I no longer expect to hear them from your mouth, the last you uttered sticking in your throat and coming near to death. But I'm glad to see you keep better society than formerly and that they who know how to esteem and treat women are not ashamed to journey in your company."

As this was said, a singularly handsome and youthful female face was thrust through an opening in the leaves, within reach of Deerslayer's paddle. Its owner smiled graciously on the young man; the frown that she cast on Hurry, though simulated and pettish, had the effect to render her beauty more striking by exhibiting the play of an expressive but capricious countenance—one that seemed to change from the soft to the severe, the mirthful to the reproving, with facility and indifference.

A second look explained the nature of the surprise. Unwittingly, the men had dropped alongside of the ark, which had been purposely concealed in bushes cut and arranged for the purpose, and Judith Hutter had merely pushed aside the leaves that lay before a window in order to show her face and speak to them.

CHAPTER IV

And that timid fawn starts not with fear,
When I steal to her secret bower;
And that young May violet to me is dear,
And I visit the silent streamlet near,
To look on the lovely flower.

BRYANT

THE ARK, as the floating habitation of the Hutters was generally called, was a very simple contrivance. A large flat, or scow, composed the buoyant part of the vessel; in its center, occupying the whole of its breadth, and about two-thirds of its length, stood a low fabric, resembling the castle in construction, though made of materials so light as barely to be bulletproof. As the sides of the scow were a little higher than usual, and the interior of the cabin had no more elevation than was necessary for comfort, this unusual addition had neither a very clumsy nor a very obtrusive appearance. It was, in short, little more than a modern canal boat, though more rudely constructed, of greater breadth than common, and bearing about it the signs of the wilderness in its bark-covered posts and roof. The scow, however, had been put together with some skill, being comparatively light, for its strength, and sufficiently manageable. The cabin was divided into two apartments, one of which served for a parlor and the sleeping room of the father, and the other was appropriated to the uses of the daughter. A very simple arrangement sufficed for the kitchen, which was in one end of the scow and removed from the cabin, standing in the open air—the ark being altogether a summer habitation.

The "and-bush," as Hurry in his ignorance of English termed it, is quite as easily explained. In many parts of the lake and river, where the banks were steep and high, the smaller trees and larger bushes, as has been already mentioned, fairly overhung the stream, their branches not unfrequently dipping into the water. In some instances they grew out in nearly horizontal lines for thirty or forty feet. The water being uniformly deepest near the shores, where the banks were highest and the nearest to a perpendicular, Hutter had found no difficulty in letting the ark drop under one of these covers, where it had been anchored with a view to conceal its position—security requiring some such precautions, in his view of the case. Once beneath the trees and bushes, a few stones fastened to the ends of the branches had caused them to bend sufficiently to dip into the river, and a few severed bushes, properly disposed, did the rest. The reader has seen that this cover was so complete as to deceive two men accustomed to the woods, and who were actually in search of those it concealed; a circumstance that will be easily understood by those who are familiar with the matted and wild luxuriance of a virgin American forest, more especially in a rich soil.

The discovery of the ark produced very different effects on our two adventurers. As soon as the canoe could be got around to the proper opening, Hurry leaped on board, and in a minute was closely engaged in a gay, and a sort of recriminating discourse with Judith, apparently forgetful of the existence of all the rest of the world. Not so with Deerslayer. He entered the ark with a slow, cautious step, examining every arrangement of the cover with curious and scrutinizing eyes. It is true, he cast one admiring glance at Judith, which was extorted by her brilliant and singular beauty, but even this could detain him but a single instant from the indulgence of his interest in Hutter's contrivances. Step by step did he look into the construction of the singular abode, investigate its fastenings and strength, ascertain its means of defense, and make every inquiry that would be likely to occur to one whose thoughts dwelt principally on such expedients. Nor was the cover neglected. Of this he examined the whole minutely, his commendation escaping him more than once in audible comments. Frontier usages admitting of this familiarity, he passed through the rooms, as he had previously done at the castle, and, opening a door, issued into the end of the scow opposite to that where he had left Hurry and Judith. Here he found the other sister, employed on some coarse needlework, seated beneath the leafy canopy of the cover.

As Deerslayer's examination was by this time ended, he dropped the butt of his rifle, and leaning on the barrel with both hands, he turned toward the girl with an interest the singular beauty of her sister had not awakened. He had gathered from Hurry's remarks that Hetty was considered to have less intellect than ordinarily falls to the share of human beings, and his education among Indians had taught him to treat those who were thus afflicted by Providence with more than common tenderness. Nor was there anything in Hetty Hutter's appearance, as so often happens, to weaken the interest her situation excited. An idiot she could not properly be termed, her mind being just enough enfeebled to lose most of those traits that are connected with the more artful qualities and to retain its ingenuousness and love of truth. It had often been remarked of this girl, by the few who had seen her and who possessed sufficient knowledge to discriminate, that her perception of the right seemed almost intuitive, while her aversion to the wrong formed so distinctive a feature of her mind as to surround her with an atmosphere of pure morality; peculiarities that are not unfrequent with persons who are termed feeble-minded; as if God had forbidden the evil spirits to invade a precinct so defenseless, with the benign purpose of extending a direct protection to those who had been left without the usual aids of humanity. Her person, too, was agreeable, having a strong resemblance to that of her sister, of which it was a subdued and humble copy. If it had none of the brilliancy of Judith's, the calm, quiet, almost holy expression of her meek countenance seldom failed to win on the observer; and few noted it long that did not begin to feel a deep and lasting interest in the girl. She had no color, in common, nor was her simple mind apt to present images that caused her cheek to brighten; though she retained a modesty so innate that it almost raised her to the unsuspecting purity of a being superior to human infirmities. Guileless, innocent, and without distrust, equally by nature and from her mode of life, Providence had nevertheless shielded her from harm by a halo of moral light, as it is said "to temper the wind to the shorn lamb."

"You are Hetty Hutter," said Deerslayer, in the way one puts a question unconsciously to himself, assuming a kindness of tone and manner that were singularly adapted to win the confidence of her he addressed. "Hurry Harry has told me of you, and I know you must be the child."

"Yes, I'm Hetty Hutter," returned the girl, in a low, sweet voice, which nature, aided by some education, had preserved from vulgarity of tone and utterance. "I'm Hetty; Judith Hutter's sister, and Thomas Hutter's youngest daughter."

"I know your history, then, for Hurry Harry talks considerable, and he is free of speech, when he can find other people's consarns to dwell on. You pass most of your life on the lake, Hetty."

"Certainly. Mother is dead; father is gone a-trapping, and Judith and I stay at home. What's *your* name?"

"That's a question more easily asked than it is answered, young woman, seeing that I'm so young and yet have borne more names than some of the greatest chiefs in all America."

"But you've *got* a name—you don't throw away one name before you come honestly by another?"

"I hope not, gal—I hope not. My names have come nat'rally and I suppose the one I bear now will be of no great lasting, since the Delawares seldom settle on a man's ra'al title until such time as he has an opportunity of showing his true natur', in the council or on the warpath—which has never behappened me, seeing, firstly, because I'm not born a redskin, and have no right to sit in *their* councilings, and am much too humble to be called on for opinions from the great of my own color; and, secondly, because this is the first war that has befallen in my time, and no inimy has yet inroaded far enough into the Colony to be reached by an arm even longer than mine."

"Tell me your names," added Hetty, looking up at him artlessly, "and maybe I'll tell you your character."

"There is some truth in that, I'll not deny, though it often fails. Men are deceived in other men's characters, and frequently give 'em names they by no means desarve. You can see the truth of this in the Mingo names, which, in their own tongue, signify the same things as the Delaware names —at least, so they tell me, for I know little of that tribe, unless it be by report—and no one can say they are as honest or as upright a nation. I put no great dependence, therefore, on names."

"Tell me *all* your names," repeated the girl earnestly, for her mind was too simple to separate things from professions, and she *did* attach importance to a name; "I want to know what to think of you."

"Well, sartain; I've no objection, and you shall hear them all. In the first place, then, I'm Christian, and white-born, like yourself, and my parents had a name that came down from father to son, as is a part of their gifts. My father was called Bumppo; I was named after him, of course, the given name being Nathaniel, or Natty, as most people saw fit to tarm it."

"Yes, yes—Natty—and Hetty—" interrupted the girl quickly, and looking up from her work again, with a smile; "you are Natty, and I'm Hetty—though you are Bumppo, and I'm Hutter. Bumppo isn't as pretty as Hutter, is it?"

"Why, that's as people fancy. Bumppo has no lofty sound, I admit, and yet men have bumped through the world with it. I did not go by this name, howsever, very long, for the Delawares soon found out, or thought they found out, that I was not given to lying, and they called me, firstly, Straighttongue."

"That's a *good* name," interrupted Hetty earnestly and in a positive manner; "don't tell me there's no virtue in names!"

"I do not say *that*, for perhaps I desarved to be so called, lies being no favorites with me, as they are with some. After a while they found out that I was quick of foot, and then they called me the 'Pigeon,' which, you know, has a swift wing and flies in a direct line."

"*That* was a *pretty* name!" exclaimed Hetty; "pigeons are pretty birds!"

"Most things that God has created are pretty, in their way, my good gal, though they get to be deformed by mankind, so as to change their natur's, as well as their appearance. From carrying messages, and striking blind trails, I got, at last, to following the hunters, when it was thought I was quicker and surer at finding the game than most lads, and then they called me the 'Lap-ear,' as, they said, I partook of the sagacity of a hound."

"That's not so pretty," answered Hetty; "I hope you didn't keep *that* name long."

"Not after I was rich enough to buy a rifle," returned the other, betraying a little pride through his usually quiet and subdued manner; "*then* it was seen I could keep a wigwam in ven'son; in time, I got the name of 'Deerslayer,' which is that I now bear; homely as some will think it, who set more valie on the scalp of a fellow mortal than on the horns of a buck."

"Well, Deerslayer, I'm not one of them," answered Hetty simply. "Judith likes soldiers, and flary coats, and fine feathers, but they're all naught to me. *She* says the officers are great, and gay, and of soft speech, but they make me shudder, for their business is to kill their fellow creatures. I like your calling better, and your last name is a very good one—better than Natty Bumppo."

"This is nat'ral, in one of your turn of mind, Hetty, and much as I should have expected. They tell me your sister is handsome—oncommon, for a mortal—and beauty is apt to seek admiration."

"Did you never see Judith?" demanded the girl, with quick earnestness; "if you never have, go at once and look at her. Even Hurry Harry isn't more pleasant to look at, though *she* is a woman, and *he* is a man."

Deerslayer regarded the girl for a moment with concern. Her pale face had flushed a little, and her eye, usually so mild and serene, brightened as she spoke, in the way to betray the inward impulses.

"Aye, Hurry Harry," he muttered to himself, as he walked through the cabin toward the other end of the boat. "This comes of good looks, if a light tongue has had no consarn in it. It's easy to see which way that poor creatur's feelin's are leanin', whatever may be the case with your Jude's."

But an interruption was put to the gallantry of Hurry, the coquetry of his mistress, the thoughts of Deerslayer, and the gentle feelings of Hetty by the sudden appearance of the canoe of the ark's owner, in the narrow opening among the bushes that served as a sort of moat to his position. It would seem that Hutter, or Floating Tom, as he was familiarly called by all the hunters who knew his habits, recognized the canoe of Hurry, for he expressed no surprise at finding him in the scow. On the contrary, his reception was such as to denote not only gratification but a pleasure, mingled with a little disappointment at his not having made his appearance some days sooner.

"I looked for you last week," he said, in a half-grumbling, half-welcoming manner, "and was disappointed uncommonly that you didn't arrive. There came a runner through to warn all the trappers and hunters that the Colony and the Canadas were again in trouble; I felt lonesome, up in these mountains, with three scalps to see to and only one pair of hands to protect them."

"That's reasonable," returned March, "and 'twas feeling like a parent. No doubt, if I had two such darters as Judith and Hetty, my exper'ence would tell the same story, though, in gin'ral, I am just as well satisfied with having the nearest neighbor fifty miles off as when he is within call."

"Notwithstanding, you didn't choose to come into the wilderness alone, now you knew that the Canada savages are likely to be stirring," returned Hutter, giving a sort of distrustful and, at the same time, inquiring glance at Deerslayer.

"Why should I? They say a bad companion on a journey helps to shorten the path, and this young man I account to be a reasonably good one. This is Deerslayer, old Tom, a noted hunter among the Delawares, and Christian-born, and Christian edicated, too, like you and me. The lad is not parfect, perhaps, but there's worse men in the country that he came from, and it's likely he'll find some that's no better, in this part of the world. Should we have occasion to defend our traps, and the territory, he'll be useful in feeding us all, for he's a reg'lar dealer in ven'son."

"Young man, you are welcome," growled Tom, thrusting a hard, bony hand toward the youth as a pledge of his sincerity. "In such times a whiteface is a friend's, and I count on you as a support. Children sometimes make a stout heart feeble, and these two daughters of mine give me more concern than all my traps, and skins, and rights in the country."

"That's nat'ral!" cried Hurry. "Yes, Deerslayer, you and I don't know it yet by experience, but on the whole I consider that as nat'ral. If we *had* darters, it's more than probable we should have some such feelin's, and I honor the man that owns 'em. As for Judith, old man, I enlist at once as her soldier, and here is Deerslayer to help you to take care of Hetty."

"Many thanks to you, Master March," returned the beauty, in a full, rich voice and with an accuracy of intonation and utterance that she shared in common with her sister, and which showed that she had been better taught than her father's life and appearance would give reason to expect; "many thanks to you; but Judith Hutter has the spirit and the experience that will make her depend more on herself than on good-looking rovers like you. Should there be need to face the savages, do you land with my father, instead of burrowing in the huts, under the show of defending us females, and——"

"Girl—girl," interrupted the father, "quiet that glib tongue of thine and hear the truth. There are savages on the lake shore already, and no man can say how near to us they may be at this very moment, or when we may hear more from them!"

"If this be true, Master Hutter," said Hurry, whose change of countenance denoted how serious he deemed the information, though it did not denote any unmanly alarm, "if this be true, your ark is in a most misfortunate position, for, though the cover did deceive Deerslayer and myself, it would hardly be overlooked by a full-blooded Injin who was out seriously in s'arch of scalps!"

"I think as you do, Hurry, and wish with all my heart we lay anywhere else, at this moment, than in this narrow, crooked stream, which has many advantages to hide in but which is almost fatal to them that are discovered. The savages are near us, moreover, and the difficulty is to get out of the river without being shot down like deer standing at a lick!"

"Are you sartain, Master Hutter, that the redskins you dread are ra'al Canadas?" asked Deerslayer, in a modest but earnest manner. "Have you seen any, and can you describe their paint?"

"I have fallen in with the signs of their being in the neighborhood, but have seen none of 'em. I was downstream a mile or so, looking to my traps, when I struck a fresh trail, crossing the corner of a swamp and moving northward. The man had not passed an hour, and I know'd it for an Indian footstep by the size of the foot and the intoe even before I found a worn moccasin, which its owner had dropped as useless. For that matter, I found the spot where he halted to make a new one, which was only a few yards from the place where he had dropped the old one."

"That doesn't look much like a redskin on the warpath!"

returned the other, shaking his head. "An exper'enced warrior, at least, would have burned, or buried, or sunk in the river such signs of his passage; and your trail is, quite likely, a peaceable trail. But the moccasin may greatly relieve my mind, if you bethought you of bringing it off. I've come here to meet a young chief myself, and his course would be much in the direction you've mentioned. The trail may have been his'n."

"Hurry Harry, you're well acquainted with this young man, I hope, who has meetings with savages in a part of the country where he has never been before?" demanded Hutter, in a tone and in a manner that sufficiently indicated the motive of the question—these rude beings seldom hesitated, on the score of delicacy, to betray their feelings. "Treachery is an Indian virtue, and the whites that live much in their tribes soon catch their ways and practices."

"True—true as the Gospel, old Tom, but not personable to Deerslayer, who's a young man of truth, if he has no other ricommend. I'll answer for his *honesty*, whatever I may do for his valor in battle."

"I should like to know his errand in this strange quarter of the country."

"That is soon told, Master Hutter," said the young man, with the composure of one who kept a clean conscience. "I think, moreover, you've a *right* to ask it. The father of two such darters, who occupies a lake after your fashion, has just the same right to inquire into a stranger's business in his neighborhood as the Colony would have to demand the reason why the Frenchers put more rijiments than common along the lines. No, no, I'll not deny your right to know why a stranger comes into your habitation or country in times as serious as these."

"If such is your way of thinking, friend, let me hear your story without more words."

"'Tis soon told, as I said afore, and shall be honestly told. I'm a young man, and, as yet, have never been on a warpath, but no sooner did the news come among the Delawares that wampum and a hatchet were about to be sent into the tribe than they wished me to go out among the people of my own color and get the exact state of things for 'em. This I did, and after delivering my talk to the chiefs, on my return, I met an officer of the Crown on the Schoharie, who had moneys to send to some of the friendly tribes that live further west. This was thought a good occasion for Chingachgook, a young chief who has never struck a foe, and myself to go on our first warpath in company, and an app'intment was made for us, by an old Delaware, to meet at the rock near the foot of this lake. I'll not deny that Chingachgook has *another* object in view, but it has no consarn with any here and is his secret, and not mine; therefore I'll say no more about it."

" 'Tis something about a young woman," interrupted Judith hastily, then laughing at her own impetuosity and even having the grace to color a little at the manner in which she had betrayed her readiness to impute such a motive. "If 'tis neither war nor a hunt, it must be love."

"Aye, it comes easy for the young and handsome, who hear so much of them feelin's, to suppose that they lie at the bottom of most proceedin's; but on that head I say nothin'. Chingachgook is to meet me at the rock an hour afore sunset tomorrow evening, after which we shall go our way together, molesting none but the King's inimies, who are lawfully our own. Knowing Hurry of old, who once trapped in our hunting grounds, and falling in with him on the Schoharie, just as he was on the p'int of starting for his summer ha'nts, we agreed to journey in company, not so much from fear of the Mingos as from good fellowship and, as he says, to shorten a long road."

"And you think the trail I saw may have been that of your friend, ahead of his time?" said Hutter.

"That's my idee—which may be wrong, but which may be right. If I saw the moccasin, however, I could tell in a minute whether it is made in the Delaware fashion or not."

"Here it is, then," said the quick-witted Judith, who had already gone to the canoe in quest of it. "Tell us what it says: friend or enemy. You look honest, and *I* believe all you say, whatever father may think."

"That's the way with you, Jude, forever finding out friends where I distrust foes," grumbled Tom. "But, speak out, young man, and tell us what you think of the moccasin."

"That's not Delaware-made," returned Deerslayer, examining the worn and rejected covering for the foot with a cautious eye. "I'm too young on a warpath to be positive, but I should say that moccasin has a northern look and comes from beyond the great lakes."

"If such is the case, we ought not to lie here a minute longer than is necessary," said Hutter, glancing through the leaves of his cover as if he already distrusted the presence of an enemy on the opposite shore of the narrow and sinuous stream. "It wants but an hour or so of night, and to move in the dark will be impossible, without making a noise that would betray us. Did you hear the echo of a piece in the mountains half an hour since?"

"Yes, old man, and heard the piece itself," answered Hurry, who now felt the indiscretion of which he had been guilty, "for the last was fired from my own shoulder."

"I feared it came from the French Indians; still, it may put them on the lookout and be a means of discovering us. You did wrong to fire, in wartime, unless there was good occasion."

"So I begin to think myself, Uncle Tom, and yet, if a man can't trust himself to let off his rifle in a wilderness that is a thousand miles square lest some inimy should hear it, where's the use in carrying one?"

Hutter now held a long consultation with his two guests, in which the parties came to a true understanding of their situation. He explained the difficulty that would exist in attempting to get the ark out of so swift and narrow a stream in the dark without making a noise that could not fail to attract Indian ears. Any strollers in their vicinity would keep near the river or the lake, but the former had swampy shores in many places and was both so crooked and so fringed with bushes that it was quite possible to move by daylight without incurring much danger of being seen. More was to be apprehended, perhaps, from the ear than from the eye, especially as long as they were in the short, straitened, and canopied reaches of the stream.

"I never drop down into this cover, which is handy to my traps and safer than the lake from curious eyes, without providing the means of getting out ag'in," continued this singular being, "and that is easier done by a pull than a push. My anchor is now lying above the suction, in the open lake, and here is a line, you see, to haul us up to it. Without some such help, a single pair of hands would make heavy work in forcing a scow like this upstream. I have a sort of a crab, too, that lightens the pull on occasion. Jude can use the oar astern, as well as myself, and, when we fear no enemy, to get out of the river gives us but little trouble."

"What should we gain, Master Hutter, by changing the position?" asked Deerslayer, with a good deal of earnestness. "This is a safe cover, and a stout defense might be made from the inside of this cabin. I've never fou't, unless in the way of tradition, but, it seems to me we might beat off twenty Mingos with palisades like them afore us."

"Aye, aye, you've never fought except in traditions—that's plain enough, young man! Did you ever see as broad a sheet of water as this above us before you came in upon it with Hurry?"

"I can't say that I ever did," Deerslayer answered modestly. "Youth is the time to l'arn, and I'm far from wishing to raise my voice in counsel afore it is justified by exper'ence."

"Well, then, I'll teach you the disadvantage of fighting in this position, and the advantage of taking to the open lake. Here, you may see, the savages will know where to aim every shot, and it would be too much to hope that *some* would not find their way through the crevices of the logs. Now, on the other hand, *we* should have nothing but a forest to aim at. Then we are not safe from fire, here, the bark of this roof being little better than so much kindling wood. The castle, too, might be entered and ransacked, in my absence, and all my possessions overrun and destroyed. Once in the lake, we can be attacked only in boats, or on rafts—shall have a fair chance with the enemy—and can protect the castle with the ark. Do you understand this reasoning, youngster?"

"It sounds well—yes, it has a rational sound, and I'll not gainsay it."

"Well, old Tom," cried Hurry, "if we are to move, the sooner we make a beginning, the sooner we shall know whether we are to have our scalps for nightcaps, or not."

As this proposition was self-evident, no one denied its justice. The three men, after a short preliminary explanation, now set about their preparations to move the ark in earnest. The slight fastenings were quickly loosened, and, by hauling on the line, the heavy craft slowly emerged from the cover. It was no sooner free from the encumbrance of the branches than it swung into the stream, sheering quite close to the western shore, by the force of the current. Not a soul on board heard the rustling of the branches as the cabin came against the bushes and trees of the western bank without a feeling of uneasiness, for no one knew at what moment, or in what place, a secret and murderous enemy might unmask himself. Perhaps the gloomy light that still struggled through the impending canopy of leaves, or found its way through the narrow, ribbonlike opening which seemed to mark, in the air above, the course of the river that flowed beneath, aided in augmenting the appearance of the danger; for it was little more than sufficient to render objects visible without giving up all their outlines at a glance. Although the sun had not absolutely set, it had withdrawn its direct rays from the valley, and the hues of evening were beginning to gather around objects that stood uncovered, rendering those within the shadows of the woods still more somber and gloomy.

No interruption followed the movement, however, and, as the men continued to haul on the line, the ark passed steadily ahead, the great breadth of the scow preventing its sinking into the water and offering much resistance to the progress of the swift element beneath its bottom. Hutter, too, had adopted a precaution, suggested by experience, which might have done credit to a seaman, and which completely prevented any of the annoyances and obstacles which otherwise would have attended the short turns of the river. As the ark descended, heavy stones, attached to the line, were dropped in the center of the stream, forming local anchors, each of which was kept from dragging by the assistance of those above it, until the uppermost of all was reached, which got its "backing" from the anchor, or grapnel, that lay well out in the lake. In consequence of this expedient, the ark floated clear of the encumbrances of the shore, against which it would otherwise have been unavoidably hauled at every turn, producing embarrassments that Hutter, singlehanded, would have found it very difficult to overcome.

Favored by this foresight, and stimulated by the apprehension of discovery, Floating Tom and his two athletic companions hauled the ark ahead with quite as much rapidity as comported with the strength of the line. At every turn in the stream, a stone was raised from the bottom, when the direction of the scow changed to one that pointed toward the stone that lay above. In this manner with the channel buoyed out for him, as a sailor might term it, did Hutter move forward, occasionally urging his friends, in a low and guarded voice, to increase their exertions, and then, as occasions offered, warning them against efforts that might, at particular moments, endanger all by too much zeal. In spite of their long familiarity with the woods, the gloomy character of the shaded river added to the uneasiness that each felt, and when the ark reached the first bend in the Susquehanna, and the eye caught a glimpse of the broader expanse of the lake, all felt a relief that perhaps none would have been willing to confess. Here the last stone was raised from the bottom and the line led directly toward the grapnel, which, as Hutter had explained, was dropped above the suction of the current.

"Thank God!" ejaculated Hurry, "*there* is daylight, and we shall soon have a chance of *seeing* our inimies, if we are to *feel* 'em."

"That is more than you or any man can say," growled Hutter. "There is no spot so likely to harbor a party as the shore around the outlet, and the moment we clear these trees and get into open water will be the most trying time, since it will leave the enemy a cover while it puts us out of one. Judith, girl—do you and Hetty leave the oar to take care of itself and go within the cabin; be mindful not to show your faces at a window, for they who will look at them won't stop to praise their beauty. And now, Hurry, we'll step into this outer room ourselves and haul through the door, where we shall all be safe, from a surprise at least. Friend Deerslayer, as the current is lighter and the line has all the strain on it that is prudent, do you keep moving from window to window, taking care not to let your head be seen, if you set any value on life. No one knows when or where we shall hear from our neighbors."

Deerslayer complied, with a sensation that had nothing in common with fear but which had all the interest of a perfectly novel and a most exciting situation. For the first time in his life he was in the vicinity of enemies, or had good reason to think so—and that, too, under all the thrilling circumstances of Indian surprises and Indian artifices. As he took his stand at a window, the ark was just passing through the narrowest part of the stream, a point where the water first entered what was properly termed the river, and where the trees fairly interlocked overhead, causing the current to rush into an arch of verdure—a feature as appropriate and peculiar to the country, perhaps, as that of Switzerland, where the rivers come rushing literally from chambers of ice.

The ark was in the act of passing the last curve of this leafy entrance as Deerslayer, having examined all that could be seen of the eastern bank of the river, crossed the room to look from the opposite window at the western. His arrival at this aperture was most opportune, for he had no sooner placed his eye at a crack than a sight met his gaze that might well have alarmed a sentinel so young and inexperienced. A sapling overhung the water in nearly half a circle, having first grown toward the light and then pressed down into this form by the weight of the snows—a circumstance of common occurrence in the American woods. On this no less than six Indians had already appeared, others standing ready to follow them, as they left room; each evidently bent on running out on the trunk and dropping on the roof of the ark as it passed beneath. This would have been an exploit of no great difficulty, the inclination of the tree admitting of an easy passage, the adjoining branches offering ample support for the hands, and the fall being too trifling to be apprehended. When Deerslayer first saw this party, it was just unmasking itself by ascending the part of the tree nearest to the earth, or that which was much the most difficult to overcome; and his knowledge of Indian habits told him at once that they were all in their war paint and belonged to a hostile tribe.

"Pull, Hurry," he cried. "Pull for your life, and as you love Judith Hutter! Pull, man, pull!"

This call was made to one that the young man knew had the strength of a giant. It was so earnest and solemn that both Hutter and March felt it was not idly given, and they applied all their force to the line simultaneously and at a most critical moment. The scow redoubled its motion and seemed to glide from under the tree as if conscious of the danger that was impending overhead. Perceiving that they were discovered, the Indians uttered the fearful war whoop and, running forward on the tree, leaped desperately toward their fancied prize. There were six on the tree, and each made the effort. All but their leader fell into the river more or less distant from the ark, as they came, sooner or later,

to the leaping place. The chief, who had taken the dangerous
post in advance, having an earlier opportunity than the
others, struck the scow just within the stern. The fall proving
so much greater than he had anticipated, he was slightly
stunned, and for a moment he remained half bent and unconscious of his situation. At this instant Judith rushed from
the cabin, her beauty heightened by the excitement that
produced the bold act, which flushed her cheek to crimson; throwing all her strength into the effort, she pushed
the intruder over the edge of the scow, headlong into the
river. This decided feat was no sooner accomplished than the
woman resumed her sway; Judith looked over the stern to
ascertain what had become of the man, and the expression of
her eyes softened to concern; next, her cheek crimsoned between shame and surprise at her own temerity; and then she
laughed in her own merry and sweet manner. All this occupied less than a minute, when the arm of Deerslayer
was thrown around her waist and she was dragged swiftly
within the protection of the cabin. This retreat was not
effected too soon. Scarcely were the two in safety when the
forest was filled with yells, and bullets began to patter against
the logs.

The ark being in swift motion all this while, it was beyond
the danger of pursuit by the time these little events had
occurred; the savages, as soon as the first burst of their
anger had subsided, ceased firing, with the consciousness
that they were expending their ammunition in vain. When the
scow came up over her grapnel, Hutter tripped the latter in a
way not to impede the motion; being now beyond the influence of the current, the vessel continued to drift ahead
until fairly in the open lake, though still near enough to the
land to render exposure to a rifle bullet dangerous. Hutter and
March got out two small sweeps, and, covered by the cabin,
they soon urged the ark far enough from the shore to leave
no inducement to their enemies to make any further attempt
to injure them.

CHAPTER V

Why, let the stricken deer go weep,
The hart ungalled play,
For some must watch, while some must sleep,
Thus runs the world away.

SHAKESPEARE

ANOTHER CONSULTATION TOOK place in the forward part of the scow, at which both Judith and Hetty were present. As no danger could now approach unseen, immediate uneasiness had given place to the concern which attended the conviction that enemies were in considerable force on the shores of the lake, and that they might be sure no practicable means of accomplishing their own destruction would be neglected. As a matter of course, Hutter felt these truths the deepest, his daughters having a habitual reliance on his resources, and knowing too little to appreciate fully all the risks they ran, while his male companions were at liberty to quit him at any moment they saw fit. His first remark showed that he had an eye to the latter circumstance, and might have betrayed, to a keen observer, the apprehension that was just then uppermost.

"We've a great advantage over the Iroquois, or the enemy, whoever they are, in being afloat," he said. "There's not a canoe on the lake that I don't know where it's hid, and now yours is here, Hurry, there are but three more on the land, and they're so snug in hollow logs that I don't believe the Indians could find them, let them try ever so long."

"There's no telling that—no one can say that," put in Deerslayer. "A hound is not more sartain on the scent than a redskin when he expects to get anything by it. Let this party see scalps afore 'em, or plunder, or honor, accordin' to their

71

idees of what honor is, and 'twill be a tight log that hides a canoe from their eyes."

"You're right, Deerslayer," cried Harry March; "you're downright Gospel in this matter, and I rej'ice that my bunch of bark is safe enough here, within reach of my arm. I calcilate they'll be at all the rest of the canoes afore tomorrow night, if they are in ra'al 'arnest to smoke you out, old Tom, and we may as well overhaul our paddles for a pull."

Hutter made no immediate reply. He looked about him in silence for quite a minute, examining the sky, the lake, and the belt of forest which enclosed it, as it might be hermetically, like one consulting their signs. Nor did he find any alarming symptoms. The boundless woods were sleeping in the deep repose of nature, the heavens were placid, but still luminous with the light of the retreating sun, while the lake looked more lovely and calm than it had before done that day. It was a scene altogether soothing and of a character to lull the passions into a species of holy calm. How far this effect was produced, however, on the party in the ark must appear in the progress of our narrative.

"Judith," called out the father, when he had taken this close but short survey of the omens, "night is at hand; find our friends food; a long march gives a sharp appetite."

"We're not starving, Master Hutter," March observed, "for we filled up just as we reached the lake, and, for one, I prefar the company of Jude even to her supper. This quiet evening is very agreeable to sit by her side."

"Natur' is natur'," objected Hutter, "and must be fed. Judith, see to the meal, and take your sister to help you. I've a little discourse to hold with you, friends," he continued, as soon as his daughters were out of hearing, "and wish the girls away. You see my situation; I should like to hear your opinions concerning what is best to be done. Three times have I been burnt out already, but that was on the shore; I've considered myself as pretty safe ever since I got the castle built, and the ark afloat. My other accidents, however, happened in peaceable times, being nothing more than such flurries as a man must meet with in the woods; but this matter looks serious, and your ideas would greatly relieve my mind."

"It's my notion, old Tom, that you, and your huts, and your traps, and your whole possessions hereaway are in desperate jippardy," returned the matter-of-fact Hurry, who saw no use in concealment. "Accordin' to my idees of valie, they're altogether not worth half as much today as they was yesterday, nor would I give more for 'em taking the pay in skins."

"Then I've children!" continued the father, making the allusion in a way that it might have puzzled even an indifferent observer to say was intended as a bait, or as an exclamation of paternal concern; "daughters, as you know, Hurry, and good girls, too, I may say, though I *am* their father."

"A man may say anything, Master Hutter, particularly when pressed by time and circumstances. You've darters, as you say, and one of them hasn't her equal on the frontiers for good looks, whatever she may have for good behavior. As for poor Hetty, she's Hetty Hutter, and that's as much as one can say about the poor thing. Give me Jude, if her conduct was only equal to her looks!"

"I see, Harry March, I can only count on you as a fair-weather friend, and I suppose that your companion will be of the same way of thinking," returned the other, with a slight show of pride that was not altogether without dignity. "Well, I must depend on Providence, which will not turn a deaf ear, perhaps, to a father's prayers."

"If you've understood Hurry, here, to mean that he intends to desart you," said Deerslayer, with an earnest simplicity that gave double assurance of its truth, "I *think* you do him injustice, as I *know* you do me, in supposing I would follow him was he so ontruehearted as to leave a family of his own color in such a strait as this. I've come on this lake, Master Hutter, to rende'vous a fri'nd, and I only wish he was here himself, as I make no doubt he will be at sunset tomorrow, when you'd have another rifle to aid you—an inexper'enced one, I'll allow, like my own, but one that has proved true so often ag'in the game, big and little, that I'll answer for its sarvice ag'in mortals."

"May I depend on *you* to stand by me and my daughters, then, Deerslayer?" demanded the old man, with a father's anxiety in his countenance.

"That may you, Floating Tom, if that's your name, and as a brother would stand by a sister—a husband his wife—or a suitor his sweetheart. In this strait you may count on me, through all adversities, and I think Hurry does discredit to his natur' and wishes, if you can't count on him."

"Not he," cried Judith, thrusting her handsome face out of the door; "his nature is hurry, as well as his name, and he'll hurry off as soon as he thinks his fine figure in danger. Neither 'old Tom' nor his 'gals' will depend much on Master March, now they know him, but *you* they will rely on, Deerslayer, for your honest face and honest heart tell us that what you promise you will perform."

This was said as much perhaps in affected scorn for Hurry as in sincerity. Still, it was not said without feeling. The fine face of Judith sufficiently proved the latter circumstance, and if the conscious March fancied that he had never seen in it a stronger display of contempt—a feeling in which the beauty was apt to indulge—than while she was looking at him, it certainly seldom exhibited more of womanly softness and sensibility than when her speaking blue eyes were turned on his traveling companion.

"Leave us, Judith," Hutter ordered sternly, before either of the young men could reply; "leave us, and do not return until you come with the venison and fish. The girl has been spoiled by the flattery of the officers who sometimes find their way up here, Master March, and you'll not think any harm of her silly words."

"You never said truer syllable, old Tom," retorted Hurry, who smarted under Judith's observations. "The devil-tongued youngsters of the garrison have proved her undoing! I scarce know Jude any longer, and shall soon take to admiring her sister, who is getting to be much more to my fancy."

"I'm glad to hear this, Harry, and look upon it as a sign that you're coming to your right senses. Hetty would make a much safer and more rational companion than Jude, and would be much the most likely to listen to your suit, as the officers have, I greatly fear, unsettled her sister's mind."

"No man need a safer wife than Hetty," said Hurry, laughing, "though I'll not answer for her being of the most rational. But no matter; Deerslayer has not misconceived me when he told you I should be found at my post. I'll not quit *you*, Uncle Tom, just now, whatever may be my feelin's and intentions respecting your eldest darter."

Hurry had a respectable reputation for prowess among his associates, and Hutter heard this pledge with a satisfaction that was not concealed. Even the great personal strength of such an aid became of moment, in moving the ark, as well as in the species of hand-to-hand conflicts, that were not unfrequent in the woods, and no commander who was hardpressed could feel more joy at hearing of the arrival of reinforcements than the borderer experienced at being told this important auxiliary was not about to quit him. A minute before, Hutter would have been well content to compromise his danger by entering into a compact to act only on the defensive, but no sooner did he feel some security on this point than the restlessness of man induced him to think of the means of carrying the war into the enemy's country.

"High prices are offered for scalps on both sides," he observed, with a grim smile, as if he felt the force of the inducement at the very time he wished to affect a superiority to earning money by means that the ordinary feelings of those who aspire to be civilized men repudiated, even while they were adopted. "It isn't right, perhaps, to take gold for human blood, and yet, when mankind is busy in killing one another, there can be no great harm in adding a little bit of skin to the plunder. What's your sentiments, Hurry, touching these p'ints?"

"That you've made a vast mistake, old man, in calling savage blood, human blood, at all. I think no more of a redskin's scalp than I do of a pair of wolf's ears, and would just as lief finger money for the one as for the other. With *white* people 'tis different, for they've a nat'ral avarsion to being scalped, whereas your Indian shaves his head in readiness for the knife and leaves a lock of hair by way of braggadocio that one can lay hold of in the bargain."

"That's manly, however, and I felt from the first that we had only to get you on our side, to have you heart and hand," returned Tom, losing all his reserve as he gained a renewed confidence in the disposition of his companion. "Something more may turn up from this inroad of the redskins than they bargained for. Deerslayer, I conclude you're of Hurry's way of thinking and look upon money 'arned in this way as being as likely to pass as money 'arned in trapping or hunting."

"I've no such feelin', nor any wish to harbor it, not I," returned the other. "My gifts are not scalpers' gifts, but such as belong to my religion and color. I'll stand by you, old man, in the ark or in the castle, the canoe or the woods, but I'll not unhumanize my natur' by falling into ways that God intended for another race. If you and Hurry have got any thoughts that lean toward the Colony's gold, go by yourselves in s'arch of it and leave the females to my care. Much as I must differ from you both on all gifts that do not properly belong to a white man, we shall agree that it is the duty of the strong to take care of the weak, especially when the last belong to them that natur' intended man to protect and console by his gentleness and strength."

"Hurry Harry, that is a lesson you might learn and practice on to some advantage," said the sweet but spirited voice of Judith from the cabin, a proof that she had overheard all that had hitherto been said.

"No more of this, Jude," called out the father angrily. "Move further off; we are about to talk of matters unfit for a woman to listen to."

Hutter did not take any steps, however, to ascertain whether he was obeyed or not, but, dropping his voice a little, he pursued the discourse.

"The young man is right, Hurry," he said, "and we can leave the children in his care. Now, my idea is just this— and I think you'll agree that it is rational and correct. There's a large party of these savages on the shore, and though I didn't tell it before the girls, for they're womanish and apt to be troublesome when anything like real work is to be done, there's women among 'em. This I know from moccasin prints, and 'tis likely they are hunters, after all, who have been out so long that they know nothing of the war, or of the bounties."

"In which case, old Tom, why was their first salute an attempt to cut all our throats?"

"We don't know that their design was so bloody. It's natural and easy for an Indian to fall into ambushes and surprises; and no doubt they wished to get on board the ark first and to make their conditions afterward. That a disapp'inted savage should fire at us is in rule, and I think nothing of that. Besides, how often have they burned me out and robbed my traps—aye, and pulled trigger on me in the most peaceful times?"

"The blackguards will do such things, I must allow, and we pay 'em off pretty much in their own c'ine. Women would not be on the warpath, sartainly, and so far there's reason in your idee."

"Nor would a hunter be in his war paint," returned Deerslayer. "I saw the Mingos and *know* that they are out on the trail of mortal men, not for beaver or deer."

"There you have it ag'in, old fellow," said Hurry. "In the way of an eye, now, I'd as soon trust this young man as trust the oldest settler in the Colony; if he says paint, why paint it was."

"Then a hunting party and a war party have met, for women must have been with 'em. It's only a few days since the runner went through with the tidings of the troubles, and it may be that warriors have come out to call in their women and children and to get an early blow."

"That would stand the courts, and is just the truth," cried Hurry. "You've got it now, old Tom, and I should like to hear what you mean to make out of it."

"The bounty," returned the other, looking up at his attentive companion in a cool, sullen manner, in which, however, heartless cupidity and indifference to the means were far more conspicuous than any feelings of animosity or revenge. "If there's women, there's children; and big and little have scalps; the Colony pays for all alike."

"More shame to it that it should do so," interrupted Deerslayer; "more shame to it that it don't understand its gifts and pay greater attention to the will of God."

"Hearken to reason, lad, and don't cry out afore you understand a case," returned the unmoved Hurry. "The savages scalp your fri'nds, the Delawares, or Mohicans, whichever they may be, among the rest; and why shouldn't we scalp? I will own it would be ag'in right for you and me, now, to go into the settlements and bring out scalps, but it's a very different matter as concerns Indians. A man shouldn't take scalps if he isn't ready to be scalped himself on fitting occasions. One good turn desarves another all the world over. That's reason, and I believe it to be good religion."

"Aye, Master Hurry," again interrupted the rich voice of Judith, "is it religion to say that one *bad* turn deserves another?"

"I'll never reason ag'in you, Judy, for you beat me with beauty, if you can't with sense. Here's the Canadas paying their Injins for scalps, and why not we pay——"

"*Our* Indians!" exclaimed the girl, laughing with a sort of melancholy merriment. "Father, Father! Think no more of this, and listen to the advice of Deerslayer, who *has* a conscience—which is more than I can say or think of Harry March."

Hutter now rose, and, entering the cabin, he compelled his daughters to go into the adjoining room, when he secured both the doors and returned. Then he and Hurry pursued the subject, but as the purport of all that was material in this discourse will appear in the narrative, it need not be related here in detail. The reader, however, can have no difficulty in comprehending the morality that presided over their conference. It was, in truth, that which, in some form or other, rules most of the acts of men, and in which the controlling principle is that one wrong will justify another. Their enemies paid for scalps, and this was sufficient to justify the Colony for retaliating. It is true, the French used the same argument, a circumstance, as Hurry took occasion to observe in answer to one of Deerslayer's objections, that proved its truth, as mortal enemies would not be likely to have recourse to the same reason unless it were a good one. But neither Hutter nor Hurry was a man likely to stick at trifles in matters connected with the right of the aborigines, since it is one of the consequences of aggression that it hardens the conscience, as the only means of quieting it. In the most peaceable state of the country, a species of warfare was carried on between the Indians, especially those of the Canadas and men of their caste, and the moment an actual and recognized warfare existed, it was regarded as the means of lawfully revenging a thousand wrongs, real and imaginary. Then, again, there was some truth and a good deal of expediency in the principle of retaliation, of which they both availed themselves in particular to answer the objections of their juster-minded and more scrupulous companion.

"You must fight a man with his own we'pons, Deerslayer," cried Hurry, in his uncouth dialect and in his dogmatic manner of disposing of all moral propositions. "If he's f'erce, you must be f'ercer; if he's stout of heart, you must be stouter. This is the way to get the better of Christian or savage: by keeping up to this trail you'll get soonest to the ind of your journey."

"That's not Moravian doctrine, which teaches that all are to be judged according to their talents or l'arning: the Injin like an Injin, and the white man like a white man. Some of their teachers say that if you're struck on the cheek, it's a duty to turn the other side of the face and take another blow, instead of seeking revenge, whereby I understand——"

"That's enough!" shouted Hurry. "That's all I want to prove a man's doctrine! How long would it take to kick a man through the Colony—in at one ind, and out at the other—on that principle?"

"Don't mistake me, March," returned the young hunter, with dignity. "I don't understand by this any more than that it's *best* to do this, if *possible*. Revenge is an Injin gift, and forgiveness a white man's. That's all. Overlook all you *can* is what's meant, and not *revenge* all you can. As for kicking, Master Hurry," and Deerslayer's sunburned cheek flushed as he continued, "into the Colony, or out of the Colony, that's neither here nor there, seeing no one proposes it, and no one would be likely to put up with it. What I wish to say is that a redskin's scalping don't justify a paleface's scalping."

"Do as you're done by, Deerslayer; that's ever the Christian parson's doctrine."

"No, Hurry, I've asked the Moravians consarning that, and it's altogether different. 'Do as you *would* be done by,' they tell me, is the *true* saying, while men practyse the *false*. They think all the Colonies wrong that offer bounties for scalps, and believe no blessing will follow the measures. Above all things, they forbid revenge."

"*That* for your Moravians!" cried March, snapping his fingers; "they're the next thing to Quakers. If you'd believe all they tell you, not even a 'rat would be skinned, out of marcy. Who ever heard of marcy on a muskrat!"

The disdainful manner of Hurry prevented a reply, and he and the old man resumed the discussion of their plans in a more quiet and confidential manner. This confidence lasted until Judith appeared, bearing the simple but savory supper. March observed, with a little surprise, that she placed the choicest bits before Deerslayer and that in the little nameless attentions it was in her power to bestow she quite obviously manifested a desire to let it be seen that she deemed him the honored guest. Accustomed, however, to the waywardness and coquetry of the beauty, this discovery gave him little concern, and he ate with an appetite that was in no degree disturbed by any moral causes. The easily digested food of the forests offering the fewest possible obstacles to the gratification of this great animal indulgence, Deerslayer, notwithstanding the hearty meal both had taken in the woods, was in no manner behind his companion in doing justice to the viands.

An hour later the scene had greatly changed. The lake was still placid and glassy, but the gloom of the hour had succeeded to the soft twilight of a summer evening, and all within the dark setting of the woods lay in the quiet repose of night. The forests gave up no song, or cry, or even murmur, but looked down from the hills on the lovely basin they encircled, in solemn stillness; the only sound that was audible was the regular dip of the sweeps, at which Hurry and Deerslayer lazily pushed, impelling the ark toward the castle. Hutter had withdrawn to the stern of the scow, in order to steer, but, finding that the young men kept even strokes and held the desired course by their own skill, he permitted the oar to drag in the water, took a seat on the end of the vessel, and lighted his pipe. He had not been thus placed many minutes ere Hetty came stealthily out of the cabin or house, as they usually termed that part of the ark, and placed herself at his feet, on a little bench that she brought with her. As this movement was by no means unusual in his feeble-minded child, the old man paid no other attention to it than to lay his hand kindly on her head, in an affectionate and approving manner, an act of grace that the girl received in meek silence.

After a pause of several minutes, Hetty began to sing. Her voice was low and tremulous, but it was earnest and solemn. The words and the time were of the simplest form, the first being a hymn that she had been taught by her mother, and the last one of those natural melodies that find favor with all classes, in every age, coming from and being addressed to the feelings. Hutter never listened to this simple strain without finding his heart and manner softened—facts that his daughter well knew, and by which she had often profited, through the sort of holy instinct that enlightens the weak of mind, more especially in their aims toward good.

Hetty's low, sweet tones had not been raised many moments when the dip of the oars ceased, and the holy strain arose singly on the breathing silence of the wilderness. As if she gathered courage with the theme, her powers appeared to increase as she proceeded, and though nothing vulgar or noisy mingled in her melody, its strength and melancholy tenderness grew on the ear until the air was filled with this simple homage of a soul that seemed almost spotless. That the men forward were not indifferent to this touching interruption was proved by their inaction; nor did their oars again dip until the last of the sweet sounds had actually died among the remarkable shores, which, at that witching hour, would waft even the lowest modulations of the human voice more than a mile. Hutter was much affected, for rude as he was by early habits, and even ruthless as he had got to be by long exposure to the practices of the wilderness, his nature was of that fearful mixture of good and evil that so generally enters into the moral composition of man.

"You are sad tonight, child," said the father, whose manner and language usually assumed some of the gentleness and elevation of the civilized life he had led in youth when he thus communed with this particular child. "We have just escaped from enemies, and ought rather to rejoice."

"You can never do it, Father!" said Hetty, in a low remonstrating manner, taking his hard, knotty hand into both her own. "You have talked long with Harry March, but neither of you have the heart to do it!"

"This is going beyond your means, foolish child; you must have been naughty enough to have listened, or you could know nothing of our talk."

"Why should you and Hurry kill people—especially women and children?"

"Peace, girl, peace. We are at war and must do to our enemies as our enemies would do to us."

"That's not it, Father! I heard Deerslayer say how it was. You must do to your enemies as you *wish* your enemies would do to you. No man wishes his enemies to kill him."

"We kill our enemies in war, girl, lest they should kill us. One side or the other must begin, and them that begin first are most apt to get the victory. You know nothing about these things, poor Hetty, and had best say nothing."

"*Judith* says it is wrong, Father, and Judith has sense, though I have none."

"Jude understands better than to talk to me of these matters, for she has sense, as you say, and knows I'll not bear it. Which would you prefer, Hetty, to have your own scalp taken and sold to the French, or that we should kill our enemies and keep them from harming us?"

"That's not it, Father! Don't kill them, nor let them kill us. Sell your skins, and get more, if you can, but don't sell human blood."

"Come, come, child, let us talk of matters you understand. Are you glad to see our old friend March back again? You like Hurry and must know that one day he may be your brother—if not something nearer."

"That can't be, Father," returned the girl, after a considerable pause. "Hurry has had one father and one mother, and people never have two."

"So much for your weak mind, Hetty. When Jude marries, her husband's father will be her father, and her husband's sister, her sister. If she should marry Hurry, then he will be your brother."

"Judith will never have Hurry," returned the girl mildly but positively; "Judith don't like Hurry."

"That's more than you can know, Hetty. Harry March is the handsomest, and the strongest, and the boldest young man that ever visits the lake, and, as Jude is the greatest beauty, I don't see why they shouldn't come together. He has as much as promised that he will enter into this job with me, on condition that I'll consent."

Hetty began to move her body back and forth and otherwise to express mental agitation, but she made no answer for more than a minute. Her father, accustomed to her manner and suspecting no immediate cause of concern, continued to smoke with the apparent phlegm which would seem to belong to that particular species of enjoyment.

"Hurry *is* handsome, Father," said Hetty, with a simple emphasis, that she might have hesitated about using had her mind been more alive to the inference of others.

"I told you so, child," muttered old Hutter, without removing the pipe from between his teeth. "He's the likeliest youth in these parts; and Jude is the likeliest young woman I've met with since her poor mother was in her best days."

"Is it wicked to be ugly, Father?"

"One might be guilty of worse things—but you're by no means ugly, though not so comely as Jude."

"Is Judith any happier for being so handsome?"

"She may be, child, and she may not be. But talk of other matters, now, for you hardly understand these, poor Hetty. How do you like our new acquaintance, Deerslayer!"

"He isn't handsome, Father. Hurry is far handsomer than Deerslayer."

"That's true, but they say he is a noted hunter! His fame had reached me before I ever saw him, and I did hope he would prove to be as stout a warrior as he is dexterous with the deer. All men are not alike, howsever, child, and it takes time, as I know by experience, to give a man a true wilderness heart."

"Have I got a wilderness heart, Father—and Hurry, is *his* heart true wilderness?"

"You sometimes ask queer questions, Hetty! Your heart is good, child, and fitter for the settlements than for the woods; while your reason is fitter for the woods than for the settlements."

"Why has Judith more reason than I, Father?"

"Heaven help thee, child—this is more than I can answer. God gives sense, and appearance, and all these things, and He grants them as he seeth fit. Dost thou wish for more sense?"

"Not I. The little I have troubles me, for when I think the hardest, then I feel the unhappiest. I don't believe thinking is good for me, though I do wish I was as handsome as Judith!"

"Why so, poor child? Thy sister's beauty may cause her trouble, as it caused her mother before her. It's no advantage, Hetty, to be so marked for anything as to become an object of envy, or to be sought after more than others."

"Mother was good, if she *was* handsome," returned the girl, the tears starting to her eyes, as usually happened when she adverted to her deceased parent.

Old Hutter, if not equally affected, was moody and silent at this allusion to his wife. He continued smoking, without appearing disposed to make any answer, until his simple-minded daughter repeated her remark, in a way to show that she felt uneasiness lest he might be inclined to deny her assertion. Then he knocked the ashes out of his pipe, and, laying his hand in a sort of rough kindness on the girl's head, he made a reply.

"Thy mother was too good for this world," he said, "though others might not think so. Her good looks did not befriend her, and you have no occasion to mourn that you are not as much like her as your sister. Think less of beauty, child, and more of your duty, and you'll be as happy on this lake as you could be in the King's palace."

"I know it, Father, but Hurry says beauty is everything in a young woman."

Hutter made an ejaculation expressive of dissatisfaction and went forward, passing through the house, in order to do so. Hetty's simple betrayal of her weakness in behalf of March gave him uneasiness on a subject concerning which he had never felt before, and he determined to come to an explanation at once with his visitor; for directness of speech and decision in conduct were two of the best qualities of this rude being, in whom the seeds of a better education seemed to be constantly struggling upward, to be choked by the fruits of a life in which his hard struggles for subsistence and security had steeled his feelings and indurated his nature. When he reached the forward end of the scow, he manifested an intention to relieve Deerslayer at the oar, directing the latter to take his own place aft. By these changes, the old man and Hurry were again left alone, while the young hunter was transferred to the other end of the ark.

Hetty had disappeared when Deerslayer reached his new post, and for some little time he directed the course of the slow-moving craft by himself. It was not long, however, before Judith came out of the cabin, as if disposed to do the honors of the place to a stranger engaged in the service of her family. The starlight was sufficient to permit objects to be plainly distinguished when near at hand, and the bright eyes of the girl had an expression of kindness in them, when they met those of the youth, that the latter was easily enabled to discover. Her rich hair shaded her spirited and yet soft countenance, even at that hour rendering it the more beautiful—as the rose is loveliest when reposing amid the shadows and contrasts of its native foliage. Little ceremony is used in the intercourse of the woods, and Judith had acquired a readiness of address by the admiration that she so generally excited which, if it did not amount to forward-

ness, certainly in no degree lent to her charms the aid of
that retiring modesty on which poets love to dwell.

"I thought I should have killed myself with laughing,
Deerslayer," the beauty abruptly but coquettishly commenced, "when I saw that Indian dive into the river! He was
a good-looking savage, too"—the girl always dwelt on personal beauty as a sort of merit—"and yet one couldn't stop
to consider whether his paint would stand water!"

"And I thought they would have killed you with their
we'pons, Judith," returned Deerslayer. "It was an awful
risk for a female to run in the face of a dozen Mingos!"

"Did *that* make *you* come out of the cabin, in spite of their
rifles, too?" asked the girl, with more real interest than she
would have cared to betray, though with an indifference of
manner that was the result of a good deal of practice united
to native readiness.

"Men ar'n't apt to see females in danger and not come to
their assistance. Even a Mingo knows that."

This sentiment was uttered with as much simplicity of
manner as of feeling, and Judith rewarded it with a smile so
sweet that even Deerslayer, who had imbibed a prejudice
against the girl in consequence of Hurry's suspicions of her
levity, felt its charm, notwithstanding half its winning influence was lost in the feeble light. It at once created a sort of
confidence between them, and the discourse was continued on
the part of the hunter without the lively consciousness of the
character of this coquette of the wilderness with which it
had certainly commenced.

"You are a man of deeds and not of words, I see plainly,
Deerslayer," continued the beauty, taking her seat near the
spot where the other stood, "and I foresee we shall be very
good friends. Hurry Harry has a tongue, and, giant as he is,
he talks more than he performs."

"March is your fri'nd, Judith, and fri'nds should be tender of each other, when apart."

"We all know what Hurry's friendship comes to! Let him
have his own way in everything and he's the best fellow in
the Colony, but 'head him off,' as you say of the deer, and he
is master of everything near him but himself. Hurry is no
favorite of mine, Deerslayer, and I daresay, if the truth was
known, and his conversation about me repeated, it would be
found that he thinks no better of me than I own I do of him."

The latter part of this speech was not uttered without uneasiness. Had the girl's companion been more sophisticated, he might have observed the averted face, the manner in which the pretty little foot was agitated, and other signs that, for some unexplained reason, the opinions of March were not quite as much matter of indifference to her as she thought fit to pretend. Whether this was no more than the ordinary working of female vanity, feeling keenly even when it affected not to feel at all, or whether it proceeded from that deeply seated consciousness of right and wrong which God himself has implanted in our breasts that we may know good from evil, will be made more apparent to the reader as we proceed in the tale. Deerslayer felt embarrassed. He well remembered the cruel imputations left by March's distrust, and while he did not wish to injure his associate's suit by exciting resentment against him, his tongue was one that literally knew no guile. To answer without saying more or less than he wished was consequently a delicate duty.

"March has his say of all things in natur', whether of fri'nd or foe," slowly and cautiously rejoined the hunter. "He's one of them that speak as they feel while the tongue's a-going, and that's sometimes different from what they'd speak if they took time to consider. Give me a Delaware, Judith, for one that reflects and ruminates on his idees! Inmity has made 'em thoughtful, and a loose tongue is no riccomend at their council fires."

"I daresay March's tongue goes free enough when it gets on the subject of Judith Hutter and her sister," said the girl, rousing herself as if in careless disdain. "Young women's good names are a pleasant matter of discourse with some that wouldn't dare to be so open-mouthed if there was a brother in the way. Master March may find it pleasant to traduce us, but sooner or later he'll repent!"

"Nay, Judith, this is taking the matter up too much in 'arnest. Hurry has never whispered a syllable ag'in the good name of Hetty, to begin with——"

"I see how it is—I see how it is," impetuously interrupted Judith. "*I* am the one he sees fit to scorch with his withering tongue!—Hetty, indeed!—Poor Hetty!" she continued, her voice sinking into low husky tones that seemed nearly to stifle her in the utterance. "*She* is beyond and above his slanderous malice! Poor Hetty! If God has created her feeble-minded, the weakness lies altogether on the side of errors of which she seems to know nothing. The earth never held a purer being than Hetty Hutter, Deerslayer."

"I can believe it—yes, I can believe *that*, Judith, and I hope 'arnestly that the same can be said of her handsome sister."

There was a soothing sincerity in the voice of Deerslayer which touched the girl's feelings; nor did the allusion to her beauty lessen the effect with one who knew only too well the power of her personal charms. Nevertheless, the still, small voice of conscience was not hushed, and it prompted the answer which she made after giving herself time to reflect.

"I daresay Hurry had some of his vile hints about the people of the garrisons," she added. "He knows they are gentlemen and can never forgive anyone for being what he feels he can never become himself."

"Not in the sense of a King's officer, Judith, sartainly, for March has no turn thataway, but in the sense of reality, why may not a beaver hunter be as respectable as a governor? Since you speak of it yourself, I'll not deny that he *did* complain of one as humble as you being as much in the company of scarlet coats and silken sashes. But 'twas jealousy that brought it out of him, and I do think that he mourned over his own thoughts as a mother would have mourned over her child."

Perhaps Deerslayer was not aware of the full meaning that his earnest language conveyed. It is certain that he did not see the color that crimsoned the whole of Judith's fine face, nor detect the uncontrollable distress that immediately after changed its hue to a deadly paleness. A minute or two elapsed in profound stillness, the splash of the water seeming to occupy all the avenues of sound, and then Judith arose and grasped the hand of the hunter, almost convulsively, with one of her own.

"Deerslayer," she said hurriedly, "I'm glad the ice is broken between us. They say that sudden friendships lead to long enmities, but I do not believe it will turn out so with us. I know not how it is—but you are the first man I ever met who did not seem to wish to flatter—to wish my ruin—to be an enemy in disguise—never mind; say nothing to Hurry, and another time we'll talk together again."

As the girl released her grasp, she vanished in the house,

leaving the astonished young man standing at the steering oar, as motionless as one of the pines on the hills. So abstracted, indeed, had his thoughts become that he was hailed by Hutter to keep the scow's head in the right direction before he remembered his actual situation.

CHAPTER VI

So spake the apostate Angel, though in pain,
Vaunting aloud, but racked with deep despair!

MILTON

SHORTLY AFTER THE disappearance of Judith, a light southerly air arose, and Hutter set a large square sail, which had
once been the flying topsail of an Albany sloop, but which,
having become threadbare in catching the breezes of Tappan,
had been condemned and sold. He had a light tough spar of
tamarack that he could raise on occasion, and with a little
contrivance his duck was spread to the wind in a sufficiently
professional manner. The effect on the ark was such as to supersede the necessity of rowing, and in about two hours the
castle was seen, in the darkness, rising out of the water, at the
distance of a hundred yards. The sail was then lowered,
and by slow degrees the scow drifted up to the building, and
was secured.

No one had visited the house since Hurry and his companion left it. The place was found in the quiet of midnight, a
sort of type of the solitude of a wilderness. As an enemy
was known to be near, Hutter directed his daughters to abstain from the use of lights, luxuries in which they seldom
indulged during the warm months, lest they might prove
beacons to direct their foes where they might be found.

"In open daylight I shouldn't fear a host of savages behind these stout logs, and they without any cover to skulk
into," added Hutter, when he had explained to his guests the
reasons why he forbade the use of lights; "for I've three or
four trusty weapons always loaded, and Killdeer, in particular, is a piece that never misses. But it's a different thing at
night. A canoe might get upon us unseen in the dark, and the

savages have so many cunning ways of attacking that I look upon it as bad enough to deal with 'em under a bright sun. I built this dwelling in order to have 'em at arm's length, in case we should ever get to blows again. Some people think it's too open and exposed, but I'm for anchoring out here, clear of underbrush and thickets, as the surest means of making a safe berth."

"You was once a sailor, they tell me, old Tom?" said Hurry, in his abrupt manner, struck by one or two expressions that the other had just used, "and some people believe you could give us strange accounts of inimies and shipwrecks, if you'd a mind to come out with all you know?"

"There are people in this world, Hurry," returned the other evasively, "who live on other men's thoughts, and some such often find their way into the woods. What I've been, or what I've seen in youth, is of less matter now than what the savages are. It's of more account to find out what will happen in the next twenty-four hours than to talk over what happened twenty-four years since."

"That's judgment, Deerslayer; yes, that's sound judgment. Here's Judith and Hetty to take care of, to say nothing of our own topknots; for my part, I can sleep as well in the dark as I could under a noonday sun. To me it's no great matter whether there is light or not to see to shut my eyes by."

As Deerslayer seldom thought it necessary to answer his companion's peculiar vein of humor, and Hutter was evidently indisposed to dwell longer on the subject, its discussion ceased with this remark. The latter had something more on his mind, however, than recollections. His daughters had no sooner left them, with an expressed intention of going to bed, than he invited his two companions to follow him again into the scow. Here the old man opened his project, keeping back the portion that he had reserved for execution by Hurry and himself.

"The great object for people posted like ourselves is to command the water," he commenced. "So long as there is no other craft on the lake, a bark canoe is as good as a man-of-war, since the castle will not be easily taken by swimming. Now, there are but five canoes remaining in these parts, two of which are mine, and one is Hurry's. These three we have with us here; one being fastened in the canoe-dock beneath the house, and the other two being alongside the scow. The other canoes are housed on the shore, in hollow logs, and the savages, who are such venomous enemies, will leave no likely place unexamined in the morning, if they're serious in s'arch of bounties——"

"Now, friend Hutter," interrupted Hurry, "the Indian don't live that can find a canoe that is suitably wintered. I've done something at this business before now, and Deerslayer here knows that I am one that can hide a craft in such a way that I can't find it myself."

"Very true, Hurry," put in the person to whom the appeal had been made, "but you overlook the sarcumstance that if you couldn't see the trail of the man who did the job, *I* *could*. I'm of Master Hutter's mind, that it's far wiser to mistrust a savage's ingenuity than to build any great expectations on his want of eyesight. If these two canoes can be got off to the castle, therefore, the sooner it's done the better."

"Will you be of the party that's to do it?" demanded Hutter, in a way to show that the proposal both surprised and pleased him.

"Sartain. I'm ready to enlist in any enterprise that's not ag'in a white man's lawful gifts. Natur' orders us to defend our lives, and the lives of others, too, when there's occasion and opportunity. I'll follow you, Floating Tom, into the Mingo camp on such an a'r'nd, and will strive to do my duty, should we come to blows; though, never having been tried in battle, I don't like to promise more than I may be able to perform. We all know our wishes, but none know their might till put to the proof."

"That's modest and suitable, lad," exclaimed Hurry. "You've never yet heard the crack of an angry rifle; and let me tell you, 'tis as different from the persuasion of one of your venison speeches as the laugh of Judith Hutter, in her best humor, is from the scolding of a Dutch housekeeper on the Mohawk. I don't expect you'll prove much of a warrior, Deerslayer, though your equal with the bucks and the does don't exist in all these parts. As for the ra'al sarvice, however, you'll turn out rather rearward, according to my consait."

"We'll see, Hurry, we'll see," returned the other meekly, so far as human eye could discover not at all disturbed by these expressed doubts concerning his conduct on a point on which men are sensitive, precisely in the degree that they feel the consciousness of demerit. "Having never been tried, I'll wait to know before I form any opinion myself, then there'll be sartainty instead of bragging. I've heard of them that was valiant afore the fight who did little in it, and of them that waited to know their own tempers, and found that they weren't as bad as some expected, when put to the proof."

"At any rate, we know you can use a paddle, young man," said Hutter, "and that's all we shall ask of you tonight. Let us waste no more time, but get into the canoe and *do* in place of talking."

As Hutter led the way in the execution of his project, the boat was soon ready, with Hurry and Deerslayer at the paddles. Before the old man embarked himself, however, he held a conference of several minutes with Judith, entering the house for that purpose; then, returning, he took his place in the canoe, which left the side of the ark at the next instant.

Had there been a temple reared to God in that solitary wilderness, its clock would have told the hour of midnight as the party set forth on their expedition. The darkness had increased, though the night was still clear, and the light of the stars sufficed for all the purposes of the adventurers. Hutter alone knew the places where the canoes were hid, and he directed the course, while his two athletic companions raised and dipped their paddles with proper caution, lest the sound should be carried to the ears of their enemies across that sheet of placid water, in the stillness of deep night. But the bark was too light to require any extraordinary efforts, and skill supplying the place of strength, in about half an hour they were approaching the shore at a point near a league from the castle.

"Lay on your paddles, men," said Hutter, in a low voice, "and let us look about us for a moment. We must now be all eyes and ears, for these vermin have noses like bloodhounds."

The shores of the lake were examined closely, in order to discover any glimmering of light that might have been left in a camp; the men strained their eyes, in the obscurity, to see if some thread of smoke was not still stealing along the mountainside as it arose from the dying embers of a fire. Nothing unusual could be traced, and as the position was at some distance from the outlet, or the spot where the savages had been met, it was thought safe to land. The paddles were plied again, and the bows of the canoe ground upon the gravelly beach with a gentle motion and a sound barely audible. Hutter and Hurry immediately landed, the former carrying his own and his friend's rifle, leaving Deerslayer in charge of the canoe. The hollow log lay a little distance up the side of the mountain, and the old man led the way toward it, using so much caution as to stop at every third or fourth step to listen if any tread betrayed the presence of a foe. The same deathlike stillness, however, reigned on the midnight scene, and the desired place was reached without an occurrence to induce alarm.

"This is it," whispered Hutter, laying a foot on the trunk of a fallen linden. "Hand me the paddles first, and draw the boat out with care, for the wretches may have left it for a bait, after all."

"Keep my rifle handy, butt toward me, old fellow," answered March. "If they attack me loaded, I shall want to unload the piece at 'em, at least. And feel if the pan is full."

"All's right," muttered the other. "Move slow when you get your load, and let me lead the way."

The canoe was drawn out of the log with the utmost care, raised by Hurry to his shoulder, and the two began to return to the shore, moving but a step at a time, lest they should tumble down the steep declivity. The distance was not great, but the descent was extremely difficult; toward the end of their little journey, Deerslayer was obliged to land and meet them, in order to aid in lifting the canoe through the bushes. With his assistance the task was successfully accomplished, and the light craft soon floated by the side of the other canoe. This was no sooner done than all three turned anxiously toward the forest and the mountain, expecting an enemy to break out of the one, or to come rushing down the other. Still the silence was unbroken, and they all embarked with the caution that had been used in coming ashore.

Hutter now steered broad off toward the center of the lake. Having got a sufficient distance from the shore, he cast his prize loose, knowing that it would drift slowly up the lake before the light, southerly air and intending to find it on his return. Thus relieved of his tow, the old man held his way down the lake, steering toward the very point where Hurry had made his fruitless attempt on the life of the deer. As the distance from this point to the outlet was less than a mile, it was like entering an enemy's country, and redoubled caution became necessary. They reached the extremity of the point, however, and landed in safety on the little gravelly beach already mentioned. Unlike the last place at which they had gone ashore, here was no acclivity to ascend, the mountains looming up in the darkness quite a quarter of a mile further west, leaving a margin of level ground between them and the strand. The point itself, though long and covered with tall trees, was nearly flat and, for some distance, only a few yards in width. Hutter and Hurry landed, as before, leaving their companion in charge of the boat.

In this instance, the dead tree that contained the canoe of which they had come in quest lay about halfway between the extremity of the narrow slip of land and the place where it joined the main shore; knowing that there was water so near him on his left, the old man led the way along the eastern side of the belt with some confidence, walking boldly, though still with caution. He had landed at the point expressly to get a glimpse into the bay, to make certain that the coast was clear; otherwise, he would have come ashore directly abreast of the hollow tree. There was no difficulty in finding the latter, from which the canoe was drawn as before, and, instead of carrying it down to the place where Deerslayer lay, it was launched at the nearest favorable spot. As soon as it was in the water, Hurry entered it and paddled round to the point, whither Hutter also proceeded, following the beach. As the three men had now in their possession all the boats on the lake, their confidence was greatly increased, and there was no longer the same feverish desire to quit the shore, or the same necessity for extreme caution. Their position on the extremity of the long, narrow bit of land added to the feeling of security, as it permitted an enemy to approach in only one direction, that in their front, and under circumstances that would render discovery, with their habitual vigilance, almost certain. The three now landed together and stood grouped in consultation on the gravelly point.

"We've fairly tree'd the scamps," said Hurry, chuckling at their success; "if they wish to visit the castle, let 'em wade or swim! Old Tom, that idee of your'n, in burrowing out in the lake, was high proof and carries a fine bead. There be men who would think the land safer than the water, but after all, reason shows it isn't, the beaver, and rats, and other l'arned creatur's taking to the last when hard-pressed. I call our position now entrenched, and set the Canadas at defiance."

"Let us paddle along this south shore," said Hutter, "and see if there's no sign of an encampment—but first, let me have a better look into the bay, for no one has been far enough around the inner shore of the point to make sure of that quarter yet."

As Hutter ceased speaking, all three moved in the direction he had named. Scarce had they fairly opened the bottom of the bay when a general start proved that their eyes had lighted on a common object at the same instant. It was no more than a dying brand, giving out its flickering and failing light, but at that hour, and in that place, it was at once as conspicuous as "a good deed in a naughty world." There was not a shadow of doubt that this fire had been kindled at an encampment of the Indians. The situation, sheltered from observation on all sides but one, and even on that except for a very short distance, proved that more care had been taken to conceal the spot than would be used for ordinary purposes, and Hutter, who knew that a spring was near at hand, as well as one of the best fishing stations on the lake, immediately inferred that this encampment contained the women and children of the party.

"That's not a warrior's encampment," he growled to Hurry; "and there's bounty enough sleeping around that fire to make a heavy division of head-money. Send the lad to the canoes, for there'll come no good of him in such an onset, and let us take the matter in hand at once, like men."

"There's judgment in your notion, old Tom, and I like it to the backbone. Deerslayer, do you get into the canoe, lad, and paddle off into the lake with the spare one, and set it adrift, as we did with the other; after which you can float along shore, as near as you can get to the head of the bay, keeping outside the point, howsever, and outside the rushes, too. You can hear us when we want you; and if there's any delay, I'll call like a loon—yes, that'll do it—the call of a loon shall be the signal. If you hear rifles, and feel like sojering, why, you may close in and see if you can make the same hand with the savages that you do with the deer."

"If my wishes could be followed, this matter would not be undertaken, Hurry———"

"Quite true—nobody denies it, boy; but your wishes *can't* be followed; that inds the matter. So just canoe yourself off into the middle of the lake, and by the time you get back there'll be movements in that camp!"

The young man set about complying with great reluctance and a heavy heart. He knew the prejudices of the frontiersmen too well, however, to attempt a remonstrance. The latter, indeed, under the circumstances might prove dangerous, as it would certainly prove useless. He paddled the canoe, therefore, silently, and with the former caution, to a spot near the center of the placid sheet of water, and set the boat just recovered adrift, to float toward the castle before the light, southerly air. This expedient had been adopted, in both cases, under the certainty that the drift could not carry the light barks more than a league or two before the return of light, when they might easily be overtaken. In order to prevent any wandering savage from using them, by swimming off and getting possession, a possible but scarcely a probable event, all the paddles were retained.

No sooner had he set the recovered canoe adrift than Deerslayer turned the bows of his own toward the point on the shore that had been indicated by Hurry. So light was the movement of the little craft, and so steady the sweep of its master's arm, that ten minutes had not elapsed ere it was again approaching the land, having, in that brief time, passed over fully half a mile of distance. As soon as Deerslayer's eye caught a glimpse of the rushes, of which there were many growing in the water a hundred feet from the shore, he arrested the motion of the canoe and anchored his boat by holding fast to the delicate but tenacious stem of one of the drooping plants. Here he remained, awaiting with an intensity of suspense that can be easily imagined the result of the hazardous enterprise.

It would be difficult to convey to the minds of those who have never witnessed it the sublimity that characterizes the silence of a solitude as deep as that which now reigned over the Glimmerglass. In the present instance, this sublimity was increased by the gloom of night, which threw its shadowy and fantastic forms around the lake, the forest, and the hills. It is not easy, indeed, to conceive of any place more favorable to heighten these natural impressions than that Deerslayer now occupied. The size of the lake brought all within the reach of human senses, while it displayed so much of the imposing scene at a single view, giving up, as it might be, at a glance, a sufficiency to produce the deepest impressions. As has been said, this was the first lake Deerslayer had ever seen. Hitherto, his experience had been limited to the courses of rivers and smaller streams, and never before had he seen so much of that wilderness which he so well loved spread before his gaze. Accustomed to the forest, however, his mind was capable of portraying all its hidden mysteries, as he looked upon its leafy surface. This was also the first time he had been on a trail where human lives depended on the issue. His ears had often drunk in the traditions of frontier warfare, but he had never yet been confronted with an enemy.

The reader will readily understand, therefore, how intense must have been the expectation of the young man as he sat in his solitary canoe, endeavoring to catch the smallest sound that might denote the course of things on shore. His training had been perfect, so far as theory could go, and his self-possession, notwithstanding the high excitement that was the fruit of novelty, would have done credit to a veteran. The visible evidences of the existence of the camp, or of the fire, could not be detected from the spot where the canoe lay, and he was compelled to depend on the sense of hearing alone. He did not feel impatient, for the lessons he had heard taught him the virtue of patience and, most of all, inculcated the necessity of wariness in conducting any covert assault on the Indians. Once he thought he heard the cracking of a dried twig, but expectation was so intense it might mislead him. In this manner minute after minute passed, until the whole time since he left his companions was extended to quite an hour. Deerslayer knew not whether to rejoice in, or to mourn over, this cautious delay, for if it augured security to his associates, it foretold destruction to the feeble and innocent.

It might have been an hour and a half after his companions and he had parted when Deerslayer was aroused by a sound that filled him equally with concern and surprise. The quavering call of a loon arose from the opposite side of the lake, evidently at no great distance from its outlet. There was no mistaking the note of this bird, which is so familiar to all who know the sounds of the American lakes. Shrill, tremulous, loud, and sufficiently prolonged, it seems the very cry of warning. It is often raised, also, at night—an exception to the habits of most of the other feathered inmates of the wilderness—a circumstance which had induced Hurry to select it as his own signal. There had been sufficient time, certainly, for the two adventurers to make their way by land from the point where they had been left to that whence the call had come, but it was not probable that they would adopt such a course. Had the camp been deserted they would have summoned Deerslayer to the shore, and, did it prove to be peopled, there could be no sufficient motive for circling it, in order to re-embark at so great a distance. Should he obey the signal and be drawn away from the landing, the lives of those who depended on him might be the forfeit—and should he neglect the call, on the supposition that it had been really made, the consequences might be equally disastrous, though from a different cause. In this indecision he waited, trusting that the call, whether feigned or natural, would be speedily renewed. Nor was he mistaken. A very few minutes elapsed before the same shrill warning cry was repeated, and from the same part of the lake. This time, being on the alert, his senses were not deceived. Although he had often heard admirable imitations of this bird, and was no mean adept himself in raising its notes, he felt satisfied that Hurry, to whose efforts in that way he had attended, could never so completely and closely follow nature. He determined, therefore, to disregard that cry and to wait for one less perfect and nearer at hand.

Deerslayer had hardly come to this determination when the profound stillness of night and solitude was broken by a cry so startling as to drive all recollection of the more melancholy call of the loon from the listener's mind. It was a shriek of agony that came either from one of the female sex, or from a boy so young as not yet to have attained a manly voice. This appeal could not be mistaken. Heart-rending terror—if not writhing agony—was in the sounds, and the anguish that had awakened them was as sudden as it was fearful. The young man released his hold of the rush and dashed his paddle into the water; to do, he knew not what—to steer, he knew not whither. A very few moments, however, removed his indecision. The breaking of branches, the cracking of dried sticks, and the fall of feet were distinctly audible; the sounds appeared to approach the water, though in a direction that led diagonally toward the shore, and a little farther north than the spot that Deerslayer had been ordered to keep near. Following this clue, the young man urged the canoe ahead, paying but little attention to the manner in which he might betray its presence. He had reached a part of the shore where its immediate bank was tolerably high and quite steep. Men were evidently threshing through the bushes and trees on the summit of this bank, following the line of the shore, as if those who fled sought a favorable place for descending. Just at this instant five or six rifles flashed, and the opposite hills gave back, as usual, the sharp reports in prolonged rolling echoes. One or two shrieks, like those which escape the bravest when suddenly overcome by unexpected anguish and alarm, followed, and then the threshing among the bushes was renewed, in a way to show that man was grappling with man.

"Slippery devil!" shouted Hurry with the fury of disappointment—"his skin's greased! I shan't grapple! Take *that* for your cunning!"

The words were followed by the fall of some heavy object among the smaller trees that fringed the bank, appearing to Deerslayer as if his gigantic associate had hurled an enemy from him in this unceremonious manner. Again the flight and pursuit were renewed, and then the young man saw a human form break down the hill and rush several yards into the water. At this critical moment the canoe was just near enough to the spot to allow this movement, which was accompanied by no little noise, to be seen; and feeling that there he must take in his companion, if anywhere, Deerslayer urged the canoe forward to the rescue. His paddle had not been raised twice when the voice of Hurry was heard filling the air with imprecations, and he rolled on the narrow beach literally loaded down with enemies. While prostrate, and almost smothered with his foes, the athletic frontiersman gave his loon call in a manner that would have excited laughter under circumstances less terrific. The figure in the water seemed suddenly to repent his own flight and rushed to the shore to aid his companion, but was met and immediately overpowered by half a dozen fresh pursuers, who just then came leaping down the bank.

"Let up, you painted riptyles—let up!" cried Hurry, too hard-pressed to be particular about the terms he used. "Isn't it enough that I am withed like a saw log that ye must choke, too!"

This speech satisfied Deerslayer that his friends were prisoners and that to land would be to share their fate. He was already within a hundred feet of the shore when a few timely strokes of the paddle not only arrested his advance but forced him off to six or eight times that distance from his enemies. Luckily for him, all of the Indians had dropped their rifles in the pursuit, or this retreat might not have been effected with impunity, though no one had noted the canoe in the first confusion of the melee.

"Keep off the land, lad," called out Hutter. "The girls depend only on you, now: you will want all your caution to escape these savages. Keep off, and God prosper you, as you aid my children!"

There was little sympathy in general between Hutter and the young man, but the bodily and mental anguish with which this appeal was made served at the moment to conceal from the latter the former's faults. He saw only the father in his sufferings, and he resolved at once to give a pledge of fidelity to his interests and to be faithful to his word.

"Put your heart at ease, Master Hutter," he called out; "the gals shall be looked to, as well as the castle. The inimy has got the shore, 'tis no use to deny, but he hasn't got the water. Providence has the charge of all, and no one can say what will come of it, but, if good will can sarve you and your'n, depend on that much. My exper'ence is small, but my will is good."

"Aye—aye, Deerslayer," returned Hurry, in his stentorian voice, which was losing some of its heartiness, notwithstanding. "Aye, aye, Deerslayer, you *mean* well enough, but what can you *do*? You're no great matter in the best of times, and such a person is not likely to turn out a miracle in the worst. If there's one savage on this lake shore there's forty, and that's an army you ar'n't the man to overcome. The best way, in my judgment, will be to make a straight course to the castle; get the gals into the canoe, with a few eatables; then strike off for the corner of the lake where we came in and take the best trail for the Mohawk. These devils won't know where to look for you for some hours, and if they did and went off hot in the pursuit, they must turn either the foot or the head of the lake to get at you. That's my judgment in the matter, and if old Tom here wishes to make his last will and testament in a manner favorable to his darters, he'll say the same."

" 'Twill never do, young man," rejoined Hutter. "The enemy has scouts out at this moment, looking for canoes, and you'll be seen and taken. Trust to the castle, and above all things, keep clear of the land. Hold out a week, and parties from the garrisons will drive the savages off."

" 'Twon't be four-and-twenty hours, old fellow, afore these foxes will be rafting off to storm your castle," interrupted Hurry, with more of the heat of argument than might be expected from a man who was bound and a captive and above whom nothing could be called free but his opinions and his tongue. "Your advice has a stout sound, but it will have a fatal tarmination. If you or I was in the house, we might hold out a few days, but remember that this lad has never seen an inimy afore tonight, and is what you yourself called settlement-conscienced; though, for my part, I think the consciences in the settlements pretty much the same as they are out here in the woods. These savages are making signs, Deerslayer, for me to encourage you to come ashore with the canoe, but that I'll never do, as it's ag'in reason and natur'. As for old Tom and myself, whether they'll scalp us tonight, keep us for the torture by fire, or carry us to Canada is more than anyone knows but the devil that advises them how to act. I've such a big and bushy head that it's quite likely they'll indivor to get two scalps off it, for the bounty is a tempting thing, or old Tom and I wouldn't be in this scrape. Aye—there they go with their signs ag'in, but if I advise you to land, may they eat me as well as roast me. No, no, Deerslayer—do you keep off where you are, and after daylight, on no account come within two hundred yards——"

This injunction of Hurry's was stopped by a hand being rudely slapped against his mouth, the certain sign that someone in the party sufficiently understood English to have at length detected the drift of his discourse. Immediately after, the whole group entered the forest, Hutter and Hurry apparently making no resistance to the movement. Just as the sounds of the cracking bushes were ceasing, however, the voice of the father was again heard.

"As you're true to my children, God prosper you, young man!" were the words that reached Deerslayer's ears; after which he found himself left to follow the dictates of his own discretion.

Several minutes elapsed, in deathlike stillness, when the party on the shore had disappeared in the woods. Owing to the distance—rather more than two hundred yards—and the obscurity, Deerslayer had been able barely to distinguish the group and to see it retiring, but even this dim connection with human forms gave an animation to the scene that was strongly in contrast to the absolute solitude that remained. Although the young man leaned forward to listen, holding his breath and condensing every faculty in the single sense of hearing, not another sound reached his ears to denote the vicinity of human beings. It seemed as if a silence that had never been broken reigned on the spot again; for an instant, even that piercing shriek which had so lately broken the stillness of the forest, or the execrations of March, would have been a relief to the feeling of desertion to which it gave rise.

This paralysis of mind and body, however, could not last long in one constituted mentally and physically like Deerslayer. Dropping his paddle into the water, he turned the head of the canoe and proceeded slowly, as one walks who thinks intently, toward the center of the lake. When he believed himself to have reached a point in a line with that where he had set the last canoe adrift, he changed his direction northward, keeping the light air as nearly on his back as possible. After paddling a quarter of a mile in this direction, a dark object became visible on the lake, a little to the right; and turning on one side for the purpose, he had soon secured his lost prize to his own boat. Deerslayer now examined the heavens, the course of the air, and the position of the two canoes. Finding nothing in either to induce a change of plan, he lay down and prepared to catch a few hours' sleep, that the morrow might find him equal to its exigencies.

Although the hardy and the tired sleep profoundly, even in scenes of danger, it was some time before Deerslayer lost his recollection. His mind dwelt on what had passed, and his half-conscious faculties kept figuring the events of the night, in a sort of waking dream. Suddenly he was up and alert, for he fancied he heard the preconcerted signal of Hurry summoning him to the shore. But all was still as the grave again. The canoes were slowly drifting northward, the thoughtful stars were glimmering in their mild glory over his head, and the forest-bound sheet of water lay embedded between its mountains, as calm and melancholy as if never troubled by the winds, or brightened by a noonday sun. Once more the loon raised his tremulous cry, near the foot of the lake, and the mystery of the alarm was explained. Deerslayer adjusted his hard pillow, stretched his form in the bottom of the canoe, and slept.

CHAPTER VII

Clear, placid Leman! Thy contrasted lake
With the wild world I dwelt in, is a thing
Which warns me, with its stillness, to forsake
Earth's troubled waters for a purer spring.
This quiet sail is as a noiseless wing
To waft me from distraction: once I loved
Torn ocean's roar, but thy soft murmuring
Sounds sweet as if a sister's voice reproved,
That I with stern delights should e'er have been so moved.

BYRON

DAY HAD FAIRLY dawned before the young man whom we have left in the situation described in the last chapter again opened his eyes. This was no sooner done than he started up and looked about him with the eagerness of one who suddenly felt the importance of accurately ascertaining his precise position. His rest had been deep and undisturbed, and when he awoke, it was with a clearness of intellect and a readiness of resources that were much needed at that particular moment. The sun had not risen, it is true, but the vault of heaven was rich with the winning softness that "brings and shuts the day," while the whole air was filled with the carols of birds, the hymns of the feathered tribe. These sounds first told Deerslayer the risks he ran. The air, for wind it could scarce be called, was still light, it is true, but it had increased a little in the course of the night, and as the canoes were mere feathers on the water, they had drifted twice the expected distance and, what was still more dangerous, had approached so near the base of the mountain that here rose precipitously from the eastern shore, as to render the carols of the birds plainly audible. This was not the worst. The third canoe had taken the same direction, and was slowly drifting toward a point where it must inevitably touch, unless turned aside by a shift of wind, or human hands. In other respects, nothing presented itself to attract attention, or to awaken alarm. The castle stood on its shoal, nearly abreast of the canoes, for the drift had amounted to miles in the course of the night, and the ark lay fastened to its piles, as both had been left so many hours before.

As a matter of course, Deerslayer's attention was first given to the canoe ahead. It was already quite near the point, and a very few strokes of the paddle sufficed to tell him that it must touch before he could possibly overtake it. Just at this moment, too, the wind inopportunely freshened, rendering the drift of the light craft much more rapid and certain. Feeling the impossibility of preventing a contact with the land, the young man wisely determined not to heat himself with unnecessary exertions; first looking to the priming of his piece, he proceeded slowly and warily toward the point, taking care to make a little circuit, that he might be exposed on only one side, as he approached.

The canoe adrift, being directed by no such intelligence, pursued its proper way and grounded on a small sunken rock at the distance of three or four yards from the shore. Just at that moment, Deerslayer had got abreast of the point, and turned the bows of his own boat to the land, first casting loose his tow, that his movements might be unencumbered. The canoe hung an instant on the rock; then it rose a hairsbreadth on an almost imperceptible swell of the water, swung around, floated clear, and reached the strand. All this the young man noted, but it neither quickened his pulses nor hastened his hand. If anyone had been lying in wait for the arrival of the waif, he must be seen, and the utmost caution in approaching the shore became indispensable; if no one was in ambush, hurry was unnecessary. The point being nearly diagonally opposite to the Indian encampment, he hoped the last, though the former was not only possible, but probable, for the savages were prompt in adopting all the expedients of their particular modes of warfare, and quite likely had many scouts searching the shores for craft to carry them off to the castle. As a glance at the lake from any height or projection would expose the smallest object on its surface, there was little hope that either of the canoes could pass unseen, and Indian sagacity needed no instruction to tell which way a boat or a log would drift, when the direction of the wind was known. As Deerslayer drew nearer and nearer to the land, the stroke of his paddle grew slower, his eye became more watchful, and his ears and nostrils almost dilated with the effort to detect any lurking danger. 'Twas a trying moment for a novice, nor was there the encouragement which even the timid sometimes feel, when conscious of being observed and commended. He was entirely alone, thrown on his own resources, and was cheered by no friendly eye, emboldened by no encouraging voice. Notwithstanding all these circumstances, the most experienced veteran in forest warfare could not have behaved better. Equally free from recklessness and hesitation, his advance was marked by a sort of philosophical prudence that appeared to render him superior to all motives but those which were best calculated to effect his purpose. Such was the commencement of a career in forest exploits that afterward rendered this man, in his way, and under the limits of his habits and opportunities, as renowned as many a hero whose name has adorned the pages of works more celebrated than legends simple as ours can ever become.

When about a hundred yards from the shore, Deerslayer rose in the canoe, gave three or four vigorous strokes with the paddle, sufficient of themselves to impel the bark to land, and then quickly laying aside the instrument of labor, he seized that of war. He was in the very act of raising the rifle when a sharp report was followed by the buzz of a bullet that passed so near his body as to cause him involuntarily to start. The next instant Deerslayer staggered and fell his whole length in the bottom of the canoe. A yell— it came from a single voice—followed, and an Indian leaped from the bushes upon the open area of the point, bounding toward the canoe. This was the moment the young man desired. He rose on the instant and leveled his own rifle at his uncovered foe, but his finger hesitated about pulling the trigger on one whom he held at such a disadvantage. This little delay, probably, saved the life of the Indian, who bounded back into the cover as swiftly as he had broken out of it. In the meantime Deerslayer had been swiftly approaching the land, and his own canoe reached the point just as his enemy disappeared. As its movements had not been directed, it touched the shore a few yards from the other boat; and though the rifle of his foe had to be loaded, there was not time to secure his prize, and to carry it beyond danger, before he would be exposed to another shot. Under the circumstances, therefore, he did not pause an instant, but dashed into the woods and sought a cover.

On the immediate point there was a small open area, partly in native grass and partly beach, but a dense fringe of bushes lined its upper side. This narrow belt of dwarf vegetation passed, one issued immediately into the high and gloomy vaults of the forest. The land was tolerably level for a few hundred feet, and then it rose precipitously in a mountainside. The trees were tall, large, and so free from underbrush that they resembled vast columns, irregularly scattered, upholding a dome of leaves. Although they stood tolerably close together, for their ages and size, the eye could penetrate to considerable distances, and bodies of men, even, might have engaged beneath their cover with concert and intelligence.

Deerslayer knew that his adversary must be employed in reloading, unless he had fled. The former proved to be the case, for the young man had no sooner placed himself behind a tree than he caught a glimpse of the arm of the Indian, his body being concealed by an oak, in the very act of forcing the leathered bullet home. Nothing would have been easier than to spring forward and decide the affair by a close assault on his unprepared foe, but every feeling of Deerslayer revolted at such a step, although his own life had just been attempted from a cover. He was yet unpracticed in the ruthless expedients of savage warfare, of which he knew nothing except by tradition and theory, and it struck him as an unfair advantage to assail an unarmed foe. His color had heightened, his eye frowned, his lips were compressed, and all his energies were collected and ready; but instead of advancing to fire, he dropped his rifle to the usual position of a sportsman in readiness to catch his aim and muttered to himself, unconscious that he was speaking—

"No, no—that may be redskin warfare, but it's not a Christian's gift. Let the miscreant charge, and then we'll take it out like men, for the canoe he *must* not and *shall* not have. No, no, let him have time to load, and God will take care of the right!"

All this time the Indian had been so intent on his own movements that he was even ignorant that his enemy was in the wood. His only apprehension was that the canoe would be recovered and carried away before he might be in readiness to prevent it. He had sought the cover from habit, but was within a few feet of the fringe of bushes, and could be at the margin of the forest in readiness to fire in a moment. The distance between him and his enemy was about fifty yards, and the trees were so arranged by nature that the line of sight was not interrupted, except by the particular trees behind which each party stood.

His rifle was no sooner loaded than the savage glanced around him and advanced incautiously as regarded the real, but stealthily as respected the fancied position of his enemy, until he was fairly exposed. Then Deerslayer stepped from behind his own cover and hailed him.

"Thisaway, redskin; thisaway if you're looking for me," he called out. "I'm young in war but not so young as to stand on an open beach to be shot down like an owl by daylight. It rests on yourself whether it's peace or war atween us, for my gifts are white gifts, and I'm not one of them that thinks it valiant to slay human mortals, singly, in the woods."

The savage was a good deal startled by this sudden discovery of the danger he ran. He had a little knowledge of English, however, and caught the drift of the other's meaning. He was also too well schooled to betray alarm, but, dropping the butt of his rifle to the earth with an air of confidence, he made a gesture of lofty courtesy. All this was done with the ease and self-possession of one accustomed to consider no man his superior. In the midst of this consummate acting, however, the volcano that raged within caused his eyes to glare and his nostrils to dilate, like those of some wild beast that is suddenly prevented from taking the fatal leap.

"Two canoe," he said, in the deep, guttural tones of his race, holding up the number of fingers he mentioned, by way of preventing mistakes; "one for you—one for me."

"No, no, Mingo, that will never do. You own neither; and neither shall you have, as long as I can prevent it. I know it's war atween your people and mine, but that's no reason why human mortals should slay each other, like savage creatur's that meet in the woods; go your way, then, and leave me to go mine. The world is large enough for us both, and when we meet fairly in battle, why, the Lord will order the fate of each of us."

"Good!" exclaimed the Indian. "My brother missionary—great talk; all about Manitou."

"Not so—not so, warrior. I'm not good enough for the Moravians and am too good for most of the other vagabonds that preach about in the woods. No, no, I'm only a hunter, as yet, though afore the peace is made, 'tis like enough there'll be occasion to strike a blow at some of your people. Still, I wish it to be done in fair fight and not in a quarrel about the ownership of a miserable canoe."

"Good! My brother very young—but he very wise. Little warrior—great talker. Chief, sometimes, in council."

"I don't know this, nor do I say it, Injin," returned Deerslayer, coloring a little at the ill-concealed sarcasm of the other's manner. "I look forward to a life in the woods, and I only hope it may be a peaceable one. All young men must go on the warpath, when there's occasion, but war isn't needfully massacre. I've seen enough of the last, this very night, to know that Providence frowns on it; I now invite you to go your own way, while I go mine, and hope that we may part fri'nds."

"Good! My brother has two scalp—gray hair under t'other. Old wisdom—young tongue."

Here the savage advanced with confidence, his hand extended, his face smiling, and his whole bearing denoting amity and respect. Deerslayer met his offered friendship in a proper spirit, and they shook hands cordially, each endeavoring to assure the other of his sincerity and desire to be at peace.

"All have his own," said the Indian: "my canoe, mine; your canoe, your'n. Go look: if your'n, you keep; if mine, I keep."

"That's just, redskin, though you must be wrong in thinking the canoe your property. However, seein' is believin', and we'll go down to the shore, where you may look with your own eyes, for it's likely you'll object to trustin' altogether to mine."

The Indian uttered his favorite exclamation of "good!" and then they walked, side by side, toward the shore. There was no apparent distrust in the manner of either, the Indian moving in advance, as if he wished to show his companion that he did not fear turning his back to him. As they reached the open ground, the former pointed toward Deerslayer's boat, and said emphatically—

"No mine—paleface canoe. *This* red man's. No want other man's canoe—want his own."

"You're wrong, redskin, you're altogether wrong. This canoe was left in old Hutter's keeping, and is his'n according to all law, red or white, till its owner comes to claim it. Here's the seats and the stitching of the bark to speak for themselves. No man ever know'd an Injin to turn off such work."

"Good! My brother little ole—big wisdom. Injin no make him. White man's work."

"I'm glad you think so, for holding out to the contrary might have made ill blood atween us, everyone having a right to take possession of his own. I'll just shove the canoe out of reach of dispute at once, as the quickest way of settling difficulties."

While Deerslayer was speaking, he put a foot against the end of the light boat, and giving a vigorous shove, he sent it out into the lake a hundred feet or more, where, taking the true current, it would necessarily float past the point, and be in no further danger of coming ashore. The savage started at this ready and decided expedient, and his companion saw that he cast a hurried and fierce glance at his own canoe, or that which contained the paddles. The change of manner, however, was but momentary, and then the Iroquois resumed his air of friendliness, and a smile of satisfaction.

"Good!" he repeated, with stronger emphasis than ever. "Young head, old mind. Know how to settle quarrel. Farewell, brother. He go to house in water—muskrat house—Injin go to camp; tell chiefs no find canoe."

Deerslayer was not sorry to hear this proposal, for he felt anxious to join the females, and he took the offered hand of the Indian very willingly. The parting words were friendly, and while the red man walked calmly toward the wood, with the rifle in the hollow of his arm, without once looking back in uneasiness or distrust, the white man moved toward the remaining canoe, carrying his piece in the same pacific manner, it is true, but keeping his eyes fastened on the movements of the other. This distrust, however, seemed to be altogether uncalled for, and, as if ashamed to have entertained it, the young man averted his look and stepped carelessly up to his boat. Here he began to push the canoe from the shore and to make his other preparations for departing. He might have been thus employed a minute when, happening to turn his face toward the land, his quick and certain eye told him at a glance the imminent jeopardy in which his life was placed. The black, ferocious eyes of the savage were glancing on him like those of the crouching tiger through a small opening in the bushes, and the muzzle of his rifle seemed already to be opening in a line with his own body.

Then, indeed, the long practice of Deerslayer as a hunter did him good service. Accustomed to fire with the deer on the bound, and often when the precise position of the animal's body had in a manner to be guessed at, he used the same expedients here. To cock and poise his rifle were the acts of a single moment and a single motion; then, aiming almost without sighting, he fired into the bushes where he knew a body ought to be in order to sustain the appalling countenance which alone was visible. There was not time to raise the piece any higher, or to take a more deliberate aim. So rapid were his movements that both parties discharged their pieces at the same instant, the concussions mingling in one report. The mountains, indeed, gave back but a single echo. Deerslayer dropped his piece and stood, with head erect, steady as one of the pines in the calm of a June morning, watching the result; while the savage gave the yell that has become historical for its appalling influence, leaped through the bushes, and came bounding across the open ground, flourishing a tomahawk. Still Deerslayer moved not, but stood with his unloaded rifle fallen against his shoulders, while, with a hunter's habits, his hands were mechanically feeling for the powder horn and charger. When about forty feet from his enemy, the savage hurled his keen weapon, but it was with an eye so vacant and a hand so unsteady and feeble that the young man caught it by the handle as it was flying past him. At that instant the Indian staggered and fell his whole length on the ground.

"I know'd it—I know'd it!" exclaimed Deerslayer, who was already preparing to force a fresh bullet into his rifle; "I know'd it must come to this as soon as I had got the range from the creatur's eyes. A man sights suddenly and fires quick when his own life's in danger; yes, I know'd it would come to this. I was about the hundredth part of a second too quick for him, or it might have been bad for me! The riptyle's bullet has just grazed my side—but, say what you will for or ag'in 'em, a redskin is by no means as sartain with powder and ball as a white man. Their gifts don't seem to lie thataway. Even Chingachgook, great as he is in other matters, isn't downright deadly with the rifle."

By this time the piece was reloaded, and Deerslayer, after tossing the tomahawk into the canoe, advanced to his victim and stood over him, leaning on his rifle, in melancholy attention. It was the first instance in which he had seen a man fall in battle—it was the first fellow creature against whom he had ever seriously raised his own hand. The sensations were novel, and regret, with the freshness of our better feelings, mingled with his triumph. The Indian was not dead, though shot directly through the body. He lay on his back, motionless, but his eyes, now full of consciousness, watched each action of his victor—as the fallen bird regards the fowler—jealous of every movement. The man probably expected the fatal blow which was to precede the loss of his scalp, or perhaps he anticipated that this latter act of cruelty would precede his death. Deerslayer read his thoughts, and he found a melancholy satisfaction in relieving the apprehensions of the helpless savage.

"No, no, redskin," he said, "you've nothing more to fear from me. I am of a Christian stock, and scalping is not of my gifts. I'll just make sartain of your rifle and then come back and do you what sarvice I can. Though here I can't stay much longer, as the crack of three rifles will be apt to bring some of your devils down upon me."

The close of this was said in a sort of a soliloquy, as the young man went in quest of the fallen rifle. The piece was found where its owner had dropped it and was immediately put into the canoe. Laying his own rifle at its side, Deerslayer then returned and stood over the Indian again.

"All inmity atween you and me's at an ind, redskin," he said, "and you may set your heart at rest on the score of the scalp, or any further injury. My gifts are white, as I've told you, and I hope my conduct will be white also!"

Could looks have conveyed all they meant, it is probable Deerslayer's innocent vanity on the subject of color would have been rebuked a little, but he comprehended the gratitude that was expressed in the eyes of the dying savage, without in the least detecting the bitter sarcasm that struggled with the better feeling.

"Water!" ejaculated the thirsty and unfortunate creature, "give poor Injin water."

"Aye, water you shall have, if you drink the lake dry. I'll just carry you down to it, that you may take your fill. This is the way, they tell me, with all wounded people— water is their greatest comfort and delight."

So saying, Deerslayer raised the Indian in his arms and carried him to the lake. Here he first helped him to take an attitude in which he could appease his burning thirst, after which he seated himself on a stone, and took the head of his wounded adversary in his own lap, and endeavored to soothe his anguish in the best manner he could.

"It would be sinful in me to tell you your time hadn't come, warrior," he commenced, "and therefore I'll not say it. You've passed the middle age already, and considerin' the sort of lives ye lead, your days have been pretty well filled. The principal thing now is to look forward to what comes next. Neither redskin nor paleface, on the whole, calculates much on sleepin' forever, but both expect to live in another world. Each has his gifts, and will be judged by 'em, and I suppose you've thought these matters over enough not to stand in need of sarmons when the trial comes. You'll find your happy hunting grounds, if you've been a just Injin; if an onjust, you'll meet your desarts in another way. I've my own idees about these things, but you're too old and exper'enced to need any explanations from one as young as I."

"Good!" ejaculated the Indian, whose voice retained its depth even as life ebbed away; "young head—ole wisdom!"

"It's sometimes a consolation, when the ind comes, to know that them we've harmed, or *tried* to harm, forgive us.

I suppose natur' seeks this relief by way of getting a pardon on 'arth, as we never can know whether He pardons, who is all in all, till judgment itself comes. It's soothing to know that *any* pardon at such times, and that, I conclude, is the secret. Now, as for myself, I overlook altogether your designs ag'in my life; first, because no harm came of 'em; next, because it's your gifts, and natur', and trainin', and I ought not to have trusted you at all; and, finally and chiefly, because I can bear no ill will to a dying man, whether heathen or Christian. So put your heart at ease, so far as I'm consarned; you know best what other matters ought to trouble you, or what ought to give you satisfaction in so trying a moment."

It is probable that the Indian had some of the fearful glimpses of the unknown state of being which God in mercy seems at times to afford to all the human race, but they were necessarily in conformity with his habits and prejudices. Like most of his people, and like too many of our own, he thought more of dying in a way to gain applause among those he left than to secure a better state of existence hereafter. While Deerslayer was speaking, his mind was a little bewildered, though he felt that the intention was good, and when he had done, a regret passed over his spirit that none of his own tribe were present to witness his stoicism, under extreme bodily suffering, and the firmness with which he met his end. With the high innate courtesy that so often distingushes the Indian warrior before he becomes corrupted by too much intercourse with the worst class of the white men, he endeavored to express his thankfulness for the other's good intentions and to let him understand that they were appreciated.

"Good!" he repeated, for this was an English word much used by the savages—"good—young head; young *heart*, too. *Old* heart tough; no shed tear. Hear Indian when he die, and no want to lie—what he call him?"

"Deerslayer is the name I bear now, though the Delawares have said that when I get back from this warpath, I shall have a more manly title, provided I can 'arn one."

"That good name for boy—poor name for warrior. He get better quick. No fear *there*"—the savage had strength sufficient, under the strong excitement he felt, to raise a hand and tap the young man on his breast—"eye sartain—

finger lightning—aim, death—great warrior soon. No Deer-slayer—Hawkeye—Hawkeye—Hawkeye. Shake hand."

Deerslayer—or Hawkeye, as the youth was then first named, for in afteryears he bore the appellation throughout all that region—Deerslayer took the hand of the savage, whose last breath was drawn in that attitude, gazing in admiration at the countenance of a stranger, who had shown so much readiness, skill, and firmness in a scene that was equally trying and novel. When the reader remembers it is the highest gratification an Indian can receive to see his enemy betray weakness, he will be better able to appreciate the conduct which had extorted so great a concession at such a moment.

"His spirit has fled!" said Deerslayer, in a suppressed, melancholy voice. "Ah's me! Well, to this we must all come sooner or later, and he is happiest, let his skin be of what color it may, who is best fitted to meet it. Here lies the body of no doubt a brave warrior, and the soul is already flying toward its heaven or hell, whether that be a happy hunting ground, a place scant of game; regions of glory, according to Moravian doctrine, or flames of fire! So it happens, too, as regards other matters! Here have old Hutter and Hurry Harry got themselves into difficulty, if they hav'n't got themselves into torment and death, and all for a bounty that luck offers to me in what many would think a lawful and suitable manner. But not a farthing of such money shall cross my hand. White I was born, and white will I die, clinging to color to the last, even though the King's Majesty, his governors, and all his councils, both at home and in the colonies, forget from what they come, and where they hope to go, and all for a little advantage in warfare. No, no—warrior, hand of mine shall never molest your scalp, and so your soul may rest in peace on the p'int of making a decent appearance, when the body comes to join it, in your own land of spirits."

Deerslayer arose as soon as he had spoken. Then he placed the body of the dead man in a sitting posture, with its back against the little rock, taking the necessary care to prevent it from falling or in any way settling into an attitude that might be thought unseemly by the sensitive, though wild notions of a savage. When this duty was performed, the young man stood gazing at the grim countenance of his fallen foe, in a sort of melancholy abstraction. As was his practice, however, a habit gained by living so much alone in the forest, he then began again to give utterance to his thoughts and feelings aloud.

"I didn't wish your life, redskin," he said, "but you left me no choice atween killing or being killed. Each party acted according to his gifts, I suppose, and blame can light on neither. You were treacherous, according to your natur' in war, and I was a little oversightful, as I'm apt to be in trusting others. Well, this is my first battle with a human mortal, though it's not likely to be the last. I have fou't most of the creatur's of the forest, such as bears, wolves, painters and catamounts, but this is the beginning with the redskins. If I was Injin born, now, I might tell of this, or carry in the scalp, and boast of the expl'ite afore the whole tribe; or, if my inimy had only been even a bear, 'twould have been nat-'ral and proper to let everybody know what had happened; but I don't well see how I'm to let even Chingachgook into this secret, so long as it can be done only by boasting with a white tongue. And why should I wish to boast of it a'ter all? It's slaying a human, although he was a savage; and how do I know that he was a just Injin, and that he has not been taken away suddenly to anything but happy hunting grounds. When it's onsartain whether good or evil has been done, the wisest way is not to be boastful—still, I *should* like Chingachgook to know that I haven't discredited the Delawares or my training!"

Part of this was uttered aloud, while part was merely muttered between the speaker's teeth; his more confident opinions enjoying the first advantage, while his doubts were expressed in the latter mode. Soliloquy and reflection received a startling interruption, however, by the sudden appearance of a second Indian on the lake shore, a few hundred yards from the point. This man, evidently another scout, who had probably been drawn to the place by the reports of the rifles, broke out of the forest with so little caution that Deerslayer caught a view of his person before he was himself discovered. When the latter event did occur, as was the case a moment later, the savage gave a loud yell, which was answered by a dozen voices from different parts of the mountainside. There was no longer any time for delay; in another minute the boat was quitting the shore under long and steady sweeps of the paddle.

As soon as Deerslayer believed himself to be at a safe distance, he ceased his efforts, permitting the little bark to drift, while he leisurely took a survey of the state of things. The canoe first sent adrift was floating before the air, quite a quarter of a mile above him, and a little nearer to the shore than he wished, now that he knew more of the savages were so near at hand. The canoe shoved from the point was within a few yards of him, he having directed his own course toward it on quitting the land. The dead Indian lay in grim quiet where he had left him, the warrior who had shown himself from the forest had already vanished, and the woods themselves were as silent and seemingly deserted as the day they came fresh from the hands of their great Creator. This profound stillness, however, lasted but a moment. When time had been given to the scouts of the enemy to reconnoiter, they burst out of the thicket upon the naked point, filling the air with yells of fury at discovering the death of their companion. These cries were immediately succeeded by shouts of delight when they reached the body and clustered eagerly around it. Deerslayer was a sufficient adept in the usages of the natives to understand the reason of the change. The yell was the customary lamentation at the loss of a warrior, the shout a sign of rejoicing that the conqueror had not been able to secure the scalp, the trophy without which a victory is never considered complete. The distance at which the canoes lay probably prevented any attempts to injure the conqueror, the American Indian, like the panther of his own woods, seldom making any effort against his foe unless tolerably certain it is under circumstances that may be expected to prove effective.

As the young man had no longer any motive to remain near the point, he prepared to collect his canoes, in order to tow them off to the castle. That nearest was soon in tow, and he proceeded in quest of the other, which was all this time floating up the lake. The eye of Deerslayer was no sooner fastened on this last boat than it struck him that it was nearer to the shore than it would have been had it merely followed the course of the gentle current of air. He began to suspect the influence of some unseen current in the water, and he quickened his exertions in order to regain possession of it before it could drift in to a dangerous proximity to the woods. On getting nearer, he thought that the canoe had a perceptible motion through the water, and, as it lay broadside to the air, that this motion was taking it toward the land. A few vigorous strokes of the paddle carried him still nearer, when the mystery was explained. Something was evidently in motion on the offside of the canoe, or that which was furthest from himself, and closer scrutiny showed that it was a naked human arm. An Indian was lying in the bottom of the canoe and was propelling it slowly but certainly to the shore, using his hand as a paddle. Deerslayer understood the whole artifice at a glance. A savage had swum off to the boat while he was occupied with his enemy on the point, got possession, and was using these means to urge it to the shore.

Satisfied that the man in the canoe could have no arms, Deerslayer did not hesitate to dash close alongside of the retiring boat, without deeming it necessary to raise his own rifle. As soon as the wash of the water, which he made in approaching, became audible to the prostrate savage, the latter sprang to his feet, and uttered an exclamation that proved how completely he was taken by surprise.

"If you've enj'yed yourself enough in that canoe, redskin," Deerslayer coolly observed, stopping his own career in sufficient time to prevent an absolute collision between the two boats—"if you've enj'yed yourself enough in that canoe, you'll do a prudent act by taking to the lake ag'in. I'm reasonable in these matters, and don't crave your blood, though there's them about that would look upon you more as a due bill for the bounty than a human mortal. Take to the lake this minute, afore we get to hot words."

The savage was one of those who did not understand a word of English, and he was indebted to the gestures of Deerslayer and to the expression of an eye that did not often deceive for an imperfect comprehension of his meaning. Perhaps, too, the sight of the rifle that lay so near the hand of the white man quickened his decision. At all events, he crouched like a tiger about to take his leap, uttered a yell, and the next instant his naked body disappeared in the water. When he rose to take breath, it was at the distance of several yards from the canoe, and the hasty glance he threw behind him denoted how much he feared the arrival of a fatal messenger from the rifle of his foe. But the young man made no indication of any hostile intention. Deliberately securing the canoe to the others, he began to paddle from the shore; by the time the Indian reached the land, and had shaken himself, like a spaniel on quitting the water, his dreaded enemy was already beyond rifle shot, on his way to the castle. As was so much his practice, Deerslayer did not fail to soliloquize on what had just occurred, while steadily pursuing his course toward the point of destination.

"Well, well"—he commenced—"'twould have been wrong to kill a human mortal without an object. Scalps are of no account with me, and life is sweet and ought not to be taken marcilessly by them that have white gifts. The savage was a Mingo, it's true, and I make no doubt he is, and will be as long as he lives, a ra'al riptyle and vagabond, but that's no reason I should forget my gifts and color. No, no—let him go; if ever we meet ag'in, rifle in hand, why then 'twill be seen which has the stoutest heart and the quickest eye. Hawkeye! That's not a bad name for a warrior, sounding much more manful and valiant than Deerslayer! 'Twouldn't be a bad title to begin with, and it has been fairly 'arned. If 'twas Chingachgook, now, he might go home and boast of his deeds, and the chiefs would name him Hawkeye in a minute; but it don't become white blood to brag, and 'tisn't easy to see how the matter can be known unless I do. Well, well—everything is in the hands of Providence; this affair as well as another; I'll trust to that for getting my desarts in all things."

Having thus betrayed what might be termed his weak spot, the young man continued to paddle in silence, making his way diligently, and as fast as his tows would allow him, toward the castle. By this time the sun had not only risen, but it had appeared over the eastern mountains, and was shedding a flood of glorious light on this as yet unchristened sheet of water. The whole scene was radiant with beauty, and no one unaccustomed to the ordinary history of the woods would fancy it had so lately witnessed incidents so ruthless and barbarous. As he approached the building of old Hutter, Deerslayer thought, or rather *felt,* that its appearance was in singular harmony with all the rest of the scene. Although nothing had been consulted but strength and security, the rude, massive logs, covered with their rough bark, the projecting roof, and the form would contribute to render the building picturesque in almost any situation, while its actual position added novelty and piquancy to its other points of interest.

When Deerslayer drew nearer to the castle, however, objects of interest presented themselves that at once eclipsed any beauties that might have distinguished the scenery of the lake, and the site of the singular edifice. Judith and Hetty stood on the platform before the door, Hurry's dooryard, awaiting his approach with manifest anxiety, the former from time to time taking a survey of his person and of the canoes through the old ship's spyglass that has been already mentioned. Never probably did this girl seem more brilliantly beautiful than at that moment, the flush of anxiety and alarm increasing her color to its richest tints, while the softness of her eyes, of charm that even poor Hetty shared with her, was deepened by intense concern. Such, at least, without pausing or pretending to analyze motives, or to draw any other very nice distinctions between cause and effect, were the opinions of the young man, as his canoes reached the side of the ark, where he carefully fastened all three before he put his foot on the platform.

CHAPTER VIII

His words are bonds, his oaths are oracles;
His love sincere, his thoughts immaculate;
His tears pure messengers sent from his heart;
His heart as far from fraud as heaven from earth.

SHAKESPEARE

NEITHER OF THE girls spoke as Deerslayer stood before them alone, his countenance betraying all the apprehension he felt on account of the two absent members of their party.

"Father!" Judith at length exclaimed, succeeding in uttering the word as it might be by a desperate effort.

"He's met with misfortune, and there's no use in concealing it," answered Deerslayer, in his direct and simpleminded manner. "He and Hurry are in Mingo hands, and Heaven only knows what's to be the tarmination. I've got the canoes safe, and that's a consolation, since the vagabonds will have to swim for it, or raft off, to come near this place. At sunset we'll be reinforced by Chingachgook, if I can manage to get him into a canoe; then, I think, we two can answer for the ark and the castle, till some of the officers in the garrisons hear of this warpath, which sooner or later must be the case, when we may look for succor from that quarter, if from no other."

"The officers!" exclaimed Judith impatiently, her color deepening and her eye expressing a lively but passing emotion. "Who thinks or speaks of the heartless gallants now? We are sufficient of ourselves to defend the castle—but what of my father and of poor Hurry Harry?"

" 'Tis natural you should feel this consarn for your own parent, Judith, and I suppose it's equally so that you should feel it for Hurry Harry, too."

Deerslayer then commenced a succinct but clear narrative

of all that occurred during the night, in no manner conceal-ing what had befallen his two companions, or his own opin-ion of what might prove to be the consequences. The girls listened with profound attention, but neither betrayed that feminine apprehension and concern which would have fol-lowed such a communication when made to those who were less accustomed to the hazards and accidents of a frontier life. To the surprise of Deerslayer, Judith seemed the most distressed, Hetty listening eagerly but appearing to brood over the facts in melancholy silence, rather than be-traying any outward signs of feeling. The former's agita-tion, the young man did not fail to attribute to the interest she felt in Hurry, quite as much as to her filial love, while Hetty's apparent indifference was ascribed to that mental darkness which, in a measure, obscured her intellect and which possibly prevented her from foreseeing all the conse-quences. Little was said, however, by either, Judith and her sister busying themselves in making the preparations for the morning meal, as they who habitually attend to such mat-ters toil on mechanically even in the midst of suffering and sorrow. The plain but nutritious breakfast was taken by all three in somber silence. The girls ate little, but Deerslayer gave proof of possessing one material requisite of a good soldier, that of preserving his appetite in the midst of the most alarming and embarrassing circumstances. The meal was nearly ended before a syllable was uttered; then, however, Judith spoke in the convulsive and hurried manner in which feeling breaks through restraint, after the latter has become more painful than even the betrayal of emotion.

"Father would have relished this fish!" she exclaimed. "He says the salmon of the lakes is almost as good as the sal-mon of the sea."

"Your father has been acquainted with the sea, they tell me, Judith," returned the young man, who could not for-bear throwing a glance of inquiry at the girl; in common with all who knew Hutter, he had some curiosity on the subject of his early history. "Hurry Harry tells me he was once a sailor."

Judith first looked perplexed; then, influenced by feelings that were novel to her in more ways than one, she became suddenly communicative, and seemingly much interested in the discourse.

"If Hurry knows anything of Father's history, I would he

had told it to me!" she cried. "Sometimes I think, too, he was once a sailor, and then again I think he was not. If that chest were open, or if it could speak, it might let us into his whole history. But its fastenings are too strong to be broken like packthread."

Deerslayer turned to the chest in question and, for the first time, examined it closely. Although discolored, and bearing proofs of having received much ill treatment, he saw that it was of materials and workmanship altogether superior to anything of the same sort he had ever before beheld. The wood was dark, rich, and had once been highly polished, though the treatment it had received left little gloss on its surface, and various scratches and indentations proved the rough collisions that it had encountered with substances still harder than itself. The corners were firmly bound with steel, elaborately and richly wrought, while the locks, of which it had no less than three, and the hinges were of a fashion and workmanship that would have attracted attention even in a warehouse of curious furniture. This chest was quite large; when Deerslayer arose and endeavored to raise an end by its massive handle, he found that the weight fully corresponded with the external appearance.

"Did you never see that chest opened, Judith?" the young man demanded with frontier freedom, for delicacy on such subjects was little felt among the people on the verge of civilization in that age, even if it be today.

"Never. Father has never opened it in my presence, if he ever opens it at all. No one here has ever seen its lid raised, unless it be Father; nor do I even know that he has ever seen it."

"Now, you're wrong, Judith," Hetty quietly answered. "Father *has* raised the lid, and *I've* seen him do it."

A feeling of manliness kept the mouth of Deerslayer shut, for while he would not have hesitated about going far beyond what would be thought the bounds of propriety in questioning the elder sister, he had just scruples about taking what might be thought an advantage of the feeble intellect of the younger. Judith, being under no such restraint, however, turned quickly to the last speaker, and continued the discourse.

"When and where did you ever see that chest opened, Hetty?"

"Here, and again and again. Father often opens it when *you* are away, though he don't in the least mind my being by and seeing all he does as well as hearing all he says."

"And what is it that he does, and what does he say?"

"That I cannot tell *you*, Judith," returned the other in a low but resolute voice. "*Father's* secrets are not *my* secrets."

"Secrets! This is stranger still, Deerslayer, that Father should tell them to Hetty and not tell them to me!"

"There's good reason for that, Judith, though you're not to know it. Father's not here to answer for himself, and I'll say no more about it."

Judith and Deerslayer looked surprised, and for a minute the first seemed pained. But suddenly recollecting herself, she turned away from her sister, as if in pity for her weakness, and addressed the young man.

"You've told but half your story," she said, "breaking off at the place where you went to sleep in the canoe—or rather where you rose to listen to the cry of the loon. We heard the call of the loons, too, and thought their cries might bring a storm, though we are little used to tempests on this lake at this season of the year."

"The winds blow and the tempests howl as God pleases, sometimes at one season and sometimes at another," answered Deerslayer; "and the loons speak accordin' to their natur'. Better would it be if men were as honest and frank. After I rose to listen to the birds, finding it could not be Hurry's signal, I lay down and slept. When the day dawned, I was up and stirring as usual, and then I went in chase of the two canoes, lest the Mingos should lay hands on 'em."

"You have not told us all, Deerslayer," said Judith earnestly. "We heard rifles under the eastern mountain; the echoes were full and long, and came so soon after the reports that the pieces must have been fired on or quite near to the shore. Our ears are used to these signs and are not to be deceived."

"They've done their duty, gal, this time; yes, they've done their duty. Rifles have been sighted this morning, aye, and triggers pulled, too, though not as often as they might have been. One warrior has gone to his happy hunting grounds, and that's the whole of it. A man of white blood and white gifts is not to be expected to boast of his expl'ites and to flourish scalps."

Judith listened almost breathlessly, and when Deerslayer,

in his quiet, modest manner, seemed disposed to quit the subject, she rose and, crossing the room, took a seat by his side. The manner of the girl had nothing forward about it, though it betrayed the quick instinct of a female's affection and the sympathizing kindness of a woman's heart. She even took the hard hand of the hunter and pressed it in both her own, unconsciously to herself, perhaps, while she looked earnestly and even reproachfully into his sunburned face.

"You have been fighting the savages, Deerslayer, singly and by yourself!" she said. "In your wish to take care of us —of Hetty—of me, perhaps, you've fought the enemy bravely, with no eye to encourage your deeds, or to witness your fall, had it pleased Providence to suffer so great a calamity!"

"I've fou't, Judith; yes, I *have* fou't the inimy, and that, too, for the first time in my life. These things must be, and they bring with 'em a mixed feelin' of sorrow and triumph. Human natur' is a fightin' natur', I suppose, as all nations kill in battle, and we must be true to our rights and gifts. What has yet been done is no great matter, but should Chingachgook come to the rock this evening, as is agreed atween us, and I get him off it onbeknown to the savages, or, if known to them, ag'in their wishes and designs, then may we all look to something like warfare afore the Mingos shall get possession of either the castle, or the ark, or yourselves."

"Who is this Chingachgook? From what place does he come, and *why* does he come *here?*"

"The questions are nat'ral and right, I suppose, though the youth has a great name already in his own part of the country. Chingachgook is a Mohican by blood, consorting with the Delawares by usage, as is the case with most of his tribe, which has long been broken up by the increase of our color. He is of the family of the great chiefs, Uncas, his father, having been the considerablest warrior and counselor of his people. Even old Tamenund honors Chingachgook, though he is thought to be yet too young to lead in war; and then the nation is so disparsed and diminished that chieftainship among 'em has got to be little more than a name. Well, this war having commenced in 'arnest, the Delaware and I rendezvous'd an app'intment, to meet this evening at sunset on the rendezvous rock at the foot of this very lake, intending to come out on our first hostile expedition ag'in the Mingos. *Why* we come exactly thisaway is our own secret, but thoughtful young men on a warpath, as you may suppose, do nothing without a calculation and a design."

"A Delaware can have no unfriendly intentions toward us," said Judith, after a moment's hesitation, "and we know you to be friendly."

"Treachery is the last crime I hope to be accused of," returned Deerslayer, hurt at the gleam of distrust that had shot through Judith's mind; "and least of all, treachery to my own color."

"No one suspects *you*, Deerslayer," the girl impetuously cried. "No—no—your honest countenance would be a sufficient surety for the truth of a thousand hearts! If all men had as honest tongues, and no more promised what they did not mean to perform, there would be less wrong done in the world, and fine feathers and scarlet cloaks would not be thought excuses for baseness and deception."

The girl spoke with strong, nay, even with convulsed feeling, and her fine eyes, usually so soft and alluring, flashed fire as she concluded. Deerslayer could not but observe this extraordinary emotion, but with the tact of a courtier, he avoided not only any allusion to the circumstance but succeeded in concealing the effect of his discovery on himself. Judith gradually grew calm again, and as she was obviously anxious to appear to advantage in the eyes of the young man, she was soon able to renew the conversation as composedly as if nothing had occurred to disturb her.

"I have no right to look into your secrets, or the secrets of your friend, Deerslayer," she continued, "and am ready to take all you say on trust. If we can really get another male ally to join us at this trying moment, it will aid us much; I am not without hope that when the savages find we are able to keep the lake, they will offer to give up their prisoners in exchange for skins, or at least for the keg of powder that we have in the house."

The young man had the words "scalps," and "bounty," on his lips, but a reluctance to alarm the feelings of the daughters prevented him from making the allusion he had intended to the probable fate of their father. Still, so little was he practiced in the arts of deception that his expressive countenance was, of itself, understood by the quick-witted Judith, whose intelligence had been sharpened by the risks and habits of her life.

"I understand what you mean," she continued hurriedly, "and what you would say, but for the fear of hurting me —us, I mean, for Hetty loves her father quite as well as I do. But this is not as we think of Indians. They never scalp an unhurt prisoner, but would rather take him away alive, unless, indeed, the fierce wish for torturing should get the mastery of them. I fear nothing for my father's scalp and little for his life. Could they steal on us in the night, we should all probably suffer in this way, but men taken in open strife are seldom injured—not, at least, until the time of torture comes."

"That's tradition, I'll allow, and it's accordin' to practice —but, Judith, do you know the 'ar'nd on which your father and Hutter went ag'in the savages?"

"I do, and a cruel errand it was! But what will you have? Men will be men, and some even that flaunt in their gold and silver, and carry the King's commission in their pockets, are not guiltless of equal cruelty." Judith's eye again flashed, but by a desperate struggle she resumed her composure. "I get warm when I think of all the wrong that men do," she added, affecting to smile, an effort in which she only succeeded indifferently well. "All this is silly. What is done is done, and it cannot be mended by complaints. But the Indians think so little of the shedding of blood, and value men so much for the boldness of their undertakings, that, did they know the business on which their prisoners came, they would be more likely to honor than to injure them for it."

"For a time, Judith; yes, I allow *that*, for a time. But, when that feelin' dies away, then will come the love of revenge. We must indivor, Chingachgook and I, we must indivor to see what we can do to get Hurry and your father free, for the Mingos will no doubt hover about this lake some days in order to make the most of their success."

"You think this Delaware can be depended on, Deerslayer?" demanded the girl thoughtfully.

"As much as I can myself. You say you do not suspect *me*, Judith?"

"*You!*" taking his hand again and pressing it between her own with a warmth that might have awakened the vanity of one less simple-minded and more disposed to dwell on his own good qualities, "I would as soon suspect a brother! I have known you but a day, Deerslayer, but it has awakened the confidence of a year. Your name, however, is not unknown to me, for the gallants of the garrisons frequently speak of the lessons you have given them in hunting, and all proclaim your honesty."

"Do they ever talk of the shooting, gal?" inquired the other eagerly, after, however, laughing in a silent but heartfelt manner. "Do they ever talk of the shooting? I want to hear nothing about my own, for if that isn't sartified to by this time, in all these parts, there's little use in being skillful and sure; but what do the officers say of their own—yes, what do they say of their own? Arms, as they call it, is their trade, and yet there's some among 'em that know very little how to use 'em!"

"Such I hope will not be the case with your friend Chingachgook, as you call him—what is the English of his Indian name?"

"Big Sarpent—so called for his wisdom and cunning. Uncas is his ra'al name—all his family being called Uncas, until they get a title that has been 'arned by deeds."

"If he has all this wisdom, we may expect a useful friend in him, unless his own business in this part of the country should prevent him from serving us."

"I see no great harm in telling you his ar'n'd, a'ter all, and, as you may find means to help us, I will let you and Hetty into the whole matter, trusting that you'll keep the secret as if it was your own. You must know that Chingachgook is a comely Injin, and is much look'd upon and admired by the young women of his tribe, both on account of his family and on account of himself. Now there is a chief that has a daughter called Wah-ta!-Wah, which is intarpreted into Hist-oh!-Hist in the English tongue, the rarest gal among the Delawares and the one most sought a'ter and craved for a wife by all the young warriors of the nation. Well Chingachgook, among others, took a fancy to Wah-ta!-Wah, and Wah-ta!-Wah took a fancy to him." Here Deerslayer paused an instant, for as he got thus far in his tale, Hetty Hutter arose, approached, and stood attentive at his knee, as a child draws near to listen to the legends of its mother. "Yes, he fancied *her,* and she fancied *him,*" resumed Deerslayer, casting a friendly and approving glance at the innocent and interested girl; "and when that is the case, and all the elders are agreed, it does not often happen that the young couple keep apart. Chingachgook couldn't well carry off such a prize without making inimies among them that wanted her as much as he did himself. A sartain Briarthorn, as we call him in English, or Yocommon, as he is tarmed in Injin, took it most to heart, and we mistrust him of having a hand in all that followed. Wah-ta!-Wah went with her father and mother two moons ago to fish for salmon on the western streams, where it is agreed by all in these parts that fish most abounds, and while thus empl'y'd the gal vanished. For several weeks we could get no tidings of her, but here, ten days since, a runner that came through the Delaware country brought us a message by which we l'arn that Wah-ta!-Wah was stolen from her people—we think, but do not know it, by Briarthorn's sarcumventions—and that she was now with the inimy, who had adopted her, and wanted her to marry a young Mingo. The message said that the party intended to hunt and forage through this region for a month or two afore it went back into the Canadas, and that if we could contrive to get on a scent in this quarter, something might turn up that would lead to our getting the maiden off."

"And how does that concern *you*, Deerslayer?" demanded Judith a little anxiously.

"It consarns me as all things that touches a fri'nd consarns a fri'nd. I'm here as Chingachgook's aid and helper, and if we can get the young maiden he likes back ag'in, it will give me almost as much pleasure as if I had got back my own sweetheart."

"And where, then, is *your* sweetheart, Deerslayer?"

"She's in the forest, Judith—hanging from the boughs of the trees, in a soft rain—in the dew on the open grass—the clouds that float about in the blue heavens—the birds that sing in the woods—the sweet springs where I slake my thirst—and in all the other glorious gifts that come from God's Providence!"

"You mean that, as yet you've never loved one of my sex, but love best your haunts and your own manner of life."

"That's it—that's just it. I am white—have a white heart, and can't, in reason, love a redskinned maiden, who must have a redskin heart and feelin's. No, no, I'm sound enough in them partic'lars and hope to remain so, at least till this war is over. I find my time too much taken up with Chingachgook's affair to wish to have one of my own on my hands afore that is settled."

"The girl that finally wins you, Deerslayer, will at least win an *honest* heart—one without treachery or guile—and that will be a victory that most of her sex ought to envy."

As Judith uttered this, her beautiful face had a resentful frown on it, while a bitter smile lingered around a mouth that no derangement of the muscles could render anything but handsome. Her companion observed the change, and though little skilled in the workings of the female heart, he had sufficient native delicacy to understand that it might be well to drop the subject.

As the hour when Chingachgook was expected still remained distant, Deerslayer had time enough to examine into the state of the defenses and to make such additional arrangements as were in his power, and which the exigency of the moment seemed to require. The experience and foresight of Hutter had left little to be done in these particulars; still, several precautions suggested themselves to the young man, who may be said to have studied the art of frontier warfare through the traditions and legends of the people among whom he had so long lived. The distance between the castle and the nearest point on the shore prevented any apprehension on the subject of rifle bullets thrown from the land. The house was within musket shot, in one sense, it was true, but aim was entirely out of the question, and even Judith professed a perfect disregard of any danger from that source. So long, then, as the party remained in possession of the fortress, they were safe, unless their assailants could find the means to come off and carry it by fire or storm, or by some of the devices of Indian cunning and Indian treachery. Against the first source of danger Hutter had made ample provision, and the building itself, the bark roof excepted, was not very combustible. The floor was scuttled in several places, and buckets provided with ropes were in daily use, in readiness for any such emergency. One of the girls could easily extinguish any fire that might be lighted, provided it had not time to make much headway. Judith, who appeared to understand all her father's schemes of defense, and who had the spirit to take no unimportant share in the execution of them, explained all these details to the young man, who was thus saved much time and labor in making his investigations.

Little was to be apprehended during the day. In possession of the canoes and of the ark, no other vessel was to be found on the lake. Nevertheless, Deerslayer well knew that a raft was soon made, and as dead trees were to be found in abundance near the water, did the savages seriously contemplate the risks of an assault, it would not be a very difficult matter to find the necessary means. The celebrated American ax, a tool that is quite unrivaled in its way, was then not very extensively known and the savages were far from expert in the use of its hatchetlike substitute; still, they had sufficient practice in crossing streams by this mode to render it certain they would construct a raft, should they deem it expedient to expose themselves to the risks of an assault. The death of their warrior might prove a sufficient incentive, or it might act as a caution, but Deerslayer thought it more than possible that the succeeding night would bring matters to a crisis, and in this precise way. This impression caused him to wish ardently for the presence and succor of his Mohican friend and to look forward to the approach of sunset with an increasing anxiety.

As the day advanced, the party in the castle matured their plans and made their preparations. Judith was active, and seemed to find a pleasure in consulting and advising with her new acquaintance, whose indifference to danger, manly devotion to herself and sister, guilelessness of manner, and truth of feeling had won rapidly on both her imagination and her affections. Although the hours appeared long in some respects to Deerslayer, Judith did not find them so, and when the sun began to descend toward the pine-clad summits of the western hills, she felt and expressed her surprise that the day should so soon be drawing to a close. On the other hand, Hetty was moody and silent. She was never loquacious, or if she occasionally became communicative, it was under the influence of some temporary excitement that served to arouse her unsophisticated mind; but for hours at a time, in the course of this all-important day, she seemed to have absolutely lost the use of her tongue. Nor did apprehension on account of her father materially affect the manner of either sister. Neither appeared seriously to dread any evil greater than captivity, and once or twice, when Hetty did speak, she intimated the expectation that Hutter would find the means to liberate himself. Although Judith was less sanguine on this head, she too betrayed the hope that propositions for a ransom would come, when the Indians discovered that the castle set their expedients and artifices at defiance. Deerslayer, however, treated these passing suggestions as the ill-digested fancies of girls, making his own arrangements as steadily and brooding over the future as seriously as if they had never fallen from their lips.

At length the hour arrived when it became necessary to proceed to the place of rendezvous appointed with the Mohican, or Delaware, as Chingachgook was more commonly called. As the plan had been matured by Deerslayer, and fully communicated to his companions, all three set about its execution in concert and intelligently. Hetty passed into the ark, and, fastening two of the canoes together, she entered one and paddled up to a sort of gateway in the palisades that surrounded the building, through which she carried both, securing them beneath the house by chains that were fastened within the building. These palisades were trunks of trees driven firmly into the mud and served the double purpose of a small enclosure that was intended to be used in this very manner, and to keep any enemy that might approach in boats at arm's-length. Canoes thus *docked* were, in a measure, hid from sight, and as the gate was properly barred and fastened, it would not be an easy task to remove them, even in the event of their being seen. Previously, however, to closing the gate, Judith also entered within the enclosure with the third canoe, leaving Deerslayer busy in securing the door and windows inside the building, over her head. As everything was massive and strong, and small saplings were used as bars, it would have been the work of an hour or two to break into the building, when Deerslayer had ended his task, even allowing the assailants the use of any tools but the ax, and to be unresisted. This attention to security arose from Hutter's having been robbed once or twice by the lawless whites of the frontiers, during some of his many absences from home.

As soon as all was fast in the inside of the dwelling, Deerslayer appeared at a trap, from which he descended into the canoe of Judith. When this was done, he fastened the door with a massive staple and stout padlock. Hetty was then received in the canoe, which was shoved outside of the palisades. The next precaution was to fasten the gate, and the keys were carried into the ark. The three were now fastened out of the dwelling, which could only be entered by violence, or by following the course taken by the young man in quitting it.

The glass had been brought outside as a preliminary step, and Deerslayer next took a careful survey of the entire shore of the lake, as far as his own position would allow. Not a living thing was visible, a few birds excepted, and even the last fluttered about in the shades of the trees, as if unwilling to encounter the heat of a sultry afternoon. All the nearest points, in particular, were subjected to severe scrutiny, in order to make certain that no raft was in preparation; the result everywhere gave the same picture of calm solitude. A few words will explain the greatest embarrassment belonging to the situation of our party. Exposed themselves to the observation of any watchful eyes, the movements of their enemies were concealed by the drapery of a dense forest. While the imagination would be very apt to people the latter with more warriors than it really contained, their own weakness must be too apparent to all who might chance to cast a glance in their direction.

"Nothing is stirring, howsever," exclaimed Deerslayer, as he finally lowered the glass, and prepared to enter the ark: "If the vagabonds do harbor mischief in their minds, they are too cunning to let it be seen; it's true, a raft may be in preparation in the woods, but it has not yet been brought down to the lake. They can't guess that we are about to quit the castle, and, if they did, they've no means of knowing where we intend to go."

"This is so true, Deerslayer," returned Judith, "that now all is ready, we may proceed at once, boldly and without the fear of being followed—else we shall be behind our time."

"No—no—the matter needs management—for, though the savages are in the dark as to Chingachgook and the rock, they've eyes and legs, and will see in what direction we steer, and will be sartain to follow us. I shall strive to baffle 'em, howsever, by heading the scow in all manner of ways, first in one quarter and then in another, until they get to be a-leg-weary and tired of tramping a'ter us."

So far as it was in his power, Deerslayer was as good as

his word. In less than five minutes after this speech was made, the whole party was in the ark and in motion. There was a gentle breeze from the north, and boldly hoisting the sail, the young man laid the head of the unwieldy craft in such a direction, as, after making a liberal but necessary allowance for leeway, would have brought it ashore a couple of miles down the lake, and on its eastern side. The sailing of the ark was never very swift, though, floating as it did on the surface, it was not difficult to get it in motion, or to urge it along over the water at the rate of some three or four miles in the hour. The distance between the castle and the rock was a little more than two leagues. Knowing the punctuality of an Indian, Deerslayer had made his calculations closely and had given himself a little more time than was necessary to reach the place of rendezvous, with a view to delay or to press his arrival, as might prove most expedient. When he hoisted the sail, the sun lay above the western hills at an elevation that promised rather more than two hours of day, and a few minutes satisfied him that the progress of the scow was such as to equal his expectations.

It was a glorious June afternoon, and never did that solitary sheet of water seem less like an arena of strife and bloodshed. The light air scarce descended as low as the bed of the lake, hovering over it, as if unwilling to disturb its deep tranquillity, or to ruffle its mirrorlike surface. Even the forests appeared to be slumbering in the sun, and a few piles of fleecy clouds had lain for hours along the northern horizon like fixtures in the atmosphere, placed there purely to embellish the scene. A few aquatic fowls occasionally skimmed along the water, and a single raven was visible, sailing high above the trees and keeping a watchful eye on the forest beneath him, in order to detect anything having life that the mysterious woods might offer as prey.

The reader will probably have observed that, amidst the frankness and abruptness of manner which marked the frontier habits of Judith, her language was superior to that used by her male companions, her own father included. This difference extended as well to pronunciation as to the choice of words and phrases. Perhaps nothing so soon betrays the education and association as the modes of speech, and few accomplishments so much aid the charm of female beauty as a graceful and even utterance, while nothing so soon produces the disenchantment that necessarily follows a discrepancy between appearance and manner as a mean intonation of voice, or a vulgar use of words. Judith and her sister were marked exceptions to all the girls of their class along that whole frontier, the officers of the nearest garrison having often flattered the former with the belief that few ladies of the towns acquitted themselves better than herself in this important particular. This was far from being literally true, but it was sufficiently near the fact to give birth to the compliment. The girls were indebted to their mother for this proficiency, having acquired from her, in childhood, an advantage that no subsequent study or labor can give without a drawback, if neglected beyond the earlier periods of life. Who that mother was, or rather had been, no one but Hutter knew. She had now been dead two summers, and as was stated by Hurry, she had been buried in the lake, whether in indulgence of a prejudice, or from a reluctance to take the trouble to dig her grave, had frequently been a matter of discussion between the rude beings of that region. Judith had never visited the spot, but Hetty was present at the interment, and she often paddled a canoe, about sunset, or by the light of the moon, to the place, and gazed down into the limpid water in the hope of being able to catch a glimpse of a form that she had so tenderly loved from infancy to the sad hour of their parting.

"Must we reach the rock exactly at the moment the sun sets?" Judith demanded of the young man, as they stood near each other, Deerslayer holding the steering oar, and she working with a needle at some ornament of dress that much exceeded her station in life and was altogether a novelty in the woods. "Will a few minutes, sooner or later, alter the matter? It will be very hazardous to remain long as near the shore as that rock!"

"That's it, Judith, that's the very difficulty! The rock's within p'int blank for a shotgun, and 'twill never do to hover about it too close and too long. When you have to deal with an Injin, you must calculate and manage, for a red natur' dearly likes sarcumvention. Now you see, Judith, that I do not steer toward the rock at all, but here to the eastward of it, whereby the savages will be tramping off in that direction, and get their legs a-wearied, and all for no advantage."

"You think, then, they see us and watch our movements, Deerslayer? I was in hopes they might have fallen back into the woods and left us to ourselves for a few hours."

"That's altogether a woman's consait. There's no letup in an Injin's watchfulness when he's on a warpath, and eyes are on us at this minute, though the lake presarves us. We must draw near the rock on a calculation and indivor to get the miscreants on a false scent. The Mingos have good noses, they tell me, but a white man's reason ought always to equalize their instinct."

Judith now entered into a desultory discourse with Deerslayer, in which the girl betrayed her growing interest in the young man, an interest that his simplicity of mind and her decision of character, sustained as it was by the consciousness awakened by the consideration her personal charms so universally produced, rendered her less anxious to conceal than might otherwise have been the case. She was scarcely forward in her manner, though there was sometimes a freedom in her glances that it required all the aid of her exceeding beauty to prevent from awakening suspicions unfavorable to her discretion, if not to her morals. With Deerslayer, however, these glances were rendered less obnoxious to so unpleasant a construction, for she seldom looked at him without discovering much of the sincerity and nature that accompany the purest emotions of woman. It was a little remarkable that, as his captivity lengthened, neither of the girls manifested any great concern for her father; but, as has been said already, their habits gave them confidence, and they looked forward to his liberation by means of a ransom, with a confidence that might in a great degree account for their apparent indifference. Once before, Hutter had been in the hands of the Iroquois, and a few skins had readily effected his release. This event, however, unknown to the sisters, had occurred in a time of peace between England and France, and when the savages were restrained, instead of being encouraged to commit their excesses, by the policy of the different colonial governments.

While Judith was loquacious and caressing in her manner, Hetty remained thoughtful and silent. Once, indeed, she drew near to Deerslayer and questioned him a little closely as to his intentions, as well as concerning the mode of effecting his purpose; but her wish to converse went no further.

As soon as her simple queries were answered—and answered they all were in the fullest and kindest manner—she withdrew to her seat and continued to work on a coarse garment that she was making for her father, sometimes humming a low melancholy air and frequently sighing.

In this manner the time passed away, and when the sun was beginning to glow behind the fringe of pines that bounded the western hill, or about twenty minutes before it actually set, the ark was nearly as low as the point where Hutter and Hurry had been made prisoners. By sheering first to one side of the lake, and then to the other, Deerslayer managed to create an uncertainty as to his object; doubtless, the savages, who were unquestionably watching his movements, were led to believe that his aim was to communicate with them, at or near this spot, and would hasten in that direction, in order to be in readiness to profit by circumstances. This artifice was well managed, since the sweep of the bay, the curvature of the lake, and the low marshy land that intervened would probably allow the ark to reach the rock before its pursuers, if really collected near the point, could have time to make the circuit that would be required to get there by land. With a view to aid this deception, Deerslayer stood as near the western shore as was at all prudent; then, causing Judith and Hetty to enter the house, or cabin, and crouching himself so as to conceal his person by the frame of the scow, he suddenly threw the head of the latter round and began to make the best of his way toward the outlet. Favored by an increase in the wind, the progress of the ark was such as to promise the complete success of this plan, though the crablike movement of the craft compelled the helmsman to keep its head looking in a direction very different from that in which it was actually moving.

CHAPTER IX

Yet art thou prodigal of smiles—
Smiles sweeter than thy frowns are stern:
Earth sends from all her thousand isles,
A shout at thy return.
The glory that comes down from thee
Bathes, in deep joy, the land and sea.

THE SKIES

IT MAY ASSIST the reader in understanding the events we are about to record if he has a rapidly sketched picture of the scene, placed before his eyes at a single view. It will be remembered that the lake was an irregularly shaped basin, of an outline that, in the main, was oval, but with bays and points to relieve its formality and ornament its shores. The surface of this beautiful sheet of water was now glittering like a gem, in the last rays of the evening sun, and the setting of the whole—hills clothed in the richest forest verdure—was lighted up with a sort of radiant smile that is best described in the beautiful lines we have placed at the head of this chapter. As the banks, with few exceptions, rose abruptly from the water, even where the mountain did not immediately bound the view, there was a nearly unbroken fringe of leaves overhanging the placid lake—the trees starting out of the acclivities, inclining to the light, until in many instances they extended their long limbs and straight trunks some forty or fifty feet beyond the line of the perpendicular. In these cases we allude only to the giants of the forest—pines of a hundred or a hundred and fifty feet in height—for of the smaller growth, very many inclined so far as to steep their lower branches in the water.

In the position in which the ark had now got, the castle was concealed from view by the projection of a point, as indeed was the northern extremity of the lake itself. A respectable mountain, forest-clad and rounded like all the rest, limited the view in that direction, stretching immediately across the whole of the fair scene, with the exception of a deep bay that passed its western end, lengthening the basin for more than a mile. The manner in which the water flowed out of the lake, beneath the leafy arches of the trees that lined the sides of the stream, has already been mentioned, and it has also been said that the rock, which was a favorite place of rendezvous throughout all that region, and where Deerslayer now expected to meet his friend, stood near this outlet, at no great distance from the shore. It was a large, isolated stone that rested on the bottom of the lake, apparently left there when the waters tore away the earth from around it in forcing for themselves a passage down the river, and which had obtained its shape from the action of the elements during the slow progress of centuries. The height of this rock could scarcely equal six feet, and, as has been said, its shape was not unlike that which is usually given to beehives or to a haycock. The latter, indeed, gives the best idea not only of its form but of its dimensions. It stood, and still stands, for we are writing of real scenes, within fifty feet of the bank and in water that was only two feet in depth, though there were seasons in which its rounded apex, if such a term can properly be used, was covered by the lake. Many of the trees stretched so far forward as almost to blend the rock with the shore, when seen from a little distance; one tall pine in particular overhung it in a way to form a noble and appropriate canopy to a seat that had held many a forest chieftain during the long succession of unknown ages in which America and all it contained existed apart in mysterious solitude, a world by itself, equally without a familiar history and without an origin that the annals of man can reach.

When distant some two or three hundred feet from the shore, Deerslayer took in his sail, and he dropped his grapnel as soon as he found the ark had drifted in a line that was directly to windward of the rock. The motion of the scow was then checked, when it was brought head to wind by the action of the breeze. As soon as this was done, Deerslayer "paid out line" and suffered the vessel to "set down" upon the rock as fast as the light air would force it to leeward. Floating entirely on the surface, this was soon effected, and the young man checked the drift when he was told that the stern of the scow was within fifteen or eighteen feet of the desired spot.

In executing this maneuver, Deerslayer had proceeded promptly, for while he did not in the least doubt that he was both watched and followed by the foe, he believed he had distracted their movements by the apparent uncertainty of his own, and he knew they could have no means of ascertaining that the rock was his aim, unless indeed one of the prisoners had betrayed him, a chance so improbable in itself as to give him no concern. Notwithstanding the celerity and decision of his movements, he did not, however, venture so near the shore without taking due precautions to effect a retreat, in the event of its becoming necessary. He held the line in his hand, and Judith was stationed at a loop on the side of the cabin next to the shore, where she could watch the beach and the rocks and give timely notice of the approach of either friend or foe. Hetty was also placed on watch, but it was to keep the trees overhead in view, lest some enemy might ascend one and, by completely commanding the interior of the scow, render the defenses of the hut or cabin useless.

The sun had disappeared from the lake and valley when Deerslayer checked the ark in the manner mentioned. Still it wanted a few minutes to the true sunset, and he knew Indian punctuality too well to anticipate any unmanly haste in his friend. The great question was whether, surrounded by enemies as he was known to be, he had escaped their toils. The occurrences of the last twenty-four hours must be a secret to him, and, like himself, Chingachgook was yet young on a warpath. It was true, he came prepared to encounter the party that withheld his promised bride, but he had no means of ascertaining the extent of the danger he ran, or the precise positions occupied by either friends or foes. In a word, the trained sagacity and untiring caution of an Indian were all he had to rely on, amid the critical risks he unavoidably ran.

"Is the rock empty, Judith?" inquired Deerslayer, as soon as he had checked the drift of the ark, deeming it imprudent to venture unnecessarily near the shore. "Is anything to be seen of the Delaware chief?"

"Nothing, Deerslayer. Neither rock, shore, tree, nor lake seems to have ever held a human form."

"Keep close, Judith—keep close, Hetty—a rifle has a prying eye, a nimble foot, and a desperate fatal tongue. Keep close then, but keep up actyve looks, and be on the alart. 'Twould grieve me to the heart did any harm befall either of you."

"And *you*, Deerslayer!" exclaimed Judith, turning her handsome face from the loop to bestow a gracious and grateful look on the young man; "do *you* 'keep close,' and have a proper care that the savages do not catch a glimpse of you! A bullet might be as fatal to *you* as to one of us; and the blow that you felt would be felt by all."

"No fear of me, Judith—no fear of me, my good gal. Do not look thisaway, although you look so pleasant and comely, but keep your eyes on the rock, and the shore, and the——"

Deerslayer was interrupted by a slight exclamation from the girl, who, in obedience to his hurried gestures as much as in obedience to his words, had immediately bent her looks again in the opposite direction.

"What is't? What is't, Judith?" he hastily demanded. "Is anything to be seen?"

"There is a man on the rock! An Indian warrior in his paint, and armed!"

"Where does he wear his hawk's feather?" eagerly added Deerslayer, relaxing his hold of the line in readiness to drift nearer to the place of rendezvous. "Is it fast to the warlock, or does he carry it above the left ear?"

"'Tis as you say, above the left ear; he smiles, too, and mutters the word 'Mohican.' "

"God be praised, 'tis the Sarpent at last!" exclaimed the young man, suffering the line to slip through his hands until hearing a light bound in the other end of the craft, he instantly checked the rope and began to haul it in again, under the assurance that his object was effected.

At that moment the door of the cabin was opened hastily, and a warrior, darting through the little room, stood at Deerslayer's side, simply uttering the exclamation "Hugh!" At the next instant Judith and Hetty shrieked, and the air was filled with the yell of twenty savages, who came leaping through

the branches down the bank, some actually falling headlong
into the water in their haste.

"Pull, Deerslayer," cried Judith, hastily barring the door,
in order to prevent an inroad by the passage through which
the Delaware had just entered. "Pull for life and death—the
lake is full of savages wading after us!"

The young man—for Chingachgook immediately came to
his friend's assistance—needed no second bidding, but they
applied themselves to their task in a way that showed how
urgent they deemed the occasion. The great difficulty was in
suddenly overcoming the *vis inertiæ* of so large a mass, for
once in motion, it was easy to cause the scow to skim the
water with all the necessary speed.

"Pull, Deerslayer, for Heaven's sake!" cried Judith again
at the loop. "These wretches rush into the water like hounds
following their prey! Ah!—the scow moves! And now the
water deepens to the armpits of the foremost; still they rush
forward, and will seize the ark!"

A slight scream, and then a joyous laugh followed from
the girl, the first produced by a desperate effort of their pursuers, and the last by its failure; the scow, which had now
got fairly in motion, gliding ahead into deep water with a
velocity that set the designs of their enemies at naught. As
the two men were prevented by the position of the cabin from
seeing what passed astern, they were compelled to inquire of
the girls into the state of the chase.

"What now, Judith? What next? Do the Mingos still follow, or are we quit of 'em for the present?" demanded Deerslayer when he felt the rope yielding, as if the scow was
going fast ahead, and heard the scream and the laugh of
the girl almost in the same breath.

"They have vanished! One, the last, is just burying himself in the bushes of the bank—there, he has disappeared in
the shadows of the trees! You have got your friend, and we
are all safe!"

The two men now made another great effort, pulled the ark
up swiftly to the grapnel, tripped it, and when the scow had
shot some distance and lost its way, they let the anchor drop
again; then, for the first time since their meeting, they ceased
their efforts. As the floating house now lay several hundred
feet from the shore, and offered a complete protection against

bullets, there was no longer any danger, or any motive for immediate exertion.

The manner in which the two friends now recognized each other was highly characteristic. Chingachgook, a noble, tall, handsome, and athletic young Indian warrior, first examined his rifle with care, opening the pan to make sure the priming was not wet; assured of this important fact, he next cast furtive but observant glances around him at the strange habitation and at the two girls; still he spoke not, and most of all did he avoid the betrayal of a womanish curiosity by asking questions.

"Judith and Hetty," said Deerslayer, with an untaught, natural courtesy, "this is the Mohican chief of whom you've heard me speak; Chingachgook, as he is called, which signifies the Big Sarpent; so named for his wisdom, and prudence, and cunning; my 'arliest and latest friend. I know'd it must be he by the hawk's feather over the left ear, most other warriors wearing 'em on the warlock."

As Deerslayer ceased speaking, he laughed heartily, excited more perhaps by the delight of having got his friend safe at his side under circumstances so trying than by any conceit that happened to cross his fancy, and exhibiting this outbreaking of feeling in a manner that was a little remarkable, since his merriment was not accompanied by any noise. Although Chingachgook both understood and spoke English, he was unwilling to communicate his thoughts in it, like most Indians, and when he had met Judith's cordial shake of the hand and Hetty's milder salute in the courteous manner that became a chief, he turned away, apparently to await the moment when it might suit his friend to enter into an explanation of his future intentions and to give a narrative of what had passed since their separation. The other understood his meaning and discovered his own mode of reasoning in the matter by addressing the girls.

"This wind will soon die away altogether, now the sun is down," he said, "and there is no need of rowing ag'in it. In half an hour or so it will either be a flat calm or the air will come off from the south shore, when we will begin our journey back ag'in to the castle; in the meanwhile, the Delaware and I will talk over matters and get correct ideas of each other's notions consarning the course we ought to take."

No one opposed this proposition, and the girls withdrew into the cabin to prepare the evening meal, while the two young men took their seats on the head of the scow and began to converse. The dialogue was in the language of the Delawares. As that dialect, however, is but little understood, even by the learned, we shall, not only on this but on all subsequent occasions, render such parts as it may be necessary to give closely into liberal English, preserving, as far as possible, the idioms and peculiarities of the respective speakers, by way of presenting the pictures in the most graphic forms to the minds of the readers.

It is unnecessary to enter into the details first related by Deerslayer, who gave a brief narrative of the facts that are already familiar to those who have read our pages. In relating these events, however, it may be well to say that the speaker touched only on the outlines, more particularly abstaining from saying anything about his encounter with, and victory over, the Iroquois, as well as to his own exertions in behalf of the deserted young women. When Deerslayer ended, the Delaware took up the narrative in turn, speaking sententiously and with great dignity. His account was both clear and short, nor was it embellished by any incidents that did not directly concern the history of his departure from the villages of his people and his arrival in the valley of the Susquehanna. On reaching the latter, which was at a point only half a mile south of the outlet, he had soon struck a trail, which gave him notice of the probable vicinity of enemies. Being prepared for such an occurrence, the object of the expedition calling him directly into the neighborhood of the party of Iroquois that was known to be out, he considered the discovery as fortunate, rather than the reverse, and took the usual precautions to turn it to account. First following the river to its source, and ascertaining the position of the rock, he met another trail, and had actually been hovering for hours on the flanks of his enemies, watching equally for an opportunity to meet his mistress and to take a scalp —and it may be questioned which he most ardently desired. He kept near the lake, and occasionally he ventured to some spot where he could get a view of what was passing on its surface. The ark had been seen and watched from the moment it hove in sight, though the young chief was necessarily ignorant that it was to be the instrument of effecting the desired junction with his friend. The uncertainty of its movements, and the fact that it was unquestionably managed by white men, led him to conjecture the truth, however, and he held himself in readiness to get on board whenever a suitable occasion might offer. As the sun drew near the horizon, he repaired to the rock, where, on emerging from the forest, he was gratified in finding the ark lying apparently in readiness to receive him. The manner of his appearance, and of his entrance into the craft, is known.

Although Chingachgook had been closely watching his enemies for hours, their sudden and close pursuit, as he reached the scow, was as much a matter of surprise to himself as it had been to his friend. He could only account for it by the fact of their being more numerous than he had at first supposed, and by their having out parties, of the existence of which he was ignorant. Their regular and permanent encampment, if the word permanent can be applied to the residence of a party that intended to remain out, in all probability, but a few weeks, was not far from the spot where Hutter and Hurry had fallen into their hands, and, as a matter of course, near a spring.

"Well, Sarpent," asked Deerslayer, when the other had ended his brief but spirited narrative, speaking always in the Delaware tongue, which, for the reader's convenience only, we render into the peculiar vernacular of the speaker.

"Well, Sarpent, as you've been scouting around these Mingos, have you anything to tell us of their captyves; the father of these young women and another, who, I somewhat conclude, is the lovyer of one of 'em."

"Chingachgook has seen them. An old man and a young warrior—the falling hemlock and the tall pine."

"You're not so much out, Delaware; you're not so much out. Old Hutter is decaying, of a sartainty, though many solid blocks might be hewn out of his trunk yet; as for Hurry Harry, so far as height and strength and comeliness go, he may be called the pride of the human forest. Were the men bound, or in any manner suffering torture? I ask on account of the young women, who, I dare to say, would be glad to know."

"It is not so, Deerslayer. The Mingos are too many to cage their game. Some watch, some sleep, some scout, some hunt. The palefaces are treated like brothers today; tomorrow they will lose their scalps."

"Yes, that's red natur', and must be submitted to! Judith and Hetty, here's comforting tidings for you, the Delaware telling me that neither your father nor Hurry Harry is in suffering; but, bating the loss of liberty, as well off as we are ourselves. Of course they are kept in the camp; otherwise they do much as they please."

"I rejoice to hear this, Deerslayer," returned Judith, "and now we are joined by your friend, I make no manner of question that we shall find an opportunity to ransom the prisoners. If there are any women in the camp, I have articles of dress that will catch their eyes; and should the worst come to the worst, we can open the good chest, which, I think, will be found to hold things that may tempt the chiefs."

"Judith," said the young man, looking up at her with a smile and an expression of earnest curiosity that, in spite of the growing obscurity, did not escape the watchful looks of the girl, "can you find it in your heart to part with your own finery to release prisoners, even though one be your own father, and the other is your sworn suitor and lovyer?"

The flush on the face of the girl arose in part from resentment, but more perhaps from a gentler and novel feeling that, with the capricious waywardness of taste, had been rapidly rendering her more sensitive to the good opinion of the youth who questioned her than to that of any other person. Suppressing the angry sensation with instinctive quickness, she answered with a readiness and truth that caused her sister to draw near to listen, though the obtuse intellect of the latter was far from comprehending the workings of a heart as treacherous, as uncertain, and as impetuous in its feelings as that of the spoiled and flattered beauty.

"Deerslayer," answered Judith, after a moment's pause, "I shall be honest with *you*. I confess that the time *has* been when what you call finery was to me the dearest thing on earth, but I begin to feel differently. Though Hurry Harry is naught to me, nor ever can be, I would give all I own to set him free. If I would do this for blustering, bullying, talking Hurry, who has nothing but good looks to recommend him, you may judge what I would do for my own father."

"This sounds well and is according to woman's gifts. Ah's me! The same feelin's is to be found among the young women of the Delawares. I've known 'em, often and often, sacrifice their vanity to their hearts. 'Tis as it should be—'tis as it should be, I suppose, in both colors. Woman was created for the feelin's, and is pretty much ruled by feelin'!"

"Would the savages let Father go, if Judith and I gave them all our best things?" demanded Hetty, in her innocent, mild manner.

"Their women might interfere, good Hetty; yes, their women might interfere with such an ind in view. But, tell me, Sarpent, how is it as to squaws among the knaves; have they many of their own women in the camp?"

The Delaware heard and understood all that passed, though with Indian gravity and finesse he had sat, with averted face, seemingly inattentive to a discourse in which he had no direct concern. Thus appealed to, however, he answered his friend in his ordinary sententious manner.

"Six," he said, holding up all the fingers of one hand, and the thumb of the other, "besides *this*." The last number denoted his betrothed, whom, with the poetry and truth of nature, he described by laying his hand on his own heart.

"Did you see her, Chief—did you get a glimpse of her pleasant countenance, or come close enough to her ear to sing in it the song she loves to hear?"

"No, Deerslayer—the trees were too many, and leaves covered their boughs like clouds hiding the heavens in a storm. But," and the young warrior turned his dark face toward his friend, with a smile on it that illuminated its fierce-looking paint and naturally stern lineaments with a bright gleam of human feeling; "Chingachgook heard the laugh of Wah-ta! Wah; he knew it from the laugh of the women of the Iroquois. It sounded in his ears like the chirp of the wren."

"Aye, trust a lovyer's ear for that, and a Delaware's ear for all sounds that are ever heard in the woods. I know not why it is so, Judith, but when young men—and I dares to say it may be all the same with young women, too—but when they get to have kind feelin's toward each other, it's wonderful how pleasant they laugh, or the speech becomes to the other person. I've seen grim warriors listening to the chattering and the laughing of young gals as if it was church music such as is heard in the old Dutch church that stands in the great street of Albany, where I've been more than once, with peltry and game."

"And *you*, Deerslayer," said Judith quickly and with more sensibility than marked her usually light and thoughtless manner; "have *you* never felt how pleasant it is to listen to the laugh of the girl you love?"

"Lord bless you, gal!—why I've never lived enough among my own color to drop into them sort of feelin's—no, never! I dares to say they are nat'ral and right, but to me there's no music so sweet as the sighing of the wind in the treetops and the rippling of a stream from a full, sparkling natyve fountain of pure fresh water; unless, indeed," he continued, dropping his head for an instant in a thoughtful manner, "it be the open mouth of a sartain hound when I'm on the track of a fat buck. As for unsartain dogs I care little for their cries, seein' they are as likely to speak when the deer is not in sight as when it is."

Judith walked slowly and pensively away, nor was there any of her ordinary calculating coquetry in the light, tremulous sigh that, unconsciously to herself, arose to her lips. On the other hand, Hetty listened with guileless attention, though it struck her simple mind as singular that the young man should prefer the melody of the woods to the songs of girls, or even to the laugh of innocence and joy. Accustomed, however, to defer in most things to her sister, she soon followed Judith into the cabin, where she took a seat and remained pondering intensely over some occurrence, or resolution, or opinion, which was a secret to all but herself. Left alone, Deerslayer and his friend resumed their discourse.

"Has the young paleface hunter been long on this lake?" demanded the Delaware, after courteously waiting for the other to speak first.

"Only since yesterday noon, Sarpent, though that has been long enough to see and do much."

The gaze that the Indian fastened on his companion was so keen that it seemed to mock the gathering darkness of the night. As the other furtively returned his look, he saw the two black eyes glistening on him, like the balls of the panther, or those of the penned wolf. He understood the meaning of this glowing gaze and answered evasively, as he fancied would best become the modesty of a white man's gifts.

" 'Tis as you suspect, Sarpent; yes, 'tis somewhat thataway. I *have* fell in with the inimy, and I suppose it may be said I've fou't them, too."

An exclamation of delight and exultation escaped the Indian; then, laying his hand eagerly on the arm of his friend, he asked if there were any scalps taken.

"That I *will* maintain, in the face of all the Delaware tribe, old Tamenund, and your father, the great Uncas, as well as the rest, is ag'in white gifts! *My* scalp is on my head, as you can see, Sarpent, and that was the only scalp that was in danger, when one side was altogether Christian and white."

"Did no warrior fall? Deerslayer did not get his name by being slow of sight, or clumsy with the rifle!"

"In that particular, Chief, you're nearer reason and therefore nearer being right. I may say one Mingo fell."

"A chief!" demanded the other, with startling vehemence.

"Nay, that's more than I know or can say. He was artful, and treacherous, and stouthearted, and may well have gained popularity enough with his people to be named to that rank. The man fou't well, though his eye wasn't quick enough for one who had had his schooling in your company, Delaware."

"My brother and friend struck the body?"

"That was uncalled for, seeing that the Mingo died in my arms. The truth may as well be said at once; he fou't like a man of red gifts, and I fou't like a man with gifts of my own color. God gave me the victory; I couldn't fly in the face of His Providence by forgetting my birth and natur'. White he made me, and white I shall live and die."

"Good! Deerslayer is a paleface and has paleface hands. A Delaware will look for the scalp, and hang it on a pole, and sing a song in his honor, when we go back to our people. The honor belongs to the tribe; it must not be lost."

"This is easy talking, but 'twill not be as easy doing. The Mingo's body is in the hands of his fri'nds and no doubt is hid in some hole, where Delaware cunning will never be able to get at the scalp."

The young man then gave his friend a succinct but clear account of the event of the morning, concealing nothing of any moment and yet touching on everything modestly and with a careful attention to avoid the Indian habit of boasting. Chingachgook again expressed his satisfaction at the honor won by his friend, and then both arose, the hour having arrived when it became prudent to move the ark further from the land.

It was now quite dark, the heavens having become clouded, and the stars hid. The north wind had ceased, as was usual, with the setting of the sun, and a light air arose from the south. This change favoring the design of Deerslayer, he lifted his grapnel, and the scow immediately and quite perceptibly began to drift more into the lake. The sail was set, when the motion of the craft increased to a rate not much less than two miles in the hour. As this superseded the necessity of rowing—an occupation that an Indian would not be likely to desire—Deerslayer, Chingachgook, and Judith seated themselves in the stern of the scow, where the first governed its movements by holding the oar. Here they discoursed on their future movements and on the means that ought to be used in order to effect the liberation of their friends.

In this dialogue Judith held a material part, the Delaware readily understanding all she said, while his own replies and remarks, both of which were few and pithy, were occasionally rendered into English by his friend. Judith rose greatly in the estimation of her companions in the half hour that followed. Prompt of resolution and firm of purpose, her suggestions and expedients partook of her spirit and sagacity, both of which were of a character to find favor with men of the frontier. The events that had occurred since their meeting, as well as her isolated and dependent situation, induced the girl to feel toward Deerslayer like the friend of a year instead of an acquaintance of a day, and so completely had she been won by his guileless truth of character and of feeling—pure novelties in our sex, as respected her own experience—that his peculiarities excited her curiosity and created a confidence that had never been awakened by any other man. Hitherto she had been compelled to stand on the defensive in her intercourse with men—with what success was best known to herself—but here had she been suddenly thrown into the society and under the protection of a youth who evidently as little contemplated evil toward herself as if he had been her brother. The freshness of his integrity, the poetry and truth of his feelings, and even the quaintness of his forms of speech all had their influence and aided in awakening an interest that she found as pure as it was sudden and deep. Hurry's fine face and manly form had never compensated for his boisterous and vulgar turn, and her intercourse with the officers had prepared her to make comparisons under which even his great natural advantages suffered. But this very intercourse with the officers who occasionally came upon the lake to fish and hunt had an effect in producing her present sentiments toward the young stranger. With them, while her vanity had been gratified and her self-love strongly awakened, she had many causes deeply to regret the acquaintance—if not to mourn over it in secret sorrow—for it was impossible for one of her quick intellect not to perceive how hollow was the association between superior and inferior, and that she was regarded as the plaything of an idle hour rather than as an equal and a friend by even the best intentioned and least designing of her scarlet-clad admirers. Deerslayer, on the other hand, had a window in his breast through which the light of his honesty was ever shining, and even his indifference to charms that so rarely failed to produce a sensation piqued the pride of the girl and gave him an interest that another, seemingly more favored by nature, might have failed to excite.

In this manner half an hour passed, during which time the ark had been slowly stealing over the water, the darkness thickening around it, though it was easy to see that the gloom of the forest at the southern end of the lake was getting to be distant, while the mountains that lined the sides of the beautiful basin were overshadowing it, nearly from side to side. There was, indeed, a narrow stripe of water in the center of the lake where the dim light that was still shed from the heavens fell upon its surface in a line extending north and south; along this faint tract—a sort of inverted Milky Way, in which the obscurity was not quite as dense as in other places—the scow held her course, he who steered well knowing that it led in the direction he wished to go. The reader is not to suppose, however, that any difficulty could exist as to the course. This would have been determined by that of the air had it not been possible to distinguish the mountains, as well as by the dim opening to the south, which marked the position of the valley in that quarter, above the plain of tall trees, by a sort of lessened obscurity; the difference between the darkness of the forest and that of the night as seen only in the air. The peculiarities at length caught the attention of

Judith and the Deerslayer, and the conversation ceased, to allow each to gaze at the solemn stillness and deep repose of nature.

" 'Tis a gloomy night," observed the girl, after a pause of several minutes. "I hope we may be able to find the castle."

"Little fear of our missing *that*, if we keep this path in the middle of the lake," returned the young man. "Natur' has made us a road here, and dim as it is, there'll be little difficulty in following it."

"Do you hear nothing, Deerslayer? It seemed as if the water was stirring quite near us!"

"Sartainly something *did* move the water, oncommon like; it must have been a fish. Them creatur's prey upon each other like men and animals on the land; one has leaped into the air and fallen back hard into his own element. 'Tis of little use, Judith, for any to strive to get out of their elements, since it's natur' to stay in 'em, and natur' will have its way. Ha! *That* sounds like a paddle, used with more than common caution!"

At this moment the Delaware bent forward and pointed significantly into the boundary of gloom, as if some object had suddenly caught his eye. Both Deerslayer and Judith followed the direction of his gesture, and each got a view of a canoe at the same instant. The glimpse of this startling neighbor was dim, and to eyes less practiced it might have been uncertain, though to those in the ark the object was evidently a canoe with a single individual in it, the latter standing erect and paddling. How many lay concealed in its bottom, of course, could not be known. Flight, by means of oars, from a bark canoe impelled by vigorous and skillful hands was utterly impracticable, and each of the men seized his rifle in expectation of a conflict.

"I can easily bring down the paddler," whispered Deerslayer, "but we'll first hail him and ask his ar'nd." Then raising his voice, he continued in a solemn manner, "Hold! If you come nearer, I must fire, though contrary to my wishes, and then sartain death will follow. Stop paddling, and answer!"

"Fire, and slay a poor, defenseless girl," returned a soft, tremulous female voice, "and God will never forgive you! Go your way, Deerslayer, and let me go mine."

"Hetty!" exclaimed the young man and Judith in a breath,

and the former sprang instantly to the spot where he had left the canoe they had been towing. It was gone, and he understood the whole affair. As for the fugitive, frightened at the menace, she ceased paddling and remained dimly visible, resembling a spectral outline of a human form, standing on the water. At the next moment the sail was lowered to prevent the ark from passing the spot where the canoe lay. This last expedient, however, was not taken in time, for the momentum of so heavy a craft and the impulsion of the air soon set her by, bringing Hetty directly to windward, though still visible, as the change in the positions of the two boats now placed her in that species of Milky Way which has been mentioned.

"What can this mean, Judith?" demanded Deerslayer. "Why has your sister taken the canoe and left us?"

"You know she is feeble-minded, poor girl! And she has her own ideas of what ought to be done. She loves her father more than most children love their parents—and then——"

"Then, what, gal? This is a trying moment, one in which truth must be spoken."

Judith felt a generous and womanly regret at betraying her sister, and she hesitated ere she spoke again. But once more urged by Deerslayer, and conscious herself of all the risks the whole party was running by the indiscretion of Hetty, she could refrain no longer.

"Then, I fear, poor, weak-minded Hetty has not been altogether able to see the vanity, and madness, and folly that lie hid behind the handsome face and fine form of Hurry Harry. She talks of him in her sleep and sometimes betrays the inclination in her waking moments."

"You think, Judith, that your sister is now bent on some mad scheme to serve her father and Hurry, which will, in all likelihood, give them riptyles, the Mingos, the mastership of a canoe?"

"Such, I fear, will turn out to be the fact, Deerslayer. Poor Hetty has hardly sufficient cunning to outwit a savage."

All this while the canoe, with the form of Hetty erect in one end of it, was dimly perceptible, though the greater drift of the ark rendered it at each instant less and less distinct. It was evident no time was to be lost, lest it should altogether disappear. The rifles were now laid aside as useless, the two men seizing the oars and sweeping the head of the scow around in the direction of the canoe. Judith, accustomed to the office, flew to the other end of the ark and placed herself at what might be called the helm. Hetty took the alarm at these preparations, which could not be made without noise, and started off like a bird that had been suddenly put up by the approach of unexpected danger.

As Deerslayer and his companion rowed with the energy of those who felt the necessity of straining every nerve, and Hetty's strength was impaired by a nervous desire to escape, the chase would have quickly terminated in the capture of the fugitive had not the girl made several short and unlooked-for deviations in her course. These turnings gave her time, and they had also the effect of gradually bringing both canoe and ark within the deeper gloom cast by the shadows from the hills. They also gradually increased the distance between the fugitive and her pursuers, until Judith called out to her companions to cease rowing, for she had completely lost sight of the canoe.

When this mortifying announcement was made, Hetty was actually so near as to understand every syllable her sister uttered; though the latter had used the precaution of speaking as low as circumstances would allow her to do and make herself heard. Hetty stopped paddling at the same moment and waited the result with an impatience that was breathless, equally from her late exertions and her desire to land. A dead silence immediately fell on the lake, during which the three in the ark were using their senses differently in order to detect the position of the canoe. Judith leaned forward to listen, in the hope of catching some sound that might betray the direction in which her sister was stealing away, while her two companions brought their eyes as near as possible to a level with the water, in order to detect any object that might be floating on its surface. All was vain, however, for neither sound nor sight rewarded their efforts. All this time, Hetty, who had not the cunning to sink into the canoe, stood erect, a finger pressed on her lips, gazing in the direction in which the voices had been heard, resembling a statue of profound and timid attention. Her ingenuity had barely sufficed to enable her to seize the canoe and to quit the ark in the noiseless manner related; and then it appeared to be momentarily exhausted. Even the doublings of the canoe had been as much the consequence of an uncertain hand and of nervous agitation as of any craftiness or calculation.

The pause continued several minutes, during which Deerslayer and the Delaware conferred together in the language of the latter. Then the oars dipped again, and the ark moved away, rowing with as little noise as possible. It steered westward, a little southerly, or in the direction of the encampment of the enemy. Having reached a point at no great distance from the shore, and where the obscurity was intense, on account of the proximity of the land, it lay there near an hour, in waiting for the expected approach of Hetty, who, it was thought, would make the best of her way to that spot as soon as she believed herself relieved from the danger of pursuit. No success rewarded this little blockade, however, neither appearance nor sound denoting the passage of the canoe. Disappointed at this failure, and conscious of the importance of getting possession of the fortress before it could be seized by the enemy, Deerslayer now took his way toward the castle with the apprehension that all his foresight in securing the canoes would be defeated by this ungarded and alarming movement on the part of the feebleminded Hetty.

Chapter X

> ——*But who in this wild wood*
> *May credit give to either eye or ear?*
> *From rocky precipice or hollow cave,*
> *'Midst the confused sound of rustling leaves,*
> *And crackling boughs, and cries of nightly birds,*
> *Returning seeming answer.*
>
> JOANNA BAILLIE

FEAR, AS MUCH as calculation, had induced Hetty to cease paddling when she found that her pursuers did not know in which direction to proceed. She remained stationary until the ark had pulled in near the encampment—as has been related in the preceding chapter—when she resumed the paddle and, with cautious strokes, made the best of her way toward the western shore. In order to avoid her pursuers, however, who, she rightly suspected, would soon be rowing along that shore themselves, the head of the canoe was pointed so far north as to bring her to land on a point that thrust itself into the lake, at the distance of near a league from the outlet. Nor was this altogether the result of a desire to escape; feeble-minded as she was, Hetty Hutter had a good deal of that instinctive caution which so often keeps those whom God has thus visited from harm. She was perfectly aware of the importance of keeping the canoes from falling into the hands of the Iroquois, and long familiarity with the lake had suggested one of the simplest expedients by which this great object could be rendered compatible with her own purpose.

The point in question was the first projection that offered on that side of the lake where a canoe, if set adrift with a southerly air, would float clear of the land, and where it would be no great violation of probabilities to suppose it might even hit the castle, the latter lying above it almost in a direct line with the wind. Such then was Hetty's intention, and she landed on the extremity of the gravelly point, beneath an overhanging oak, with the express intention of shoving the canoe off from the shore, in order that it might drift up toward her father's insulated abode. She knew, too, from the logs that occasionally floated about the lake that, did it miss the castle and its appendages, the wind would be likely to change before the canoe could reach the northern extremity of the lake, and that Deerslayer might have an opportunity of regaining it in the morning, when no doubt he would be earnestly sweeping the surface of the water and the whole of its wooded shores with the glass. In all this, too, Hetty was less governed by any chain of reasoning than by her habits, the latter often supplying the defects of mind in human beings, as they perform the same office for animals of the inferior classes.

The girl was quite an hour finding her way to the point, the distance and the obscurity equally detaining her, but she was no sooner on the gravelly beach than she prepared to set the canoe adrift, in the manner mentioned. While in the act of pushing it from her, she heard low voices that seemed to come from among the trees behind her. Startled at this unexpected danger, Hetty was on the point of springing into the canoe again, in order to seek safety in flight, when she thought she recognized the tones of Judith's melodious voice. Bending forward so as to catch the sounds more directly— they evidently came from the water—she then understood that the ark was approaching from the south, so close in with the western shore as necessarily to cause it to pass the point within twenty yards of the spot where she stood. Here, then, was all she could desire: the canoe was shoved off into the lake, leaving its late occupant alone on the narrow strand.

When this act of self-devotion was performed, Hetty did not retire. The foliage of the overhanging trees and bushes would have almost concealed her person, had there been light, but in that obscurity it was utterly impossible to discover any object thus shaded at the distance of a few feet. Flight, too was perfectly easy, as twenty steps would effectually bury her in the forest. She remained, therefore, watching with intense anxiety the result of her expedient, intending to call the attention of the others to the canoe with her

voice, should they appear to pass without observing it. The
ark approached under its sail again, Deerslayer standing in
its bow, with Judith near him, and the Delaware at the helm.
It would seem that, in the bay below, it had got too close to
the shore in the lingering hope of intercepting Hetty, for as
it came nearer, the latter distinctly heard the directions that
the young man forward gave to his companion, in order to
clear the point.

"Lay her head more off the shore, Delaware," said Deerslayer for the third time, speaking in English, that his fair
companion might understand his words; "lay her head well
offshore. We have got embayed here and needs keep the
mast clear of the trees. Judith, there's a canoe!"

The last words were uttered with great earnestness, and
Deerslayer's hand was on his rifle ere they were fairly out
of his mouth. But the truth flashed on the mind of the quick-
witted girl, and she instantly told her companion that the
boat *must* be that in which her sister had fled.

"Keep the scow straight, Delaware; steer as straight as
your bullet flies when sent ag'in a buck; there—I have it."

The canoe was seized and immediately secured again to
the side of the ark. At the next moment the sail was lowered,
and the motion of the ark arrested by means of the oars.

"Hetty!" called out Judith, concern, even affection, betraying itself in her tones. "Are you within hearing, sister—
for God's sake answer, and let me hear the sound of your
voice again! Hetty! Dear Hetty!"

"I'm here, Judith—here on the shore, where it will be useless to follow me, as I will hide in the woods."

"Oh, Hetty, what is't you do! Remember, 'tis drawing
near midnight, and the woods are filled with savages and
wild beasts!"

"Neither will harm a poor half-witted girl, Judith. God is
as much with me here as he would be in the ark, or in the
hut. I am going to help my father and poor Hurry Harry,
who will be tortured and slain unless someone cares for
them."

"We all care for them and intend tomorrow to send them a
flag of truce to buy their ransom. Come back then, sister;
trust to us, who have better heads than you and who will do
all we can for Father."

"I know your head is better than mine, Judith, for mine is

very weak, to be sure, but I must go to Father and poor Hurry. Do you and Deerslayer keep the castle, sister; leave me in the hands of God."

"God is with us all, Hetty—in the castle, or on the shore —Father as well as ourselves; it is sinful not to trust to His goodness. You can do nothing in the dark, will lose your way in the forest and perish for want of food."

"God will not let that happen to a poor child that goes to serve her father, sister. I must try and find the savages."

"Come back for this night only; in the morning we will put you ashore and leave you to do as you may think right."

"You *say* so, Judith, and you *think* so, but you would not. Your heart would soften, and you'd see tomahawks and scalping knives in the air. Besides, I've got a thing to tell the Indian chief that will answer all our wishes, and I'm afraid I may forget it if I don't tell it to him at once. You'll see that he will let Father go as soon as he hears it!"

"Poor Hetty! What can *you* say to a ferocious savage that will be likely to change his bloody purpose!"

"That which will frighten him and make him let Father go," returned the simple-minded girl positively. "You'll see, sister; you'll see how soon it will bring him to, like a gentle child!"

"Will you tell *me*, Hetty, what you intend to say?" asked Deerslayer. "I know the savages well and can form some idee how far fair words will be likely, or not, to work on their bloody natur's. If it's not suited to the gifts of a redskin, 'twill be of no use, for reason goes by gifts, as well as conduct."

"Well, then," answered Hetty, dropping her voice to a low, confidential tone; for the stillness of the night and the nearness of the ark permitted her to do this and still to be heard. "Well, then, Deerslayer, as you seem a good and honest young man, I will tell *you*. I mean not to say a word to any of the savages until I get face to face with their head chief, let them plague me with as many questions as they please; no—I'll answer none of them, unless it be to tell them to lead me to their wisest man. Then, Deerslayer, I'll tell him that God will not forgive murder and thefts, and that if Father and Hurry did go after the scalps of the Iroquois, he must return good for evil, for so the Bible commands, else he will go into everlasting punishment. When he hears this and feels it to be true, as feel it he must, how long will it be before he sends Father and Hurry and me to the shore opposite the castle, telling us all three to go our way in peace?"

The last question was put in a triumphant manner, and then the simple-minded girl laughed at the impression she never doubted that her project had made on her auditors. Deerslayer was dumfounded at this proof of guileless feebleness of mind, but Judith had suddenly bethought her of a means of counteracting this wild project, by acting on the very feelings that had given it birth. Without adverting to the closing question, or the laugh, therefore, she hurriedly called to her sister by name, as one suddenly impressed with the importance of what she had to say. But no answer was given to the call.

By the snapping of twigs, and the rustling of leaves, Hetty had evidently quitted the shore, and was already burying herself in the forest. To follow would have been bootless, since the darkness, as well as the dense cover that the woods everywhere afforded, would have rendered her capture next to impossible, there was also the never-ceasing danger of falling into the hands of their enemies. After a short and melancholy discussion, therefore, the sail was again set, and the ark pursued its course toward its habitual moorings, Deerslayer silently felicitating himself on the recovery of the canoe and brooding over his plans for the morrow. The wind rose as the party quitted the point, and in less than an hour they reached the castle. Here all was found as it had been left, and the reverse of the ceremonies had to be taken in entering the building that had been used on quitting it. Judith occupied a solitary bed that night, bedewing the pillow with her tears as she thought of the innocent and hitherto neglected creature who had been her companion from childhood; bitter regrets came over her mind from more causes than one, as the weary hours passed away, making it nearly morning before she lost her recollection in sleep. Deerslayer and the Delaware took their rest in the ark, where we shall leave them enjoying the deep sleep of the honest, the healthful, and fearless, to return to the girl we have last seen in the midst of the forest.

When Hetty left the shore, she took her way unhesitatingly into the woods with a nervous apprehension of being followed. Luckily, this course was the best she could have hit on to effect her own purpose, since it was the only one that led her from the point. The night was so intensely dark, beneath the branches of the trees, that her progress was very slow, and the direction she went altogether a matter of chance, after the first few yards. The formation of the ground, however, did not permit her to deviate far from the line in which she desired to proceed. On one hand, it was soon bounded by the acclivity of the hill, while the lake on the other served as a guide. For two hours did this singlehearted and simple-minded girl toil through the mazes of the forest, sometimes finding herself on the brow of the bank that bounded the water, and at others struggling up an ascent that warned her to go no further in that direction, since it necessarily ran at right angles to the course on which she wished to proceed. Her feet often slid from beneath her, and she got many falls, though none to do her injury; but by the end of the period mentioned, she had become so weary as to want strength to go any further. Rest was indispensable, and she set about preparing a bed with the readiness and coolness of one to whom the wilderness presented no unnecessary terrors. She knew that wild beasts roamed through all the adjacent forest, but animals that preyed on the human species were rare, and of dangerous serpents there were literally none. These facts had been taught her by her father, and whatever her feeble mind received at all, it received so confidingly as to leave her no uneasiness from any doubts or skepticism. To her the sublimity of the solitude in which she was placed was soothing rather than appalling, and she gathered a bed of leaves with as much indifference to the circumstances that would have driven the thoughts of sleep entirely from the minds of most of her sex as if she had been preparing her place of nightly rest beneath the paternal roof.

As soon as Hetty had collected a sufficient number of the dried leaves to protect her person from the damps of the ground, she kneeled beside the humble pile, clasped her raised hands in an attitude of deep devotion, and in a soft, low, but audible voice repeated the Lord's Prayer. This was followed by those simple and devout verses, so familiar to children, in which she recommended her soul to God, should it be called away to another state of existence ere the return of morning. This duty done, she lay down and disposed herself to sleep. The attire of the girl, though suited to the season, was sufficiently warm for all ordinary purposes, but the forest is ever cool, and the nights of that elevated region of country have always a freshness about them that renders clothing more necessary than is commonly the case in the summers of a low latitude. This had been foreseen by Hetty, who had brought with her a coarse, heavy mantle, which, when laid over her body, answered all the useful purposes of a blanket. Thus protected, she dropped asleep in a few minutes, as tranquilly as if watched over by the guardian care of that mother who had so recently been taken from her forever—affording, in this particular, a most striking contrast between her own humble couch and the sleepless pillow of her sister.

Hour passed after hour in a tranquillity as undisturbed and a rest as sweet as if angels expressly commissioned for that object watched around the bed of Hetty Hutter. Not once did her soft eyes open, until the gray of the dawn came struggling through the tops of the trees, falling on their lids and, united to the freshness of a summer's morning, giving the usual summons to awake. Ordinarily, Hetty was up ere the rays of the sun tipped the summits of the mountains, but on this occasion her fatigue had been so great and her rest was so profound that the customary warnings failed of their effect. The girl murmured in her sleep, threw an arm forward, smiled as gently as an infant in its cradle, but still slumbered. In making this unconscious gesture, her hand fell on some object that was warm, and, in the half-unconscious state in which she lay, she connected the circumstance with her habits. At the next moment, a rude attack was made on her side, as if a rooting animal were thrusting its snout beneath with a desire to force her position; then, uttering the name of "Judith," she awoke. As the startled girl arose to a sitting attitude, she perceived that some dark object sprang from her, scattering the leaves and snapping the fallen twigs in its haste. Opening her eyes and recovering from the first confusion and astonishment of her situation, Hetty perceived a cub of the common American brown bear balancing itself on its hinder legs and still looking toward her, as if doubtful whether it would be safe to trust itself near her person again. The first impulse of Hetty, who had been mistress of several of these cubs, was to run and seize the little creature as a prize, but a loud growl warned her of the danger of such a procedure. Recoiling a few steps, the girl looked hurriedly around and perceived the dam watching her movements, with fiery eyes, at no great distance. A hollow tree that had once been the home of bees having recently fallen, the mother, with two more cubs, was feasting on the dainty food that this accident had placed within her reach, while the first kept a jealous eye on the situation of its truant and reckless young.

It would exceed all the means of human knowledge to pretend to analyze the influences that govern the acts of the lower animals. On this occasion, the dam, though proverbially fierce when its young is thought to be in danger, manifested no intention to attack the girl. It quitted the honey and advanced to a place within twenty feet of her, where it raised itself on its hinder legs and balanced its body in a sort of angry, growling discontent, but approached no nearer. Happily, Hetty did not fly. On the contrary, though not without terror, she knelt with her face toward the animal and, with clasped hands and uplifted eyes, repeated the prayer of the previous night. This act of devotion was not the result of alarm; it was a duty she never neglected to perform ere she slept, and when the return of consciousness awoke her to the business of the day. As the girl arose from her knees, the bear dropped on her feet again and, collecting its cubs around her, permitted them to draw their natural sustenance. Hetty was delighted with this proof of tenderness in an animal that has but a very indifferent reputation for the gentler feelings, and as a cub would quit its mother to frisk and leap about in wantonness, she felt a strong desire again to catch it up in her arms and play with it. But admonished by the growl, she had self-command sufficient not to put this dangerous project in execution; and recollecting her errand among the hills, she tore herself away from the group and proceeded on her course, along the margin of the lake, of which she now caught glimpses again through the trees. To her surprise, though not to her alarm, the family of bears arose and followed her steps, keeping a short distance behind her, apparently watching every movement, as if they had a near interest in all she did.

In this manner, escorted by the dam and cubs, the girl proceeded nearly a mile, thrice the distance she had been able to achieve in the darkness during the same period of time.

She then reached a brook that had dug a channel for itself into the earth, and went brawling into the lake, between steep and high banks covered with trees. Here Hetty performed her ablutions; then, drinking of the pure mountain water, she went her way, refreshed and lighter of heart, still attended by her singular companions. Her course now lay along a broad and nearly level terrace, which stretched from the top of the bank that bounded the water to a low acclivity that rose to a second and irregular platform above. This was at a part of the valley where the mountains ran obliquely, forming the commencement of a plain that spread between the hills, southward of the sheet of water. Hetty knew by this circumstance that she was getting near to the encampment, and had she not, the bears would have given her warning of the vicinity of human beings. Snuffing the air, the dam refused to follow any further, though the girl looked back and invited her to come by childish signs and even by direct appeals made in her own sweet voice. It was while making her way slowly through some bushes in this manner, with averted face and eyes riveted on the immovable animals, that the girl suddenly found her steps arrested by a human hand that was laid lightly on her shoulder.

"Where go?" said a soft female voice, speaking hurriedly and in concern. "Indian—red man—savage—wicked warrior —thataway."

This unexpected salutation alarmed the girl no more than the presence of the fierce inhabitants of the woods. It took her a little by surprise, it is true, but she was in a measure prepared for some such meeting, and the creature who stopped her was as little likely to excite terror as any who ever appeared in the guise of an Indian. It was a girl not much older than herself, whose smile was sunny as Judith's in her brightest moments, whose voice was melody itself, and whose accents and manner had all the rebuked gentleness that characterizes the sex among a people who habitually treat their women as the attendants and servitors of the warriors. Beauty among the women of the aboriginal Americans, before they have become exposed to the hardships of wives and mothers, is by no means uncommon. In this particular the original owners of the country were not unlike their more civilized successors, *nature* appearing to have bestowed that delicacy of mien and outline that forms so great a charm in the youthful female, but of which they are so early deprived—and that, too, as much by the habits of domestic life as from any other cause.

The girl who had so suddenly arrested the steps of Hetty, was dressed in a calico mantle that effectually protected all the upper part of her person, while a short petticoat of blue cloth edged with gold lace, which fell no lower than her knees, leggings of the same, and moccasins of deerskin completed her attire. Her hair fell in long, dark braids down her shoulders and back, and was parted above a low, smooth forehead in a way to soften the expression of eyes that were full of archness and natural feeling. Her face was oval, with delicate features; the teeth were even and white; while the mouth expressed a melancholy tenderness, as if it wore that peculiar meaning in intuitive perception of the fate of a being who was doomed from birth to endure a woman's sufferings, relieved by a woman's affections. Her voice, as has been already intimated, was soft as the sighing of the night air, a characteristic of the females of her race, but which was so conspicuous in herself as to have procured for her the name of Wah-ta!-Wah, which, rendered into English, means Hist-oh!-Hist.

In a word, this was the betrothed of Chingachgook, who, having succeeded in lulling their suspicions, was permitted to wander around the encampment of her captors. This indulgence was in accordance with the general policy of the red man, who well knew, moreover, that her trail could have been followed in the event of flight. It will also be remembered that the Iroquois, or Hurons, as it would be better to call them, were entirely ignorant of the proximity of her lover; a fact, indeed, that she did not know herself.

It is not easy to say which manifested the most self-possession at this unexpected meeting, the paleface or the red girl. But though a little surprised, Wah-ta!-Wah was the most willing to speak and far the readier in foreseeing consequences as well as in devising means to avert them. Her father, during her childhood, had been much employed as a warrior by the authorities of the colony; dwelling for several years near the forts, she had caught a knowledge of the English tongue, which she spoke in the usual abbreviated manner of an Indian, but fluently and without any of the ordinary reluctance of her people.

"Where go?" repeated Wah-ta!-Wah, returning the smile of Hetty, in her own gentle, winning manner. "*Wicked* warrior thataway—*good* warrior far off."

"What's your name?" asked Hetty, with the simplicity of a child.

"Wah-ta!-Wah, I no Mingo—good Delaware—Yengeese * friend. Mingo cruel, and love scalp for blood—Delaware love him for honor. Come here, where no eyes."

Wah-ta!-Wah now led her companion toward the lake, descending the bank so as to place its overhanging trees and bushes between them and any probable observers; nor did she stop until they were both seated, side by side, on a fallen log, one end of which actually lay buried in the water.

"*Why* you come for?" the young Indian eagerly inquired. "*Where* you come from?"

Hetty told her tale in her own simple and truth-loving manner. She explained the situation of her father and stated her desire to serve him and, if possible, to procure his release.

"Why your father come to Mingo camp in night?" asked the Indian girl, with a directness which, if not borrowed from the other, partook largely of its sincerity. "He know it wartime, and he no boy—he no want beard—no want to be told Iroquois carry tomahawk, and knife, and rifle. Why he come nighttime, seize *me* by hair, and try to scalp Delaware girl?"

"You!" said Hetty, almost sickening with horror; "did he seize *you*—did he try to scalp *you?*"

"Why no? Delaware scalp sell for much as Mingo scalp. Governor no tell difference. Wicked t'ing for paleface to scalp. No his gifts, as good Deerslayer alway tell me."

---

* It is singular there should be any question concerning the origin of the well-known sobriquet of "Yankees." Nearly all the old writers who speak of the Indians first known to the colonists make them pronounce the word "English" as "Yengeese." Even at this day, it is a provincialism of New England to say "*En*glish" instead of "*In*glish," and there is a close conformity of sound between "*En*glish" and "Yengeese," more especially if the latter word, as was probably the case, be pronounced short. The transition from "Yengeese," thus pronounced, to "Yankees" is quite easy. If the former is pronounced "Yangis," it is almost identical with "Yankees," and Indian words have seldom been spelt as they are pronounced. Thus the scene of this tale is spelled "Ot*sego*" and is properly pronounced "Ot*sago*." The liquids of the Indians would easily convert "En" into "Yen."

"And do *you* know the Deerslayer?" said Hetty, coloring with delight and surprise, forgetting her regrets at the moment in the influence of this new feeling. "I know him, too. He is now in the ark, with Judith and a Delaware who is called the Big Serpent. A bold and handsome warrior is this Serpent, too!"

In spite of the rich, deep color that nature had bestowed on the Indian beauty, the telltale blood deepened on her cheeks, until the blush gave new animation and intelligence to her jet-black eyes. Raising a finger in an attitude of warning, she dropped her voice, already so soft and sweet, nearly to a whisper as she continued the discourse.

"Chingachgook!" returned the Delaware girl, sighing out the harsh name in sounds so softly guttural as to cause it to reach the ear in melody. "His father, Uncas—great chief of the Mahicanni—next to old Tamenund! More as warrior, not so much gray hair, and less at council fire. *You* know Serpent?"

"He joined us last evening and was in the ark with me for two or three hours before I left it. I'm afraid, Hist"—Hetty could not pronounce the Indian name of her new friend, but having heard Deerslayer give her this familiar appellation, she used it without any of the ceremony of civilized life— "I'm afraid he has come after scalps as well as my poor father and Hurry Harry!"

"Why he shouldn't, ha? Chingachgook red warrior, very red—scalp make his honor—be sure he take him."

"Then," said Hetty earnestly, "he will be as wicked as any other. God will not pardon in a red man what he will not pardon in a white man."

"No true," returned the Delaware girl, with a warmth that nearly amounted to passion; "no true, I tell you! The Manitou smile and please when he see young warrior come back from the warpath with two, ten, hundred scalp on a pole! Chingachgook father take scalp, grandfather take scalp —all old chief take scalp, and Chingachgook take as many scalp as he can carry himself!"

"Then, Hist, his sleep of nights must be terrible to think of! No one can be cruel and hope to be forgiven."

"No cruel—plenty forgiven," returned Wah-ta!-Wah, stamping her little foot on the stony strand and shaking her head in a way to show how completely feminine feeling, in

one of its aspects, had got the better of feminine feeling in
another. "I tell you, Serpent brave; he go home this time with
four, yes, *two* scalp."

"And is that his errand here? Did he really come all this
distance, across mountains and valleys, rivers and lakes, to
torment his fellow creatures and do so wicked a thing?"

This question at once appeased the growing ire of the half-
offended Indian beauty. It completely got the better of the
prejudices of education and turned all her thoughts to a
gentler and more feminine channel. At first, she looked
around her suspiciously, as if distrusting eavesdroppers; then
she gazed wistfully into the face of her attentive companion;
after which this exhibition of girlish coquetry and womanly
feeling terminated by her covering her face with both her
hands and laughing in a strain that might well be termed
the melody of the woods. Dread of discovery, however, soon
put a stop to this naïve exhibition of feeling, and removing
her hands, this creature of impulses gazed again wistfully
into the face of her companion, as if inquiring how far she
might trust a stranger with her secret. Although Hetty had no
claim to her sister's extraordinary beauty, many thought her
countenance the more winning of the two. It expressed all
the undisguised sincerity of her character, and it was totally
free from any of the unpleasant physical accompaniments
that so frequently attend mental imbecility. It is true that one
accustomed to closer observation than common might have
detected the proofs of her feebleness of intellect in the
language of her sometimes vacant eyes, but they were signs
that attracted sympathy by their total want of guile, rather
than by any other feeling. The effect on Hist, to use the
English and more familiar translation of the name, was
favorable, and yielding to an impulse of tenderness, she
threw her arms around Hetty and embraced her with an
outpouring emotion so natural that it was only equaled by
its warmth.

"*You* good," whispered the young Indian; "you good, I
know. It's so long since Wah-ta!-Wah have a friend—a
sister—anybody to speak her heart to! You Hist friend; don't
I say trut'!"

"I never had a friend," answered Hetty, returning the
warm embrace with unfeigned earnestness; "I've a sister, but
no friend. Judith loves me, and I love Judith, but that's

natural and as we are taught in the Bible; but I *should* like to have a *friend!* I'll be your friend, with all my heart, for I like your voice, and your smile, and your way of thinking in everything except about the scalps——"

"No t'ink more of him—no say more of scalp," interrupted Hist soothingly. "You paleface, I redskin; we bring up different fashion. Deerslayer and Chingachgook great friend, and no the same color; Hist and—what your name, pretty paleface?"

"I am called Hetty, though when they spell the name in the Bible, they always spell it Esther."

"What that make?—no good, no harm. No need to spell name at all. Moravian try to make Wah-ta!-Wah spell, but no won't let him. No good for Delaware girl to know too much —know more than warrior sometime; that great shame. My name Wah-ta!-Wah—that say Hist in your tongue. You call him, Hist—I call him, Hetty."

These preliminaries settled to their mutual satisfaction, the two girls began to discourse of their several hopes and projects. Hetty made her new friend more fully acquainted with her intentions in behalf of her father; and, to one in the least addicted to prying into the affairs of others, Hist would have betrayed her own feelings and expectations in connection with the young warrior of her own tribe. Enough was revealed on both sides, however, to let each party get a tolerable insight into the views of the other, though enough still remained in mental reservation to give rise to the following questions and answers, with which the interview in effect closed. As the quickest-witted, Hist was the first with her interrogatories. Folding an arm about the waist of Hetty, she bent her head so as to look up playfully into the face of the other; and, laughing, as if her meaning were to be extracted from her looks, she spoke more plainly.

"Hetty got broder as well as fader?" she said. "Why no talk of broder as well as fader?"

"I have no brother, Hist. I had one once, they say, but he is dead many a year and lies buried in the lake, by the side of Mother."

"No got broder—got a young warrior; love him almost as much as fader, eh? Very handsome and brave-looking; fit to be chief if he *good* as he *seem* to be."

"It's wicked to love any man as well as I love my father,

and so I strive not to do it, Hist," returned the conscientious Hetty, who knew not how to conceal an emotion by an approach to an untruth as venial as an evasion, though powerfully tempted by female shame to err; "though I sometimes think that wickedness will get the better of me, if Hurry comes so often to the lake. I *must* tell you the truth, dear Hist, because you ask me, but I should fall down and die in the woods if he knew it!"

"Why he no ask you himself? Brave-looking—why not bold-speaking? Young warrior ought to ask young girl; no make young girl speak first. Mingo girls too shame for *that*."

This was said indignantly and with the generous warmth a young female of spirit would be apt to feel at what she deemed an invasion of her sex's most valued privilege. It had little influence on the simple-minded, but also just-minded Hetty, who, though inherently feminine in all her impulses, was much more alive to the workings of her own heart than to any of the usages with which convention has protected the sensitiveness of her sex.

"Ask me *what?*" the startled girl demanded, with a suddenness that proved how completely her fears had been aroused. "Ask me if I like him as well as I do my own father? Oh, I hope he will never put such a question to *me*, for I should have to answer, and that would *kill* me!"

"No—no—no kill, *quite* almost," returned the other, laughing in spite of herself. "Make blush come—make shame come, too—but he no stay great while; then feel happier than ever. Young warrior must tell young girl he want to make wife, else never can live in his wigwam."

"Hurry don't want to marry me—nobody will ever want to marry me, Hist."

"How you can know? P'r'aps everybody want to marry you, and by-and-by tongue say what heart feel. Why nobody want to marry you?"

"I am not full-witted, they say. Father often tells me this; and so does Judith sometimes, when she is vexed; but I shouldn't so much mind them as I did Mother. *She* said so *once,* and then she cried as if her heart would break; and so I *know* I'm not full-witted."

Hist gazed at the gentle, simple girl for quite a minute without speaking; then the truth appeared to flash all at once on the mind of the young Indian maid. Pity, reverence, and tenderness seemed struggling together in her breast; then, rising suddenly, she indicated a wish to her companion that she would accompany her to the camp, which was situated at no great distance. This unexpected change, from the precaution that Hist had previously manifested a desire to use in order to prevent being seen, to an open exposure of the person of her friend, arose from the perfect conviction that no Indian would harm a being whom the Great Spirit had disarmed by depriving it of its strongest defense, reason. In this respect, nearly all unsophisticated nations resemble each other, appearing to offer spontaneously, by a feeling creditable to human nature, that protection by their own forbearance which has been withheld by the inscrutable wisdom of Providence. Wah-ta!-Wah, indeed, knew that in many tribes the mentally imbecile and the mad were held in a species of religious reverence, receiving from the untutored inhabitants of the forest respect and honors, instead of the contumely and neglect that it is their fortune to meet with among the more pretending and sophisticated.

Hetty accompanied her new friend without apprehension or reluctance. It was her wish to reach the camp, and sustained by her motives, she felt no more concern for the consequences than did her companion herself, now the latter was apprised of the character of the protection that the paleface maiden carried with her. Still, as they proceeded slowly along a shore that was tangled with overhanging bushes, Hetty continued the discourse, assuming the office of interrogating, which the other had instantly dropped as soon as she ascertained the character of the mind to which her questions had been addressed.

"But *you* are not half-witted," said Hetty, "and there's no reason why the Serpent should not marry *you*."

"Hist prisoner, and Mingo got big ear. No speak of Chingachgook when they by. Promise Hist that, good Hetty."

"I know—I know," returned Hetty, half-whispering in her eagerness to let the other see she understood the necessity of caution. "I know—Deerslayer and the Serpent mean to get you away from the Iroquois, and you wish me not to tell the secret."

"How you know?" said Hist hastily, vexed at the moment that the other was not even more feeble-minded than was actually the case. "How you know? Better not talk of any but fader and Hurry; Mingo understand *dat;* he no understand *t'udder.* Promise you no talk about what you no understand."

"But I *do* understand this, Hist, and so I *must* talk about it. Deerslayer as good as told Father all about it in my presence, and as nobody told me not to listen, I overheard it all, as I did Hurry's and Father's discourse about the scalps."

"Very bad for paleface to talk about scalps, and very bad for young woman to hear! Now you love Hist, I know, Hetty, and so, among Injins, when love hardest never talk most."

"That's not the way among white people, who talk most about them they love best. I suppose it's because I'm only half-witted that I don't see the reason why it should be so different among red people."

"That what Deerslayer call gift. One gift to talk, t'udder gift to hold tongue. Hold-tongue your gift, among Mingos. If Sarpent want to see Hist, so Hetty want to see Hurry. Good girl never tell secret of friend."

Hetty understood this appeal, and she promised the Delaware girl not to make any allusion to the presence of Chingachgook, or to the motive of his visit to the lake.

"Maybe he get off Hurry and fader as well as Hist, if let him have his way," whispered Wah-ta!-Wah to her companion in a confiding, flattering way, just as they got near enough to the encampment to hear the voices of several of their own sex, who were apparently occupied in the usual toils of women of their class. "T'ink of dat, Hetty, and put two, twenty finger on mouth. No get friends free without Sarpent do it."

A better expedient could not have been adopted to secure the silence and discretion of Hetty than that which was now presented to her mind. As the liberation of her father and the young frontiersman was the great object of her adventure, she felt the connection between it and the services of the Delaware, and with an innocent laugh, she nodded her head and, in the same suppressed manner, promised a due attention to the wishes of her friend. Thus assured, Hist tarried no longer but immediately and openly led the way into the encampment of her captors.

CHAPTER XI

THAT THE PARTY to which Hist compulsorily belonged was not one that was regularly on the warpath was evident by the presence of females. It was a small fragment of a tribe that had been hunting and fishing within the English limits, where it was found by the commencement of hostilities, and, after passing the winter and spring by living on what was strictly the property of its enemies, it chose to strike a hostile blow before it finally retired. There was also deep Indian sagacity in the maneuver which had led them so far into the territory of their foes. When the runner arrived who announced the breaking out of hostilities between the English and French—a struggle that was certain to carry with it all the tribes that dwelt within the influence of the respective belligerents—this particular party of the Iroquois were posted on the shores of the Oneida, a lake that lies some fifty miles nearer to their own frontier than that which is the scene of our tale. To have fled in a direct line for the Canadas would have exposed them to the dangers of a direct pursuit, and the chiefs had determined to adopt the expedient of penetrating deeper into a region that had now become dangerous, in the hope of being able to retire in the rear of their pursuers, instead of having them on their trail. The presence of the women had induced the attempt of this ruse, the strength of these feebler members of the party being unequal to the effort of escaping from the pursuit of warriors. When the

173

reader remembers the vast extent of the American wilderness at that early day, he will perceive that it was possible for even a tribe to remain months undiscovered in particular portions of it; nor was the danger of encountering a foe, the usual precautions being observed, as great in the woods as it is on the high seas in a time of active warfare.

The encampment being temporary, it offered to the eye no more than the rude protection of a bivouac, relieved in some slight degree by the ingenious expedients which suggested themselves to the readiness of those who passed their lives amid similar scenes. One fire that had been kindled against the roots of a living oak sufficed for the whole party, the weather being too mild to require it for any purpose but cooking. Scattered around this center of attraction were some fifteen or twenty low huts—perhaps kennels would be a better word—into which their different owners crept at night, and which were also intended to meet the exigencies of a storm. These little huts were made of the branches of trees put together with some ingenuity, and they were uniformly topped with bark that had been stripped from fallen trees, of which every virgin forest possesses hundreds in all stages of decay. Of furniture, they had next to none. Cooking utensils of the simplest sort were lying near the fire; a few articles of clothing were to be seen in or around the huts; rifles, horns, and pouches leaned against the trees, or were suspended from the lower branches; and the carcasses of two or three deer were stretched to view on the same natural shambles.

As the encampment was in the midst of a dense wood, the eye could not take in its *tout ensemble* at a glance, but hut after hut started out of the gloomy picture as one gazed about him in quest of objects. There was no center, unless the fire might be so considered—no open area where the possessors of this rude village might congregate—but all was dark, covert, and cunning, like its owners. A few children strayed from hut to hut, giving the spot a little the air of domestic life, and the suppressed laugh and low voices of the women occasionally broke in upon the deep stillness of the somber forest. As for the men, they either ate, slept, or examined their arms. They conversed but little, and then usually apart, or in groups withdrawn from the females; whilst an air of untiring, innate watchfulness and apprehension of danger seemed to be blended even with their slumbers.

As the two girls came near the encampment, Hetty uttered a slight exclamation on catching a view of the person of her father. He was seated on the ground with his back to a tree, and Hurry stood near him, indolently whittling a twig. Apparently, they were as much at liberty as any others in or about the camp, and one unaccustomed to Indian usages would have mistaken them for visitors, instead of supposing them to be captives. Wah-ta!-Wah led her new friend quite near them and then modestly withdrew, that her own presence might be no restraint on her feelings. But Hetty was not sufficiently familiar with caresses or outward demonstrations of fondness to indulge in any outbreaking of feeling. She merely approached and stood at her father's side without speaking, resembling a silent statue of filial affection. The old man expressed neither alarm nor surprise at her sudden appearance. In these particulars he had caught the stoicism of the Indians, well knowing that there was no more certain mode of securing their respect than by imitating their self-command. Nor did the savages themselves betray the least sign of surprise at this sudden appearance of a stranger among them. In a word, this arrival produced much less visible sensation, though occurring under circumstances so peculiar, than would be seen in a village of higher pretensions to civilization, did an ordinary traveler drive up to the door of its principal inn. Still a few warriors collected, and it was evident, by the manner in which they glanced at Hetty as they conversed together, that she was the subject of their discourse, and probable that the reasons of her unlooked-for appearance were matters of discussion. This phlegm of manner is characteristic of the North American Indian—some say of his white successor also— but in this case, much should be attributed to the peculiar situation in which the party was placed. The force in the ark, the presence of Chingachgook excepted, was well known; no tribe or body of troops was believed to be near; and vigilant eyes were posted around the entire lake, watching, day and night, the slightest movement of those whom it would not be exaggerated now to term the besieged.

Hutter was inwardly much moved by the conduct of Hetty, though he affected so much indifference of manner. He recollected her gentle appeal to him before he left the ark, and misfortune rendered that of weight which might have been forgotten amid the triumph of success. Then he knew the simple, singlehearted fidelity of his child and understood why she had come and the total disregard of self that reigned in all her acts.

"This is not well, Hetty," he said, deprecating the consequences to the girl herself more than any other evil. "These are fierce Iroquois and are as little apt to forget an injury as a favor."

"Tell me, Father," returned the girl, looking furtively about her, as if fearful of being overheard, "did God let you do the cruel errand on which you came? I want much to know this, that I may speak to the Indians plainly if he did not."

"You should not have come hither, Hetty; these brutes will not understand your nature or your intentions!"

"How was it, Father? Neither you nor Hurry seems to have anything that looks like scalps."

"If that will set your mind at peace, child, I can answer you no. I had caught the young creatur' who came here with you, but her screeches soon brought down upon me a troop of the wildcats that was too much for any single Christian to withstand. If that will do you any good, we are as innocent of having taken a scalp this time as I make no doubt we shall also be innocent of receiving the bounty."

"Thank you for that, Father! Now I can speak boldly to the Iroquois, and with an easy conscience. I hope Hurry, too, has not been able to harm any of the Indians?"

"Why, as to that matter, Hetty," returned the individual in question, "you've put it pretty much in the natyve character of the religious truth. Hurry has not been *able,* and that is the long and short of it. I've seen many squalls, old fellow, both on land and on the water, but never did I feel one as lively and as snappish as that which come down upon us night afore last, in the shape of an Indian hurrah-boys! Why, Hetty, you're no great matter at a reason or an idee that lies a little deeper than common, but you're human and have some human notions—now I'll just ask you to look at these circumstances. Here was old Tom, your father, and myself bent on a legal operation, as is to be seen in the words of the law and the proclamation, thinking no harm, when we were set upon by critturs that were more like a pack of hungry wolves than mortal savages even, and there they had us tethered like two sheep in less time than it has taken me to tell you the story."

"You are free, now, Hurry," returned Hetty, glancing timidly at the fine, unfettered limbs of the young giant. "You have no cords or withes to pain your arms or legs now."

"Not I, Hetty. Natur' is natur', and freedom is natur', too. My limbs have a free look, but that's pretty much the amount of it, sin' I can't use them in the way I should like. Even these trees have eyes—aye, and tongues, too, for, was the old man here or I to start one single rod beyond our jail limits, sarvice would be put on the bail afore we could 'gird up our loins' for a race; and like as not four or five rifle bullets would be traveling after us, carrying so many invitations to curb our impatience. There isn't a jail in the Colony as tight as this we are now in, for I've tried the vartue of two or three on 'em, and I know the mater'als they are made of, as well as the men that made 'em, takin' down being the next step in schoolin' to puttin' up in all such fabrications."

Lest the reader should get an exaggerated opinion of Hurry's demerits from this boastful and indiscreet revelation, it may be well to say that his offenses were confined to assaults and batteries, for several of which he had been imprisoned, when, as he has just said, he often escaped by demonstrating the flimsiness of the constructions in which he was confined by opening for himself doors in spots where the architects had neglected to place them. But Hetty had no knowledge of jails and little of the nature of crime beyond what her unadulterated and almost instinctive perceptions of right and wrong taught her, and this sally of the rude being who had spoken was lost upon her. She understood his general meaning, however, and answered in reference to that alone.

"It's so best, Hurry," she said. "It is best Father and you should be quiet and peaceable till I have spoken to the Iroquois, when all will be well and happy. I don't wish either of you to follow, but leave me to myself. As soon as all is settled and you are at liberty to go back to the castle, I will come and let you know it."

Hetty spoke with so much simple earnestness, seemed so

confident of success, and wore so high an air of moral feeling and truth that both the listeners felt more disposed to attach an importance to her mediation than might otherwise have happened. When she manifested an intention to quit them, therefore, they offered no obstacle, though they saw she was about to join the group of chiefs who were consulting apart, seemingly on the manner and motive of her own sudden appearance.

When Hist—for so we love best to call her—quitted her companion, she strayed near one or two of the elder warriors who had shown her most kindness in her captivity—the principal man of whom had even offered to adopt her as his child, if she would consent to become a Huron. In taking this direction the shrewd girl did so to invite inquiry. She was too well trained in the habits of her people to obtrude the opinions of one of her sex and years on men and warriors, but nature had furnished a tact and ingenuity that enabled her to attract the attention she desired without wounding the pride of those whom it was her duty to defer to and respect. Even her affected indifference stimulated curiosity, and Hetty had hardly reached the side of her father before the Delaware girl was brought within the circle of the warriors by a secret but significant gesture. Here she was questioned as to the presence of her companion and the motives that had brought her to the camp. This was all that Hist desired. She explained the manner in which she had detected the weakness of Hetty's reason, rather exaggerating than lessening the deficiency in her intellect, and then she related, in general terms, the object of the girl in venturing among her enemies. The effect was all that the speaker expected, her account investing the person and character of their visitor with a sacredness and respect that she well knew would prove her protection. As soon as her own purpose was attained, Hist withdrew to a distance, where, with female consideration and a sisterly tenderness, she set about the preparation of a meal to be offered to her new friend as soon as the latter might be at liberty to partake of it. While thus occupied, however, the ready girl in no degree relaxed in her watchfulness, noting every change of countenance among the chiefs, every movement of Hetty, and the smaller occurrences that could be likely to affect her own interests or that of her new friend.

As Hetty approached the chiefs, they opened their little

circle with an ease and deference of manner that would have done credit to men of more courtly origin. A fallen tree lay near, and the oldest of the warriors made a quiet sign for the girl to be seated on it, taking his place at her side with the gentleness of a father. The others arranged themselves around the two with grave dignity, and then the girl, who had sufficient observation to perceive that such a course was expected of her, began to reveal the object of her visit. The moment she opened her mouth to speak, however, the old chief gave a gentle sign for her to forbear, said a few words to one of his juniors, and then waited in silent patience until the latter had summoned Hist to the party. This interruption proceeded from the chief's having discovered that there existed a necessity for an interpreter, few of the Hurons present understanding the English language, and they but imperfectly.

Wah-ta!-Wah was not sorry to be called upon to be present at the interview, and least of all in the character in which she was now wanted. She was aware of the hazards she ran in attempting to deceive one or two of the party; but was nonetheless resolved to use every means that offered and to practice every artifice that an Indian education could supply to conceal the facts of the vicinity of her betrothed and of the errand on which he had come. One unpracticed in the expedients and opinions of savage life would not have suspected the readiness of invention, the wariness of action, the high resolution, the noble impulses, the deep self-devotion, and the feminine disregard of self, where the affections were concerned, that lay concealed beneath the demure looks, the mild eyes, and the sunny smiles of this young Indian beauty. As she approached them, the grim old warriors regarded her with pleasure, for they had a secret pride in the hope of engrafting so rare a scion on the stock of their own nation, adoption being as regularly practiced and as distinctly recognized among the tribes of America as it ever had been among those nations that submit to the sway of the civil law.

As soon as Hist was seated by the side of Hetty, the old chief desired her to ask "the fair young paleface" what had brought her among the Iroquois, and what they could do to serve her.

"Tell them, Hist, who I am—Thomas Hutter's youngest

daughter; Thomas Hutter, the oldest of their two prisoners; he who owns the castle and the ark, and who has the best right to be thought the owner of these hills and that lake, since he has dwelt so long, and trapped so long, and fished so long among them. They'll know whom you mean by Thomas Hutter, if you tell them *that*. And then tell them that I've come here to convince them they ought not to harm Father and Hurry, but let them go in peace, and to treat them as brothers, rather than as enemies. Now tell them all this plainly, Hist, and fear nothing for yourself or me; God will protect us."

Wah-ta!-Wah did as the other desired; taking care to render the words of her friend as literally as possible into the Iroquois tongue, a language she used with a readiness almost equal to that with which she spoke her own. The chiefs heard this opening explanation with grave decorum, the two who had a little knowledge of English intimating their satisfaction with the interpreter by furtive but significant glances of the eyes.

"And, now, Hist," continued Hetty, as soon as it was intimated to her that she might proceed, "I wish you to tell these red men, word for word, what I am about to say. Tell them first, that Father and Hurry came here with an intention to take as many scalps as they could; for the wicked governor and the province have offered money for scalps—whether of warriors or women, men, or children—and the love of gold was too strong for their hearts to withstand it. Tell them this, dear Hist, just as you have heard it from me, word for word."

Wah-ta!-Wah hesitated about rendering this speech as literally as had been desired, but detecting the intelligence of those who understood English, and apprehending even a greater knowledge than they actually possessed, she found herself compelled to comply. Contrary to what a civilized man would have expected, the admission of the motives and of the errands of their prisoners produced no visible effect on either the countenances or the feelings of the listeners. They probably considered the act meritorious, and that which neither of them would have hesitated to perform in his own person, he would not be apt to censure in another.

"And now, Hist," resumed Hetty, as soon as she perceived

that her first speeches were understood by the chiefs, "you can tell them more. They know that Father and Hurry did not succeed, and therefore they can bear them no grudge for any harm that has been done. If they had slain their children and wives, it would not alter the matter, and I'm not certain that what I am about to tell them would not have more weight had there been mischief done. But ask them first, Hist, if they know there is a God who reigns over the whole earth and is ruler and chief of all who live, let them be red or white, or what color they may?"

Wah-ta!-Wah looked a little surprised at this question, for the idea of the Great Spirit is seldom long absent from the mind of an Indian girl. She put the question as literally as possible, however, and received a grave answer in the affirmative.

"This is right," continued Hetty, "and my duty will now be light. This Great Spirit, as you call our God, has caused a book to be written, which we call a Bible, and in this book have been set down all His commandments, and His holy will and pleasure, and the rules by which all men are to live, and directions how to govern the thoughts even, and the wishes, and the will. Here, this is one of these holy books, and you must tell the chiefs what I am about to read to them from its sacred pages."

As Hetty concluded, she reverently unrolled a small English Bible from its envelope of coarse calico, treating the volume with the sort of external respect that a Romanist would be apt to show to a religious relic. As she slowly proceeded in her task, the grim warriors watched each movement with riveted eyes, and when they saw the little volume appear, a slight expression of surprise escaped one or two of them. But Hetty held it out toward them in triumph, as if she expected the sight would produce a visible miracle; then, without betraying either surprise or mortification at the stoicism of the Indian, she turned eagerly to her new friend in order to renew the discourse.

"This is the sacred volume, Hist," she said, "and these words, and lines, and verses, and chapters all came from God."

"Why Great Spirit no send book to Injin, too?" demanded Hist, with the directness of a mind that was totally unsophisticated.

"Why?" answered Hetty, a little bewildered by a question so unexpected. "Why?—Ah! You know the Indians don't know how to read."

If Hist was not satisfied with this explanation, she did not deem the point of sufficient importance to be pressed. Simply bending her body in gentle admission of the truth of what she heard, she sat patiently awaiting the further arguments of the paleface enthusiast.

"You can tell these chiefs that throughout this book men are ordered to forgive their enemies, to treat them as they would brethren, and never to injure their fellow creatures, more especially on account of revenge, or any evil passion. Do you think you can tell them this so that they will understand it, Hist?"

"Tell him well enough, but he no very easy to understand."

Hist then conveyed the ideas of Hetty in the best manner she could to the attentive Indians, who heard her words with some such surprise as an American of our own times would be apt to betray at a suggestion that the great modern, but vacillating ruler of things human, public opinion, might be wrong. One or two of their number, however, having met with missionaries, said a few words in explanation, and then the group gave all its attention to the communications that were to follow. Before Hetty resumed, she inquired earnestly of Hist if the chiefs had understood her, and receiving an evasive answer, was fain to be satisfied.

"I will now read to the warriors some of the verses that it is good for them to know," continued the girl, whose manner grew more solemn and earnest as she proceeded; "and they will remember that they are the words of the Great Spirit. First, then, ye are commanded to *'Love thy neighbor as thyself.'* Tell them *that*, dear Hist."

"Neighbor for Injin no mean paleface," answered the Delaware girl, with more decision than she had hitherto thought it necessary to use. "Neighbor mean Iroquois for Iroquois, Mohican for Mohican, paleface for paleface. No need tell chief anything else."

"You forget, Hist, these are the words of the Great Spirit, and the chiefs must obey them as well as others. Here is another commandment: *'Whosoever shall smite thee on the right cheek, turn to him the other also.'* "

"What that mean?" demanded Hist, with the quickness of lightning.

Hetty explained that it was an order not to resent injuries, but rather to submit to receive fresh wrongs from the offender.

"And hear this too, Hist," she added: " *'Love your enemies, bless them that curse you, do good to them that hate you, and pray for them which despitefully use you and persecute you.'* "

By this time Hetty had become excited; her eye gleamed with the earnestness of her feelings, her cheeks flushed, and her voice, usually so low and modulated, became stronger and more impressive. With the Bible she had been early made familiar by her mother, and she now turned from passage to passage with surprising rapidity, taking care to cull such verses as taught the sublime lessons of Christian charity and Christian forgiveness. To translate half of what she said, in her pious earnestness, Wah-ta!-Wah would have found impracticable had she made the effort, but wonder held her tongue-tied equally with the chiefs, and the young, simple-minded enthusiast had fairly become exhausted with her own efforts before the other opened her mouth again to utter a syllable. Then, indeed, the Delaware girl gave a brief translation of the substance of what had been both read and said, confining herself to one or two of the more striking of the verses, those that had struck her own imagination as the most paradoxical, and which certainly would have been the most applicable to the case, could the uninstructed minds of the listeners embrace the great moral truths they conveyed.

It will be scarcely necessary to tell the reader the effect that such novel duties would be likely to produce among a group of Indian warriors, with whom it was a species of religious principle never to forget a benefit or to forgive an injury. Fortunately, the previous explanations of Hist had prepared the minds of the Hurons for something extravagant, and most of that which to them seemed inconsistent and paradoxical was accounted for by the fact that the speaker possessed a mind that was constituted differently from those of most of the human race. Still, there were one or two old men who had heard similar doctrines from the missionaries, and they felt a desire to occupy an idle moment by pursuing a subject that they found so curious.

"This is the Good Book of the palefaces," observed one of these chiefs, taking the volume from the unresisting hand of Hetty, who gazed anxiously at his face while he turned the leaves, as if she expected to witness some visible results from the circumstance. "This is the law by which my white brethren profess to live?"

Hist, to whom this question was addressed, if it might be considered as addressed to anyone in particular, answered simply in the affirmative, adding that both the French of the Canadas and the Yengeese of the British provinces equally admitted its authority and affected to revere its principles.

"Tell my young sister," said the Huron, looking directly at Hist, "that I will open my mouth and say a few words."

"The Iroquois chief go to speak—my paleface friend listen," said Hist.

"I rejoice to hear it!" exclaimed Hetty. "God has touched his heart, and he will now let Father and Hurry go!"

"This is the paleface law," resumed the chief. "It tells him to do good to them that hurt him; when his brother asks him for his rifle, to give him the powder horn, too. Such is the paleface law?"

"Not so—not so," answered Hetty earnestly, when these words had been interpreted. "There is not a word about rifles in the whole book, and powder and bullets give offense to the Great Spirit."

"Why, then, does the paleface use them? If he is ordered to *give* double to him that asks only for one thing, why does he *take* double from the poor Indians, who ask for *no* thing? He comes from beyond the rising sun, with his book in his hand, and he teaches the red man to read it; but why does he forget himself all it says? When the Indian gives, he is never satisfied, and now he offers gold for the scalps of our women and children, though he calls us beasts if we take the scalp of a warrior killed in open war. My name is Rivenoak."

When Hetty had got this formidable question fairly presented to her mind in the translation, and Hist did her duty with more than usual readiness on this occasion, it scarcely need be said that she was sorely perplexed. Abler heads than that of this poor girl have frequently been puzzled by questions of a similar drift, and it is not surprising that, with all her own earnestness and sincerity, she did not know what answer to make.

"What shall I tell them, Hist?" she asked imploringly. "I *know* that all I have read from the book is true, and yet it wouldn't seem so, would it, by the conduct of those to whom the book was given?"

"Give 'em paleface reason," returned Hist ironically; "that always good for one side; though be bad for t'other."

"No, no, Hist, there can't be two sides to truth—and yet it does seem strange! I'm certain I have read the verses right, and no one would be so wicked as to print the word of God wrong. *That* can never be, Hist."

"Well, to poor Injin girl it seem everything *can* be to pale-faces," returned the other coolly. "One time 'ey say white, and one time 'ey say black. Why, *never can be?*"

Hetty was more and more embarrassed until, overcome with the apprehension that she had failed in her object and that the lives of her father and Hurry would be the forfeit of some blunder of her own, she burst into tears. From that moment the manner of Hist lost all its irony and cool indifference, and she became the fond, caressing friend again. Throwing her arms around the afflicted girl, she attempted to soothe her sorrows by the scarcely ever failing remedy of female sympathy.

"Stop cry—no cry," she said, wiping the tears from the face of Hetty, as she would have performed the same office for a child, and stopping to press her, occasionally, to her own warm bosom with the affection of a sister; "why you so trouble? You no make he book, if he be wrong; and you no make he paleface, if he be wicked. There wicked red man and wicked white man—no color all good—no color all wicked. Chiefs know *that* well enough."

Hetty soon recovered from this sudden burst of grief, and then her mind reverted to the purpose of her visit, with its singlehearted earnestness. Perceiving that the grim-looking chiefs were still standing around her in grave attention, she hoped that another effort to convince them of the right might be successful.

"Listen, Hist," she said, struggling to suppress her sobs and to speak distinctly; "tell the chiefs that it matters not what the wicked do—right is right—the words of the Great

Spirit are the words of the Great Spirit—and no one can go harmless for doing an evil act because another has done it before him! *'Render good for evil,'* says this book, and that is the law for the red man as well as for the white man."

"Never hear such law among Delaware, or among Iroquois," answered Hist soothingly. "No good to tell chiefs any such law as *dat.* Tell 'em somet'ing they believe."

Hist was about to proceed, notwithstanding, when a tap on the shoulder, from the finger of the oldest chief, caused her to look up. She then perceived that one of the warriors had left the group, and was already returning to it with Hutter and Hurry. Understanding that the two last were to become parties in the inquiry, she became mute, with the unhesitating obedience of an Indian woman. In a few seconds the prisoners stood face to face with the principal men of the captors.

"Daughter," said the senior chief to the young Delaware, "ask this graybeard why he came into our camp?"

The question was put by Hist, in her own imperfect English, but in a way that was easy to be understood. Hutter was too stern and obdurate, by nature, to shrink from the consequences of any of his acts, and he was also too familiar with the opinions of the savages not to understand that nothing was to be gained by equivocation, or an unmanly dread of their anger. Without hesitating, therefore, he avowed the purpose with which he had landed, merely justifying it by the fact that the government of the province had bid high for scalps. This frank avowal was received by the Iroquois with evident satisfaction, not so much, however, on account of the advantage it gave them in a moral point of view, as by proving that they had captured a man worthy of occupying their thoughts and of becoming a subject of their revenge. Hurry, when interrogated, confessed the truth, though he would have been more disposed to concealment than his sterner companion, did the circumstances very well admit of its adoption. But he had tact enough to discover that equivocation would be useless at that moment, and he made a merit of necessity by imitating a frankness, which, in the case of Hutter, was the offspring of habits of indifference, acting on a disposition that was always ruthless and reckless of personal consequences.

As soon as the chiefs had received the answers to their

questions, they walked away in silence, like men who deemed the matter disposed of, all Hetty's dogmas being thrown away on beings trained in violence from infancy to manhood. Hetty and Hist were now left alone with Hutter and Hurry, no visible restraint being placed on the movements of either, though all four, in fact, were vigilantly and unceasingly watched. As respects the men, care was had to prevent them from getting possession of any of the rifles that lay scattered about, their own included—and there all open manifestations of watchfulness ceased. But they, who were so experienced in Indian practices, knew too well how great was the distance between appearances and reality to become the dupes of this seeming carelessness. Although both thought incessantly on the means of escape, and this without concert, each was aware of the uselessness of attempting any project of the sort that was not deeply laid and promptly executed. They had been long enough in the encampment, and were sufficiently observant to have ascertained that Hist, also, was a sort of captive; presuming on the circumstance, Hutter spoke in her presence more openly than he might otherwise have thought it prudent to do, inducing Hurry to be equally unguarded by his example.

"I'll not blame you, Hetty, for coming on this errand, which was well meant, if not very wisely planned," commenced the father, seating himself by the side of his daughter and taking her hand, a sign of affection that this rude being was accustomed to manifest to this particular child; "but preaching and the Bible are not the means to turn an Indian from his ways. Has Deerslayer sent any message, or has he any scheme by which he thinks to get us free?"

"Aye, that's the substance of it!" put in Hurry. "If you can help us, gal, to half a mile of freedom, or even a good start of a short quarter, I'll answer for the rest. Perhaps the old man may want a little more, but for one of my height and years *that* will meet all objections."

Hetty looked distressed, turning her eyes from one to the other, but she had no answer to give to the question of the reckless Hurry.

"Father," she said, "neither Deerslayer nor Judith knew of my coming until I had left the ark. They are afraid the Iroquois will make a raft and try to get off to the hut, and think more of defending *that* than of coming to aid you."

"No—no—no," said Hist hurriedly, though in a low voice, and with her face bent toward the earth, in order to conceal from those whom she knew to be watching them the fact of her speaking at all. "No, no no, Deerslayer different man. He no t'ink of defending 'self, with friend in danger. Help one another, and all get to hut."

"This sounds well, old Tom," said Hurry, winking and laughing, though he too used the precaution to speak low. "Give me a ready-witted squaw for a fri'nd, and though I'll not downright defy an Iroquois, I think I would defy the devil."

"No talk loud," said Hist. "Some Iroquois got Yengeese tongue, and all got Yengeese ear."

"Have we a friend in you, young woman?" inquired Hutter, with an increasing interest in the conference. "If so, you may calculate on a solid reward; and nothing will be easier than to send you to your own tribe, if we can once fairly get you off with us to the castle. Give us the ark and the canoes, and we can command the lake, in spite of all the savages in the Canadas. Nothing but artillery could drive us out of the castle, if we can get back to it."

"S'pose 'ey come ashore to take scalp?" retorted Hist, with cool irony, at which the girl appeared to be more expert than is common for her sex.

"Aye, aye—that was a mistake; but there is little use in lamentations, and less still, young woman, in flings."

"Father," said Hetty, "Judith thinks of breaking open the big chest, in hopes of finding something in *that* which may buy your freedom of the savages."

A dark look came over Hutter at the announcement of this fact, and he muttered his dissatisfaction in a way to render it intelligible enough.

"What for no break open chest?" put in Hist. "Life sweeter than old chest—scalp sweeter than old chest. If no tell darter to break him open, Wah-ta!-wah no help him to run away."

"Ye know not what ye ask—ye are but silly girls, and the wisest way for ye both is to speak of what ye understand and to speak of nothing else. I little like this cold neglect of the savages, Hurry; it's a proof that they think of something serious, and if we are to do anything, we must do it soon. Can we count on this young woman, think you?"

"Listen," said Hist quickly, and with an earnestness that proved how much her feelings were concerned; "Wah-ta!-wah no Iroquois—all over Delaware—got Delaware heart—Delaware feeling. She prisoner, too. One prisoner help t'udder prisoner. No good to talk more, now. Darter stay with fader—Wah-ta!-wah come and see friend—all look right—*then* tell what he do."

This was said in a low voice, but distinctly, and in a manner to make an impression. As soon as it was uttered, the girl arose and left the group, walking composedly toward the hut she occupied, as if she had no further interest in what might pass between the palefaces.

CHAPTER XII

She speaks much of her father; says she hears
There's tricks i' the world; and hems, and beats her heart;
Spurns enviously at straws: speaks things in doubt,
That carry but half sense; her speech is nothing,
Yet the unsuspected use of it doth move
The hearers to collection;——

SHAKESPEARE

WE LEFT THE occupants of the castle and the ark buried in sleep. Once or twice, in the course of the night, it is true, Deerslayer or the Delaware arose and looked out upon the tranquil lake, when, finding all safe, each returned to his pallet and slept like a man who was not easily deprived of his natural rest. At the first signs of the dawn, the former arose, however, and made his personal arrangements for the day, though his companion, whose nights had not been tranquil or without disturbance of late, continued on his blanket until the sun had fairly risen. Judith, too, was later than common that morning, for the earlier hours of the night had brought her little of either refreshment or sleep. But ere the sun had shown himself over the eastern hills, these too were up and afoot; even the tardy, in that region, seldom remained on their pallets after the appearance of the great luminary.

Chingachgook was in the act of arranging his forest toilet, when Deerslayer entered the cabin of the ark and threw him a few coarse, but light summer vestments that belonged to Hutter.

"Judith hath given me them for your use, Chief," said the latter, as he cast the jacket and trousers at the feet of the Indian; "for it's ag'in all prudence and caution to be seen in your war dress and paint. Wash off all them fiery

190

streaks from your cheeks, put on these garments, and here is a hat, such as it is, that will give you an awful oncivilized sort of civilization, as the missionaries call it. Remember that Hist is at hand, and what we do for the maiden must be done while we are doing for others. I know it's ag'in your gifts and your natur' to wear clothes, unless they are cut and carried in a red man's fashion, but make a vartue of necessity and put these on at once, even if they do rise a little in your throat."

Chingachgook, or the Serpent, eyed the vestments with strong disgust, but he saw the usefulness of the disguise, if not its absolute necessity. Should the Iroquois discover a red man in or about the castle, it might, indeed, place them more on their guard and give their suspicions a direction toward their female captive. Anything was better than a failure, as it regarded his betrothed, and after turning the different garments around and around, examining them with a species of grave irony, affecting to draw them on in a way that defeated itself, and otherwise manifesting the reluctance of a young savage to confine his limbs in the usual appliances of civilized life, the chief submitted to the directions of his companion and finally stood forth, so far as the eye could detect, a red man in color alone. Little was to be apprehended from this last peculiarity, however, the distance from the shore and the want of glasses preventing any very close scrutiny, and Deerslayer himself, though of a brighter and fresher tint, had a countenance that was burned by the sun to a hue scarcely less red than that of his Mohican companion. The awkwardness of the Delaware in his new attire caused his friend to smile more than once that day, but he carefully abstained from the use of any of those jokes which would have been bandied among white men on such an occasion; the habits of a chief, the dignity of a warrior on his first path, and the gravity of the circumstances in which they were placed united to render so much levity out of season.

The meeting at the morning meal of the three islanders, if we may use the term, was silent, grave, and thoughtful. Judith showed by her looks that she had passed an unquiet night, while the two men had the future before them, with its unseen and unknown events. A few words of courtesy passed between Deerslayer and the girl in the course of the breakfast, but no allusion was made to their situation. At length, Judith, whose heart was full and whose novel feelings disposed her to entertain sentiments more gentle and tender than common, introduced the subject, and this in a way to show how much of her thoughts it had occupied in the course of the last sleepless night.

"It would be dreadful, Deerslayer," the girl abruptly exclaimed, "should anything serious befall my father and Hetty! We cannot remain quietly here and leave them in the hands of the Iroquois, without bethinking us of some means of serving them."

"I'm ready, Judith, to sarve them and all others who are in trouble, could the way to do it be pointed out. It's no trifling matter to fall into redskin hands, when men set out on an a'r'nd like that which took Hutter and Hurry ashore—that I know as well as another—and I wouldn't wish my worst inimy in such a strait, much less them with whom I've journeyed, and eat, and slept. Have you any scheme that you would like to have the Sarpent and me indivor to carry out?"

"I know of no other means to release the prisoners than by bribing the Iroquois. They are not proof against presents, and we might offer enough, perhaps, to make them think it better to carry away what to them will be rich gifts than to carry away poor prisoners—if, indeed, they should carry them away at all!"

"This is well enough, Judith; yes, it's well enough, if the inimy is to be bought, and we can find articles to make the purchase with. Your father has a convenient lodge, and it is most cunningly placed, though it doesn't seem overstocked with riches that will be likely to buy his ransom. There's the piece he calls Killdeer might count for something, and I understand there's a keg of powder about, which might be a makeweight, sartain; and yet two able-bodied men are not to be bought off for a trifle—besides——"

"Besides what?" demanded Judith impatiently, observing that the other hesitated to proceed, probably from a reluctance to distress her.

"Why, Judith, the Frenchers offer bounties as well as our own side; and the price of two scalps would purchase a keg of powder and a rifle; though I'll not say one of the latter altogether as good as Killdeer there, which your father va'nts as oncommon and onequaled, like. But fair powder, and a pretty sartain rifle; then the red men are not the expartest in firearms and don't always know the difference atwixt that which is ra'al and that which is seeming."

"This is horrible!" muttered the girl, struck by the homely manner in which her companion was accustomed to state his facts. "But you overlook my own clothes, Deerslayer; they, I think, might go far with the women of the Iroquois."

"No doubt they would; no doubt they would, Judith," returned the other, looking at her keenly, as if he would ascertain whether she were really capable of making such a sacrifice. "But are you sartain, gal, you could find it in your heart to part with your own finery for such a purpose? Many is the man who has thought he was valiant till danger stared him in the face; I've known them too that consaited they were kind and ready to give away all they had to the poor, when they've been listening to other people's hardheartedness, but whose fists have clenched as tight as the riven hickory, when it came to downright offerings of their own. Besides, Judith, you're handsome—oncommon in that way, one might obsarve and do no harm to the truth—and they that have beauty like to have that which will adorn it. Are you sartain you could find it in your heart to part with your own finery?"

The soothing allusion to the personal charms of the girl was well-timed to counteract the effect produced by the distrust that the young man expressed of Judith's devotion to her filial duties. Had another said as much as Deerslayer, the compliment would most probably have been overlooked in the indignation awakened by the doubts, but even the unpolished sincerity that so often made this simple-minded hunter bare his thoughts had a charm for the girl; and, while she colored, and for an instant her eyes flashed fire, she could not find it in her heart to be really angry with one whose very soul seemed truth and manly kindness. Look her reproaches she did; but conquering the desire to retort, she succeeded in answering in a mild and friendly manner.

"You must keep all your favorable opinions for the Delaware girls, Deerslayer, if you seriously think thus of those of your own color," she said, affecting to laugh. "But, *try* me; if you find that I regret either ribbon or feather, silk or muslin, then may you think what you please of my heart and say what you think."

"That's justice! The rarest thing to find on 'arth is a truly just man. So says Tamenund, the wisest prophet of the Delawares, and so all must think that have occasion to see, and talk, and act among mankind. I love a just man, Sarpent; his eyes are never covered with darkness toward his inimies, while they are all sunshine and brightness toward his fri'nds. He uses the reason that God has given him, and he uses it with a feelin' of his being ordered to look at, and to consider things as they *are*, and not as he *wants* them to be. It's easy enough to find men who *call* themselves just, but it's wonderfully oncommon to find them that are the very thing, in fact. How often have I seen Indians, gal, who believed they were lookin' into a matter agreeable to the will of the Great Spirit when, in truth, they were only striving to act up to their own will and pleasure, and this, half of the time, with a temptation to go wrong that could no more be seen by themselves than the stream that runs in the next valley can be seen by us through yonder mountain; though any looker-on might have discovered it as plainly as we can discover the parch that are swimming around this hut."

"Very true, Deerslayer," rejoined Judith, losing every trace of displeasure in a bright smile; "very true; and I hope to see you act on this love of justice in all matters in which I am concerned. Above all, I hope you will judge for yourself and not believe every evil story that a prating idler like Hurry Harry may have to tell that goes to touch the good name of any young woman who may not happen to have the same opinions of his face and person that the blustering gallant has of himself."

"Hurry Harry's ideas do not pass for gospel with me, Judith, but even worse than he may have eyes and ears," returned the other gravely.

"Enough of this!" exclaimed Judith, with flashing eye and a flush that mounted to her temples, "and more of my father and his ransom. 'Tis as you say, Deerslayer; the Indians will not be likely to give up their prisoners without a heavier bribe than my clothes can offer, and Father's rifle and powder. There is the chest."

"Aye, there is the chist, as you say, Judith; and when the question gets to be between a secret and a scalp, I should think most men would prefar keeping the last. Did your father ever give you any downright command consarning that chist?"

"Never. He has always appeared to think its locks, and its steel bands, and its strength its best protection."

" 'Tis a rare chist, and altogether of curious build," returned Deerslayer, rising and approaching the thing in question, on which he seated himself, with a view to examine it with greater ease. "Chingachgook, this is no wood that comes of any forest that you or I have ever trailed through! 'Tisn't the black walnut, and yet it's quite as comely, if not more so, did the smoke and the treatment give it fair play."

The Delaware drew near, felt of the wood, examined its grain, endeavored to indent the surface with a nail, and passed his hand curiously over the steel bands, the heavy padlocks, and the other novel peculiarities of the massive box.

"No—nothing like this grows in these regions," resumed Deerslayer. "I've seen all the oaks, both the maples, the elms, the basswood, all the walnuts, the butternuts, and every tree that has a substance and color, wrought into some form or other, but never have I before seen such a wood as this! Judith, the chist itself would buy your father's freedom; or Iroquois cur'osity isn't as strong as redskin cur'osity, in general, especially in the matter of woods."

"The purchase might be cheaper made, perhaps, Deerslayer. The chest is full, and it would be better to part with half than to part with the whole. Besides, Father—I know not why —but Father values that chest highly."

"He would seem to prize what it holds more than the chist itself, judging by the manner in which he treats the outside and secures the inside. Here are three locks, Judith; is there no key?"

"I've never seen one, and yet key there must be, since Hetty told us *she* had often seen the chest opened."

"Keys no more lie in the air, or float on the water, than humans, gal; if there is a key, there must be a place in which it is kept."

"That is true, and it might not be difficult to find it, did we dare to search!"

"This is for you, Judith, it is altogether for you. The chist is your'n, or your father's, and Hutter is your father, not mine. Cur'osity is a woman's, not a man's failing, and there you have got all the reasons before you. If the chist has articles for ransom, it seems to me they would be wisely used in redeeming their owner's life, or even in saving his scalp, but that is a matter for your judgment, and not for ourn. When the lawful owner of a trap, or a buck, or a canoe, isn't present, his next of kin becomes his riprisenta-tyve, by all the laws of the woods. We therefore leave you to say whether the chist shall or shall not be opened."

"I hope you do not believe I can hesitate when my father's life's in danger, Deerslayer!"

"Why, it's pretty much putting a scolding ag'in tears and mourning. It's not onreasonable to foretell that old Tom may find fault with what you've done when he sees himself once more in his hut here, but there's nothing unusual in men's falling out with what has been done for their own good; I dare to say that even the moon would seem a different thing from what it now does, could we look at it from the other side."

"Deerslayer, if we can find the key, I will authorize you to open the chest and to take such things from it as you may think will buy Father's ransom."

"First find the key, gal; we'll talk of the rest a'terward. Sarpent, you've eyes like a fly and a judgment that's seldom out; can you help us in calculating where Floating Tom would be apt to keep the key of a chist that he holds to be as private as this?"

The Delaware had taken no part in the discourse until he was thus directly appealed to, when he quitted the chest, which had continued to attract his attention, and cast about him for the place in which a key would be likely to be concealed under such circumstances. As Judith and Deerslayer were not idle the while, the whole three were soon engaged in an anxious and spirited search. As it was certain that the desired key was not to be found in any of the common drawers or closets, of which there were several in the building, none looked there, but all turned their inquiries to those places that struck them as ingenious hiding places, more likely to be used for such a purpose. In this manner the outer room was thoroughly but fruitlessly examined; then they entered the sleeping apartment of Hutter. This part of the rude building was better furnished than the rest of the structure, containing several articles that had been especially devoted to the service of the deceased wife of its owner, but as Judith had all the rest of the keys, it was soon rummaged, without bringing to light the particular key desired.

They now entered the bedroom of the daughters. Chingachgook was immediately struck with the contrast between the articles, and the arrangement of that side of the room that might be called Judith's, and that which more properly belonged to Hetty. A slight exclamation escaped him, and pointing in each direction, he alluded to the fact in a low voice, speaking to his friend in the Delaware tongue.

"As you think, Sarpent," answered Deerslayer, whose remarks we always translate into English, preserving as much as possible of the peculiar phraseology and manner of the man. " 'Tis just so, as anyone may see, and 'tis all founded in natur'. One sister loves finery, some say, overmuch, while t'other is as meek and lowly as God ever created goodness and truth. Yet, after all, I daresay that Judith has her vartues and Hetty has her failin's."

"And the 'Feeble-mind' has seen the chest opened?" inquired Chingachgook, with curiosity in his glance.

"Sartain; that much I've heard from her own lips; for that matter, so have you. It seems her father doesn't misgive *her* discretion, though he does that of his eldest darter."

"Then the key is hid only from the Wild Rose?" for so Chingachgook had begun gallantly to term Judith, in his private discourse with his friend.

"That's it! That's just it! One he trusts, and the other he doesn't. There's red and white in that, Sarpent, all tribes and nations agreeing in trusting some and refusing to trust other some. It depends on character and judgment."

"Where could a key be put, so little likely to be found by the Wild Rose, as among coarse clothes?"

Deerslayer started, and turning to his friend with admiration expressed in every lineament of his face, he fairly laughed, in his silent but hearty manner, at the ingenuity and readiness of the conjecture.

"Your name's well bestowed, Sarpent—yes, 'tis well bestowed! Sure enough, where would a lover of finery be so little likely to s'arch as among garments as coarse and unseemly as these of poor Hetty? I dares to say Judith's delicate fingers haven't touched a bit of cloth as rough and oncomely as that petticoat, now, since she first made acquaintance with the officers! Yet, who knows? The key may be as likely to be on the same peg as in any other place. Take down the garment, Delaware, and let us see if you are ra'ally a prophet."

Chingachgook did as desired, but no key was found. A coarse pocket, apparently empty, hung on the adjoining peg, and this was next examined. By this time the attention of Judith was called in that direction, and she spoke hurriedly, like one who wished to save unnecessary trouble.

"These are only the clothes of poor Hetty, dear simple girl!" she said. "Nothing we seek would be likely to be there."

The words were hardly out of the handsome mouth of the speaker when Chingachgook drew the desired key from the pocket. Judith was too quick of apprehension not to understand the reason a hiding place so simple and exposed had been used. The blood rushed to her face—as much with resentment, perhaps, as with shame—and she bit her lip, though she continued silent. Deerslayer and his friend now discovered the delicacy of men of native refinement, neither smiling, or even by a glance betraying how completely he understood the motives and ingenuity of this clever artifice. The former, who had taken the key from the Indian, led the way into the adjoining room and, applying it to a lock, ascertained that the right instrument had actually been found. There were three padlocks, each of which, however, was easily opened by this single key. Deerslayer removed them all, loosened the hasps, raised the lid a little to make certain it was loose, and then he drew back from the chest several feet, signing to his friend to follow.

"This is a family chist, Judith," he said, "and 'tis like to hold family secrets. The Sarpent and I will go into the ark, and look to the canoes, and paddles, and oars, while you can examine it by yourself and find out whether anything that will be a makeweight in a ransom is or is not among the articles. When you've got through, give us a call, and we'll all sit in council together, touching the valie of the articles."

"Stop, Deerslayer," exclaimed the girl, as he was about to withdraw; "not a single thing will I touch—I will not even raise the lid—unless you are present. Father and Hetty have seen fit to keep the inside of this chest a secret from me, and I am much too proud to pry into their hidden treasures, unless it were for their own good. But on no account will I open the chest alone. Stay with me, then; I want witnesses of what I do."

"I rather think, Sarpent, that the gal is right! Confidence and reliance beget security, but suspicion is like to make us all wary. Judith has a right to ask us to be present, and should the chist hold any of Master Hutter's secrets, they will fall into the keeping of two as close-mouthed young men as are to be found. We *will* stay with you, Judith—but first let us take a look at the lake and the shore, for this chist will not be emptied in a minute."

The two men now went out on the platform, and Deerslayer swept the shore with the glass, while the Indian gravely turned his eye on the water and the woods in quest of any sign that might betray the machinations of their enemies. Nothing was visible, and assured of their temporary security, the three collected around the chest again with the avowed object of opening it.

Judith had held this chest, and its unknown contents, in a species of reverence as long as she could remember. Neither her father nor her mother ever mentioned it in her presence, and there appeared to be a silent convention that in naming the different objects that occasionally stood near it, or even lay on its lid, care should be had to avoid any allusion to the chest itself. Habit rendered this so easy and so much a matter of course that it was only quite recently the girl had begun even to muse on the singularity of the circumstance. But there had never been sufficient intimacy between Hutter and his eldest daughter to invite confidence. At times, he was kind, but in general, with her more especially, he was stern and morose. Least of all had his authority been exercised in a way to embolden his child to venture on the liberty she was about to take without many misgivings of the consequences, although the liberty proceeded from a desire to serve himself. Then Judith was not altogether free from a little superstition on the subject of this chest, which had stood a sort of tabooed relic before her eyes from childhood to the present hour. Nevertheless, the time had come when it would seem that this mystery was to be explained, and that under circumstances, too, which left her very little choice in the matter.

Finding that both her companions were watching her

movements in grave silence, Judith placed a hand on the lid and endeavored to raise it. Her strength, however, was insufficient, and it appeared to the girl, who was fully aware that all the fastenings were removed, that she was resisted in an unhallowed attempt by some supernatural power.

"I cannot raise the lid, Deerslayer," she said; "had we not better give up the attempt and find some other means of releasing the prisoners?"

"Not so, Judith; not so, gal. No means are as sartain and easy as a good bribe," answered the other. "As for the lid, 'tis held by nothing but its own weight, which is prodigious for so small a piece of wood, loaded with iron as it is."

As Deerslayer spoke, he applied his own strength to the effort and succeeded in raising the lid against the timbers of the house, where he took care to secure it by a sufficient prop. Judith fairly trembled as she cast her first glance at the interior, and she felt a temporary relief in discovering that a piece of canvas that was carefully tucked in around the edges effectually concealed all beneath it. The chest was apparently well stored, however, the canvas lying within an inch of the lid.

"Here's a full cargo," said Deerslayer, eyeing the arrangement, "and we had needs go to work leisurely and at our ease. Sarpent, bring some stools, while I spread this blanket on the floor, and then we'll begin work orderly and in comfort."

The Delaware complied; Deerslayer civilly placed a stool for Judith, took one himself, and commenced the removal of the canvas covering. This was done deliberately and in as cautious a manner as if it were believed that fabrics of a delicate construction lay hidden beneath. When the canvas was removed, the first articles that came in view were some of the habiliments of the male sex. These were of fine materials, and according to the fashions of the age, were gay in colors and rich in ornaments. One coat, in particular, was of scarlet, and had buttonholes worked in gold thread. Still it was not military but was part of the attire of a civilian of condition at a period when social rank was rigidly respected in dress. Chingachgook could not refrain from an exclamation of pleasure, as soon as Deerslayer opened this coat and held it up to view; notwithstanding all his trained self-command, the splendor of the vestment was too much for the philosophy of an Indian. Deerslayer turned quickly, and he regarded his friend with a momentary displeasure, as this burst of weakness escaped him; then he soliloquized, as was his practice whenever any strong feeling suddenly got the ascendancy.

" 'Tis his gift! Yes, 'tis the gift of a redskin to love finery, and he is not to be blamed. This is an extr'ornary garment, too, and extr'ornary things get up extr'ornary feelin's. I think this will do, Judith, for the Indian heart is hardly to be found in all America that can withstand colors like these and glitter like that. If this coat was ever made for your father, you've come honestly by the taste for finery, you have."

"That coat was never made for Father," answered the girl quickly. "It is much too long, while Father is short and square."

"Cloth was plenty, if it was, and glitter cheap," answered Deerslayer, with his silent, joyous laugh. "Sarpent, this garment was made for a man of your size, and I should like to see it on your shoulders."

Chingachgook, nothing loath, submitted to the trial, throwing aside the coarse and threadbare jacket of Hutter to deck his person in a coat that was originally intended for a gentleman. The transformation was ludicrous, but as men are seldom struck with incongruities in their own appearance any more than in their own conduct, the Delaware studied this change in a common glass, by which Hutter was in the habit of shaving, with grave interest. At that moment he thought of Hist, and we owe it to truth to say, though it may militate a little against the stern character of a warrior to own it, that he wished he could be seen by her in his present improved aspect.

"Off with it, Sarpent—off with it," resumed the inflexible Deerslayer. "Such garments as little become you as they would become me. Your gifts are for paint, and hawk's feathers, and blankets, and wampum; and mine are for doublets of skins, tough leggings, and sarviceable moccasins. I say moccasins, Judith, for though white, living as I do in the woods, it's necessary to take to some of the practyces of the woods, for comfort's sake and cheapness."

"I see no reason, Deerslayer, why one man may not wear a scarlet coat as well as another," returned the girl. "I wish I could see *you* in this handsome garment."

"See me in a coat fit for a lord! Well, Judith, if you wait till that day, you'll wait until you see me beyond reason and memory. No—no—gal, my gifts are my gifts, and I'll live and die in 'em, though I never bring down another deer or spear another salmon. What have I done that you should wish to see *me* in such a flaunting coat, Judith?"

"Because I think, Deerslayer, that the false-tongued and falsehearted young gallants of the garrison ought not alone to appear in fine feathers, but that truth and honesty have *their* claims to be honored and exalted."

"And what exaltification—" the reader will have remarked that Deerslayer had not very critically studied his dictionary —"would it be to me, Judith, to be bedizened and bescarleted like a Mingo chief that has just got his presents up from Quebec? No—no—I'm well as I am, and if not, I can be no better. Lay the coat down on the blanket, Sarpent, and let us look further into the chist."

The tempting garment, one surely that was never intended for Hutter, was laid aside, and the examination proceeded. The male attire, all of which corresponded with the coat in quality, was soon exhausted, and then succeeded female. A beautiful dress of brocade, a little the worse from negligent treatment, followed, and this time open exclamations of delight escaped the lips of Judith. Much as the girl had been addicted to dress, and favorable as had been her opportunities of seeing some little pretension in that way among the wives of the different commandants and other ladies of the forts, never before had she beheld a tissue or tints to equal those that were now so unexpectedly placed before her eyes. Her rapture was almost childish; nor would she allow the inquiry to proceed until she had attired her person in a robe so unsuited to her habits and her abode. With this end, she withdrew into her own room, where, with hands practiced in such offices, she soon got rid of her own neat gown of linen and stood forth in the gay tints of the brocade. The dress happened to fit the fine, full person of Judith, and certainly it had never adorned a being better qualified by natural gifts to do credit to its really rich hues and fine texture. When she returned, both Deerslayer and Chingachgook, who had passed the brief time of her absence in taking a second look at the male garments, arose in surprise, each permitting exclamations of wonder and pleasure to escape him in a way so unequivocal as to add new luster to the eyes of Judith, by flushing her cheeks with a glow of triumph. Affecting, however, not to notice the impression she had made, the girl seated herself with the stateliness of a queen, desiring that the chest might be looked into further.

"I don't know a better way to treat with the Mingos, gal," cried Deerslayer, "than to send you ashore as you be, and to tell 'em that a queen has arrived among 'em! They'll give up old Hutter, and Hurry, and Hetty, too, at such a spectacle!"

"I thought your tongue too honest to flatter, Deerslayer," returned the girl, gratified at this admiration more than she would have cared to own. "One of the chief reasons of my respect for you was your love for truth."

"And 'tis truth, solemn truth, Judith, and nothing else. Never did eyes of mine gaze on as glorious a lookin' creatur' as you be yourself at this very moment! I've seen beauties in my time, too, both white and red, and them that was renowned and talked of, far and near, but never have I beheld one that could hold any comparison with what you are at this blessed instant, Judith. Never."

The glance of delight which the girl bestowed on the frank-speaking hunter in no degree lessened the effect of her charms, and as the humid eyes blended with it a look of sensibility, perhaps Judith never appeared more truly lovely than at what the young man had called that "blessed instant." He shook his head, held it suspended a moment over the open chest like one in doubt, and then proceeded with the examination.

Several of the minor articles of female dress came next, all of a quality to correspond with the gown. These were laid at Judith's feet, in silence, as if she had a natural claim to their possession. One or two, such as gloves and lace, the girl caught up and appended to her already rich attire in affected playfulness, but with the real design of decorating her person as far as circumstances would allow. When these two remarkable suits, male and female they might be termed, were removed, another canvas covering separated the remainder of the articles from the part of the chest which they had occupied. As soon as Deerslayer perceived this arrangement, he paused, doubtful of the propriety of proceeding any further.

"Every man has his secrets, I suppose," he said, "and all men have a right to their enj'yment. We've got low enough in this chist, in my judgment, to answer our wants, and it seems to me we should do well by going no further and by letting Master Hutter have to himself and his own feelin's all that's beneath this cover."

"Do you mean, Deerslayer, to offer these clothes to the Iroquois as ransom?" demanded Judith quickly.

"Sartain. What are we prying into another man's chist for, but to sarve its owner in the best way we can? This coat, alone, would be very apt to gain over the head chief of the riptyles, and if his wife or darter should happen to be out with him, that there gownd would soften the heart of any woman that is to be found atween Albany and Montreal. I do not see that we want a larger stock in trade than them two articles."

"To you it may seem so, Deerslayer," returned the disappointed girl, "but of what use could a dress like this be to any Indian woman? She could not wear it among the branches of the trees; the dirt and smoke of the wigwam would soon soil it; and how would a pair of red arms appear thrust through these short, laced sleeves!"

"All very true, gal, and you might go on and say it is altogether out of time, and place, and season in this region at all. What is it to us how the finery is treated, so long as it answers our wishes? I do not see that your father can make any use of such clothes, and it's lucky he has things that are of no valie to himself that will bear a high price with others. We can make no better trade for him than to offer these duds for his liberty. We'll throw in the light frivol'ties and get Hurry off in the bargain!"

"Then you think, Deerslayer, that Thomas Hutter has no one in his family—no child—no daughter—to whom this dress may be thought becoming, and whom you could wish to see in it once and a while, even though it should be at long intervals, and only in playfulness?"

"I understand you, Judith—yes, I now understand your meaning, and I think I can say, your wishes. That you are as glorious in that dress as the sun when it rises or sets in a soft October day, I'm ready to allow; and that you greatly become it is a good deal more sartain than that it becomes you. There's gifts in clothes as well as in other things. Now

I do not think that a warrior on his first path ought to lay on the same awful paints as a chief that has had this vartue tried, and knows from exper'ence he will not disgrace his pretensions. So it is with all of us, red or white. You are Thomas Hutter's darter, and that gownd was made for the child of some governor, or a lady of high station, and it was intended to be worn among fine furniture and in rich company. In my eyes, Judith, a modest maiden never looks more becoming than when becomingly clad, and nothing is suitable that is out of character. Besides, gal, if ther's a creatur' in the colony that can afford to do without finery and to trust to her own good looks and sweet countenance, it's yourself."

"I'll take off the rubbish this instant, Deerslayer," cried the girl, springing up to leave the room, "and never do I wish to see it on any human being again."

"So it is with 'em all, Sarpent," said the other, turning to his friend and laughing, as soon as the beauty had disappeared. "They like finery, but they like their natyve charms most of all. I'm glad the gal has consented to lay aside her furbelows, howsever, for it's ag'in reason for one of her class to wear 'em; and then she *is* handsome enough, as I call it, to go alone. Hist would show oncommon likely, too, in such a gownd, Delaware!"

"Wah-ta!-Wah is a redskin girl, Deerslayer," returned the Indian. "Like the young of the pigeon, she is to be known by her own feathers. I should pass by without knowing her, were she dressed in such a skin. It's wisest always to be so clad that our friends need not ask us for our names. The 'Wild Rose' is very pleasant, but she is no sweeter for so many colors."

"That's it! That's natur', and the true foundation for love and protection. When a man stops to pick a wild strawberry, he does not expect to find a melon, and when he wishes to gather a melon, he's disapp'inted if it proves to be a squash—though squashes *be* often brighter to the eye than melons. That's it, and it means, stick to your gifts and your gifts will stick to you."

The two men had now a little discussion together, touching the propriety of penetrating any further into the chest of Hutter, when Judith reappeared, divested of her robes, and in her own simple linen frock again.

"Thank you, Judith," said Deerslayer, taking her kindly

by the hand, "for I know it went a little ag'in the nat'ral
cravings of woman to lay aside so much finery as it might
be in a lump. But you're more pleasing to the eye as you
stand, you be, than if you had a crown on your head and
jewels dangling from your hair. The question now is whether
to lift this covering, to see what will be ra'ally the best bargain we can make for Master Hutter, for we must do as we
think *he* would be willing to do, did he stand here in our
places."

Judith looked very happy. Accustomed as she was to adula-
tion, the humble homage of Deerslayer had given her more
true satisfaction than she had ever yet received from the
tongue of man. It was not the terms in which this admiration had been expressed, for *they* were simple enough, that
produced so strong an impression; nor yet their novelty, or
their warmth of manner, nor any of those peculiarities that
usually give value to praise; but it was the unflinching truth
of the speaker that carried his words so directly to the heart
of the listener. This is one of the great advantages of plain
dealing and frankness. The habitual and wily flatterer may
succeed until his practices recoil on himself and, like other
sweets, his aliment cloys by its excess; but he who deals
honestly, though he often necessarily offend, possesses a
power of praising that no quality but sincerity can bestow,
since his words go directly to the heart, finding their support
in the understanding. Thus it was with Deerslayer and
Judith; so soon and so deeply did this simple hunter impress
those who knew him with a conviction of his unbending
honesty, that all he uttered in commendation was as certain to please, as all he uttered in the way of rebuke was as
certain to rankle and excite enmity where his character had
not awakened a respect and affection that in another sense
rendered it painful. In afterlife, when the career of this untutored being brought him in contact with officers of rank
and others entrusted with the care of the interests of the
state, this same influence was exerted on a wider field; even
generals listening to his commendations with a glow of pleasure that it was not always in the power of their official supe-
riors to awaken. Perhaps Judith was the first individual of his
own color who fairly submitted to this natural consequence
of truth and fair-dealing, on the part of Deerslayer. She had
actually pined for his praise, and she had now received it;

and that in the form which was most agreeable to her weaknesses and habits of thought. The result will appear in the course of the narrative.

"If we knew all that chest holds, Deerslayer," returned the girl, when she had a little recovered from the immediate effect produced by his commendations of her personal appearance, "we could better determine on the course we ought to take."

"That's not onreasonable, gal, though it's more a paleface than a redskin gift, to be prying into other people's secrets."

"Curiosity is natural, and it is expected that all human beings should have human failings. Whenever I've been at the garrisons, I've found that most in and about them had a longing to learn their neighbor's secrets."

"Yes, and sometimes to fancy them, when they couldn't find 'em out! That's the difference atween an Indian gentleman and a white gentleman. The Sarpent, here, would turn his head aside, if he found himself onknowingly lookin' into another chief's wigwam; whereas, in the settlements, while all pretend to be great people, most prove they've got betters, by the manner in which they talk of their consarns. I'll be bound, Judith, you wouldn't get the Sarpent, there, to confess there was another in the tribe so much greater than himself, as to become the subject of his idees, and to empl'y his tongue in conversations about his movements, and ways, and food, and all the other little matters that occupy a man when he's not empl'y'd in his greater duties. He who does this is but little better than a blackguard in the grain, and them that encourages him is pretty much of the same kidney, let them wear coats as fine as they may, or of what dye they please."

"But this is not another man's wigwam; it belongs to my father. These are his things, and they are wanted in his service."

"That's true, gal, that's true, and it carries weight with it. Well, when all is before us, we may, indeed, best judge which to offer for the ransom and which to withhold."

Judith was not altogether as disinterested in her feelings as she affected to be. She remembered that the curiosity of Hetty had been indulged in connection with this chest, while her own had been disregarded, and she was not sorry to possess an opportunity of being placed on a level with her less gifted sister in this one particular. It appearing to be admitted all around that the inquiry into the contents of the chest ought to be renewed, Deerslayer proceeded to remove the second covering of canvas.

The articles that lay uppermost, when the curtain was again raised on the secrets of the chest, were a pair of pistols, curiously inlaid with silver. Their value would have been considerable in one of the towns, though as weapons, in the woods, they were a species of arms seldom employed; never, indeed, unless it might be by some officer from Europe, who visited the colonies, as many were then wont to do, so much impressed with the superiority of the usages of London as to fancy they were not to be laid aside on the frontiers of America. What occurred on the discovery of these weapons will appear in the succeeding chapter.

CHAPTER XIII

An oaken, broken, elbow chair;
A candle-cup without an ear;
A battered, shattered, ash bedstead;
A box of deal without a lid;
A pair of tongs, but out of joint;
A back-sword poker, without point:
A dish which might good meat afford once;
An Ovid, and an old Concordance.

DEAN SWIFT'S *Inventory*

No SOONER DID Deerslayer raise the pistols than he turned
to the Delaware and held them up for his admiration.

"Child gun," said the Serpent, smiling, while he handled
one of the instruments as if it had been a toy.

"Not it, Sarpent; not it. 'Tis made for a man, and would
satisfy a giant if rightly used. But stop; white men are remarkable for their carelessness in putting away firearms in
chists and corners. Let me look if care has been given to
these."

As Deerslayer spoke, he took the weapon from the hand of
his friend and opened the pan. The last was filled with priming, caked like a bit of cinder, by time, moisture, and com-
pression. An application of the ramrod showed that both
the pistols were charged, although Judith could testify that
they had probably lain for years in the chest. It is not easy to
portray the surprise of the Indian at this discovery, for he
was in the practice of renewing his priming daily and of
looking to the contents of his piece at other short intervals.

"This is white neglect," said Deerslayer, shaking his head,
"and scarce a season goes by that someone in the settlements
doesn't suffer from it. It's extr'ornary too, Judith—yes, it's
downright extr'ornary—that the owner shall fire his piece at
a deer, or some other game, or perhaps at an inimy, and

twice out of three times he'll miss, but let him catch an accident with one of these forgotten charges, and he makes it sartain death to a child, or a brother, or a fri'nd! Well, we shall do a good turn to the owner if we fire these pistols for him; and as they're novelties to you and me, Sarpent, we'll try our hands at a mark. Freshen that priming, and I'll do the same with this, and then we'll see who is the best man with a pistol; as for the rifle, that's long been settled atween us."

Deerslayer laughed heartily at his own conceit, and in a minute or two they were both standing on the platform, selecting some object in the ark for their target. Judith was led by curiosity to their side.

"Stand back, gal, stand a little back; these we'pons have been long loaded," said Deerslayer, "and some accident may happen in the discharge."

"Then *you* shall not fire them! Give them both to the Delaware—or it would be better to unload them without firing."

"That's ag'in usage—and some people say ag'in manhood, though I hold to no such silly doctrine. We must fire 'em, Judith; yes, we must fire 'em; though I foresee that neither will have any great reason to boast of his skill."

Judith, in the main, was a girl of great personal spirit, and her habits prevented her from feeling any of the terror that is apt to come over her sex at the report of firearms. She had discharged many a rifle and had even been known to kill a deer, under circumstances that were favorable to the effort. She submitted, therefore, falling a little back by the side of Deerslayer, giving the Indian the front of the platform to himself. Chingachgook raised the weapon several times, endeavored to steady it by using both hands, changed his attitude from one that was awkward to another still more so, and finally drew the trigger with a sort of desperate indifference, without having, in reality, secured any aim at all. The consequence was that, instead of hitting the knot which had been selected for the mark, he missed the ark altogether, the bullet skipping along the water like a stone that was thrown by hand.

"Well done, Sarpent—well done," cried Deerslayer, laughing with his noiseless glee. "You've hit the lake, and that's an expl'ite, for some men! I know'd it, and as much as said it, here, to Judith, for your short we'pons don't belong to redskin gifts. You've hit the lake, and that's better than only hitting the air! Now, stand back, and let us see what white gifts can do with a white we'pon. A pistol isn't a rifle, but color is color."

The aim of Deerslayer was both quick and steady, and the report followed almost as soon as the weapon rose. Still the pistol hung fire, as it is termed, and fragments of it flew in a dozen directions, some falling on the roof of the castle, others in the ark, and one in the water. Judith screamed, and when the two men turned anxiously toward the girl, she was as pale as death, trembling in every limb.

"She's wounded—yes, the poor gal's wounded, Sarpent, though one couldn't foresee it, standing where she did. We'll lead her into a seat, and we must do the best for her that our knowledge and skill can afford."

Judith allowed herself to be supported to a seat, swallowed a mouthful of the water that the Delaware offered to her in a gourd, and, after a violent fit of trembling that seemed ready to shake her fine frame to dissolution, she burst into tears.

"The pain must be borne, poor Judith—yes, it must be borne," said Deerslayer soothingly; "though I am far from wishing you not to weep, for weeping often lightens galish feelin's. Where can she be hurt, Sarpent? I see no signs of blood, nor any rent of skin or garments."

"I am uninjured, Deerslayer," stammered the girl through her tears. "It's fright—nothing more, I do assure you; and, God be praised, no one, I find, has been harmed by the accident."

"This is extr'ornary!" exclaimed the unsuspecting and simple-minded hunter. "I thought, Judith, you'd been above settlement weaknesses, and that you was a gal not to be frightened by the sound of a bursting we'pon. No—I didn't think you so skeary! *Hetty* might well have been startled, but you've too much judgment and reason to be frightened when the danger's all over. They're pleasant to the eye, Chief, and changeful, but very unsartain in their feelin's!"

Shame kept Judith silent. There had been no acting in her agitation, but all had fairly proceeded from sudden and uncontrollable alarm—an alarm that she found almost as inexplicable to herself as it proved to be to her companions.

Wiping away the traces of tears, however, she smiled again, and was soon able to join in the laugh at her own folly.

"And you, Deerslayer," she at length succeeded in saying, "are you, indeed, altogether unhurt? It seems almost miraculous that a pistol should have burst in your hand, and you escape without the loss of a limb, if not of life!"

"Such wonders ar'n't oncommon, at all, among wornout arms. The first rifle they gave me played the same trick, and yet I lived through it, though not as onharmless as I've got out of this affair. Thomas Hutter is master of one pistol less than he was this morning, but as it happened in trying to sarve him, there's no ground of complaint. Now, draw near and let us look further into the inside of the chist."

Judith, by this time, had so far got the better of her agitation as to resume her seat, and the examination went on. The next article that offered was enveloped in cloth, and, on opening it, it proved to be one of the mathematical instruments that were then in use among seamen, possessing the usual ornaments and fastenings in brass. Deerslayer and Chingachgook expressed their admiration and surprise at the appearance of the unknown instrument, which was bright and glittering, having apparently been well cared for.

"This goes beyond the surveyors, Judith," Deerslayer exclaimed, after turning the instrument several times in his hands. "I've seen all their tools often—and wicked and heartless enough are they, for they never come into the forest but to lead the way to waste and destruction—but none of them have as designing a look as this! I fear me, after all, that Thomas Hutter has journeyed into the wilderness with no fair intentions toward its happiness. Did you ever see any of the cravings of a surveyor about your father, gal?"

"He is no surveyor, Deerslayer, nor does he know the use of that instrument, though he seems to own it. Do you suppose that Thomas Hutter ever wore that coat? It is as much too large for him as this instrument is beyond his learning."

"That's it—that must be it, Sarpent; the old fellow, by some onknown means, has fallen heir to another man's goods! They say he has been a mariner, and no doubt this chist and all it holds—Ha! What have we here? This far outdoes the brass and black wood of the tool!"

Deerslayer had opened a small bag from which he was

taking, one by one, the pieces of a set of chessmen. They were of ivory, much larger than common, and exquisitely wrought. Each piece represented the character or thing after which it is named; the knights being mounted; the castles stood on elephants; and even the pawns possessed the heads and busts of men. The set was not complete, and a few fractures betrayed bad usage, but all that was left had been carefully put away and preserved. Even Judith expressed wonder as these novel objects were placed before her eyes, and Chingachgook fairly forgot his Indian dignity in admiration and delight. The latter took up each piece and examined it with never-tiring satisfaction, pointing out to the girl the more ingenious and striking portions of the workmanship. But the elephants gave him the greatest pleasure. The "hughs" that he uttered as he passed his fingers over their trunks and ears and tails were very distinct; nor did he fail to note the pawns, which were armed as archers. This exhibition lasted several minutes, during which time Judith and the Indian had all the rapture to themselves. Deerslayer sat silent, thoughtful, and even gloomy, though his eyes followed each movement of the two principal actors, noting every new peculiarity about the pieces as they were held up to view. Not an exclamation of pleasure nor a word of condemnation passed his lips. At length his companions observed his silence, and then, for the first time since the chessmen had been discovered, did he speak.

"Judith," he asked earnestly, but with a concern that amounted almost to tenderness of manner, "did your parents ever talk to you of religion?"

The girl colored, and the flashes of crimson that passed over her beautiful countenance were like the wayward tints of a Neapolitan sky in November. Deerslayer had given her so strong a taste for truth, however, that she did not waver in her answer, replying simply and with sincerity:

"My *mother* did, often," she said; "my father *never*. I thought it made my mother sorrowful to speak of our prayers and duties, but my father has never opened his mouth on such matters before or since her death."

"That I can believe—that I can believe. He has no God—no such God as it becomes a man of white skin to worship, or even a redskin. Them things are idols!"

Judith started, and for a moment she seemed seriously hurt. Then she reflected, and in the end she laughed.

"And you think, Deerslayer, that these ivory toys are my father's gods? I have heard of idols, and know what they are."

"Them are idols!" repeated the other positively. "Why should your father keep 'em if he doesn't worship 'em?"

"Would he keep his gods in a bag and locked up in a chest? No, no, Deerslayer, my poor father carries his god with him wherever he goes, and that is in his own cravings. These things may really be idols—I think they are, myself, from what I have heard and read of idolatry—but they have come from some distant country, like all the other articles, and have fallen into Thomas Hutter's hands when he was a sailor."

"I'm glad of it—I am downright glad to hear it, Judith, for I do not think I could have mustered the resolution to strive to help a white idolator out of his difficulties! The old man is of my color and nation, and I wish to sarve him, but as one who denied all his gifts in the way of religion, it would have come hard to do so. That animal seems to give you great satisfaction, Sarpent, thought it's an idolatrous head, at the best."

"It is an elephant," interrupted Judith. "I've often seen pictures of such animals at the garrisons, and mother had a book in which there was a printed account of the creature. Father burned that, with all the other books, for he said mother loved reading too well. This was not long before mother died, and I've sometimes thought that the loss hastened her end."

This was said equally without levity and without any deep feeling. It was said without levity, for Judith was saddened by her recollections, and yet she had been too much accustomed to live for self and for the indulgence of her own vanities to feel her mother's wrongs very heavily. It required extraordinary circumstances to awaken a proper sense of her situation and to stimulate the better feelings of this beautiful but misguided girl, and these circumstances had not yet occurred in her brief existence.

"Elephant, or no elephant, 'tis an idol," returned the hunter, "and not fit to remain in Christian keeping."

"Good for Iroquois!" said Chingachgook, parting with one

of the castles with reluctance as his friend took it from him to replace it in the bag. "Elephon buy whole tribe—buy Delaware, almost!"

"Aye, that it would, as anyone who comprehends redskin natur' must know," answered Deerslayer; "but the man that passes false money, Sarpent, is as bad as he who makes it. Did you ever know a just Injin that wouldn't scorn to sell a coonskin for the true marten, or to pass off a mink for a beaver. I know that a few of these idols, perhaps *one* of them elephants, would go far toward buying Thomas Hutter's liberty, but it goes ag'in conscience to pass such counterfeit money. Perhaps no Injin tribe, hereaway, is downright idolaters, but there's some that come so near it that white gifts ought to be particular about encouraging them in their mistake."

"If idolatry is a *gift*, Deerslayer, and *gifts* are what you seem to think them, idolatry in such people can hardly be a sin," said Judith, with more smartness than discrimination.

"God grants no such gifts to any of his creatur's, Judith," returned the hunter seriously. "*He* must be adored, under some name or other, and not creatur's of brass or ivory. It matters not whether the Father of all is called God or Manitou, Deity or Great Spirit, he is nonetheless our common Maker and Master; nor does it count for much whether the souls of the just go to Paradise or happy hunting grounds, since He may send each his own way, as suits His own pleasure and wisdom; but it curdles my blood when I find human mortals so bound up in darkness and consait as to fashion the 'arth, or wood, or bones—things made by their own hands—into motionless, senseless effigies, and then fall down before them and worship 'em as a Deity!"

"After all, Deerslayer, these pieces of ivory may not be idols at all. I remember, now, to have seen one of the officers at the garrison with a set of fox and geese made in some such a design as these; and here is something hard, wrapped in cloth, that may belong to your idols."

Deerslayer took the bundle the girl gave him, and unrolling it, he found the board within. Like the pieces, it was large, rich, and inlaid with ebony and ivory. Putting the whole in conjunction, the hunter, though not without many misgivings, slowly came over to Judith's opinion, and finally admitted that the fancied idols must be merely the curiously carved men of some unknown game. Judith had the tact to use her victory with great moderation, nor did she once, even in the most indirect manner, allude to the ludicrous mistake of her companion.

This discovery of the uses of the extraordinary-looking little images settled the affair of the proposed ransom. It was agreed generally—and all understood the weaknesses and tastes of Indians—that nothing could be more likely to tempt the cupidity of the Iroquois than the elephants, in particular. Luckily, the whole of the castles were among the pieces, and these four tower-bearing animals it was finally determined should be the ransom offered. The remainder of the men, and, indeed, all the rest of the articles in the chest, were to be kept out of view and to be resorted to only as a last appeal. As soon as these preliminaries were settled, everything but those intended for the bribe was carefully replaced in the chest, and all the covers were "tucked in" as they had been found; it was quite possible, could Hutter have been put in possession of the castle again, that he might have passed the remainder of his days in it, without even suspecting the invasion that had been made on the privacy of the chest. The rent pistol would have been the most likely to reveal the secret, but this was placed by the side of its fellow, and all were pressed down as before—some half a dozen packages in the bottom of the chest not having been opened at all. When this was done, the lid was lowered, the padlocks replaced, and the key turned. The latter was then replaced in the pocket from which it had been taken.

More than an hour was consumed in settling the course proper to be pursued and in returning everything to its place. The pauses to converse were frequent, and Judith, who experienced a lively pleasure in the open, undisguised admiration with which Deerslayer's honest eye gazed at her handsome face, found the means to prolong the interview with a dexterity that seems to be innate in female coquetry. Deerslayer, indeed, appeared to be the first who was conscious of the time that had been thus wasted, and to call the attention of his companions to the necessity of doing something toward putting the plan of ransoming into execution. Chingachgook had remained in Hutter's bedroom, where the elephants were laid, to feast his eyes with the images of animals so wonderful and so novel. Perhaps an instinct told him that his presence would not be as acceptable to his companions as this holding himself aloof, for Judith had not much reserve in the manifestations of her preferences, and the Delaware had not got so far as one betrothed without acquiring some knowledge of the symptoms of the master passion.

"Well, Judith," said Deerslayer, rising, after the interview had lasted much longer than even he himself suspected, " 'tis pleasant conversing with you and settling all these matters, but duty calls us another way. All this time, Hurry and your father, not to say Hetty——"

The word was cut short in the speaker's mouth, for, at that critical moment, a light step was heard on the platform or courtyard, a human figure darkened the doorway, and the person last mentioned stood before him. The low exclamation that escaped Deerslayer and the slight scream of Judith were hardly uttered when an Indian youth, between the ages of fifteen and seventeen, stood beside her. These two entrances had been made with moccasined feet and consequently almost without noise, but unexpected and stealthy as they were, they had not the effect to disturb Deerslayer's self-possession. His first measure was to speak rapidly in Delaware to his friend, cautioning him to keep out of sight, while he stood on his guard; the second was to step to the door to ascertain the extent of the danger. No one else, however, had come, and a simple contrivance, in the shape of a raft, that lay floating at the side of the ark at once explained the means that had been used in bringing Hetty off. Two dead, dry, and consequently buoyant logs of pine were bound together with pins and withes, and a little platform of riven chestnut had been rudely placed on their surfaces. Here Hetty had been seated on a billet of wood, while the young Iroquois had rowed the primitive and slow-moving, but perfectly safe craft from the shore. As soon as Deerslayer had taken a close survey of this raft, and satisfied himself nothing else was near, he shook his head, and muttered in his soliloquizing way——

"This comes of prying into another man's chist! Had we been watchful and keen-eyed, such a surprise could never have happened; and getting this much from a boy teaches us what we may expect when the old warriors set themselves fairly about their sarcumventions. It opens the way, hows-

ever, to a treaty for the ransom, and I will hear what Hetty
has to say."

Judith, as soon as her surprise and alarm had a little
abated, discovered a proper share of affectionate joy at the
return of her sister. She folded her to her bosom and kissed
her, as had been her wont in the days of their childhood and
innocence. Hetty herself was less affected, for to her there
was no surprise, and her nerves were sustained by the purity
and holiness of her purpose. At her sister's request she took
a seat and entered into an account of her adventures since
they had parted. Her tale commenced just as Deerslayer returned, and he also became an attentive listener, while the
young Iroquois stood near the door, seemingly as indifferent
to what was passing as one of its posts.

The narrative of the girl was sufficiently clear until she
reached the time where we left her in the camp, after the
interview with the chiefs and at the moment when Hist
quitted her in the abrupt manner already stated. The sequel
of the story may be told in her own language.

"When I read the texts to the chiefs, Judith, you could not
have seen that they made any changes on their minds," she
said, "but if seed is planted, it *will* grow. God planted the
seeds of all the trees——"

"Aye, that did he—that did he," muttered Deerslayer;
"and a goodly harvest has followed."

"God planted the seeds of all the trees," continued Hetty,
after a moment's pause, "and you see to what a height and
shade they have grown! So it is with the Bible. You may
read a verse this year, and forget it, and it will come back
to you a year hence, when you least expect to remember it."

"And did you find anything of this among the savages,
poor Hetty?"

"Yes, Judith, and sooner and more fully than I had even
hoped. I did not stay long with Father and Hurry, but went
to get my breakfast with Hist. As soon as we had done, the
chiefs came to us, and *then* we found the fruits of the seed
that had been planted. They said what I had read from the
good book was right—it *must* be right—it sounded *right*, like
a sweet bird singing in their ears, and they told me to come
back and say as much to the great warrior who had slain
one of their braves; to tell it to you and to say how happy
they should be to come to church here, in the castle, or to

come out in the sun and hear me read more of the sacred volume; to tell you that they wish you would lend them some canoes, that they can bring Father and Hurry and their women to the castle, that we might all sit on the platform there and listen to the singing of the paleface Manitou—there, Judith, did you ever know of anything that so plainly shows the power of the Bible as *that?*"

"If it were true, 'twould be a miracle, indeed, Hetty. But all this is no more than Indian cunning and Indian treachery, striving to get the better of us by management, when they find it is not to be done by force."

"Do you doubt the Bible, sister, that you judge the savages so harshly?"

"I do not doubt the Bible, poor Hetty, but I much doubt an Indian and an Iroquois. What do you say to this visit, Deerslayer?"

"First let me talk a little with Hetty," returned the party appealed to. "Was this raft made a'ter you had got your breakfast, gal, and did you walk from the camp to the shore opposite to us, here?"

"Oh, no, Deerslayer. The raft was ready made, and in the water—could that have been by a miracle, Judith?"

"Yes—yes—an Indian miracle," rejoined the hunter. "They're expart enough in them sort of miracles. And you found the raft ready made to your hands, and in the water, and in waiting like for its cargo?"

"It was all as you say. The raft was near the camp, and the Indians put me on it, and had ropes of bark, and they dragged me to the place opposite to the castle, and then they told that young man to row me off, here."

"And the woods are full of the vagabonds, waiting to know what is to be the upshot of the miracle. We comprehend this affair, now, Judith—but I'll first get rid of this young Canadian bloodsucker, and then we'll settle our own course. Do you and Hetty leave us together, first bringing me the elephants, which the Sarpent is admiring; for 'twill never do to let this loping deer be alone a minute, or he'll borrow a canoe without asking."

Judith did as desired, first bringing the pieces and retiring with her sister into their own room. Deerslayer had acquired some knowledge of most of the Indian dialects of that region, and he knew enough of the Iroquois to hold a dialogue in the language. Beckoning to the lad, therefore, he caused him to take a seat on the chest, when he placed two of the castles suddenly before him. Up to that moment, this youthful savage had not expressed a single intelligible emotion or fancy. There were many things in and about the place that were novelties to him, but he had maintained his self-command with philosophical composure. It is true, Deerslayer had detected his dark eye scanning the defenses and the arms, but the scrutiny had been made with such an air of innocence, in such a gaping, indolent, boyish manner, that no one but a man who had himself been taught in a similar school would have even suspected his object. The instant, however, the eyes of the savage fell upon the wrought ivory and the images of the wonderful, unknown beasts, surprise and admiration got the mastery of him. The manner in which the natives of the South Sea Islands first beheld the toys of civilized life has been often described, but the reader is not to confound it with the manner of an American Indian under similar circumstances. In this particular case, the young Iroquois, or Huron, permitted an exclamation of rapture to escape him, and then he checked himself, like one who had been guilty of an indecorum. After this, his eyes ceased to wander but became riveted on the elephants, one of which, after a short hesitation, he even presumed to handle. Deerslayer did not interrupt him for quite ten minutes, knowing that the lad was taking such note of the curiosities as would enable him to give the most minute and accurate description of their appearance to his seniors on his return. When he thought sufficient time had been allowed to produce the desired effect, the hunter laid a finger on the naked knee of the youth and drew his attention to himself.

"Listen," he said, "I want to talk with my young friend from the Canadas. Let him forget that wonder for a minute."

"Where t'other pale brother?" demanded the boy, looking up and letting the idea that had been most prominent in his mind, previously to the introduction of the chessmen, escape him involuntarily.

"He sleeps—or if he isn't fairly asleep, he is in the room where the men do sleep," returned Deerslayer. "How did my young friend know there was another?"

"See him from the shore. Iroquois have got long eyes—see beyond the clouds—see the bottom of the great spring!"

"Well, the Iroquois are welcome. Two palefaces are pris-oners in the camp of your fathers, boy."

The lad nodded, treating the circumstance with great apparent indifference, though a moment after he laughed, as if exulting in the superior address of his own tribe.

"Can you tell me, boy, what your chiefs intend to do with these captyves; or haven't they yet made up their minds?"

The lad looked a moment at the hunter with a little surprise; then he coolly put the end of his forefinger on his own head, just above the left ear, and passed it around his crown, with an accuracy and readiness that showed how well he had been drilled in the peculiar art of his race.

"When?" demanded Deerslayer, whose gorge rose at this cool demonstration of indifference to human life. "And why not take them to your wigwams?"

"Road too long and full of palefaces. Wigwam full, and scalps sell high. Small scalp, much gold."

"Well, that explains it—yes, that does explain it. There's no need of being any plainer. Now, you know, lad, that the oldest of your prisoners is the father of these two young women; the other is the suitor of one of them. The gals nat'rally wish to save the scalps of such fri'nds, and they will give them two ivory creatur's as ransom; one for each scalp. Go back and tell this to your chiefs, and bring me the answer before the sun sets."

The boy entered zealously into this project, and with a sincerity that left no doubt of his executing his commission with intelligence and promptitude. For a moment he forgot his love of honor and all his clannish hostility to the British and their Indians, in his wish to have such a treasure in his tribe, and Deerslayer was satisfied with the impression he had made. It is true, the lad proposed to carry one of the elephants with him, as a specimen of the other, but to this his brother negotiator was too sagacious to consent, well knowing that it might never reach its destination if confided to such hands. This little difficulty was soon arranged, and the boy prepared to depart. As he stood on the platform, ready to step aboard the raft, he hesitated and turned short with a proposal to borrow a canoe, as the means most likely to shorten the negotiation. Deerslayer quietly refused the request, and, after lingering a little longer, the boy rowed slowly away from the castle, taking the direction of a thicket on the shore that lay less than half a mile distant. Deer-slayer seated himself on a stool and watched the progress of the ambassador, sometimes closely scanning the whole line of shore, as far as eye could reach; then, placing an elbow on a knee, he remained a long time with his chin resting on the hand.

During the interview between Deerslayer and the lad, a different scene took place in the adjoining room. Hetty had inquired for the Delaware, and being told why and where he remained concealed, she joined him. The reception which Chingachgook gave his visitor was respectful and gentle. He understood her character, and no doubt his disposition to be kind to such a being was increased by the hope of learning some tidings of his betrothed. As soon as the girl entered, she took a seat and invited the Indian to place himself near her; then she continued silent, as if she thought it decorous for him to question her, before she consented to speak on the subject she had on her mind. But, as Chingachgook did not understand this feeling, he remained respectfully atten-tive to anything she might be pleased to tell him.

"You are Chingachgook—the Great Serpent of the Dela-wares, arn't you?" the girl at length commenced, in her own simple way, losing her self-command in the desire to proceed, but anxious first to make sure of the individual.

"Chingachgook," returned the Delaware with grave dig-nity. "That say Great Sarpent in Deerslayer tongue."

"Well, that is my tongue. Deerslayer, and Father, and Judith, and I, and poor Hurry Harry—do you know Henry March, Great Serpent? I know you don't, however, or *he* would have spoken of *you*, too."

"Did any tongue name Chingachgook, Drooping Lily?"—for so the chief had named poor Hetty. "Was his name sung by a little bird among the Iroquois?"

Hetty did not answer at first, but with that indescribable feeling that awakens sympathy and intelligence among the youthful and unpracticed of her sex, she hung her head, and the blood suffused her cheek ere she found her tongue. It would have exceeded her stock of intelligence to explain this embarrassment, but though poor Hetty could not reason on every emergency, she could always feel. The color slowly receded from her cheek, and the girl looked up archly at the

Indian, smiling with the innocence of a child, mingled with the interest of a woman.

"My sister, the Drooping Lily, hear such bird!" Chingachgook added, and this with a gentleness of tone and manner that would have astonished those who sometimes heard the discordant cries that often came from the same throat—these transitions from the harsh and guttural to the soft and melodious not being infrequent in ordinary Indian dialogues. "My sister's ears were open—has she lost her tongue?"

"You *are* Chingachgook—you *must* be, for there is no other red man here—and she thought Chingachgook would come."

"Chin-gach-gook," pronouncing the name slowly and dwelling on each syllable; "Great Sarpent, Yengeese tongue."

"Chin-gach-gook," repeated Hetty, in the same deliberate manner. "Yes, so Hist called it, and you *must* be the chief."

"Wah-ta!-Wah," added the Delaware.

"Wah-ta!-Wah, or Hist-oh!-Hist. I think Hist prettier than Wah, and so I call her Hist."

"Wah very sweet in Delaware ears!"

"You make it sound differently from me. But never mind; I *did* hear the bird you speak of sing, Great Serpent."

"Will my sister say words of song? What she sing most—how she look—often she laugh?"

"She sang Chin-gach-gook oftener than anything else, and she laughed heartily when I told how the Iroquois waded into the water after us and couldn't catch us. I hope these logs haven't ears, Serpent!"

"No fear logs; fear sister next room. No fear Iroquois; Deerslayer stuff his eyes and ears with strange beast."

"I understand you, Serpent, and I understand Hist. Sometimes I think I'm not half as feeble-minded as they say I am. Now, do you look up at the roof and I'll tell you all. But you frighten me, you look so eager when I speak of Hist."

The Indian controlled his looks and affected to comply with the simple request of the girl.

"Hist told me to say, in a very low voice, that you mustn't trust the Iroquois in anything. They are more artful than any Indians she knows. Then she says that there is a large bright star that comes over the hill about an hour after dark—Hist had pointed out the planet Jupiter, without knowing it—and just as that star comes in sight, she will be on the point where I landed last night, and that you must come for her, in a canoe."

"Good—Chingachgook understand well enough, now, but he understand better if my sister sing to him ag'in."

Hetty repeated her words, more fully explaining what star was meant and mentioning the part of the point where he was to venture ashore. She now proceeded in her own unsophisticated way to relate her intercourse with the Indian maid and to repeat several of her expressions and opinions that gave great delight to the heart of her betrothed. She particularly renewed her injunctions to be on their guard against treachery, a warning that was scarcely needed, however, as addressed to men as wary as those to whom it was sent. She also explained, with sufficient clearness—for on all such subjects the mind of the girl seldom failed her—the present state of the enemy and the movements they had made since morning. Hist had been on the raft with her until it quitted the shore, and was now somewhere in the woods, opposite to the castle, and did not intend to return to the camp until night approached, when she hoped to be able to slip away from her companions, as they followed the shore on their way home, and conceal herself on the point. No one appeared to suspect the presence of Chingachgook, though it was necessarily known that an Indian had entered the ark the previous night, and it was suspected that he had since appeared in and about the castle in the dress of a paleface. Still some little doubt existed on the latter point, for, as this was the season when white men might be expected to arrive, there was some fear that the garrison of the castle was increasing by these ordinary means. All this had Hist communicated to Hetty while the Indians were dragging them along shore; the distance, which exceeded six miles, affording abundance of time.

"Hist don't know, herself, whether they suspect her or not, or whether they suspect *you*, but she hopes neither is the case. And now, Serpent, since I have told you so much from your betrothed," continued Hetty, unconsciously taking one of the Indian's hands and playing with the fingers, as a child is often seen to play with those of a parent, "you must let me tell you something from myself. When you marry Hist, you must be kind to her, and smile on her, as you do now on me, and not look cross, as some of the chiefs do at their squaws. Will you promise this?"

"Always good to Wah—too tender to twist hard, else she break."

"Yes, and smile, too; you don't know how much a girl craves smiles from them she loves. Father scarce smiled on me once while I was with him—and, Hurry—yes—Hurry talked loud, and laughed, but I don't think *he* smiled once either. You know the difference between a smile and a laugh?"

"Laugh, best. Hear Wah laugh, think bird sing?"

"I know that; her laugh *is* pleasant, but *you* must smile. And then, Serpent, you mustn't make her carry burdens and hoe corn, as so many Indians do, but treat her more as the palefaces treat their wives."

"Wah-ta!-Wah no paleface—got red skin, red heart, red feelin's. All red; no paleface. *Must* carry papoose."

"Every woman is willing to carry her child," said Hetty, smiling, "and there is no harm in *that*. But you must love Hist, and be gentle, and good to her, for she is gentle and good herself."

Chingachgook gravely bowed, and then he seemed to think this part of the subject might be dismissed. Before there was time for Hetty to resume her communications, the voice of Deerslayer was heard calling on his friend, in the outer room. At this summons the Serpent arose to obey, and Hetty joined her sister.

CHAPTER XIV

"A stranger animal," cries one,
"Sure never lived beneath the sun;
A lizard's body, lean and long,
A fish's head, a serpent's tongue,
Its foot, with triple claw disjoined;
And what a length of tail behind!"

MERRICK

THE FIRST ACT of the Delaware on rejoining his friend was to proceed gravely to disencumber himself of his civilized attire and to stand forth an Indian warrior again. The protest of Deerslayer was met by his communicating the fact that the presence of an Indian in the hut was known to the Iroquois, and that his maintaining the disguise would be more likely to direct suspicions to his real object than if he came out openly as a member of a hostile tribe. When the latter understood the truth, and was told that he had been deceived in supposing the chief had succeeded in entering the ark undiscovered, he cheerfully consented to the change, since further attempt at concealment was useless. A gentler feeling than the one avowed, however, lay at the bottom of the Indian's desire to appear as a son of the forest. He had been told that Hist was on the opposite shore, and nature so far triumphed over all distinctions of habit, and tribes, and people as to reduce this young savage warrior to the level of a feeling which would have been found in the most refined inhabitant of a town, under similar circumstances. There was a mild satisfaction in believing that she he loved could see him, and as he walked out on the platform in his scanty native attire, an Apollo of the wilderness, a hundred of the tender fancies that fleet through lovers' brains beset his imagination and softened his heart.

226

All this was lost on Deerslayer, who was no great adept in the mysteries of Cupid, but whose mind was far more occupied with the concerns that forced themselves on his attention than with any of the truant fancies of love. He soon recalled his companion, therefore, to a sense of their actual condition by summoning him to a sort of council of war, in which they were to settle their future course. In the dialogue that followed, the parties mutually made each other acquainted with what had passed in their several interviews. Chingachgook was told the history of the treaty about the ransom, and Deerslayer heard the whole of Hetty's communications. The latter listened with generous interest to his friend's hopes and promised cheerfully all the assistance he could lend.

" 'Tis our main ar'n'd, Sarpent, as you know, this battling for the castle and old Hutter's darters coming in as a sort of accident. Yes—yes—I'll be actyve in helping little Hist, who's not only one of the best and handsomest maidens of the tribe, but the *very* best and handsomest. I've always encouraged you, Chief, in that liking; it's proper, too, that a great and ancient race like your'n shouldn't come to an end. If a woman of red skin and red gifts could get to be near enough to me to wish her for a wife, I'd s'arch for just such another, but that can *never* be; no, that can *never* be. I'm glad Hetty has met with Hist, howsever, for though the first is a little short of wit and understanding, the last has enough for both. Yes, Sarpent," laughing heartily, "put 'em together and two smarter gals isn't to be found in all York Colony!"

"I will go to the Iroquois camp," returned the Delaware gravely. "No one knows Chingachgook but Wah, and a treaty for lives and scalps should be made by a chief! Give me the strange beasts, and let me take a canoe."

Deerslayer dropped his head and played with the end of a fish pole in the water, as he sat dangling his legs over the edge of the platform, like a man who was lost in thought by the sudden occurrence of a novel idea. Instead of directly answering the proposal of his friend, he began to soliloquize; a circumstance, however, that in no manner rendered his words more true, as he was remarkable for saying what he thought, whether the remarks were addressed to himself or to anyone else.

"Yes—yes," he said, "this must be what they call love! I've heard say that it sometimes upsets reason altogether, leaving a young man as helpless, as to calculation and caution, as a brute beast. To think that the Sarpent should be so lost to reason, and cunning, and wisdom! We must, sartainly, manage to get Hist off, and have 'em married as soon as we get back to the tribe, or this war will be of no more use to the chief than a hunt a little oncommon and extr'ornary. Yes—yes—he'll never be the man he was till this matter is off his mind and he comes to his senses, like all the rest of mankind. Sarpent, you can't be in airnest, and therefore I shall say but little to your offer. But you're a chief, and will soon be sent out on the warpath at the head of parties, and I'll just ask if you'd think of putting your forces into the inimy's hands afore the battle is fou't?"

"Wah!" ejaculated the Indian.

"Aye—Wah!—I know well enough it's Wah, and altogether Wah! Ra'ally, Sarpent, I'm consarned and mortified about you! I never heard so weak an idea come from a chief, and he, too, one that's already got a name for being wise, young and inexper'enced as he is. Canoe you shan't have, so long as the v'ice of fri'ndship and warning can count for anything."

"My paleface friend is right. A cloud came over the face of Chingachgook, and weakness got into his mind, while his eyes were dim. My brother has a good memory for good deeds and a weak memory for bad. He will forget."

"Yes, that's easy enough. Say no more about it, Chief, but if another of them clouds blow near you, do your endivor to get out of its way. Clouds are bad enough in the weather, but when they come to the reason, it gets to be serious. Now, sit down by me here and let us calculate our movements a little, for we shall soon either have a truce and a peace, or we shall come to an actyve and bloody war. You see the vagabonds can make logs sarve their turn as well as the best raftsmen on the rivers, and it would be no great expl'ite for them to invade us in a body. I've been thinking of the wisdom of putting all old Tom's stores into the ark, of barring and locking up the castle, and of taking to the ark altogether. That is movable, and by keeping the sail up and shifting places, we might worry through a great many nights without them Canada wolves finding a way into our sheepfold."

Chingachgook listened to this plan with approbation. Did the negotiation fail, there was now little hope that the night would pass without an assault; and the enemy had sagacity enough to understand, that, in carrying the castle, they would probably become masters of all it contained, the offered ransom included, and still retain the advantages they had hitherto gained. Some precaution of the sort appeared to be absolutely necessary, for now the numbers of the Iroquois were known, a night attack could scarcely be successfully met. It would be impossible to prevent the enemy from getting possession of the canoes and the ark, and the latter itself would be a hold in which the assailants would be as effectually protected against bullets as were those in the building. For a few minutes both the men thought of sinking the ark in the shallow water, of bringing the canoes into the house, and of depending altogether on the castle for protection. But reflection satisfied them that, in the end, this expedient would fail. It was so easy to collect logs on the shore and to construct a raft of almost any size that it was certain the Iroquois, now they had turned their attention to such means, would resort to them seriously, so long as there was the certainty of success by perseverance. After deliberating maturely and placing all the considerations fairly before them, the two young beginners in the art of forest warfare settled down into the opinion that the ark offered the only available means of security. This decision was no sooner come to than it was communicated to Judith. The girl had no serious objection to make, and all four set about the measures necessary to carrying the plan into execution.

The reader will readily understand that Floating Tom's worldly goods were of no great amount. A couple of beds, some wearing apparel, the arms and ammunition, a few cooking utensils, and the mysterious but half-examined chest formed the principal items. These were all soon removed, the ark having been hauled on the eastern side of the building, so that the transfer could be made without being seen from the shore. It was thought unnecessary to disturb the heavier and coarser articles of furniture, as they were not required in the ark and were of but little value in themselves. As great caution was necessary in removing the different objects, most of which were passed out of a window with a view to conceal what was going on, it required two or three hours before all could be effected. By the expiration of that time the raft made its appearance, moving from the shore. Deerslayer immediately had recourse to the glass, by the aid of which he perceived that two warriors were on it, though they appeared to be unarmed. The progress of the raft was slow; a circumstance that formed one of the great advantages that would be possessed by the scow in any future collision between them, the movements of the latter being comparatively swift and light. As there was time to make the dispositions for the reception of the two dangerous visitors, everything was prepared for them long before they had got near enough to be hailed. The Serpent and the girls retired into the building, where the former stood near the door, well provided with rifles, while Judith watched the proceedings without through a loop. As for Deerslayer, he had brought a stool to the edge of the platform, at the point toward which the raft was advancing, and taken his seat, with his rifle leaning carelessly between his legs.

As the raft drew nearer, every means possessed by the party in the castle was resorted to in order to ascertain if their visitors had any firearms. Neither Deerslayer nor Chingachgook could discover any, but Judith, unwilling to trust to simple eyesight, thrust the glass through the loop and directed it toward the hemlock boughs that lay between the two logs of the raft, forming a sort of flooring, as well as a seat for the use of the rowers. When the heavy-moving craft was within fifty feet of him, Deerslayer hailed the Hurons, directing them to cease rowing, it not being his intention to permit them to land. Compliance, of course, was necessary, and the two grim-looking warriors instantly quitted their seats, though the raft continued slowly to approach until it had driven in much nearer to the platform.

"Are ye chiefs?" demanded Deerslayer, with dignity. "Are ye chiefs?—or have the Mingos sent me warriors without names, on such an ar'n'd? If so, the sooner ye go back, the sooner the one will be likely to come that a warrior can talk with."

"Hugh!" exclaimed the elder of the two on the raft, rolling his glowing eyes over the different objects that were visible in and about the castle, with a keenness that showed how little escaped him. "My brother is very proud, but Rivenoak (we use the literal translation of the term, writing as we do in English) is a name to make a Delaware turn pale."

"That's true, or it's a lie, Rivenoak, as it may be, but I am not likely to turn pale, seeing that I was born pale. What's your ar'n'd, and why do you come among light bark canoes on logs that are not even dug out?"

"The Iroquois are not ducks, to walk on water! Let the palefaces give them a canoe, and they'll come in a canoe."

"That's more rational than likely to come to pass. We have but four canoes, and being four persons, that's only one for each of us. We thank you for the offer, howsever, though we ask leave not to accept it. You are welcome, Iroquois, on your logs!"

"Thanks—my young paleface warrior—he has got a name —how do the chiefs call him?"

Deerslayer hesitated a moment, and a gleam of pride and human weakness came over him. He smiled, muttered between his teeth, and then looking up proudly, he said:

"Mingo, like all are young and actyve, I've been known by different names at different times. One of your warriors, whose spirit started for the happy grounds of your people as lately as yesterday morning, thought I desarved to be known by the name of Hawkeye, and this because my sight happened to be quicker than his own, when it got to be life or death atween us."

Chingachgook, who was attentively listening to all that passed, heard and understood this proof of passing weakness in his friend, and on a future occasion he questioned him more closely concerning the transaction on the point where Deerslayer had first taken human life. When he had got the whole truth, he did not fail to communicate it to the tribe, from which time the young hunter was universally known among the Delawares by an appellation so honorably earned. As this, however, was a period posterior to all the incidents of this tale, we shall continue to call the young hunter by the name under which he has been first introduced to the reader. Nor was the Iroquois less struck with the vaunt of the white man. He knew of the death of his comrade and had no difficulty in understanding the allusion, the intercourse between the conqueror and his victim on that occasion having been seen by several savages on the shore of the lake, who had been stationed at different points just within the margin of the bushes to watch the drifting canoes, and who had not time to reach the scene of action ere the victor had retired. The effect on this rude being of the forest was an exclamation of surprise; then such a smile of courtesy and wave of the hand succeeded as would have done credit to Asiatic diplomacy. The two Iroquois spoke to each other in low terms, and both drew near the end of the raft that was closest to the platform.

"My brother, Hawkeye, has sent a message to the Hurons," resumed Rivenoak, "and it has made their hearts very glad. They hear he has images of beasts with two tails! Will he show them to his friends?"

"Inimies would be truer," returned Deerslayer, "but sound isn't sense and does little harm. Here is one of the images; I toss it to you under faith of treaties. If it's not returned, the rifle will settle the p'int atween us."

The Iroquois seemed to acquiesce in the conditions, and Deerslayer arose and prepared to toss one of the elephants to the raft, both parties using all the precaution that was necessary to prevent its loss. As practice renders men expert in such things, the little piece of ivory was soon successfully transferred from one hand to the other, and then followed another scene on the raft in which astonishment and delight got the mastery of Indian stoicism. These two grim old warriors manifested even more feeling as they examined the curiously wrought chessman than had been betrayed by the boy, for in the case of the latter, recent schooling had interposed its influence, while the men, like all who are sustained by well-established characters, were not ashamed to let some of their emotions be discovered. For a few minutes they apparently lost the consciousness of their situation in the intense scrutiny they bestowed on a material so fine, work so highly wrought, and an animal so extraordinary. The lip of the moose is, perhaps, the nearest approach to the trunk of the elephant that is to be found in the American forest, but this resemblance was far from being sufficiently striking to bring the new creature within the range of their habits and ideas, and the more they studied the image, the greater was their astonishment. Nor did these children of the forest mistake the structure on the back of the elephant for a part of the animal. They were familiar with horses and oxen, and had seen towers in the Canadas, and found nothing surprising in creatures of burden. Still, by a very natural association, they supposed the carving meant to represent that the animal they saw was of a strength sufficient to carry a fort on its back, a circumstance that in no degree lessened their wonder.

"Has my paleface brother any more such beasts?" at last the senior of the Iroquois asked in a sort of petitioning manner.

"There's more where them came from, Mingo," was the answer; "one is enough, however, to buy off fifty scalps."

"One of my prisoners is a great warrior—tall as a pine—strong as the moose—active as a deer—fierce as the panther. Someday he'll be a great chief and lead the army of King George!"

"Tut—tut—Mingo; Hurry Harry is Hurry Harry, and you'll never make more than a corporal of him, if you do that. He's tall enough, of a sartainty, but that's of no use, as he only hits his head ag'in the branches as he goes through the forest. He's strong, too, but a strong body isn't a strong head, and the king's generals are not chosen for their sinews. He's swift, if you will, but a rifle bullet is swifter. And as for f'erceness, it's no great ricommend to a soldier, they that think they feel the stoutest, often givin' out at the pinch. No—no—you'll never make Hurry's scalp pass for more than a good head of curly hair, and a rattlepate beneath it!"

"My old prisoner very wise—king of the lake—great warrior, wise counselor!"

"Well, there's them that might gainsay all this, too, Mingo. A very wise man wouldn't be apt to be taken in so foolish a manner as befell Master Hutter, and if he gives good counsel, he must have listened to very bad in that affair. There's only one king of this lake, and he's a long way off and isn't likely ever to see it. Floating Tom is some such king of this region, as the wolf that prowls through the woods is king of the forest. A beast with two tails is well worth two such scalps!"

"But my brother has another beast? He will give two," holding up as many fingers, "for old father."

"Floating Tom is no father of mine, but he'll fare none the worse for that. As for giving two beasts for his scalp, and each beast with two tails, it is quite beyond reason. Think yourself well off, Mingo, if you make a much worse trade."

By this time the self-command of Rivenoak had got the better of his wonder, and he began to fall back on his usual habits of cunning, in order to drive the best bargain he could. It would be useless to relate more than the substance of the desultory dialogue that followed, in which the Indian manifested no little management, in endeavoring to recover the ground lost under the influence of surprise. He even affected to doubt whether any original for the image of the beast existed and asserted that the oldest Indian had never heard a tradition of any such animal. Little did either of them imagine at the time that long ere a century elapsed, the progress of civilization would bring even much more extraordinary and rare animals into that region, as curiosities to be gazed at by the curious, and that the particular beast about which the disputants contended would be seen laving its sides and swimming in the very sheet of water on which they had met.* As is not uncommon on such occasions, one of the parties got a little warm in the course of the discussion, for Deerslayer met all the arguments and prevarications of his subtle opponent with his own cool directness of manner and unmoved love of truth. What an elephant was he knew little better than the savage, but he perfectly understood that the carved pieces of ivory must have some such value in the eyes of an Iroquois as a bag of gold, or a package of beaver skins, would in those of a trader. Under the circumstances, therefore, he felt it to be prudent not to concede too much at first, since there existed a nearly unconquerable obstacle to making the transfers, even after the contracting parties had actually agreed upon the terms. Keeping this difficulty in view, he held the extra chessmen in reserve as a means of smoothing any difficulty in the moment of need.

At length the savage pretended that further negotiation was useless, since he could not be so unjust to his tribe as to part with the honor and emoluments of two excellent, full-grown male scalps for a consideration so trifling as a toy like that he had seen—and he prepared to take his departure. Both parties now felt as men are wont to feel when a bargain

---

* The Otsego is a favorite place for the caravankeepers to let their elephants bathe. The writer has seen two at a time, since the publication of this book, swimming about in company.

that each is anxious to conclude is on the eve of being broken off in consequence of too much pertinacity in the way of management. The effect of the disappointment was very different, however, on the respective individuals. Deerslayer was mortified and filled with regret, for he not only felt for the prisoners, but he also felt deeply for the two girls. The conclusion of the treaty, therefore, left him melancholy and full of regret. With the savage, his defeat produced the desire of revenge. In a moment of excitement, he loudly announced his intention to say no more, and he felt equally enraged with himself and with his cool opponent, that he had permitted a paleface to manifest more indifference and self-command than an Indian chief. When he began to urge his raft away from the platform, his countenance lowered, and his eye glowed even while he affected a smile of amity and a gesture of courtesy, at parting.

It took some little time to overcome the *vis inertiæ* of the logs, and while this was doing by the silent Indian, Rivenoak stalked over the hemlock boughs that lay between the logs, in sullen ferocity, eyeing keenly the while the hut, the platform, and the person of his late disputant. Once he spoke in low, quick terms to his companion, and he stirred the boughs with his feet, like an animal that is restive. At that moment the watchfulness of Deerslayer had a little abated, for he sat musing on the means of renewing the negotiation without giving too much advantage to the other side. It was, perhaps, fortunate for him that the keen and bright eyes of Judith were as vigilant as ever. At the instant when the young man was least on his guard, and his enemy was the most on the alert, she called out in a warning voice to the former, most opportunely giving the alarm.

"Be on your guard, Deerslayer," the girl cried. "I see rifles, with the glass, beneath the hemlock brush, and the Iroquois is loosening them with his feet!"

It would seem that the enemy had carried their artifices so far as to employ an agent who understood English. The previous dialogue had taken place in his own language, but it was evident, by the sudden manner in which his feet ceased their treacherous occupation, and in which the countenance of Rivenoak changed from sullen ferocity to a smile of courtesy, that the call of the girl was understood. Signing to his companion to cease his efforts to set the logs in motion, he advanced to the end of the raft which was nearest to the platform and spoke.

"Why should Rivenoak and his brother leave any cloud between them?" he said. "They are both wise, both brave, and both generous; they ought to part friends. One beast shall be the price of one prisoner."

"And, Mingo," answered the other, delighted to renew the negotiation on almost any terms and determined to clench the bargain if possible by a little extra liberality, "you'll see that a paleface knows how to pay a full price, when he trades with an open heart and an open hand. Keep the beast that you had forgotten to give back to me, as you was about to start, and which I forgot to ask for, on account of consarn at parting in anger. Show it to your chiefs. When you bring us our fri'nds two more shall be added to it—and"—hesitating a moment in distrust of the expediency of so great a concession, then deciding in its favor—"and, if we see them afore the sun sets, we may find a fourth to make up an even number."

This settled the matter. Every gleam of discontent vanished from the dark countenance of the Iroquois, and he smiled as graciously, if not as sweetly, as Judith Hutter herself. The piece already in his possession was again examined, and an ejaculation of pleasure showed how much he was pleased with this unexpected termination of the affair. In point of fact, both he and Deerslayer had momentarily forgotten what had become of the subject of their discussion, in the warmth of their feelings, but such had not been the case with Rivenoak's companion. This man retained the piece, and had fully made up his mind, were it claimed under such circumstances as to render its return necessary, to drop it in the lake, trusting to his being able to find it again at some future day. This desperate expedient, however, was no longer necessary, and after repeating the terms of agreement and professing to understand them, the two Indians finally took their departure, moving slowly toward the shore.

"Can any faith be put in such wretches?" asked Judith, when she and Hetty had come out on the platform, and were standing at the side of Deerslayer, watching the dull movement of the logs. "Will they not rather keep the toy they have and send us off some bloody proofs of their getting the better of us in cunning, by way of boasting? I've heard of acts as bad as this."

"No doubt, Judith; no manner of doubt, if it wasn't for Indian natur'. But I'm no judge of a redskin if that two-tailed beast doesn't set the whole tribe in some such stir as a stick raises in a beehive! Now, there's the Sarpent, a man with narves like flint and no more cur'osity in everyday consarns than is befitting prudence. Why, he was so overcome with the sight of the creatur', carved as it is in bone, that I felt ashamed for him! That's just their gifts, however, and one can't well quarrel with a man for his gifts, when they are lawful. Chingachgook will soon get over his weakness, and remember that he's a chief, and that he comes of a great stock, and has a renowned name to support and uphold; but, as for yonder scamps, there'll be no peace among 'em, until they think they've got possession of everything of the natur' of that bit of carved bone that's to be found among Thomas Hutter's stores!"

"They only know of the elephants and can have no hopes about the other things."

"That's true, Judith; still, covetousness is a craving feelin'. They'll say, if the palefaces have these curious beasts with two tails, who knows but they've got some with three, or, for that matter, with four! That's what the schoolmasters call nat'ral arithmetic, and 'twill be sartain to beset the feelin's of savages. They'll never be easy till the truth is known."

"Do you think, Deerslayer," inquired Hetty, in her simple and innocent manner, "that the Iroquois won't let Father and Hurry go? I read to them several of the very best verses in the whole Bible, and you see what they have done already."

The hunter, as he always did, listened kindly and even affectionately to Hetty's remarks; then he mused a moment in silence. There was something like a flush on his cheek as he answered, after quite a minute had passed.

"I don't know whether a white man ought to be ashamed or not to own he can't read, but such is my case, Judith. You are skillful, I find, in all such matters, while I have only studied the hand of God, as it is seen in the hills and the valleys, the mountaintops, the streams, the forest, and the springs. Much l'arning may be got in this way, as well as out of books, and yet I sometimes think it is a white man's gift to read! When I hear from the mouths of the Moravians the words of which Hetty speaks, they raise a longing in my mind, and I think I *will* know how to read 'em myself; but the game in summer, and the traditions, and lessons in war, and other matters have always kept me behindhand."

"Shall I teach you, Deerslayer?" asked Hetty earnestly. "I'm weak-minded, they say, but I can read as well as Judith. It might save your life, to know how to read the Bible to the savages, and it will certainly save your soul, for Mother told me *that* again and again!"

"Thankee, Hetty—yes, thankee, with all my heart. There are like to be too stirring times for much idleness; but, after it's peace, and I come to see you ag'in on this lake, then I'll give myself up to it, as if 'twas pleasure and profit in a single business. Perhaps I ought to be ashamed, Judith, that 'tis so, but truth is truth. As for these Iroquois, 'tisn't very likely they'll forget a beast with two tails on account of a varse or two from the Bible. I rather expect they'll give up the prisoners and trust to some sarcumvention or other to get 'em back ag'in, with us and all in the castle, and the ark in the bargain. Howsever, we must humor the vagabonds first, to get your father and Hurry out of their hands, and next, to keep the peace atween us, until such time as the Sarpent there can make out to get off his betrothed wife. If there's any sudden outbreakin' of anger and ferocity, the Indians will send off all their women and children to the camp at once, whereas, by keeping 'em calm and trustful, we may manage to meet Hist at the spot she has mentioned. Rather than have the bargain fall through now, I'd throw in half a dozen of them effigy bow-and-arrow men, such as we've in plenty in the chist."

Judith cheerfully assented, for she would have resigned even the flowered brocade, rather than not redeem her father and please Deerslayer.

The prospects of success were now so encouraging as to raise the spirits of all in the castle, though a due watchfulness on the movements of the enemy was maintained. Hour passed after hour, notwithstanding, and the sun had once more begun to fall toward the summits of the western hills, and yet no signs were seen of the return of the raft. By dint of sweeping the shore with the glass, Deerslayer at length discovered a place in the dense and dark woods where, he entertained no doubt, the Iroquois were assembled in considerable numbers. It was near the thicket whence the raft had issued, and a little rill that trickled into the lake announced the vicinity of a spring. Here, then, the savages were probably holding their consultation, and the decision was to be made that went to settle the question of life or death for the prisoners. There was one ground for hope in spite of the delay, however, that Deerslayer did not fail to place before his anxious companions. It was far more probable that the Indians had left their prisoners in the camp than that they had encumbered themselves by causing them to follow through the woods a party that was out on a merely temporary excursion. If such was the fact, it required considerable time to send a messenger the necessary distance and to bring the two white men to the spot where they were to embark. Encouraged by these reflections, a new stock of patience was gathered, and the declension of the sun was viewed with less alarm.

The result justified Deerslayer's conjecture. Not long before the sun had finally disappeared, the two logs were seen coming out of the thicket again; as it drew near, Judith announced that her father and Hurry, both of them pinioned, lay on the bushes in the center. As before, the Indians were rowing. The latter seemed to be conscious that the lateness of the hour demanded unusual exertions, and contrary to the habits of their people, who are ever averse to toil, they labored hard at the rude substitutes for oars. In consequence of this diligence the raft occupied its old station in about half the time that had been taken in the previous visits.

Even after the conditions were so well understood, and matters had proceeded so far, the actual transfer of the prisoners was not a duty to be executed without difficulty. The Iroquois were compelled to place great reliance on the good faith of their foes, though it was reluctantly given, and was yielded to necessity rather than to confidence. As soon as Hutter and Hurry should be released the party in the castle numbered two to one, as opposed to those on the raft, and escape by flight was out of the question, as the former had three bark canoes, to say nothing of the defenses of the house and the ark. All this was understood by both parties, and it is probable the arrangement never could have been completed had not the honest countenance and manner of Deerslayer wrought their usual effect on Rivenoak.

"My brother knows I put faith in *him*," said the latter as he advanced with Hutter, whose legs had been released to enable the old man to ascend to the platform. "One scalp —one more beast."

"Stop, Mingo," interrupted the hunter, "keep your prisoner a moment. I have to go and seek the means of payment."

This excuse, however, though true in part, was principally a fetch. Deerslayer left the platform, and entering the house, he directed Judith to collect all the arms and to conceal them in her own room. He then spoke earnestly to the Delaware, who stood on guard as before near the entrance of the building, put the three remaining castles in his pocket, and returned.

"You are welcome back to your old abode, Master Hutter," said Deerslayer, as he helped the other up on the platform, slyly passing into the hand of Rivenoak at the same time another of the castles. "You'll find your darters right glad to see you, and here's Hetty come herself to say as much in her own behalf."

Here the hunter stopped speaking and broke out into a hearty fit of his silent and peculiar laughter. Hurry's legs were just released, and he had been placed on his feet. So tightly had the ligatures been drawn that the use of his limbs was not immediately recovered, and the young giant presented, in good sooth, a very helpless and somewhat ludicrous picture. It was this unusual spectacle, particularly the bewildered countenance, that excited the merriment of Deerslayer.

"You look like a girdled pine in a clearin', Hurry Harry, that is rocking in a gale," said Deerslayer, checking his unseasonable mirth more from delicacy to the others than from any respect to the liberated captive. "I'm glad, however, to see that you haven't had your hair dressed by any of the Iroquois barbers in your late visit to their camp."

"Harkee, Deerslayer," returned the other a little fiercely; "it will be prudent for you to deal less in mirth and more in friendship on this occasion. Act like a Christian, for once, and not like a laughing gal in a country school when the master's back is turned, and just tell me whether there's any feet or not at the end of these legs of mine. I think I can see them, but as for feelin', they might as well be down on the banks of the Mohawk as where they seem to be."

"You've come off whole, Hurry, and that's not a little," answered the other, secretly passing to the Indian the remainder of the stipulated ransom and making an earnest sign, at the same moment, for him to commence his retreat. "You've come off whole, feet and all, and are only a little numb from a tight fit of the withes. Natur' 'll soon set the blood in motion, and then you may begin to dance, to celebrate what I call a most wonderful and onexpected deliverance from a den of wolves."

Deerslayer released the arms of his friends, as each landed, and the two were now stamping and limping about on the platform, growling and uttering denunciations as they endeavored to help the returning circulation. They had been tethered too long, however, to regain the use of their limbs in a moment; and the Indians being quite as diligent on their return as on their advance, the raft was fully a hundred yards from the castle when Hurry, turning accidentally in that direction, discovered how fast it was getting beyond the reach of his vengeance. By this time he could move with tolerable facility, though still numb and awkward. Without considering his own situation, however, he seized the rifle that leaned against the shoulder of Deerslayer and attempted to cock and present it. The young hunter was too quick for him. Seizing the piece he wrenched it from the hands of the giant; not, however, until it had gone off in the struggle, when pointed directly upward. It is probable that Deerslayer could have prevailed in such a contest, on account of the condition of Hurry's limbs, but the instant the gun went off, the latter yielded and stumped toward the house, raising his legs at each step quite a foot from the ground, from an uncertainty of the actual position of his feet. But he had been anticipated by Judith. The whole stock of Hutter's arms, which had been left in the building as a resource in the event of a sudden outbreaking of hostilities, had been removed, and was already secreted, agreeably to Deerslayer's directions. In consequence of this precaution, no means offered by which March could put his designs in execution.

Disappointed in his vengeance, Hurry seated himself, and like Hutter, for half an hour he was too much occupied in endeavoring to restore the circulation and in regaining the use of his limbs to indulge in any other reflections. By the end of this time the raft had disappeared, and night was beginning to throw her shadows once more over the whole sylvan scene. Before darkness had completely set in, and while the girls were preparing the evening meal, Deerslayer related to Hutter an outline of the events that had taken place and gave him a history of the means he had adopted for the security of his children and property.

CHAPTER XV

THE CALM OF evening was again in singular contrast, while its gathering gloom was in as singular unison with the passions of men. The sun was set, and the rays of the retiring luminary ceased to gild the edges of the few clouds that had sufficient openings to admit the passage of its fading light. The canopy overhead was heavy and dense, promising another night of darkness, but the surface of the lake was scarcely disturbed by a ripple. There was a little air, though it scarce deserved to be termed wind. Still, being damp and heavy, it had a certain force. The party in the castle were as gloomy and silent as the scene. The two ransomed prisoners felt humbled and dishonored, but their humility partook of the rancor of revenge. They were far more disposed to remember the indignity with which they had been treated during the last few hours of their captivity than to feel grateful for the previous indulgence. Then that keen-sighted monitor conscience, by reminding them of the retributive justice of all they had endured, goaded them rather to turn the tables on their enemies than to accuse themselves. As for the others, they were thoughtful equally from regret and joy. Deerslayer and Judith felt most of the former sensation, though from very different causes, while Hetty for the moment was perfectly happy. The Delaware had also lively pictures of felicity in the prospect of so soon regaining his betrothed. Under such circumstances, and in this mood, all were taking the evening meal.

"Old Tom!" cried Hurry, bursting into a fit of boisterous laughter, "you looked amazin'ly like a tethered bear as you was stretched on them hemlock boughs, and I only wonder you didn't growl more. Well, it's over, and syth's and lamentations won't mend the matter! There's the blackguard Rivenoak, he that brought us off, has an oncommon scalp, and I'd give as much for it myself as the Colony. Yes, I feel as rich as the governor in these matters now, and will lay down with them doubloon for doubloon. Judith, darling, did you mourn for me much when I was in the hands of the Philipsteins?"

The last were a family of German descent on the Mohawk to whom Hurry had a great antipathy and whom he had confounded with the enemies of Judea.

"Our tears have raised the lake, Harry March, as you might have seen by the shore!" returned Judith, with a feigned levity that she was far from feeling. "That Hetty and I should have grieved for Father was to be expected, but we fairly rained tears for you."

"We *were* sorry for poor Hurry, as well as for Father, Judith!" put in her innocent and unconscious sister.

"True, girl, true, but we feel sorrow for everybody that's in trouble, you know," returned the other in a quick, admonitory manner and a low tone. "Nevertheless, we are glad to see you, Master March, and out of the hands of the Philipsteins, too."

"Yes, they're a bad set, and so is the other brood of 'em, down on the river. It's a wonderment to me how you got us off, Deerslayer; and I forgive you the interference that prevented my doin' justice on that vagabond, for this small sarvice. Let us into the secret, that we may do you the same good turn, at need. Was it by lying, or by coaxing?"

"By neither, Hurry, but by buying. We paid a ransom for you both, and that, too, at a price so high you had well be on your guard ag'in another captyvement, lest our stock of goods shouldn't hold out."

"A ransom! Old Tom has paid the fiddler, then, for nothing of mine would have bought off the hair, much less the skin. I didn't think men as keen set as them vagabonds would let a fellow up so easy, when they had him fairly at a close hug and floored. But money is money, and somehow it's unnat'ral hard to withstand. Injin, or white man, 'tis pretty much the same. It must be owned, Judith, there's a considerable of human natur' in mankind ginirally, arter all!"

Hutter now rose, and signing to Deerslayer, he led him to an inner room, where, in answer to his questions, he first learned the price that had been paid for his release. The old man expressed neither resentment nor surprise at the inroad that had been made on his chest, though he did manifest some curiosity to know how far the investigation of its contents had been carried. He also inquired where the key had been found. The habitual frankness of Deerslayer prevented any prevarication, and the conference soon terminated by the return of the two to the outer room, or that which served for the double purpose of parlor and kitchen.

"I wonder if it's peace or war between us and the savages!" exclaimed Hurry, just as Deerslayer, who had paused for a single instant, listened attentively, and was passing through the outer door without stopping. "This givin' up captives has a friendly look, and when men have traded together, on a fair and honorable footing, they ought to part fri'nds, for that occasion, at least. Come back, Deerslayer, and let us have your judgment, for I'm beginnin' to think more of you, since your late behavior, than I used to do."

"There's an answer to your question, Hurry, since you're in such haste to come ag'in to blows."

As Deerslayer spoke, he threw on the table, on which the other was reclining with one elbow, a sort of miniature fagot, composed of a dozen sticks bound tightly together with a deerskin thong. March seized it eagerly, and holding it close to a blazing knot of pine that lay on the hearth, and which gave out all the light there was in the room, ascertained that the ends of the several sticks had been dipped in blood.

"If this isn't plain English," said the reckless frontiersman, "it's plain Injin! Here's what they call a dicliration of war, down at York, Judith. How did you come by this defiance, Deerslayer?"

"Fairly enough. It lay, not a minut' since, in what you call Floatin' Tom's dooryard."

"How came it there? It never fell from the clouds, Judith,

as little toads sometimes do, and then it don't rain. You
must prove where it come from, Deerslayer, or we shall
suspect some design to skear them that would have lost their
wits long ago, if fear could drive 'em away."

Deerslayer had approached a window, and cast a glance
out of it on the dark aspect of the lake. As if satisfied with
what he beheld, he drew near Hurry and took the bundle of
sticks into his own hand, examining it attentively.

"Yes, this is an Indian declaration of war, sure enough,"
he said, "and it's a proof how little you're suited to be on
the path it has traveled, Harry March, that it has got here,
and you never the wiser as to the means. The savages may
have left the scalp on your head, but they must have taken off
the *ears;* else you'd have heard the stirring of the water made
by the lad as he come off ag'in, on his two logs. His ar'n'd
was to throw these sticks at our door, as much as to say,
we've struck the warpost since the trade, and the next thing
will be to strike *you.*"

"The prowling wolves! But hand me that rifle, Judith, and
I'll send an answer back to the vagabonds through their messenger."

"Not while I stand by, Master March," coolly put in Deerslayer, motioning for the other to forbear. "Faith is faith,
whether given to a redskin or to a Christian. The lad lighted
a knot and came off fairly, under its blaze, to give us this
warning, and no man here should harm him while empl'yed
on such an ar'n'd. There's no use in words, for the boy is too
cunning to leave the knot burning, now his business is done,
and the night is already too dark for a rifle to have any
sartainty."

"That may be true enough, as to a gun, but there's virtue
still in a canoe," answered Hurry, passing toward the door
with enormous strides, carrying a rifle in his hands. "The
being doesn't live that shall stop me from following and
bringing back that riptyle's scalp. The more on 'em that you
crush in the egg, the fewer there'll be to dart at you in the
woods!"

Judith trembled like the aspen, she scarce knew why herself, though there was the prospect of a scene of violence;
for, if Hurry was fierce and overbearing in the consciousness of his vast strength, Deerslayer had about him the calm
determination that promises greater perseverance, and a reso-

lution more likely to effect its object. It was the stern, resolute eye of the latter, rather than the noisy vehemence of the first, that excited her apprehensions. Hurry soon reached the spot where the canoe was fastened, but not before Deerslayer had spoken in a quick, earnest voice to the Serpent, in Delaware. The latter had been the first, in truth, to hear the sounds of the oars, and he had gone upon the platform in jealous watchfulness. The light satisfied him that a message was coming, and when the boy cast his bundle of sticks at his feet, it neither moved his anger nor induced surprise. He merely stood at watch, rifle in hand, to make certain that no treachery lay behind the defiance. As Deerslayer now called to him, he stepped into the canoe and, quick as thought, removed the paddles. Hurry was furious when he found that he was deprived of the means of proceeding. He first approached the Indian with loud menaces, and even Deerslayer stood aghast at the probable consequences. March shook his sledge-hammer fists and flourished his arms, as he drew near the Indian, and all expected he would attempt to fell the Delaware to the earth; one of them, at least, was well aware that such an experiment would be followed by immediate bloodshed. But even Hurry was awed by the stern composure of the chief, and he, too, knew that such a man was not to be outraged with impunity; he therefore turned to vent his rage on Deerslayer, where he foresaw no consequences so terrible. What might have been the result of this second demonstration, if completed, is unknown, since it was never made.

"Hurry," said a gentle, soothing voice at his elbow, "it's wicked to be so angry, and God will not overlook it. The Iroquois treated you well, and they didn't take *your* scalp, though you and Father wanted to take *theirs*."

The influence of mildness on passion is well known. Hetty, too, had earned a sort of consideration that had never before been enjoyed by her, through the self-devotion and decision of her recent conduct. Perhaps her established mental imbecility, by removing all distrust of a wish to control, aided her influence. Let the cause be as questionable as it might, the effect was sufficiently certain. Instead of throttling his old fellow traveler, Hurry turned to the girl and poured out a portion of his discontent, if none of his anger, in her attentive ears.

" 'Tis too bad, Hetty!" he exclaimed; "as bad as a county jail, or a lack of beaver, to get a creatur' into your very trap and then to see it get off. As much as six first-quality skins in valie has paddled off on them clumsy logs, when twenty strokes of a well-turned paddle would overtake 'em. I say in valie, for as to the boy in the way of natur', he is only a boy and is worth neither more nor less than one. Deerslayer, you've been ontrue to your fri'nds in letting such a chance slip through my fingers as well as your own."

The answer was given quietly, but with a voice as steady as a fearless nature and the consciousness of rectitude could make it. "I should have been ontrue to the right, had I done otherwise," returned the Deerslayer steadily; "and neither you nor any other man has authority to demand that much of me. The lad came on a lawful business, and the meanest redskin that roams the woods would be ashamed of not respecting his ar'n'd. But he's now far beyond your reach, Master March, and there's little use in talking, like a couple of women, of what can no longer be helped."

So saying, Deerslayer turned away, like one resolved to waste no more words on the subject, while Hutter pulled Harry by the sleeve and led him into the ark. There they sat long in private conference. In the meantime, the Indian and his friend had their secret consultation, for though it wanted some three or four hours to the rising of the star, the former could not abstain from canvassing his scheme and from opening his heart to the other. Judith, too, yielded to her softer feelings and listened to the whole of Hetty's artless narrative of what occurred after she had landed. The woods had few terrors for either of these girls, educated as they had been, and accustomed as they were to look out daily at their rich expanse, or to wander beneath their dark shades, but the elder sister felt that she would have hesitated about thus venturing alone into an Iroquois camp. Concerning Hist, Hetty was not very communicative. She spoke of her kindness and gentleness and of the meeting in the forest, but the secret of Chingachgook was guarded with a shrewdness and fidelity that many a sharper-witted girl might have failed to display.

At length the several conferences were broken up by the reappearance of Hutter on the platform. Here he assembled the whole party and communicated as much of his intentions

as he deemed expedient. Of the arrangement made by Deerslayer, to abandon the castle during the night and to take
refuge in the ark, he entirely approved. It struck him, as it
had the others, as the only effectual means of escaping destruction. Now that the savages had turned their attention
to the construction of rafts, no doubt could exist of their
at least making an attempt to carry the building, and the
message of the bloody sticks sufficiently showed their confidence in their own success. In short, the old man viewed
the night as critical, and he called on all to get ready as
soon as possible, in order to abandon the dwelling, temporarily at least, if not forever.

These communications made, everything proceeded promptly and with intelligence: the castle was secured in the
manner already described, the canoes were withdrawn from
the dock and fastened to the ark by the side of the other;
the few necessaries that had been left in the house were
transferred to the cabin, the fire was extinguished, and all
embarked.

The vicinity of the hills, with their drapery of pines,
had the effect to render nights that were obscure darker
than common on the lake. As usual, however, a belt of
comparative light was stretched through the center of the
sheet, while it was within the shadows of the mountains
that the gloom rested most heavily on the water. The island or castle stood in this belt of comparative light, but
still the night was so dark as to cover the departure of
the ark. At the distance of an observer on the shore, her
movements could not be seen at all, more particularly as a
background of dark hillside filled up the perspective of
every view that was taken diagonally or directly across the
water. The prevalent wind on the lakes of that region is
west, but owing to the avenues formed by the mountains,
it is frequently impossible to tell the true direction of the
currents, as they often vary within short distances and brief
differences of time. This is truer in light, fluctuating puffs of
air than in steady breezes, though the squalls of even the
latter are familiarly known to be uncertain and baffling
in all mountainous regions and narrow waters. On the present occasion, Hutter himself (as he shoved the ark from
her berth at the side of the platform) was at a loss to
pronounce which way the wind blew. In common, this

difficulty was solved by the clouds, which, floating high above the hilltops, as a matter of course obeyed the currents, but now the whole vault of heaven seemed a mass of gloomy wall. Not an opening of any sort was visible, and Chingachgook was already trembling lest the nonappearance of the star might prevent his betrothed from being punctual to her appointment. Under these circumstances, Hutter hoisted his sail, seemingly with the sole intention of getting away from the castle, as it might be dangerous to remain much longer in its vicinity. The air soon filled the cloth, and when the scow was got under command, and the sail was properly trimmed, it was found that the direction was southerly, inclining toward the eastern shore. No better course offering for the purposes of the party, the singular craft was suffered to skim the surface of the water in this direction for more than an hour, when a change in the currents of the air drove them over toward the camp.

Deerslayer watched all the movements of Hutter and Harry with jealous attention. At first he did not know whether to ascribe the course they held to accident or to design, but he now began to suspect the latter. Familiar as Hutter was with the lake, it was easy to deceive one who had little practice on the water, and let his intentions be what they might, it was evident, ere two hours had elapsed, that the ark had got over sufficient space to be within a hundred rods of the shore, directly abreast of the known position of the camp. For a considerable time previously to reaching this point, Hurry, who had some knowledge of the Algonquin language, had been in close conference with the Indian, and the result was now announced by the latter to Deerslayer, who had been a cold, not to say distrusted looker-on of all that passed.

"My old father and my young brother, the Big Pine"—for so the Delaware had named March—"want to see Huron scalps at their belts," said Chingachgook to his friend. "There is room for some on the girdle of the Serpent, and his people will look for them when he goes back to his village. Their eyes must not be left long in a fog, but they must see what they look for. I know that my brother has a white hand; he will not strike even the dead. He will wait for us; when we come back, he will not hide his face from shame for his friend. The great Serpent of the Mohicans must be worthy to go on the warpath with Hawkeye."

"Aye, aye, Sarpent, I see how it is; that name's to stick, and in time, I shall get to be known by it instead of Deerslayer; well, if such honors will come, the humblest of us all must be willing to abide by 'em. As for your looking for scalps, it belongs to your gifts, and I see no harm in it. Be marciful, Sarpent, howsever; be marciful, I beseech of you. It surely can do no harm to a redskin's honor to show a little marcy. As for the old man, the father of two young women, who might ripen better feelin's in his heart, and Harry March here, who, pine as he is, might better bear the fruit of a more Christianized tree—as for *them* two, I leave them in the hands of the white man's God. Wasn't it for the bloody sticks, no man should go ag'in the Mingos this night, seein' that it would dishonor our faith and characters, but them that crave blood can't complain if blood is shed at their call. Still, Sarpent, you can be *marciful*. Don't begin your career with the wails of women and the cries of children. Bear yourself so that Hist will smile, not weep, when she meets you. Go, then, and the Manitou presarve you!"

"My brother will stay here with the scow. Wah will soon be standing on the shore waiting, and Chingachgook must hasten."

The Indian then joined his two co-adventurers, and first lowering the sail, they all three entered a canoe and left the side of the ark. Neither Hutter nor March spoke to Deerslayer concerning their object, or the probable length of their absence. All this had been confided to the Indian, who had acquitted himself of the trust with characteristic brevity. As soon as the canoe was out of sight, and that occurred ere the paddles had given a dozen strokes, Deerslayer made the best dispositions he could to keep the ark as nearly stationary as possible; then he sat down in the end of the scow, to chew the cud of his own bitter reflections. It was not long, however, before he was joined by Judith, who sought every occasion to be near him, managing her attack on his affections with the address that was suggested by native coquetry, aided by no little practice, but which received much of its most dangerous power from the touch of feeling that threw around her manner, voice, accents, thoughts, and acts, the indescribable witchery of natural tenderness. Leaving the young hunter exposed to these dangerous assailants, it has become our more immediate business to follow the party in the canoe to the shore.

The controlling influence that led Hutter and Hurry to repeat their experiment against the camp was precisely that which had induced the first attempt, a little heightened, perhaps, by the desire of revenge. But neither of these two rude beings, so ruthless in all things that touched the rights and interests of the red man, though possessing veins of human feeling on other matters, was much actuated by any other desire than a heartless longing for profit. Hurry had felt angered at his sufferings when first liberated, it is true, but that emotion soon disappeared in the habitual love of gold, which he sought with the reckless avidity of a needy spendthrift, rather than with the ceaseless longings of a miser. In short, the motive that urged them both so soon to go against the Hurons was a habitual contempt of their enemy, acting on the unceasing cupidity of prodigality. The additional chances of success, however, had their place in the formation of the second enterprise. It was known that a large portion of the warriors—perhaps all—were encamped for the night abreast of the castle, and it was hoped that the scalps of helpless victims would be the consequence. To confess the truth, Hutter in particular—he who had just left two daughters behind him—expected to find few besides women and children in the camp. This fact had been but slightly alluded to in his communications with Hurry, and with Chingachgook it had been kept entirely out of view. If the Indian thought of it at all, it was known only to himself.

Hutter steered the canoe; Hurry had manfully taken his post in the bows; Chingachgook stood in the center. We say stood, for all three were so skilled in the management of that species of frail bark as to be able to keep erect positions in the midst of the darkness. The approach to the shore was made with great caution, and the landing effected in safety. The three now prepared their arms and began their tigerlike approach upon the camp. The Indian was on the lead, his two companions treading in his footsteps, with a stealthy cautiousness of manner that rendered their progress almost literally noiseless. Occasionally a dried twig snapped under the heavy weight of the gigantic Hurry, or the blundering clumsiness of the old man, but had the Indian walked on air, his step could not have seemed lighter. The great object was first to discover the position of the fire, which was known to be the center of the whole encampment. At length the keen eye of Chingachgook caught a glimpse of this important guide. It was glimmering at a distance among the trunks of trees. There was no blaze, but merely a single smoldering brand, as suited the hour, the savages usually retiring and rising with the revolutions of the sun.

As soon as a view was obtained of this beacon, the progress of the adventurers became swifter and more certain. In a few minutes they got to the edge of the circle of little huts. Here they stopped to survey their ground and to concert their movements. The darkness was so deep as to render it difficult to distinguish anything but the glowing brand, the trunks of the nearest trees, and the endless canopy of leaves that veiled the clouded heaven. It was ascertained, however, that a hut was quite near, and Chingachgook attempted to reconnoiter its interior. The manner in which the Indian approached the place that was supposed to contain enemies resembled the wily advances of the cat on the bird. As he drew near, he stooped to his hands and knees, for the entrance was so low as to require this attitude even as a convenience. Before trusting his head inside, however, he listened long to catch the breathing of sleepers. No sound was audible, and this human Serpent thrust his head in at the door, or opening, as another serpent would have peered in on the nest. Nothing rewarded the hazardous experiment, for after feeling cautiously with a hand, the place was found to be empty.

The Delaware proceeded in the same guarded manner to one or two more of the huts, finding all in the same situation. He then returned to his companions and informed them that the Hurons had deserted their camp. A little further inquiry corroborated this fact, and it only remained to return to the canoe. The different manner in which the adventurers bore the disappointment is worthy of a passing remark. The chief, who had landed solely with the hope of acquiring renown, stood stationary, leaning against a tree, waiting the pleasure of his companions. He was mortified, and a little surprised, it is true, but he bore all with dignity, falling back for support on the sweeter expectations that still lay in reserve for that evening. It was true, he could not now hope to meet his mistress with the proofs of his daring and skill on his person, but he might still hope to meet her, and the warrior who was zealous in the search might always hope to be honored. On the other hand, Hutter and Hurry, who had been chiefly instigated by the basest of all human motives, the thirst of gain, could scarce control their feelings. They went prowling among the huts, as if they expected to find some forgotten child or careless sleeper; and again and again did they vent their spite on the insensible huts, several of which were actually torn to pieces and scattered about the place. Nay, they even quarreled with each other, and fierce reproaches passed between them. It is possible some serious consequences might have occurred had not the Delaware interfered to remind them of the danger of being so unguarded and of the necessity of returning to the ark. This checked the dispute, and in a few minutes they were paddling sullenly back to the spot where they hoped to find that vessel.

It has been said that Judith took her place at the side of Deerslayer soon after the adventurers departed. For a short time the girl was silent, and the hunter was ignorant which of the sisters had approached him, but he soon recognized the rich, full-spirited voice of the elder, as her feelings escaped in words.

"This is a terrible life for women, Deerslayer!" she exclaimed. "Would to Heaven I could see an end of it!"

"The life is well enough, Judith," was the answer, "being pretty much as it is used or abused. What would you wish to see in its place?"

"I should be a thousand times happier to live nearer to civilized beings—where there are farms and churches, and houses built as it might be by Christian hands, and where my sleep at night would be sweet and tranquil! A dwelling near one of the forts would be far better than this dreary place where we live!"

"Nay, Judith, I can't agree too lightly in the truth of all this. If forts are good to keep off inimies, they sometimes hold inimies of their own. I don't think 'twould be for your good, or the good of Hetty, to live near one, and if

I *must* say what I think, I'm afeard you are a little too near as it is." Deerslayer went on in his own steady, earnest manner, for the darkness concealed the tints that colored the cheeks of the girl almost to the brightness of crimson, while her own great efforts suppressed the sounds of the breathing that nearly choked her. "As for farms, they have their uses, and there's them that like to pass their lives on 'em; but what comfort can a man look for in a clearin' that he can't find in double quantities in the forest? If air, and room, and light are a little craved, the windrows and the streams will furnish 'em, or here are the lakes for such as have bigger longings in that way; but where are you to find your shades, and laughing springs, and leaping brooks, and vinerable trees a thousand years old in a clearin'? You don't find *them*, but you find their disabled trunks, marking the 'arth like headstones in a graveyard. It seems to me that the people who live in such places must be always thinkin' of their own inds and of univarsal decay—and that, too, not of the decay that is brought about by time and natur', but the decay that follows waste and violence. Then, as to churches, they are good, I suppose, else wouldn't good men uphold 'em. But they are not altogether necessary. They call 'em the temples of the Lord, but, Judith, the whole 'arth is a temple of the Lord to such as have the right mind. Neither forts nor churches make people happier of themselves. Moreover, all is contradiction in the settlements, while all is concord in the woods. Forts and churches almost always go together, and yet they're downright contradictions, churches being for peace and forts for war. No, no—give me the strong places of the wilderness, which is the trees, and the churches, too, which are arbors raised by the hand of natur'."

"Woman is not made for scenes like these, Deerslayer; scenes of which we shall have no end as long as this war lasts."

"If you mean women of white color, I rather think you're not far from the truth, gal; but as for the females of the red men, such visitations are quite in character. Nothing would make Hist, now, the bargained wife of yonder Delaware, happier than to know that he is at this moment prowling around his nat'ral inimies, striving after a scalp."

"Surely, surely, Deerslayer, she cannot be a woman and

not feel concern when she thinks the man she loves is in danger!"

"She doesn't think of the danger, Judith, but of the honor; and when the heart is desperately set on such feelin's, why, there is little room to crowd in fear. Hist is a kind, gentle, laughing, pleasant creatur', but she loves honor as well as any Delaware gal I ever know'd. She's to meet the Sarpent an hour hence, on the p'int where Hetty landed, and no doubt she has her anxiety about it, like any other woman; but she'd be all the happier did she know that her lover was at this moment waylaying a Mingo for his scalp."

"If you really believe this, Deerslayer, no wonder you lay so much stress on gifts. Certain am I that no white girl could feel anything but misery while she believed her betrothed in danger of his life! Nor do I suppose even you, unmoved and calm as you ever seem to be, could be at peace if you believed *your* Hist in danger."

"That's a different matter—'tis altogether a different matter, Judith. Woman is too weak and gentle to be intended to run such risks, and man *must* feel for her. Yes, I rather think that's as much red natur' as it's white. But I have no Hist, nor am I like to have, for I hold it wrong to mix colors anyway except in friendship and sarvices."

"In that you are and feel as a white man should! As for Hurry Harry, I do think it would be all the same to him whether his wife were a squaw or a governor's daughter, provided she was a little comely and could help to keep his craving stomach full."

"You do March injustice, Judith; yes, you do. The poor fellow dotes on *you*, and when a man has ra'ally set his heart on such a creatur', it isn't a Mingo, or even a Delaware gal, that'll be likely to unsettle his mind. You may laugh at such men as Hurry and I, for we're rough and unteached in the way of books and other knowledge, but we've our good p'ints as well as our bad ones. An honest heart is not to be despised, gal, even though it be not varsed in all the niceties that please a female fancy."

"*You*, Deerslayer! And *do* you—*can* you, for an instant, suppose I place *you* by the side of Harry March? No, no. I am not so far gone in dullness as that. No one—man or woman—could think of naming your honest heart, manly nature, and simple truth with the boisterous selfishness, greedy avarice, and overbearing ferocity of Henry March. The very best that can be said of him is to be found in his name of Hurry-scurry, which, if it means no great harm, means no great good. Even my father, following his feelings with the other, as he is doing at this moment, well knows the difference between you. This I *know*, for he has said as much to me in plain language."

Judith was a girl of quick sensibilities and of impetuous feelings, and being under few of the restraints that curtail the manifestations of maiden emotions among those who are educated in the habits of civilized life, she sometimes betrayed the latter with a freedom that was so purely natural as to place it as far above the wiles of coquetry as it was superior to its heartlessness. She had now even taken one of the hard hands of the hunter and pressed it between both her own with a warmth and earnestness that proved how sincere was her language. It was perhaps fortunate that she was checked by the very excess of her feelings, since the same power might have urged her on to avow *all* that her father had said—the old man not having been satisfied with making a comparison favorable to Deerslayer, as between the hunter and Hurry, but having actually, in his blunt, rough way, briefly advised his daughter to cast off the latter entirely and to think of the former as a husband. Judith would not willingly have said this to any other man, but there was so much confidence awakened by the guileless simplicity of Deerslayer that one of her nature found it a constant temptation to overstep the bounds of habit. She went no further, however, immediately relinquishing the hand and falling back on a reserve that was more suited to her sex and, indeed, to her natural modesty.

"Thankee, Judith, thankee with all my heart," returned the hunter, whose humility prevented him from placing any flattering interpretation on either the conduct or the language of the girl. "Thankee as much as if it was all true. Harry's sightly—yes, he's as sightly as the tallest pine of these mountains, and the Sarpent has named him accordingly; howsever, some fancy good looks, and some fancy good conduct, only. Hurry has one advantage, and it depends on himself whether he'll have t'other or—Heark! That's your father's voice, gal, and he speaks like a man who's riled at something."

"God save us from any more of these horrible scenes!"

exclaimed Judith, bending her face to her knees and endeavoring to exclude the discordant sounds by applying her hands to her ears. "I sometimes wish I had no father!"

This was bitterly said, and the repinings which extorted the words were bitterly felt. It is impossible to say what might next have escaped her had not a gentle, low voice spoken at her elbow.

"Judith, I ought to have read a chapter to Father and Hurry!" said the innocent but terrified speaker, "and *that* would have kept them from going again on such an errand. Do you call to them, Deerslayer, and tell them I want them, and that it will be good for them both if they'll return and hearken to my words."

"Ah's me! Poor Hetty, you little know the cravin's for gold and revenge if you believe they are so easily turned aside from their longin's! But this is an oncommon business in more ways than one, Judith! I hear your father and Hurry growling like bears, and yet no noise comes from the mouth of the young chief. There's an ind of secresy, and yet his whoop, which ought to ring in the mountains, accordin' to rule in such sarcumstances, is silent!"

"Justice may have alighted on him, and his death have saved the lives of the innocent."

"Not it—not it—the Sarpent is not the one to suffer if *that's* to be the law. Sartainly there has been no onset, and 'tis most likely that the camp's deserted and the men are coming back disapp'inted. That accounts for the growls of Hurry and the silence of the Sarpent."

Just at this instant a fall of a paddle was heard in the canoe, for vexation made March reckless. Deerslayer felt convinced that his conjecture was true. The sail being down, the ark had not drifted far, and ere many minutes he heard Chingachgook, in a low, quiet tone, directing Hutter how to steer in order to reach it. In less time than it takes to tell the fact, the canoe touched the scow, and the adventurers entered the latter. Neither Hutter nor Hurry spoke of what had occurred. But the Delaware, in passing his friend, merely uttered the words "fire's out," which, if not literally true, sufficiently explained the truth to his listener.

It was now a question as to the course to be steered. A short, surly conference was held, when Hutter decided that the wisest way would be to keep in motion as the means most likely to defeat any attempt at a surprise—announcing his own and March's intention to requite themselves for the loss of sleep during their captivity by lying down. As the air still baffled and continued light, it was finally determined to sail before it, let it come in what direction it might, so long as it did not blow the ark upon the strand. This point settled, the released prisoners helped to hoist the sail, and then they threw themselves on two of the pallets, leaving Deerslayer and his friend to look after the movements of the craft. As neither of the latter was disposed to sleep, on account of the appointment with Hist, this arrangement was acceptable to all parties. That Judith and Hetty remained up also in no manner impaired the agreeable features of this change.

For some time the scow rather drifted than sailed along the western shore, following a light, southerly current of the air. The progress was slow—not exceeding a couple of miles in the hour—but the two men perceived that it was not only carrying them toward the point they desired to reach, but at a rate that was quite as fast as the hour yet rendered necessary. But little was said the while even by the girls, and that little had more reference to the rescue of Hist than to any other subject. The Indian was calm to the eye, but as minute after minute passed his feelings became more and more excited, until they reached a state that might have satisfied the demands of even the most exacting mistress. Deerslayer kept the craft as much in the bays as was prudent, for the double purpose of sailing within the shadows of the woods and of detecting any signs of an encampment they might pass on the shore. In this manner they doubled one low point, and were already in the bay that was terminated north by the goal at which they aimed. The latter was still a quarter of a mile distant when Chingachgook came silently to the side of his friend and pointed to a place directly ahead. A small fire was glimmering just within the verge of the bushes that lined the shore on the southern side of the point—leaving no doubt that the Indians had suddenly removed their camp to the very place, or at least the very projection of land, where Hist had given them the rendezvous!

CHAPTER XVI

I hear thee babbling to the vale
Of sunshine and of flowers,
But unto me thou bring'st a tale
Of visionary hours.

WORDSWORTH

THE DISCOVERY MENTIONED at the close of the preceding chapter was of great moment in the eyes of Deerslayer and his friend. In the first place, there was the danger, almost the certainty, that Hutter and Hurry would make a fresh attempt on this camp should they awake and ascertain its position. Then there was the increased risk of landing to bring off Hist; and there were the general uncertainty and additional hazards that must follow from the circumstance that their enemies had begun to change their positions. As the Delaware was aware that the hour was near when he ought to repair to the rendezvous, he no longer thought of trophies torn from his foes; one of the first things arranged between him and his associate was to permit the two others to sleep on, lest they should disturb the execution of their plans by substituting some of their own. The ark moved slowly, and it would have taken fully a quarter of an hour to reach the point, at the rate at which they were going, thus affording time for a little forethought. The Indians, in the wish to conceal their fire from those who were thought to be still in the castle, had placed it so near the southern side of the point as to render it extremely difficult to shut it in by the bushes, though Deerslayer varied the direction of the scow, both to the right and to the left, in the hope of being able to effect that object.

"There's one advantage, Judith, in finding that fire so near the water," he said, while executing these little maneuvers; "it shows the Mingos believe we are in the hut, and our coming on 'em from this quarter will be an onlooked-for event.

But 'tis lucky Harry March and your father are asleep, else we should have 'em prowling after scalps ag'in. Ha! There —the bushes are beginning to shut in the fire—and now it can't be seen at all!"

Deerslayer waited a little to make certain that he had at last gained the desired position; then he gave the signal agreed on, and Chingachgook let go the grapnel and lowered the sail.

The situation in which the ark now lay had its advantages and its disadvantages. The fire had been hid by sheering toward the shore, and the latter was nearer perhaps than was desirable. Still, the water was known to be very deep farther off in the lake, and anchoring in deep water, under the circumstances in which the party was placed, was to be avoided, if possible. It was also believed no raft could be within miles; and, though the trees in the darkness appeared almost to overhang the scow, it would not be easy to get off to her without using a boat. The intense darkness that prevailed so close in with the forest, too, served as an effectual screen, and so long as care was had not to make a noise, there was little or no danger of being detected. All these things Deerslayer pointed out to Judith, instructing her as to the course she was to follow in the event of an alarm, for it was thought to the last degree inexpedient to arouse the sleepers, unless it might be in the greatest emergency.

"And now, Judith, as we understand one another, it is time the Sarpent and I had taken to the canoe," the hunter concluded. "The star has not risen yet, it's true, but it soon must, though none of us are likely to be any the wiser for it, tonight, on account of the clouds. Howsever, Hist has a ready mind, and she's one of them that doesn't always need to have a thing afore her to see it. I'll warrant you she'll not be either two minutes or two feet out of the way, unless them jealous vagabonds, the Mingos, have taken the alarm and put her as a stool pigeon to catch us; or have hid her away in order to prepare her mind for a Huron instead of a Mohican husband."

"Deerslayer," interrupted the girl earnestly, "this is a most dangerous service; why do *you* go on it at all?"

"Anan! Why you know, gal, we go to bring off Hist, the Sarpent's betrothed—the maid he means to marry, as soon as we get back to the tribe."

"That is all right for the Indian—but *you* do not mean

to marry Hist—*you* are not betrothed, and why should *two* risk their lives and liberties to do that which one can just as well perform?"

"Ah!—now I understand you, Judith—yes, now I begin to take the idee. You think as Hist is the Sarpent's betrothed, as they call it, and not mine, it's altogether his affair; and as one man can paddle a canoe, he ought to be left to go after his gal alone! But you forget this is our ar'n'd here, on the lake, and it would not tell well to forget an ar'n'd just at the pinch. Then, if love does count for so much with some people, particularly with young women, fri'ndship counts for something, too, with other some. I dares to say the Delaware can paddle a canoe by himself and can bring off Hist by himself, and perhaps he would like that quite as well as to have me with him, but he couldn't sarcumvent sarcumventions, or stir up an ambushment, or fight with the savages, and get his sweetheart at the same time, as well by himself as if he had a fri'nd with him, to depend on, even if that fri'nd is no better than myself. No—no—Judith, you wouldn't desart one that counted on *you*, at such a moment, and you can't in reason expect me to do it."

"I fear—I believe you are right, Deerslayer, yet I wish you were not to go! Promise me one thing, at least, and that is not to trust yourself among the savages, or to do anything more than to save the girl. That will be enough for once, and with that you ought to be satisfied."

"Lord bless you, gal, one would think it was Hetty that's talking, not the quick-witted and wonderful Judith Hutter! But fright makes the wise silly and the strong weak. Yes, I've seen proofs of that time and ag'in! Well, it's kind and softhearted in you, Judith, to feel this consarn for a fellow creatur', and I shall always say that you are kind and of true feelin's, let them that invy your good looks tell as many idle stories of you as they may."

"Deerslayer!" hastily said the girl, interrupting him, though nearly choked by her emotions, "do you believe all you hear about a poor motherless girl? Is the foul tongue of Hurry Harry to blast my life?"

"Not it, Judith—not it. I've told Hurry it wasn't manful to backbite them he couldn't win by fair means, and that even an Indian is always tender, touching a young woman's good name."

"If I had a brother, he wouldn't dare to do it!" exclaimed Judith, her eyes flashing fire. "But finding me without any protector but an old man, whose ears are getting to be as dull as his feelings, he has his way as he pleases."

"Not exactly that, Judith; no, not exactly that, neither! *No* man, brother or stranger, would stand by and see as fair a gal as yourself hunted down without saying a word in her behalf. Hurry's in 'arnest in wanting to make you his wife, and the little he does let out ag'in you comes more from jealousy, like, than from anything else. Smile on him when he awakes, and squeeze his hand only half as hard as you squeezed mine a bit ago, and my life on it, the poor fellow will forget everything but your comeliness. Hot words don't always come from the heart, but oftener from the stomach than anywhere else. Try him, Judith, when he wakes, and see the vartue of a smile."

Deerslayer laughed, in his own manner, as he concluded, and then he intimated to the patient-looking, but really impatient Chingachgook his readiness to proceed. As the young man entered the canoe, the girl stood immovable as stone, lost in the musings that the language and manner of the other were likely to produce. The simplicity of the hunter had completely put her at fault, for in her narrow sphere Judith was an expert manager of the other sex, though in the present instance she was far more actuated by impulses, in all she had said and done, than by calculation. We shall not deny that some of Judith's reflections were bitter, though the sequel of the tale must be referred to, in order to explain how merited, or how keen were her sufferings.

Chingachgook and his paleface friend set forth on their hazardous and delicate enterprise with a coolness and method that would have done credit to men who were on their twentieth instead of being on their first warpath. As suited his relation to the pretty fugitive in whose service they were engaged, the Indian took his place in the head of the canoe, while Deerslayer guided its movements in the stern. By this arrangement, the former would be the first to land and, of course, the first to meet his mistress. The latter had taken his post without comment, but in secret influenced by the reflection that one who had so much at stake as the Indian might not possibly guide the canoe with the same steadiness and intelligence as another who had more com-

mand of his feelings. From the instant they left the side of
the ark, the movements of the two adventurers were like the
maneuvers of highly drilled soldiers who for the first time
were called on to meet the enemy in the field. As yet,
Chingachgook had never fired a shot in anger, and the debut
of his companion in warfare is known to the reader. It is
true, the Indian had been hanging about his enemy's camp
for a few hours, on his first arrival, and he had even once
entered it, as related in the last chapter, but no consequences had followed either experiment. Now, it was certain that an important result was to be effected, or a mortifying failure was to ensue. The rescue, or the continued
captivity of Hist, depended on the enterprise. In a word, it
was virtually the maiden expedition of these two ambitious
young forest soldiers, and while one of them set forth, impelled by sentiments that usually carry men so far, both had all
their feelings of pride and manhood enlisted in their success.

Instead of steering in a direct line to the point, then distant from the ark less than a quarter of a mile, Deerslayer
laid the head of his canoe diagonally toward the center of
the lake, with a view to obtain a position from which he
might approach the shore, having his enemies in his front
only. The spot where Hetty had landed and where Hist had
promised to meet them, moreover, was on the upper side of
the projection rather than on the lower, and to reach it
would have required the adventurers to double nearly the
whole point, close in with the shore, had not this preliminary
step been taken. So well was the necessity for this measure
understood that Chingachgook quietly paddled on, although
it was adopted without consulting him and apparently was
taking him in a direction nearly opposite to that one might
think he most wished to go. A few minutes sufficed, however,
to carry the canoe the necessary distance when both the
young men ceased paddling, as it were by instinctive consent, and the boat became stationary.

The darkness increased rather than diminished, but it was
still possible, from the place where the adventurers lay, to
distinguish the outlines of the mountains. In vain did the
Delaware turn his head eastward to catch a glimpse of the
promised star, for notwithstanding that the clouds broke a
little near the horizon in that quarter of the heavens, the
curtain continued so far drawn as effectually to conceal all

behind it. In front, as was known by the formation of land above and behind it, lay the point, at a distance of about a thousand feet. No signs of the castle could be seen, nor could any movement in that quarter of the lake reach the ear. The latter circumstance might have been equally owing to the distance, which was several miles, or to the fact that nothing was in motion. As for the ark, though scarcely further from the canoe than the point, it lay so completely buried in the shadows of the shore that it would not have been visible even had there been many degrees more of light than actually existed.

The adventurers now held a conference in low voices, consulting together as to the probable time. Deerslayer thought it wanted yet some minutes to the rising of the star, while the impatience of the chief caused him to fancy the night further advanced and to believe that his betrothed was already waiting his appearance on the shore. As might have been expected, the opinion of the latter prevailed, and his friend disposed himself to steer for the place of rendezvous. The utmost skill and precaution now became necessary in the management of the canoe. The paddles were lifted and returned to the water in a noiseless manner, and when within a hundred yards of the beach, Chingachgook took in his altogether, laying his hand on his rifle in its stead. As they got still more within the belt of darkness that girded the woods, it was seen that they were steering too far north, and the course was altered accordingly. The canoe now seemed to move by instinct, so cautious and deliberate were all its motions. Still it continued to advance, until its bows grated on the gravel of the beach, at the precise spot where Hetty had landed, and whence her voice had issued, the previous night, as the ark was passing. There was, as usual, a narrow strand, but bushes fringed the woods and, in most places, overhung the water.

Chingachgook stepped upon the beach and cautiously examined it, for some distance, on each side of the canoe. In order to do this, he was often obliged to wade to his knees in the lake. No Hist rewarded his search. When he returned, he found his friend also on the shore. They next conferred in whispers, the Indian apprehending that they must have mistaken the place of rendezvous. Deerslayer thought it was probable they had mistaken the hour. While he was yet

speaking, he grasped the arm of the Delaware, caused him
to turn his head in the direction of the lake, and pointed
toward the summits of the eastern mountains. The clouds
had broken a little, apparently behind rather than above the
hills, and the selected star was glittering among the branches
of a pine. This was every way a flattering omen, and the
young men leaned on their rifles, listening intently for the
sound of approaching footsteps. Voices they often heard,
and mingled with them were the suppressed cries of children
and the low but sweet laugh of Indian women. As the native
Americans are habitually cautious and seldom break out
in loud conversation, the adventurers knew by these
facts that they must be very near the encampment. It was
easy to perceive that there was a fire within the woods by
the manner in which some of the upper branches of the trees
were illuminated, but it was not possible, where they stood,
to ascertain exactly how near it was to themselves. Once or
twice it seemed as if stragglers from around the fire were
approaching the place of rendezvous, but these sounds were
either altogether illusion, or those who had drawn near returned again without coming to the shore. A quarter of an
hour was passed in this state of intense expectation and
anxiety, when Deerslayer proposed that they should circle
the point in the canoe and, by getting a position close in
where the camp could be seen, reconnoiter the Indians and
thus enable themselves to form some plausible conjectures
for the nonappearance of Hist. The Delaware, however, reso-
lutely refused to quit the spot, plausibly enough offering as
a reason the disappointment of the girl, should she arrive in
his absence. Deerslayer felt for his friend's concern and
offered to make the circuit of the point by himself, leaving
the latter concealed in the bushes to await the occurrence of
any fortunate event that might favor his views. With this
understanding, then, the parties separated.

As soon as Deerslayer was at his post again, in the stern
of the canoe, he left the shore with the same precautions
and in the same noiseless manner as he had approached it.
On this occasion he did not go far from the land, the bushes
affording a sufficient cover, by keeping as close in as possible. Indeed, it would not have been easy to devise any
means more favorable to reconnoitering around an Indian
camp than those afforded by the actual state of things.

The formation of the point permitted the place to be circled on three of its sides, and the progress of the boat was so noiseless as to remove any apprehensions from an alarm through sound. The most practiced and guarded foot might stir a bunch of leaves or snap a dried stick in the dark, but a bark canoe could be made to float over the surface of smooth water almost with the instinctive readiness, and certainly with the noiseless movements, of an aquatic bird.

Deerslayer had got nearly in a line between the camp and the ark before he caught a glimpse of the fire. This came upon him suddenly and a little unexpectedly, at first causing an alarm, lest he had incautiously ventured within the circle of light it cast. But, perceiving at a second glance that he was certainly safe from detection so long as the Indians kept near the center of the illumination, he brought the canoe to a state of rest, in the most favorable position he could find, and commenced his observations.

We have written much, but in vain, concerning this extraordinary being, if the reader requires now to be told that, untutored as he was in the learning of the world, and simple as he ever showed himself to be in all matters touching the subtleties of conventional taste, he was a man of strong, native, poetical feeling. He loved the woods for their freshness, their sublime solitudes, their vastness, and the impress that they everywhere bore of the divine hand of their Creator. He rarely moved through them without pausing to dwell on some peculiar beauty that gave him pleasure, though seldom attempting to investigate the causes, and never did a day pass without his communing in spirit, and this, too, without the aid of forms or language, with the infinite source of all he saw, felt, and beheld. Thus constituted in a moral sense, and of a steadiness that no danger could appall or any crisis disturb, it is not surprising that the hunter felt a pleasure at looking on the scene he now beheld that momentarily caused him to forget the object of his visit. This will more fully appear when we describe it.

The canoe lay in front of a natural vista, not only through the bushes that lined the shore but of the trees also, that afforded a clear view of the camp. It was by means of this same opening that the light had been first seen from the ark. In consequence of their recent change of ground, the Indians had not yet retired to their huts, but had been delayed by their preparations, which included lodging as well as food. A large fire had been made, as much to answer the purpose of torches as for the use of their simple cookery, and at this precise moment it was blazing high and bright, having recently received a large supply of dried brush. The effect was to illuminate the arches of the forest and to render the whole area occupied by the camp as light as if hundreds of tapers were burning. Most of the toil had ceased, and even the hungriest child had satisfied its appetite. In a word, the time was that moment of relaxation and general indolence which is apt to succeed a hearty meal, and when the labors of the day have ended. The hunters and the fishermen had been equally successful, and food, that one great requisite of savage life, being abundant, every other care appeared to have subsided in the sense of enjoyment dependent on this all-important fact.

Deerslayer saw at a glance that many of the warriors were absent. His acquaintance, Rivenoak, however, was present, being seated in the foreground of a picture that Salvator Rosa would have delighted to draw, his swarthy features illuminated as much by pleasure as by the torchlike flame, while he showed another of the tribe one of the elephants that had caused so much sensation among his people. A boy was looking over his shoulder in dull curiosity, completing the group. More in the background, eight or ten warriors lay half recumbent on the ground, or sat with their backs inclining against trees, so many types of indolent repose. Their arms were near them, sometimes leaning against the same trees as themselves, or were lying across their bodies, in careless preparation. But the group that most attracted the attention of Deerslayer was that composed of the women and children. All the females appeared to be collected together, and almost as a matter of course, their young were near them. The former laughed and chatted in their rebuked and quiet manner, though one who knew the habits of the people might have detected that everything was not going on in its usual train. Most of the young women seemed to be lighthearted enough, but one old hag was seated apart, with a watchful, soured aspect, which the hunter at once knew betokened that some duty of an unpleasant character had been assigned her by the chiefs. What that duty was he had no means of knowing, but he felt satisfied it must be in some measure connected with her own sex, the aged among the women generally being chosen for such offices and no other.

As a matter of course, Deerslayer looked eagerly and anxiously for the form of Hist. She was nowhere visible, though the light penetrated to considerable distances in all directions around the fire. Once or twice he started, as he thought he recognized her laugh, but his ears were deceived by the soft melody that is so common to the Indian female voice. At length the old woman spoke loud and angrily, and then he caught a glimpse of one or two dark figures, in the background of trees, which turned, as if obedient to the rebuke, and walked more within the circle of the light. A young warrior's form first came fairly into view, then followed two youthful females, one of whom proved to be the Delaware girl. Deerslayer now comprehended it all. Hist was watched, possibly by her young companion, certainly by the old woman. The youth was probably some suitor of either her or her companion, but even his discretion was distrusted under the influence of his admiration. The known vicinity of those who might be supposed to be her friends, and the arrival of a strange red man on the lake, had induced more than the usual care, and the girl had not been able to slip away from those who watched her, in order to keep her appointment. Deerslayer traced her uneasiness by her attempting, once or twice, to look up through the branches of the trees, as if endeavoring to get glimpses of the star she had herself named as the sign for meeting. All was vain, however, and after strolling about the camp a little longer, in affected indifference, the two girls quitted their male escort and took seats among their own sex. As soon as this was done, the old sentinel changed her place to one more agreeable to herself, a certain proof that she had hitherto been exclusively on watch.

Deerslayer now felt greatly at a loss how to proceed. He well knew that Chingachgook could never be persuaded to return to the ark without making some desperate effort for the recovery of his mistress, and his own generous feelings well disposed him to aid in such an undertaking. He thought he saw the signs of an intention among the females to retire for the night; and should he remain, and the fire continue to give out its light, he might discover the particular hut, or arbor, under which Hist reposed, a circumstance that would be of infinite use in their future proceedings. Should he remain, however, much longer where he was, there was great danger that the impatience of his friend would drive him into some act of imprudence. At each instant, indeed, he expected to see the swarthy form of the Delaware appearing in the background, like the tiger prowling around the fold. Taking all things into consideration, therefore, he came to the conclusion it would be better to rejoin his friend and endeavor to temper his impetuosity by some of his own coolness and discretion. It required but a minute or two to put this plan in execution, the canoe returning to the strand some ten or fifteen minutes after it had left it.

Contrary to his expectations, perhaps, Deerslayer found the Indian at his post, from which he had not stirred, fearful that his betrothed might arrive during his absence. A conference followed, in which Chingachgook was made acquainted with the state of things in the camp. When Hist named the point as the place of meeting, it was with the expectation of making her escape from the old position and of repairing to a spot that she expected to find without any occupants, but the sudden change of localities had disconcerted all her plans. A much greater degree of vigilance than had been previously required was now necessary, and the circumstance that an aged woman was on watch also denoted some special grounds of alarm. All these considerations, and many more that will readily suggest themselves to the reader, were briefly discussed before the young men came to any decision. The occasion, however, being one that required acts instead of words, the course to be pursued was soon chosen.

Disposing of the canoe in such a manner that Hist must see it, should she come to the place of meeting previously to their return, the young men looked to their arms and prepared to enter the wood. The whole projection into the lake contained about two acres of land, and the part that formed the point, and on which the camp was placed, did not compose a surface of more than half that size. It was principally covered with oaks, which, as is usual in the American forests, grew to a great height without throwing out a branch and then arched in a dense and rich foliage. Beneath, except the fringe of thick bushes along the shore, there was very little underbrush, though, in consequence of their shape, the trees were closer together than is common in regions where the ax has been freely used, resembling tall, straight, rustic columns, upholding the usual canopy of leaves. The surface of the land was tolerably even, but it had a small rise near its center, which divided it into a northern and southern half. On the latter the Hurons had built their fire, profiting by the formation to conceal it from their enemies, who, it will be remembered, were supposed to be in the castle, which bore northerly. A brook also came brawling down the sides of the adjacent hills and found its way into the lake on the southern side of the point. It had cut for itself a deep passage through some of the higher portions of the ground, and, in later days, when the spot has become subjected to the uses of civilization, by its windings and shaded banks, it has become no mean accessory in contributing to the beauty of the place. This brook lay west of the encampment, and its waters found their way into the great reservoir of that region on the same side, quite near to the spot chosen for the fire. All these peculiarities, so far as circumstances allowed, had been noted by Deerslayer and explained to his friend.

The reader will understand that the little rise in the ground that lay behind the Indian encampment greatly favored the secret advance of the two adventurers. It prevented the light of the fire diffusing itself on the ground directly in the rear, although the land fell away toward the water, so as to leave what might be termed the left, or eastern flank of the position unprotected by this covering. We have said "unprotected," though that is not properly the word, since the knoll behind the huts and the fire offered a cover for those who were now stealthily approaching, rather than any protection to the Indians. Deerslayer did not break through the fringe of bushes immediately abreast of the canoe, which might have brought him too suddenly within the influence of the light, since the hillock did not extend to the water, but he followed the beach northerly until he had got nearly on the opposite side of the tongue of land, which brought him under the shelter of the low acclivity and, consequently, more in shadow.

As soon as the friends emerged from the bushes, they stopped to reconnoiter. The fire was still blazing behind the little ridge, casting its light upward into the tops of the trees,

producing an effect that was more pleasing than advanta-
geous. Still, the glare had its uses, for while the background
was in obscurity, the foreground was in strong light, exposing the savages and concealing their foes. Profiting by
the latter circumstance, the young men advanced cautiously
toward the ridge, Deerslayer in front, for he insisted on this
arrangement, lest the Delaware should be led by his feelings
into some indiscretion. It required but a moment to reach
the foot of the little ascent, and then commenced the most
critical part of the enterprise. Moving with exceeding caution, and trailing his rifle, both to keep its barrel out of view
and in readiness for service, the hunter put foot before foot,
until he had got sufficiently high to overlook the summit, his
own head being alone brought into the light. Chingachgook
was at his side, and both paused to take another close
examination of the camp. In order, however, to protect themselves against any straggler in the rear, they placed their
bodies against the trunk of an oak, standing on the side next
the fire.

The view that Deerslayer now obtained of the camp was
exactly the reverse of that he had perceived from the water.
The dim figures which he had formerly discovered must have
been on the summit of the ridge, a few feet in advance of
the spot where he was now posted. The fire was still blazing
brightly, and around it were seated on logs thirteen warriors,
which accounted for all whom he had seen from the canoe.
They were conversing with much earnestness among themselves, the image of the elephant passing from hand to hand.
The first burst of savage wonder had abated, and the question now under discussion was the probable existence, the history and habits of so extraordinary an animal. We have not
leisure to record the opinions of these rude men on a subject
so consonant to their lives and experience, but little is haz-
arded in saying that they were quite as plausible, and far
more ingenious, than half the conjectures that precede the
demonstrations of science. However much they may have
been at fault as to their conclusions and inferences, it is certain that they discussed the questions with a zealous and
most undivided attention. For the time being, all else was
forgotten, and our adventurers could not have approached
at a more fortunate instant.

The females were collected near each other, much as

Deerslayer had last seen them, nearly in a line between the place where he now stood and the fire. The distance from the oak against which the young men leaned and the warriors was about thirty yards; the women may have been half that number of yards nigher. The latter, indeed, were so near as to make the utmost circumspection as to motion and noise indispensable. Although they conversed in their low, soft voices, it was possible, in the profound stillness of the woods, even to catch passages of the discourse, and the lighthearted laugh that escaped the girls might occasionally have reached the canoe. Deerslayer felt the tremor that passed through the frame of his friend when the latter first caught the sweet sounds that issued from the plump, pretty lips of Hist. He even laid a hand on the shoulder of the Indian, as a sort of admonition to command himself. As the conversation grew more earnest, each leaned forward to listen.

"The Hurons have more curious beasts than that," said one of the girls contemptuously, for, like the men, they conversed of the elephant and his qualities. "The Delawares will think this creature wonderful, but tomorrow no Huron tongue will talk of it. Our young men will find him if the animal dares to come near our wigwams!"

This was in fact addressed to Wah-ta!-Wah, though she who spoke uttered her words with an assumed diffidence and humility that prevented her looking at the other.

"The Delawares are so far from letting such creatures come into their country," returned Hist, "that no one has even seen their images there! Their young men would frighten away the *images* as well as the *beasts*."

"The Delaware young men!—the nation is women—even the deer walk when they hear their hunters coming! Who has ever heard the name of a young Delaware warrior?"

This was said in good humor and with a laugh, but it was also said bitingly. That Hist so felt it was apparent by the spirit betrayed in her answer.

"Who has ever heard the name of a young Delaware!" she repeated earnestly. "Tamenund, himself, though now as old as the pines on the hill, or as the eagles in the air, was once young; his name was heard from the great salt lake to the sweet waters of the west. What is the family of Uncas? Where is another as great, though the palefaces have plowed up its graves and trodden on its bones? Do the eagles fly as high, is the deer as swift, or the panther as brave? Is there no young warrior of that race? Let the Huron maidens open their eyes wider, and they may see one called Chingachgook, who is as stately as a young ash and as tough as the hickory."

As the girl used her figurative language and told her companions to "open their eyes and they would see" the Delaware, Deerslayer thrust his fingers into the sides of his friend and indulged in a fit of his hearty, benevolent laughter. The other smiled, but the language of the speaker was too flattering and the tones of her voice too sweet for him to be led away by any accidental coincidence, however ludicrous. The speech of Hist produced a retort, and the dispute, though conducted in good humor and without any of the coarse violence of tone and gesture that often impairs the charms of the sex in what is called civilized life, grew warm and slightly clamorous. In the midst of this scene the Delaware caused his friend to stoop so as completely to conceal himself, and then he made a noise so closely resembling the little chirrup of the smallest species of the American squirrel that Deerslayer himself, though he had heard the imitation a hundred times, actually thought it came from one of the little animals skipping about over his head. The sound is so familiar in the woods that none of the Hurons paid it the least attention. Hist, however, instantly ceased talking and sat motionless. Still, she had sufficient self-command to abstain from turning her head. She had heard the signal by which her lover so often called her from the wigwam to the stolen interview, and it came over her senses and her heart, as the serenade affects the maiden in the land of song.

From that moment Chingachgook felt certain that his presence was known. This was effecting much, and he could now hope for a bolder line of conduct on the part of his mistress than she might dare to adopt under an uncertainty of his situation. It left no doubt of her endeavoring to aid him in his effort to release her. Deerslayer arose as soon as the signal was given, and though he had never held that sweet communion which is known only to lovers, he was not slow to detect the great change that had come over the manner of the girl. She still affected to dispute, though it was no longer with spirit and ingenuity, but what she said was uttered more as a lure to draw her antagonists on to an easy conquest than with any hopes of succeeding herself. Once or twice, it is true, her native readiness suggested a retort or an argument that raised a laugh and gave her a momentary advantage, but these little sallies, the offspring of mother wit, served the better to conceal her real feelings and to give to the triumph of the other party a more natural air than it might have possessed without them. At length the disputants became wearied, and they rose in a body as if about to separate. It was now that Hist, for the first time, ventured to turn her face in the direction whence the signal had come. In doing this, her movements were natural but guarded, and she stretched her arm and yawned, as if overcome with a desire to sleep. The chirrup was again heard, and the girl felt satisfied as to the position of her lover, though the strong light in which she herself was placed, and the comparative darkness in which the adventurers stood, prevented her from seeing their heads, the only portions of their forms that appeared above the ridge at all. The tree against which they were posted had a dark shadow cast upon it by the intervention of an enormous pine that grew between it and the fire, a circumstance which alone would have rendered objects within its cloud invisible at any distance. This Deerslayer well knew, and it was one of the reasons why he had selected this particular tree.

The moment was near when it became necessary for Hist to act. She was to sleep in a small hut, or bower, that had been built near the spot where she stood, and her companion was the aged hag already mentioned. Once within the hut, with this sleepless old woman stretched across the entrance, as was her nightly practice, the hope of escape was nearly destroyed—and she might, at any moment, be summoned to her bed. Luckily, at this instant, one of the warriors called to the old woman by name and bade her bring him water to drink. There was a delicious spring on the northern side of the point; the hag took a gourd from a branch and, summoning Hist to her side, moved toward the summit of the ridge, intending to descend and cross the point to the natural fountain. All this was seen and understood by the adventurers, and they fell back into the obscurity, concealing their persons by trees, until the two females had passed them. In walking, Hist was held tightly by the hand. As she moved by the tree that hid Chingachgook and his friend, the former felt for his tomahawk, with the intention to bury it in the brain of the woman. But the other saw the hazard of such a measure, since a single scream might bring all the warriors upon them, and he was averse to the act on considerations of humanity. His hand, therefore, prevented the blow. Still, as the two moved past, the chirrup was repeated, and the Huron woman stopped and faced the tree whence the sounds seemed to proceed, standing, at the moment, within six feet of her enemies. She expressed her surprise that a squirrel should be in motion at so late an hour and said it boded evil. Hist answered that she had heard the same squirrel three times within the last twenty minutes, and that she supposed it was waiting to obtain some of the crumbs left from the late supper. This explanation appeared satisfactory, and they moved toward the spring, the men following stealthily and closely. The gourd was filled, and the old woman was hurrying back, her hand still grasping the wrist of the girl, when she was suddenly seized so violently by the throat as to cause her to release her captive and to prevent her making any sound other than a sort of gurgling, suffocating noise. The Serpent passed his arm around the waist of his mistress and dashed through the bushes with her, on the north side of the point. Here he immediately turned along the beach and ran toward the canoe. A more direct course could have been taken, but it might have led to a discovery of the place of embarking.

Deerslayer kept playing on the throat of the old woman, like the keys of an organ, occasionally allowing her to breathe, and then compressing his fingers again nearly to strangling. The brief intervals for breath, however, were well improved, and the hag succeeded in letting out a screech or two that served to alarm the camp. The tramp of the warriors as they sprang from the fire was plainly audible, and at the next moment three or four of them appeared on the top of the ridge, drawn against the background of light, resembling the dim shadows of the phantasmagoria. It was now quite time for the hunter to retreat. Tripping up the heels of his captive, and giving her throat a parting squeeze, quite as much in resentment at her indomitable efforts to sound the alarm as from any policy, he left her on her back and moved toward the bushes, his rifle at a poise, and his head over his shoulders, like a lion at bay.

CHAPTER XVII

There, ye wise saints, behold your light, your star,
Ye would be dupes and victims, and ye are,
Is it enough? or, must I, while a thrill
Lives in your sapient bosoms, cheat you still?

MOORE

THE FIRE, THE CANOE, and the spring near which Deerslayer commenced his retreat would have stood in the angles of a triangle of tolerably equal sides. The distance from the fire to the boat was a little less than the distance from the fire to the spring, while the distance from the spring to the boat was about equal to that between the two points first named. This, however, was in straight lines—a means of escape to which the fugitives could not resort. They were obliged to have recourse to a detour in order to get the cover of the bushes, and to follow the curvature of the beach. Under these disadvantages, then, the hunter commenced his retreat—disadvantages that he felt to be so much the greater from his knowledge of the habits of all Indians, who rarely fail in cases of sudden alarm, more especially when in the midst of cover, immediately to throw out flankers with a view to meet their foes at all points and, if possible, to turn their rear. That some such course was now adopted, he believed from the tramp of feet, which not only came up the ascent, as related, but were also heard, under the faint impulse, diverging not only toward the hill in the rear, but toward the extremity of the point, in a direction opposite to that he was about to take himself. Promptitude consequently became a matter of the last importance, as the parties might meet on the strand before the fugitive could reach the canoe.

Notwithstanding the pressing nature of the emergency, Deerslayer hesitated a single instant ere he plunged into the

James Fenimore Cooper

bushes that lined the shore. His feelings had been awakened by the whole scene, and a sternness of purpose had come over him to which he was ordinarily a stranger. Four dark figures loomed on the ridge, drawn against the brightness of the fire, and an enemy might have been sacrificed at a glance. The Indians had paused to gaze into the gloom in search of the screeching hag, and with many a man less given to reflection than the hunter, the death of one of them would have been certain. Luckily, he was more prudent. Although the rifle dropped a little toward the foremost of his pursuers, he did not aim or fire, but disappeared in the cover. To gain the beach, and to follow it around to the place where Chingachgook was already in the canoe with Hist, anxiously waiting his appearance, occupied but a moment. Laying his rifle in the bottom of the canoe, Deerslayer stooped to give the latter a vigorous shove from the shore, when a powerful Indian leaped through the bushes, alighting like a panther on his back. Everything was now suspended by a hair, a false step ruining all. With a generosity that would have rendered a Roman illustrious throughout all time—but which, in the career of one so simple and humble, would have been forever lost to the world, but for this unpretending legend—Deerslayer threw all his force into a desperate effort, shoved the canoe off with a power that sent it a hundred feet from the shore as it might be in an instant, and fell forward into the lake himself, face downward, his assailant necessarily following him.

Although the water was deep within a few yards of the beach, it was not more than breast high as close in as the spot where the two combatants fell. Still, this was quite sufficient to destroy one who had sunk under the great disadvantages in which Deerslayer was placed. His hands were free, however, and the savage was compelled to relinquish his hug to keep his own face above the surface. For half a minute there was a desperate struggle, like the floundering of an alligator that has just seized some powerful prey, and then both stood erect, grasping each other's arms, in order to prevent the use of the deadly knife in the darkness. What might have been the issue of this severe personal struggle cannot be known, for half a dozen savages came leaping into the water to the aid of their friend, and Deerslayer yielded himself a prisoner with a dignity that was as remarkable as his self-devotion.

To quit the lake and lead their new captive to the fire occupied the Indians but another minute. So much engaged were they all with the struggle and its consequences that the canoe was unseen, though it still lay so near the shore as to render every syllable that was uttered perfectly intelligible to the Delaware and his betrothed; the whole party left the spot, some continuing the pursuit after Hist, along the beach, though most proceeded to the light. Here Deerslayer's antagonist so far recovered his breath and his recollection, for he had been throttled nearly to strangulation, as to relate the manner in which the girl had got off. It was now too late to assail the other fugitives, for no sooner was his friend led into the bushes than the Delaware placed his paddle into the water, and the light canoe glided noiselessly away, holding its course toward the center of the lake, until safe from shot, after which it sought the ark.

When Deerslayer reached the fire, he found himself surrounded by no less than eight grim savages, among whom was his old acquaintance Rivenoak. As soon as the latter caught a glimpse of the captive's countenance, he spoke apart to his companions, and a low but general exclamation of pleasure and surprise escaped them. They knew that the conqueror of their late friend, he who had fallen on the opposite side of the lake, was in their hands, and subject to their mercy or vengeance. There was no little admiration mingled in the ferocious looks that were thrown on the prisoner, an admiration that was as much excited by his present composure as by his past deeds. This scene may be said to have been the commencement of the great and terrible reputation that Deerslayer, or Hawkeye, as he was afterward called, enjoyed among all the tribes of New York and Canada; a reputation that was certainly more limited in its territorial and numerical extent than those which are possessed in civilized life, but which was compensated for what it wanted in these particulars, perhaps, by its greater justice and the total absence of mystification and management.

The arms of Deerslayer were not pinioned, and he was left the free use of his hands, his knife having been first removed. The only precaution that was taken to secure his person was untiring watchfulness, and a strong rope of bark that passed from ankle to ankle, not so much to prevent his walking as to place an obstacle in the way of his attempting to escape by any sudden leap. Even this extra provision against flight was not made until the captive had been brought to the light and his character ascertained. It was, in fact, a compliment to his prowess, and he felt proud of the distinction. That he might be bound when the warriors slept he thought probable, but to be bound in the moment of capture showed that he was already, and thus early, attaining a name. While the young Indians were fastening the rope, he wondered if Chingachgook would have been treated in the same manner, had he too fallen into the hands of the enemy. Nor did the reputation of the young paleface rest altogether on his success in the previous combat, or in his discriminating and cool manner of managing the late negotiation, for it had received a great accession by the occurrences of the night. Ignorant of the movements of the ark, and of the accident that had brought their fire into view, the Iroquois attributed the discovery of their new camp to the vigilance of so shrewd a foe. The manner in which he ventured upon the point, the abstraction or escape of Hist, and most of all the self-devotion of the prisoner, united to the readiness with which he had sent the canoe adrift, were so many important links in the chain of facts on which his growing fame was founded. Many of these circumstances had been seen, some had been explained, and all were understood.

While this admiration and these honors were so unreservedly bestowed on Deerslayer, he did not escape some of the penalties of his situation. He was permitted to seat himself on the end of a log, near the fire, in order to dry his clothes, his late adversary standing opposite, now holding articles of his own scanty vestments to the heat, and now feeling his throat, on which the marks of his enemy's fingers were still quite visible. The rest of the warriors consulted together, near at hand, all those who had been out having returned to report that no signs of any other prowlers near the camp were to be found. In this state of things, the old woman, whose name was Shebear, in plain English, approached Deerslayer with her fists clenched and her eyes flashing fire. Hitherto she had been occupied with screaming, an employment at which she had played her part with no small degree of success, but having succeeded in effectually alarming all within reach of a pair of lungs that had been strengthened by long practice, she next turned her attention to the injuries her own person had sustained in the struggle. These were in no manner material, though they were of a nature to arouse all the fury of a woman who had long ceased to attract by means of the gentler qualities, and who was much disposed to revenge the hardships she had so long endured as the neglected wife and mother of savages on all who came within her power. If Deerslayer had not permanently injured her, he had temporarily caused her to suffer, and she was not a person to overlook a wrong of this nature on account of its motive.

"Skunk of the palefaces," commenced this exasperated and semipoetic fury, shaking her fist under the nose of the impassable hunter, "you are not even a woman. Your friends, the Delawares, are only women, and you are their sheep. Your own people will not own you, and no tribe of red *men* would have you in their wigwams; you skulk among petticoated warriors. *You* slay our brave friend who has left us?—no—his great soul scorned to fight you and left his body rather than have the shame of slaying *you!* But the blood that you spilled when the spirit was not looking on has not sunk into the ground. It must be buried in your groans—what music do I hear? Those are not the wailings of a red man!—no red warrior groans so much like a hog. They come from a paleface throat—a Yengeese bosom—and sound as pleasant as girls singing. Dog—skunk—woodchuck —mink—hedgehog—pig—toad—spider—Yengee—"

Here the old woman, having expended her breath and exhausted her epithets, was fain to pause a moment, though both her fists were shaken in the prisoner's face and the whole of her wrinkled countenance was filled with fierce resentment. Deerslayer looked upon these impotent attempts to arouse him as indifferently as a gentleman in our own state of society regards the vituperative terms of a blackguard: the one party feeling that the tongue of an old woman could never injure a warrior, and the other knowing that mendacity and vulgarity can only permanently affect those who resort to their use; but he was spared any further attack at present by the interposition of Rivenoak, who shoved aside the hag, bidding her quit the spot, and prepared to take his seat at the side of his prisoner. The old woman withdrew, but the hunter well understood that he was to be the subject of all her means of annoyance, if not of positive injury, so long as he remained in the power of his enemies; for nothing rankles so deeply as the consciousness that an attempt to irritate has been met by contempt, a feeling that is usually the most passive of any that is harbored in the human breast. Rivenoak quietly took the seat we have mentioned, and, after a short pause, he commenced a dialogue, which we translate, as usual, for the benefit of those readers who have not studied the North American languages.

"My paleface friend is very welcome," said the Indian, with a familiar nod and a smile so covert it required all Deerslayer's vigilance to detect, and not a little of his philosophy to detect unmoved; "he is welcome. The Hurons keep a hot fire to dry the white man's clothes."

"I thank you, Huron, or Mingo, as I most like to call you," returned the other; "I thank you for the welcome, and I thank you for the fire. Each is good in its way, and the last is very good, when one has been in a spring as cold as the Glimmerglass. Even Huron warmth may be pleasant, at such a time, to a man with a Delaware heart."

"The paleface—but my brother has a name? So great a warrior would not have lived without a name?"

"Mingo," said the hunter, a little of the weakness of human nature exhibiting itself in the glance of his eye and the color on his cheek, "Mingo, *your* brave called me Hawkeye, I suppose on account of a quick and sartain aim, when he was lying with his head in my lap, afore his spirit started for the happy hunting grounds."

" 'Tis a good name! The hawk is sure of his blow. Hawkeye is not a woman; why does he live with the Delawares?"

"I understand you, Mingo, but we look on all that as a sarcumvention of some of your subtle devils, and deny the charge. Providence placed me among the Delawares young; and, 'bating what Christian usages demand of my color and gifts, I hope to live and die in their tribe. Still, I do not mean to throw away altogether my natyve rights, and shall strive to do a paleface's duty in redskin society."

"Good; a Huron is a redskin, as well as a Delaware. Hawkeye is more of a Huron than of a woman."

"I suppose you know, Mingo, your own meaning; if you don't, I make no question, 'tis well known to Satan. But if you wish to get anything out of me, speak plainer, for bargains cannot be made blindfolded or tongue-tied."

"Good; Hawkeye has not a forked tongue, and he likes to say what he thinks. He is an acquaintance of the Muskrat"—this was a name by which all the Indians designated Hutter—"and he has lived in his wigwam; but he is not a friend. He wants no scalps, like a miserable Indian, but fights like a stouthearted paleface. The Muskrat is neither white nor red; neither a beast nor a fish. He is a water snake; sometimes in the spring and sometimes on the land. He looks for scalps like an outcast. Hawkeye can go back and tell him how he has outwitted the Hurons, how he has escaped, and when his eyes are in a fog, when he can't see as far as from his cabin to the woods, then Hawkeye can open the door for the Hurons. And how will the plunder be divided? Why, Hawkeye will carry away the most, and the Hurons will take what he may choose to leave behind him. The scalps can go to Canada, for a paleface has no satisfaction in *them*."

"Well, well, Rivenoak—for so I hear 'em tarm you—this is plain English enough, though spoken in Iroquois. I understand all you mean, now, and must say it outdevils even Mingo deviltry! No doubt, 'twould be easy enough to go back and tell the Muskrat that I had got away from you, and gain some credit, too, by the expl'ite."

"Good; that is what I want the paleface to do."

"Yes—yes—that's plain enough. I know what you want me to do, without more words. When inside the house, and eating the Muskrat's bread, and laughing and talking with his pretty darters, I might put his eyes into so thick a fog that he couldn't even see the door, much less the land."

"Good! Hawkeye should have been born a Huron! His blood is not more than half white!"

"There you're out, Huron; yes, there you're as much out as if you mistook a wolf for a catamount. I'm white in blood, heart, natur', and gifts, though a little redskin in feelin's and habits. But when old Hutter's eyes are well befogged, and his pretty darters, perhaps, in a deep sleep, and Hurry Harry, the Great Pine, as you Indians tarm him, is dreaming of anything but mischief, and all suppose Hawkeye is acting as a faithful sentinel, all I have to do is to set a torch somewhere in sight for a signal, open the door, and let in the Hurons to knock 'em all on the head."

"Surely my brother is mistaken; he *cannot* be white! He is worthy to be a great chief among the Hurons!"

"That is true enough, I dares to say, if he could do all this. Now, hearkee, Huron, and for once hear a few honest words from the mouth of a plain man. I am a Christian born, and them that come of such a stock and that listen to the words that were spoken to their fathers, and will be spoken to their children, until 'arth and all it holds perishes, can never lend themselves to such wickedness. Sarcumventions in war may be, and *are*, lawful, but sarcumventions, and deceit, and treachery among fri'nds are fit only for the paleface devils. I know that there are white men enough to give you this wrong idee of our natur', but such are ontrue to their blood and gifts, and ought to be, if they are not, outcasts and vagabonds. No upright paleface could do what you wish, and to be as plain with you as I wish to be, in my judgment no upright Delaware either; with a Mingo it may be different."

The Huron listened to his rebuke with obvious disgust; but he had his ends in view, and was too wily to lose all chance of effecting them by a precipitate avowal of resentment. Affecting to smile, he seemed to listen eagerly, and he then pondered on what he had heard.

"Does Hawkeye love the Muskrat?" he abruptly demanded; "or does he love his daughters?"

"Neither, Mingo. Old Tom is not a man to gain my love; as for the darters, they are comely enough to gain the liking of any young man; but there's reason ag'in any very great love for either. Hetty is a good soul, but natur' has laid a heavy hand on her mind, poor thing!"

"And the Wild Rose!" exclaimed the Huron—for the fame of Judith's beauty had spread among those who could travel the wilderness as well as the highway, by means of old eagles' nests, rocks, and riven trees, known to them by report and tradition, as well as among the white borderers—"Is she not sweet enough to be put in the bosom of my brother?"

Deerslayer had far too much of the innate gentleman to insinuate aught against the fair fame of one who, by nature and position, was so helpless; and as he did not choose to utter an untruth, he preferred being silent. The Huron mistook the motive and supposed that disappointed affection lay at the bottom of his reserve. Still bent on corrupting or bribing his captive in order to obtain possession of the treasures with which his imagination filled the castle, he persevered in his attack.

"Hawkeye is talking with a friend," he continued. "He knows that Rivenoak is a man of his word, for they have traded together, and trade opens the soul. My friend has come here on account of a little string, held by a girl, that can pull the whole body of the stoutest warrior?"

"You are nearer the truth now, Huron, than you've been afore, since we began to talk. This is true. But one end of that string was not fast to my heart, nor did the Wild Rose hold the other."

"This is wonderful! Does my brother love in his head and not in his heart? And can the Feeble Mind pull so hard against so stout a warrior?"

"There it is ag'in; sometimes right and sometimes wrong! The string you mean is fast to the heart of a great Delaware —one of the Mohican stock in fact, living among the Delawares since the dispersion of his own people, and of the family of Uncas—Chingachgook by name, or Great Sarpent. He has come here, led by the string, and I've followed, or rather come afore, for I got here first pulled by nothing stronger than fri'ndship, which is strong enough for such as are not niggardly of their feelin's and are willing to live a little for their fellow creatur's, as well as for themselves."

"But a string has two ends—one is fast to the mind of a Mohican, and the other——?"

"Why, the other was here close to the fire, half an hour since. Wah-ta!-Wah held it in her hand, if she didn't hold it to her heart."

"I understand what you mean, my brother," returned the Indian gravely, for the first time catching a direct clue to the adventures of the evening. "The Great Serpent being strongest, pulled the hardest, and Hist was forced to leave us."

"I don't think there was much pulling about it," answered the other, laughing, always in his silent manner, with as much heartiness as if he were not a captive and in danger of torture or death. "I don't think there was much pulling about it; no, I don't. Lord help you, Huron, he likes the gal, and the gal likes him, and it surpassed Huron sarcumventions to keep two young people apart, when there was so strong a feelin' to bring 'em together."

"And Hawkeye and Chingachgook came into our camp on this errand only?"

"That's a question that'll answer itself, Mingo! Yes, if a question could talk, it would answer itself to your perfect satisfaction. For what else should we come? And yet, it isn't exactly so, neither, for we didn't come into your camp at all, but only as far as that pine, there, that you see on the other side of the ridge, where we stood watching your movements and conduct as long as we liked. When we were ready, the Sarpent gave his signal, and then all went just as it should, down to the moment when yonder vagabond leaped upon my back. Sartain; we came for that, and for no other purpose, and we got what we came for; there's no use in pretending otherwise. Hist is off with a man who's the next thing to her husband, and come what will to me, *that's* one good thing determined."

"What sign or signal told the young maiden that her lover was nigh?" asked the old Huron, with more curiosity than it was usual for him to betray.

Deerslayer laughed again and seemed to enjoy the success of the exploit with as much glee as if he had not been its victim.

"Your squirrels are great gadabouts, Mingo!" he cried, still laughing; "yes, they're sartainly great gadabouts! When other folks' squirrels are at home and asleep, yourn keep in motion among the trees and chirrup and sing in a way that even a Delaware gal can understand their music! Well, there's four-legged squirrels, and there's two-legged squirrels, and give me the last when there's a good tight string atween two hearts. If one brings 'em together, t'other tells when to pull hardest."

The Huron looked vexed, though he succeeded in suppressing any violent exhibition of resentment. He soon quitted his prisoner and, joining the rest of his warriors, communicated the substance of what he had learned. As in his own case admiration was mingled with anger at the boldness and success of their enemies. Three or four of them ascended the little acclivity and gazed at the tree where it was understood the adventurers had posted themselves, and one even descended and examined for footprints around its roots, in order to make sure that the statement was true. The result confirmed the story of the captive, and they all returned to the fire with increased wonder and respect. The messenger, who had arrived with some communication from the party above while the two adventurers were watching the camp, was now dispatched with some answer, and doubtless bore with him the intelligence of all that had happened.

Down to this moment, the young Indian who had been seen walking in company with Hist and another female had made no advances to any communication with Deerslayer. He had held himself aloof from his friends even, passing near the bevy of younger women who were clustering together, apart as usual, and conversed in low tones on the subject of the escape of their late companion. Perhaps it would be true to say that these last were pleased as well as vexed at what had just occurred. Their female sympathies were with the lovers, while their pride was bound up in the success of their own tribe. It is possible, too, that the superior personal advantages of Hist rendered her dangerous to some of the younger part of the group, and they were not sorry to find she was no longer in the way of their own ascendency. On the whole, however, the better feeling was most prevalent, for neither the wild condition in which they lived, the clannish prejudices of tribes, nor their hard fortunes as Indian women could entirely conquer the inextinguishable leaning of their sex to the affections. One of the girls even laughed at the disconsolate look of the swain who might fancy himself deserted, a circumstance that seemed suddenly to arouse his energies and induced him to move toward the log on which the prisoner was still seated, drying his clothes.

"This is Catamount!" said the Indian, striking his hand boastfully on his naked breast as he uttered the words, in a manner to show how much weight he expected them to carry.

"This is Hawkeye," quietly returned Deerslayer, adopting the name by which he knew he would be known in future among all the tribes of the Iroquois. "My sight is keen: is my brother's leap long?"

"From here to the Delaware villages. Hawkeye has stolen my wife: he must bring her back, or his scalp will hang on a pole and dry in my wigwam."

"Hawkeye has stolen nothing, Huron. He doesn't come of a thieving breed, nor has he thieving gifts. Your wife, as you call Wah-ta!-Wah, will never be the wife of any redskin of the Canadas; her mind is in the cabin of a Delaware, and her body has gone to find it. The catamount is actyve, I know, but its legs can't keep pace with a woman's wishes."

"The Serpent of the Delawares is a dog; he is a poor bull-pout that keeps in the water; he is afraid to stand on the hard earth like a brave Indian!"

"Well, well, Huron, that's pretty impudent, considering it's not an hour since the Sarpent stood within a hundred feet of you, and would have tried the toughness of your skin with a rifle bullet, when I pointed you out to him, hadn't I laid the weight of a little judgment on his hand. You may take in timersome gals in the settlements with your catamount whine, but the ears of a man can tell truth from ontruth."

"Hist laughs at him! She sees he is lame, and a poor hunter, and he has never been on a warpath. She will take a man for a husband, not a fool."

"How do you know that, Catamount? How do you know that?" returned Deerslayer, laughing. "She has gone into the lake, you see, and maybe she prefers a trout to a mongrel cat. As for warpaths, neither the Sarpent nor I have much exper'ence, we are ready to own, but if you don't call this one, you must tarm it what the gals in the settlements tarm it, the high road to matrimony. Take my advice, Catamount, and s'arch for a wife among the Huron women; you'll never get one with a willing mind from among the Delawares."

Catamount's hand felt for his tomahawk, and when the fingers reached the handle, they worked convulsively, as if their owner hesitated between policy and resentment. At this critical moment Rivenoak approached and, by a gesture of authority, induced the young man to retire, assuming his former position himself on the log, at the side of Deerslayer. Here he continued silent for a little time, maintaining the grave reserve of an Indian chief.

"Hawkeye is right," the Iroquois at length began; "his sight is so strong that he can see truth in a dark night, and our eyes have been blinded. He is an owl, darkness hiding nothing from him. He ought not to strike his friends. He is right."

"I'm glad you think so, Mingo," returned the other, "for a traitor, in my judgment, is worse than a coward. I care as little for the Muskrat as one paleface ought to care for another, but I care too much for him to ambush him in the way you wished. In short, according to my ideas, any sarcumvention, except open-war sarcumventions, are ag'in both law and what we whites call 'gospel,' too."

"My paleface brother is right; he is no Indian to forget his Manitou and his color. The Hurons know that they have a great warrior for their prisoner, and they will treat him as one. If he is to be tortured, his torments shall be such as no common man can bear; if he is to be treated as a friend, it will be the friendship of chiefs."

As the Huron uttered this extraordinary assurance of consideration, his eye furtively glanced at the countenance of his listener, in order to discover how he stood the compliment; though his gravity and apparent sincerity would have prevented any man but one practiced in artifices from detecting his motives. Deerslayer belonged to the class of the unsuspicious, and acquainted with the Indian notions of what constituted respect, in matters connected with the treatment of captives, he felt his blood chill at the announcement, even while he maintained an aspect so steeled that his quick-sighted enemy could discover in it no signs of weakness.

"God has put me in your hands, Huron," the captive at length answered, "and I suppose you will act your will on me. I shall not boast of what I can do, under torment, for I've never been tried, and no man can say till he has been, but I'll do my endivors not to disgrace the people among whom I got my training. Howsever, I wish you now to bear witness that I'm altogether of white blood, and, in a nat'ral way, of white gifts, too, so, should I be overcome and forget myself, I hope you'll lay the fault where it properly belongs, and in no manner put it on the Delawares, or their allies and friends the Mohicans. We're all created with more or less weakness, and I'm afeard it's a paleface's to give in under great bodily torment, when a redskin will sing his songs and boast of his deeds in the very teeth of his foes!"

"We shall see. Hawkeye has a good countenance, and he is tough—but why should he be tormented when the Hurons love him? He is not born their enemy, and the death of one warrior will not cast a cloud between them forever."

"So much the better, Huron, so much the better. Still I don't wish to owe anything to a mistake about each other's meaning. It is so much the better that you bear no malice for the loss of a warrior who fell in war, and yet it is ontrue that there is no inmity—lawful inmity I mean, atween us. So far as I have redskin feelin's at all, I've Delaware feelin's, and I leave you to judge for yourself how far they are likely to be fri'ndly to the Mingos—"

Deerslayer ceased, for a sort of specter stood before him that put a stop to his words, and, indeed, caused him for a moment to doubt the fidelity of his boasted vision. Hetty Hutter was standing at the side of the fire, as quietly as if she belonged to the tribe.

As the hunter and the Indian sat watching the emotions that were betrayed in each other's countenance, the girl had approached unnoticed, doubtless ascending from the beach on the southern side of the point, or that next to the spot where the ark had anchored, and had advanced to the fire with the fearlessness that belonged to her simplicity, and which was certainly justified by the treatment formerly received from the Indians. As soon as Rivenoak perceived the girl she was recognized, and calling to two or three of the younger warriors, the chief sent them out to reconnoiter, lest her appearance should be the forerunner of another attack. He then motioned to Hetty to draw near.

"I hope your visit is a sign that the Sarpent and Hist are in safety, Hetty," said Deerslayer, as soon as the girl had complied with the Huron's request. "I don't think you'd come ashore ag'in on the ar'n'd that brought you here afore."

"Judith told me to come this time, Deerslayer," Hetty replied. "She paddled me ashore herself, in a canoe, as soon as the Serpent had shown her Hist and told his story. How handsome Hist is tonight, Deerslayer, and how much happier she looks than when she was with the Hurons!"

"That's natur', gal; yes, that may be set down as human natur'. She's with her betrothed and no longer fears a Mingo husband. In my judgment, Judith herself would lose most of her beauty if she thought she was to bestow it all on a Mingo! Content is a great fortifier of good looks; and I'll warrant you, Hist is contented enough, now she is out of the hands of these miscreants and with her chosen warrior! Did you say that your sister told you to come ashore—why should Judith do that?"

"She bid me come to see you and to try and persuade the

savages to take more elephants to let you off; but I've brought the Bible with me—*that* will do more than all the elephants in Father's chest!"

"And your father, good little Hetty—and Hurry; did they know of your ar'n'd?"

"Nothing. Both are asleep, and Judith and the Serpent thought it best they should not be woke, lest they might want to come again after scalps, when Hist had told them how few warriors and how many women and children there were in the camp. Judith would give me no peace till I had come ashore to see what had happened to *you*."

"Well, that's remarkable as consarns Judith! Why should she feel so much unsartainty about me? Ah, I see how it is now; yes, I see into the whole matter now. You must understand, Hetty, that your sister is oneasy lest Harry March should wake and come blundering here into the hands of the inimy ag'in, under some idee that, being a traveling comrade, he ought to help me in this matter! Hurry is a blunderer, I will allow, but I don't think he'd risk as much for my sake as he would for his own."

"Judith don't care for Hurry, though Hurry cares for her," replied Hetty innocently but quite positively.

"I've heard you say as much as that afore; yes, I've heard that from you afore, gal; and yet it isn't true. One don't live in a tribe not to see something of the way in which liking works in a woman's heart. Though no way given to marrying myself, I've been a looker-on among the Delawares, and this is a matter in which paleface and redskin gifts are all as one the same. When the feelin' begins, the young woman is thoughtful and has no eyes or ears onless for the warrior that has taken her fancy; then follows melancholy and sighing and such sort of actions; after which, especially if matters don't come to plain discourse, she often flies around to backbiting and fault-finding, blaming the youth for the very things she likes best in him. Some young creatur's are forward in this way of showing their love, and I'm of opinion Judith is one of 'em. Now, I've heard her as much as deny that Hurry was good-looking, and the young woman who could do *that* must be far gone indeed."

"The young woman who liked Hurry would own that he is handsome. *I* think Hurry *very* handsome, Deerslayer, and I'm sure everybody must think so that has eyes. Judith don't like Harry March, and that's the reason she finds fault with him."

"Well—well—my good little Hetty, have it your own way, if we should talk from now till winter, each would think as at present, so there's no use in words. I must believe that Judith is much wrapped up in Hurry and that, sooner or later, she'll have him; and this, too, all the more from the manner in which she abuses him; and I dare to say, you think just the contrary. But mind what I now tell you, gal, and pretend not to know it," continued this being, who was so obtuse on a point on which men are usually quick enough to make discoveries, and so acute in matters that would baffle the observation of much the greater portion of mankind; "I see how it is with them vagabonds. Rivenoak has left us, you see, and is talking yonder with his young men; and though too far to be *heard*, I can *see* what he is telling them. Their orders is to watch your movements, and to find where the canoe is to meet you, to take you back to the ark, and then to seize all and what they can. I'm sorry Judith sent you, for I suppose she wants you to go back ag'in."

"All that's settled, Deerslayer," returned the girl in a low, confidential, and meaning manner; "you may trust me to outwit the best Indian of them all. I know I am feeble-minded, but I've got *some* sense, and you'll see how I'll use it in getting back, when my errand is done!"

"Ah's me! Poor girl; I'm afeard all that's easier said than done. They're a venomous set of riptyles, and their p'ison's none the milder for the loss of Hist. Well, I'm glad the Sarpent was the one to get off with the gal, for now ther'll be two happy, at least; whereas, had *he* fallen into the hands of the Mingos, there'd be two miserable and another far from feelin' as a man likes to feel."

"Now you put me in mind of a part of my errand that I had almost forgotten, Deerslayer. Judith told me to ask you what you thought the Hurons would do with you if you couldn't be bought off, and what *she* had best do to serve you. Yes, this was the most important part of the errand— what she had best do in order to serve you."

"That's as *you* think, Hetty, but it's no matter. Young women are apt to lay most stress on what most touches their feelin's; but no matter; have it your own way, so you be but careful not to let the vagabonds get the mastery of a canoe. When you get back to the ark, tell 'em to keep close and to keep moving too, most especially at night. Many hours can't go by without the troops on the river hearing of this party, and then your fri'nds may look for relief. 'Tis but a day's march from the nearest garrison, and true soldiers will never lie idle with the foe in their neighborhood. This is my advice, and you may say to your father and Hurry that scalp-hunting will be a poor business now, as the Mingos are up and awake, and nothing can save 'em 'till the troops come, except keeping a good belt of water atween 'em and the savages."

"What shall I tell Judith about you, Deerslayer? I know she will send me back again, if I don't bring her the truth about *you*."

"Then tell her the *truth*. I see no reason Judith Hutter shouldn't hear the *truth* about me as well as a *lie*. I'm a captyve in Indian hands, and Providence only knows what will come of it! Hark'ee, Hetty"—dropping his voice and speaking still more confidentially—"you *are* a little weak-minded, it must be allowed, but you know something of Injins. Here I am in their hands, after having slain one of their stoutest warriors, and they've been endivoring to work upon me, through fear of consequences, to betray your father and all in the ark. I understand the blackguards as well as if they told it all out plainly with their tongues. They hold up avarice afore me on one side, and fear on t'other, and think honesty will give way atween 'em both. But let your father and Hurry know 'tis all useless; as for the Sarpent, *he* knows it already."

"But what shall I tell *Judith?* She will certainly send me back if I don't satisfy her mind."

"Well, tell Judith the same. No doubt the savages will try the torments to make me give in and to revenge the loss of their warrior, but I must hold out ag'in nat'ral weakness in the best manner I can. You may tell Judith to feel no consarn on my account—it will come hard, I know, seeing that a white man's gifts don't run to boasting and singing under torment, for he generally feels smallest when he suffers most—but you may tell her not to have any consarn. I think I shall make out to stand it; and she may rely on this, let me give in as much as I may, and prove completely that I am white, by wailings, and howlings, and even tears, yet I'll never fall so far as to betray my fri'nds. When it gets to burning holes in the flesh with heated ramrods, and to hacking the body, and tearing the hair out by the roots, natur' may get the upper hand, so far as groans and complaints are consarned, but there the triumph of the vagabonds will ind; nothing short of God's abandoning him to the devils can make an honest man ontrue to his color and duty."

Hetty listened with great attention, and her mild but speaking countenance manifested a strong sympathy in the anticipated agony of the supposititious sufferer. At first she seemed at a loss how to act; then, taking a hand of Deerslayer's, she affectionately recommended to him to borrow her Bible and to read it while the savages were inflicting their torments. When the other honestly admitted that it exceeded his power to read, she even volunteered to remain with him and to perform this holy office in person. The offer was gently declined, and Rivenoak being about to join them, Deerslayer requested the girl to leave him, first enjoining her again to tell those in the ark to have full confidence in his fidelity. Hetty now walked away and approached the group of females with as much confidence and self-possession as if she were a native of the tribe. On the other hand, the Huron resumed his seat by the side of his prisoner, the one continuing to ask questions with all the wily ingenuity of a practical Indian counselor, the other baffling him by the very means that are known to be the most efficacious in defeating the finesse of the more pretending diplomacy of civilization, or by confining his answers to the truth, and the truth only.

CHAPTER XVIII

Thus died she; never more on her
Shall sorrow light, or shame. She was not made
Through years or moons the inner weight to bear,
Which colder hearts endure till they are laid
By age in earth; her days and pleasures were
Brief but delightful—such as had not stayed
Long with her destiny; but she sleeps well
By the sea-shore whereon she loved to dwell.

BYRON

THE YOUNG MEN who had been sent out to reconnoiter, on the sudden appearance of Hetty, soon returned to report their want of success in making any discovery. One of them had even been along the beach as far as the spot opposite to the ark, but the darkness completely concealed that vessel from his notice. Others had examined in different directions, and everywhere the stillness of night was added to the silence and solitude of the woods. It was consequently believed that the girl had come alone, as on her former visit, and on some similar errand. The Iroquois were ignorant that the ark had left the castle, and there were movements projected, if not in the course of actual execution by this time, which also greatly added to the sense of security. A watch was set, therefore, and all but the sentinels disposed themselves to sleep.

Sufficient care was had to the safekeeping of the captive without inflicting on him any unnecessary suffering; as for Hetty, she was permitted to find a place among the Indian girls in the best manner she could. She did not find the friendly offices of Hist, though her character not only bestowed impunity from pain and captivity, but procured for her a consideration and an attention that placed her, on the score of comfort, quite on a level with the wild but gentle beings around her. She was supplied with a skin, and made her own bed on a pile of boughs a little apart from the huts. Here she was soon in a profound sleep, like all around her.

There were now thirteen men in the party, and three kept watch at a time. One remained in shadow, not far from the fire, however. His duty was to guard the captive, to take care that the fire neither blazed up so as to illuminate the spot, nor yet became wholly extinguished, and to keep an eye generally on the state of the camp. Another passed from one beach to the other, crossing the base of the point, while the third kept moving slowly around the strand on its outer extremity, to prevent a repetition of the surprise that had already taken place that night. This arrangement was far from being usual among savages, who ordinarily rely more on the secrecy of their movements than on vigilance of this nature, but it had been called for by the peculiarity of the circumstances in which the Hurons were now placed. Their position was known to their foes, and it could not easily be changed at an hour which demanded rest. Perhaps, too, they placed most of their confidence on the knowledge of what they believed to be passing higher up the lake, and which, it was thought, would fully occupy the whole of the palefaces, who were at liberty, with their solitary Indian ally. It was also probable Rivenoak was aware that, in holding his captive, he had in his own hands the most dangerous of all his enemies.

The precision with which those accustomed to watchfulness, or lives of disturbed rest, sleep is not the least of the phenomena of our mysterious being. The head is no sooner on the pillow than consciousness is lost; and yet, at a necessary hour the mind appears to arouse the body as promptly as if it had stood sentinel over it the while. There can be no doubt that they who are thus roused awake by the influence of thought over matter, though the mode in which this influence is exercised must remain hidden from our curiosity until it shall be explained, should that hour ever arrive, by the entire enlightenment of the soul on the subject of all human mysteries. Thus it was with Hetty Hutter. Feeble as the immaterial portion of her existence was thought to be, it was sufficiently active to cause her to open her eyes at midnight. At that hour she awoke, and leaving her bed of skin and boughs, she walked innocently and openly to the embers of the fire, stirring the latter, as the coolness of the night and the woods, in connection with an exceedingly unsophisticated bed, had a little chilled her. As the flame shot up, it lighted the swarthy countenance of the Huron on watch, whose dark eyes glistened under its light, like the balls of the panther that is pursued to his den with burning brands. But Hetty felt no fear, and she approached the spot where the Indian stood. Her movements were so natural and so perfectly devoid of any of the stealthiness of cunning or deception that he imagined she had merely arisen on account of the coolness of the night, a common occurrence in a bivouac, and the one of all others, perhaps, the least likely to excite suspicion. Hetty spoke to him, but he understood no English. She then gazed near a minute at the sleeping captive and moved slowly away in a sad and melancholy manner.

The girl took no pains to conceal her movements. Any ingenious expedient of this nature quite likely exceeded her powers; still, her step was habitually light and scarcely audible. As she took the direction of the extremity of the point, or the place where she had landed in the first adventure, and where Hist had embarked, the sentinel saw her light form gradually disappear in the gloom without uneasiness or changing his own position. He knew that others were on the lookout, and he did not believe that one who had twice come into the camp voluntarily, and had already left it openly, would take refuge in flight. In short, the conduct of the girl excited no more attention than that on any person of feeble intellect would excite in civilized society, while her person met with more consideration and respect.

Hetty certainly had no very distinct notions of the localities, but she found her way to the beach, which she reached on the same side of the point as that on which the camp had been made. By following the margin of the water, taking a northern direction, she soon encountered the Indian who paced the strand as sentinel. This was a young warrior, and when he heard her light tread coming along the gravel, he approached swiftly, though with anything but menace in his manner. The darkness was so intense that it was not easy to discover forms, within the shadows of the woods, at the distance of twenty feet, and quite impossible to distinguish persons until near enough to touch them. The young Huron manifested disappointment when he found whom he had met, for, truth to say, he was expecting his favorite, who had promised to relieve the *ennui* of a midnight watch with her presence. This man was also ignorant of English, but he was at no loss to understand why the girl should be up at that hour. Such things were usual in an Indian village and camp, where sleep is as irregular as the meals. Then poor Hetty's known imbecility, as in most things connected with the savages, stood her friend on this occasion. Vexed at his disappointment, and impatient of the presence of one he thought an intruder, the young warrior signed for the girl to move forward, holding the direction of the beach. Hetty complied, but as she walked away, she spoke aloud in English, in her usual soft tones, which the stillness of the night made audible at some little distance.

"If you took me for a Huron girl, warrior," she said, "I don't wonder you are so little pleased. I am Hetty Hutter, Thomas Hutter's daughter, and have never met any man at night, for Mother always said it was wrong, and modest young women should never do it; modest young women of the palefaces, I mean; for customs are different in different parts of the world, I know. No, no, I'm Hetty Hutter, and wouldn't meet even Hurry Harry, though he should fall down on his knees and ask me! Mother said it was wrong."

By the time Hetty had said this, she reached the place where the canoes had come ashore, and owing to the curvature of the land and the bushes, would have been completely hid from the sight of the sentinel, had it been broad day. But another footstep caught the lover's ear, and he was already nearly beyond the sound of the girl's silvery voice. Still Hetty, bent only on her own thoughts and purposes, continued to speak, though the gentleness of her tones prevented the sounds from penetrating far into the woods. On the water they were more widely diffused.

"Here I am, Judith," she added, "and there is no one near me. The Huron on watch has gone to meet his sweetheart, who is an Indian girl, you know, and never had a Christian mother to tell her how wrong it is to meet a man at night—"

Hetty's voice was hushed by a "hist!" that came from the water, and then she caught a dim view of the canoe, which approached noiselessly and soon grated on the shingle with its bow. The moment the weight of Hetty was felt in the

light craft, the canoe withdrew, stern foremost, as if possessed
of life and volition, until it was a hundred yards from the
shore. Then it turned, and making a wide sweep, as much to
prolong the passage as to get beyond the sound of voices, it
held its way toward the ark. For several minutes nothing
was uttered; but, believing herself to be in a favorable position to confer with her sister, Judith, who alone sat in the
stern, managing the canoe with a skill little short of that of a
man, began a discourse which she had been burning to
commence ever since they quitted the point.

"Here we are safe, Hetty," she said, "and may talk without the fear of being overheard. You must speak low, however, for sounds are heard far on the water in a still night.
I was so close to the point, some of the time while you were
on it, that I have heard the voices of the warriors, and I
heard your shoes on the gravel of the beach even before you
spoke."

"I don't believe, Judith, the Hurons know I have left them."

"Quite likely they do not, for a lover makes a poor sentry,
unless it be to watch for his sweetheart! But tell me, Hetty,
did you see and speak with Deerslayer?"

"Oh, yes—there he was seated near the fire, with his legs
tied, though they left his arms free to move them as he
pleased."

"Well, what did he tell you, child? Speak quick; I am
dying to know what message he sent me."

"What did he tell me? Why, what do you think, Judith;
he told me that he couldn't read! Only think of that! A
white man, and not know how to read his Bible, even! He
never could have had a mother, sister!"

"Never mind *that*, Hetty. All men can't read; though Mother
knew so much, and taught us so much, Father knows very
little about books, and he can barely read the Bible, you
know."

"Oh! I never thought fathers *could* read much, but *mothers*
ought all to read, else how can they teach their children?
Depend on it, Judith, Deerslayer could never have had a
mother, else he would know how to read."

"Did you tell him *I* sent you ashore, Hetty, and how much
concern I feel for his misfortune?" asked the other impatiently.

"I believe I did, Judith, but you know I am feeble-minded,

and I may have forgotten. I *did* tell him you brought me
ashore. And he told me a great deal that I was to say to you,
which I remember well, for it made my blood run cold to
hear him. He told me to say that his friends—I suppose you
are one of them, sister—?"

"How can you torment me thus, Hetty! Certainly, I am
one of the truest friends he has on earth."

"Torment you! Yes, now I remember all about it. I am
glad you used that word, Judith, for it brings it all back to
my mind. Well, he said he might be *tormented* by the
savages, but he would try to bear it as becomes a Christian white
man, and that no one need be afeard—why does Deerslayer
call it afeard, when Mother has always taught us to say afraid?"

"Never mind, dear Hetty, never mind *that* now," cried the
other, almost gasping for breath. "Did Deerslayer really tell
you that he thought the savages would put him to the
torture? Recollect well now, Hetty, for this is a most awful
and serious thing."

"Yes, he did; and I remember it by your speaking about
my tormenting you. Oh! I felt very sorry for him, and
Deerslayer took all so quietly and without noise! Deerslayer is
not as handsome as Hurry Harry, Judith, but he is more quiet."

"He's worth a million Hurrys! Yes, he's worth all the
young men who ever came upon the lake put together,"
said Judith, with an energy and positiveness that caused
her sister to wonder. "He is *true*. There is no lie about
Deerslayer. *You*, Hetty, may not know what a merit it is in
a man to have truth, but when you get—no—I hope you
will never know it. Why should one like you be ever made
to learn the hard lesson to distrust and hate!"

Judith bowed her face, dark as it was, and unseen as she
must have been by any eye but that of Omniscience, between her hands and groaned. This sudden paroxysm of
feeling, however, lasted but for a moment, and she continued more calmly, still speaking frankly to her sister,
whose intelligence and whose discretion in anything that
related to herself she did not in the least distrust. Her voice,
however, was low and husky, instead of having its former
clearness and animation.

"It is a hard thing to fear truth, Hetty," she said, "and
yet do I more dread Deerslayer's truth than any enemy!
One cannot tamper with such truth—so much honesty—such

obstinate uprightness! But we are not altogether unequal, sister—Deerslayer and I? He is not altogether my superior?"

It was not usual for Judith so far to demean herself as to appeal to Hetty's judgment. Nor did she often address her by the title of sister, a distinction that is commonly given by the junior to the senior, even where there is perfect equality in all other respects. As trifling departures from habitual deportment oftener strike the imagination than more important changes, Hetty perceived the circumstances and wondered at them in her own simple way.

Her ambition was a little quickened, and the answer was as much out of the usual course of things as the question, the poor girl attempting to refine beyond her strength.

"Superior, Judith!" she repeated with pride. "In what *can* Deerslayer be *your* superior? Are you not Mother's child—and does he know how to read—and wasn't Mother before any woman in all this part of the world? I should think, so far from supposing himself *your* superior, he would hardly believe himself *mine*. You are handsome, and he is ugly——"

"No, not ugly, Hetty," interrupted Judith. "Only plain. But his honest face has a look in it that is far better than beauty. In my eyes Deerslayer is handsomer than Hurry Harry."

"Judith Hutter, you frighten me! Hurry is the handsomest mortal in the world—even handsomer than you are yourself, because a man's good looks, you know, are always better than a woman's good looks."

This little innocent touch of natural taste did not please the elder sister at the moment, and she did not scruple to betray it.

"Hetty, you now speak foolishly, and had better say no more on this subject," she answered. "Hurry is not the handsomest mortal in the world, by many; and there are officers in the garrisons"—Judith stammered at the words—"there are officers in the garrisons near us far comelier than he. But, why do you think me the equal of Deerslayer—speak of *that*, for I do not like to hear you show so much admiration of a man like Hurry Harry, who has neither feelings, manners, nor conscience. *You* are too good for *him*, and he ought to be told it at once."

"*I!* Judith, how you forget! Why *I* am not beautiful and am feeble-minded."

"You are *good*, Hetty, and that is more than can be said of Henry March. He may have a *face*, and a *body*, but he has no *heart*. But enough of this, for the present. Tell me what raises me to an equality with Deerslayer."

"To think of you asking me this, Judith! He can't read, and you can. He don't know how to talk, but speaks worse than Hurry even—for, sister, Hurry doesn't always pronounce his words right! Did you ever notice *that?*"

"Certainly, he is as coarse in speech as in everything else. But I fear you flatter me, Hetty, when you think I can be justly called the equal of a man like Deerslayer. It is true, I have been better taught; in one sense am more comely; and perhaps might look higher; but then his truth—his truth—makes a fearful difference between us! Well, I will talk no more of this, and we will bethink us of the means of getting him out of the hands of the Hurons. We have Father's chest in the ark, Hetty, and might try the temptation of more elephants, though I fear such baubles will not buy the liberty of a man like Deerslayer. I am afraid Father and Hurry will not be as willing to ransom Deerslayer as Deerslayer was to ransom them!"

"Why not, Judith? Hurry and Deerslayer are friends, and friends should always help one another."

"Alas, poor Hetty, you little know mankind! Seeming friends are often more to be dreaded than open enemies, particularly by females. But you'll have to land in the morning and try again what can be done for Deerslayer. Tortured he *shall* not be, while Judith Hutter lives and can find means to prevent it."

The conversation now grew desultory, and was drawn out, until the elder sister had extracted from the younger every fact that the feeble faculties of the latter permitted her to retain and to communicate. When Judith was satisfied—though she could never be said to be satisfied, whose feelings seemed to be so interwoven with all that related to the subject as to have excited a nearly inappeasable curiosity—but when Judith could think of no more questions to ask, without resorting to repetition, the canoe was paddled toward the scow. The intense darkness of the night and the deep shadows which the hills and forest cast upon the water rendered it difficult to find the vessel, anchored, as it had been, as close to the shore as a regard to safety rendered prudent. Judith was expert in the management of a bark canoe, the lightness of which demanded skill rather than strength, and she forced her own little vessel swiftly over the water the moment she had ended her conference with Hetty and had come to the determination to return. Still no ark was seen. Several times the sisters fancied they saw it, looming up in the obscurity, like a low black rock, but on each occasion it was found to be either an optical illusion, or some swell of the foliage on the shore. After a search that lasted half an hour, the girls were forced to the unwelcome conviction that the ark had departed.

Most young women would have felt the awkwardness of their situation, in a physical sense, under the circumstances in which the sisters were left, more than any apprehensions of a different nature. Not so with Judith, however, and even Hetty felt more concern about the motives that might have influenced her father and Hurry than any fears for her own safety.

"It cannot be, Hetty," said Judith, when a thorough search had satisfied them both that no ark was to be found, "it cannot be that the Indians have rafted, or swum off, and surprised our friends as they slept?"

"I don't believe that Hist and Chingachgook would sleep until they had told each other all they had to say after so long a separation—do you, sister?"

"Perhaps not, child. There was much to keep them awake, but one Indian may have been surprised even when not asleep, especially as his thoughts may have been on other things. Still, we should have heard a noise, for in a night like this an oath of Hurry Harry's would have echoed in the eastern hills like a clap of thunder."

"Hurry *is* sinful and thoughtless about his words, Judith," Hetty meekly and sorrowfully answered.

"No—no; 'tis impossible the ark could be taken and I not hear the noise. It is not an hour since I left it, and the whole time I have been attentive to the smallest sound. And yet it is not easy to believe a father would willingly abandon his children!"

"Perhaps Father has thought us in our cabin asleep, Judith, and has moved away to go home. You know we often move the ark in the night."

"This is true, Hetty, and it must be as you suppose. There

is a little more southern air than there was, and they have gone up the lake—"

Judith stopped, for as the last word was on her tongue, the scene was suddenly lighted, though only for a single instant, by a flash. The crack of a rifle succeeded, and then followed the roll of the echo along the eastern mountains. Almost at the same moment a piercing female cry arose in the air in a prolonged shriek. The awful stillness that succeeded was, if possible, more appalling than the fierce and sudden interruption of the deep silence of midnight. Resolute as she was both by nature and habit, Judith scarce breathed, while poor Hetty hid her face and trembled.

"That was a woman's cry, Hetty," said the former solemnly, "and it was a cry of anguish! If the ark has moved from this spot, it can only have gone north with this air, and the gun and shriek came from the point. Can anything have befallen Hist?"

"Let us go and see, Judith; she may want our assistance —for, besides herself, there are none but men in the ark."

It was not a moment for hesitation, and ere Judith had ceased speaking her paddle was in the water. The distance to the point in a direct line was not great, and the impulses under which the girls worked were too exciting to allow them to waste the precious moments in useless precautions. They paddled incautiously for them, but the same excitement kept others from noting their movements. Presently a glare of light caught the eye of Judith through an opening in the bushes, and steering by it she so directed the canoe as to keep it visible, while she got as near the land as was either prudent or necessary.

The scene that was now presented to the observation of the girls was within the woods, on the side of the declivity so often mentioned and in plain view from the boat. Here all in the camp were collected, some six or eight carrying torches of fat-pine, which cast a strong but funereal light on all beneath the arches of the forest. With her back supported against a tree, and sustained on one side by the young sentinel whose remissness had suffered Hetty to escape, sat the female whose expected visit had produced his delinquency. By the glare of the torch that was held near her face, it was evident that she was in the agonies of death, while the blood that trickled from her bared bosom betrayed the nature of the injury she had received. The pungent, peculiar smell of gunpowder, too, was still quite perceptible in the heavy, damp night air. There could be no question that she had been shot. Judith understood it all at a glance. The streak of light had appeared on the water a short distance from the point, and either the rifle had been discharged from a canoe hovering near the land, or it had been fired from the ark in passing. An incautious exclamation or laugh may have produced the assault, for it was barely possible that the aim had been assisted by any other agent than sound. As to the effect, that was soon still more apparent, the head of the victim dropping and the body sinking in death. Then all the torches but one were extinguished—a measure of prudence—and the melancholy train that bore the body to the camp was just to be distinguished by the glimmering light that remained.

Judith sighed heavily and shuddered as her paddle again dipped and the canoe moved cautiously around the point. A sight had afflicted her senses, and now haunted her imagination, that was still harder to be borne than even the untimely fate and passing agony of the deceased girl. She had seen, under the strong glare of all the torches, the erect form of Deerslayer, standing, with commiseration and, as she thought, with shame depicted on his countenance, near the dying female. He betrayed neither fear nor backwardness, *himself*, but it was apparent by the glances cast at him by the warriors that fierce passions were struggling in *their* bosoms. All this seemed to be unheeded by the captive, but it remained impressed on the memory of Judith throughout the night.

No canoe was met hovering near the point. A stillness and darkness, as complete as if the silence of the forest had never been disturbed, or the sun had never shone on that retired region, now reigned on the point, and on the gloomy water, the slumbering woods, and even the murky sky. No more could be done, therefore, than to seek a place of safety, and this was only to be found in the center of the lake. Paddling, in silence, to that spot, the canoe was suffered to drift northerly, while the girls sought such repose as their situation and feelings would permit.

CHAPTER XIX

Stand to your arms, and guard the door—all's lost
Unless that fearful bell be silenced soon.
The officer hath missed his path, or purpose,
Or met some unforeseen and hideous obstacle.
Anselmo, with thy company proceed
Straight to the tower; the rest remain with me.

MARINO FALIERO

THE CONJECTURE OF Judith Hutter concerning the manner in which the Indian girl had met her death was accurate in the main. After sleeping several hours, her father and March awoke. This occurred a few minutes after she had left the ark to go in quest of her sister, and when of course Chingachgook and his betrothed were on board. From the Delaware the old man learned the position of the camp, and the recent events, as well as the absence of his daughters. The latter gave him no concern, for he relied greatly on the sagacity of the eldest and the known impunity with which the younger passed among the savages. Long familiarity with danger, too, had blunted his sensibilities. Nor did he seem much to regret the captivity of Deerslayer, for while he knew how material his aid might be in a defense, the difference in their views on the morality of the woods had not left much sympathy between them. He would have rejoiced to know the position of the camp before it had been alarmed by the escape of Hist, but it would be too hazardous now to venture to land; and he reluctantly relinquished for the night the ruthless designs that captivity and revenge had excited him to entertain. In this mood Hutter took a seat in the head of the scow, where he was quickly joined by Hurry, leaving the Serpent and Hist in quiet possession of the other extremity of the vessel.

"Deerslayer has shown himself a boy in going among the savages at this hour and letting himself fall into their hands like a deer that tumbles into a pit," growled the old man, perceiving as usual the mote in his neighbor's eyes while he overlooked the beam in his own. "If he is left to pay for his stupidity with his own flesh, he can blame no one but himself."

"That's the way of the world, Old Tom," returned Hurry. "Every man must meet his own debts and answer for his own sins. I'm amazed, however, that a lad as skillful and watchful as Deerslayer should have been caught in such a trap! Didn't he know any better than to go prowling about a Huron camp, at midnight, with no place to retreat to but a lake? Or did he think himself a buck that, by taking to the water, could throw off the scent and swim himself out of difficulty? I had a better opinion of the boy's judgment, I'll own; but we must overlook a little ignorance in a raw hand. I say, Master Hutter, do you happen to know what has become of the gals? I see no signs of Judith or Hetty, though I've been through the ark and looked into all its living creatur's."

Hutter briefly explained the manner in which his daughters had taken to the canoe, as it had been related by the Delaware, as well as the return of Judith after landing her sister and her second departure.

"This comes of a smooth tongue, Floating Tom," exclaimed Hurry, grating his teeth in pure resentment—"this comes of a smooth tongue, and a silly gal's inclinations—and you had best look into the matter! You and I were both prisoners"—Hurry could recall that circumstance *now*—"you and I were both prisoners, and yet Judith never stirred an inch to do us any service! She is bewitched with this lank-looking Deerslayer, and he, and she, and you, and all of us had best look to it. I am not a man to put up with such a wrong quietly, and do say, all the parties had best look to it! Let's up kedge, old fellow, and move nearer to this point, and see how matters are getting on."

Hutter had no objections to this movement, and the ark was got under way in the usual manner, care being taken to make no noise. The wind was passing northward, and the sail soon swept the scow so far up the lake as to render the dark outlines of the trees that clothed the point dimly visible. Floating Tom steered, and he sailed along as near the land as the depth of the water and the overhanging branches would allow. It was impossible to distinguish anything that stood within the shadows of the shore, but the forms of the sail and of the hut were discerned by the young sentinel on the beach, who has already been mentioned. In the moment of sudden surprise, a deep Indian exclamation escaped him. In that spirit of recklessness and ferocity that formed the essence of Hurry's character, this man dropped his rifle and fired. The ball was sped by accident, or by that overruling Providence which decides the fates of all, and the girl fell. Then followed the scene with the torches, which has just been described.

At the precise moment when Hurry committed this act of unthinking cruelty, the canoe of Judith was within a hundred feet of the spot from which the ark had so lately moved. Her own course has been described, and it has now become our office to follow that of her father and his companions. The shriek announced the effects of the random shot of March, and it also proclaimed that the victim was a woman. Hurry himself was startled at these unlooked-for consequences, and for a moment he was sorely disturbed by conflicting sensations. At first he laughed, in reckless and rude-minded exultation, and then conscience, that moniter planted in our breasts by God and which receives its more general growth from the training bestowed in the tillage of childhood, shot a pang to his heart. For a minute the mind of this creature, equally of civilization and barbarism, was a sort of chaos as to feeling, not knowing what to think of its own act; then the obstinacy and pride of one of his habits interposed to assert their usual ascendency. He struck the butt of his rifle on the bottom of the scow with a species of defiance and began to whistle a low air with an affectation of indifference. All this time the ark was in motion, and it was already opening the bay above the point, and was consequently quitting the land.

Hurry's companions did not view his conduct with the same indulgence as that with which he appeared disposed to regard it himself. Hutter growled out his dissatisfaction, for the act led to no advantage, while it threatened to render the warfare more vindictive than ever, and none censure motiveless departures from the right more severely than the mercenary and unprincipled. Still, he commanded himself, the captivity of Deerslayer rendering the arm of the offender of double consequence to him at that moment. Chingachgook arose, and for a single instant the ancient animosity of tribes was forgotten in a feeling of color, but he recollected himself in season to prevent any of the fierce consequences that for a passing moment he certainly meditated. Not so with Hist. Rushing through the hut, or cabin, the girl stood at the side of Hurry, almost as soon as his rifle touched the bottom of the scow, and with a fearlessness that did credit to her heart, she poured out her reproaches with the generous warmth of a woman.

"What for you shoot?" she said. "What Huron gal do dat you kill her? What you t'ink Manitou *say?* What you t'ink Manitou *feel?* What Iroquois *do?* No get honor—no get camp—no get prisoner—no get battle—no get scalp—no get not'ing at all. Blood come after blood! How you feel your wife killed? Who pity you when tear come for moder or sister? You big as great pine—Huron gal little slender birch—why you fall on her and crush her? You t'ink Huron forget it? No, redskin never forget. Never forget friend; never forget enemy. Red man Manitou in *dat.* Why you so wicked, great paleface?"

Hurry had never been so daunted as by this close and warm attack of the Indian girl. It is true that she had a powerful ally in his conscience, and while she spoke earnestly, it was in tones so feminine as to deprive him of any pretext for unmanly anger. The softness of her voice added to the weight of her remonstrance by lending to the latter an air of purity and truth. Like most vulgar-minded men, he had only regarded the Indians through the medium of their coarser and fiercer characteristics. It had never struck him that the affections are human; that even high principles —modified by habits and prejudices, but not the less elevated within their circle—can exist in the savage state; and that the warrior who is most ruthless in the field can submit to the softest and gentlest influences in the moments of domestic quiet. In a word, it was the habit of his mind to regard all Indians as being only a slight degree removed from the wild beasts that roamed the woods, and to feel disposed to treat them accordingly, whenever interest or caprice supplied a motive or an impulse. Still, though daunted by these reproaches, the handsome barbarian could hardly be said to be penitent. He was too much rebuked by conscience to suffer an outbreak of temper to escape him, and perhaps he felt that he had already committed an act that might justly bring his manhood in question. Instead of resenting, or answering the simple but natural appeal of Hist, he walked away like one who disdained entering into a controversy with a woman.

In the meanwhile the ark swept onward, and by the time the scene with the torches was enacting beneath the trees, it had reached the open lake; Floating Tom causing it to sheer further from the land with a sort of instinctive dread of retaliation. An hour now passed in gloomy silence, no one appearing disposed to break it. Hist had retired to her pallet, and Chingachgook lay sleeping in the forward part of the scow. Hutter and Hurry alone remained awake, the former at the steering oar, while the latter brooded over his own conduct with the stubbornness of one little given to a confession of his errors and the secret goadings of the worm that never dies. This was at the moment when Judith and Hetty reached the center of the lake, and had lain down to endeavor to sleep in their drifting canoe.

The night was calm, though so much obscured by clouds. The season was not one of storms, and those which did occur in the month of June on that embedded water, though frequently violent, were always of short continuance. Nevertheless, there was the usual current of heavy, damp night air, which, passing over the summits of the trees, scarcely appeared to descend so low as the surface of the glassy lake, but kept moving a short distance above it, saturated with the humidity that constantly arose from the woods and apparently never proceeding far in any one direction. The currents were influenced by the formation of the hills, as a matter of course—a circumstance that rendered even fresh breezes baffling, and which reduced the feebler efforts of the night air to a sort of capricious and fickle sighings of the woods. Several times the head of the ark pointed east, and once it was actually turned toward the south again, but on the whole, it worked its way north, Hutter making always a fair wind, if wind it could be called, his principal motive appearing to be a wish to keep in motion, in order to defeat any treacherous design of his enemies. He now felt some little concern about his daughters, and perhaps as much about the canoe, but on the whole, this uncertainty did not much disturb him, as he had the reliance already mentioned on the intelligence of Judith.

It was the season of the shortest nights, and it was not long before the deep obscurity which precedes the day began to yield to the returning light. If any earthly scene could be presented to the senses of man that might soothe his passions and temper his ferocity, it was that which grew upon the eyes of Hutter and Hurry as the hours advanced, changing night to morning. There were the usual soft tints of the sky in which neither the gloom of darkness nor the brilliancy of the sun prevails, and under which objects appear more unearthly and, we might add, holy than at any other portion of the twenty-four hours. The beautiful and soothing calm of eventide has been extolled by a thousand poets, and yet it does not bring with it the far-reaching and sublime thoughts of the half hour that precedes the rising of a summer's sun. In the one case the panorama is gradually hid from the sight, while in the other its objects start out from the unfolding picture, first dim and misty, then marked in in solemn background; next seen in the witchery of an *increasing,* a thing as different as possible from the *decreasing* twilight, and finally mellow, distinct, and luminous as the rays of the great center of light diffuse themselves in the atmosphere. The hymns of birds, too, have no novel counterpart in the retreat to the roost, or the flight to the nest, and these invariably accompany the advent of the day, until the appearance of the sun itself

Bathes in deep joy, the land and sea.

All this, however, Hutter and Hurry witnessed without experiencing any of that calm delight which the spectacle is wont to bring when the thoughts are just and the aspirations pure. They not only witnessed it, but they witnessed it under circumstances that had a tendency to increase its power and to heighten its charms. Only one solitary object became visible, in the returning light, that had received its form or uses from human taste or human desires, which as often deform as beautify a landscape. This was the castle, all the rest being native and fresh from the hand of God. That singular residence, too, was in keeping with the natural objects of the view, starting out from the gloom—quaint, picturesque, and ornamental. Nevertheless, the whole was lost on the observers, who knew no feeling of poetry, had lost their sense of natural devotion in lives of obdurate and narrow selfishness, and had little other sympathy with nature than that which originated with her lowest wants.

As soon as the light was sufficiently strong to allow of a distinct view of the lake, and more particularly of its shores, Hutter turned the head of the ark directly toward the castle, with the avowed intention of taking possession for the day at least, as the place most favorable for meeting his daughters and for carrying on his operations against the Indians. By this time, Chingachgook was up, and Hist was heard stirring among the furniture of the kitchen. The place for which they steered was distant only a mile, and the air was sufficiently favorable to permit it to be neared by means of the sail. At this moment, too, to render the appearances generally auspicious, the canoe of Judith was seen floating northward in the broadest part of the lake, having actually passed the scow in the darkness, in obedience to no other power than that of the elements. Hutter got his glass and took a long and anxious survey to ascertain if his daughters were in the light craft or not, and a slight exclamation like that of joy escaped him as he caught a glimpse of what he rightly conceived to be a part of Judith's dress above the top of the canoe. At the next instant, the girl arose, and was seen gazing about her, like one assuring herself of her situation. A minute later, Hetty was seen on her knees, in the other end of the canoe, repeating the prayers that had been taught her in childhood by a misguided but repentant mother. As Hutter laid down the glass, still drawn to its focus, the Serpent raised it to his eye and turned it toward the canoe. It was the first time he had ever used such an instrument, and Hist understood by his "hugh!" the expression of his face, and his entire mien that something wonderful had excited his admiration. It is well known that the American Indians, more particularly those of superior character and stations, singularly maintain their self-possession and stoicism in the midst of the flood of marvels that present themselves in their occasional visits to the abodes of civilization; Chingachgook had imbibed enough of this impassibility to suppress any very undignified manifestation of surprise. With Hist, however, no such law was binding, and when her lover managed to bring the glass in a line with a canoe, and her eye was applied to the smaller end, the girl started back in alarm; then she clapped her hands with delight, and a laugh, the usual attendant of untutored admiration, followed. A few minutes sufficed to enable this quick-witted girl to manage the instrument for herself, and she directed it at every prominent object that struck her fancy. Finding a rest in one of the windows, she and the Delaware first surveyed the lake, then the shores, the hills, and finally the castle attracted their attention. After a long, steady gaze at the latter, Hist took away her eye and spoke to her lover in a low, earnest manner. Chingachgook immediately placed his eye to the glass, and his look even exceeded that of his betrothed, in length and intensity. Again they spoke together confidentially, appearing to compare opinions, after which the glass was laid aside, and the young warrior quitted the cabin to join Hutter and Hurry.

The ark was slowly but steadily advancing, and the castle was materially within half a mile, when Chingachgook joined the two white men in the stern of the scow. His manner was calm, but it was evident to the others, who were familiar with the habits of the Indians, that he had something to communicate. Hurry was generally prompt to speak, and according to custom, he took the lead on this occasion.

"Out with it, redskin," he cried, in his usual rough manner. "Have you discovered a chipmunk in a tree, or is there a salmon trout swimming under the bottom of the scow? You find what a paleface can do in the way of eyes, now, Sarpent, and mustn't wonder that they can see the land of the Indians from afar off."

"No good to go to castle," put in Chingachgook with emphasis, the moment the other gave him an opportunity of speaking. "Huron there."

"The Devil he is! If this should turn out to be true, Floating Tom, a pretty trap were we about to pull down on our heads! Huron there!—well, this may be so, but no signs can I see of anything near or about the old hut but logs, water, and bark—'bating two or three windows and one door."

Hutter called for the glass and took a careful survey of the spot before he ventured an opinion at all; then he somewhat cavalierly expressed his dissent from that given by the Indian.

"You've got this glass wrong end foremost, Delaware," continued Hurry; "neither the old man nor I can see any trail in the lake."

"No trail—water make no trail," said Hist eagerly. "Stop boat—no go too near—Huron there!"

"Aye, that's it! Stick to the same tale and more people will believe you. I hope, Sarpent, you and your gal will agree in telling the same story arter marriage as well as you do now. Huron there!—whereabouts is he to be seen—in the padlock, or the chains, or the logs? There isn't a jail in the Colony that has a more lock-up look about it than old Tom's *chiente;* and I know something about jails from exper'ence."

"No see moccasin," said Hist impatiently, "why no *look*—and see him."

"Give me the glass, Harry," interrupted Hutter, "and lower the sail. It is seldom that an Indian woman meddles, and when she does, there is generally a cause for it. There *is,* truly, a moccasin floating against one of the piles, and it may or may not be a sign that the castle hasn't escaped visitors in our absence. Moccasins are no rarities, however, for I wear 'em myself, and Deerslayer wears 'em, and you wear 'em, March; and for that matter, so does Hetty, quite as often as she wears shoes; though I never yet saw Judith trust her pretty foot in a moccasin."

Hurry had lowered the sail, and by this time the ark was within two hundred yards of the castle, setting in nearer and nearer each moment, but at a rate too slow to excite any uneasiness. Each now took the glass in turn, and the castle and everything near it was subjected to a scrutiny still more rigid than ever. There the moccasin lay, beyond a question, floating so lightly and preserving its form so well that it was scarcely wet. It had caught by a piece of the rough bark of one of the piles on the exterior of the water palisade that formed the dock already mentioned, which circumstance alone prevented it from drifting away before the air. There were many modes, however, of accounting for the presence of the moccasin without supposing it to have been dropped by an enemy. It might have fallen from the platform even while Hutter was in possession of the place and drifted to the spot where it was now seen, remaining unnoticed until detected by the acute vision of Hist. It might have drifted from a distance up or down the lake, and accidentally become attached to the pile or palisade. It might have been thrown from a window and alighted in that particular place; or it might certainly have fallen from a scout or an assailant during the past night, who was obliged to abandon it to the lake in the deep obscurity which then prevailed.

All these conjectures passed from Hutter to Hurry, the former appearing disposed to regard the omen as a little sinister, while the latter treated it with his usual reckless disdain. As for the Indian, he was of opinion that the moccasin should be viewed as one would regard a trail in the woods which might or might not equally prove to be threatening. Hist, however, had something available to propose. She declared her readiness to take a canoe, proceed to the palisade, and bring away the moccasin, when its ornaments would show whether it came from the Canadas or not. Both the white men were disposed to accept this offer, but the Delaware interfered to prevent the risk. If such a service was to be undertaken, it best became a warrior to expose himself in its execution, and he gave his refusal to let his betrothed proceed much in the quiet but brief manner in which an Indian husband issues his commands.

"Well, then, Delaware, go yourself if you're so tender of your squaw," put in the unceremonious Hurry. "That moccasin must be had, or Floating Tom will keep off here at arm's length till the hearth cools in his cabin. It's but a little deerskin arter all, and cut thisaway or thataway, it's not a skearcrow to frighten true hunters from their game. What say you, Sarpent, shall you or I canoe it?"

"Let red man go. Better eyes than paleface—know Huron trick better, too."

"That I'll gainsay, to the hour of my death! A white man's eyes, and a white man's nose, and for that matter his sight and ears, are all better than an Injin's, when fairly tried. Time and ag'in have I put that to the proof, and what is proved is sartain. Still I suppose the poorest vagabond going, whether Delaware or Huron, can find his way to yonder hut and back ag'in; and so, Sarpent, use your paddle and welcome."

Chingachgook was already in the canoe, and he dipped the implement the other named into the water just as Hurry's limber tongue ceased. Wah-ta!-Wah saw the departure of her warrior on this occasion with the submissive silence of an Indian girl, but with most of the misgivings and apprehensions of her sex. Throughout the whole of the past night, and down to the moment when they used the glass together in the hut, Chingachgook had manifested as much manly tenderness toward his betrothed as one of the most refined sentiments could have shown under similar circumstances, but now every sign of weakness was lost in an appearance of stern resolution. Although Hist timidly endeavored to catch his eye as the canoe left the side of the ark, the pride of a warrior would not permit him to meet her fond and anxious looks. The canoe departed, and not a wandering glance rewarded her solicitude.

Nor were the Delaware's care and gravity misplaced, under the impressions with which he proceeded on this enterprise. If the enemy had really gained possession of the building, he was obliged to put himself under the very muzzles of their rifles, as it were, and this too without the protection of any of that cover which forms so essential an ally in Indian warfare. It is scarcely possible to conceive of a service more dangerous, and had the Serpent been fortified by the experience of ten more years—or had his friend, the Deerslayer, been present—it would never have been attempted, the advantages in no degree compensating for the risk. But the pride of an Indian chief was acted on by the rivalry of color, and it is not unlikely that the presence of the very creature from whom his ideas of manhood prevented his receiving a single glance, overflowing as he was with the love she so well merited, had no small influence on his determination.

Chingachgook paddled steadily toward the palisades, keeping his eye on the different loops of the building. Each instant he expected to see the muzzle of a rifle protruded, or to hear its sharp crack, but he succeeded in reaching the piles in safety. Here he was, in a measure, protected, having the heads of the palisades between him and the hut; the chances of any attempt on his life, while thus covered, were greatly diminished. The canoe had reached the piles with its head inclining northward, at a short distance from the moccasin. Instead of turning to pick up the latter, the Delaware slowly made the circuit of the whole building, deliberately examining every object that should betray the presence of enemies, or the commission of violence. Not a single sign could be discovered, however, to confirm the suspicions that had been awakened. The stillness of desertion pervaded the building; not a fastening was displaced; not a window had been broken. The door looked as secure as at the hour when it was closed by Hutter, and even the gate of the dock had all the customary fastenings. In short, the most wary and jealous eye could detect no other evidence of the visit of enemies than that which was connected with the appearance of the floating moccasin.

The Delaware was now greatly at a loss how to proceed. At one moment, as he came round in front of the castle, he was on the point of stepping up on the platform, and of applying his eye to one of the loops, with a view of taking a direct personal inspection of the state of things within; but he hesitated. Though of little experience in such matters, himself, he had heard so much of Indian artifices through traditions, had listened with such breathless interest to the narration of the escapes of the elder warriors, and, in short, was so well schooled in the theory of his calling, that it was almost as impossible for him to make any gross blunder on such an occasion, as it was for a well-grounded scholar, who had commenced correctly, to fail in solving his problem in mathematics. Relinquishing the momentary intention to land, the chief slowly pursued his course round the palisades. As he approached the moccasin—having now nearly completed the circuit of the building—he threw the ominous article into the canoe, by a dexterous and almost imperceptible movement of his paddle. He was now ready to depart; but retreat was even more dangerous than the approach, as the eye could no longer be riveted on the loops. If there was really anyone in the castle, the motive of the Delaware in reconnoitering must be understood; and it was the wisest way, however perilous it might be, to retire with an air of confidence, as if all distrust were terminated by the examination. Such, accordingly, was the course adopted by the Indian, who paddled deliberately away, taking the direction of the ark, suffering no nervous impulse to quicken the motions of his arms, or to induce him to turn even a furtive glance behind him.

No tender wife, reared in the refinements of the highest

civilization, ever met a husband on his return from the field, with more of sensibility in her countenance than Hist discovered as she saw the Great Serpent of the Delawares step, unharmed, into the ark. Still, she repressed her emotions, though the joy that sparkled in her dark eyes, and the smile that lighted her pretty mouth spoke a language that her betrothed could understand.

"Well, Sarpent," cried Hurry, always the first to speak, "what news from the muskrats? Did they show their teeth, as you surrounded their dwelling?"

"I no like him," sententiously returned the Delaware. "Too still. So still, can see silence!"

"That's downright Injin—as if anything could make less noise than nothing! If you've no better reason than this to give, Old Tom had better hoist his sail and go and get his breakfast under his own roof. What has become of the moccasin?"

"Here," returned Chingachgook, holding up his prize for the general inspection.

The moccasin was examined, and Hist confidently pronounced it to be Huron, by the manner in which the porcupine's quills were arranged on its front. Hutter, and the Delaware, too, were decidedly of the same opinion. Admitting all this, however, it did not necessarily follow that its owners were in the castle. The moccasin might have drifted from a distance, or it might have fallen from the foot of some scout who had quitted the place when his errand was accomplished. In short, it explained nothing, while it awakened so much distrust.

Under the circumstances, Hutter and Hurry were not men to be long deterred from proceeding by proofs as slight as that of the moccasin. They hoisted the sail again, and the ark was soon in motion, heading toward the castle. The wind, or air, continued light, and the movement was sufficiently slow to allow of a deliberate survey of the building as the scow approached.

The same deathlike silence reigned, and it was difficult to fancy that anything possessing animal life could be in or around the place. Unlike the Serpent, whose imagination had acted through his traditions until he was ready to perceive an artificial in a natural stillness, the others saw nothing to apprehend in a tranquillity that, in truth, merely denoted the repose of inanimate objects. The accessories of the scene, too, were soothing and calm, rather than exciting. The day had not yet advanced so far as to bring the sun above the horizon, but the heavens, the atmosphere, and the woods and lake were all seen under that softened light which immediately precedes his appearance and which, perhaps, is the most witching period of the four-and-twenty hours. It is the moment when everything is distinct, even the atmosphere seeming to possess a liquid lucidity, the hues appearing gray and softened, with the outlines of objects diffused, and the perspective just as moral truths that are presented in their simplicity without the meretricious aids of ornament or glitter. In a word, it is the moment when the senses seem to recover their powers in the simplest and most accurate forms, like the mind emerging from the obscurity of doubts into the tranquillity and peace of demonstration. Most of the influence that such a scene is apt to produce on those who are properly constituted in a moral sense was lost on Hutter and Hurry, but both the Delawares, though too much accustomed to witness the loveliness of morningtide to stop to analyze their feelings, were equally sensible of the beauties of the hour, though it was probably in a way unknown to themselves. It disposed the young warrior to peace, and never had he felt less longings for the glory of the combat than when he joined Hist in the cabin the instant the scow rubbed against the side of the platform. From the indulgence of such gentle emotions, however, he was aroused by a rude summons from Hurry, who called on him to come forth and help to take in the sail and to secure the ark.

Chingachgook obeyed, and by the time he had reached the head of the scow, Hurry was on the platform, stamping his feet, like one glad to touch what, by comparison, might be called terra firma, and proclaiming his indifference to the whole Huron tribe in his customary noisy, dogmatical manner. Hutter had hauled a canoe up to the head of the scow, and was already about to undo the fastenings of the gate, in order to enter within the dock. March had no other motive in landing than a senseless bravado, and having shaken the door in a manner to put its solidity to the proof, he joined Hutter in the canoe and began to aid him in opening the gate. The reader will remember that this mode of entrance was rendered necessary by the manner in which the owner of this singular residence habitually secured it whenever it was left empty; more particularly at moments when danger was apprehended. Hutter had placed a line in the Delaware's hand, on entering the canoe, intimating that the other was to fasten the ark to the platform and to lower the sail. Instead of following these directions, however, Chingachgook left the sail standing, and throwing the bight of the rope over the head of a pile, he permitted the ark to drift around until it lay against the defenses in a position where it could be entered only by means of a boat, or by passing along the summits of the palisades—the latter being an exploit that required some command of the feet, and which was not to be attempted in the face of a resolute enemy.

In consequence of this change in the position of the scow, which was effected before Hutter had succeeded in opening the gate of his dock, the ark and the castle lay, as sailors would express it, yardarm and yardarm, kept asunder some ten or twelve feet by means of the piles. As the scow pressed close against the latter, their tops formed a species of breastwork that rose to the height of a man's head, covering in a certain degree the parts of the scow that were not protected by the cabin. The Delaware surveyed this arrangement with great satisfaction, and as the canoe of Hutter passed through the gate into the dock, he thought that he might defend his position against any garrison in the castle for a sufficient time, could he but have had the helping arm of his friend Deerslayer. As it was, he felt comparatively secure and no longer suffered the keen apprehensions he had lately experienced in behalf of Hist.

A single shove sent the canoe from the gate to the trap beneath the castle. Here Hutter found all fast, neither padlock, nor chain, nor bar having been molested. The key was produced, the locks removed, the chain loosened, and the trap pushed upward. Hurry now thrust his head in at the opening; the arms followed, and the colossal legs rose without any apparent effort. At the next instant, his heavy foot was heard stamping in the passage above—that which separated the chambers of the father and daughters, and into which the trap opened. He then gave a shout of triumph.

"Come on, old Tom," the reckless woodsman called out from within the building. "Here's your tenement, safe and sound; aye, and as empty as a nut that has passed half an hour in the paws of a squirrel! The Delaware brags of being able to *see* silence; let him come here, and he may *feel* it in the bargain."

"Any silence where you are, Hurry Harry," returned Hutter, thrusting his head in at the hole as he uttered the last word, which instantly caused his voice to sound smothered to those without—"any silence where you are ought to be both seen and felt, for it's unlike any other silence."

"Come, come—old fellow; hoist yourself up, and we'll open doors and windows and let in the fresh air to brighten up matters. Few words, in troublesome times, make men the best fri'nds. Your darter Judith is what I call a misbehaving young woman, and the hold of the whole family on me is so much weakened by her late conduct that it wouldn't take a speech as long as the ten commandments to send me off to the river, leaving you and your traps, your ark and your children, your manservants and your maidservants, your oxen and your asses, to fight this battle with the Iroquois by yourselves. Open that window, Floating Tom, and I'll blunder through and do the same job to the front door."

A moment of silence succeeded, and a noise like that produced by the fall of a heavy body followed. A deep execration from Hurry succeeded, and then the whole interior of the building seemed alive. The noises that now so suddenly —and, we may add, so unexpectedly, even to the Delaware —broke the stillness within could not be mistaken. They resembled those that would be produced by a struggle between tigers in a cage. Once or twice the Indian yell was given, but it seemed smothered, and as if it proceeded from exhausted or compressed throats, and in a single instance, a deep and another shockingly revolting execration came from the throat of Hurry. It appeared as if bodies were constantly thrown upon the floor with violence, as often rising to renew the struggle. Chingachgook felt greatly at a loss what to do. He had all the arms in the ark, Hutter and Hurry having proceeded without their rifles, but there was no means of using them, or of passing them to the hands of their owners. The combatants were literally caged, rendering it almost as impossible, under the circumstances, to get out as to get into the building. Then there was Hist to embarrass his movements and to cripple his efforts. With a view to relieve himself from this disadvantage, he told the girl to take the remaining canoe and to join Hutter's daughters, who were incautiously but deliberately approaching, in order to save herself and to warn the others of their danger. But the girl positively and firmly refused to comply. At that moment, no human power, short of an exercise of superior physical force, could have induced her to quit the ark. The exigency of the moment did not admit of delay, and the Delaware, seeing no possibility of serving his friends, cut the line and, by a strong shove, forced the scow some twenty feet clear of the piles. Here he took the sweeps and succeeded in getting a short distance to windward, if any direction could be thus termed in so light an air, but neither the time nor his skill at the oars allowed the distance to be great. When he ceased rowing, the ark might have been a hundred yards from the platform, and half that distance to the southward of it, the sail being lowered. Judith and Hetty had now discovered that something was wrong, and were stationary a thousand feet further north.

All this while the furious struggle continued within the house. In scenes like these, events thicken in less time than they can be related. From the moment when the first fall was heard within the building to that when the Delaware ceased his awkward attempts to row, it might have been three or four minutes, but it had evidently served to weaken the combatants. The oaths and execrations of Hurry were no longer heard, and even the struggles had lost some of their force and fury; nevertheless, they still continued with unabated perseverance. At this instant the door flew open and the fight was transferred to the platform, the light, and the open air.

A Huron had undone the fastenings of the door, and three or four of his tribe rushed after him upon the narrow space, as if glad to escape from some terrible scene within. The body of another followed, pitched headlong through the door with terrific violence. Then March appeared, raging like a lion at bay, and for an instant freed from his numerous enemies. Hutter was already a captive and bound. There was now a pause in the struggle which resembled a lull in a tempest. The necessity of breathing was common to all, and the combatants stood watching each other, like mastiffs that have been driven from their holds and are waiting for a favorable opportunity of renewing them. We shall profit by this pause to relate the manner in which the Indians had obtained possession of the castle; and this the more willingly because it may be necessary to explain to the reader why a conflict which had been so close and fierce should have also been so comparatively bloodless.

Rivenoak and his companion, particularly the latter, who had appeared to be a subordinate and occupied solely with his raft, had made the closest observations in their visits to the castle; even the boy had brought away minute and valuable information. By these means the Hurons obtained a general idea of the manner in which the place was constructed and secured, as well as of details that enabled them to act intelligently in the dark. Notwithstanding the care that Hutter had taken to drop the ark on the east side of the building, when he was in the act of transferring the furniture from the former to the latter, he had been watched in a way to render the precaution useless. Scouts were on the lookout on the eastern as well as on the western shore of the lake, and the whole proceeding had been noted. As soon as it was dark, rafts like that already described approached from both shores to reconnoiter, and the ark had passed within fifty feet of one of them without its being discovered, the men it held lying at their length on the logs, so as to blend themselves and their slow-moving machine with the water. When these two sets of adventurers drew near the castle, they encountered each other, and after communicating their respective observations, they unhesitatingly approached the building. As had been expected, it was found empty. The rafts were immediately sent for a reinforcement to the shore, and two of the savages remained to profit by their situation. These men succeeded in getting on the roof and, by removing some of the bark, in entering what might be termed the garret. Here they were found by their companions. Hatchets now opened a hole through the square logs of the upper floor, through which no less than eight of the most athletic of the Indians dropped into the room beneath. Here they were left, well supplied with arms and provisions, either to stand a siege, or to make a sortie, as the case might require. The night was passed in sleep, as is usual with Indians in a state of inactivity. The returning day brought them a view of the approach of the ark, through the loops, the only manner in which light and air were now admitted, the windows being closed most effectually with plank, rudely fashioned to fit. As soon as it was ascertained that the two white men were about to enter by the trap, the chief, who directed the proceedings of the Hurons, took his measures accordingly. He removed all the arms from his own people, even to the knives, in distrust of savage ferocity, when awakened by personal injuries, and he hid them where they could not be found without a search. Ropes of bark were then prepared, and taking their stations in the three different rooms, they all waited for the signal to fall upon their intended captives. As soon as the party had entered the building, men without replaced the bark of the roof, removed every sign of their visit with care, and then departed for the shore. It was one of these who had dropped his moccasin, which he had not been able to find again, in the dark. Had the death of the girl been known, it is probable nothing could have saved the lives of Hurry and Hutter, but that event occurred after the ambush was laid, and at a distance of several miles from the encampment near the castle. Such were the means that had been employed to produce the state of things we shall continue to describe.

CHAPTER XX

Now all is done that man can do,
And all is done in vain!
My love! my native land, adieu,
For I must cross the main;
My dear,
For I must cross the main.

SCOTTISH BALLAD

IN THE LAST chapter we left the combatants breathing in their narrow lists. Accustomed to the rude sports of wrestling and jumping then so common in America, more especially on the frontiers, Hurry possessed an advantage, in addition to his prodigious strength, that had rendered the struggle less unequal than it might otherwise appear to be. This alone had enabled him to hold out so long against so many enemies, for the Indian is by no means remarkable for his skill or force in athletic exercises. As yet, no one had been seriously hurt, though several of the savages had received severe falls; and he, in particular, who had been thrown bodily upon the platform, might be said to be temporarily *hors de combat*. Some of the rest were limping, and March himself had not entirely escaped from bruises, though want of breath was the principal loss that both sides wished to repair.

Under circumstances like those in which the parties were placed, a truce, let it come from what cause it might, could not well be of long continuance. The arena was too confined, and the distrust of treachery too great, to admit of this. Contrary to what might be expected in his situation, Hurry was the first to recommence hostilities. Whether this proceeded from policy or an idea that he might gain some advantage by making a sudden and unexpected assault, or was the fruit of irritation and his undying hatred of an Indian, it is impossible to say. His onset was furious, however, and at first it carried all before it. He seized the nearest Huron by the waist, raised him entirely from the platform, and hurled him into the water as if he had been a child. In half a minute, two more were at his side, one of whom received a grave injury by falling on the friend who had just preceded him. But four enemies remained, and in a hand-to-hand conflict, in which no arms were used but those which nature had furnished, Hurry believed himself fully able to cope with that number of redskins.

"Hurrah, Old Tom!" he shouted; "the rascals are taking to the lake, and I'll soon have 'em all swimming!" As these words were uttered, a violent kick in the face sent back the injured Indian, who had caught at the edge of the platform and was endeavoring to raise himself to its level, helplessly and hopelessly into the water. When the affray was over, his dark body was seen, through the limpid element of the Glimmerglass, lying, with outstretched arms, extended on the bottom of the shoal on which the castle stood, clinging to the sands and weeds as if life were to be retained by this frenzied grasp of death. A blow sent into the pit of another's stomach doubled him up like a worm that had been trodden on; but two able-bodied foes remained to be dealt with. One of these, however, was not only the largest and strongest of the Hurons, but he was also the most experienced of the warriors present, and that one whose sinews were the best strung in fights and by marches on the warpath. This man fully appreciated the gigantic strength of his opponent, and had carefully husbanded his own. He was also equipped in the best manner for such a conflict, standing in nothing but his breechcloth, the model of a naked and beautiful statue of agility and strength. To grasp him required additional dexterity and unusual force. Still, Hurry did not hesitate; but the kick that had actually destroyed one fellow creature was no sooner given than he closed in with this formidable antagonist, endeavoring to force him into the water also. The struggle that succeeded was truly frightful. So fierce did it immediately become, and so quick and changeful were the evolutions of the athletes, that the remaining savage had no chance for interfering, had he possessed the desire; but wonder and apprehension held him spellbound. He was an inexperienced youth, and his blood curdled as he witnessed the fell strife of human passions, exhibited, too, in an unaccustomed form.

Hurry first attempted to throw his antagonist. With this view he seized him by the throat and an arm and tripped with the quickness and force of an American borderer. The effect was frustrated by the agile movements of the Huron, who had clothes to grasp by and whose feet avoided the attempt with a nimbleness equal to that with which it was made. Then followed a sort of melee, if such a term can be applied to a struggle between two in which no efforts were distinctly visible, the limbs and bodies of the combatants assuming so many attitudes and contortions as to defeat observation. This confused but fierce rally lasted less than a minute, however, when Hurry, furious at having his strength baffled by the agility and nakedness of his foe, made a desperate effort, which sent the Huron from him, hurling his body violently against the logs of the hut. The concussion was so great as momentarily to confuse the latter's faculties. The pain, too, extorted a deep groan—an unusual concession to agony to escape a red man in the heat of battle. Still, he rushed forward again to meet his enemy, conscious that his safety rested on his resolution. Hurry now seized the other by the waist, raised him bodily from the platform, and fell with his own great weight on the form beneath. This additional shock so far stunned the sufferer that his gigantic white opponent now had him completely at his mercy. Passing his hands round the throat of his victim, he compressed them with the strength of a vice, fairly doubling the head of the Huron over the edge of the platform, until the chin was uppermost, with the infernal strength he expended. An instant sufficed to show the consequences. The eyes of the sufferer seemed to start forward, his tongue protruded, and his nostrils dilated nearly to splitting. At this instant a rope of bark, having an eye, was passed dexterously within the two arms of Hurry; the end threaded the eye, forming a noose, and his elbows were drawn together behind his back with a power that all his gigantic strength could not resist. Reluctantly, even under such circumstances, did the exasperated borderer see his hands drawn from their deadly grasp, for all the evil passions were then in the ascendant. Almost at the same instant, a similar fastening secured his ankles, and his body was rolled to the center of the platform as helplessly, and as cavalierly, as if it were a log of wood. His rescued antagonist, however, did not rise, for while he began again to breathe, his head still hung helplessly over the edge of the logs, and it was thought at first that his neck was dislocated. He recovered gradually only, and it was hours before he could walk. Some fancied that neither his body nor his mind ever totally recovered from this near approach to death.

Hurry owed his defeat and capture to the intensity with which he had concentrated all his powers on his fallen foe. While thus occupied, the two Indians he had hurled into the water mounted to the heads of the piles along which they passed and joined their companion on the platform. The latter had so far rallied his faculties as to have got the ropes, which were in readiness for use as the others appeared, and they were applied in the manner related, as Hurry lay pressing his enemy down with his whole weight, intent only on the horrible office of strangling him. Thus were the tables turned in a single moment; he who had been so near achieving a victory that would have been renowned for ages, by means of tradition, throughout all that region, lying helpless, bound, and a captive. So fearful had been the efforts of the paleface, and so prodigious the strength he exhibited, that even as he lay, tethered like a sheep before them, they regarded him with respect, and not without dread. The helpless body of their stoutest warrior was still stretched on the platform; and, as they cast their eyes toward the lake in quest of the comrade that had been hurled into it so unceremoniously, and of whom they had lost sight in the confusion of the fray, they perceived his lifeless form clinging to the grass on the bottom, as already described. These several circumstances contributed to render the victory of the Hurons almost as astounding to themselves as a defeat.

Chingachgook and his betrothed witnessed the whole of this struggle from the ark. When the three Hurons were about to pass the cords around the arms of the prostrate Hurry, the Delaware sought his rifle, but before he could use it, the white man was bound, and the mischief was done. He might still bring down an enemy, but to obtain the scalp was impossible; and the young chief, who would so freely risk his own life to obtain such a trophy, hesitated about

taking that of a foe without such an object in view. A glance
at Hist and the recollection of what might follow checked
any transient wish for revenge. The reader has been told
that Chingachgook could scarcely be said to know how to
manage the oars of the ark at all, however expert he might
be in the use of the paddle. Perhaps there is no manual
labor at which men are so bungling and awkward as in their
first attempts to pull an oar, even the experienced mariner,
or boatman, breaking down in his efforts to figure with the
celebrated rullock of the gondolier. In short, it is temporarily
an impracticable thing for a beginner to succeed with a
single oar, but in this case it was necessary to handle two
at the same time, and those of great size. Sweeps, or large
oars, however, are sooner rendered of use by the raw hand
than lighter implements, and this was the reason that the
Delaware had succeeded in moving the ark as well as he
did in a first trial. That trial, notwithstanding, sufficed to
produce distrust, and he was fully aware of the critical
situation in which Hist and himself were now placed, should
the Hurons take to the canoe that was still lying beneath
the trap, and come against them. At one moment he thought
of putting Hist into the canoe in his own possession and of
taking to the eastern mountain, in the hope of reaching the
Delaware villages by direct flight. But many considerations
suggested themselves to put a stop to this indiscreet step.
It was almost certain that scouts watched the lake on both
sides, and no canoe could possibly approach the shore without being seen from the hills. Then a trail could not be concealed from Indian eyes, and the strength of Hist was
unequal to a flight sufficiently sustained to outstrip the pursuit of trained warriors. This was a part of America in
which the Indians did not know the use of horses, and
everything would depend on the physical energies of the
fugitives. Last, but far from being least, were the thoughts
connected with the situation of Deerslayer, a friend who was
not to be deserted in his extremity.

Hist, in some particulars, reasoned and even felt differently, though she arrived at the same conclusions. Her own
danger disturbed her less than her concern for the two sisters, in whose behalf her womanly sympathies were now
strongly enlisted. The canoe of the girls, by the time the
struggle on the platform had ceased, was within three hun-

dred yards of the castle, and here Judith ceased paddling, the evidences of strife first becoming apparent to the eyes. She and Hetty were standing erect, anxiously endeavoring to ascertain what had occurred, but unable to satisfy their doubts, from the circumstance that the building, in a great measure, concealed the scene of action.

The parties in the ark and in the canoe were indebted to the ferocity of Hurry's attack for their momentary security. In any ordinary case, the girls would have been immediately captured; a measure easy of execution now that the savages had a canoe, were it not for the rude check the audacity of the Hurons had received in the recent struggle. It required some little time to recover from the effects of this violent scene, and this so much the more because the principal man of the party, in the way of personal prowess at least, had been so great a sufferer. Still, it was of the last importance that Judith and her sister should seek immediate refuge in the ark, where the defenses offered a temporary shelter at least; and the first step was to devise the means of inducing them to do so. Hist showed herself in the stern of the scow and made many gestures and signs, in vain, in order to induce the girls to make a circuit to avoid the castle and to approach the ark from the eastward. But these signs were distrusted or misunderstood. It is probable Judith was not yet sufficiently aware of the real state of things to put full confidence in either party. Instead of doing as desired, she rather kept more aloof, paddling slowly back to the north, or into the broadest part of the lake, where she could command the widest view and had the fairest field for flight before her. At this instant the sun appeared above the pines of the eastern range of mountains, and a light southerly breeze arose, as was usual enough at that season and hour.

Chingachgook lost no time in hoisting the sail. Whatever might be in reserve for him, there could be no question that it was every way desirable to get the ark at such a distance from the castle as to reduce his enemies to the necessity of approaching the former in the canoe, which the chances of war had so inopportunely, for his wishes and security, thrown into their hands. The appearance of the opening duck seemed first to arouse the Hurons from their apathy, and by the time the head of the scow had fallen off before the wind, which it did unfortunately in the wrong direction, bringing it within a few yards of the platform, Hist found it necessary to warn her lover of the importance of covering his person against the rifles of his foes. This was a danger to be avoided under all circumstances, and so much the more because the Delaware found that Hist would not take to the cover herself, so long as he remained exposed. Accordingly Chingachgook abandoned the scow to its own movements, forced Hist into the cabin, the doors of which he immediately secured, and then he looked about him for the rifles.

The situation of the parties was now so singular as to merit a particular description. The ark was within sixty yards of the castle, a little to the southward, or to windward of it, with its sail full, and the steering oar abandoned. The latter, fortunately, was loose, so that it produced no great influence on the crablike movements of the unwieldy craft. The sail being set, as sailors term it, flying, or having no braces, the air forced the yard forward, though both sheets were fast. The effect was threefold on a boat with a bottom that was perfectly flat and that drew merely some three or four inches of water. It pressed the head slowly around to leeward, it forced the whole fabric bodily in the same direction at the same time, and the water that unavoidably gathered under the lee also gave the scow a forward movement. All these changes were exceedingly slow, however, for the wind was not only light, but it was baffling as usual, and twice or thrice the sail shook. Once it was absolutely taken aback.

Had there been any keel to the ark, it would inevitably have run foul of the platform, bows on, when it is probable nothing could have prevented the Hurons from carrying it, more particularly as the sail would have enabled them to approach under cover. As it was, the scow wore slowly round, barely clearing that part of the building. The piles projecting several feet, *they* were not cleared, but the head of the slow-moving craft caught between two of them by one of its square corners, and hung. At this moment the Delaware was vigilantly watching through a loop for an opportunity to fire, while the Hurons kept within the building, similarly occupied. The exhausted warrior reclined against the hut, there having been no time to remove him, and Hurry lay, almost as helpless as a log, tethered like a sheep on its way to the slaughter, near the middle of the platform. Chingachgook could have slain the first at any moment, but his scalp would have been safe, and the young chief disdained to strike a blow that could lead to neither honor nor advantage.

"Run out one of the poles, Sarpent, if Sarpent you be," said Hurry, amid the groans that the tightness of the ligatures was beginning to extort from him. "Run out one of the poles, and shove the head of the scow off, and you'll drift clear of us—and, when you've done that good turn for *yourself,* just finish this gagging blackguard for *me.*"

The appeal of Hurry, however, had no other effect than to draw the attention of Hist to his situation. This quick-witted creature comprehended it at a glance. His ankles were bound with several turns of stout bark rope, and his arms above the elbows were similarly secured behind his back, barely leaving him a little play of the hands and wrists. Putting her mouth near a loop, she said in a low but distinct voice:

"Why you don't roll here, and fall in scow? Chingachgook shoot Huron if he chase!"

"By the Lord, gal, that's a judgmatical thought, and it shall be tried, if the starn of your scow will come a little nearer. Put a bed at the bottom for me to fall on."

This was said at a happy moment, for, tired of waiting, all the Indians made a rapid discharge of their rifles, almost simultaneously, injuring no one, though several bullets passed through the loops. Hist had heard part of Hurry's words, but most of what he said was lost in the sharp reports of the firearms. She undid the bar of the door that led to the stern of the scow, but did not dare to expose her person. All this time the head of the ark hung, but by a gradually decreasing hold, as the other end swung slowly round, nearer and nearer to the platform. Hurry, who now lay with his face toward the ark, occasionally writhing and turning over like one in pain, evolutions he had performed ever since he was secured, watched every change, and at last he saw that the whole vessel was free, and was beginning to grate slowly along the sides of the piles. The attempt was desperate, but it seemed the only chance for escaping torture and death, and it suited the reckless daring of the man's character. Waiting to the last moment, in order that the stern of the scow might fairly rub against the platform, he began to writhe again, as if in intolerable suffering, execrating all Indians in general, and the Hurons in particular, and then he suddenly and rapidly rolled over and over, taking the direction of the stern of the scow. Unfortunately, Hurry's shoulders required more space to revolve in than his feet, and by the time he reached the edge of the platform, his direction had so far changed as to carry him clear of the ark altogether; and the rapidity of his revolutions, and the emergency, admitting of no delay, he fell into the water. At this instant, Chingachgook, by an understanding with his betrothed, drew the fire of the Hurons again, not a man of whom saw the manner in which one whom they knew to be effectually tethered had disappeared. But Hist's feelings were strongly interested in the success of so bold a scheme, and she watched the movements of Hurry as the cat watches the mouse. The moment he was in motion she foresaw the consequences, and this the more readily as the scow was now beginning to move with some steadiness, and she bethought her of the means of saving him. With a sort of instinctive readiness, she opened the door at the very moment the rifles were ringing in her ears; protected by the intervening cabin, she stepped into the stern of the scow in time to witness the fall of Hurry into the lake. Her foot was unconsciously placed on the end of one of the sheets of the sail, which was fastened aft, and catching up all the spare rope with the awkwardness but also with the generous resolution of a woman, she threw it in the direction of the helpless Hurry. The line fell on the head and body of the sinking man, and he not only succeeded in grasping separate parts of it with his hands, but he actually got a portion of it between his teeth. Hurry was an expert swimmer, and tethered as he was, he resorted to the very expedient that philosophy and reflection would have suggested. He had fallen on his back, and instead of floundering and drowning himself by desperate efforts to walk on the water, he permitted his body to sink as low as possible, and was already submerged, with the exception of his face, when the line reached him. In this situation he might possibly have remained until rescued by the Hurons, using his hands as fishes use their fins, had he received no other succor; but the movement of the ark soon tightened the rope, and of course he was dragged gently ahead, holding even pace with the scow. The motion aided in keeping his face above the surface of the water, and it would have been possible for one accustomed to endurance to have been towed a mile in this singular but simple manner.

It has been said that the Hurons did not observe the sudden disappearance of Hurry. In his present situation he was not only hid from view by the platform, but as the ark drew slowly ahead, impelled by a sail that was now filled, he received the same friendly service from the piles. The Hurons, indeed, were too intent on endeavoring to slay their Delaware foe by sending a bullet through some one of the loops or crevices of the cabin to bethink them at all of one whom they fancied so thoroughly tied. Their great concern was the manner in which the ark rubbed past the piles, although its motion was lessened at least one half by the friction, and they passed into the northern end of the castle, in order to catch opportunities of firing through the loops of that part of the building. Chingachgook was similarly occupied, and remained as ignorant as his enemies of the situation of Hurry. As the ark grated along, the rifles sent their little clouds of smoke from one cover to the other, but the eyes and movements of the opposing parties were too quick to permit any injury to be done. At length one side had the mortification, and the other the pleasure, of seeing the scow swing clear of the piles altogether, when it immediately moved away, with a materially accelerated motion, toward the north.

Chingachgook now first learned from Hist the critical condition of Hurry. To have exposed either of their persons in the stern of the scow would have been certain death, but, fortunately, the sheet to which the man clung led forward to the foot of the sail. The Delaware found means to unloosen it from the cleat aft, and Hist, who was already forward for that purpose, immediately began to pull upon the line. At this moment Hurry was towing fifty or sixty feet astern, with nothing but his face above water. As he was dragged out clear of the castle and the piles, he was first perceived by the Hurons, who raised a hideous yell and commenced a fire on what may very well be termed the "floating mass." It was at the same instant, that Hist began to pull upon the line forward—a circumstance that probably saved Hurry's life, aided by his own self-possession and border readiness. The first bullet struck the water directly on the spot where the broad chest of the young giant was visible through the pure element, and might have pierced his heart had the angle at which it was fired been less acute. Instead of penetrating the lake, however, it glanced from its smooth surface, rose, and actually buried itself in the logs of the cabin, near the spot at which Chingachgook had shown himself the minute before, while clearing the line from the cleat. A second, and a third, and a fourth bullet followed, all meeting with the same resistance from the surface of the water, though Hurry sensibly felt the violence of the blows they struck upon the lake so immediately above and so near his breast. Discovering their mistake, the Hurons now changed their plan and aimed at the uncovered face, but by this time Hist was pulling on the line, the target advanced, and the deadly missiles still fell upon the water. In another moment the body was dragged past the end of the scow and became concealed. As for the Delaware and Hist, they worked perfectly covered by the cabin, and in less time than it requires to tell it they had hauled the huge frame of Hurry to the place they occupied. Chingachgook stood in readiness with his keen knife, and bending over the side of the scow, he soon severed the bark that bound the limbs of the borderer. To raise him high enough to reach the edge of the boat and to aid him in entering were less easy tasks, as Hurry's arms were still nearly useless, but both were done in time, when the liberated man staggered forward and fell, exhausted and helpless, into the bottom of the scow. Here we shall leave him to recover his strength and the due circulation of his blood, while we proceed with the narrative of events that crowd upon us too fast to admit of any postponement.

The moment the Hurons lost sight of the body of Hurry, they gave a common yell of disappointment, and three of the most active of their number ran to the trap and entered the canoe. It required some little delay, however, to embark with their weapons, to find the paddles, and, if we may use a phrase so purely technical, "to get out of dock." By this time Hurry was in the scow, and the Delaware had his rifles again in readiness. As the ark necessarily sailed before the wind, it had got by this time quite two hundred yards from the castle, and was sliding away each instant, further and further, though with a motion so easy as scarcely to stir the water. The canoe of the girls was quite a quarter of a mile distant from the ark, obviously keeping aloof, in ignorance

of what had occurred and in apprehension of the consequences of venturing too near. They had taken the direction
of the eastern shore, endeavoring at the same time to get to
windward of the ark and, in a manner, between the two
parties, as if distrusting which was to be considered a friend
and which an enemy. The girls, from long habit, used the
paddles with great dexterity; Judith, in particular, had often
sportively gained races in trials of speed with the youths that
occasionally visited the lake.

When the three Hurons emerged from behind the palisades and found themselves on the open lake, and under the
necessity of advancing unprotected on the ark, if they
persevered in the original design, their ardor sensibly cooled.
In a bark canoe, they were totally without cover, and Indian discretion was entirely opposed to such a sacrifice of
life as would most probably follow any attempt to assault
an enemy entrenched as effectually as the Delaware. Instead
of following the ark, therefore, these three warriors inclined
toward the eastern shore, keeping at a safe distance from the
rifles of Chingachgook. But this maneuver rendered the position of the girls exceedingly critical. It threatened to place
them, if not between two fires, at least between two dangers,
or what they conceived to be dangers; instead of permitting
the Hurons to enclose her in what she fancied a sort of net,
Judith immediately commenced her retreat in a southern
direction, at no very great distance from the shore. She did
not dare to land; if such an expedient were to be resorted to
at all, she could only venture on it in the last extremity. At
first the Indians paid little or no attention to the other canoe,
for, fully apprised of its contents, they deemed its capture
of comparatively little moment, while the ark, with its
imaginary treasures, the persons of the Delaware and of
Hurry, and its means of movement on a large scale, was
before them. But this ark had its dangers as well as its
temptations, and after wasting nearly an hour in vacillating
evolutions, always at a safe distance from the rifle, the
Hurons seemed suddenly to take their resolution and began
to display it by giving eager chase to the girls.

When this last design was adopted, the circumstances of
all parties, as connected with their relative positions, were
materially changed. The ark had sailed and drifted quite
half a mile, and was nearly that distance due north of the

castle. As soon as the Delaware perceived that the girls avoided him, unable to manage his unwieldy craft, and knowing that flight from a bark canoe, in the event of pursuit, would be a useless expedient if attempted, he had lowered his sail, in the hope it might induce the sisters to change their plan and to seek refuge in the scow. This demonstration produced no other effect than to keep the ark nearer to the scene of action and to enable those in her to become witnesses of the chase. The canoe of Judith was about a quarter of a mile south of that of the Hurons, a little nearer to the east shore, and about the same distance to the southward of the castle as it was from the hostile canoe, a circumstance which necessarily put the last nearly abreast of Hutter's fortress. With the several parties thus situated, the chase commenced.

At the moment when the Hurons so suddenly changed their mode of attack, their canoe was not in the best possible racing trim. There were but two paddles, and the third man was so much extra and useless cargo. Then the difference in weight between the sisters and the other two men, more especially in vessels so extremely light, almost neutralized any difference that might proceed from the greater strength of the Hurons and rendered the trial of speed far from being as unequal as it might seem. Judith did not commence her exertions until the near approach of the other canoe rendered the object of the movement certain, and then she excited Hetty to aid her with her utmost skill and strength.

"Why should we run, Judith?" asked the simple-minded girl; "the Hurons have never harmed *me,* nor do I think they ever will."

"That may be true as to you, Hetty, but it will prove very different with me. Kneel down and say your prayer, and rise and do your utmost to help escape. Think of me, dear girl, too, as you pray."

Judith gave these directions from a mixed feeling; first, because she knew that her sister ever sought the support of her Great Ally, in trouble; and next, because a sensation of feebleness and dependence suddenly came over her own proud spirit in that moment of apparent desertion and trial. The prayer was quickly said, however, and the canoe was soon in rapid motion. Still, neither party resorted to their greatest exertions from the outset, both knowing that the chase was likely to be arduous and long. Like two vessels of war that are preparing for an encounter, they seemed desirous of first ascertaining their respective rates of speed, in order that they might know how to graduate their exertions, previous to the great effort. A few minutes sufficed to show the Hurons that the girls were expert and that it would require all their skill and energies to overtake them.

Judith had inclined toward the eastern shore at the commencement of the chase with a vague determination of landing and flying to the woods as a last resort, but as she approached the land, the certainty that scouts must be watching her movements made her reluctance to adopt such an expedient unconquerable. Then she was still fresh, and had sanguine hopes of being able to tire out her pursuers. With such feelings, she gave a sweep with her paddle, and sheered off from the fringe of dark hemlocks, beneath the shades of which she was so near entering, and held her way again, more toward the center of the lake. This seemed the instant favorable for the Hurons to make their push, as it gave them the entire breadth of the sheet to do it in; and this, too, in the widest part, as soon as they had got between the fugitives and the land. The canoes now flew, Judith making up for what she wanted in strength by her great dexterity and self-command. For half a mile the Indians gained no material advantage, but the continuance of so great exertions for so many minutes sensibly affected all concerned. Here the Indians resorted to an expedient that enabled them to give one of their party time to breathe, by shifting their paddles from hand to hand, and this, too, without sensibly relaxing their efforts. Judith occasionally looked behind her, and she saw this expedient practiced. It caused her immediately to distrust the result, since her powers of endurance were not likely to hold out against those of men who had the means of relieving each other; still she persevered, allowing no very visible consequences immediately to follow the change.

As yet, the Indians had not been able to get nearer to the girls than two hundred yards, though they were what seamen would term "in their wake," or in a direct line behind them, passing over the same track of water. This made the pursuit what is technically called a "stern chase," which is proverbially a "long chase," the meaning of which is that in consequence of the relative positions of the parties, no change becomes apparent except that which is a direct gain in the nearest possible approach. "Long" as this species of chase is admitted to be, however, Judith was enabled to perceive that the Hurons were sensibly drawing nearer and nearer, before she had gained the center of the lake. She was not a girl to despair, but there was an instant when she thought of yielding, with the wish of being carried to the camp where she knew the Deerslayer to be a captive; but the considerations connected with the means she hoped to be able to employ in order to procure his release immediately interposed, in order to stimulate her to renewed exertions. Had there been anyone there to note the progress of the two canoes, he would have seen that of Judith flying swiftly away from its pursuers, as the girl gave it freshly impelled speed, while her mind was thus dwelling on her own ardent and generous schemes. So material, indeed, was the difference in the rate of going between the two canoes for the next five minutes that the Hurons began to be convinced all their powers must be exerted, or they would suffer the disgrace of being baffled by women. Making a furious effort, under the mortification of such a conviction, one of the stronger of their party broke his paddle at the very moment when he had taken it from the hand of a comrade to relieve him. This at once decided the matter, a canoe containing three men, and having but one paddle, being utterly unable to overtake fugitives like the daughters of Thomas Hutter.

"There, Judith!" exclaimed Hetty, who saw the accident —"I hope, now, you will own that praying is useful! The Hurons have broke a paddle, and they never *can* overtake us."

"I never denied it, poor Hetty, and sometimes wish, in bitterness of spirit, that I had prayed more myself, and thought less of my beauty. As you say, we are now safe, and need only go a little south, and take breath."

This was done, the enemy giving up the pursuit as suddenly as a ship that has lost an important spar, the instant the accident occurred. Instead of following Judith's canoe, which was now lightly skimming over the water toward the south, the Hurons turned their bows toward the castle, where they soon arrived and landed. The girls, fearful that some spare paddles might be found in or about the buildings, continued on; nor did they stop until so distant from their enemies as to give them every chance of escape, should the chase be renewed. It would seem that the savages meditated no such design, but at the end of an hour their canoe, filled with men, was seen quitting the castle and steering toward the shore. The girls were without food, and they now drew nearer to the buildings and the ark, having finally made up their minds, from its maneuvers, that the latter contained friends.

Notwithstanding the seeming desertion of the castle, Judith approached it with extreme caution. The ark was now quite a mile to the northward, but sweeping up toward the buildings; this, too, with a regularity of motion that satisfied Judith a white man was at the oars. When within a hundred yards of the building, the girls began to encircle it, in order to make sure that it was empty. No canoe was nigh, and this emboldened them to draw nearer and nearer, until they had gone around the piles and reached the platform.

"Do you go into the house, Hetty," said Judith, "and see that the savages are gone. They will not harm you; and if any of them are still here, you can give me the alarm. I do not think they will fire on a poor defenseless girl, and I at least may escape, until I shall be ready to go among them of my own accord."

Hetty did as desired—Judith retiring a few yards from the platform the instant her sister landed, in readiness for flight. But the last was unnecessary, not a minute elapsing before Hetty returned to communicate that all was safe.

"I've been in all the rooms, Judith," said the latter earnestly, "and they are empty, except Father's; he is in his own chamber, sleeping, though not as quietly as we could wish."

"Has anything happened to Father?" demanded Judith, as her foot touched the platform, speaking quick, for her nerves were in a state to be easily alarmed.

Hetty seemed concerned, and she looked furtively about her, as if unwilling anyone but a child should hear what she had to communicate, and even that *she* should learn it abruptly.

"You know how it is with Father sometimes, Judith," she said. "When overtaken with liquor, he doesn't always know what he says or does—and he seems to be overtaken with liquor now."

"That is strange! Would the savages have drunk with him

and then leave him behind? But 'tis a grievous sight to a child, Hetty, to witness such a failing in a parent, and we will not go near him till he wakes."

A groan from the inner room, however, changed this resolution, and the girls ventured near a parent, whom it was no unusual thing for them to find in a condition that lowers a man to the level of brutes. He was seated, reclining in a corner of a narrow room, with his shoulders supported by the angle, and his head fallen heavily on his chest. Judith moved forward, with a sudden impulse, and removed a canvas cap that was forced so low on his head as to conceal his face and, indeed, all but his shoulders. The instant this obstacle was taken away, the quivering and raw flesh, the bared veins and muscles, and all the other disgusting signs of mortality as they are revealed by tearing away the skin, showed he had been scalped, though still living.

Chapter XXI

Lightly they'll talk of the spirit that's gone,
And o'er his cold ashes upbraid him;
But nothing he'll reck, if they'll let him sleep on,
In the grave where a Briton has laid him.

DISPUTED

THE READER MUST imagine the horror that daughters would experience at unexpectedly beholding the shocking spectacle that was placed before the eyes of Judith and Esther, as related in the close of the last chapter. We shall pass over the first emotions, the first acts of filial piety, and proceed with the narrative by imagining rather than relating most of the revolting features of the scene. The mutilated and ragged head was bound up, the unseemly blood was wiped from the face of the sufferer, the other appliances required by appearances and care were resorted to, and there was time to inquire into the more serious circumstances of the case. The facts were never known until years later, in all their details, simple as they were; but they may as well be related here, as it can be done in a few words. In the struggle with the Hurons, Hutter had been stabbed by the knife of the old warrior who had used the discretion to remove the arms of everyone but himself. Being hard pushed by his sturdy foe, his knife settled the matter. This occurred just as the door was opened and Hurry burst out upon the platform, as has been previously related. This was the secret of neither party's having appeared in the subsequent struggle, Hutter having been literally disabled, and his conqueror being ashamed to be seen with the traces of blood about him, after having used so many injunctions to convince his young warriors of the necessity of taking their prisoners alive. When the three Hurons returned from the chase, and it was determined to abandon the castle and join the party on the land, Hutter was simply scalped, to secure the usual trophy, and was left to die by inches, as has been done in a thousand similar instances by the ruthless warriors of this part of the American continent. Had the injury of Hutter been confined to his head, he might have recovered, however; it was the blow of the knife that proved mortal.

There are moments of vivid consciousness, when the stern justice of God stands forth in colors so prominent as to defy any attempts to veil them from the sight, however unpleasant they may appear, or however anxious we may be to avoid recognizing it. Such was now the fact with Judith and Hetty, who both perceived the decrees of a retributive Providence, in the manner of their father's suffering, as a punishment for his own recent attempts on the Iroquois. This was seen and felt by Judith with the keenness of perception and sensibility that were suited to her character, while the impression made on the simpler mind of her sister was perhaps less lively, though it might well have proved more lasting.

"Oh, Judith!" exclaimed the weak-minded girl as soon as their first care had been bestowed on the sufferer. "Father went for scalps himself, and now where is his own? The Bible might have foretold this dreadful punishment!"

"Hush—Hetty—hush, poor sister—he opens his eyes; he may hear and understand you. 'Tis as you say and think, but 'tis too dreadful to speak of!"

"Water—" ejaculated Hutter, as it might be by a desperate effort that rendered his voice frightfully deep and strong for one as near death as he evidently was. "Water—foolish girls—will you let me die of thirst?"

Water was brought and administered to the sufferer—the first he had tasted in hours of physical anguish. It had the double effect of clearing his throat and of momentarily reviving his sinking system. His eyes opened with that anxious, distended gaze which is apt to accompany the passage of a soul surprised by death, and he seemed disposed to speak.

"Father—" said Judith, inexpressibly pained by his deplorable situation, and this so much the more from her ignorance of what remedies ought to be applied. "Father, can we do anything for you? Can Hetty and I relieve your pain?"

"Father!" slowly repeated the old man. "No, Judith—no, Hetty—I'm no father. *She* was your mother, but I'm no father. Look in the chest—'tis all there—give me more water."

The girls complied, and Judith, whose early recollections extended further back than her sister's, and who on every account had more distinct impressions of the past, felt an uncontrollable impulse of joy as she heard these words. There had never been much sympathy between her reputed father and herself, and suspicions of this very truth had often glanced across her mind, in consequence of dialogues she had overheard between Hutter and her mother. It might be going too far to say she had never loved him, but it is not so to add that she rejoiced it was no longer a duty. With Hetty the feeling was different. Incapable of making all the distinctions of her sister, her very nature was full of affection, and she *had* loved her reputed parent, though far less tenderly than the real parent, and it grieved her now to hear him declare he was not naturally entitled to that love. She felt a double grief, as if his death and his words together were twice depriving her of parents. Yielding to her feelings, the poor girl went aside and wept.

The very opposite emotions of the two girls kept both silent for a long time. Judith gave water to the sufferer frequently, but she forbore to urge him with questions, in some measure out of consideration for his condition but; if truth must be said, quite as much lest something he should add in the way of explanation might disturb her pleasing belief that she was not Thomas Hutter's child. At length Hetty dried her tears and came and seated herself on a stool by the side of the dying man, who had been placed at his length on the floor, with his head supported by some worn vestments that had been left in the house.

"Father," she said—"you let me *call* you Father, though you say you are not one—Father, shall I read the Bible to you? Mother always said the Bible was good for people in trouble. She was often in trouble herself, and then she made me read the Bible to her—for Judith wasn't as fond of the Bible as I am—and it always did her good. Many is the time I've known Mother begin to listen with the tears streaming from her eyes and end with smiles and gladness. Oh, Father, you don't know how much good the Bible can do, for you've never tried it; now, I'll read a chapter, and it will soften your heart, as it softened the hearts of the Hurons."

While poor Hetty had so much reverence for, and faith in, the virtue of the Bible, her intellect was too shallow to enable her fully to appreciate its beauties, or to fathom its profound and sometimes mysterious wisdom. That instinctive sense of right, which appeared to shield her from the commission of wrong and even cast a mantle of moral loveliness and truth around her character, could not penetrate abstrusities, or trace the nice affinities between cause and effect, beyond their more obvious and indisputable connection, though she seldom failed to see the latter and to defer to all their just consequences. In a word, she was one of those who feel and act correctly, without being able to give a logical reason for it, even admitting revelation as her authority. Her selections from the Bible, therefore, were commonly distinguished by the simplicity of her own mind and were oftener marked for containing images of known and palpable things than for any of the higher cast of moral truths with which the pages of that wonderful book abound—wonderful and unequaled, even without referring to its divine origin, as a work replete with the profoundest philosophy, expressed in the noblest language. Her mother, with a connection that will probably strike the reader, had been fond of the book of Job, and Hetty had, in a great measure, learned to read by the frequent lessons she had received from the different chapters of this venerable and sublime poem—now believed to be the oldest book in the world. On this occasion the poor girl was submissive to her training, and she turned to that well-known part of the sacred volume with the readiness with which the practiced counsel would cite his authorities from the stores of legal wisdom. In selecting the particular chapter, she was influenced by the caption, and she chose that which stands in our English version as, *"Job excuseth his desire of death."* This she read steadily, from beginning to end, in a sweet, low, and plaintive voice, hoping devoutly that the allegorical and abstruse sentences might convey to the heart of the sufferer the consolation he needed. It is another peculiarity of the comprehensive wisdom of the Bible that scarce a chapter, unless it be strictly narrative, can be turned to that does not contain some searching truth that is applicable to the condition of every human heart, as well as to the temporal state of its owner, either through the workings of that heart or even in a still more direct form. In this instance, the very opening sentence—*"Is there not an appointed time to man on earth?"*—was startling, and as Hetty proceeded, Hutter applied, or fancied he could apply, many aphorisms and figures to his own worldly and mental condition. As life is ebbing fast, the mind clings eagerly to hope, when it is not absolutely crushed by despair. The solemn words, *"I have sinned; what shall I do unto thee, O thou preserver of men? Why hast thou set me as a mark against thee, so that I am a burden to myself?"* struck Hutter more perceptibly than the others; and, though too obscure for one of his blunted feelings and obtuse mind either to feel or to comprehend in their fullest extent, they had a directness of application to his own state that caused him to wince under them.

"Don't you feel better now, Father?" asked Hetty, closing the volume. "Mother was always better when she had read the Bible."

"Water," returned Hutter, "give me water, Judith. I wonder if my tongue will always be so hot! Hetty, isn't there something in the Bible about cooling the tongue of a man who was burning in hellfire?"

Judith turned away, shocked, but Hetty eagerly sought the passage, which she read aloud to the conscience-stricken victim of his own avaricious longings.

"That's it, poor Hetty; yes, that's it. My tongue wants cooling, *now;* what will it be *hereafter?*"

This appeal silenced even the confiding Hetty, for she had no answer ready for a confession so fraught with despair. Water, so long as it could relieve the sufferer, it was in the power of the sisters to give, and, from time to time it was offered to the lips of the sufferer, as he asked for it. Even Judith prayed. As for Hetty, as soon as she found that her efforts to make her father listen to her texts were no longer rewarded with success, she knelt at his side and devoutly repeated the words which the Saviour has left behind him as a model for human petitions. This she continued to do, at intervals, as long as it seemed to her that the act could benefit the dying man. Hutter, however, lingered longer than the girls had believed possible when they first found him.

At times he spoke intelligibly, though his lips oftener moved in utterance of sounds that carried no distinct impressions to the mind. Judith listened intently, and she heard the words "husband," "death," "pirate," "law," "scalps," and several others of a similar import, though there was no sentence to tell the precise connection in which they were used. Still they were sufficiently expressive to be understood by one whose ears had not escaped all the rumors that had been circulated to her reputed father's discredit, and whose comprehension was as quick as her faculties were attentive.

During the whole of the painful hour that succeeded, neither of the sisters bethought her sufficiently of the Hurons to dread their return. It seemed as if their desolation and grief placed them above the danger of such an interruption; when the sound of oars was at length heard, even Judith, who alone had any reason to apprehend the enemy, did not start but at once understood that the ark was near. She went upon the platform fearlessly, for should it turn out that Hurry was not there, and that the Hurons were masters of the scow also, escape was impossible. Then she had the sort of confidence that is inspired by extreme misery. But there was no cause for any new alarm—Chingachgook, Hist, and Hurry all standing in the open part of the scow, cautiously examining the building to make certain of the absence of the enemy. They, too, had seen the departure of the Hurons, as well as the approach of the canoe of the girls to the castle, and presuming on the latter fact, March had swept the scow up to the platform. A word sufficed to explain that there was nothing to be apprehended, and the ark was soon moored in her old berth.

Judith said not a word concerning the condition of her father, but Hurry knew her too well not to understand that something was more than usually wrong. He led the way, though with less of his confident, bold manner than usual, into the house, and penetrating to the inner room, found Hutter lying on his back, with Hetty sitting at his side, fanning him with pious care. The events of the morning had sensibly changed the manner of Hurry. Notwithstanding his skill as a swimmer and the readiness with which he had adopted the only expedient that could possibly save him, the helplessness of being in the water, bound hand and foot, had produced some such an effect on him as the near approach of punishment is known to produce on most criminals, leaving a vivid impression of the horrors of death upon his mind, and this, too, in connection with a picture of bodily helplessness, the daring of this man being far more the offspring of vast physical powers than of the energy of the will, or even of natural spirit. Such heroes invariably lose a large portion of their courage with the failure of their strength, and though Hurry was now unfettered and as vigorous as ever, events were too recent to permit the recollection of his late deplorable condition to be at all weakened. Had he lived a century, the occurrences of the few momentous minutes during which he was in the lake would have produced a chastening effect on his character, if not always on his manner.

Hurry was not only shocked when he found his late associate in this desperate situation, but he was greatly surprised. During the struggle in the building, he had been far too much occupied himself to learn what had befallen his comrade, and as no deadly weapon had been used in his particular case, but every effort had been made to capture him without injury, he naturally believed that Hutter had been overcome, while he owed his own escape to his great bodily strength and to a fortunate concurrence of extraordinary circumstances. Death, in the silence and solemnity of a chamber, was a novelty to him. Though accustomed to scenes of violence, he had been unused to sit by the bedside and watch the slow beating of the pulse as it gradually grew weaker and weaker. Notwithstanding the change in his feelings, the manners of a life could not be altogether cast aside in a moment, and the unexpected scene extorted a characteristic speech from the borderer.

"How now, old Tom," he said, "have the vagabonds got you at an advantage, where you're not only down, but are likely to be kept down! I thought you a captyve, it's true, but never supposed you so hard run as this!"

Hutter opened his glassy eyes and stared wildly at the speaker. A flood of confused recollections rushed on his wavering mind at the sight of his late comrade. It was evident that he struggled with his own images and knew not the real from the unreal.

"Who are you?" he asked in a husky whisper, his failing strength refusing to aid him in a louder effort of his voice.

"Who are you? You look like the mate of the *Snow*—he was a giant, too, and near overcoming us."

"I'm your mate, Floating Tom, and your comrade, but have nothing to do with any snow. It's summer now, and Harry March always quits the hills as soon after the frosts set in as is convenient."

"I know you—Hurry-scurry—I'll sell you a scalp! A sound one, and of a full-grown man—what'll you give?"

"Poor Tom! That scalp business hasn't turned out at all profitable, and I've pretty much concluded to give it up and to follow a less bloody calling."

"Have you got any scalp? Mine's gone—how does it feel to have a scalp? I know how it feels to lose one—fire and flames about the brain—and a wrenching at the heart—no, no—kill *first,* Hurry, and scalp *afterward.*"

"What does the old fellow mean, Judith? He talks like one that is getting tired of the business as well as myself. Why have you bound up his head? Or have the savages tomahawked him about the brains?"

"They have done that for *him* which you and he, Harry March, would have so gladly done for *them*. His skin and hair have been torn from his head to gain money from the Governor of Canada, as you would have torn theirs from the heads of the Hurons to gain money from the Governor of York."

Judith spoke with a strong effort to appear composed, but it was neither in her nature, nor in the feeling of the moment, to speak altogether without bitterness. The strength of her emphasis, indeed, as well as her manner, caused Hetty to look up reproachfully.

"These are high words to come from Thomas Hutter's darter, as Thomas Hutter lies dying before her eyes," retorted Hurry.

"God be praised for that! Whatever reproach it may bring on my poor mother, I am *not* Thomas Hutter's daughter."

"Not Thomas Hutter's darter! Don't disown the old fellow in his last moments, Judith, for *that's* a sin the Lord will never overlook. If you're not Thomas Hutter's darter, whose darter be you?"

This question rebuked the rebellious spirit of Judith, for in getting rid of a parent whom she felt it was a relief to find she might own she had never loved, she overlooked

the important circumstance that no substitute was ready to
supply his place.

"I cannot tell you, Harry, who my father was," she answered more mildly. "I hope he was an honest man, at least."

"Which is more than you think was the case with old
Hutter? Well, Judith, I'll not deny that hard stories were
in circulation consarning Floating Tom, but who is there that
doesn't get a scratch when an inimy holds the rake? There's
them that say hard things of *me,* and even *you,* beauty as
you be, don't always escape."

This was said with a view to set up a species of com-
munity of character between the parties, and, as the poli-
ticians are wont to express it, with ulterior intentions. What
might have been the consequences with one of Judith's known
spirit, as well as her assured antipathy to the speaker, it is not
easy to say, for just then Hutter gave unequivocal signs
that his last moment was nigh. Judith and Hetty had stood
by the dying bed of their mother, and neither needed a
monitor to warn them of the crisis, and every sign of resentment vanished from the face of the first. Hutter opened
his eyes and even tried to feel about him with his hands,
a sign that sight was failing. A minute later his breathing
grew ghastly; a pause totally without respiration followed;
and then succeeded the last, long-drawn sigh, on which the
spirit is supposed to quit the body. This sudden termination
of the life of one who had hitherto filled so important a
place in the narrow scene on which he had been an actor
put an end to all discussion.

The day passed by without further interruption, the
Hurons, though possessed of a canoe, appearing so far satisfied with their success as to have relinquished all immediate designs on the castle. It would not have been a safe
undertaking, indeed, to approach it under the rifles of those
it was now known to contain, and it is probable that the
truce was more owing to this circumstance than to any
other. In the meanwhile, the preparations were made for
the interment of Hutter. To bury him on the land was
impracticable, and it was Hetty's wish that his body should
lie by the side of that of her mother, in the lake. She had
it in her power to quote one of his speeches, in which he
himself had called the lake the "family burying ground,"
and luckily this was done without the knowledge of her

sister, who would have opposed the plan, had she known it, with unconquerable disgust. But Judith had not meddled with the arrangement, and every necessary disposition was made without her privity or advice.

The hour chosen for the rude ceremony was just as the sun was setting, and a moment and a scene more suited to paying the last office to one of calm and pure spirit could not have been chosen. There are a mystery and a solemn dignity in death that dispose the living to regard the remains of even a malefactor with a certain degree of reverence. All worldly distinctions have ceased; it is thought that the veil has been removed and that the character and destiny of the departed are now as much beyond human opinions as they are beyond human ken. In nothing is death more truly a leveler than in this, since, while it may be impossible absolutely to confound the great with the low, the worthy with the unworthy, the mind feels it to be arrogance to assume a right to judge of those who are believed to be standing at the judgment seat of God. When Judith was told that all was ready, she went upon the platform, passive to the request of her sister, and then she first took heed of the arrangement. The body was in the scow, enveloped in a sheet, and quite a hundredweight of stones, which had been taken from the fireplace, were enclosed with it in order that it might sink. No other preparation seemed to be thought necessary, though Hetty carried her Bible beneath her arm.

When all were on board the ark, this singular habitation of the man whose body it now bore to its final abode was set in motion. Hurry was at the oars. In his powerful hands, indeed, they seemed little more than a pair of sculls which were wielded without effort, and as he was expert in their use, the Delaware remained a passive spectator of the proceedings. The progress of the ark had something of the stately solemnity of a funeral procession, the dip of the oars being measured and the movement slow and steady. The wash of the water, as the blades rose and fell, kept time with the efforts of Hurry, and might have been likened to the measured tread of mourners. Then the tranquil scene was in beautiful accordance with a rite that ever associates with itself the idea of God. At that instant the lake had not even a single ripple on its glassy surface, and the broad panorama of woods seemed to look down on the holy tranquillity of the hour and ceremony in melancholy stillness. Judith was affected to tears, and even Hurry, though he hardly knew why, was troubled. Hetty preserved the outward signs of tranquillity, but her inward grief greatly surpassed that of her sister, since her affectionate heart loved more from habit and long association than from the usual connections of sentiment and taste. She was sustained by religious hope, however, which in her simple mind usually occupied the space that worldly feelings filled in that of Judith, and she was not without an expectation of witnessing some open manifestation of divine power on an occasion so solemn. Still, she was neither mystical nor exaggerated, her mental imbecility denying both. Nevertheless, her thoughts had generally so much of the purity of a better world about them that it was easy for her to forget earth altogether and to think only of heaven. Hist was serious, attentive, and interested, for she had often seen the interments of the palefaces, though never one that promised to be as peculiar as this, while the Delaware, though grave and also observant in his demeanor, was stoical and calm.

Hetty acted as pilot, directing Hurry how to proceed to find that spot in the lake which she was in the habit of terming "mother's grave." The reader will remember that the castle stood near the southern extremity of a shoal that extended near half a mile northerly, and it was at the furthest end of this shallow water that Floating Tom had seen fit to deposit the remains of his wife and child. His own were now in the course of being placed at their side. Hetty had marks on the land by which she usually found the spot, although the position of the buildings, the general direction of the shoal, and the beautiful transparency of the water all aided her, the latter even allowing the bottom to be seen. By these means the girl was enabled to note their progress, and at the proper time she approached March, whispering—

"Now, Hurry, you can stop rowing. We have passed the stone on the bottom, and mother's grave is near."

March ceased his efforts, immediately dropping the kedge, and taking the warp in his hand in order to check the scow. The ark turned slowly around under this restraint, and when it was quite stationary, Hetty was seen at its stern, pointing into the water, the tears streaming from her eyes in ungovernable natural feeling. Judith had been present at the interment of her mother, but she had never visited the spot since. This neglect proceeded from no indifference to the memory of the deceased—for she had loved her *mother*, and bitterly had she found occasion to mourn her loss—but she was averse to the contemplation of death, and there had been passages in her own life since the day of that interment which increased this feeling and rendered her, if possible, still more reluctant to approach the spot that contained the remains of one whose severe lessons of female morality and propriety had been deepened and rendered doubly impressive by remorse for her own failings. With Hetty, the case had been very different. To her simple and innocent mind, the remembrance of her mother brought no other feeling than one of gentle sorrow, a grief that is so often termed luxurious, even, because it associates with itself the images of excellence and the purity of a better state of existence. For an entire summer she had been in the habit of repairing to the place after nightfall, and carefully anchoring her canoe so as not to disturb the body, she would sit and hold fancied conversations with the deceased, sing sweet hymns to the evening air, and repeat the orisons that the being who now slumbered below had taught her in infancy. Hetty had passed her happiest hours in this indirect communion with the spirit of her mother, the wildness of Indian traditions and Indian opinions unconsciously to herself mingling with the Christian lore received in childhood. Once she had even been so far influenced by the former as to have bethought her of performing some of those physical rites at her mother's grave, which the red men are known to observe, but the passing feeling had been obscured by the steady, though mild light of Christianity, which never ceased to burn in her gentle bosom. Now her emotions were merely the natural outpourings of a daughter that wept for a mother whose love was indelibly impressed on the heart, and whose lessons had been too earnestly taught to be easily forgotten by one who had so little temptation to err.

There was no other priest than nature at that wild and singular funeral rite. March cast his eyes below, and through the transparent medium of the clear water, which was al-

most as pure as air, he saw what Hetty was accustomed
to call "mother's grave." It was a low, straggling mound of
earth, fashioned by no spade, out of a corner of which
gleamed a bit of the white cloth that formed the shroud
of the dead. The body had been lowered to the bottom,
and Hutter brought earth from the shore and let it fall
upon it until all was concealed. In this state the place had
remained until the movement of the waters revealed the
solitary sign of the uses of the spot that has just been mentioned.

Even the most rude and brawling are chastened by the
ceremonies of a funeral. March felt no desire to indulge
his voice in any of its coarse outbreakings, and was disposed to complete the office he had undertaken in decent
sobriety. Perhaps he reflected on the retribution that had
alighted on his late comrade, and bethought him of the
frightful jeopardy in which his own life had so lately been
placed. He signified to Judith that all was ready, received
her directions to proceed, and, with no other assistant than
his own vast strength, raised the body and bore it to the
end of the scow. Two parts of a rope were passed beneath
the legs and shoulders, as they are placed beneath coffins,
and then the corpse was slowly lowered beneath the surface
of the lake.

"Not *there*—Harry March—no, not *there*," said Judith,
shuddering involuntarily. "Do not lower it quite so near
the spot where mother lies!"

"Why not, Judith?" asked Hetty earnestly. "They lived together in life, and should lie together in death."

"No—no—Harry March, further off—further off. Poor
Hetty, you know not what you say. Leave me to order this."

"I know I am weak-minded, Judith, and that you are
clever—but surely a husband should be placed near a wife.
Mother always said that this was the way they bury in
Christian churchyards."

This little controversy was conducted earnestly but in
smothered voices, as if the speakers feared that the dead
might overhear them. Judith could not contend with her
sister at such a moment, but a significant gesture from
her induced March to lower the body at a little distance
from that of his wife; then he withdrew the cords, and the
act was performed.

"There's an end of Floating Tom!" exclaimed Hurry, bending over the scow and gazing through the water at the body. "He was a brave companion on a scout and a notable hand with traps. Don't weep, Judith—don't be overcome, Hetty, for the righteousest of us all must die, and when the time comes, lamentations and tears can't bring the dead to life. Your father will be a loss to you, no doubt—most fathers are a loss, especially to onmarried darters—but there's a way to cure that evil, and you're both too young and handsome to live long without finding it out. When it's agreeable to hear what an honest and onpretending man has to say, Judith, I should like to talk a little with you, apart."

Judith had scarce attended to this rude attempt of Hurry's at consolation, although she necessarily understood its general drift and had a tolerably accurate notion of its manner. She was weeping at the recollection of her mother's early tenderness, and painful images of long-forgotten lessons and neglected precepts were crowding her mind. The words of Hurry, however, recalled her to the present time, and abrupt and unseasonable as was their import, they did not produce those signs of distaste that one might have expected, from the girl's character. On the contrary, she appeared to be struck with some sudden idea, gazed intently for a moment at the young man, dried her eyes, and led the way to the other end of the scow, signifying her wish for him to follow. Here she took a seat and motioned for March to place himself at her side. The decision and earnestness with which all this was done a little intimidated her companion, and Judith found it necessary to open the subject herself.

"You wish to speak to me of marriage, Harry March," she said, "and I have come here, over the grave of my parents, as it might be—no, no—over the grave of my poor, dear, dear mother to hear what you have to say."

"This is oncommon, and you have a skearful way with you this evening, Judith," answered Hurry, more disturbed than he would have cared to own; "but truth is truth, and it shall come out, let what will follow. You well know, gal, that I've long thought you the comeliest young woman my eyes ever beheld, and that I've made no secret of that fact, either here on the lake, out among the hunters and trappers, or in the settlements."

"Yes—yes, I've heard this before, and I suppose it to be true," answered Judith, with a sort of feverish impatience.

"When a young man holds such language of any particular young woman, it's reasonable to calculate he sets store by her."

"True—true, Hurry—all this you've told me again and again."

"Well, if it's agreeable, I should think a woman couldn't hear it too often. They all tell me this is the way with your sex—that nothing pleases them more than to repeat, over and over, for the hundredth time, how much you like 'em, unless it be to talk to 'em of their good looks!"

"No doubt—we like both, on most occasions: but this is an uncommon moment, Hurry, and vain words should not be too freely used. I would rather hear you speak plainly."

"You shall have your own way, Judith, and I some suspect you always will. I've often told you that I not only like you better than any other young women going—or for that matter, better than *all* the young women going—but you must have obsarved, Judith, that I've never asked you, in up-and-down tarms, to marry me."

"I have observed both," returned the girl, a smile struggling about her beautiful mouth in spite of the singular and engrossing intentness which caused her cheeks to flush and lighted her eyes with a brilliancy that was almost dazzling. "I have observed both and have thought the last remarkable for a man of Harry March's decision and fearlessness."

"There's been a reason, gal, and it's one that troubles me even now—nay, don't flush up so, and look fierylike, for there are thoughts which will stick long in any man's mind, as there be words that will stick in his throat—but then, ag'in, there's feelin's that will get the better of 'em all, and to these feelin's I find I must submit. You've no longer a father, or a mother, Judith, and it's morally impossible that you and Hetty could live here alone, allowing it was peace and the Iroquois was quiet; but as matters stand, not only would you starve, but you'd both be prisoners, or scalped, afore a week was out. It's time to think of a change and a husband, and if you'll accept of me, all that's past shall be forgotten, and there's an end on't."

Judith had difficulty in repressing her impatience until this rude declaration and offer were made, which she evidently wished to hear and which she now listened to with a willingness that might well have excited hope. She hardly allowed the young man to conclude, so eager was she to bring him to the point and so ready to answer.

"There, Hurry, that's enough," she said, raising a hand, as if to stop him. "I understand you as well as if you were to talk a month. You prefer me to other girls, and you wish me to become your wife."

"You put it in better words than I can do, Judith, and I wish you to fancy them said, just as you most like to hear 'em."

"They're plain enough, Hurry, and 'tis fitting they should be so. This is no place to trifle or deceive in. Now listen to my answer, which shall be, in every tittle, as sincere as your offer. There is a reason, March, why I should never——"

"I suppose I understand you, Judith, but if I'm willing to overlook that reason, it's no one's consarn but mine. Now don't brighten up like the sky at sundown, for no offense is meant, and none should be taken."

"I do not brighten up, and will *not* take offense," said Judith, struggling to repress her indignation in a way she had never found it necessary to exert before. "There is a reason why I should not, *cannot*, ever be your wife, Hurry, that you seem to overlook, and which it is my duty now to tell you, as plainly as you have asked me to consent to become so. I do not, and I am certain that I never shall, love you well enough to marry you. No man can wish for a wife who does not prefer him to all other men, and when I tell you this frankly, I suppose you yourself will thank me for my sincerity."

"Oh, Judith, them flaunting, gay, scarlet-coated officers of the garrisons have done all this mischief!"

"Hush, March, do not calumniate a daughter over her mother's grave. Do not, when I only wish to treat you fairly, give me reason to call for evil on your head, in bitterness of heart! Do not forget that I am a woman, and that you are a man, and that I have neither father nor brother to revenge your words."

"Well, there is something in the last, and I'll say no more. Take time, Judith, and think better on this."

"I want no time; my mind has long been made up, and I have only waited for you to speak plainly, to answer plainly.

We now understand each other, and there is no use in saying any more."

The impetuous earnestness of the girl awed the young man, for never before had he seen her so serious and determined. In most of their previous interviews she had met his advances with evasion or sarcasm, but these Hurry had mistaken for female coquetry and had supposed might easily be converted into consent. The struggle had been with himself, about offering; he had never seriously believed it possible that Judith would refuse to become the wife of the handsomest man on all that frontier. Now that the refusal came, and that in terms so decided as to put all caviling out of the question, if not absolutely dumfounded, he was so much mortified and surprised as to feel no wish to attempt to change her resolution.

"The Glimmerglass has now no great call for me," he exclaimed after a minute's silence. "Old Tom is gone; the Hurons are as plenty on shore as pigeons in the woods, and altogether it is getting to be an onsuitable place."

"Then leave it. You see it surrounded by dangers, and there is no reason why you should risk your life for others. Nor do I know that you can be of any service to us. Go tonight; we'll never accuse you of having done anything forgetful or unmanly."

"If I do go, 'twill be with a heavy heart on your account, Judith; I would rather take you with me."

"That is not to be spoken of any longer, March; but I will land you in one of the canoes as soon as it is dark, and you can strike a trail for the nearest garrison. When you reach the fort, if you send a party—"

Judith smothered the words, for she felt that it was humiliating to be thus exposing herself to the comments and reflections of one who was not disposed to view her conduct in connection with all in these garrisons with an eye of favor. Hurry, however, caught the idea, and without perverting it, as the girl dreaded, he answered to the purpose.

"I understand *what* you would say, and *why* you don't say it," he replied. "If I get safe to the fort, a party shall start on the trail of these vagabonds, and I'll come with it myself, for I should like to see you and Hetty in a place of safety before we part forever."

"Ah, Harry March, had you always spoken thus, felt

thus, my feelings toward you might have been different!"

"Is it too late now, Judith? I'm rough and a woodsman, but we all change under different treatment from what we have been used to."

"It *is* too late, March. I can never feel toward you, or any other man but *one*, as you would wish to have me. There, I've said enough, surely, and you will question me no further. As soon as it is dark, I or the Delaware will put you on the shore; you will make the best of your way to the Mohawk and the nearest garrison and send all you can to our assistance. And, Hurry, we are now friends, and I may trust you, may I not?"

"Sartain, Judith, though our fri'ndship would have been all the warmer could you look upon me as I look upon you."

Judith hesitated, and some powerful emotion was struggling within her. Then, as if determined to look down all weaknesses and accomplish her purposes at every hazard, she spoke more plainly.

"You will find a captain of the name of Warley at the nearest post," she said, pale as death and even trembling as she spoke; "I think it likely he will wish to head the party; I would greatly prefer it should be another. If Captain Warley *can* be kept back, 'twould make me very happy."

"That's easier said than done, Judith, for those officers do pretty much as they please. The major will order, and captains, and lieutenants, and ensigns must obey. I know the officer you mean; a red-faced, gay, oh!-be-joyful sort of a gentleman, who swallows Madeira enough to drown the Mohawk, and yet a pleasant talker. All the gals in the valley admire him, and they say he admires all the gals. I don't wonder he is your dislike, Judith, for he's a very gin'ral lover, if he isn't a gin'ral officer."

Judith did not answer, though her frame shook, and her color changed from pale to crimson and from crimson back again to the hue of death.

"Alas, my poor mother!" she ejaculated mentally, instead of uttering it aloud. "We are over thy grave, but little dost thou know how much thy lessons have been forgotten; thy care neglected; thy love defeated."

As this goading of the worm that never dies was felt, she arose and signified to Hurry that she had no more to communicate.

CHAPTER XXII

———That point
In misery, which makes the oppressed man
Regardless of his own life, makes him too
Lord of the oppressor's———

COLERIDGE

ALL THIS TIME Hetty had remained seated in the head of the scow, looking sorrowfully into the water which held the body of her mother as well as that of the man whom she had been taught to consider her father. Hist stood near her in gentle quiet, but had no consolation to offer in words. The habits of her people taught her reserve in this respect, and the habits of her sex induced her to wait patiently for a moment when she might manifest some soothing sympathy by means of acts, rather than of speech. Chingachgook held himself a little aloof, in grave reserve, looking like a warrior but feeling like a man.

Judith joined her sister with an air of dignity and solemnity it was not her practice to show, and though the gleamings of anguish were still visible on her beautiful face, when she spoke, it was firmly and without tremor. At that instant Hist and the Delaware withdrew, moving toward Hurry, in the other end of the boat.

"Sister," said Judith kindly, "I have much to say to you. We will get into this canoe, and paddle off to a distance from the ark—the secrets of two orphans ought not to be heard by every ear."

"Certainly, Judith, by the ears of their parents. Let Hurry lift the grapnel, and move away with the ark, and leave us here, near the graves of Father and Mother, to say what we may have to say."

"Father!" repeated Judith slowly, the blood for the first

360

time since her parting with March, mounting to her cheeks; "He was no father of ours, Hetty! *That* we had from his own mouth, and in his dying moments."

"Are you glad, Judith, to find you had no father? He took care of us, and fed us, and clothed us, and loved us; a father could have done no more. I don't understand why he wasn't a father."

"Never mind, dear child, but let us do as you have said. It may be well to remain here and let the ark move a little away. Do you prepare the canoe, and I will tell Hurry and the Indians our wishes."

This was soon and simply done, the ark moving with measured strokes of the sweeps a hundred yards from the spot, leaving the girls floating seemingly in air, above the place of the dead, so buoyant was the light vessel that held them, and so limpid the element by which it was sustained.

"The death of Thomas Hutter," Judith commenced after a short pause had prepared her sister to receive her communications, "has altered all our prospects, Hetty. If he was *not* our father, we are *sisters* and must feel alike and live together."

"How do I know, Judith, that you wouldn't be as glad to find I am not your sister as you are in finding that Thomas Hutter, as you call him, was not your father? I am only half-witted, and few people like to have half-witted relations; and then I'm not handsome—at least, not as handsome as you—and you may wish a handsomer sister."

"No, no, Hetty. *You* and you only are my sister—my heart, and my love for you, tell me that—and Mother was my mother—of that, too, am I glad and proud, for she was a mother to be proud of—but Father was not father!"

"Hush, Judith! His spirit may be near; it would grieve it to hear his children talking so, and that, too, over his very grave. Children should never grieve parents, Mother often told me, and especially when they are dead!"

"Poor Hetty! They are happily removed beyond all cares on our accounts. Nothing that *I* can do or say will cause Mother any sorrow *now*—there is some consolation in that, at least!—and nothing *you* can say or do will make her smile, as she used to smile on your good conduct when living."

"You don't know that, Judith. Spirits can see, and Mother may see as well as any spirit. She always told us that God saw all we did and that we should do nothing to offend *him,* and now *she* has left us, I strive to do nothing that can displease *her.* Think how her spirit would mourn and feel sorrow, Judith, did it see either of us doing what is not right; and spirits *may* see, after all, especially the spirits of parents that feel anxious about their children."

"Hetty, Hetty—you know not what you say!" murmured Judith, almost livid with emotion. "The dead *cannot* see and know nothing of what passes here! But we will not talk of this any longer. The bodies of Mother and Thomas Hutter lie together in the lake, and we will hope that the spirits of both are with God. That we, the children of one of them, remain on earth is certain; it is now proper to know what we are to do in future."

"If we are not Thomas Hutter's children, Judith, no one will dispute our right to his property. We have the castle, and the ark, and the canoes, and the woods, and the lakes, the same as when he was living, and what can prevent us from staying here and passing our lives just as we ever have done?"

"No, no—poor sister. This can no longer be. Two girls would not be safe here, even should these Hurons fail in getting us into their power. Even Father had as much as he could sometimes do to keep peace upon the lake, and we should fail altogether. We must quit this spot, Hetty, and remove into the settlements."

"I am sorry you think so, Judith," returned Hetty, dropping her head on her bosom and looking thoughtfully down at the spot where the funeral pile of her mother could just be seen. "I am *very* sorry to hear it. I would rather stay here where, if I wasn't born, I've passed my life. I don't like the settlements—they are full of wickedness and heartburnings, while God dwells unoffended in these hills! I love the trees, and the mountains, and the lake, and the springs—all that His bounty has given us—and it would grieve me sorely, Judith, to be forced to quit them. You are handsome and not at all half-witted, and one day you will marry, and then you will have a husband, and I a brother, to take care of us, if women can't really take care of themselves in such a place as this."

"Ah! If this *could* be so, Hetty, then, indeed, I could *now* be a thousand times happier in these woods than in the settlements! *Once* I did not feel thus, but *now* I do. Yet where is the man to turn this beautiful place into such a Garden of Eden for us?"

"Harry March loves you, sister," returned poor Hetty, unconsciously picking the bark off the canoe as she spoke. "He would be glad to be your husband, I'm sure, and a stouter and a braver youth is not to be met with the whole country around."

"Harry March and I understand each other, and no more need be said about *him*. There is one—but no matter. It is all in the hands of Providence, and we must shortly come to some conclusion about our future manner of living. Remain here—that is, remain here alone, we cannot—and perhaps no occasion will ever offer for remaining in the manner you think of. It is time, too, Hetty, we should learn all we can concerning our relations and family. It is not probable we are altogether without relations, and they may be glad to see us. The old chest is now our property, and we have a right to look into it and learn all we can by what it holds. Mother was so very different from Thomas Hutter that, now I know we are not his children, I burn with a desire to know whose children we can be. There are papers in that chest, I am certain, and those papers may tell us all about our parents and natural friends."

"Well, Judith, you know best, for you are cleverer than common, Mother always said, and I am only half-witted. Now Father and Mother are dead, I don't much care for any relations but you, and don't think I could love them I never saw as well as I ought. If you don't like to marry Hurry, I don't see who you can choose for a husband, and then I fear we shall have to quit the lake after all."

"What do you think of Deerslayer, Hetty?" asked Judith, bending forward like her unsophisticated sister and endeavoring to conceal her embarrassment in a similar manner. "Would he not make a brother-in-law to your liking?"

"Deerslayer!" repeated the other, looking up in unfeigned surprise. "Why, Judith, Deerslayer isn't in the least comely, and is altogether unfit for one like you!"

"He is not ill-looking, Hetty, and beauty in a man is not of much matter."

"Do you think so, Judith? I know that beauty is of no great matter, in man or woman, in the eyes of God; Mother has often told me so, when she thought I might have been sorry I was not as handsome as you—though she needn't have been uneasy on that account, for I never coveted anything that is yours, sister; but tell me so she did; still, beauty is very pleasant to the eye, in both. I think, if I were a man, I should pine more for good looks than I do as a girl. A handsome man is a more pleasing sight than a handsome woman."

"Poor child! You scarce know what you say or what you mean! Beauty in our sex is something, but in man it passes for little. To be sure, a man ought to be tall, but others are tall as well as Hurry; and active—I think I know those that are more active; and strong—well, he hasn't all the strength in the world; and brave—I am certain I can name a youth who is braver."

"This is strange, Judith. I didn't think the earth held a handsomer, or a stronger, or a more active, or a braver man than Hurry Harry. I am sure *I* never met his equal in either of these things."

"Well, well, Hetty—say no more of this. I dislike to hear *you* talking in this manner. 'Tis not suitable to your innocence, and truth, and warmhearted sincerity. Let Harry March go. He quits us tonight, and no regret of mine will follow him, unless it be that he has stayed so long and to so little purpose."

"Ah, Judith, that is what I've long feared, and I did *so* hope he might be my brother-in-law!"

"Never mind it now; let us talk of our poor mother and of Thomas Hutter."

"Speak kindly, then, sister, for you can't be quite certain that spirits don't both hear and see. If Father wasn't father, he was good to us and gave us food and shelter. We can't put any stones over their graves here in the water to tell people all this, and so we ought to say it it with our tongues."

"They will care little for that, girl. 'Tis a great consolation to know, Hetty, that if Mother ever did commit any heavy fault when young, she lived sincerely to repent of it; no doubt her sins were forgiven her."

" 'Tisn't right, Judith, for children to talk of their parents' sins. We had better talk of our own."

"Talk of your sins, Hetty! If there ever was a creature on earth without sin, it is you! I wish I could say or think the same of myself; but we shall see. No one knows what changes affection for a good husband can make in a woman's heart. I don't think, child, I have even now the same love for finery I once had."

"It would be a pity, Judith, if you did think of clothes over your parents' graves! We will never quit this spot, if you say so, and will let Hurry go where he pleases."

"I am willing enough to consent to the last, but cannot answer for the first, Hetty. We must live, in future, as becomes respectable young women, and cannot remain here to be the talk and jest of all the rude and foul-tongued trappers and hunters that may come upon the lake. Let Hurry go by himself, and then I'll find the means to see Deerslayer, when the future shall be soon settled. Come, girl, the sun has set and the ark is drifting away from us; let us paddle up to the scow and consult with our friends. This night I shall look into the chest, and tomorrow shall determine what we are to do. As for the Hurons, now we can use our stores without fear of Thomas Hutter, they will be easily bought off. Let me get Deerslayer once out of their hands, and a single hour shall bring things to an understanding."

Judith spoke with decision, and she spoke with authority, a habit she had long practiced toward her feeble-minded sister. But while thus accustomed to have her way by the aid of manner and a readier command of words, Hetty occasionally checked her impetuous feelings and hasty acts by the aid of those simple moral truths that were so deeply engrafted in all her own thoughts and feelings, shining through both with a mild and beautiful luster that threw a sort of holy halo around so much of what she both said and did. On the present occasion, this healthful ascendency of the girl of weak intellect over her of a capacity that, in other situations, might have become brilliant and admired, was exhibited in the usual simple and earnest manner.

"You forget, Judith, what has brought us here," she said reproachfully. "This is Mother's grave, and we have just laid the body of Father by her side. We have done wrong to talk so much of ourselves at such a spot, and ought now to pray God to forgive us and ask *Him* to teach us where we are to go and what we are to do."

Judith involuntarily laid aside her paddle, while Hetty dropped on her knees and was soon lost in her devout but simple petitions. Her sister did not pray. This she had long ceased to do directly, though anguish of spirit frequently wrung from her mental and hasty appeals to the great source of benevolence for support, if not for a change of spirit. Still, she never beheld Hetty on her knees that a feeling of tender recollection, as well as of profound regret at the deadness of her own heart, did not come over her. Thus had she herself done in childhood and even down to the hour of her ill-fated visits to the garrisons; and she would willingly have given worlds, at such moments, to be able to exchange her present sensations for that confiding faith, those pure aspirations, and the gentle hope that shone through every lineament and movement of her otherwise less-favored sister. All she could do, however, was to drop her head to her bosom and assume in her attitude some of that devotion in which her stubborn spirit refused to unite.

When Hetty rose from her knees, her countenance had a glow and serenity that rendered a face that was always agreeable positively handsome. Her mind was at peace, and her conscience acquitted her of a neglect of duty.

"Now you may go, if you want to, Judith," she said. "God has been kind to me and lifted a burden off my heart. Mother had many such burdens, she used to tell me, and she always took them off in this way. 'Tis the only way, sister, such things can be done. You may raise a stone, or a log, with your hands, but the heart *must* be lightened by prayer. I don't think you pray as often as you used to do when younger, Judith!"

"Never mind—never mind, child," answered the other huskily; " 'tis no matter, now. Mother is gone, and Thomas Hutter is gone, and the time has come when we must think and act for ourselves."

As the canoe moved slowly away from the place under the gentle impulsion of the elder sister's paddle, the younger sat musing, as was her wont whenever her mind was perplexed by any idea more abstract and difficult of comprehension than common.

"I don't know what you mean by future, Judith," she at length suddenly observed. "Mother used to call heaven the future, but you seem to think it means next week, or to-morrow!"

"It means both, dear sister—everything that is yet to come, whether in this world or another. It is a solemn word, Hetty, and most so, I fear, to them that think the least about it. Mother's future is eternity; ours may yet mean what will happen while we live in this world—is not that a canoe just passing behind the castle? Here, more in the direction of the point, I mean; it is hid, now; but certainly I saw a canoe stealing behind the logs."

"I've seen it some time," Hetty quietly answered, for the Indians had few terrors for her, "but I did not think it right to talk about such things over Mother's grave. The canoe came from the camp, Judith, and was paddled by a single man; he seemed to be Deerslayer, and no Iroquois."

"Deerslayer!" returned the other, with much of her native impetuosity. "That can't be! Deerslayer is a prisoner, and I have been thinking of the means of setting him free. Why did you fancy it Deerslayer, child?"

"You can look for yourself, sister; there comes the canoe in sight again, on this side of the hut."

Sure enough, the light boat had passed the building, and was now steadily advancing toward the ark, the persons on board of which were already collecting in the head of the scow to receive their visitor. A single glance sufficed to assure Judith that her sister was right and that Deerslayer was alone in the canoe. His approach was so calm and leisurely, however, as to fill her with wonder, since a man who had effected his escape from enemies, by either artifice or violence, would not be apt to move with the steadiness and deliberation with which his paddle swept the water. By this time the day was fairly departing, and objects were already seen dimly under the shores. In the broad lake, however, the light still lingered, and around the immediate scene of the present incidents, which was less shaded than most of the sheet, being in its broadest part, it cast a glare that bore some faint resemblance to the warm tints of an Italian or Grecian sunset. The logs of the hut and ark had a sort of purple hue, blended with the growing obscurity, and the bark of the hunter's boat was losing its distinctness, in colors richer but more mellowed than those it showed under a bright sun. As the two canoes approached each other—for Judith and her sister had plied their paddles so as to intercept the unexpected visitor ere he reached the ark—even Deerslayer's sunburned countenance wore a brighter aspect than common, under the pleasing tints that seemed to dance in the atmosphere. Judith fancied that delight at meeting her had some share in this unusual and agreeable expression. She was not aware that her own beauty appeared to more advantage than common from the same natural cause, nor did she understand what it would have given her so much pleasure to know, that the young man actually thought her, as she drew near, the loveliest creature of her sex, his eyes had ever dwelt on.

"Welcome—welcome, Deerslayer!" exclaimed the girl as the canoes floated at each other's sides. "We have had a melancholy—a frightful day—but your return is, at least, one misfortune the less. Have the Hurons become more humane and let you go, or have you escaped from the wretches by your own courage and skill?"

"Neither, Judith—neither one nor t'other. The Mingos are Mingos still, and will live and die Mingos; it is not likely their natur's will ever undergo much improvement. Well, they've *their* gifts, and we've our'n, Judith, and it doesn't much become either to speak ill of what the Lord has created, though if the truth must be said, I find it a sore trial to think kindly or to talk kindly of them vagabonds. As for outwitting them, that might have been done, and it *was* done, too, atween the Sarpent, yonder, and me, when we were on the trail of Hist"—here the hunter stopped to laugh in his own silent fashion—"but it's no easy matter to sarcumvent the sarcumvented. Even the fa'ans get to know the tricks of the hunters afore a single season is over, and an Indian whose eyes have once been opened by a sarcumvention never shuts them ag'in in precisely the same spot. I've known whites to do that, but never a redskin. What they l'arn comes by practice, and not by books, and of all schoolmasters, exper'ence gives lessons that are the longest remembered."

"All this is true, Deerslayer; but if you have not escaped from the savages, how came you here?"

"That's a nat'ral question, and charmingly put. You *are* wonderful handsome this evening, Judith, or Wild Rose, as the Sarpent calls you, and I may as well say it, since I honestly think it. You may well call them Mingos savages, too, for savage enough do they feel, and savage enough will they act, if you once give them an opportunity. They feel their loss here, in the late scrimmage, to their hearts' cores, and are ready to revenge it on any creatur' of English blood that may fall in their way. Nor, for that matter, do I much think they would stand at taking their satisfaction out of a Dutchman."

"They have killed Father; that ought to satisfy their wicked cravings for blood," observed Hetty reproachfully.

"I know it, gal—I know the whole story—partly from what I've seen from the shore, since they brought me up from the point, and partly from their threats ag'in myself, and their other discourse. Well, life is unsartain at the best, and we all depend on the breath of our nostrils for it from day to day. If you've lost a staunch fri'nd, as I make no doubt you have, Providence will raise up new ones in his stead, and since our acquaintance has begun in this oncommon manner, I shall take it as a hint that it will be a part of my duty in futur', should the occasion offer, to see you don't suffer for want of food in the wigwam. I can't bring the dead to life, but as to feeding the living, there's few on all this frontier can outdo me, though I say it in the way of pity and consolation like, and in no particular in the way of boasting!"

"We understand you, Deerslayer," returned Judith hastily, "and take all that falls from your lips as it is meant, in kindness and friendship. Would to heaven all men had tongues as true and hearts as honest!"

"In that respect men *do* differ, of a sartainty, Judith. I've known them that wasn't to be trusted any further than you can see them, and others ag'in whose messages, sent with a small piece of wampum, perhaps, might just as much be depended on as if the whole business was finished afore your face. Yes, Judith, you never said truer words than when you said some men might be depended on and some others might not."

"You are an unaccountable being, Deerslayer," returned the girl, not a little puzzled by the childish simplicity of character that the hunter so often betrayed—a simplicity so striking that it frequently appeared to place him nearly on a level with the fatuity of poor Hetty, though always relieved by the beautiful moral truth that shone through all that this unfortunate girl both said and did. "You are a most unaccountable man, and I often do not know how to understand you. But never mind, just now; you have forgotten to tell us by what means you are here."

"I!—oh! That's not very onaccountable, if I am myself, Judith. I'm out on furlough."

"Furlough! That word has a meaning among the soldiers that I understand; I cannot tell what it signifies when used by a prisoner."

"It means just the same. You're right enough; the soldiers do use it, and just in the same way as I use it. A furlough is when a man has leave to quit a camp, or a garrison, for a sartain specified time, at the end of which he is to come back and shoulder his musket, or submit to his torments, just as he may happen to be a soldier or a captyve. Being the last, I must take the chances of a prisoner."

"Have the Hurons suffered you to quit them in this manner, without watch or guard?"

"Sartain—I couldn't have come in any other manner, unless, indeed, it had been by a bold rising, or a sarcumvention."

"What pledge have they that you will ever return?"

"My word," answered the hunter simply. "Yes, I own I gave 'em *that*, and big fools would they have been to let me come without it! Why, in that case, I shouldn't have been obliged to go back and ondergo any deviltries their fury may invent, but might have shouldered my rifle, and made the best of my way to the Delaware villages. But, Lord, Judith, they know'd this, just as well as you and I do, and would no more let me come away without a promise to go back than they would let the wolves dig up the bones of their fathers!"

"Is it possible you mean to do this act of extraordinary self-destruction and recklessness?"

"Anan!"

"I ask if it can be possible that you expect to be able to put yourself again in the power of such ruthless enemies by keeping your word?"

Deerslayer looked at his fair questioner for a moment with stern displeasure. Then the expression of his honest and guileless face suddenly changed, lighting as by a quick illumination of thought, after which he laughed in his ordinary manner.

"I didn't understand you, at first, Judith; no, I didn't. You believe that Chingachgook and Hurry Harry won't suffer it, but you don't know mankind thoroughly yet, I see. The Delaware would be the last man on 'arth to offer any objections to what he knows is a duty; as for March, he doesn't care enough about any creatur' but himself to spend many words on such a subject. If he did, 'twould make no great difference, howsever; but not he—for he thinks more of his gains than of even his own word. As for my promises, or your'n, Judith, or anybody else's, they give him no consarn. Don't be under any oneasiness, therefore, gal; I shall be allowed to go back according to the furlough; and if difficulties was made, I've not been brought up, and edicated, as one may say, in the woods, without knowing how to look 'em down."

Judith made no answer for some little time. All her feelings as a woman—and as a woman who, for the first time in her life, was beginning to submit to that sentiment which has so much influence on the happiness or misery of her sex—revolted at the cruel fate that she fancied Deerslayer was drawing down upon himself, while the sense of right, which God has implanted in every human breast, told her to admire an integrity as indomitable and unpretending as that which the other so unconsciously displayed. Argument, she felt, would be useless, nor was she, at that moment, disposed to lessen the dignity and high principle that were so striking in the intentions of the hunter by any attempt to turn him from his purpose. That something might yet occur to supersede the necessity for this self-immolation she tried to hope, and then she proceeded to ascertain the facts in order that her own conduct might be regulated by her knowledge of circumstances.

"When is your furlough out, Deerslayer?" she asked, after both canoes were heading toward the ark and moving, with scarcely a perceptible effort of the paddles, through the water.

"Tomorrow noon; not a minute afore; and you may depend on it, Judith, I shan't quit what I call Christian company to go and give myself up to them vagabonds an instant sooner than is downright necessary. They begin to fear a visit from the garrisons, and wouldn't lengthen the time a moment; and it's pretty well understood atween us that, should I fail in my ar'n'd, the torments are to take place when the sun begins to fall, that they may strike upon their home trail as soon as it is dark."

This was said solemnly, as if the thought of what was believed to be in reserve duly weighed on the prisoner's mind, and yet so simply and without a parade of suffering as rather to repel than to invite any open manifestations of sympathy.

"Are they bent on revenging their losses?" Judith asked faintly, her own high spirit yielding to the influence of the other's quiet but dignified integrity of purpose.

"Downright, if I can judge of Indian inclinations by the symptoms. They think, howsever, I don't suspect their designs, I do believe; but one that has lived so long among men of redskin gifts is no more likely to be misled in Injin feelin's than a true hunter is like to lose his trail, or a staunch hound his scent. My own judgment is greatly ag'in my own escape, for I see the women are a good deal enraged on behalf of Hist, though I say it, perhaps, that shouldn't say it—seein' that I had a considerable hand myself in getting the gal off. Then there was a cruel murder in their camp last night, and that shot might just as well have been fired into my breast. Howsever, come what will, the Sarpent and his wife will be safe, and that is some happiness, in any case."

"Oh, Deerslayer, they will think better of this, since they have given you until tomorrow noon to make up your mind!"

"I judge not, Judith; yes, I judge not. An Injin is an Injin, gal, and it's pretty much hopeless to think of swarving him when he's got the scent and follows it with his nose in the air. The Delawares, now, are a half-christianized tribe —not that I think such sort of Christians much better than your whole-blooded disbelievers—but, nevertheless, what good half-christianizing can do to a man some among 'em have got, and yet revenge clings to their hearts like the wild creepers here to the tree! Then I slew one of the best and boldest of their warriors, they say, and it *is* too much to expect that they should captivate the man who did this deed in the very same scouting on which it was performed, and they take no account of the matter. Had a month or so gone by, their feelin's would have been softened down, and we might have met in a more friendly way; but it is as it is. Judith, this is talking of nothing but myself and my own consarns, when you have had trouble enough, and may want to consult a fri'nd a little about your own matters. Is the old man laid in the water, where I should think his body would like to rest?"

"It is, Deerslayer," answered Judith almost inaudibly. "That duty has just been performed. You are right in thinking that I wish to consult a friend, and that friend is yourself. Hurry Harry is about to leave us; when he is gone, and we have got a little over the feelings of this solemn office, I hope you will give me an hour alone. Hetty and I are at a loss what to do."

"That's quite natural, coming as things have, suddenly and fearfully. But here's the ark, and we'll say more of this when there is a better opportunity."

CHAPTER XXIII

The winde is great upon the highest hilles;
The quiet life is in the dale below;
Who tread on ice shall slide against their willes;
They want not cares, that curious arts should know;
Who lives at ease and can content him so,
Is perfect wise, and sets us all to schoole:
Who hates this lore may well be called a foole.

CHURCHYARD

THE MEETING BETWEEN Deerslayer and his friends in the ark was grave and anxious. The two Indians, in particular, read in his manner that he was not a successful fugitive, and a few sententious words sufficed to let them comprehend the nature of what their friend had termed his "furlough." Chingachgook immediately became thoughtful, while Hist, as usual, had no better mode of expressing her sympathy than by those little attentions which mark the affectionate manner of woman.

In a few minutes, however, something like a general plan for the proceedings of the night was adopted, and to the eye of an uninstructed observer, things would be thought to move in their ordinary train. It was now getting to be dark, and it was decided to sweep the ark up to the castle and secure it in its ordinary berth. This decision was come to in some measure on account of the fact that all the canoes were again in the possession of their proper owners, but principally from the security that was created by the representations of Deerslayer. He had examined the state of things among the Hurons, and felt satisfied that they meditated no further hostilities during the night, the loss they had met having indisposed them to further exertions for the moment. Then, he had a proposition to make—the object of his visit—and if this were accepted, the war would at once terminate between the parties, and it was improbable that the Hurons would anticipate the failure of a project on which their chiefs had apparently set their hearts by having recourse to violence previously to the return of their messenger.

As soon as the ark was properly secured, the different members of the party occupied themselves in their several peculiar manners, haste in council or in decision no more characterizing the proceedings of the border whites than it did those of their red neighbors. The women busied themselves in preparations for the evening meal, sad and silent, but ever attentive to the first wants of nature.

Hurry set about repairing his moccasins by the light of a blazing knot; Chingachgook seated himself in gloomy thought; while Deerslayer proceeded, in a manner equally free from affectation and concern, to examine "Killdeer," the rifle of Hutter that has been already mentioned, and which subsequently became so celebrated in the hands of the individual who was now making a survey of its merits. The piece was a little longer than usual, and had evidently been turned out from the workshop of some manufacturer of a superior order. It had a few silver ornaments, though on the whole it would have been deemed a plain piece by most frontiersmen; its great merit consisting in the accuracy of its bore, the perfection of the details, and the excellence of the metal. Again and again did the hunter apply the breech to his shoulder and glance his eye along the sights, and as often did he poise his body and raise the weapon slowly, as if about to catch an aim at a deer, in order to try the weight and to ascertain its fitness for quick and accurate firing. All this was done by the aid of Hurry's torch, simply, but with an earnestness and abstraction that would have been found touching by any spectator who happened to know the real situation of the man.

" 'Tis a glorious we'pon, Hurry!" Deerslayer at length exclaimed, "and it may be thought a pity that it has fallen into the hands of women. The hunters have told me of its expl'ites, and by all I have heard I should set it down as sartain death in exper'enced hands. Hearken to the tick of this lock—a wolf trap hasn't a livelier spring; pan and cock speak together, like two singing masters undertaking a psalm in meetin'. I never *did* see so true a bore, Hurry, that's sartain."

"Aye, Old Tom used to give the piece a character, though he wasn't the man to particularize the ra'al natur' of any sort of firearms in practice," returned March, passing the deer's thongs through the moccasin with the coolness of a cobbler. "He was no marksman, that we must all allow, but he had his good p'ints as well as his bad ones. I have had hopes that Judith might consait the idee of giving Killdeer to me."

"There's no saying what young women may do, that's a truth, Hurry, and I suppose you're as likely to own the rifle as another. Still, when things are so very near perfection, it's a pity not to reach it entirely."

"What do you mean by that? Would not that piece look as well on my shoulder as on any man's?"

"As for looks, I say nothing. You are both good-looking and might make what is called a good-looking couple. But the true p'int is as to conduct. More deer would fall in one day, by that piece, in some men's hands than would fall in a week in your'n, Hurry! I've seen you try; you remember the buck, t'other day?"

"That buck was out of season, and who wishes to kill venison out of season? I was merely trying to frighten the creatur', and I think you will own that he was pretty well skeared, at any rate."

"Well, well, have it as you say. But this is a lordly piece, and would make a steady hand and quick eye the King of the Woods."

"Then keep it, Deerslayer, and become King of the Woods," said Judith earnestly, who had heard the conversation, and whose eye was never long averted from the honest countenance of the hunter. "It can never be in better hands than it is at this moment; there I hope it will remain these fifty years."

"Judith, you can't be in 'arnest!" exclaimed Deerslayer, taken so much by surprise as to betray more emotion than it was usual for him to manifest on ordinary occasions. "Such a gift would be fit for a ra'al king to make—yes, and for a ra'al king to receive."

"I never was more in earnest in my life, Deerslayer, and I am as much in earnest in the wish as in the gift."

"Well, gal, well, we'll find time to talk of this ag'in. You mustn't be downhearted, Hurry, for Judith is a sprightly young woman, and she has a quick reason; she knows that the credit of her father's rifle is safer in my hands than it can possibly be in your'n, and therefore you mustn't be downhearted. In other matters, more to your liking, too, you'll find she'll give you the preference."

Hurry growled out his dissatisfaction, but he was too intent on quitting the lake and in making his preparations to waste his breath on a subject of this nature. Shortly after, the supper was ready; it was eaten in silence, as is so much the habit of those who consider the table as merely a place of animal refreshment. On this occasion, however, sadness and thought contributed their share to the general desire not to converse, for Deerslayer was so far an exception to the usages of men of his cast as not only to wish to hold discourse on such occasions, but as often to create a similar desire in his companions.

The meal ended, and the humble preparations removed, the whole party assembled on the platform to hear the expected intelligence from Deerslayer on the subject of his visit. It had been evident he was in no haste to make his communications, but the feelings of Judith would no longer admit of delay. Stools were brought from the ark and the hut, and the whole six placed themselves in a circle, near the door, watching each other's countenances as best they could by the scanty means that were furnished by a lovely, starlit night. Along the shore, beneath the mountains, lay the usual body of gloom, but in the broad lake no shadow was cast, and a thousand mimic stars were dancing in the limpid element that was just stirred enough by the evening air to set them all in motion.

"Now, Deerslayer," commenced Judith, whose impatience resisted further restraint; "tell us all the Hurons have to say, and the reason why they have sent you on parole, to make us some offer."

"Furlough, Judith; furlough is the word; and it carries the same meaning with a captyve at large as it does with a soldier who has leave to quit his colors. In both cases the word is passed to come back—and now I remember to have heard that's the ra'al signification, 'furlough' meaning a 'word' passed for the doing of anything, or the like. Parole,

I rather think, is Dutch and has something to do with the tattoos of the garrisons. But this makes no great difference, since the vartue of a pledge lies in the idea, not in the word. Well, then, if the message must be given, it must, and perhaps there is no use in putting it off. Hurry will soon be wanting to set out on his journey to the river, and the stars rise and set just as if they cared for neither Injin nor message. Ah's me! 'Tisn't a pleasant, and I know it's a useless ar'n'd, but it must be told."

"Hearkee, Deerslayer," put in Hurry a little authoritatively; "you're a sensible man in a hunt, and as good a fellow on a march as a sixty-miler-a-day could wish to meet with, but you're oncommon slow about messages, especially them that you think won't be likely to be well received. When a thing is to be told, why, tell it, and don't hang back like a Yankee lawyer pretending he can't understand a Dutchman's English, just to get a double fee out of him."

"I understand you, Hurry, and well are you named to-night, seeing you've no time to lose. But let us come at once to the p'int, seeing that's the object of this council— for council it may be called, though women have seats among us. The simple fact is this. When the party came back from the castle, the Mingos held a council, and bitter thoughts were uppermost, as was plainly to be seen by their gloomy faces. No one likes to be beaten, a redskin as little as a paleface. Well, when they had smoked upon it, and made their speeches, and their council fire had burnt low, the matter came out. It seems the elders among 'em consaited I was a man to be trusted on a furlough. They're wonderful obsarvant, them Mingos; *that* their worst inimies must allow; but they consaited I was such a man; and it isn't often," added the hunter, with a pleasing consciousness that his previous life justified this implicit reliance on his good faith, "it isn't often they consait anything so good of a paleface; but so they did with me, and therefore they didn't hesitate to speak their minds, which is just this: You see the state of things. The lake and all on it, they fancy, lie at their marcy. Thomas Hutter is deceased, and as for Hurry, they've got the idea he has been near enough to death today not to wish to take another look at him this summer. Therefore, they account all your forces as reduced to Chingachgook and the two young women, and while they know the Delaware to be of a high race, and a born warrior, they know he's now on his first warpath. As for the gals, of course they set them down much as they do women in gin'ral."

"You mean that they despise us!" interrupted Judith, with eyes that flashed so brightly as to be observed by all present.

"That will be seen in the ind. They hold that all on the lake lies at their marcy, and therefore they send by me this belt of wampum"—showing the article in question to the Delaware, as he spoke—"with these words: Tell the Sarpent, they say, that he has done well for a beginner; he may now strike across the mountains for his own villages, and no one shall look for his trail. If he has found a scalp, let him take it with him; the Huron braves have hearts and can feel for a young warrior who doesn't wish to go home empty-handed. If he is nimble, he is welcome to lead out a party in pursuit. Hist, howsever, must go back to the Hurons; when she left them in the night, she carried away, by mistake, that which doesn't belong to her."

"That *can't* be true!" said Hetty earnestly. "Hist is no such girl—but one that gives everybody his due—"

How much more she would have said in remonstrance cannot be known, inasmuch as Hist, partly laughing and partly hiding her face in shame, put her own hand across the speaker's mouth in a way to check the words.

"You don't understand Mingo messages, poor Hetty," resumed Deerslayer, "which seldom mean what lies exactly uppermost. Hist has brought away with her the inclinations of a young Huron, and they want her back again, that the poor young man may find them where he last saw them! The Sarpent, they say, is too promising a young warrior not to find as many wives as he wants, but this one he cannot have. That's their meaning, and nothing else, as I understand it."

"They are very obliging and thoughtful in supposing a young woman can forget all her own inclinations in order to let this unhappy youth find his!" said Judith ironically, though her manner became more bitter as she proceeded. "I suppose a woman is a woman, let her color be white or red, and your chiefs know little of a woman's heart, Deerslayer, if they think it can ever forgive when wronged, or ever forget when it fairly loves."

"I suppose that's pretty much the truth with some women,

Judith, though I've known them that could do both. The next message is to you. They say the Muskrat, as they call your father, has dove to the bottom of the lake; that he will never come up again; and that his young will soon be in want of wigwams, if not of food. The Huron huts, they think, are better than the huts of York; they wish you to come and try them. Your color is white, they own, but they think young women who've lived so long in the woods would lose their way in the clearin's. A great warrior among them has lately lost his wife, and he would be glad to put the Wild Rose on her bench at his fireside. As for the Feeble-mind, she will always be honored and taken care of by red warriors. Your father's goods, they think, ought to go to enrich the tribe, but your own property, which is to include everything of a female natur', will go, like that of all wives, into the wigwam of the husband. Moreover, they've lost a young maiden by violence lately, and 'twill take two palefaces to fill her seat."

"And do *you* bring such a message to *me?*" exclaimed Judith, though the tone in which the words were uttered had more in it of sorrow than of anger. "Am I a girl to be an Indian's slave?"

"If you wish my honest thoughts on this p'int, Judith, I shall answer that I don't think you'll willingly ever become any man's slave, redskin or white. You're not to think hard, howsever, of my bringing the message, as near as I could, in the very words in which it was given to me. Them was the conditions on which I got my furlough, and a bargain is a bargain, though it is made with a vagabond. I've told you what *they've* said, but I've not yet told you what I think you ought, one and all, to answer."

"Aye, let's hear that, Deerslayer," put in Hurry. "My cur'osity is up on that consideration, and I should like right well to hear your idees of the reasonableness of the reply. For my part, though, my own mind is pretty much settled on the p'int of my own answer, which shall be made known as soon as necessary."

"And so is mine, Hurry, on all the different heads, and on no one is it more sartainly settled than on your'n. If I was you, I should say—'Deerslayer, tell them scamps they don't know Harry March! He is human, and having a white skin he has also a white natur', which natur' won't let him desart females of his own race and gifts in their greatest need. So set me down as one that will refuse to come into your treaty, though you should smoke a hogshead of tobacco over it."

March was a little embarrassed at this rebuke, which was uttered with sufficient warmth of manner and with a point that left no doubt of the meaning. Had Judith encouraged him, he would not have hesitated about remaining to defend her and her sister, but under the circumstances a feeling of resentment rather urged him to abandon them. At all events, there was not a sufficiency of chivalry in Hurry Harry to induce him to hazard the safety of his own person, unless he could see a direct connection between the probable consequences and his own interests. It is no wonder, therefore, that his answer partook equally of his intention and of the reliance he so boastingly placed on his gigantic strength, which, if it did not always make him courageous, usually made him impudent as respects those with whom he conversed.

"Fair words make long friendships, Master Deerslayer," he said a little menacingly. "You're but a stripling, and you know by exper'ence what you are in the hands of a man. As you're not me, but only a go-between sent by the savages to us Christians, you may tell your empl'yers that they do know Harry March, which is a proof of their sense as well as his. He's human enough to follow human natur', and that tells him to see the folly of one man's fighting a whole tribe. If females desart him, they must expect to be desarted *by* him, whether they're of his own gifts or another man's gifts. Should Judith see fit to change her mind, she's welcome to my company to the river, and Hetty with her; but shouldn't she come to this conclusion, I start as soon as I think the enemy's scouts are beginning to nestle themselves in among the brush and leaves for the night."

"Judith will *not* change her mind, and she does not ask your company, Master March," returned the girl, with spirit.

"That p'int's settled, then," resumed Deerslayer, unmoved by the other's warmth. "Hurry Harry must act for himself and do that which will be most likely to suit his own fancy. The course he means to take will give him an easy race, if it don't give him an easy conscience. Next comes the question with Hist—what say you, gal?—will you desart your duty, too, and go back to the Mingos and take a Huron husband; and all, not for the love of the man you're to marry, but for the love of your own scalp?"

"Why you talk so to Hist?" demanded the girl, half offended. "You t'ink a redskin girl made like captain's lady, to laugh and joke with any officer that come?"

"What I think, Hist, is neither here nor there, in this matter. I must carry back your answer, and in order to do so, it is necessary that you should send it. A faithful messenger gives his ar'n'd, word for word."

Hist no longer hesitated to speak her mind fully. In the excitement she rose from her bench, and naturally recurring to that language in which she expressed herself the most readily, she delivered her thoughts and intentions beautifully and with dignity in the tongue of her own people.

"Tell the Hurons, Deerslayer," she said, "that they are as ignorant as moles; they don't know the wolf from the dog. Among my people, the rose dies on the stem where it budded; the tears of the child fall on the graves of its parents; the corn grows where the seed has been planted. The Delaware girls are not messengers, to be sent like belts of wampum from tribe to tribe. They are honeysuckles that are sweetest in their own woods; their own young men carry them away in their bosoms because they are fragrant; they are sweetest when plucked from their native stems. Even the robin and the marten come back, year after year, to their old nests; shall a woman be less truehearted than a bird? Set the pine in the clay, and it will turn yellow; the willow will not flourish on the hill; the tamarack is healthiest in the swamp; the tribes of the sea love best to hear the winds that blow over the salt water. As for a Huron youth, what is he to a maiden of the Lenni Lenape? He may be fleet, but her eyes do not follow him in the race; they look back toward the lodges of the Delawares. He may sing a sweet song for the girls of Canada, but there is no music for Wah but in the tongue she has listened to from childhood. Were the Huron born of the people that once roamed the shores of the salt lake, it would be in vain, unless he were of the family of Uncas. The young pine will rise to be as high as any of its fathers. Wah-ta!-Wah has but one heart, and it can love but one husband."

Deerslayer listened to this characteristic message, which

was given with an earnestness suited to the feelings from which it sprang, with undisguised delight, meeting the ardent eloquence of the girl, as she concluded, with one of his own heartfelt, silent, and peculiar fits of laughter.

"That's worth all the wampum in the woods!" he exclaimed. "You don't understand it, I suppose, Judith; but if you'll look into your feelin's, and fancy that an inimy had sent to tell you to give up the man of your ch'ice, and to take up with another that wasn't the man of your ch'ice, you'll get the substance of it, I'll warrant! Give me a woman for ra'al eloquence, if they'll only make up their minds to speak what they *feel*. By speakin', I don't mean chatterin', howsever; for most of them will do *that* by the hour; but comin' out with their honest, deepest feelin's, in proper words. And now, Judith, having got the answer of a redskin girl, it is fit I should get that of a paleface, if, indeed, a countenance that is as blooming as your'n can in any wise so be tarmed. You are well named the Wild Rose, and so far as color goes, Hetty ought to be called the Honeysuckle."

"Did this language come from one of the garrison gallants, I should deride it, Deerslayer; but coming from *you*, I know it can be depended on," returned Judith, deeply gratified by his unmeditated and characteristic compliments. "It is too soon, however, to ask my answer; the Great Serpent has not yet spoken."

"The Sarpent? Lord; I could carry back his speech without hearing a word of it! I didn't think of putting the question to him at all, I will allow; though 'twould be hardly right either, seeing that truth is truth, and I'm bound to tell these Mingos the fact, and nothing else. So, Chingachgook, let us hear *your* mind on this matter—are you inclined to strike across the hills toward your village, to give up Hist to a Huron, and to tell the chiefs at home, that if they're actyve and successful they may possibly get *on* the end of the Iroquois trail some two or three days a'ter the inimy has got *off* of it?"

Like his betrothed, the young chief arose, that his answer might be given with due distinctness and dignity. Hist had spoken with her hands crossed upon her bosom, as if to suppress the emotions within; but the warrior stretched an arm before him, with a calm energy that aided in giving emphasis to his expressions.

"Wampum should be sent for wampum," he said, "a message must be answered by a message. Hear what the Great Serpent of the Delawares has to say to the pretended wolves from the great lakes, that are howling through our woods. They are no wolves; they are dogs that have come to get their tails and ears cropped by the hands of the Delawares. They are good at stealing young women: bad at keeping them. Chingachgook takes his own where he finds it; he asks leave of no cur from the Canadas. If he has a tender feeling in his heart, it is no business of the Hurons. He tells it to her who most likes to know it; he will not bellow it in the forest for the ears of those that only understand yells of terror. What passes in his lodge is not for the chiefs of his own people to know; still less for Mingo rogues—"

"Call 'em vagabonds, Sarpent," interrupted Deerslayer, unable to restrain his delight—"yes, just call 'em up-and-down vagabonds, which is a word easily intarpreted, and the most hateful to all their ears, it's so true. Never fear me; I'll give 'em your message, syllable for syllable, sneer for sneer, idee for idee, scorn for scorn—and they desarve no better at your hands. Only call 'em vagabonds, once or twice, and that will set the sap mounting in 'em, from their lowest roots to the uppermost branches."

"Still less for Mingo vagabonds!" resumed Chingachgook, quite willingly complying with his friend's request. "Tell the Huron dogs to howl louder, if they wish a Delaware to find them in the woods, where they burrow like foxes, instead of hunting like warriors. When they had a Delaware maiden in their camp, there was a reason for hunting them up; now they will be forgotten, unless they make a noise. Chingachgook don't like the trouble of going to his villages for more warriors; he can strike their runaway trail; unless they hide it under ground, he will follow it to Canada, alone. He will keep Wah-ta!-Wah with him to cook his game; they two will be Delawares enough to scare all the Hurons back to their own country."

"That's a grand dispatch, as the officers call them things!" cried Deerslayer; " 'twill set all the Huron blood in motion; most particularly that part where he tells 'em Hist, too, will keep on their heels till they're fairly driven out of the country. Ah's me! Big words arn't always big deeds, notwithstanding. The Lord send that we be able to be only one half as good as we promise to be. And now, Judith, it's your turn to speak, for them miscreants will expect an answer from each person, poor Hetty, perhaps, excepted."

"And why not Hetty, Deerslayer? She often speaks to the purpose; the Indians may respect her words, for they feel for people in her condition."

"That is true, Judith, and quick-thoughted in you. The redskins *do* respect misfortunes of all kinds, and Hetty's in particular. So, Hetty, if you have anything to say, I'll carry it to the Hurons as faithfully as if it was spoken by a schoolmaster or a missionary."

The girl hesitated a moment, and then she answered in her own gentle, soft tones, as earnestly as any who had preceded her.

"The Hurons can't understand the difference between white people and themselves," she said, "or they wouldn't ask Judith and me to go and live in their villages. God has given one country to the red men, and another to us. He meant us to live apart. Then Mother always said that we should never dwell with any but Christians, if possible, and *that* is a reason why we can't go. This lake is ours, and we won't leave it. Father's and Mother's graves are in it, and even the worst Indians love to stay near the graves of their fathers. I will come and see them again, if they wish me to to, and read more out of the Bible to them, but I can't quit Father's and Mother's graves."

"That will do—that will do, Hetty, just as well as if you sent them a message twice as long," interrupted the hunter. "I'll tell 'em all you've said and all you mean, and I'll answer for it, that they'll be easily satisfied. Now, Judith, your turn comes next, and then this part of my ar'n'd will be tarminated for the night."

Judith manifested a reluctance to give her reply that had awakened a little curiosity in the messenger. Judging from her known spirit, he had never supposed the girl would be less true to her feelings and principles than Hist or Hetty, and yet there was a visible wavering of purpose that rendered him slightly uneasy. Even now, when directly required to speak, she seemed to hesitate; nor did she open her lips until the profound silence told her how anxiously her words were expected. Then, indeed, she spoke, but it was doubtingly and with reluctance.

"Tell me, first—tell *us*, first, Deerslayer," she commenced, repeating the words merely to change the emphasis. "What effect will our answers have on *your* fate? If you are to be the sacrifice of our spirit, it would have been better had we all been more wary as to the language we use. What, then, are likely to be the consequences to yourself?"

"Lord, Judith, you might as well ask me which way the wind will blow next week, or what will be the age of the next deer that will be shot! I can only say that their faces look a little dark upon me, but it doesn't thunder every time a black cloud rises, nor does every puff of wind blow up rain. That's a question, therefore, much more easily put than answered."

"So is this message of the Iroquois to me," answered Judith, rising, as if she had determined on her own course for the present. "My answer shall be given, Deerslayer, after you and I have talked together alone, when the others have laid themselves down for the night."

There was a decision in the manner of the girl that disposed Deerslayer to comply, and this he did the more readily as the delay could produce no material consequences, one way or the other. The meeting now broke up, Hurry announcing his resolution to leave them speedily. During the hour that was suffered to intervene, in order that the darkness might deepen before the frontiersman took his departure, the different individuals occupied themselves in their customary modes, the hunter, in particular, passing most of the time in making further inquiries into the perfection of the rifle already mentioned.

The hour of nine soon arrived, however, and then it had been determined that Hurry should commence his journey. Instead of making his adieus frankly and in a generous spirit, the little he thought it necessary to say was uttered sullenly and in coldness. Resentment at what he considered Judith's obstinacy was blended with mortification at the career he had run since reaching the lake; as is usual with the vulgar and narrow-minded, he was more disposed to reproach others with his failures than to censure himself. Judith gave him her hand, but it was quite as much in gladness as with regret, while the two Delawares were not sorry to find he was leaving them. Of the whole party, Hetty alone betrayed any real feeling. Bashfulness and the timidity of her sex and character kept even her aloof, so that Hurry entered the canoe, where Deerslayer was already waiting for him, before she ventured near enough to be observed. Then, indeed, the girl came into the ark and approached its end just as the little bark was turning from it, with a movement so light and steady as to be almost imperceptible. An impulse of feeling now overcame her timidity, and Hetty spoke.

"Goodbye, Hurry"—she called out in her sweet voice— "goodbye, dear Hurry. Take care of yourself in the woods, and don't stop once till you reach the garrison. The leaves on the trees are scarcely plentier than the Hurons around the lake, and they'd not treat a strong man like you as kindly as they treat me."

The ascendency which March had obtained over this feeble-minded but right-thinking and right-feeling girl arose from a law of nature. Her senses had been captivated by his personal advantages, and her moral communications with him had never been sufficiently intimate to counteract an effect that must have been otherwise lessened, even with one whose mind was as obtuse as her own. Hetty's instinct of right, if such a term can be applied to one who seemed taught by some kind spirit how to steer her course with unerring accuracy between good and evil, would have revolted at Hurry's character on a thousand points, had there been opportunities to enlighten her; but while he conversed and trifled with her sister, at a distance from herself, his perfection of form and feature had been left to produce their influence on her simple imagination and naturally tender feelings without suffering by the alloy of his opinions and coarseness. It is true, she found him rough and rude, but her father was that, and most of the other men she had seen, and that which she believed to belong to all of the sex struck her less unfavorably in Hurry's character than it might otherwise have done. Still, it was not absolutely love that Hetty felt for Hurry, nor do we wish so to portray it, but merely that awakening sensibility and admiration, which, under more propitious circumstances, and always supposing no untoward revelations of character on the part of the young man had supervened to prevent it, might soon have

ripened into that engrossing feeling. She felt for him an incipient tenderness, but scarcely any passion. Perhaps the
nearest approach to the latter that Hetty had manifested
was to be seen in the sensitiveness which had caused her to
detect March's predilection for her sister, for among Judith's
many admirers, this was the only instance in which the dull
mind of the girl had been quickened into an observation of
the circumstance.

Hurry received so little sympathy at his departure that
the gentle tones of Hetty, as she thus called after him,
sounded soothingly. He checked the canoe and, with one
sweep of his powerful arm, brought it back to the side of
the ark. This was more than Hetty, whose courage had risen
with the departure of her hero, expected, and she now shrank
timidly back at his unexpected return.

"You're a good gal, Hetty, and I can't quit you without
shaking hands," said March kindly. "Judith, a'ter all, isn't
worth as much as you, though she may be a trifle better
looking. As to wits, if honesty and fair dealing with a young
man is a sign of sense in a young woman, you're worth a
dozen Judiths—aye, and for that matter, most young women
of my acquaintance."

"Don't say anything against Judith, Harry," returned
Hetty imploringly. "Father's gone, and Mother's gone, and
nobody's left but Judith and me, and it isn't right for sisters
to speak evil, or to hear evil, of each other. Father's in the
lake, and so is Mother, and we should all fear God, for
we don't know when we may be in the lake, too."

"That sounds reasonable, child, as does most you say.
Well, if we ever meet again, Hetty, you'd find a fri'nd in
me, let your sister do what she may. I was no great fri'nd of
your mother, I'll allow, for we didn't think alike on most
p'ints; but then your father, Old Tom, and I fitted each other
as remarkably as a buckskin garment will fit any reasonable-
built man. I've always been unanimous of opinion that old
Floating Tom Hutter, at the bottom, was a good fellow, and
will maintain that ag'in all inimies for his sake, as well as
for your'n."

"Goodbye, Hurry," said Hetty, who now wanted to hasten
the young man off as ardently as she had wished to keep him
only the moment before, though she could give no clearer
account of the latter than of the former feeling; "goodbye,

Hurry; take care of yourself in the woods; don't halt till you reach the garrison. I'll read a chapter in the Bible for you, before I go to bed, and think of you in my prayers."

This was touching a point on which March had no sympathies, and without more words he shook the girl cordially by the hand and re-entered the canoe. In another minute the two adventurers were a hundred feet from the ark, and half a dozen had not elapsed before they were completely lost to view. Hetty sighed deeply and rejoined her sister and Hist.

For some time Deerslayer and his companion paddled ahead in silence. It had been determined to land Hurry at the precise point where he is represented, in the commencement of our tale, as having embarked, not only as a place little likely to be watched by the Hurons, but because he was sufficiently familiar with the signs of the woods at that spot to thread his way through them in the dark. Thither, then, the light craft proceeded, being urged as diligently and as swiftly as two vigorous and skillful canoemen could force their little vessel through, or rather *over*, the water. Less than a quarter of an hour sufficed for the object, and at the end of that time, being within the shadows of the shore and quite near the point they sought, each ceased his efforts in order to make their parting communications out of earshot of any straggler who might happen to be in the neighborhood.

"You will do well to persuade the officers at the garrison to lead out a party ag'in these vagabonds as soon as you get in, Hurry," Deerslayer commenced; "and you'll do better if you volunteer to guide it up yourself. You know the paths, and the shape of the lake, and the natur' of the land, and can do it better than a common, gin'ralizing scout. Strike at the Huron camp first and follow the signs that will then show themselves. A few looks at the hut and the ark will satisfy you as to the state of the Delaware and the women; at any rate, there'll be a fine opportunity to fall on the Mingo trail and to make a mark on the memories of the blackguards that they'll be apt to carry with 'em a long time. It won't be likely to make much difference with me, since *that* matter will be determined afore tomorrow's sun has set, but it may make a great change in Judith and Hetty's hopes and prospects!"

"And as for yourself, Nathaniel," Hurry inquired with more interest than he was accustomed to betray in the welfare of others—"and as for yourself, what do you think is likely to turn up?"

"The Lord, in his wisdom, only can tell, Henry March! The clouds look black and threatening, and I keep my mind in a state to meet the worst. Vengeful feelin's are uppermost in the hearts of the Mingos, and any little disapp'intment about the plunder, or the prisoners, or Hist may make the torments sartain. The Lord, in his wisdom, can only detarmine my fate, or you'rn!"

"This is a black business and ought to be put a stop to in some way or other," answered Hurry, confounding the distinctions between right and wrong, as is usual with selfish and vulgar men. "I heartily wish old Hutter and I had scalped every creatur' in their camp the night we first landed with that capital object! Had you not held back, Deerslayer, it might have been done; then you wouldn't have found yourself, at the last moment, in the desperate condition you mention."

" 'Twould have been better had you said you wished you had never attempted to do what it little becomes any white man's gifts to undertake, in which case, not only might we have kept from coming to blows, but Thomas Hutter would now have been living, and the hearts of the savages would be less given to vengeance. The death of that young woman, too, was oncalled for, Henry March, and leaves a heavy load on our names, if not on our consciences!"

This was so apparent, and it seemed so obvious to Hurry himself, at the moment, that he dashed his paddle into the water and began to urge the canoe toward the shore, as if bent only on running away from his own lively remorse. His companion humored this feverish desire for change, and in a minute or two the bows of the boat grated lightly on the shingle of the beach. To land, shoulder his pack and rifle, and to get ready for his march occupied Hurry but an instant, and with a growling adieu he had already commenced his march, when a sudden twinge of feeling brought him to a dead stop and, immediately after, to the other's side.

"You cannot mean to give yourself up ag'in to them murdering savages, Deerslayer!" he said, quite as much in angry remonstrance as with generous feeling. " 'Twould be the act of a madman or a fool!"

"There's them that thinks it madness to keep their words, and there's them that don't, Hurry Harry. You may be one of the first, but I'm one of the last. No redskin breathing shall have it in his power to say that a Mingo minds his word more than a man of white blood and white gifts in anything that consarns me. I'm out on a furlough, and if I've strength and reason, I'll go in on a furlough afore noon tomorrow!"

"What's an Injin, or a word passed, or a furlough taken from creatur's like them that have neither souls nor names?"

"If they've got neither souls nor names, you and I have both, Harry March, and one is accountable for the other. This furlough is not, as you seem to think, a matter altogether atween me and the Mingos, seeing it is a solemn bargain made atween me and God. He who thinks that he can say what he pleases in his distress, and that 'twill all pass for nothing because 'tis uttered in the forest and into red men's ears, knows little of his situation, and hopes, and wants. The words are said to the ears of the Almighty. The air is His breath, and the light of the sun is little more than a glance of His eye. Farewell, Harry; we may not meet ag'in, but I would wish you never to treat a furlough, or any other solemn thing that your Christian God has been called on to witness, as a duty so light that it may be forgotten according to the wants of the body, or even according to the cravings of the spirit."

March was now glad again to escape. It was quite impossible that he could enter into the sentiments that ennobled his companion, and he broke away from both with an impatience that caused him secretly to curse the folly that could induce a man to rush, as it were, on his own destruction. Deerslayer, on the contrary, manifested no such excitement. Sustained by his principles, inflexible in the purpose of acting up to them, and superior to any unmanly apprehension, he regarded all before him as a matter of course and no more thought of making any unworthy attempt to avoid it than a Moslem thinks of counteracting the decrees of Providence. He stood calmly on the shore, listening to the reckless tread with which Hurry betrayed his progress through the bushes, shook his head in dissatisfaction at the want of caution, and then stepped quietly into his canoe. Before he dropped the paddle again into the water, the young man gazed about him at the scene presented by the starlit night. This was the spot where he had first laid his eyes on the beautiful sheet of water on which he floated. If it was then glorious in the bright light of summer's noontide, it was now sad and melancholy under the shadows of night. The mountains rose around it, like black barriers to exclude the outer world, and the gleams of pale light that rested on the broader parts of the basin were no bad symbols of the faintness of the hopes that were so dimly visible in his own future. Sighing heavily, he pushed the canoe from the land and took his way back, with steady diligence, toward the ark and the castle.

CHAPTER XXIV

Thy secret pleasures turned to open shame;
Thy private feasting to a public fast;
Thy smoothing titles to a ragged name;
Thy sugared tongue to bitter wormwood taste;
Thy violent vanities can never last.

RAPE OF LUCRECE

JUDITH WAS ON the platform, awaiting the return of Deer-slayer with stifled impatience, when the latter reached the hut. Hist and Hetty were both in a deep sleep on the bed usually occupied by the two daughters of the house, and the Delaware was stretched on the floor of the adjoining room, his rifle at his side, and a blanket over him, already dreaming of the events of the last few days. There was a lamp burning in the ark, for the family was accustomed to indulge in this luxury on extraordinary occasions, and possessed the means, the vessel being of a form and material to render it probable it had once been an occupant of the chest.

As soon as the girl got a glimpse of the canoe, she ceased her hurried walk up and down the platform and stood ready to receive the young man whose return she had now been anxiously expecting for some time. She helped him to fasten the canoe and, by aiding in the other little similar employments, manifested her desire to reach a moment of liberty as soon as possible. When this was done, in answer to an inquiry of his, she informed him of the manner in which their companions had disposed of themselves. He listened attentively, for the manner of the girl was so earnest and impressive as to apprise him that she had something on her mind of more than common concern.

"And now, Deerslayer," Judith continued, "you see I have lighted the lamp and put it in the cabin of the ark. That is never done with us, unless on great occasions, and I consider this night as the most important of my life. Will you follow me and see what I have to show you—hear what I have to say?"

The hunter was a little surprised, but making no objections, both were soon in the scow, in the room that contained the light. Here two stools were placed at the side of the chest, with the lamp on another, and a table nearby to receive the different articles as they might be brought to view. This arrangement had its rise in the feverish impatience of the girl, which could brook no delay that it was in her power to obviate. Even all the padlocks were removed, and it only remained to raise the heavy lid and to expose the treasures of this long-secreted hoard.

"I see, in part, what all this means," observed Deerslayer; "yes, I see through it, in part. But why is not Hetty present? Now Thomas Hutter is gone, she is one of the owners of these cur'osities, and ought to see them opened and handled."

"Hetty sleeps," answered Judith hastily. "Happily for her, fine clothes and riches have no charms. Besides, she has this night given her share of all that the chest may hold to me, that I may do with it as I please."

"Is poor Hetty compass enough for that, Judith?" demanded the just-minded young man. "It's a good rule, and a righteous one, never to take when those that give don't know the valie of their gifts, and such as God has visited heavily in their wits ought to be dealt with as carefully as children that haven't yet come to their understandings."

Judith was hurt at this rebuke, coming from the person it did, but she would have felt it far more keenly, had not her conscience fully acquitted her of any unjust intentions toward her feeble-minded but confiding sister. It was not a moment, however, to betray any of her usual mountings of the spirit, and she smothered the passing sensation in the desire to come to the great object she had in view.

"Hetty will not be wronged," she mildly answered; "she even knows not only what I am about to do, Deerslayer, but *why* I do it. So take your seat, raise the lid of the chest, and this time we will go to the bottom. I shall be disappointed if something is not found to tell us more of the history of Thomas Hutter and my mother."

"Why Thomas Hutter, Judith, and not your father? The

dead ought to meet with as much reverence as the living!"

"I have long suspected that Thomas Hutter was not *my* father, though I did think he might have been Hetty's, but now we know he was the father of neither. He acknowledged that much in his dying moments. I am old enough to remember better things than we have seen on this lake, though they are so faintly impressed on my memory that the earlier part of my life seems like a dream."

"Dreams are but miserable guides when one has to determine about realities, Judith," returned the other admonishingly. "Fancy nothing and hope nothing on their account; though I've known chiefs that thought 'em useful."

"I expect nothing for the future from them, my good friend, but cannot help remembering what has been. This is idle, however, when half an hour of examination may tell us all, or even more than I want to know."

Deerslayer, who comprehended the girl's impatience, now took his seat and proceeded once more to bring to light the different articles that the chest contained. As a matter of course, all that had been previously examined were found where they had been last deposited, and they excited much less interest or comment than when formerly exposed to view. Even Judith laid aside the rich brocade with an air of indifference, for she had a far higher aim before her than the indulgence of vanity and was impatient to come at the still hidden, or rather unknown, treasures.

"All these we have seen before," she said, "and will not stop to open. The bundle under your hand, Deerslayer, is a fresh one; that we will look into. God send it may contain something to tell poor Hetty and myself who we really are."

"Aye, if some bundles could speak, they might tell wonderful secrets," returned the young man, deliberately undoing the folds of another piece of coarse canvas in order to come at the contents of the roll that lay on his knees; "though this doesn't seem to be one of that family, seeing 'tis neither more nor less than a sort of flag—though of what nation, it passes my l'arnin' to say."

"That flag must have some meaning to it," Judith hurriedly interposed. "Open it wider, Deerslayer, that we may see the colors."

"Well, I pity the ensign that has to shoulder this cloth and to parade it about in the field. Why 'tis large enough,

Judith, to make a dozen of them colors the King's officers set so much store by. These can be no ensign's colors, but a gin'ral's!"

"A ship might carry it, Deerslayer, and ships I know do use such things. Have you never heard any fearful stories about Thomas Hutter's having once been concerned with the people they call buccaneers?"

"Buck-and-near! Not I—not I—I never heard him mentioned as good at a buck, far off or nearby. Hurry Harry did tell me something about its being supposed that he had formerly, in some way or other, dealings with sartain sea-robbers; but, Lord, Judith, it can't surely give you any satisfaction to make out that ag'in your mother's own husband, though he isn't your father?"

"Anything will give me satisfaction that tells me who I am and helps to explain the dreams of childhood. My mother's husband! Yes, he must have been that, though why a woman like *her* should have chosen a man like *him* is more than mortal reason can explain. You never saw Mother, Deerslayer, and can't feel the vast, vast difference there was between them!"

"Such things *do* happen, howsever—yes, they *do* happen—though why Providence lets them come to pass is more than I understand. I've knew the f'ercest warriors with the gentlest wives of any in the tribe, and awful scolds fall to the lot of Injins fit to be missionaries."

"That was not it, Deerslayer, that was not it. Oh! If it should prove that—no; I cannot wish she should not have been his wife at all. *That* no daughter can wish for her own mother! Go on, now, and let us see what the square-looking bundle holds."

Deerslayer complied, and he found that it contained a small trunk of pretty workmanship, but fastened. The next point was to find a key, but search proving ineffectual, it was determined to force the lock. This Deerslayer soon effected by the aid of an iron instrument, and it was found that the interior was nearly filled with papers. Many were letters; some fragments of manuscripts, memorandums, accounts, and other similar documents. The hawk does not pounce upon the chicken with a more sudden swoop than Judith sprang forward to seize this mine of hitherto concealed knowledge. Her education, as the reader will have perceived, was far superior to her situation in life, and her eye glanced over page after page of the letters with a readiness that her schooling supplied and with an avidity that found its origin in her feelings. At first, it was evident that the girl was gratified, and, we may add, with reason; for the letters, written by females, in innocence and affection, were of a character to cause her to feel proud of those with whom she had every reason to think she was closely connected by the ties of blood. It does not come within the scope of our plan to give more of these epistles, however, than a general idea of their contents, and this will best be done by describing the effect they produced on the manner, appearance, and feeling of her who was so eagerly perusing them.

It has been said already that Judith was much gratified with the letters that first met her eye. They contained the correspondence of an affectionate and intelligent mother to an absent daughter, with such allusions to the answers as served, in a great measure, to fill up the vacuum left by the replies. They were not without admonitions and warnings, however, and Judith felt the blood mounting to her temples, and a cold shudder succeeding, as she read one in which the propriety of the daughter's indulging in as much intimacy, as had evidently been described in one of the daughter's own letters, with an officer "who came from Europe, and who could hardly be supposed to wish to form an honorable connection in America," was rather coldly commented on by the mother. What rendered it singular was the fact that the signatures had been carefully cut from every one of these letters, and wherever a name occurred in the body of the epistles, it had been erased with so much diligence as to render it impossible to read it. They had all been enclosed in envelopes, according to the fashion of the age, and not an address either was to be found. Still, the letters themselves had been religiously preserved, and Judith thought she could discover traces of tears remaining on several. She now remembered to have seen the little trunk in her mother's keeping, previously to her death, and she supposed it had first been deposited in the chest, along with the other forgotten, or concealed objects, when the letters could no longer contribute to that parent's grief or happiness.

Next came another bundle, and these were filled with the protestations of love, written with passion certainly, but also with that deceit which men so often think it justifiable to use to the other sex. Judith had shed tears abundantly over the first packet, but now she felt a sentiment of indignation and pride better sustaining her. Her hand shook, however, and cold shivers again passed through her frame as she discovered a few points of strong resemblance between these letters and some it had been her own fate to receive. Once, indeed, she laid the packet down, bowed her head to her knees, and seemed nearly convulsed. All this time Deerslayer sat, a silent but attentive observer of everything that passed. As Judith read a letter, she put it into his hands to hold, until she could peruse the next; but this seemed in no degree to enlighten her companion, as he was totally unable to read. Nevertheless, he was not entirely at fault in discovering the passions that were contending in the bosom of the fair creature by his side, and as occasional sentences escaped her in murmurs, he was nearer the truth, in his divinations or conjectures, than the girl would have been pleased at discovering.

Judith had commenced with the earliest letters, luckily for a ready comprehension of the tale they told, for they were carefully arranged in chronological order, and to anyone who would take the trouble to peruse them, they would have revealed a sad history of gratified passion, coldness, and, finally, of aversion. As she obtained the clue to their import, her impatience could not admit of delay, and she soon got to glancing her eyes over a page, by way of coming at the truth in the briefest manner possible. By adopting this expedient, one to which all who are eager to arrive at results without encumbering themselves with details are so apt to resort, Judith made a rapid progress in this melancholy revelation of her mother's failings and punishment. She saw that the period of her own birth was distinctly referred to, and even learned that the homely name she bore was given her by the father of whose person she retained so faint an impression as to resemble a dream. This name was not obliterated from the text of the letters, but stood as if nothing was to be gained by erasing it. Hetty's birth was mentioned once, and in that instance the name was the mother's; but ere this period was reached came the signs of coldness, shadowing forth the desertion that was so soon to follow. It was in this stage of the correspondence that her mother had recourse to the plan of copying her own epistles. They were but few, but were eloquent with the feelings of blighted affection and contrition. Judith sobbed over them until again and again she felt compelled to lay them aside from sheer physical inability to see, her eyes being literally obscured with tears. Still she returned to the task with increasing interest, and finally succeeded in reaching the end of the latest communication that had probably ever passed between her parents.

All this occupied fully an hour, for near a hundred letters were glanced at, and some twenty had been closely read. The truth now shone clear upon the acute mind of Judith, so far as her own birth and that of Hetty were concerned. She sickened at the conviction, and for the moment, the rest of the world seemed to be cut off from her, and she had now additional reasons for wishing to pass the remainder of her life on the lake, where she had already seen so many bright and so many sorrowing days.

There yet remained more letters to examine. Judith found these were a correspondence between her mother and Thomas Hovey. The originals of both parties were carefully arranged, letter and answer, side by side, and they told the early history of the connection between the ill-assorted pair far more plainly than Judith wished to learn it. Her mother made the advances toward a marriage, to the surprise, not to say horror, of her daughter, and she actually found a relief when she discovered traces of what struck her as insanity, or a morbid disposition, bordering on that dire calamity, in the earlier letters of that ill-fated woman. The answers of Hovey were coarse and illiterate, though they manifested a sufficient desire to obtain the hand of a woman of singular personal attractions, and whose great error he was willing to overlook for the advantage of possessing one every way so much his superior, and who, it also appeared, was not altogether destitute of money. The remainder of this part of the correspondence was brief, and it was soon confined to a few communications on business, in which the miserable wife hastened the absent husband in his preparations to abandon a world which there was a sufficient reason to think was as dangerous to one of the parties as it was disagreeable to the other. But a single expression had escaped her mother, by which Judith could get a clue to the motives that had induced her to marry Hovey, or Hutter; and this she found was that feeling of resentment which so often tempts the injured to inflict wrongs on themselves, by way of heaping coals on the heads of those through whom they have suffered. Judith had enough of the spirit of that mother to comprehend this sentiment, and for a moment did she see the exceeding folly which permitted such revengeful feelings to get the ascendency.

There what may be called the historical part of the papers ceased. Among the loose fragments, however, was an old newspaper that contained a proclamation offering a reward for the apprehension of certain freebooters by name, among which was that of Thomas Hovey. The attention of the girl was drawn to the proclamation, and to this particular name, by the circumstance that black lines had been drawn under both in ink. Nothing else was found among the papers that could lead to a discovery of either the name or the place of residence of the wife of Hutter. All the dates, signatures, and addresses had been cut from the letters, and wherever a word occurred in the body of the communications that might furnish a clue, it was scrupulously erased. Thus Judith found all her hopes of ascertaining who her parents were defeated, and she was obliged to fall back on her own resources and habits for everything connected with the future. Her recollection of her mother's manners, conversation, and sufferings filled up many a gap in the historical facts she had now discovered, and the truth in its outlines stood sufficiently distinct before her to take away all desire, indeed, to possess any more details. Throwing herself back in her seat, she simply desired her companion to finish the examination of the other articles in the chest, as it might yet contain something of importance.

"I'll do it, Judith; I'll do it," returned the patient Deerslayer; "but if there's many more letters to read, we shall see the sun ag'in afore you've got through with the reading of them! Two good hours have you been looking at them bits of papers!"

"They tell me of my parents, Deerslayer, and have settled my plans for life. A girl may be excused who reads about her *own* father and mother, and that too for the first time in her life! I am sorry to have kept you waiting."

"Never mind me, gal; never mind me. It matters little

whether I sleep or watch; but though you be pleasant to look at, and are so handsome, Judith, it is not altogether agreeable to sit so long to behold you shedding tears. I know that tears don't kill, and that some people are better for shedding a few now and then—especially women—but I'd rather see you smile any time, Judith, than see you weep."

This gallant speech was rewarded with a sweet, though a melancholy smile, and then the girl again desired her companion to finish the examination of the chest. The search necessarily continued some time, during which Judith collected her thoughts and regained her composure. She took no part in the search, leaving everything to the young man, looking listlessly herself, at the different articles that came uppermost. Nothing further of much interest or value, however, was found. A sword or two, such as were then worn by gentlemen, some buckles of silver, or so richly plated as to appear silver, and a few handsome articles of female dress composed the principal discoveries. It struck both Judith and the Deerslayer, notwithstanding, that some of these things might be made useful in effecting a negotiation with the Iroquois, though the latter saw a difficulty in the way that was not so apparent to the former. The conversation was first renewed in connection with this point.

"And now, Deerslayer," said Judith, "we may talk of yourself and of the means of getting you out of the hands of the Hurons. Any part, or all of what you have seen in the chest, will be cheerfully given by me and Hetty to set you at liberty."

"Well, that's ginerous,—yes, 'tis downright freehearted, and freehanded and ginerous. This is the way with women; when they take up a fri'ndship, they do nothing by halves, but are as willing to part with their property as if it had no valie in their eyes. Howsever, while I thank you both, just as much as if the bargain was made and Rivenoak or any of the other vagabonds was here to accept and close the treaty, there's two principal reasons why it can never come to pass, which may be as well told at once, in order no onlikely expectations may be raised in you, or any onjustifiable hopes in me."

"What reason *can* there be, if Hetty and I are willing to part with the trifles for your sake, and the savages are willing to receive them?"

"That's it, Judith—you've got the ideas, but they're a little out of their places, as if a hound should take the back'ard instead of the leading scent. That the Mingos will be willing to receive them things, or any more like 'em you may have to offer, is probable enough, but whether they'll pay valie for 'em is quite another matter. Ask yourself, Judith, if anyone should send you a message to say that, for such or such a price, you and Hetty might have that chist and all it holds, whether you'd think it worth your while to waste many words on the bargain?"

"But this chest and all it holds are already ours; there is no reason why we should purchase what is already our own."

"Just so the Mingos calculate! They say the chist is theirs already; or as good as theirs, and they'll not thank anybody for the key."

"I understand you, Deerslayer; surely we are yet in possession of the lake, and we can keep possession of it until Hurry sends troops to drive off the enemy. This we may certainly do, provided you will stay with us, instead of going back and giving yourself up a prisoner again, as you now seem determined on."

"That Hurry Harry should talk in this way is natr'al and according to the gifts of the man. He knows no better, and therefore he is little likely to feel or to act any better; but, Judith, I put it to your heart and conscience—would you, *could* you think of me as favorably as I hope and believe you now do, was I to forget my furlough and not go back to the camp?"

"To think *more* favorably of you than I now do, Deerslayer, would not be easy; but I might continue to think *as* favorably—at least it seems so—I hope I could; for a world wouldn't tempt me to let you do anything that might change my real opinion of you."

"Then don't try to entice me to overlook my furlough, gal! A furlough is a sacred thing among warriors and men that carry their lives in their hands, as we of the forests do, and what a grievous disapp'intment would it be to old Tamenund, and to Uncas, the father of the Sarpent, and to my other fri'nds in the tribe, if I was so to disgrace myself on my very first warpath! This you will parceive, moreover, Judith, is without laying any stress on nat'ral gifts and a white man's duties, to say nothing of conscience. The last is king with me, and I try never to dispute his orders."

"I believe you are right, Deerslayer," returned the girl, after a little reflection and in a saddened voice; "a man like *you* ought not to act as the selfish and dishonest would be apt to act; *you* must indeed go back. We will talk no more of this, then; should I persuade you to anything for which you would be sorry hereafter, my own regret would not be less than yours. You shall not have it to say, Judith—I scarce know by what name to call myself now!"

"And why not?—why not, gal? Children take the names of their parents nat'rally and by a sort of gift, like; and why shouldn't you and Hetty do as others have done afore ye? Hutter was the old man's name, and Hutter should be the name of his darters—at least until you are given away in lawful and holy wedlock."

"I am Judith, and Judith only," returned the girl positively, "until the law gives me a right to another name. Never will I use that of Thomas Hutter again; nor, with my consent, shall Hetty! Hutter was not his own name, I find, but had he a thousand rights to it, it would give none to me. *He* was not my father, thank heaven, though I may have no reason to be proud of him that *was!*"

"This is strange," said Deerslayer, looking steadily at the excited girl, anxious to know more but unwilling to inquire into matters that did not properly concern him; "yes, this is very strange and oncommon! Thomas Hutter wasn't Thomas Hutter, and his darters weren't his darters! Who, then, could Thomas Hutter be, and who are his darters?"

"Did you never hear anything whispered against the former life of this person, Deerslayer?" demanded Judith. "Passing, as I did, for his child, such reports reached even me."

"I'll not deny it, Judith; no, I'll not deny it. Sartain things have been said, as I've told you, but I'm not very credible as to reports. Young as I am, I've lived long enough to l'arn there's two sorts of characters in the world—them that is 'arned by deeds, and them that is 'arned by tongues—and so I prefer to see and judge for myself, instead of letting every jaw that chooses to wag become my judge. Hurry Harry spoke pretty plainly of the whole family, as we journeyed thisaway; and he did hint something consarning Thomas Hutter's having been a free liver on the water, in his younger days. By free liver, I mean that he made free to live on other men's goods."

"He told you he was a pirate—there is no need of mincing matters between friends. Read that, Deerslayer, and you will see that he told you no more than the truth. This Thomas Hovey was the Thomas Hutter you knew, as is seen by these letters."

As Judith spoke, with a flushed cheek and eyes dazzling with the brilliancy of excitement, she held the newspaper toward her companion, pointing to the proclamation of a Colonial governor, already mentioned.

"Bless you, Judith!" answered the other, laughing; "you might as well ask me to print that—or for that matter to write it. My edication has been altogether in the woods; the only book I read, or care about reading, is the one which God has opened afore all his creatur's in the noble forests, broad lakes, rolling rivers, blue skies, and the winds, and tempests, and sunshine, and other glorious marvels of the land! This book I can read, and I find it full of wisdom and knowledge."

"I crave your pardon, Deerslayer," said Judith earnestly, more abashed than was her wont, in finding that she had inadvertently made an appeal that might wound her companion's pride. "I had forgotten your manner of life, and least of all did I wish to hurt your feelings."

"Hurt my feelin's!—why should it hurt my feelin's to ask me to read when I can't read? I'm a hunter—and, I may now begin to say, a warrior—and no missionary, and therefore books and papers are of no account with such as I. No, no, Judith"—and here the young man laughed cordially—"not even for wads, seeing that your true deerkiller always uses the hide of a fa'an, if he's got one, or some other bit of leather suitably prepared. There's some that *do* say all that stands in print is true, in which case I'll own an unl'arned man must be somewhat of a loser; nevertheless, it can't be truer than that which God has printed with His own hand, in the sky, and the woods, and the rivers, and the springs."

"Well, then, Hutter, or Hovey, was a pirate, and being no father of mine, I cannot wish to call him one. His name shall no longer be my name."

"If you dislike the name of that man, there's the name

of your mother, Judith. Her name may sarve you just as good a turn."

"I do not know it. I've looked through those papers, Deerslayer, in the hope of finding some hint by which I might discover who my mother was, but there is no more trace of the past in that respect than the bird leaves in the air."

"That's both oncommon and onreasonable. Parents are bound to give their offspring a name, even though they give 'em nothing else. Now, I come of a humble stock, though we have white gifts and a white natur', but we are not so poorly off as to have no name. Bumppo we are called, and I've heard it said," a touch of human vanity glowing on his cheek, "that the time has been when the Bumppos had more standing and note among mankind than they have just now."

"They never deserved them more, Deerslayer, and the name is a good one; either Hetty or myself would a thousand times rather be called Hetty Bumppo or Judith Bumppo than to be called Hetty or Judith Hutter."

"That's a moral impossible," returned the hunter good-humoredly, "unless one of you should so far demean herself as to marry me."

Judith could not refrain from smiling when she found how simply and naturally the conversation had come around to the very point at which she had aimed to bring it. Although far from unfeminine or forward either in her feelings or her habits, the girl was goaded by a sense of wrongs not altogether merited, incited by the helplessness of a future that seemed to contain no resting place, and still more influenced by feelings that were as novel to her as they proved to be active and engrossing. The opening was too good, therefore, to be neglected, though she came to the subject with much of the indirectness and, perhaps, justifiable address of a woman.

"I do not think Hetty will ever marry, Deerslayer," she said, "if your name is to be borne by either of us, it must be borne by me."

"There's been handsome women, too, they tell me, among the Bumppos, Judith, afore now, and should you take up with the name, oncommon as you be, in this particular, them that knows the family won't be altogether surprised."

"This is not talking as becomes either of us, Deerslayer, for whatever is said on such a subject beyween man and woman should be said seriously and in sincerity of heart. Forgetting the shame that ought to keep girls silent until spoken to, in most cases, I will deal with you as frankly as I know one of your generous nature will most like to be dealt by. Can you—do you think, Deerslayer, that you could be happy with such a wife as a woman like myself would make?"

"A woman like you, Judith! But where's the sense in trifling about such a thing? A woman like you, that is handsome enough to be a captain's lady, and fine enough, and, so far as I know, edication enough, would be little apt to think of becoming my wife. I suppose young gals that feel themselves to be smart and know themselves to be handsome find a sartain satisfaction in passing their jokes ag'in them that's neither, like a poor Delaware hunter."

This was said good-naturedly, but not without a betrayal of feeling which showed that something like mortified sensibility was blended with the reply. Nothing could have occurred more likely to awaken all Judith's generous regrets, or to aid her in her purpose, by adding the stimulant of a disinterested desire to atone to her other impulses, and clothing all under a guise so winning and natural as greatly to lessen the unpleasant feature of a forwardness unbecoming the sex.

"You do me injustice if you suppose I have any such thought or wish," she answered earnestly. "Never was I more serious in my life, or more willing to abide by any agreement that we may make tonight. I have had many suitors, Deerslayer—nay, scarce an unmarried trapper or hunter has been in at the lake these four years who has not offered to take me away with him, and I fear some that were married, too——"

"Aye, I'll warrant that!" interrupted the other. "I'll warrant all that! Take 'em as a body, Judith, 'arth don't hold a set of men more given to theirselves, and less given to God and the law."

"Not one of them would I—could I listen to; happily for myself, perhaps, has it been that such was the case. There have been well-looking youths among them, too, as you may have seen in your acquaintance, Henry March."

"Yes, Harry is sightly to the eye, though, to my idees, less so to the judgment. I thought at first you meant to have him, Judith, I did, but afore he went, it was easy enough to verify that the same lodge wouldn't be big enough for you both."

"You have done me justice in that at least, Deerslayer. Hurry is a man I could never marry, though he were ten times more comely to the eye and a hundred times more stout of heart than he really is."

"Why not, Judith—why not? I own I'm cur'ous to know why a youth like Hurry shouldn't find favor with a maiden like you."

"Then you shall know, Deerslayer," returned the girl, gladly availing herself of the opportunity of extolling the qualities which had so strongly interested her in her listener —hoping by these means covertly to approach the subject nearest her heart. "In the first place, looks in a man are of no importance with a woman, provided he is manly, and not disfigured or deformed."

"There I can't altogether agree with you," returned the other thoughtfully, for he had a very humble opinion of his own personal appearance. "I have noticed that the comeliest warriors commonly get the best-looking maidens of the tribe for wives; the Sarpent, yonder, who is sometimes wonderful in his paint, is a gin'ral favorite with all the Delaware young women, though he takes to Hist himself as if she was the only beauty on 'arth."

"It may be so with Indians, but it is different with white girls. So long as a young man has a straight and manly frame that promises to make him able to protect a woman and to keep want from the door, it is all they ask of the figure. Giants like Hurry may do for grenadiers, but are of little account as lovers. Then as to the face, an honest look, one that answers for the heart within, is of more value than any shape, or color, or eyes, or teeth, or trifles like them. The last may do for girls, but who thinks of them at all in a hunter, or a warrior, or a husband! If there are women so silly, Judith's not among them."

"Well, this is wonderful! I always thought that handsome liked handsome, as riches love riches!"

"It may be so with you men, Deerslayer, but it is not always so with us women. We like stouthearted men, but we wish to see them modest, sure on a hunt or the warpath, ready to die for the right and unwilling to yield to the wrong. Above all, we wish for honesty—tongues that are not used to say what the mind does not mean, and hearts that feel a little for others as well as for themselves. A true-hearted girl could die for such a husband, while the boaster and the double-tongued suitor gets to be as hateful to the sight as he is to the mind."

Judith spoke bitterly and with her usual force, but her listener was too much struck with the novelty of the sensations he experienced to advert to her manner. There was something so soothing to the humility of a man of his temperament to hear qualities that he could not but know he possessed himself thus highly extolled by the loveliest female he had ever beheld that, for the moment, his faculties seemed suspended in a natural and excusable pride. Then it was that the idea of the possibility of such a creature as Judith becoming his companion for life first crossed his mind. The image was so pleasant and so novel that he continued completely absorbed by it for more than a minute, totally regardless of the beautiful reality that was seated before him, watching the expression of his upright and truth-telling countenance with a keenness that gave her a very fair, if not an absolutely accurate clue to his thoughts. Never before had so pleasing a vision floated before the mind's eye of the young hunter, but accustomed most to practical things and little addicted to submitting to the power of his imagination, even while possessed of so much true poetical feeling in connection with natural objects in particular, he soon recovered his reason and smiled at his own weakness, as the fancied picture faded from his mental sight and left him the simple, untaught, but highly moral being he was, seated in the ark of Thomas Hutter, at midnight, with the lovely countenance of its late owner's reputed daughter beaming on him with anxious scrutiny by the light of the solitary lamp.

"You're wonderful handsome, and enticing, and pleasing to look on, Judith!" he exclaimed, in his simplicity, as fact resumed its ascendency over fancy. "Wonderful! I don't remember ever to have seen so beautiful a gal, even among the Delawares, and I'm not astonished that Hurry Harry went away soured as well as disapp'inted!"

"Would you have had me, Deerslayer, become the wife of such a man as Henry March?"

"There's that which is in his favor, and there's that which is ag'in him. To my taste, Hurry wouldn't make the best of husbands, but I fear that the tastes of most young women hereaway wouldn't be so hard upon him."

"No—no—Judith without a name would never consent to be called Judith March! Anything would be better than *that!*"

"Judith Bumppo wouldn't sound as well, gal, and there's many names that would fall short of March in pleasing the ear."

"Ah, Deerslayer, the pleasantness of the sound in such cases does not come through the ear, but through the heart. Everything is agreeable when the heart is satisfied. Were Natty Bumppo Henry March, and Henry March Natty Bumppo, I might think the name of March better than it is: or were he you, I should fancy the name of Bumppo horrible!"

"That's just it—yes, that's the reason of the matter. Now, I'm nat'rally avarse to sarpents, and I hate even the word—which, the missionaries tell me, comes from human natur' on account of a sartain sarpent at the creation of the 'arth that outwitted the first woman—yet ever since Chingachgook has 'arned the title he bears, why the sound is as pleasant to my ears as the whistle of the whippoorwill of a calm evening—it is. The feelin's make all the difference in the world, Judith, in the natur' of sounds; aye, even in that of looks, too."

"This is so true, Deerslayer, that I am surprised you should think it remarkable that a girl, who may have some comeliness herself, should not think it necessary that her husband should have the same advantage, or what you fancy an advantage. To me, looks in a man are nothing, provided his countenance be as honest as his heart."

"Yes, honesty is a great advantage, in the long run, and they that are the most apt to forget it, in the beginning, are the most apt to l'arn it in the ind. Nevertheless, there's more, Judith, that look to present profit than to the benefit that is to come after a time. One they think a sartainty, and the other an onsartainty. I'm glad, howsever, that *you* look at the thing in its true light and not in the way in which so many is apt to deceive themselves."

"I do thus look at it, Deerslayer," returned the girl with emphasis, still shrinking with a woman's sensitiveness from a direct offer of her hand, "and can say, from the bottom of my heart, that I would rather trust my happiness to a man whose truth and feelings may be depended on than to a false-tongued and falsehearted wretch that had chests of gold and houses and lands—yes, though he were even seated on a throne!"

"These are brave words, Judith; they're downright brave words; but do you think that the feelin's would keep 'em company, did the ch'ice actually lie afore you? If a gay gallant in a scarlet coat stood on one side, with his head smelling like a deer's foot, his face smooth and blooming as your own, his hands as white and soft as if God hadn't bestowed 'em that man might live by the sweat of his brow, and his step as lofty as dancing teachers and a light heart could make it—and on the other side stood one that has passed his days in the open air till his forehead is as red as his cheek, had cut his way through swamps and bushes till his hand was as rugged as the oaks he slept under, had trodden on the scent of game till his step was as stealthy as the catamount's, and had no other pleasant odor about him than such as natur' gives in the free air and the forest—now, if both these men stood here as suitors for your feelin's, which do you think would win your favor?"

Judith's fine face flushed, for the picture that her companion had so simply drawn of a gay officer of the garrisons had once been particularly grateful to her imagination, though experience and disappointment had not only chilled all her affections, but given them a backward current, and the passing image had a momentary influence on her feelings; but the mounting color was succeeded by a paleness so deadly as to make her appear ghastly.

"As God is my judge," the girl solemnly answered, "did both these men stand before me, as I may say one of them does, my choice, if I know my own heart, would be the latter. I have no wish for a husband who is any way better than myself."

"This is pleasant to listen to and might lead a young man, in time, to forget his own onworthiness, Judith! Howsever, you hardly think all that you say. A man like me is too rude and ignorant for one that has had such a mother to teach her; vanity is nat'ral, I do believe, but vanity like that would surpass reason!"

"Then you do not know of what a woman's heart is capable! Rude *you* are not, Deerslayer! Nor can one be called ignorant that has studied what is before his eyes as closely as you have done. When the affections are concerned, all things appear in their pleasantest colors, and trifles are overlooked, or are forgotten. When the heart feels a sunshine, nothing is gloomy—even dull-looking objects seeming gay and bright—and so it would be between you and the woman who should love you, even though your wife might happen in some matters to possess what the world calls the advantage over you."

"Judith, you come of people altogether above mine in the world, and onequal matches, like onequal fri'ndships, can't often tarminate kindly. I speak of this matter altogether as a fanciful thing, since it's not very likely that *you*, at least, would be able to treat it as a matter that can ever come to pass."

Judith fastened her deep blue eyes on the open, frank countenance of her companion, as if she would read his soul. Nothing there betrayed any covert meaning, and she was obliged to admit to herself that he regarded the conversation as argumentative, rather than positive, and that he was still without any active suspicion that her feelings were seriously involved in the issue. At first she felt offended; then she saw the injustice of making the self-abasement and modesty of the hunter a charge against him; this novel difficulty gave a piquancy to the state of affairs that rather increased her interest in the young man. At that critical instant, a change of plan flashed on her mind, and with a readiness of invention that is peculiar to the quick-witted and ingenious, she adopted a scheme by which she hoped effectually to bind him to her person. This scheme partook equally of her fertility of invention and of the decision and boldness of her character. That the conversation might not terminate too abruptly, however, or any suspicion of her design exist, she answered the last remark of Deerslayer as earnestly and as truly as if her original intention remained unaltered.

"I, certainly, have no reason to boast of parentage, after what I have seen this night," said the girl, in a saddened voice. "I had a mother, it is true, but of her name, even, I am ignorant; as for my father, it is better perhaps that I should never know who he was, lest I speak too bitterly of him!"

"Judith," said Deerslayer, taking her hand kindly and with a manly sincerity that went directly to the girl's heart, " 'tis better to say no more tonight. Sleep on what you've seen and felt; in the morning, things that now look gloomy may look more cheerful. Above all, never do anything in bitterness, or because you feel as if you'd like to take revenge on yourself for other people's backslidings. All that has been said or done atween us this night is your secret, and shall never be talked of by me, even with the Sarpent; and you may be sartain if he can't get it out of me, no man can. If your parents have been faulty, let the darter be less so; remember that you're young, and the youthful may always hope for better times; that you're more quick-witted than usual, and such gin'rally get the better of difficulties; and that as for beauty, you're oncommon; this is an advantage with all. It is time to get a little rest, for tomorrow is like to prove a trying day to some of us."

Deerslayer arose as he spoke, and Judith had no choice but to comply. The chest was closed and secured, and they parted in silence, she to take her place by the side of Hist and Hetty, and he to seek a blanket on the floor of the cabin he was in. It was not five minutes ere the young man was in a deep sleep, but the girl continued awake for a long time. She scarce knew whether to lament or to rejoice at having failed in making herself understood. On the one hand, were her womanly sensibilities spared; on the other, was the disappointment of defeated, or at least of delayed expectations, and the uncertainty of a future that looked so dark. Then came the new resolution and the bold project for the morrow; and when drowsiness finally shut her eyes, they closed on a scene of success and happiness that was pictured by the fancy, under the influence of a sanguine temperament and a happy invention.

CHAPTER XXV

But, mother, now a shade has past
  Athwart my brightest visions here,
A cloud of darkest gloom has wrapt
  The remnant of my brief career!
No song, no echo can I win;
The sparkling fount has dried within.

MARGARET DAVIDSON

HIST AND HETTY arose with the return of light, leaving Judith still buried in sleep. It took but a minute for the first to complete her toilet. Her long, coal-black hair was soon adjusted in a simple knot, the calico dress belted tight to her slender waist, and her little feet concealed in their gaudily-ornamented moccasins. When attired, she left her companion employed in household affairs and went herself on the platform, to breathe the pure air of the morning. Here she found Chingachgook studying the shores of the lake, the mountains, and the heavens with the sagacity of a man of the woods and the gravity of an Indian.

The meeting between the two lovers was simple but affectionate. The chief showed a manly kindness, equally removed from boyish weakness and haste, while the girl betrayed in her smile and half-averted looks the bashful tenderness of her sex. Neither spoke, unless it were with the eyes, though each understood the other as fully as if a vocabulary of words and protestations had been poured out. Hist seldom appeared to more advantage than at that moment, for just from her rest and ablutions, there was a freshness about her youthful form and face that the toils of the wood do not always permit to be exhibited by even the juvenile and pretty. Then Judith had not only imparted some of her own skill in the toilet during their short intercourse, but she had actually bestowed a few well-selected ornaments from her own stores that contributed not a little to set off the natural graces of the Indian maid. All this the lover saw and felt, and for a moment his countenance was illuminated with a look of pleasure; but it soon grew grave again and became saddened and anxious. The stools used the previous night were still standing on the platform; placing two against the walls of the hut, he seated himself on one, making a gesture to his companion to take the other. This done, he continued thoughtful and silent for quite a minute, maintaining the reflecting dignity of one born to take his seat at the council fire, while Hist was furtively watching the expression of his face, patient and submissive, as became a woman of her people. Then the young warrior stretched his arm before him, as if to point out the glories of the scene at that witching hour when the whole panorama, as usual, was adorned by the mellow distinctness of early morning, sweeping with his hand slowly over lake, hills, and heavens. The girl followed the movement with pleased wonder, smiling as each new beauty met her gaze.

"Hugh!" exclaimed the chief, in admiration of a scene so unusual even to him, for this was the first lake he had ever beheld. "This is the country of the Manitou! It is too good for Mingos, Hist, but the curs of that tribe are howling in packs through the woods. They think that the Delawares are asleep, over the mountains."

"All but one of them is, Chingachgook. There is one here, and he is of the blood of Uncas!"

"What is one warrior against a tribe? The path to our villages is very long and crooked, and we shall travel it under a cloudy sky. I am afraid, too, Honeysuckle of the Hills, that we shall travel it alone!"

Hist understood the allusion, and it made her sad— though it sounded sweet to her ears to be compared, by the warrior she so loved, to the most fragrant and the pleasantest of all the wildflowers of her native woods. Still, she continued silent, as became her when the allusion was to a grave interest that men could best control, though it exceeded the power of education to conceal the smile that gratified feeling brought to her pretty mouth.

"When the sun is thus," continued the Delaware, pointing

to the zenith by simply casting upward a hand and finger by a play of the wrist, "the great hunter of our tribe will go back to the Hurons to be treated like a bear that they roast and skin, even on full stomachs."

"The Great Spirit may soften their hearts and not suffer them to be so bloody-minded. I have lived among the Hurons, and know them. They have hearts, and will not forget their own children, should they fall into the hands of the Delawares."

"A wolf is forever howling; a hog will always eat. They have lost warriors; even their women will call out for vengeance. The paleface has the eyes of an eagle and can see into a Mingo's heart; he looks for no mercy. There is a cloud over his spirit, though it is not before his face."

A long, thoughtful pause succeeded, during which Hist stealthily took the hand of the chief, as if seeking his support, though she scarce ventured to raise her eyes to a countenance that was now literally becoming terrible, under the conflicting passions and stern resolution that were struggling in the breast of its owner.

"What will the son of Uncas do?" the girl at length timidly asked. "He is a chief, and is already celebrated in council, though so young; what does his heart tell him is wisest? Does the head, too, speak the same words as the heart?"

"What does Wah-ta!-Wah say, at a moment when my dearest friend is in danger. The smallest birds sing the sweetest; it is always pleasant to hearken to their songs. I wish I could hear the Wren of the Woods in my difficulty; its note would reach deeper than the ear."

Again Hist experienced the profound gratification that the language of praise can always awaken when uttered by those we love. The "Honeysuckle of the Hills" was a term often applied to the girl by the young men of the Delawares, though it never sounded so sweet in her ears as from the lips of Chingachgook; but the latter alone had ever styled her the Wren of the Woods. With him, however, it had got to be a familiar phrase, and it was past expression pleasant to the listener, since it conveyed to her mind the idea that her advice and sentiments were as acceptable to her future husband as the tones of her voice and modes of conveying them were agreeable, uniting the two things most prized by an Indian girl, as coming from her betrothed, admiration for a valued physical advantage, with respect for her opinion. She pressed the hand she held between both her own, and answered:

"Wah-ta!-Wah says that neither she nor the Great Serpent could ever laugh again, or ever sleep without dreaming of the Hurons, should the Deerslayer die under a Mingo tomahawk, and they do nothing to save him. She would rather go back and start on her long path alone than let such a dark cloud pass before her happiness."

"Good! The husband and the wife will have but one heart; they will see with the same eyes and feel with the same feelings."

What further was said need not be related here. That the conversation was of Deerslayer and his hopes has been seen already, but the decision that was come to will better appear in the course of the narrative. The youthful pair were yet conversing when the sun appeared above the tops of the pines, and the light of a brilliant American day streamed down into the valley, bathing "in deep joy" the lake, the forests, and the mountainsides. Just at this instant Deerslayer came out of the cabin of the ark and stepped upon the platform. His first look was at the cloudless heavens; then his rapid glance took in the entire panorama of land and water, when he had leisure for a friendly nod at his friends and a cheerful smile for Hist.

"Well," he said, in his usual composed manner and pleasant voice, "he that sees the sun set in the west and wakes arly enough in the morning will be sartain to find him coming back ag'in in the east, like a buck that is hunted around his ha'nts. I daresay, now, Hist, you've beheld this time and ag'in, and yet it never entered into your galish mind to ask the reason?"

Both Chingachgook and his betrothed looked up at the luminary with an air that betokened sudden wonder, and then they gazed at each other, as if to seek the solution of the difficulty. Familiarity deadens the sensibilities, even as connected with the gravest natural phenomena, and never before had these simple beings thought of inquiring into a movement that was of daily occurrence, however puzzling it might appear on investigation. When the subject was thus suddenly started, it struck both alike and at the same instant, with some such force as any new and brilliant proposition in the natural sciences would strike the scholar. Chingachgook alone saw fit to answer.

"The palefaces know everything," he said; "can they tell us why the sun hides his face, when he goes back, at night?"

"Aye, that is downright redskin l'arnin'," returned the other, laughing, though he was not altogether insensible to the pleasure of proving the superiority of his race by solving the difficulty, which he set about doing, in his own peculiar manner. "Hark'ee, Sarpent," he continued more gravely, though too simply for affectation; "this is easierly explained than an Indian brain may fancy. The sun, while he seems to keep traveling in the heavens, never budges, but it is the 'arth that turns round; and anyone can understand, if he is placed on the side of a mill wheel, for instance, when it's in motion, that he must sometimes see the heavens, while he is at other times under water. There's no great secret in that, but plain natur', the difficulty being in setting the 'arth in motion."

"How does my brother know that the earth turns round?" demanded the Indian. "Can he see it?"

"Well, that's been a puzzler, I will own, Delaware, for I've often tried, but never could fairly make it out. Sometimes I've consaited that I could, and then ag'in I've been obliged to own it an onpossibility. Howsever, turn it does, as all my people say, and you ought to believe 'em, since they can foretell eclipses and other prodigies that used to fill the tribes with terror, according to your own traditions of such things."

"Good. This is true; no red man will deny it. When a wheel turns, my eyes can see it—they do not see the earth turn."

"Aye, that's what I call sense obstinacy! Seeing is believing, they say, and what they can't see, some men won't in the least give credit to. Nevertheless, Chief, that isn't quite as good reason as it may at first seem. You believe in the Great Spirit, I know, and yet, I conclude, it would puzzle you to show where you see Him!"

"Chingachgook can see Him everywhere—everywhere in *good* things—the Evil Spirit in *bad*. Here, in the lake; there, in the forest; yonder, in the clouds; in Hist, in the son of

Uncas, in Tamenund, in Deerslayer. The Evil Spirit is in the Mingos. That I know; I do not see the earth turn round."

"I don't wonder they call you the Sarpent, Delaware; no, I don't! There's always a meaning in your words, and there's often a meaning in your countenance, too! Not withstanding, your answers doesn't quite meet my idee. That God is obsarvable in all nat'ral objects is allowable, but then he is not parceptible in the way I mean. *You* know there is a Great Spirit by his works, and the palefaces know that the 'arth turns round by its works. This is the reason of the matter, though how it is to be explained is more than I can exactly tell you. This I know: all my people consait that fact, and what all the palefaces consait is very likely to be true."

"When the sun is in the top of that pine tomorrow, where will my brother Deerslayer be?"

The hunter started, and he looked intently, though totally without alarm, at his friend. Then he signed for him to follow and led the way into the ark, where he might pursue the subject unheard by those whose feelings he feared might get the mastery over their reason. Here he stopped and pursued the conversation in a more confidential tone.

" 'Twas a little onreasonable in you, Sarpent," he said, "to bring up such a subject afore Hist, and when the young woman of my own color might overhear what was said. Yes, 'twas a little more onreasonable than most things that you do. No matter; Hist didn't comprehend, and the other didn't hear. Howsever, the question is easier put than answered. No mortal can say where he will be when the sun rises tomorrow. I will ask you the same question, Sarpent, and should like to hear what answer you can give."

"Chingachgook will be with his friend, Deerslayer; if he be in the land of spirits, the Great Serpent will crawl at his side; if beneath yonder sun, its warmth and light shall fall on both."

"I understand you, Delaware," returned the other, touched with the simple self-devotion of his friend. "Such language is as plain in one tongue as in another; it comes from the heart, and goes to the heart, too. 'Tis well to think so, and it may be well to *say* so, for that matter, but it would not be well to *do* so, Sarpent. You are no longer alone in life, for though you have the lodges to change and other ceremonies to go through afore Hist becomes your lawful wife, yet are you as good as married in all that bears on the feelin's, and joy, and misery. No, no; Hist must not be desarted because a cloud is passing atween you and me a little onexpectedly and a little darker than we may have looked for."

"Hist is a daughter of the Mohicans: she knows how to obey her husband. Where he goes she will follow. *Both* will be with the Great Hunter of the Delawares when the sun shall be in the pine tomorrow."

"The Lord bless and protect you! Chief, this is downright madness. Can either or both of you alter a Mingo natur'? Will your grand looks, or Hist's tears and beauty, change a wolf into a squirrel, or make a catamount as innocent as a fa'an! No, Sarpent, you will think better of this matter, and leave me in the hands of God. A'ter all, it's by no means sartain that the scamps design the torments, for they may yet be pitiful and bethink them of the wickedness of such a course—though it *is* but a hopeless expectation to look forward to a Mingo's turning aside from evil, and letting marcy get uppermost in his heart. Nevertheless, no one knows to a sartainty what will happen, and young creatur's like Hist ar'n't to be risked on unsartainties. This marrying is altogether a different undertaking from what some young men fancy. Now, if you was single, or as good as single, Delaware, I should expect you to be actyve and stirring about the camp of the vagabonds from sunrise to sunset, sarcumventing and contriving, as restless as a hound off the scent, and doing all manner of things to help me and to distract the inimy; but two are often feebler than one, and we must take things as they are and not as we want 'em to be."

"Listen, Deerslayer," returned the Indian, with an emphasis so decided as to show how much he was in earnest. "If Chingachgook was in the hands of the Hurons, what would my paleface brother do? Sneak off to the Delaware villages and say to the chiefs, and old men, and young warriors—'See; here is Wah-ta!-wah; she is safe, but a little tired; and here is the Son of Uncas, not as tired as the Honeysuckle, being stronger, but just as safe.' Would he do this?"

"Well, that's oncommon ingen'ous; it's cunning enough for

a Mingo himself. The Lord only knows what put it into your head to ask such a question. What would I do? Why, in the first place, Hist wouldn't be likely to be in my company at all, for she would stay as near you as possible, and therefore all that part about *her* couldn't be said without talking nonsense. As for her being tired, that would fall through, too, if she didn't go, and no part of your speech would be likely to come from me: so you see, Sarpent, reason is ag'in you, and you may as well give it up, since to hold out ag'in reason is no way becoming a chief of your character and repitation."

"My brother is not himself; he forgets that he is talking to one who has sat at the council fires of his nation," returned the other kindly. "When men speak, they should say that which does not go in at one side of the head and out at the other. Their words shouldn't be feathers, so light that a wind which does not ruffle the water can blow them away. He has not answered my question; when a chief puts a question, his friend should not talk of other things."

"I understand you, Delaware; I understand well enough what you mean, and truth won't allow me to say otherwise. Still, it's not as easy to answer as you seem to think, for this plain reason. You wish me to say what I would do if I had a betrothed, as you have, here on the lake, and a fri'nd yonder, in the Huron camp, in danger of the torments. That's it, isn't it?"

The Indian bowed his head silently and always with unmoved gravity, though his eye twinkled at the sight of the other's embarrassment.

"Well, I never had a betrothed, never had the kind of feelin's toward any young woman that you have toward Hist, though the Lord knows my feelin's kind enough toward 'em all! Still, my heart, as they call it, in such matters isn't touched, and therefore I can't say what I would do. A fri'nd pulls strong; that I know by exper'ence, Sarpent; but by all that I've seen and heard consarning love, I'm led to think that a betrothed pulls stronger."

"True; but the betrothed of Chingachgook does not pull toward the lodges of the Delawares; she pulls toward the camp of the Hurons."

"She's a noble gal, for all her little feet and hands that an't bigger than a child's, and a voice that's as pleasant as a mocker's; she's a noble gal, and like the stock of her sires! Well, what is it, Sarpent?—for I conclude she hasn't changed her mind and means to give herself up and turn Huron wife. What is it you want?"

"Wah-ta!-wah will never live in the wigwam of an Iroquois," answered the Delaware drily. "She has little feet, but they can carry her to the villages of her people; she has small hands, too, but her mind is large. My brother will see what we can do when the time shall come, rather than let him die under Mingo torments."

"Attempt nothing heedlessly, Delaware," said the other earnestly. "I suppose you must and will have your way; on the whole, it's right you should, for you'd neither be happy unless something was undertaken. But attempt nothing heedlessly. I didn't expect you'd quit the lake while my matter remained in unsartainty; but remember, Sarpent, that no torments that Mingo ingenuity can invent, no ta'ntings and revilings, no burnings and roastings and nail-tearings, nor any other onhuman contrivance, can so soon break down my spirit as to find that you and Hist have fallen into the power of the inimy in striving to do something for my good."

"The Delawares are prudent. The Deerslayer will not find them running into a strange camp with their eyes shut."

Here the dialogue terminated. Hetty announced that the breakfast was ready, and the whole party were soon seated around the simple board, in the usual primitive manner of borderers. Judith was the last to take her seat, pale, silent, and betraying in her countenance that she had passed a painful if not a sleepless night. At this meal scarce a syllable was exchanged, all the females manifesting want of appetite, though the two men were unchanged in this particular. It was early when the party arose, and there still remained several hours before it would be necessary for the prisoner to leave his friends. The knowledge of this circumstance, and the interest all felt in his welfare, induced the whole to assemble on the platform again, in the desire to be near the expected victim, to listen to his discourse, and, if possible, to show their interest in him by anticipating his wishes. Deerslayer himself, so far as human eyes could penetrate, was wholly unmoved, conversing cheerfully and naturally, though he avoided any direct allusion to the expected and great event of the day. If any evidence could be discovered of his thoughts reverting to that painful subject at all, it was in the manner in which he spoke of death and the last great change.

"Grieve not, Hetty," he said—for it was while consoling this simple-minded girl for the loss of her parents that he thus betrayed his feelings—"since God has app'inted that all must die. Your parents, or them you fancied your parents, which is the same thing, have gone afore you; this is only in the order of natur', my good gal, for the aged go first and the young follow. But one that had a mother like your'n, Hetty, can be at no loss to hope the best as to how matters will turn out in another world. The Delaware here and Hist believe in happy hunting grounds and have idees befitting their notions and gifts as redskins, but we who are of white blood hold altogether to a different doctrine. Still, I rather conclude our heaven is their land of spirits and that the path which leads to it will be traveled by all colors alike. 'Tis onpossible for the wicked to enter on it, I will allow; but fri'nds can scarce be separated, though they are not of the same race on 'arth. Keep up your spirits, poor Hetty, and look forward to the day when you will meet your mother ag'in, and that without pain or sorrowing."

"I do expect to see Mother," returned the truth-telling and simple girl, "but what will become of Father?"

"That's a nonplusser, Delaware," said the hunter in the Indian dialect; "yes, that is a downright nonplusser! The Muskrat was not a saint on 'arth, and it's fair to guess he'll not be much of one hereafter! Howsever, Hetty"—dropping into the English by an easy transition—"we must all hope for the best. That is wisest, and it is much the easiest to the mind, if one can only do it, I ricommend to you trusting to God and putting down all misgivings and fainthearted feelin's. It's wonderful, Judith, how different people have different notions about the futur', some fancying one change and some fancying another. I've known white teachers that have thought all was spirit hereafter, and them ag'in that believed the body will be transported to another world, much as the redskins themselves imagine, and that we shall walk about in the flesh, and know each other, and talk together, and be fri'nds there as we've been fri'nds here."

"Which of these opinions is most pleasing to *you*, Deerslayer?" asked the girl, willing to indulge his melancholy mood, and far from being free from its influence herself. "Would it be disagreeable to think that you should meet all who are now on this platform in another world? Or have you known enough of us here to be glad to see us no more?"

"The last would make death a bitter portion; yes, it would. It's eight good years since the Sarpent and I began to hunt together, and the thought that we were never to meet ag'in would be a hard thought to me. He looks forward to the time when he shall chase a sort of spirit deer, in company, on plains where there's no thorns, or brambles, or marshes, or other hardships to overcome; whereas, I can't fall into all these notions, seeing that they appear to be ag'in reason. Spirits can't eat, nor have they any use for clothes, and deer can only rightfully be chased to be slain, or slain, unless it be for the venison or the hides. Now I find it hard to suppose that blessed spirits can be put to chasing game without an object, tormenting the dumb animals just for the pleasure and agreeableness of their own amusements. I never yet pulled a trigger on buck or doe, Judith, unless when food or clothes was wanting."

"The recollection of which, Deerslayer, must now be a great consolation to you."

"It is the thought of such things, my fri'nds, that enables a man to keep his furlough. It might be done without it, I own; for the worst redskins sometimes do their duty in this matter; but it makes that which might otherwise be hard, easy, if not altogether to our liking. Nothing truly makes a bolder heart than a light conscience."

Judith turned paler than ever, but she struggled for self-command and succeeded in obtaining it. The conflict had been severe, however, and it left her so little disposed to speak that Hetty pursued the subject. This was done in the simple manner natural to the girl.

"It would be cruel to kill the poor deer," she said, "in this world or any other, when you don't want their venison or their skins. No good white man and no good red man would do it. But it's wicked for a Christian to talk about chasing anything in Heaven. Such things are not done before the face of God, and the missionary that teaches these doctrines can't be a true missionary. He must be a wolf in sheep's clothing. I suppose you know what a sheep is, Deer-slayer?"

"That I do, gal; and a useful creature it is to such as like cloths better than skins for winter garments. I understand the natur' of sheep, though I've had but little to do with 'em —and the natur' of wolves too, and can take the idee of a wolf in the fleece of a sheep, though I think it would be likely to prove a hot jacket for such a beast in the warm months."

"And sin and hypocrisy are hot jackets, as *they* will find who put them on," returned Hetty positively, "so the wolf would be no worse off than the sinner. Spirits don't hunt, nor trap, nor fish, nor do anything that vain men undertake, since they've none of the longings of this world to feed. Oh, Mother told me all that years ago, and I didn't wish to hear it denied."

"Well, my good Hetty, in that case you'd better not broach your doctrine to Hist when she and you are alone and the young Delaware maiden is inclined to talk religion. It's her fixed idee, I know, that the good warriors do nothing but hunt and fish in the other world, though I don't believe that she fancies any of them are brought down to trapping, which is no empl'yment for a brave. But of hunting and fishing, accordin' to her notion, they've their fill, and that, too, over the most agreeablest hunting grounds and among game that is never out of season, and which is just actyve and instinctyve enough to give a pleasure to death. So I wouldn't ricommend it to you to start Hist on that idee."

"Hist can't be so wicked as to believe any such thing," returned the other earnestly. "No Indian hunts after he is dead."

"No wicked Indian, I grant you; no wicked Indian sartainly. He is obliged to carry the ammunition, and to look on without sharing in the sport, and to cook, and to light the fires, and to do everything that isn't manful. Now mind, I don't tell you these are my idees, but they are Hist's idees, and therefore for the sake of peace, the less you say to her ag'in 'em the better."

"And what are your ideas of the fate of an Indian in the other world?" demanded Judith, who had just found her voice.

"Ah, gal, anything but that! I am too Christianized to

expect anything so fanciful as hunting and fishing after death; nor do I believe there is one Manitou for the redskin and another for a paleface. You find different colors on 'arth, as anyone may see, but you don't find different natur's. Different gifts, but only one natur'."

"In what is a gift different from a nature? Is not nature itself a gift from God?"

"Sartain; that's quick-thoughted and creditable, Judith, though the main idee is wrong. A natur' is the creatur' itself; its wishes, wants, idees, and feelin's, as all are born in him. This natur' never can be changed in the main, though it may undergo some increase or lessening. Now, gifts come of sarcumstances. Thus, if you put a man in a town, he gets town gifts; in a settlement, settlement gifts; in a forest, gifts of the woods. A soldier has soldierly gifts, and a missionary preaching gifts. All these increase and strengthen until they get to fortify natur', as it might be, and excuse a thousand acts and idees. Still, the creatur' is the same at the bottom, just as a man who is clad in regimentals is the same as the man that is clad in skins. The garments make a change to the eye and some change in the conduct, perhaps, but none in the man. Herein lies the apology for gifts, seein' that you expect different conduct from one in silks and satins from one in homespun, though the Lord, who didn't make the dresses but who made the creatur's themselves, looks only at His own work. This isn't ra'al missionary doctrine, but it's as near it as a man of white color need be. Ah's me! Little did I think to be talking of such matters today, but it's one of our weaknesses never to know what will come to pass. Step into the ark with me, Judith, for a minute. I wish to converse with you."

Judith complied with a willingness she could scarce conceal. Following the hunter into the cabin, she took a seat on a stool, while the young man brought Killdeer, the rifle she had given him, out of a corner, and placed himself on another, with the weapon laid upon his knees. After turning the piece around and around and examining its lock and its breech with a sort of affectionate assiduity, he laid it down and proceeded to the subject which had induced him to desire the interview.

"I understand you, Judith, to say that you gave me this rifle," he said. "I agreed to take it because a young woman can have no particular use for firearms. The we'pon has a great name, and it desarves it, and ought of right to be carried by some known and sure hand, for the best reputation may be lost by careless and thoughtless handling."

"Can it be in better hands than those in which it is now, Deerslayer? Thomas Hutter seldom missed with it: with you it must turn out to be——"

"Sartain death!" interrupted the hunter, laughing. "I once know'd a beaver man that had a piece he called by that very name, but 'twas all boastfulness, for I've seen Delawares that were as true with arrows at a short range. Howsever, I'll not deny my gifts—for *this* is a gift, Judith, and not natur'—but I'll not deny my gifts, and therefore allow that the rifle couldn't well be in better hands than it is at present. But how long will it be likely to remain there? Atween us, the truth may be said, though I shouldn't like to have it known to the Sarpent and Hist; but to *you* the truth may be spoken, since *your* feelin's will not be as likely to be tormented by it as those of them that have known me longer and better. How long am I like to own this rifle or any other? That is a serious question for our thoughts to rest on, and should that happen which is so likely to happen, Killdeer would be without an owner."

Judith listened with apparent composure, though the conflict within came near overpowering her. Appreciating the singular character of her companion, however, she succeeded in appearing calm, though, had not his attention been drawn exclusively to the rifle, a man of his keenness of observation could scarce have failed to detect the agony of mind with which the girl had hearkened to his words. Her great self-command, notwithstanding, enabled her to pursue the subject in a way still to deceive him.

"What would you have me do with the weapon," she asked, "should that which you seem to expect take place?"

"That's just what I wanted to speak to you about, Judith —that's just it. There's Chingachgook, now, though far from being parfect sartainty with a rifle—for few redskins ever get to be *that*—though far from being parfect sartainty, he is respectable and is coming on. Nevertheless, he is my fri'nd, and all the better fri'nd, perhaps, because there never can be any hard feelin's atween us, touchin' our gifts, his'n bein' red and mine bein' altogether white. Now, I should like to leave Killdeer to the Sarpent, should anything happen to keep me from doing credit and honor to your precious gift, Judith."

"Leave it to whom you please, Deerslayer; the rifle is your own, to do with as you please; Chingachgook shall have it, should you never return to claim it, if that be your wish."

"Has Hetty been consulted in this matter? Property goes from the parent to the children, and not to one child in partic'lar."

"If you place your right on that of the law, Deerslayer, I fear none of us can claim to be the owner. Thomas Hutter was no more the father of Esther than he was the father of Judith. Judith and Esther we are, truly, having no other name."

"There may be law in that, but there's no great reason, gal. Accordin' to the custom of families, the goods are your'n, and there's no one here to gainsay it. If Hetty would only say that she is willing, my mind would be quite at ease in the matter. It's true, Judith, that your sister has neither your beauty nor your wit, but we should be the tenderest of the rights and welfare of the most weak-minded."

The girl made no answer, but, placing herself at a window, she summoned her sister to her side. When the question was put to Hetty, her simple-minded and affectionate nature cheerfully assented to the proposal to confer on Deerslayer a full right of ownership to the much-coveted rifle. The latter now seemed perfectly happy, for the time being, at least, and after again examining and re-examining his prize, he expressed a determination to put its merits to a practical test before he left the spot. No boy could have been more eager to exhibit the qualities of his trumpet or his crossbow than this simple forester was to prove those of his rifle. Returning to the platform, he first took the Delaware aside and informed him that this celebrated piece was to become his property in the event of anything serious befalling himself.

"This is a new reason why you should be wary, Sarpent, and not run into any oncalculated danger," the hunter added, "for it will be a victory of itself, to a tribe, to own such a piece as this! The Mingos will turn green with envy, and what is more, they will not ventur' heedlessly near a village where it is known to be kept. So look well to it, Delaware, and remember that you've now to watch over a thing that has all the valie of a creatur', without its failin's. Hist may be, and should be precious to you, but Killdeer will have the love and veneration of your whole people."

"One rifle like another, Deerslayer," returned the Indian in English, the language used by the other, a little hurt at his friend's lowering his betrothed to the level of a gun. "All kill; all wood and iron. Wife dear to heart; rifle good to shoot."

"And what is a man in the woods, without something to shoot with?—a miserable trapper, or a forlorn broom and basketmaker, at the best. Such a man may hoe corn and keep soul and body together, but he can never know the savory morsels of venison, or tell a bear's ham from a hog's. Come, my fri'nd, such another occasion may never offer ag'in, and I feel a strong craving for a trial with this celebrated piece. You shall bring out your own rifle, and I will just sight Killdeer in a careless way, in order that we may know a few of its secret vartues."

As this proposition served to relieve the thoughts of the whole party, by giving them a new direction, while it was likely to produce no unpleasant result, everyone was willing to enter into it, the girls bringing forth the firearms with an alacrity bordering on cheerfulness. Hutter's armory was well supplied, possessing several rifles, all of which were habitually kept loaded, in readiness to meet any sudden demand for their use. On the present occasion it only remained to freshen the primings, and each piece was in a state for service. This was soon done, as all assisted in it, the females being as expert in this part of the system of defense as their male companions.

"Now, Sarpent, we'll begin in an humble way, using old Tom's commoners first and coming to your we'pon and Killdeer as the winding-up observations," said Deerslayer, delighted to be again, weapon in hand, ready to display his skill. "Here's birds in abundance, some in, and some over the lake, and they keep at just a good range, hovering around the hut. Speak your mind, Delaware, and p'int out the creatur' you wish to alarm. Here's a diver, nearest in, off to the eastward, and that's a creatur' that buries itself at the flash, and will be like enough to try both piece and powder."

Chingachgook was a man of few words. No sooner was

the bird pointed out to him than he took his aim and fired. The duck dived at the flash, as had been expected, and the bullet skipped harmlessly along the surface of the lake, first striking the water within a few inches of the spot where the bird had so lately swum. Deerslayer laughed cordially and naturally, but at the same time he threw himself into an attitude of preparation and stood keenly, watching the sheet of placid water. Presently a dark spot appeared, and then the duck arose to breathe, and shook its wings. While in this act, a bullet passed directly through its breast, actually turning it over lifeless, on its back. At the next moment Deerslayer stood with the breech of his rifle on the platform, as tranquil as if nothing had happened, though laughing in his own peculiar manner.

"There's no great trial of the pieces in that!" he said, as if anxious to prevent a false impression of his own merit. "No, that proof's neither for nor ag'in the rifles, seeing it was all quickness of hand and eye. I took the bird at a disadvantage, or he might have got under again, afore the bullet reached him. But the Sarpent is too wise to mind such tricks, having long been used to them. Do you remember the time, Chief, when you thought yourself sartain of the wild goose, and I took him out of your very eyes, as it might be, with a little smoke! Howsever such things pass for nothing atween fri'nds, and young folk will have their fun, Judith. Aye, here's just the bird we want, for it's as good for the fire as it is for the aim, and nothing should be lost that can be turned to just account. There, farther north, Delaware."

The latter looked in the required direction, and he soon saw a large black duck, floating in stately repose on the water. At that distant day, when so few men were present to derange the harmony of the wilderness, all the smaller lakes with which the interior of New York so abounds were places of resort for the migratory aquatic birds, and this sheet, like the others, had once been much frequented by all the varieties of the duck, by the goose, the gull, and the loon. On the appearance of Hutter, the spot was comparatively deserted for other sheets, more retired and remote, though some of each species continued to resort thither, as indeed they do to the present hour. At that instant, a hundred birds were visible from the castle, sleeping on the water, or laving their feathers in the limpid element, though no other offered so favorable a mark as that Deerslayer had just pointed out to his friend. Chingachgook, as usual, speared his words and proceeded to execution. This time his aim was more careful than before, and his success in proportion. The bird had a wing crippled, and fluttered along the water screaming, materially increasing its distance from its enemies.

"That bird must be put out of pain," exclaimed Deerslayer, the moment the animal endeavored to rise on the wing, "and this is the rifle and the eye to do it."

The duck was still floundering along when the fatal bullet overtook it, severing the head from the neck as neatly as if it had been done with an ax. Hist had indulged in a low cry of delight at the success of the young Indian, but now she affected to frown and resent the greater skill of his friend. The chief, on the contrary, uttered the usual exclamation of pleasure, and his smile proved how much he admired and how little he envied.

"Never mind the gal, Sarpent; never mind Hist's feelin's, which will neither choke nor drown, slay nor beautify," said Deerslayer, laughing. " 'Tis nat'ral for women to enter into their husband's victories and defeats, and you are as good as man and wife, so far as prejudice and friendship go. Here is a bird overhead that will put the pieces to the proof; I challenge you to an upward aim, with a flying target. That's a ra'al proof, and one that needs sartain rifles, as well as sartain eyes."

The species of eagle that frequents the water and lives on fish was also present, and one was hovering at a considerable height above the hut, greedily watching for an opportunity to make a swoop, its hungry young elevating their heads from a nest that was in sight in the naked summit of a dead pine. Chingachgook silently turned a new piece against this bird and, after carefully watching his time, fired. A wider circuit than common denoted that the messenger had passed through the air at no great distance from the bird, though it missed its object. Deerslayer, whose aim was not more true than it was quick, fired as soon as it was certain his friend had missed, and the deep swoop that followed left it momentarily doubtful whether the eagle was hit or not. The marksman himself, however, proclaimed his own want of success, calling on his friend to seize another rifle, for he saw signs on the part of the bird of an intention to quit the spot.

"I made him wink, Sarpent; I do think his feathers were ruffled, but no blood has yet been drawn, nor is that old piece fit for so nice and quick a sight. Quick, Delaware, you've now a better rifle; Judith, bring out Killdeer, for this is the occasion to try his merits, if he has 'em!"

A general movement followed, each of the competitors got ready, and the girls stood in eager expectation of the result. The eagle had made a wide circuit after his low swoop, and fanning his way upward, once more hovered nearly over the hut, at a distance even greater than before. Chingachgook gazed at him and then expressed his opinion of the impossibility of striking a bird at that great height, and while he was so nearly perpendicular as to the range. But a low murmur from Hist produced a sudden impulse, and he fired. The result showed how well he had calculated, the eagle not even varying his flight, sailing around and around in his airy circle, and looking down, as if in contempt, at his foes.

"Now, Judith," cried Deerslayer, laughing, with glistening and delighted eyes, "we'll see if Killdeer isn't Killeagle, too! Give me room, Sarpent, and watch the reason of the aim, for by reason anything may be l'arned."

A careful sight followed, and was repeated again and again, the bird continuing to rise higher and higher. Then followed the flash and the report. The swift messenger sped upward, and at the next instant, the bird turned on its side and came swooping down, now struggling with one wing and then with the other, sometimes whirling in a circuit, next fanning desperately as if conscious of its injury, until, having described several complete circles around the spot, it fell heavily into the end of the ark. On examining the body, it was found that the bullet had pierced it about halfway between one of its wings and the breastbone.

Chapter XXVI

Upon two stony tables, spread before her,
She leaned her bosom, more than stony hard;
There slept the impartial judge, and strict restorer
Of wrong or right, with pain or with reward;
There hung the score of all our debts, the card
Where good, and bad, and life, and death, were painted,
Was never heart of mortal so untainted,
But when the roll was read, with thousand terrors fainted.

GILES FLETCHER

"WE'VE DONE AN unthoughtful thing, Sarpent—yes, Judith, we've done an unthoughtful thing in taking life with an object no better than vanity!" exclaimed Deerslayer, when the Delaware held up the enormous bird, by its wings, and exhibited the dying eyes riveted on its enemies with the gaze that the helpless ever fasten on their destroyers. " 'Twas more becomin' two boys to gratify their feelin's in this onthoughtful manner than two warriors on a warpath, even though it be their first. Ah's me! Well, as a punishment I'll quit you at once, and when I find myself alone with them bloody-minded Mingos, it's more than like I'll have occasion to remember that life is sweet, even to the beasts of the woods and the fowls of the air. Here, Judith; there's Killdeer; take him back ag'in, and keep him for some hand that's more desarving to own such a piece."

"I know of none as deserving as your own, Deerslayer," answered the girl in haste; "none but yours shall keep the rifle."

"If it depended on skill, you might be right enough, gal, but we should know *when* to use firearms as well as *how* to use 'em. I haven't l'arnt the first duty yet, it seems, so keep the peace till I have. The sight of a dyin' and distressed creatur', even though it be only a bird, brings wholesome

432

thoughts to a man who don't know how soon his own time may come, and who *is* pretty sartain that it will come afore the sun sets; I'd give back all my vain feelin's and rej'icin's in hand and eye if that poor eagle was only on its nest ag'in with its young, praisin' the Lord, for anything that we can know about the matter, for health and strength!"

The listeners were confounded with this proof of sudden repentance in the hunter, and that, too, for an indulgence so very common that men seldom stop to weigh its consequences or the physical suffering it may bring on the unoffending and helpless. The Delaware understood what was said, though he scarce understood the feelings which had prompted the words, and by way of disposing of the difficulty, he drew his keen knife and severed the head of the sufferer from its body.

"What a thing is power!" continued the hunter, "and what a thing it is to have it and not to know how to use it! It's no wonder, Judith, that the great so often fail of their duties, when even the little and the humble find it so hard to do what's right and not to do what's wrong. Then, how one evil act brings others a'ter it! Now, wasn't it for this furlough of mine, which must soon take me back to the Mingos, I'd find this creatur's nest, if I traveled the woods a fortnight—though an eagle's nest is soon found by them that understands the bird's natur'—but I'd travel a fortnight rather than not find it, just to put the young, too, out of their pain."

"I'm glad to hear you say this, Deerslayer," observed Hetty, "and God will be more apt to remember your sorrow for what you've done than the wickedness itself. I thought how wicked it was to kill harmless birds while you were shooting and meant to tell you so, but—I don't know how it happened—I was so curious to see if you *could* hit an eagle at so great a height that I forgot altogether to speak till the mischief was done."

"That's it; that's just it, my good Hetty. We can all see our faults and mistakes when it's too late to help them! Howsever, I'm glad you didn't speak, for I don't think a word or two would have stopped me just at that moment; and so the sin stands in its nakedness, not aggravated by any unheeded calls to forbear. Well, well, bitter thoughts are hard to be borne at all times, but there's times when they're harder than at others."

Little did Deerslayer know, while thus indulging in feelings that were natural to the man and so strictly in accordance with his own unsophisticated and just principles, that, in the course of the inscrutable Providence which so uniformly and yet so mysteriously covers all events with its mantle, the very fault he was disposed so severely to censure, was to be made the means of determining his own earthly fate. The mode and the moment in which he was to feel the influence of this interference it would be premature to relate, but both will appear in the course of the succeeding chapters. As for the young man, he now slowly left the ark, like one sorrowing for his misdeeds, and seated himself in silence on the platform. By this time the sun had ascended to some height, and its appearance, taken in connection with his present feelings, induced him to prepare to depart. The Delaware got the canoe ready for his friend as soon as apprised of his intention, while Hist busied herself in making the few arrangements that were thought necessary to his comfort. All this was done without ostentation but in a way that left Deerslayer fully acquainted with, and equally disposed to appreciate, the motive. When all was ready, both returned to the side of Judith and Hetty—neither of whom had moved from the spot where the young hunter sat.

"The best fri'nds must often part," the last began, when he saw the whole party grouped around him. "Yes, fri'ndship can't alter the ways of Providence, and let our feelin's be as they may, we must part. I've often thought there's moments when our words dwell longer on the mind than common, and when advice is remembered, just because the mouth that gives it isn't likely to give it ag'in. No one knows what will happen in the world, and therefore it may be well, when fri'nds separate under a likelihood that the parting may be long, to say a few words in kindness, as a sort of keepsakes. If all but one will go into the ark, I'll talk to each in turn, and what is more, I'll listen to what you may have to say back ag'in; for it's a poor counselor that won't take as well as give."

As the meaning of the speaker was understood, the two Indians immediately withdrew as desired, leaving the sisters, however, still standing at the young man's side. A look of Deerslayer's induced Judith to explain.

"You can advise Hetty as you land," she said hastily, "I intend that she shall accompany you to the shore."

"Is this wise, Judith? It's true that, under common sarcumstances, a feeble mind is a great protection among redskins, but when their feelin's are up, and they're bent on revenge, it's hard to say what may come to pass. Besides——"

"What were you about to say, Deerslayer?" asked Judith, whose gentleness of voice and manner amounted nearly to tenderness, though she struggled hard to keep her emotions and apprehensions in subjection.

"Why, simply that there are sights and doin's that one even as little gifted with reason and memory as Hetty, here, might better not witness. So, Judith, you would do well to let me land alone and to keep your sister back."

"Never fear for me, Deerslayer," put in Hetty, who comprehended enough of the discourse to know its general drift; "I'm feeble-minded, and that, they say, is an excuse for going anywhere, and what that won't excuse will be overlooked on account of the Bible I always carry. It is wonderful, Judith, how all sorts of men, the trappers as well as the hunters, red men as well as white, Mingos as well as Delawares, do reverence and fear the Bible!"

"I think you have not the least ground to fear any injury, Hetty," answered the sister, "and therefore I shall insist on your going to the Huron camp with our friend. Your being there can do no harm, not even to yourself, and may do great good to Deerslayer."

"This is not a moment, Judith, to dispute, and so have the matter your own way," returned the young man. "Get yourself ready, Hetty, and go into the canoe, for I've a few parting words to say to your sister, which can do you no good."

Judith and her companion continued silent until Hetty had so far complied as to leave them alone, when Deerslayer took up the subject as if it had been interrupted by some ordinary occurrence, and in a very matter-of-fact way.

"Words spoken at parting, and which may be the last we ever hear from a fri'nd, are not soon forgotten," he repeated, "and so, Judith, I intend to speak to you like a brother, seein' I'm not old enough to be your father. In the first place, I wish to caution you ag'in your inimies, of which two may be said to ha'nt your very footsteps and to beset your ways. The first is oncommon good looks, which is as dangerous a foe to some young women as a whole tribe of Mingos could prove, and which calls for great watchfulness; not to admire and praise, but to distrust and sarcumvent. Yes, good looks may be sarcumvented and fairly outwitted, too. In order to do this, you've only to remember that they melt like the snows, and when once gone, they never come back ag'in. The seasons come and go, Judith; if we have winter, with storms and frosts, and spring, with chills and leafless trees, we have summer, with its sun and glorious skies, and fall, with its fruits and a garment thrown over the forest that no beauty of the town could rummage out of all the shops in America. 'Arth is an eternal round, the goodness of God bringing back the pleasant when we've had enough of the onpleasant. But it's not so with good looks. *They* are lent for a short time in youth, to be used and not abused, and as I never met with a young woman to whom Providence has been as bountiful as it has to you, Judith, in this partic'lar, I warn you, as it might be with my dyin' breath, to beware of the inimy—fri'nd or inimy, as we deal with the gift."

It was so grateful to Judith to hear these unequivocal admissions of her personal charms that much would have been forgiven to the man who made them, let him be who he might. But at that moment, and from a far better feeling, it would not have been easy for Deerslayer seriously to offend her, and she listened with a patience which, had it been foretold only a week earlier, it would have excited her indignation to hear.

"I understand your meaning, Deerslayer," returned the girl, with a meekness and humility that a little surprised her listener, "and hope to be able to profit by it. But you have mentioned only one of the enemies I have to fear; who, or what, is the other?"

"The other is givin' way afore your own good sense and judgment, I find, Judith; yes, he's not as dangerous as I supposed. Howsever, havin' opened the subject, it will be as well to end it honestly. The first inimy you have to be watchful of, as I've already told you, Judith, is oncommon good looks, and the next is an oncommon knowledge of the sarcumstance. If the first is bad, the last doesn't, in any way, mend the matter, so far as safety and peace of mind are consarned."

How much longer the young man would have gone on in his simple and unsuspecting, but well-intentioned manner, it might not be easy to say, had he not been interrupted by his listener's bursting into tears and giving way to an outbreak of feeling which was so much the more violent from the fact that it had been with so much difficulty suppressed. At first her sobs were so violent and uncontrollable that Deerslayer was a little appalled, and he was abundantly repentant from the instant that he discovered how much greater was the effect produced by his words than he had anticipated. Even the austere and exacting are usually appeased by the signs of contrition, but the nature of Deerslayer did not require proofs of intense feeling so strong, in order to bring him down to a level with the regrets felt by the girl herself. He arose as if an adder had stung him, and the accents of the mother that soothes her child were scarcely more gentle and winning than the tones of his voice, as he now expressed his contrition at having gone so far.

"It was well meant, Judith," he said, "but it was not intended to hurt your feelin's so much. I have overdone the advice, I see; yes, I've overdone it, and I crave your pardon for the same. Fri'ndship's an awful thing! Sometimes it chides us for not having done enough, and then ag'in it speaks in strong words for havin' done too much. Howsever, I acknowledge I've overdone the matter, and as I've a ra'al and strong regard for you, I rej'ice to say it, inasmuch as it proves how much better you are than my own vanity and consaits had made you out to be."

Judith now removed her hands from her face, her tears had ceased, and she unveiled a countenance so winning, with the smile which rendered it even radiant, that the young man gazed at her for a moment with speechless delight.

"Say no more, Deerslayer," she hastily interposed; "it pains me to hear you find fault with yourself. I know my own weakness all the better, now I see that you have discovered it; the lesson, bitter as I have found it for a moment, shall not be forgotten. We will not talk any longer of these things, for I do not feel myself brave enough for the undertaking, and I should not like the Delawares, or Hist, or even Hetty to notice my weakness. Farewell, Deerslayer, may God bless and protect you as your honest heart deserves blessing and protection, and as I must think He will."

Judith had so far regained the superiority that properly belonged to her better education, high spirit, and surpassing personal advantages as to preserve the ascendency she had thus accidentally obtained, and effectually prevented any return to the subject that was as singularly interrupted as it had been singularly introduced. The young man permitted her to have everything her own way, and when she pressed his hard hand in both her own, he made no resistance, but submitted to the homage as quietly, and with quite as matter of course a manner, as a sovereign would have received a similar tribute from a subject, or the mistress from her suitor. Feeling had flushed the face and illuminated the whole countenance of the girl, and her beauty was never more resplendent than when she cast a parting glance at the youth. That glance was filled with anxiety, interest, and gentle pity. At the next instant she darted into the hut and was seen no more, though she spoke to Hist from a window to inform her that their friend expected her appearance.

"You know enough of redskin natur', and redskin usages, Wah-ta!-Wah, to see the condition I am in on account of this furlough," commenced the hunter, in Delaware, as soon as the patient and submissive girl of that people had moved quietly to his side; "you will therefore best onderstand how onlikely I am ever to talk with you ag'in. I've but little to say, but that little comes from long livin' among your people and from havin' obsarved and noted their usages. The life of a woman is hard at the best, but I must own, though I'm not opinionated in favor of my own color, that it is harder among the red men than it is among the palefaces. This is a p'int on which Christians may well boast, if boasting can be set down for Christianity in any manner or form, which I rather think it cannot. Howsever, all women have their trials. Red women have their'n in what I should call the nat'ral way, while white women take 'em inoculated like. Bear your burden, Hist, becomingly, and remember, if it be a little toilsome, how much lighter it is than that of most Indian women. I know the Sarpent well—what I call cordially—and he will never be a tyrant to anything he loves, though he will expect to be treated himself like a Mohican chief. There will be cloudy days in your lodge, I suppose, for they happen under all usages and among all people, but by keepin' the windows of the heart open, there will always be room for the sunshine to enter. You come of a great stock yourself, and so does Chingachgook. It's not very likely that either will ever forget the sarcumstance and do anything to disgrace your forefathers. Nevertheless, likin' is a tender plant and never thrives long when watered with tears. Let the 'arth around your married happiness be moistened by the dews of kindness."

"My pale brother is very wise; Wah will keep in her mind all that his wisdom tells her."

"That's judicious and womanly, Hist. Care in listening and stouteheartedness in holding to good counsel is a wife's great protection. And, now, ask the Sarpent to come and speak with me for a moment, and carry away with you all my best wishes and prayers. I shall think of you, Hist, and of your intended husband, let what may come to pass, and always wish you well, here and hereafter, whether the last is to be according to Indian idees or Christian doctrines."

Hist shed no tear at parting. She was sustained by the high resolution of one who had decided on her course; but her dark eyes were luminous with the feelings that glowed within, and her pretty countenance beamed with an expression of determination that was in marked and singular contrast to its ordinary gentleness. It was but a minute ere the Delaware advanced to the side of his friend with the light, noiseless tread of an Indian.

"Come thisaway, Sarpent, here more out of sight of the women," commenced the Deerslayer, "for I've several things to say that mustn't so much as be suspected, much less overheard. *You* know too well the natur' of furloughs and Mingos to have any doubts or misgivin's consarnin' what is likely to happen when I get back to the camp. On them two p'ints, therefore, a few words will go a great way. In the first place, Chief, I wish to say a little about Hist, and the manner in which you red men treat your wives. I suppose it's accordin' to the gifts of your people that the women should work and the men hunt, but there's such a thing as moderation in all matters. As for huntin', I see no good reason why any limits need be set to *that*, but Hist comes of too good a stock to toil like a common drudge. One of your means and standin' need never want for corn, or potatoes, or anything that the fields yield; therefore, I hope the hoe will never be put into the hands of any wife of your'n.

You know I am not quite a beggar, and all I own, whether in ammunition, skins, arms, or calicoes, I give to Hist, should I not come back to claim them by the end of the season. This will set the maiden up and will buy labor for her for a long time to come. I suppose I needn't tell you to love the young woman, for that you do already, and whomsoever the man ra'ally loves he'll be likely enough to cherish. Nevertheless, it can do no harm to say that kind words never rankle, while bitter words do. I know you're a man, Sarpent, that is less apt to talk in his own lodge than to speak at the council fire, but forgetful moments may overtake us all, and the practyce of kind doin' and kind talkin' is a wonderful advantage in keepin' peace in a cabin, as well as on a hunt."

"My ears are open," returned the Delaware gravely; "the words of my brother have entered so far that they never can fall out again. They are like rings that have no end and cannot drop. Let him speak on; the song of the wren and the voice of a friend never tire."

"I will speak a little longer, Chief, but you will excuse it for the sake of old companionship, should I now talk about myself. If the worst comes to the worst, it's not likely there'll be much left of me but ashes, so a grave would be useless and a sort of vanity. On that score I'm no way partic'lar, though it might be well enough to take a look at the remains of the pile, and should any bones or pieces be found, 'twould be more decent to gather them together and bury them than to let them lie for the wolves to gnaw at and howl over. These matters can make no great difference in the ind, but men of white blood and Christian feelin's have rather a gift for graves."

"It shall be done as my brother says," returned the Indian gravely. "If his mind is full, let him empty it in the bosom of a friend."

"Thank you, Sarpent; my mind's easy enough; yes, it's tolerable easy. Idees will come uppermost that I'm not apt to think about in common, it's true, but by striving ag'in some and lettin' others come out, all will be right in the long run. There's one thing, howsever, Chief, that *does* seem to be *on*reasonable, and ag'in natur', though the missionaries say it's true; and bein' of my religion and color, I feel bound to believe them. They say an Injin may torment and tortur' the body to the heart's content, and scalp, and cut, and tear, and burn, and consume all his inventions and deviltries, until nothin' is left but ashes, and they shall be scattered to the four winds of heaven, yet, when the trumpet of God shall sound, all will come together ag'in, and the man will stand forth in his flesh the same creatur' as to looks, if not as to feelin's, that he was afore he was harmed!"

"The missionaries are good men; they mean well," returned the Delaware courteously; "they are not great medicines. They think all they say, Deerslayer; that is no reason why warriors and orators should be all ears. When Chingachgook shall see the father of Tamenund standing in his scalp, and paint, and warlock, then will he believe the missionaries."

"Seein' *is* believin', of a sartainty. Ah's me! And some of us may see these things sooner than we thought. I comprehend your meanin' about Tamenund's father, Sarpent, and the idee's a close idee. Tamenund is now an elderly man— say eighty, every day of it—and his father was scalped, and tormented, and burned when the present prophet was a youngster. Yes, if one could see *that* come to pass, there wouldn't be much difficulty in yieldin' faith to all that the missionaries say. Howsever, I'm not ag'in the opinion now, for you must know, Sarpent, that the great principle of Christianity is to believe *without* seeing, and a man should always act up to his religion and principles, let them be what they may."

"That is strange for a wise nation," said the Delaware, with emphasis. "The red man looks hard, that he may *see* and understand."

"Yes, that's plauserble and is agreeable to mortal pride, but it's not as deep as it seems. If we could understand *all* we see, Sarpent, there might be not only sense but safety in refusin' to give faith to any *one* thing that we might find oncomprehensible, but when there's so many things about which it may be said we know nothing at all, why, there's little use and no reason in bein' difficult touchin' anyone in partic'lar. For my part, Delaware, all my thoughts haven't been on the game, when outlyin' in the hunts and scoutin's of our youth. Many's the hour I've passed, pleasantly enough, too, in what is tarmed conterplation by my people. On such occasions the mind is actyve, though the body seems lazy and listless. An open spot on a mountainside, where a wide look can be had at the heavens and the 'arth, is a most judicious place for a man to get a just idee of the power of the Maritou, and of his own littleness. At such times there isn't any great disposition to find fault with little difficulties in the way of comprehension, as there are so many big ones to hide them. Believin' comes easy enough to me at such times, and if the Lord made man first out of 'arth, as they tell me it is written in the Bible, then turns him into dust at death, I see no great difficulty in the way to bringin' him back in the body, though ashes be the only substance left. These things lie beyond our understandin', though they may and do lie so close to our feelin's. But of all the doctrines, Sarpent, that which disturbs me, and disconsarts my mind the most, is the one which teaches us to think that a pale-face goes to one heaven and a redskin to another; it may separate in death them which lived much together and loved each other well in life!"

"Do the missionaries teach their white brethren to think it is so?" demanded the Indian, with serious earnestness. "The Delawares believe that good men and brave warriors will hunt together in the same pleasant woods, let them belong to whatever tribe they may; that all the unjust Indians, and cowards, will have to sneak in with the dogs and the wolves to get venison for their lodges."

" 'Tis wonderful how many consaits mankind have consarnin' happiness and misery hereafter!" exclaimed the hunter, borne away by the power of his own thoughts. "Some believe in burnin's and flames, and some think punishment is to eat with the wolves and dogs. Then, ag'in, some fancy heaven to be only the carryin' out of their own 'arthly longin's, while others fancy it all gold and shinin' lights! Well, I've an idee of my own, in that matter, which is just this, Sarpent. Whenever I've done wrong, I've gin'rally found 'twas owin' to some blindness of the mind, which hid the right from view, and when sight has returned, then has come sorrow and repentance. Now, I consait that, after death, when the body is laid aside, or, if used at all, is purified and without its longin's, the spirit sees all things in their ra'al light and never becomes blind to truth and justice. Such bein' the case, all that has been done in life is beheld as plainly as the sun is seen at noon; the good brings joy while the evil brings sorrow. There's nothin' onreasonable in that, but it's agreeable to every man's experience."

"I thought the palefaces believed *all* men were wicked; who then could ever find the white man's heaven?"

"That's ingen'ous, but it falls short of the missionary teachin's. You'll be Christianized one day, I make no doubt, and then 'twill all come plain enough. You must know, Sarpent, that there's been a great deed of salvation done that, by God's help, enables all men to find a pardon for their wickedness, and *that* is the essence of the white man's religion. I can't stop to talk this matter over with you any longer, for Hetty's in the canoe, and the furlough takes me away; but the time will come, I hope, when you'll *feel* these things; for, after all, they must be *felt* rather than reasoned about. Ah's me! Well, Delaware, there's my hand; you know it's that of a fri'nd, and will shake it as such, though it never has done you one half the good its owner wishes it had."

The Indian took the offered hand and returned its pressure warmly. Then falling back on his acquired stoicism of manner, which so many mistake for constitutional indifference, he drew up in reserve and prepared to part from his friend with dignity. Deerslayer, however, was more natural; nor would he have at all cared about giving way to his feelings, had not the recent conduct and language of Judith give him some secret, though ill-defined apprehensions of a scene. He was too humble to imagine the truth concerning the actual feelings of that beautiful girl, while he was too observant not to have noted the struggle she had maintained with herself, and which had so often led her to the very verge of discovery. That something extraordinary was concealed in her breast he thought obvious enough, and through a sentiment of manly delicacy that would have done credit to the highest human refinement, he shrank from any exposure of her secret that might subsequently cause regret to the girl herself. He therefore determined to depart now, and that without any further manifestations of feeling either from himself or from others.

"God bless you, Sarpent—God bless you!" cried the hunter as the canoe left the side of the platform. "Your Manitou and my God only know when and where we shall meet ag'in; I shall count it a great blessing, and a full reward for any little good I may have done on 'arth, if we shall be permitted to know each other and to consort together hereafter as we have so long done in these pleasant woods afore us!"

Chingachgook waved his hand. Drawing the light blanket he wore over his head, as a Roman would conceal his grief in his robes, he slowly withdrew into the ark, in order to indulge his sorrow and his musings alone. Deerslayer did not speak again until the canoe was halfway to the shore. Then he suddenly ceased paddling at an interruption that came from the mild, musical voice of Hetty.

"Why do *you* go back to the Hurons, Deerslayer?" demanded the girl. "They say *I* am feeble-minded, and such they never harm; but you have as much sense as Hurry Harry; and more too, Judith thinks, though I don't see how that can well be."

"Ah, Hetty, afore we land I must converse a little with you, child; and that, too, on matters touching your own welfare, principally. Stop paddling—or, rather, that the Mingos needn't think we are plotting and contriving, and so treat us accordingly, just dip your paddle lightly, and give the canoe a little motion and no more. That's just the idee and the movement; I see you're ready enough at an appearance, and might be made useful at a sarcumvention, if it was lawful now to use one—that's just the idee and the movement! Ah's me! Desait and a false tongue are evil things and altogether onbecoming our color, Hetty, but it *is* a pleasure and a satisfaction to outdo the contrivances of a redskin in the strife of lawful warfare. My path has been short, and is like soon to have an end, but I can see that the wanderings of a warrior arn't altogether among brambles and difficulties. There's a bright side to a warpath, as well as to most other things, if we'll only have the wisdom to see it and the ginerosity to own it."

"And why should your warpath, as you call it, come so near to an end, Deerslayer?"

"Because, my good girl, my furlough comes so near to an end. They're likely to have pretty much the same tarmination as regards time—one following on the heels of the other as a matter of course."

"I don't understand your meaning, Deerslayer," returned the girl, looking a little bewildered. "Mother always said people ought to speak more plainly to me than to most other persons because I'm feeble-minded. Those that are feeble-minded don't understand as easily as those that have sense."

"Well then, Hetty, the simple truth is this. You know that I'm now a captyve to the Hurons, and captyves can't do, in all things, as they please———"

"But how can you be a captive," eagerly interrupted the girl, "when you are out here on the lake, in Father's bark canoe, and the Indians are in the woods, with no canoe at all? *That* can't be true, Deerslayer!"

"I wish with all my heart and soul, Hetty, that you was right and that I was wrong, instead of your bein' all wrong and my bein' only too near the truth. Free as I seem to your eyes, gal, I'm bound hand and foot, in ra'ality."

"Well, it *is* a great misfortune not to have sense! Now, I can't see, or understand, that you are a captive, or bound in any manner. If you are bound, with what are your hands and feet fastened?"

"With a furlough, gal; that's a thong that binds tighter than any chain. One *may* be broken, but the other can't. Ropes and chains allow of knives, and desait, and contrivances, but a furlough can be neither cut, slipped, nor sarcumvented."

"What sort of a thing is a furlough, then, if it be stronger than hemp or iron? I never saw a furlough."

"I hope you may never feel one, gal; the tie is altogether in the feelin's in these matters, and therefore is to be felt and not seen. You can understand what it is to give a promise, I dare to say, good little Hetty?"

"Certainly. A promise is to say you will do a thing, and that binds you to be as good as your word. Mother always kept her promises to me, and then she said it would be wicked if I didn't keep my promises to her and to everybody else."

"You have had a good mother in some matters, child, whatever she may have been in other some. That is a promise, and as you say, it must be kept. Now, I fell into the hands of the Mingos last night, and they let me come off to see my fri'nds and send messages in to my own color, if any such feel consarn on my account, on condition that I shall be back when the sun is up today, and take whatever their revenge and hatred can contrive, in the way of torments, in satisfaction for the life of a warrior that fell by my rifle, as well as for that of the young woman shot by Hurry, and other disapp'intments met with on and about this lake. What is called a promise atween a mother and darter, or even atween strangers, in the settlements is called a furlough, when given by one soldier to another on a warpath. And now I suppose you understand my situation, Hetty?"

The girl made no answer for some time, but she ceased paddling altogether, as if the novel idea distracted her mind too much to admit of other employment. Then she resumed the dialogue earnestly and with solicitude.

"Do you think the Hurons will have the heart to do what you say, Deerslayer?" she asked. "I have found them kind and harmless."

"That's true enough as consarns one like you, Hetty, but it's a very different affair when it comes to an open inimy, and he too the owner of a pretty sartain rifle. I don't say that they bear me special malice on account of any expl'its already performed, for that would be bragging, as it might be, on the varge of the grave, but it's no vanity to believe that they know one of their bravest and cunnin'est chiefs fell by my hands. Such bein' the case, the tribe would reproach them if they failed to send the spirit of a paleface to keep the company of the spirit of their red brother—always supposin' that he can catch it. I look for no marcy, Hetty, at their hands, and my principal sorrow is that such a calamity should befall me on my first warpath: that it would come sooner or later, every soldier counts on and expects."

"The Hurons shall *not* harm you, Deerslayer," cried the girl, much excited. " 'Tis wicked as well as cruel; I have the Bible here to tell them so. Do you think I would stand by and see you tormented?"

"I hope not, my good Hetty, I hope not; and, therefore, when the moment comes, I expect you will move off and not be a witness of what you can't help, while it would grieve you. But I haven't stopped the paddles to talk of my own afflictions and difficulties, but to speak a little plainly to you, gal, consarnin' your own matters."

"What can you have to say to me, Deerslayer! Since Mother died, few talk to me of such things."

"So much the worse, poor gal; yes, 'tis so much the worse, for one of your state of mind needs frequent talking to in order to escape the snares and desaits of this wicked world.

You haven't forgotten Hurry Harry, gal, so soon, I calculate?"

"I!—I forget Henry March!" exclaimed Hetty, starting. "Why should I forget him, Deerslayer, when he is our friend, and only left us last night? Then, the large bright star that Mother loved so much to gaze at was just over the top of yonder tall pine on the mountain as Hurry got into the canoe, and when you landed him on the point near the east bay, it wasn't more than the length of Judith's handsomest ribbon above it."

"And how can you know how long I was gone, or how far I went to land Hurry, seein' you were not with us, and the distance was so great, to say nothing of the night?"

"Oh! I knew when it was well enough," returned Hetty positively. "There's more ways than one for counting time and distance. When the mind is engaged, it is better than any clock. Mine is feeble, I know, but it goes true enough in all that touches poor Hurry Harry. Judith will never marry March, Deerslayer."

"That's the p'int, Hetty; that's the very p'int I want to come to. I suppose you know that it's nat'ral for young people to have kind feelin's for one another, more especially when one happens to be a youth and t'other a maiden. Now one of your years and mind, gal, that has neither father nor mother, and who lives in a wilderness frequented by hunters and trappers, needs to be on her guard against evils she little dreams of."

"What harm can it be to think well of a fellow creature?" returned Hetty simply, though the conscious blood was stealing to her cheeks in spite of a spirit so pure that it scarce knew why it prompted the blush. "The Bible tells us to love them who despitefully use us, and why shouldn't we like them that do not?"

"Ah! Hetty, the love of the missionaries isn't the sort of likin' I mean. Answer me one thing, child: do you believe yourself to have mind enough to become a wife and a mother?"

"That's not a proper question to ask a young woman, Deerslayer, and I'll not answer it," returned the girl, in a reproving manner—much as a parent rebukes a child for an act of indiscretion. "If you have anything to say about Hurry, I'll hear *that*—but you must not speak evil of him; he is absent, and 'tis unkind to talk evil of the absent."

"Your mother has given you so many good lessons, Hetty, that my fears for you are not as great as they were. Nevertheless, a young woman without parents, in your state of mind, and who is not without beauty, must always be in danger in such a lawless region as this. I would say nothin' amiss of Hurry, who, in the main, is not a bad man for one of his callin', but you ought to know one thing, which it may not be altogether pleasant to tell you but which must be said. March has a desperate likin' for your sister Judith."

"Well, what of that? Everybody admires Judith, she's so handsome, and Hurry has told me again and again how much he wishes to marry her. But that will never come to pass, for Judith don't like Hurry. She likes another and talks about him in her sleep, though you need not ask me who he is, for all the gold in King George's crown, and all the jewels, too, wouldn't tempt me to tell you his name. If sisters can't keep each other's secrets, who can?"

"Sartainly; I do not wish you to tell me, Hetty, nor would it be any advantage to a dyin' man to know. What the tongue says when the mind's asleep, neither head nor heart is answerable for."

"I wish I knew why Judith talks so much about officers, and honest hearts, and false tongues, but I suppose she don't like to tell me, as I'm feeble-minded. Isn't it odd, Deerslayer, that Judith don't like Hurry—he, who is the bravest-looking youth that ever comes upon the lake and is as handsome as she is herself. Father always said they would be the comeliest couple in the country, though Mother didn't fancy March any more than Judith. There's no telling what will happen, they say, until things actually come to pass."

"Ah's me! Well, poor Hetty, 'tis of no great use to talk to them that can't understand you, and so I'll say no more about what I did wish to speak of, though it lay heavy on my mind. Put the paddle in motion ag'in, gal, and we'll push for the shore, for the sun is nearly up and my furlough is almost out."

The canoe now glided ahead, holding its way toward the point where Deerslayer well knew that his enemies expected him, and where he now began to be afraid he might not arrive in season to redeem his plighted faith. Hetty, perceiving his impatience, without very clearly comprehending its cause, however, seconded his efforts in a way that soon rendered their timely return no longer a matter of doubt. Then, and then only, did the young man suffer his exertions to flag, and Hetty began again to prattle in her simple, confiding manner, though nothing further was uttered that it may be thought necessary to relate.

CHAPTER XXVII

ONE EXPERIENCED IN the signs of the heavens would have seen that the sun wanted but two or three minutes of the zenith when Deerslayer landed on the point where the Hurons were now encamped, nearly abreast of the castle. This spot was similar to the one already described, with the exception that the surface of the land was less broken and less crowded with trees. Owing to these two circumstances, it was all the better suited to the purpose for which it had been selected, the space beneath the branches bearing some resemblance to a densely wooded lawn. Favored by its position and its spring, it had been much resorted to by savages and hunters, and the natural grasses had succeeded their fires, leaving an appearance of sward in places, a very unusual accompaniment of the virgin forest. Nor was the margin of water fringed with bushes, as on so much of its shore, but the eye penetrated the woods immediately on reaching the strand, commanding nearly the whole area of the projection.

If it was a point of honor with the Indian warrior to redeem his word, when pledged to return and meet his death at a given hour, so was it a point of characteristic pride to show no womanish impatience, but to reappear as nearly as possible at the appointed moment. It was well not to exceed the grace accorded by the generosity of the enemy, but it was better to meet it to a minute. Something of this dramatic effect mingles with most of the graver usages of the American aborigines, and, no doubt, like the prevalence of a similar feeling among people more sophisticated and refined, may be referred to a principle of nature. We all love the wonderful, and when it comes attended by chivalrous self-devotion and a rigid regard to honor, it presents itself to our admiration in a shape doubly attractive. As respects Deerslayer, though he took a pride in showing his white blood by often deviating from the usages of the red men, he frequently dropped into their customs, and oftener into their feelings, unconsciously to himself, in consequence of having no other arbiters to appeal to than their judgments and tastes. On the present occasion, he would have abstained from betraying a feverish haste by a too speedy return, since it would have contained a tacit admission that the time asked for was more than had been wanted; but, on the other hand, had the idea occurred to him, he would have quickened his movements a little, in order to avoid the dramatic appearance of returning at the precise instant set as the utmost limit of his absence. Still, accident had interfered to defeat the last intention, for when the young man put his foot on the point and advanced with a steady tread toward the group of chiefs that was seated in grave array on a fallen tree, the oldest of their number cast his eye upward at an opening in the trees and pointed out to his companions the startling fact that the sun was just entering a space that was known to mark the zenith. A common but low exclamation of surprise and admiration escaped every mouth, and the grim warriors looked at each other, some with envy and disappointment, some with astonishment, at the precise accuracy of their victim, and others with a more generous and liberal feeling. The American Indian always deemed his moral victories the noblest, prizing the groans and yielding of his victim under torture more than the trophy of his scalp—and the trophy itself more than his life. To slay, and not to bring off the proof of victory, indeed, was scarcely deemed honorable, even these rude and fierce tenants of the forest, like their more nurtured brethren of the court and the camp, having set up for themselves imaginary and arbitrary points of honor, to supplant the conclusions of the right and the decisions of reason.

The Hurons had been divided in their opinions concerning

the probability of their captive's return. Most among them, indeed, had not expected it possible for a paleface to come back voluntarily and meet the known penalties of an Indian torture, but a few of the seniors expected better things from one who had already shown himself so singularly cool, brave, and upright. The party had come to its decision, however, less in the expectation of finding the pledge redeemed than in the hope of disgracing the Delawares by casting into their teeth the delinquency of one bred in their villages. They would have greatly preferred that Chingachgook should be their prisoner and prove the traitor, but the paleface scion of the hated stock was no bad substitute for their purposes, failing in their designs against the ancient stem. With a view to render the triumph as signal as possible, in the event of the hour's passing without the reappearance of the hunter, all the warriors and scouts of the party had been called in, and the whole band, men, women, and children, was now assembled at this single point to be a witness of the expected scene. As the castle was in plain view, and by no means distant, it was easily watched by daylight, and it being thought that its inmates were now limited to Hurry, the Delaware, and the two girls, no apprehensions were felt of their being able to escape unseen. A large raft, having a breastwork of logs, had been prepared, and was in actual readiness to be used against either ark or castle, as occasion might require, so soon as the fate of Deerslayer was determined, the seniors of the party having come to the opinion that it was getting to be hazardous to delay their departure for Canada beyond the coming night. In short, the band waited merely to dispose of this single affair, ere it brought matters to a crisis and prepared to commence its retreat toward the distant waters of Ontario.

It was an imposing scene, into which Deerslayer now found himself advancing. All the older warriors were seated on the trunk of the fallen tree, waiting his approach with grave decorum. On the right stood the young men, armed, while the left was occupied by the women and children. In the center was an open space of considerable extent, always canopied by leaves, but from which the underbrush, dead wood, and other obstacles had been carefully removed. The more open area had probably been much used by former parties, for this was the place where the appearance of a sward was the most decided. The arches of the woods, even at high noon, cast their somber shadows on the spot, which the brilliant rays of the sun that struggled through the leaves contributed to mellow and, if such an expression can be used, to illuminate. It was probably from a similar scene that the mind of man first got its idea of the effects of Gothic tracery and churchly hues; this temple of nature producing some such effect, so far as light and shadows were concerned, as the well-known offspring of human invention.

As was not unusual among the tribes and wandering bands of the aborigines, two chiefs shared in nearly equal degrees the principal and primitive authority that was wielded over these children of the forest. There were several who might claim the distinction of being chief men, but the two in question were so much superior to all the rest in influence that, when they agreed, no one disputed their mandates, and when they were divided, the band hesitated, like men who had lost their governing principle of action. It was also in conformity with practice—perhaps we might add, in conformity with nature, that one of the chiefs was indebted to his mind for his influence, whereas the other owed his distinction altogether to qualities that were physical. One was a senior, well known for eloquence in debate, wisdom in council, and prudence in measures, while his great competitor, if not his rival, was a brave, distinguished in war, notorious for ferocity, and remarkable, in the way of intellect, for nothing but the cunning and expedients of the warpath. The first was Rivenoak, who has already been introduced to the reader, while the last was called le Panthère, in the language of the Canadas, or the Panther, to resort to the vernacular of the English colonies. The appellation of the fighting chief was supposed to indicate the qualities of the warrior, agreeably to a practice of the red man's nomenclature: ferocity, cunning, and treachery being, perhaps, the distinctive features of his character. The title had been received from the French, and was prized so much the more from that circumstance, the Indian submitting profoundly to the greater intelligence of his paleface allies, in most things of this nature. How well the sobriquet was merited will be seen in the sequel.

Rivenoak and the Panther sat side by side, awaiting the approach of their prisoner, as Deerslayer put his moccasined foot on the strand; nor did either move or utter a syllable until the young man had advanced into the center of the area, and proclaimed his presence with his voice. This was done firmly, though in the simple manner that marked the character of the individual.

"Here I am, Mingos," he said, in the dialect of the Delawares, a language that most present understood; "here I am, and there is the sun. One is not more true to the laws of natur' than the other has proved true to his word. I am your prisoner; do with me what you please. My business with man and 'arth is settled; nothing remains now but to meet the white man's God, accordin' to a white man's duties and gifts."

A murmur of approbation escaped even the women at this address, and for an instant there was a strong and pretty general desire to adopt into the tribe one who owned so brave a spirit. Still there were dissenters from this wish, among the principal of whom might be classed the Panther, and his sister, le Sumac, so called from the number of her children, who was the widow of le Loup Cervier, now known to have fallen by the hand of the captive. Native ferocity held one in subjection, while the corroding passion of revenge prevented the other from admitting any gentler feeling at the moment. Not so with Rivenoak. This chief arose, stretched his arm before him in a gesture of courtesy, and paid his compliments with an ease and dignity that a prince might have envied. As, in that band, his wisdom and eloquence were confessedly without rivals, he knew that on himself would properly fall the duty of first replying to the speech of the paleface.

"Paleface, you are honest," said the Huron orator. "My people are happy in having captured a man and not a skulking fox. We now know you; we shall treat you like a brave. If you have slain one of our warriors and helped to kill others, you have a life of your own ready to give away in return. Some of my young men thought that the blood of a paleface was too thin, that it would refuse to run under the Huron knife. You will show them it is not so; your heart is stout as well as your body. It is a pleasure to make such a prisoner; should my warriors say that the death of le Loup Cervier ought not to be forgotten, that he cannot travel toward the land of spirits alone, and that his enemy must be sent to overtake him, they will remember that he fell by the hand of a brave, and send you after him with such signs of our friendship as shall not make him ashamed to keep your company. I have spoken; you know what I have said."

"True enough, Mingo, all true as the gospel," returned the simple-minded hunter; "you *have* spoken, and I *do* know not only what you have *said*, but, what is still more important, what you *mean*. I dare to say your warrior, the Lynx, was a stouthearted brave, and worthy of your fri'ndship and respect, but I do not feel unworthy to keep his company, without any passport from your hands. Nevertheless, here I am, ready to receive judgment from your council, if, indeed, the matter was not determined among you afore I got back."

"My old men would not sit in council over a paleface until they saw him among them," answered Rivenoak, looking around him a little ironically; "they said it would be like sitting in council over the winds; they go where they will and come back as they see fit, and not otherwise. There was one voice that spoke in your favor, Deerslayer, but it was alone, like the song of the wren whose mate has been struck by the hawk."

"I thank that voice whosever it may have been, Mingo, and will say it was as true a voice, as the rest were lying voices. A furlough is as binding on a paleface, if he be honest, as it is on a redskin; and was it not so, I would never bring disgrace on the Delawares, among whom I may be said to have received my edication. But words are useless and lead to braggin' feelin's; here I am; act your will on me."

Rivenoak made a sign of acquiescence, and then a short conference was privately held among the chiefs. As soon as the latter ended, three or four young men fell back from among the armed group and disappeared. Then it was signified to the prisoner that he was at liberty to go at large on the point until a council was held concerning his fate. There was more of seeming than of real confidence, however, in this apparent liberality, inasmuch as the young men mentioned already formed a line of sentinels across the breadth of the point, inland, and escape from any other part was out of the question. Even the canoe was removed beyond this line of sentinels, to a spot where it was considered safe from any sudden attempt. These precautions did not proceed from a failure of confidence, but from the circumstance that the prisoner had now complied with all the required conditions of his parole, and it would have been considered a commendable and honorable exploit to escape from his foes. So nice, indeed, were the distinctions drawn by the savages, in cases of this nature, that they often gave their victims a chance to evade the torture, deeming it as creditable to the captors to overtake, or to outwit a fugitive, when his exertions were supposed to be quickened by the extreme jeopardy of his situation, as it was for him to get clear from so much extraordinary vigilance.

Nor was Deerslayer unconscious or forgetful of his rights and of his opportunities. Could he now have seen any probable opening for an escape, the attempt would not have been delayed a minute. But the case seemed desperate. He was aware of the line of sentinels, and felt the difficulty of breaking through it unharmed. The lake offered no advantages, as the canoe would have given his foes the greatest facilities for overtaking him; else would he have found it no difficult task to swim as far as the castle. As he walked about the point, he even examined the spot to ascertain if it offered no place of concealment, but its openness, its size, and the hundred watchful glances that were turned toward him, even while those who made them affected not to see him, prevented any such expedient from succeeding. The dread and disgrace of failure had no influence on Deerslayer, who deemed it ever a point of honor to reason and feel like a white man, rather than as an Indian, and who felt it a sort of duty to do all he could that did not involve a dereliction from principle in order to save his life. Still he hesitated about making the effort, for he also felt that he ought to see the chance of success before he committed himself.

In the meantime the business of the camp appeared to proceed in its regular train. The chiefs consulted apart, admitting no one but the Sumac to their councils; for she, the widow of the fallen warrior, had an exclusive right to be heard on such an occasion. The young men strolled about in indolent listlessness, awaiting the result with Indian impatience, while the females prepared the feast that was to celebrate the termination of the affair, whether it proved fortunate or otherwise for our hero. No one betrayed feeling, and an indifferent observer, beyond the extreme watchfulness of the sentinels, would have detected no extraordinary movement or sensation to denote the real state of things. Two or three old women put their heads together, and it appeared unfavorably to the prospect of Deerslayer, by their scowling looks and angry gestures, but a group of Indian girls were evidently animated by a different impulse, as was apparent by stolen glances that expressed pity and regret. In this condition of the camp an hour soon glided away.

Suspense is, perhaps, the feeling, of all others that is most difficult to be supported. When Deerslayer landed, he fully expected in the course of a few minutes to undergo the tortures of an Indian revenge, and he was prepared to meet his fate manfully, but the delay proved far more trying than the nearer approach of suffering, and the intended victim began seriously to meditate some desperate effort at escape, as it might be from sheer anxiety to terminate the scene, when he was suddenly summoned to appear, once more, in front of his judges, who had already arranged the band in its former order in readiness to receive him.

"Killer of the Deer," commenced Rivenoak, as soon as his captive stood before him, "my aged men have listened to wise words; they are ready to speak. You are a man whose fathers came from beyond the rising sun; we are children of the setting sun; we turn our faces toward the Great Sweet Lakes when we look toward our villages. It may be a wise country and full of riches toward the morning, but it is very pleasant toward the evening. We love most to look in that direction. When we gaze at the east we feel afraid, canoe after canoe bringing more and more of your people in the track of the sun, as if their land was so full as to run over. The red men are few already; they have need of help. One of our best lodges has lately been emptied by the death of its master; it will be a long time before his son can grow big enough to sit in his place. There is his widow! She will want venison to feed her and her children, for her sons are yet like the young of the robin before they quit the nest. By your hand has this great calamity befallen her. She has two duties; one to le Loup Cervier, and one to his children. Scalp for scalp, life for life, blood for blood, is one law; to feed her young another. We know you, Killer of the Deer. You are honest; when you say a thing, it is so. You have but one tongue, and that is not forked like a snake's. Your head is never hid in the grass; all can see it. What you say, that will you do. You are just. When you have done wrong, it is your wish to do right again as soon as you can. Here is the Sumac; she is alone in her wigwam, with children crying around her for food—yonder is a rifle; it is loaded and ready to be fired. Take the gun; go forth and shoot a deer; bring the venison and lay it before the widow of le Loup Cervier; feed her children; call yourself her husband. After which, your heart will no longer be Delaware but Huron; le Sumac's ears will not hear the cries of her children; my people will count the proper number of warriors.

"I feared this, Rivenoak," answered Deerslayer, when the other had ceased speaking; "yes, I did dread that it would come to this. Howsever, the truth is soon told, and that will put an end to all expectations on this head. Mingo, I'm white, and Christian-born; 'twould ill become me to take a wife, under redskin forms, from among heathen. That which I wouldn't do in peaceable times and under a bright sun, still less would I do behind clouds, in order to save my life. I may never marry; most likely Providence, in putting me up here in the woods, has intended I should live single, without a lodge of my own: but should such a thing come to pass, none but a woman of my own color and gifts shall darken the door of my wigwam. As for feeding the young of your dead warrior, I would do that cheerfully, could it be done without discredit, but it cannot, seeing that I can never live in a Huron village. Your own young men must find the Sumac in venison, and the next time she marries, let her take a husband whose legs are not long enough to overrun territory that don't belong to him. We fou't a fair battle, and he fell; in this there is nothin' but what a brave expects, and should be ready to meet. As for getting a Mingo heart, as well might you expect to see gray hairs on a boy, or the blackberry growing on the pine. No, no, Huron; my gifts are white, so far as wives are consarned; it is Delaware in all things touchin' Injins."

These words were scarcely out of the mouth of Deerslayer before a common murmur betrayed the dissatisfaction with which they had been heard. The aged women, in particular, were loud in their expressions of disgust, and the gentle Sumac herself, a woman quite old enough to be our hero's mother, was not the least pacific in her denunciations. But all the other manifestations of disappointment and discontent were thrown into the background by the fierce resentment of the Panther. This grim chief had thought it a degradation to permit his sister to become the wife of a paleface of the Yengeese at all, and had only given a reluctant consent to the arrangement—one by no means unusual among the Indians, however—at the earnest solicitations of the bereaved widow; and it goaded him to the quick to find his condescension slighted, the honor he had with so much regret been persuaded to accord condemned. The animal from which he got his name does not glare on his intended prey with more frightful ferocity than his eyes gleamed on the captive, nor was his arm backward in seconding the fierce resentment that almost consumed his breast.

"Dog of the palefaces!" he exclaimed in Iroquois, "go yell among the curs of your own evil hunting grounds!"

The denunciation was accompanied by an appropriate action. Even while speaking his arm was lifted and the tomahawk hurled. Luckily the loud tones of the speaker had drawn the eye of Deerslayer toward him, else would that moment have probably closed his career. So great was the dexterity with which this dangerous weapon was thrown, and so deadly the intent, that it would have riven the skull of the prisoner, had he not stretched forth an arm and caught the handle in one of its turns with a readiness quite as remarkable as the skill with which the missile had been hurled. The projectile force was so great, notwithstanding, that when Deerslayer's arm was arrested, his hand was raised above and behind his own head; and in the very attitude necessary to return the attack. It is not certain whether the circumstance of finding himself unexpectedly in this menacing posture and armed, tempted the young man to retaliate, or whether sudden resentment overcame his forbearance and prudence. His eye kindled, however, and a small red spot appeared on each cheek, while he cast all his energy into the effort of his arm and threw back the weapon at his assailant. The unexpectedness of this blow contributed to its success, the Panther neither raising an arm nor bending his head to avoid it. The keen little ax struck the victim in a perpendicular line with the nose, directly between the eyes, literally braining him on the spot. Sallying forward, as the serpent darts at its enemy even while receiving its own death wound, this man of powerful frame fell his length into the open area formed by the circle, quivering in death. A common rush to his relief left the captive for a single instant quite without the crowd, and willing to make one desperate effort for life, he bounded off with the activity of a deer. There was but a breathless instant, then the whole band, old and young, women and children, abandoning the lifeless body of the Panther where it lay, raised the yell of alarm and followed in pursuit.

Sudden as had been the event which induced Deerslayer to make this desperate trial of speed, his mind was not wholly unprepared for the fearful emergency. In the course of the past hour, he had pondered well on the chances of such an experiment and had shrewdly calculated all the details of success and failure. At the first leap, therefore, his body was completely under the direction of an intelligence that turned all its efforts to the best account and prevented everything like hesitation or indecision at the important instant of the start. To this alone was he indebted for the first great advantage, that of getting through the line of sentinels unharmed. The manner in which this was done, though sufficiently simple, merits a description.

Although the shores of the point were not fringed with bushes, as was the case with most of the others on the lake, it was owing altogether to the circumstance that the spot had been so much used by hunters and fishermen. This fringe commenced on what might be termed the mainland, and was as dense as usual, extending in long lines both north and south. In the latter direction, then, Deerslayer held his way, and as the sentinels were a little without the commencement of this thicket before the alarm was clearly communicated to them, the fugitive had gained its cover. To run among the bushes, however, was out of the question, and Deerslayer held his way for some forty or fifty yards in the water, which was barely knee deep, offering as great an obstacle to the speed of his pursuers as it did to his own. As soon as a favorable spot presented, he darted through the line of bushes and issued into the open woods.

Several rifles were discharged at Deerslayer while in the water, and more followed as he came out into the comparative exposure of the clear forest. But the direction of his line of flight, which partially crossed that of the fire, the haste with which the weapons had been aimed, and the general confusion that prevailed in the camp prevented any harm from being done. Bullets whistled past him, and many cut twigs from the branches at his side, but not one touched even his dress. The delay caused by these fruitless attempts was of great service to the fugitive, who had gained more than a hundred yards on even the leading men of the Hurons, ere something like concert and order had entered into the chase. To think of following with rifle in hand was out of the question, and after emptying their pieces in vague hopes of wounding their captive, the best runners of the Indians threw them aside, calling out to the women and boys to recover and load them again, as soon as possible.

Deerslayer knew too well the desperate nature of the struggle in which he was engaged to lose one of the precious moments. He also knew that his only hope was to run in a straight line, for as soon as he began to turn, or double, the greater number of his pursuers would put escape out of the question. He held his way, therefore, in a diagonal direction up the acclivity, which was neither very high nor very steep, in this part of the mountain, but which was sufficiently toilsome for one contending for life to render it painfully oppressive. There, however, he slackened his speed to recover breath, proceeding even at a quick walk, or a slow trot, along the more difficult parts of the way. The Hurons were whooping and leaping behind him; but this he disregarded, well knowing they must overcome the difficulties he had surmounted, ere they could reach the elevation to which he had attained. The summit of the first hill was now quite near him, and he saw, by the formation of the land, that a deep glen intervened before the base of a second hill could be reached. Walking deliberately to the summit, he glanced eagerly about him in every direction in quest of a cover. None offered in the ground, but a fallen tree lay near him, and desperate circumstances required desperate remedies. This tree lay in a line parallel to the glen, at the brow of the hill; to leap on it, and then to force his person as close as possible under its lower side, took but a moment. Previously to disappearing from his pursuers, however, Deerslayer stood on the height and gave a cry of triumph, as if exulting at the sight of the descent that lay before him. In the next instant he was stretched beneath the tree.

No sooner was this expedient adopted than the young man ascertained how desperate had been his own efforts by the violence of the pulsations in his frame. He could hear his heart beat, and his breathing was like the action of a bellows in quick motion. Breath was gained, however, and the heart soon ceased to throb as if about to break through its confinement. The footsteps of those who toiled up the opposite side of the acclivity were now audible, and presently voices and treads announced the arrival of the pursuers. The foremost shouted as they reached the height; then, fearful that their enemy would escape under favor of the descent, each leaped upon the fallen tree and plunged into the ravine, trusting to get a sight of the pursued, ere he reached the bottom. In this manner, Huron followed Huron, until Natty began to hope the whole had passed. Others succeeded, however, until quite forty had leaped over the tree; and then he counted them, as the surest mode of ascertaining how many could be behind. Presently all were in the bottom of the glen, quite a hundred feet below him, and some had even ascended part of the opposite hill, when it became evident an inquiry was making as to the direction he had taken. This was the critical moment, and one of nerves less steady, or of a training that had been neglected, would have seized it to rise and fly. Not so with Deerslayer. He still lay quiet, watching with jealous vigilance every movement below and fast regaining his breath.

The Hurons now resembled a pack of hounds at fault. Little was said, but each man ran about examining the dead leaves, as the hound hunts for the lost scent. The great number of moccasins that had passed made the examination difficult, though the intoe of an Indian was easily to be distinguished from the freer and wider step of a white man. Believing that no more pursuers remained behind, and hoping to steal away unseen, Deerslayer suddenly threw himself over the tree and fell on the upper side. This achievement appeared to be effected successfully, and hope beat high in the bosom of the fugitive. Rising to his hands and feet after a moment lost in listening to the sounds in the glen, in order to ascertain if he had been seen, the young man next scrambled to the top of the hill, a distance of only ten yards, in the expectation of getting its brow between him and his pursuers, and himself so far under cover. Even this was effected, and he rose to his feet, walking swiftly but steadily along the summit in a direction opposite to that in which he had first fled. The nature of the calls in the glen, however, soon made him uneasy, and he sprang upon the summit, again, in order to reconnoiter. No sooner did he reach the height than he was seen, and the chase renewed. As it was better footing on the level ground, Deerslayer now avoided the side hill, holding his flight along the ridge, while the Hurons, judging from the general formation of the land, saw that the ridge would soon melt into the hollow, and kept to the latter, as the easiest mode of heading the fugitive. A few, at the same time, turned south, with a view to prevent his escaping in that direction, while some crossed his trail toward the water, in order to prevent his retreat by the lake, running southerly.

The situation of Deerslayer was now more critical than it ever had been. He was virtually surrounded on three sides, having the lake on the fourth. But he had pondered well on all the chances and took his measures with coolness, even while at the top of his speed. As is generally the case with the vigorous bordermen, he could outrun any single Indian among his pursuers, who were principally formidable to him on account of their numbers and the advantages they possessed in position, and he would not have hesitated to break off in a straight line at any spot, could he have got the whole band again fairly behind him. But no such chance did, or indeed could now offer, and when he found that he was descending toward the glen, by the melting away of the ridge, he turned short, at right angles to his previous course, and went down the declivity with tremendous velocity, holding his way toward the shore. Some of his pursuers came panting up the hill, in direct chase, while most still kept on, in the ravine, intending to head him at its termination.

Deerslayer had now a different, though a desperate project in view. Abandoning all thoughts of escape by the woods, he made the best of his way toward the canoe. He knew where it lay: could it be reached, he had only to run the gauntlet of a few rifles, and success would be certain. None of the warriors had kept their weapons, which would have retarded their speed, and the risk would come either from the uncer-

tain hands of the women, or from those of some well-grown
boy—though most of the latter were already out in hot pursuit. Everything seemed propitious to the execution of this
plan, and the course being a continued descent, the young
man went over the ground at a rate that promised a speedy
termination to his toil.

As Deerslayer approached the point, several women and
children were passed, but though the former endeavored to
cast dried branches between his legs, the terror inspired by
his bold retaliation on the redoubted Panther was so great
that none dared come near enough seriously to molest him.
He went by all triumphantly and reached the fringe of
bushes. Plunging through these, our hero found himself once
more in the lake and within fifty feet of the canoe. Here he
ceased to run, for he well understood that his breath was now
all-important to him. He even stooped, as he advanced, and
cooled his parched mouth by scooping up water in his hand
to drink. Still the moments pressed, and he soon stood at
the side of the canoe. The first glance told him that the paddles had been removed! This was a sore disappointment after
all his efforts, and for a single moment he thought of turning and of facing his foes by walking with dignity into the
center of the camp again. But an infernal yell, such as the
American savage alone can raise, proclaimed the quick approach of the nearest of his pursuers, and the instinct of life
triumphed. Preparing himself duly, and giving a right direction to its bows, he ran off into the water bearing the canoe
before him, threw all his strength and skill into a last effort,
and cast himself forward so as to fall into the bottom of the
light craft, without materially impeding its way. Here he remained on his back, both to regain his breath and to cover
his person from the deadly rifle. The lightness, which was
such an advantage in paddling the canoe, now operated unfavorably. The material was so like a feather that the
boat had no momentum; else would the impulse in that
smooth and placid sheet have impelled it to a distance from
the shore that would have rendered paddling with the hands
safe. Could such a point once be reached, Deerslayer thought
he might get far enough out to attract the attention of
Chingachgook and Judith, who would not fail to come to his
relief with other canoes, a circumstance that promised everything. As the young man lay in the bottom of the canoe,

he watched its movements by studying the tops of the trees on the mountainside, and judged of his distance by the time and the motion. Voices on the shore were now numerous, and he heard something said about manning the raft, which fortunately for the fugitive lay at a considerable distance on the other side of the point.

Perhaps the situation of Deerslayer had not been more critical that day than it was at this moment. It certainly had not been one half as tantalizing. He lay perfectly quiet for two or three minutes, trusting to the single sense of hearing, confident that the noise in the lake would reach his ears, did anyone venture to approach by swimming. Once or twice he fancied that the element was stirred by the cautious movement of an arm, and then he perceived it was the wash of the water on the pebbles of the strand; for, in mimicry of the ocean, it is seldom that those little lakes are so totally tranquil as not to possess a slight heaving and setting on their shores. Suddenly all the voices ceased, and a deathlike stillness pervaded the spot, a quietness as profound as if all lay in the repose of inanimate life. By this time the canoe had drifted so far as to render nothing visible to Deerslayer, as he lay on his back, except the blue void of space, and a few of those brighter rays that proceed from the effulgence of the sun, marking his proximity. It was not possible to endure this uncertainty long. The young man well knew that the profound stillness foreboded evil, the savages never being so silent as when about to strike a blow, resembling the stealthy foot of the panther ere he takes his leap. He took out a knife, and was about to cut a hole through the bark in order to get a view of the shore, when he paused from a dread of being seen in the operation, which would direct the enemy where to aim their bullets. At this instant a rifle *was* fired, and the ball pierced both sides of the canoe, within eighteen inches of the spot where his head lay. This was close work, but our hero had too lately gone through that which was closer to be appalled. He lay still half a minute longer, and then he saw the summit of an oak coming slowly within his narrow horizon.

Unable to account for this change, Deerslayer could restrain his impatience no longer. Hitching his body along with the utmost caution, he got his eye at the bullethole, and fortunately commanded a very tolerable view of the point.

The canoe, by one of those imperceptible impulses that so often decide the fate of men as well as the course of things, had inclined southerly, and was slowly drifting down the lake. It was lucky that Deerslayer had given it a shove sufficiently vigorous to send it past the end of the point ere it took this inclination, or it must have gone ashore again. As it was, it drifted so near it as to bring the tops of two or three trees within the range of the young man's view, as has been mentioned, and, indeed, to come in quite as close proximity with the extremity of the point as was at all safe. The distance could not much have exceeded a hundred feet, though fortunately a light current of air from the southwest began to set it slowly offshore.

Deerslayer now felt the urgent necessity of resorting to some expedient to get further from his foes and, if possible, to apprise his friends of his situation. The distance rendered the last difficult, while the proximity to the point rendered the first indispensable. As was usual in such craft, a large, round, smooth stone was in each end of the canoe for the double purpose of seats and ballast; one of these was within reach of his feet. The stone he contrived to get so far between his legs as to reach it with his hands, and then he managed to roll it to the side of its fellow in the bows, where the two served to keep the trim of the light boat, while he worked his own body as far aft as possible. Before quitting the shore, and as soon as he perceived that the paddles were gone, Deerslayer had thrown a bit of dead branch into the canoe, and this was within reach of his arm. Removing the cap he wore, he put it on the end of this stick, and just let it appear over the edge of the canoe, as far as possible from his own person. This ruse was scarcely adopted before the young man had a proof how much he had underrated the intelligence of his enemies. In contempt of an artifice so shallow and commonplace, a bullet was fired directly through another part of the canoe, which actually raised his skin. He dropped the cap, and instantly raised it immediately over his head, as a safeguard. It would seem that this second artifice was unseen, or what was more probable, the Hurons, feeling certain of recovering their captive, wished to take him alive.

Deerslayer lay passive a few minutes longer, his eye at the bullethole, however, and much did he rejoice at seeing that he was drifting gradually further and further from the shore. When he looked upward, the treetops had disappeared, but he soon found that the canoe was slowly turning, so as to prevent his getting a view of anything at his peephole but of the two extremities of the lake. He now bethought him of the stick, which was crooked, and offered some facilities for rowing, without the necessity of rising. The experiment succeeded, on trial, better even than he had hoped, though his great embarrassment was to keep the canoe straight. That his present maneuver was seen soon became apparent by the clamor on the shore, and a bullet entering the stern of the canoe, traversed its length, whistling between the arms of our hero, and passed out at the head. This satisfied the fugitive that he was getting away with tolerable speed and induced him to increase his efforts. He was making a stronger push than common when another messenger from the point broke the stick outboard and at once deprived him of his oar. As the sound of voices seemed to grow more and more distant, however, Deerslayer determined to leave all to the drift, until he believed himself beyond the reach of bullets. This was nervous work, but it was the wisest of all the expedients that offered; and the young man was encouraged to persevere in it by the circumstance that he felt his face fanned by the air, a proof that there was a little more wind.

CHAPTER XXVIII

Nor widows' tears, nor tender orphans' cries
Can stop th' invaders' force;
Nor swelling seas, nor threatening skies,
Prevent the pirate's course:
Their lives to selfish ends decreed,
Through blood and rapine they proceed;
No anxious thoughts of ill-repute,
Suspend the impetuous and unjust pursuit;
But power and wealth obtained, guilty and great,
Their fellow-creatures' fears they raise, or urge their hate.

CONGREVE

BY THIS TIME Deerslayer had been twenty minutes in the canoe, and he began to grow a little impatient for some signs of relief from his friends. The position of the boat still prevented his seeing in any direction, unless it were up or down the lake; and, though he knew that his line of sight must pass within a hundred yards of the castle, it, in fact, passed that distance to the westward of the buildings. The profound stillness troubled him also, for he knew not whether to ascribe it to the increasing space between him and the Indians, or to some new artifice. At length, wearied with fruitless watchfulness, the young man turned himself on his back, closed his eyes, and awaited the result in determined acquiescence. If the savages could so completely control their thirst for revenge, he was resolved to be as calm as themselves and to trust his fate to the interposition of the currents and air.

Some additional ten minutes may have passed in this quiescent manner, on both sides, when Deerslayer thought he heard a slight noise, like a low rubbing against the bottom of his canoe. He opened his eyes of course, in expectation of seeing the face or arm of an Indian rising from the water, and found that a canopy of leaves was impending directly

468

over his head. Starting to his feet, the first object that met his eye was Rivenoak, who had so far aided the slow progress of the boat as to draw it on the point, the grating on the strand being the sound that had first given our hero the alarm. The change in the drift of the canoe had been altogether owing to the baffling nature of the light currents of air, aided by some eddies in the water.

"Come," said the Huron, with a quiet gesture of authority to order his prisoner to land; "my young friend has sailed about till he is tired; he will forget how to run again, unless he uses his legs."

"You've the best of it, Huron," returned Deerslayer, stepping steadily from the canoe and passively following his leader to the open area of the point; "Providence has helped you in an onexpected manner. I'm your prisoner ag'in, and I hope you'll allow that I'm as good at breaking jail as I am at keeping furloughs."

"My young friend is a moose!" exclaimed the Huron. "His legs are very long; they have given my young men trouble. But he is not a fish; he cannot find his way in the lake. We did not shoot him; fish are taken in nets, and not killed by bullets. When he turns moose again, he will be treated like a moose."

"Aye, have your talk, Rivenoak; make the most of your advantage. 'Tis your right, I suppose, and I know it is your gift. On that p'int there'll be no words atweeen us, for all men must and ought to follow their gifts. Howsever, when your women begin to ta'nt and abuse me, as I suppose will soon happen, let 'em remember that if a paleface struggles for life so long as it's lawful and manful, he knows how to loosen his hold on it decently, when he feels that the time has come. I'm your captyve; work your will on me."

"My brother has had a long run on the hills and a pleasant sail on the water," returned Rivenoak more mildly, smiling, at the same time, in a way that his listener knew denoted pacific intentions. "He has seen the woods; he has seen the water; which does he like best? Perhaps he has seen enough to change his mind and make him hear reason."

"Speak out, Huron. Something is in your thoughts, and the sooner it is said, the sooner you'll get my answer."

"That is straight! There is no turning in the talk of my paleface friend, though he is a fox in running. I will speak to him; his ears are now open wider than before, and his eyes are not shut. The Sumac is poorer than ever. Once she had a brother and a husband. She had children, too. The time came, and the husband started for the happy hunting grounds without saying farewell; he left her alone with his children. This he could not help, or he would not have done it; le Loup Cervier was a good husband. It was pleasant to see the venison, and wild ducks, and geese, and bear's meat that hung in his lodge in winter. It is now gone; it will not keep in warm weather. Who shall bring it back again? Some thought the brother would not forget his sister, and that, next winter, he would see that the lodge should not be empty. We thought this; but the Panther yelled and followed the husband on the path of death. They are now trying which shall first reach the happy hunting grounds. Some think the Lynx can run fastest, and some think the Panther can jump the furthest. The Sumac thinks both will travel so fast and so far that neither will ever come back. Who shall feed her and her young? The man who told her husband and her brother to quit her lodge, that there might be room for him to come into it. He is a great hunter, and we know that the woman will never want."

"Aye, Huron, this is soon settled, accordin' to your notions, but it goes sorely ag'in the grain of a white man's feelin's. I've heard of men's saving their lives thisaway, and I've know'd them that would prefer death to such a sort of captivity. For my part, I do not seek my end, nor do I seek matrimony."

"The paleface will think of this while my people get ready for the council. He will be told what will happen. Let him remember how hard it is to lose a husband and a brother. Go: when we want him, the name of Deerslayer will be called."

This conversation had been held with no one near but the speakers. Of all the band that had so lately thronged the place, Rivenoak alone was visible. The rest seemed to have totally abandoned the spot. Even the furniture, clothes, arms, and other property of the camp had entirely disappeared, and the place bore no other proofs of the crowd that had so lately occupied it than the traces of their fires and resting places and the trodden earth that still showed the marks of their feet. So sudden and unexpected a change caused

Deerslayer a good deal of surprise and some uneasiness, for he had never known it to occur, in the course of his experience among the Delawares. He suspected, however, and rightly, that a change of encampment was intended, and that the mystery of the movement was resorted to in order to work on his apprehensions.

Rivenoak walked up the vista of trees, as soon as he ceased speaking, leaving Deerslayer by himself. The chief disappeared behind the covers of the forest, and one unpracticed in such scenes might have believed the prisoner left to the dictates of his own judgment. But the young man, while he felt a little amazement at the dramatic aspect of things, knew his enemies too well to fancy himself at liberty, or a free agent. Still, he was ignorant how far the Hurons meant to carry their artifices, and he determined to bring the question as soon as practicable to the proof. Affecting an indifference he was far from feeling, he strolled about the area, gradually getting nearer and nearer to the spot where he had landed, when he suddenly quickened his pace, though carefully avoiding all appearance of flight, and, pushing aside the bushes, he stepped upon the beach. The canoe was gone, nor could he see any traces of it after walking to the northern and southern verges of the point and examining the shores in both directions. It was evidently removed beyond his reach and knowledge, and under circumstances to show that such had been the intention of the savages.

Deerslayer now better understood his actual situation. He was a prisoner on the narrow tongue of land, vigilantly watched beyond a question, and with no other means of escape than that of swimming. He again thought of this last expedient, but the certainty that the canoe would be sent in chase, and the desperate nature of the chances of success, deterred him from the undertaking. While on the strand, he came to a spot where the bushes had been cut and thrown into a small pile. Removing a few of the upper branches, he found beneath them the dead body of the Panther. He knew that it was kept until the savages might find a place to inter it, when it would be beyond the reach of the scalping knife. He gazed wistfully toward the castle, but there all seemed to be silent and desolate, and a feeling of loneliness and desertion came over him to increase the gloom of the moment.

"God's will be done!" murmured the young man, as he walked sorrowfully away from the beach, entering again beneath the arches of the wood; "God's will be done, on 'arth as it is in heaven! I did hope that my days would not be numbered so soon! But it matters little, a'ter all. A few more winters, and a few more summers, and 'twould have been over, accordin' to natur'. Ah's me! The young and actyve seldom think death possible, till he grins in their faces and tells 'em the hour is come!"

While this soliloquy was being pronounced, the hunter advanced into the area, where, to his surprise, he saw Hetty alone, evidently awaiting his return. The girl carried the Bible under her arm, and her face, over which a shadow of gentle melancholy was usually thrown, now seemed sad and downcast. Moving nearer, Deerslayer spoke.

"Poor Hetty," he said; "times have been so troublesome of late that I'd altogether forgotten you; we meet, as it might be, to mourn over what is to happen. I wonder what has become of Chingachgook and Wah?"

"Why did you kill the Huron, Deerslayer?" returned the girl reproachfully. "Don't you know your commandments, which say, 'Thou shalt not kill!' They tell me you have now slain the woman's husband and brother."

"It's true, my good Hetty, 'tis gospel truth, and I'll not deny what has come to pass. But, you must remember, gal, that many things are lawful in war which would be onlawful in peace. The husband was shot in open fight— or open so far as I was consarned, while he had a better cover than common—and the brother brought his end on himself by casting his tomahawk at an unarmed prisoner. Did you witness that deed, gal?"

"I saw it and was sorry it happened, Deerslayer, for I hoped you wouldn't have returned blow for blow, but good for evil."

"Ah, Hetty, that may do among the missionaries, but 'twould make an onsartain life in the woods. The Panther craved my blood, and he was foolish enough to throw arms into my hands at the very moment he was striving a'ter it. 'Twould have been ag'in natur' not to raise a hand in such a trial, and 'twould have done discredit to my training and gifts. No, no; I'm as willing to give every man his own as another, and so I hope you'll testify to them that will be likely to question you as to what you've seen this day."

"Deerslayer, do you mean to marry Sumac, now she has neither husband nor brother to feed her?"

"Are such your ideas of matrimony, Hetty? Ought the young to wive with the old—the paleface with the redskin—the Christian with the heathen? It's ag'in reason and natur', and so you'll see, if you think of it a moment."

"I've always heard Mother say," returned Hetty, averting her face, more from a feminine instinct than from any consciousness of wrong, "that people should never marry until they loved each other better than brothers and sisters—and I suppose that is what you mean. Sumac *is* old and you *are* young."

"Aye, and she's red and I'm white. Besides, Hetty, suppose you was a wife, now, having married some young man of your own years, and state, and color—Hurry Harry, for instance"—Deerslayer selected this example simply from the circumstance that he was the only young man known to both—"and that he had fallen on a warpath, would you wish to take to your bosom for a husband the man that slew him?"

"Oh! no, no, no," returned the girl, shuddering. "*That* would be wicked as well as heartless! No Christian girl could or would do that. I never shall be the wife of Hurry, I know, but were he my husband, no man should ever be it again after his death."

"I thought it would get to this, Hetty, when you come to understand sarcumstances. 'Tis a moral impossibility that I should ever marry Sumac, and though Injin weddin's have no priests and not much religion, a white man who knows his gifts and duties can't profit by that and so make his escape at the fitting time. I do think death would be more nat'ral like, and welcome, than wedlock with this woman."

"Don't say it too loud," interrupted Hetty impatiently. "I suppose she will not like to hear it. I'm sure Hurry would rather marry even me than suffer torments, though I *am* feeble-minded, and I am sure it would kill me to think he'd prefer death to being my husband."

"Aye, gal; you an't Sumac, but a comely young Christian

with a good heart, pleasant smile, and kind eye. Hurry might be proud to get you, and that, too, not in misery and sorrow, but in his best and happiest days. Howsever, take my advice and never talk to Hurry about these things; he's only a borderer, at the best."

"I wouldn't tell him for the world!" exclaimed the girl, looking about her like one affrighted and blushing she knew not why. "Mother always said young women shouldn't be forward and speak their minds before they're asked; oh, I never forget what mother told me. 'Tis a pity Hurry is so handsome, Deerslayer; I do think fewer girls would like him then, and he would sooner know his own mind."

"Poor gal, poor gal, it's plain enough how it is; but the Lord will bear in mind one of your simple heart and kind feelin's! We'll talk no more of these things; if you had reason, you'd be sorrowful at having let others so much into your secret. Tell me, Hetty, what has become of all the Hurons, and why they let you roam about the p'int, as if you, too, was a prisoner?"

"I'm no prisoner, Deerslayer, but a free girl, and go when and where I please. Nobody dare hurt *me!* If they did, God would be angry—as I can show them in the Bible. No—no—Hetty Hutter is not afraid; *she's* in good hands. The Hurons are up yonder in the woods and keep a good watch on us both, I'll answer for it, since all the women and children are on the lookout. Some are burying the body of the poor girl who was shot, so that the enemy and the wild beasts can't find it. I told 'em that Father and Mother lay in the lake, but I wouldn't let them know in what part of it, for Judith and I don't want any of their heathenish company in our burying ground."

"Ah's me! Well, it *is* an awful dispatch to be standing here, alive and angry, and with the feelin's up and furious, one hour, and then to be carried away at the next and put out of sight of mankind in a hole in the 'arth. No one knows what will happen to him on a warpath, that's sartain."

Here the stirring of leaves and the cracking of dried twigs interrupted the discourse and apprised Deerslayer of the approach of his enemies. The Hurons closed around the spot that had been prepared for the coming scene, and in the center of which the intended victim now stood, in a circle —the armed men being so distributed among the feebler

members of the band that there was no safe opening
through which the prisoner could break. But the latter no
longer contemplated flight, the recent trial having satisfied
him of his inability to escape when pursued so closely by
numbers. On the contrary, all his energies were aroused in
order to meet his expected fate with a calmness that
should do credit to his color and his manhood, one equally
removed from recreant alarm and savage boasting.

When Rivenoak reappeared in the circle, he occupied his
old place at the head of the area. Several of the elder warriors stood near him, but now that the brother of Sumac
had fallen, there was no longer any recognized chief present whose influence and authority offered a dangerous rivalry
to his own. Nevertheless, it is well known that little which
could be called monarchical or despotic entered into the
politics of the North American tribes, although the first
colonists, bringing with them to this hemisphere the notions
and opinions of their own countries, often dignified the
chief men of those primitive nations with the titles of kings
and princes. Hereditary influence did certainly exist, but
there is much reason to believe it existed rather as a consequence of hereditary merit and acquired qualifications than
as a birthright. Rivenoak, however, had not even this claim
—having risen to consideration purely by the force of
talents, sagacity, and, as Bacon expresses it in relation to all
distinguished statesmen, "by a union of great and mean
qualities," a truth of which the career of the profound Eng-
lishman himself furnishes so apt an illustration.

Next to arms, eloquence offers the great avenue to popu-
lar favor, whether it be in civilized or savage life, and
Rivenoak had succeeded, as so many have succeeded before
him, quite as much by rendering fallacies acceptable to his
listeners as by any profound or learned expositions of truth,
or the accuracy of his logic. Nevertheless, he had influence,
and was far from being altogether without just claims to its
possession. Like most men who reason more than they feel,
the Huron was not addicted to the indulgence of the mere
ferocious passions of his people: he had been commonly
found on the side of mercy in all the scenes of vindictive
torture and revenge that had occurred in his tribe since his
own attainment to power. On the present occasion, he was
reluctant to proceed to extremities, although the provocation

was so great; still, it exceeded his ingenuity to see how that alternative could well be avoided. Sumac resented her rejection more than she did the deaths of her husband and brother, and there was little probability that the woman would pardon a man who had so unequivocally preferred death to her embraces. Without her forgiveness, there was scarce a hope that the tribe could be induced to overlook its loss, and even to Rivenoak himself, much as he was disposed to pardon, the fate of our hero now appeared to be almost hopelessly sealed.

When the whole band was arrayed around the captive, a grave silence, so much the more threatening from its profound quiet, pervaded the place. Deerslayer perceived that the women and boys had been preparing splinters of the fat pine roots, which he well knew were to be stuck into his flesh and set in flames, while two or three of the young men held the thongs of bark with which he was to be bound. The smoke of a distant fire announced that the burning brands were in preparation, and several of the elder warriors passed their fingers over the edges of their tomahawks, as if to prove their keenness and temper. Even the knives seemed loosened in their sheaths, impatient for the bloody and merciless work to begin.

"Killer of the Deer," recommended Rivenoak, certainly without any signs of sympathy or pity in his manner, though with calmness and dignity; "Killer of the Deer, it is time that my people knew their minds. The sun is no longer over our heads; tired of waiting on the Hurons, he has begun to fall near the pines on this side of the valley. He is traveling fast toward the country of our French fathers; it is to warn his children that their lodges are empty, and that they ought to be at home. The roaming wolf has his den, and he goes to it when he wishes to see his young. The Iroquois are not poorer than the wolves. They have villages, and wigwams, and fields of corn; the good spirits will be tired of watching them alone. My people must go back and see to their own business. There will be joy in the lodges when they hear our whoop from the forest! It will be a sorrowful whoop; when it is understood, grief will come after it. There will be one scalp whoop, but there will be only one. We have the fur of the Muskrat; his body is among the fishes. Deerslayer must say whether another scalp shall be on our pole. Two lodges are empty; a scalp, living or dead, is wanted at each door."

"Then take 'em dead, Huron," firmly, but altogether without dramatic boasting, returned the captive. "My hour is come, I do suppose; and what must be, must. If you are bent on the tortur', I'll do my indivors to bear up ag'in it, though no man can say how far his natur' will stand pain, until he's been tried."

"The paleface cur begins to put his tail between his legs!" cried a young and garrulous savage, who bore the appropriate title of the Corbeau Rouge; a sobriquet he had gained from the French, by his facility in making unseasonable noises, and an undue tendency to hear his own voice; "he is no warrior; he has killed the Loup Cervier when looking behind him not to see the flash of his own rifle. He grunts like a hog, already; when the Huron women begin to torment him, he will cry like the young of the catamount. He is a Delaware woman, dressed in the skin of a Yengeese!"

"Have your say, young man; have your say," returned Deerslayer, unmoved; "you know no better, and I can overlook it. Talking may aggravate women, but can hardly make knives sharper, fire hotter, or rifles more sartain."

Rivenoak now interfered, reproving the Red Crow for his premature interference and then directing the proper persons to bind the captive. This expedient was adopted, not from any apprehensions that he would escape, or from any necessity that was yet apparent, of his being unable to endure the torture with his limbs free, but from an ingenious design of making him feel his helplessness and of gradually sapping his resolution, by undermining it, as it might be, little by little. Deerslayer offered no resistance. He submitted his arms and legs, freely if not cheerfully, to the ligaments of bark, which were bound around them, by order of the chief, in a way to produce as little pain as possible. These directions were secret, and given in a hope that the captive would finally save himself from any serious bodily suffering, by consenting to take the Sumac for a wife. As soon as the body of Deerslayer was withed in bark sufficiently to create a lively sense of helplessness, he was literally carried to a young tree, and bound against it, in a way that effectually prevented him from moving, as well as from falling. The hands were laid flat against the legs, and thongs were passed over all, in a way nearly to incorporate the prisoner with the tree. His cap was then removed, and he was left half-standing, half-sustained by his bonds, to face the coming scene in the best manner he could.

Previously to proceeding to anything like extremities, it was the wish of Rivenoak to put his captive's resolution to the proof, by renewing the attempt at a compromise. This could be effected only in one manner, the acquiescence of the Sumac being indispensably necessary to a compromise of her right to be revenged. With this view, then, the woman was next desired to advance, and to look to her own interest; no agent being considered as efficient as the principal herself in this negotiation. The Indian females, when girls, are usually mild and submissive, with musical tones, pleasant voices, and merry laughs; but toil and suffering generally deprive them of most of these advantages by the time they have reached an age which the Sumac had long before passed. To render their voices harsh, it would seem to require active, malignant passions, though when excited their screams can rise to a sufficiently conspicuous degree of discordancy to assert their claim to possess this distinctive peculiarity of the sex. The Sumac was not altogether without feminine attraction, however, and had so recently been deemed handsome in her tribe, as not to have yet learned the full influence that time and exposure produce on man as well as on woman. By an arrangement of Rivenoak's some of the women around her had been employing the time in endeavoring to persuade the bereaved widow that there was still a hope Deerslayer might be prevailed on to enter her wigwam, in preference to entering the world of spirits, and this, too, with a success that previous symptoms scarcely justified. All this was the result of a resolution on the part of the chief to leave no proper means unemployed, in order to get the greatest hunter that was then thought to exist in all that region, transferred to his own nation, as well as a husband for a woman who he felt would be likely to be troublesome, were any of her claims to the attention and care of the tribe overlooked.

In conformity with this scheme the Sumac had been secretly advised to advance into the circle, and to make her appeal to the prisoner's sense of justice before the band had recourse to the last experiment. The woman, nothing loath, consented; for there was some such attraction, in becoming the wife of a noted hunter, among the females of the tribes, as is experienced by the sex in more refined life when they bestow their hands on the affluent. As the duties of a mother were thought to be paramount to all other considerations, the widow felt none of that embarrassment in preferring her claims, to which even a female fortune hunter among ourselves might be liable. When she stood forth before the whole party, therefore, the children that she led by the hand fully justified all she did.

"You see me before you, cruel paleface," the woman commenced; "your spirit must tell you my errand. I have found *you;* I cannot find le Loup Cervier, nor the Panther; I have looked for them in the lake, in the woods, in the clouds. I cannot say where they have gone."

"No man knows, good Sumac, no man knows," interposed the captive. "When the spirit leaves the body it passes into a world beyond our knowledge, and the wisest way for them that are left behind is to hope for the best. No doubt both your warriors have gone to the happy hunting grounds, and at the proper time you will see 'em ag'in in their improved state. The wife and sister of braves must have looked forward to some such tarmination of their 'arthly careers."

"Cruel paleface, what had my warriors done that you should slay them? They were the best hunters and the boldest young men of their tribe; the Great Spirit intended that they should live until they withered like the branches of the hemlock, and fell of their own weight."

"Nay, nay, good Sumac," interrupted the Deerslayer, whose love of truth was too indomitable to listen to such hyperbole with patience, even though it came from the torn breast of a widow—"Nay, nay, good Sumac, this is a little outdoing redskin privileges. Young man was neither, any more than you can be called a young woman; and as to the Great Spirit's intending that they should fall otherwise than they did, that's a grievous mistake, inasmuch as what the Great Spirit intends is sartain to come to pass. Then, ag'in, it's plain enough neither of your fri'nds did me any harm: I raised my hand ag'in 'em on account of what they were *striving* to do, rather than what they did. This is nat'ral law, 'to do, lest you should be done by.' "

"It is so. Sumac has but one tongue; she can tell but
one story. The paleface struck the Hurons, lest the Hurons
should strike him. The Hurons are a just nation; they will
forget it. The chiefs will shut their eyes, and pretend not to
have seen it. The young men will believe the Panther and
the Lynx have gone to far-off hunts; and the Sumac will take
her children by the hand, and go into the lodge of the paleface, and say, 'See; these are *your* children—they are also
mine; feed us, and we will live with you.' "

"The tarms are onadmissible, woman; and, though I feel
for your losses, which must be hard to bear, the tarms
cannot be accepted. As to givin' you ven'son, in case we
lived near enough together, that would be no great expl'ite;
but as for becomin' your husband, and the father of your
children, to be honest with you, I feel no callin' thataway."

"Look at this boy, cruel paleface; he has no father to
teach him to kill the deer, or to take scalps. See this girl;
what young man will come to look for a wife in a lodge
that has no head? There are more among my people in the
Canadas, and the Killer of Deer will find as many mouths
to feed as his heart can wish for."

"I tell you, woman," exclaimed Deerslayer, whose imagination was far from seconding the appeal of the widow, and
who began to grow restive under the vivid pictures she was
drawing, "all this is nothing to me. People and kindred
must take care of their own fatherless, leaving them that
have no children to their own loneliness. As for me, I have
no offspring, and I want no wife. Now, go away, Sumac;
leave me in the hands of your chiefs; for my color, and
gifts, and natur' itself cry out ag'in the idee of taking
you for a wife."

It is unnecessary to expatiate on the effect of this downright refusal of the woman's proposals. If there was anything
like tenderness in her bosom—and no woman was, probably,
ever entirely without that feminine quality—it all disappeared at this plain announcement. Fury, rage, mortified
pride, and a volcano of wrath, burst out at one explosion,
converting her into a sort of maniac, as it might be at the
touch of a magician's wand. Without deigning a reply in
words, she made the arches of the forest ring with screams,
and then flew forward at her victim, seizing him by the
hair, which she appeared resolute to draw out by the roots.

It was some time before her grasp could be loosened. Fortunately for the prisoner, her rage was blind, since his total helplessness left him entirely at her mercy; had it been better directed, it might have proved fatal before any relief could have been offered. As it was, she did succeed in wrenching out two or three handfuls of hair, before the young men could tear her away from her victim.

The insult that had been offered to the Sumac was deemed an insult to the whole tribe; not so much, however, on account of any respect that was felt for the woman, as on account of the honor of the Huron nation. Sumac, herself, was generally considered to be as acid as the berry from which she derived her name; and now that her great supporters, her husband and brother, were both gone, few cared about concealing their aversion. Nevertheless, it had become a point of honor to punish the paleface who disdained a Huron woman, and more particularly, one who coolly preferred death to relieving the tribe from the support of a widow and her children. The young men showed an impatience to begin to torture, that Rivenoak understood; and as his elder associates manifested no disposition to permit any longer delay, he was compelled to give the signal for the infernal work to proceed.

CHAPTER XXIX

The ugly bear now minded not the stake,
Nor how the cruel mastiffs do him tear;
The stag lay still, unroused from the brake,
The foamy boar feared not the hunter's spear;
All thing was still in desert, bush, and briar.

EARL OF DORSET

IT WAS ONE of the common expedients of the savages, on such occasions, to put the nerves of their victims to the severest proofs. On the other hand, it was a matter of Indian pride to betray no yielding to terror or pain, but for the prisoner to provoke his enemies to such acts of violence as would soonest produce death. Many a warrior had been known to bring his own sufferings to a more speedy termination by taunting reproaches and reviling language, when he found that his physical system was giving way under the agony of sufferings produced by a hellish ingenuity that might well eclipse all that has been said of the infernal devices of religious persecution. This happy expedient of taking refuge from the ferocity of his foes in their passions was denied Deerslayer, however, by his peculiar notions of the duty of a white man, and he had stoutly made up his mind to endure everything, in preference to disgracing his color.

No sooner did the young men understand that they were at liberty to commence than some of the boldest and most forward among them sprang into the arena, tomahawk in hand. Here they prepared to throw that dangerous weapon, the object being to strike the tree as near as possible to the victim's head without absolutely hitting him. This was so hazardous an experiment that none but those who were

482

known to be exceedingly expert with the weapon were allowed to enter the lists at all, lest an early death interfere with the expected entertainment. In the truest hands, it was seldom that the captive escaped injury in these trials, and it often happened that death followed, even when the blow was not premeditated. In the particular case of our hero, Rivenoak and the older warriors were apprehensive that the example of the Panther's fate might prove a motive with some fiery spirit, suddenly to sacrifice his conqueror, when the temptation of effecting it in precisely the same manner, and possibly with the identical weapon with which the warrior had fallen, offered. This circumstance, of itself, rendered the ordeal of the tomahawk doubly critical for the Deerslayer.

It would seem, however, that all who now entered what we shall call the lists were more disposed to exhibit their own dexterity than to resent the deaths of their comrades. Each prepared himself for the trial with the feelings of rivalry rather than with the desire for vengeance, and for the first few minutes the prisoner had little more connection with the result than grew out of the interest that necessarily attached itself to a living target. The young men were eager, instead of being fierce, and Rivenoak thought he still saw signs of being able to save the life of the captive, when the vanity of the young men had been gratified, always admitting that it was not sacrificed to the delicate experiments that were about to be made.

The first youth who presented himself for the trial was called the Raven, having as yet had no opportunity of obtaining a more warlike sobriquet. He was remarkable for high pretension rather than for skill or exploits, and those who knew his character thought the captive in imminent danger when he took his stand, and poised the tomahawk. Nevertheless, the young man was good-natured, and no thought was uppermost in his mind other than the desire to make a better cast than any of his fellows. Deerslayer got an inkling of this warrior's want of reputation by the injunctions that he had received from the seniors, who, indeed, would have objected to his appearing in the arena at all, but for an influence derived from his father, an aged warrior of great merit, who was then in the lodges of the tribe. Still, our hero maintained an appearance of self-possession. He had made up his mind that his hour was come, and it would have been a mercy, instead of a calamity, to fall by the unsteadiness of the first hand that was raised against him. After a suitable number of flourishes and gesticulations that promised much more than he could perform, the Raven let the tomahawk quit his hand. The weapon whirled through the air with the usual evolutions, cut a chip from the sapling to which the prisoner was bound, within a few inches of his cheek, and stuck in a large oak that grew several yards behind him. This was decidedly a bad effort, and a common sneer proclaimed as much, to the great mortification of the young man. On the other hand, there was a general but suppressed murmur of admiration at the steadiness with which the captive stood the trial. The head was the only part he could move, and this had been purposely left free, that the tormentors might have the amusement, and the tormented endure the shame, of dodging and otherwise attempting to avoid the blows. Deerslayer disappointed these hopes by a command of nerve that rendered his whole body as immovable as the tree to which he was bound. Nor did he even adopt the natural and usual expedient of shutting his eyes: the firmest and oldest warrior of the red men never having more disdainfully denied himself this advantage under similar circumstances.

The Raven had no sooner made his unsuccessful and puerile effort than he was succeeded by le Daim-Mose, or the Moose, a middle-aged warrior who was particularly skillful in the use of the tomahawk, and from whose attempt the spectators confidently looked for gratification. This man had none of the good nature of the Raven, but he would gladly have sacrificed the captive to his hatred of the palefaces generally, were it not for the greater interest he felt in his own success as one particularly skillful in the use of this weapon. He took his stand quietly but with an air of confidence, poised his little ax but a single instant, advanced a foot with a quick motion, and threw. Deerslayer saw the keen instrument whirling toward him and believed all was over; still he was not touched. The tomahawk had actually bound the head of the captive to the tree by carrying before it some of his hair, having buried itself deep beneath the soft bark. A general yell expressed the delight of the spectators, and the Moose felt his heart soften a little toward the prisoner, whose steadiness of nerve alone enabled him to give this evidence of his consummate skill.

Le Daim-Mose was succeeded by the Bounding Boy, or le Garçon qui Bondi, who came leaping into the circle like a hound or a goat at play. This was one of those elastic youths whose muscles seemed always in motion, and who either affected, or who from habit was actually unable to move in any other manner, than by showing the antics just mentioned. Nevertheless, he was both brave and skillful, and had gained the respect of his people by deeds in war as well as success in the hunts. A far nobler name would long since have fallen to his share, had not a Frenchman of rank inadvertently given him this sobriquet, which he religiously preserved as coming from his great father, who lived beyond the wide salt lake. The Bounding Boy skipped about in front of the captive, menacing him with his tomahawk, now on one side and now on another, and then again in front, in the vain hope of being able to extort some sign of fear by this parade of danger. At length Deerslayer's patience became exhausted by all this mummery, and he spoke for the first time since the trial had actually commenced.

"Throw away, Huron!" he cried, "or your tomahawk will forget its ar'n'd. Why do you keep loping about like a fa'an that's showing its dam how well it can skip, when you're a warrior grown, yourself, and a warrior grown defies you and all your silly antics? Throw, or the Huron gals will laugh in your face."

Although not intended to produce such an effect, the last words aroused the "Bounding" warrior to fury. The same nervous excitability which rendered him so active in his person made it difficult to repress his feelings, and the words were scarcely past the lips of the speaker than the tomahawk left the hand of the Indian. It was cast without good will, and with a fierce determination to slay. Had the intention been less deadly, the danger might have been greater. The aim was uncertain, and the weapon glanced near the cheek of the captive, slightly cutting the shoulder in its evolutions. This was the first instance in which any other object than that of terrifying the prisoner and of displaying skill had been manifested, and the Bounding Boy was immediately led from the arena and was warmly rebuked for his intemperate haste, which had come so near defeating all the hopes of the band.

To this irritable person succeeded several other young warriors, who not only hurled the tomahawk but who cast the knife, a far more dangerous experiment, with reckless indifference; yet they always manifested a skill that prevented any injury to the captive. Several times Deerslayer was grazed, but in no instance did he receive what might be termed a wound. The unflinching firmness with which he faced his assailants, more especially in the sort of rally with which this trial terminated, excited a profound respect in the spectators, and when the chiefs announced that the prisoner had well withstood the trials of the knife and the tomahawk, there was not a single individual in the band who really felt any hostility toward him, with the exception of Sumac and the Bounding Boy. These two discontented spirits got together, it is true, feeding each other's ire, but, as yet, their malignant feelings were confined very much to themselves, though there existed the danger that the others, ere long, could not fail to be excited by their own efforts into that demoniacal state which usually accompanied all similar scenes among the red men.

Rivenoak now told his people that the paleface had proved himself to be a man. He might live with the Delawares, but he had not been made woman with that tribe. He wished to know whether it was the desire of the Hurons to proceed any further. Even the gentlest of the females, however, had received too much satisfaction in the late trials to forgo their expectations of a gratifying exhibition, and there was but one voice in the request to proceed. The politic chief, who had some such desire to receive so celebrated a hunter into his tribe as a European minister has to devise a new and available means of taxation, sought every plausible means of arresting the trial in season, for he well knew, if permitted to go far enough to arouse the more ferocious passions of the tormentors, it would be as easy to dam the waters of the great lakes of his own region as to attempt to arrest them in their bloody career. He therefore called four or five of the best marksmen to him and bid them put the captive to the proof of the rifle, while at the same time he cautioned them touching the necessity of their maintaining their own credit, by the closest attention to the manner of exhibiting their skill.

When Deerslayer saw the chosen warriors step into the

circle, with their arms prepared for service, he felt some such relief as the miserable sufferer who has long endured the agonies of disease feels at the certain approach of death. Any trifling variance in the aim of this formidable weapon would prove fatal, since, the head being the target, or rather the point it was desired to graze without injury, an inch or two of difference in the line of projection must at once determine the question of life or death.

In the torture by the rifle there was none of the latitude permitted that appeared in the case of even Gesler's apple, a hairsbreadth being, in fact, the utmost limits that an expert marksman would allow himself on an occasion like this. Victims were frequently shot through the head by too eager or unskillful hands, and it often occurred that, exasperated by the fortitude and taunts of the prisoner, death was dealt intentionally in a moment of ungovernable irritation. All this Deerslayer well knew, for it was in relating the traditions of such scenes, as well as of the battles and victories of their people, that the old men beguiled the long winter evenings in their cabins. He now fully expected the end of his career and experienced a sort of melancholy pleasure in the idea that he was to fall by a weapon as much beloved as the rifle. A slight interruption, however, took place before the business was allowed to proceed.

Hetty Hutter witnessed all that passed, and the scene at first had pressed upon her feeble mind in a way to paralyze it entirely, but by this time she had rallied, and was growing indignant at the unmerited suffering the Indians were inflicting on her friend. Though timid and shy as the young of the deer on so many occasions, this right-feeling girl was always intrepid in the cause of humanity, the lessons of her mother, and the impulses of her own heart—perhaps we might say the promptings of that unseen and pure spirit that seemed ever to watch over and direct her actions—uniting to keep down the apprehensions of woman and to impel her to be bold and resolute. She now appeared in the circle, gentle, feminine, even bashful in mien, as usual, but earnest in her words and countenance, speaking like one who knew herself to be sustained by the high authority of God.

"Why do you torment Deerslayer, red men?" she asked. "What has he done that you trifle with his life? Who has given you the right to be his judges? Suppose one of your knives or tomahawks had hit him; what Indian among you all could cure the wound you would make? Besides, in harming Deerslayer, you injure your own friend; when Father and Hurry Harry came after your scalps, he refused to be of the party and stayed in the canoe by himself. You are tormenting your friend, in tormenting this young man!"

The Hurons listened with grave attention, and one among them who understood English translated what had been said into their native tongue. As soon as Rivenoak was made acquainted with the purport of her address, he answered it in his own dialect, the interpreter conveying it to the girl in English.

"My daughter is very welcome to speak," said the stern old orator, using gentle intonations and smiling as kindly as if addressing a child. "The Hurons are glad to hear her voice; they listen to what she says. The Great Spirit often speaks to men with such tongues. This time her eyes have not been open wide enough to see all that has happened. Deerslayer did not come for our scalps, that is true; why did he not come? Here they are, on our heads; the warlocks are ready to be taken hold of; a bold enemy ought to stretch out his hand to seize them. The Iroquois are too great a nation to punish men that take scalps. What they do themselves, they like to see others do. Let my daughter look around her and count my warriors. Had I as many hands as four warriors, their fingers would be fewer than my people, when they came into your hunting grounds. Now a whole hand is missing. Where are the fingers? Two have been cut off by this paleface; my Hurons wish to see if he did this by means of a stout heart or by treachery, like a skulking fox, or like a leaping panther."

"You know yourself, Huron, how one of them fell. I saw it, and you all saw it, too. 'Twas too bloody to look at; but it was not Deerslayer's fault. Your warrior sought his life, and he defended himself. I don't know whether the good book says that it was right, but all men will do that. Come, if you want to know which of you can shoot best, give Deerslayer a rifle, and then you will find how much more expert he is than any of your warriors; yes, than *all* of them together!"

Could one have looked upon such a scene with indifference, he would have been amused at the gravity with which the savages listened to the translation of this unusual request. No taunt, no smile mingled with their surprise, for Hetty had a character and a manner too saintly to subject her infirmity to the mockings of the rude and ferocious. On the contrary, she was answered with respectful attention.

"My daughter does not always talk like a chief at a council fire," returned Rivenoak, "or she would not have said this. Two of my warriors have fallen by the blows of our prisoner; their grave is too small to hold a third. The Hurons do not like to crowd their dead. If there is another spirit about to set out for the far-off world, it must not be the spirit of a Huron; it must be the spirit of a paleface. Go, daughter, and sit by Sumac, who is in grief; let the Huron warriors show how well they can shoot; let the paleface show how little he cares for their bullets."

Hetty's mind was unequal to a sustained discussion, and accustomed to defer to the directions of her seniors, she did as told, seating herself passively on a log by the side of the Sumac and averting her face from the painful scene that was occurring within the circle.

The warriors, as soon as this interruption had ceased, resumed their places and again prepared to exhibit their skill, as there was a double object in view, that of putting the constancy of the captive to the proof and that of showing how steady were the hands of the marksmen under circumstances of excitement. The distance was small and, in one sense, safe. But in diminishing the distance taken by the tormentors, the trial to the nerves of the captive was essentially increased. The face of Deerslayer, indeed, was just removed sufficiently from the ends of the guns to escape the effects of the flash, and his steady eye was enabled to look directly into their muzzles, as it might be, in anticipation of the fatal messenger that was to issue from each. The cunning Hurons well knew this fact, and scarce one leveled his piece without first causing it to point as near as possible at the forehead of the prisoner, in the hope that his fortitude would fail him and that the band would enjoy the triumph of seeing a victim quail under their ingenious cruelty. Nevertheless, each of the competitors was still careful not to injure, the disgrace of striking prematurely being second only to that of failing altogether in attaining the object. Shot after shot was made, all the bullets coming in close proximity to the Deerslayer's head without touching it. Still, no one could detect even the twitching of a muscle on the part of the captive, or the slightest winking of an eye. This indomitable resolution, which so much exceeded everything of its kind that any present had before witnessed, might be referred to three distinct causes. The first was resignation to his fate, blended with natural steadiness of deportment, for our hero had calmly made up his mind that he must die, and preferred this mode to any other; the second was his great familiarity with this particular weapon, which deprived it of all the terror that is usually connected with the mere form of the danger; and the third was this familiarity carried out in practice, to a degree so nice as to enable the intended victim to tell, within an inch, the precise spot where each bullet must strike, for he calculated its range by looking in at the bore of the piece. So exact was Deerslayer's estimation of the line of fire that his pride of feeling finally got the better of his resignation, and when five or six had discharged their bullets into the tree, he could not refrain from expressing his contempt at their want of hand and eye.

"You may call this shooting, Mingos," he exclaimed, "but we've squaws among the Delawares, and I have known Dutch gals on the Mohawk, that could outdo your greatest indivors. Ondo these arms of mine, put a rifle into my hands, and I'll pin the thinnest warlock in your party to any tree you can show me, and this at a hundred yards: aye, or at two hundred, if the object can be seen, nineteen shots in twenty: or for that matter, twenty in twenty, if the piece is creditable and trusty!"

A low menacing murmur followed this cool taunt, the ire of the warriors kindled at listening to such a reproach from one who so far disdained their efforts as to refuse even to wink, when a rifle was discharged as near his face as could be done without burning it. Rivenoak perceived that the moment was critical, and still retaining his hope of adopting so noted a hunter into his tribe, the politic old chief interposed in time, probably, to prevent an immediate resort to that portion of the torture which must necessarily have produced death, through extreme bodily suffering, if in no other manner. Moving into the center of the irritated group, he addressed them with his usual wily logic and plausible manner, at once suppressing the fierce movement that had commenced.

"I see how it is," he said. "We have been like the palefaces when they fasten their doors at night, out of fear of the red man. They use so many bars that the fire comes and burns them before they can get out. We have bound the Deerslayer too tight; the thongs keep his limbs from shaking and his eyes from shutting. Loosen him; let us see what his own body is really made of."

It is often the case, when we are thwarted in a cherished scheme, that any expedient, however unlikely to succeed, is gladly resorted to, in preference to a total abandonment of the project. So it was with the Hurons. The proposal of the chief found instant favor, and several hands were immediately at work cutting and tearing the ropes of bark from the body of our hero. In half a minute Deerslayer stood as free from bonds as when, an hour before, he had commenced his flight on the side of the mountain. Some little time was necessary that he should recover the use of his limbs, the circulation of the blood having been checked by the tightness of the ligatures, and this was accorded to him by the politic Rivenoak, under the pretense that his body would be more likely to submit to apprehension if its true tone were restored, though really with a view to give time to the fierce passions which had been awakened in the bosoms of his young men to subside. This ruse succeeded, and Deerslayer, by rubbing his limbs, stamping his feet, and moving about, soon regained the circulation, recovering all his physical powers as effectually as if nothing had occurred to disturb them.

It is seldom men think of death in the pride of their health and strength. So it was with Deerslayer. Having been helplessly bound, and, as he had every reason to suppose, so lately on the very verge of the other world, to find himself so unexpectedly liberated, in possession of his strength, and with a full command of limb, acted on him like a sudden restoration to life, reanimating hopes that he had once absolutely abandoned. From that instant all his plans changed. In this he simply obeyed a law of nature, for while we have wished to represent our hero as being resigned to his fate, it has been far from our intention to represent him as anxious to die. From the instant that his buoyancy of feeling revived, his thoughts were keenly bent on the various projects that presented themselves as modes of evading the designs of his enemies, and he again became the quick-witted, ingenious, and determined woodsman, alive to all his own powers and resources. The change was so great that his mind resumed its elasticity, and, no longer thinking of submission, it dwelt only on the devices of the sort of warfare in which he was engaged.

As soon as Deerslayer was released, the band divided itself in a circle around him, in order to hedge him in, and the desire to break down his spirit grew in them, precisely as they saw proofs of the difficulty there would be in subduing it. The honor of the band was now involved in the issue, and even the sex lost all its sympathy with suffering, in the desire to save the reputation of the tribe. The voices of the girls, soft and melodious as nature had made them, were heard mingling with the menaces of the men, and the wrongs of Sumac suddenly assumed the character of injuries inflicted on every Huron female. Yielding to this rising tumult, the men drew back a little, signifying to the females that they left the captive for a time in their hands, it being a common practice, on such occasions, for the women to endeavor to throw the victim into a rage by their taunts and revilings, and then to turn him suddenly over to the men in a state of mind that was little favorable to resisting the agony of bodily suffering. Nor was this party without the proper instruments for effecting such a purpose. Sumac had a notoriety as a scold, and one or two crones, like the She Bear, had come out with the party, most probably as the conservators of its decency and moral discipline, such things occurring in savage as well as civilized life. It is unnecessary to repeat all that ferocity and ignorance could invent for such a purpose, the only difference between this outbreaking of feminine anger and a similar scene among ourselves consisting in the figures of speech and the epithets; the Huron women called their prisoner by the names of the lower and least respected animals that were known to themselves.

But Deerslayer's mind was too much occupied to permit him to be disturbed by the abuse of excited hags, and their rage necessarily increasing with his indifference, as his indifference increased with their rage, the furies soon rendered themselves impotent by their own excesses. Perceiving that

the attempt was a complete failure, the warriors interfered
to put a stop to this scene, and this so much the more, because preparations were now seriously making for the commencement of the real tortures, or that which would put the
fortitude of the sufferer to the test of severe bodily pain. A
sudden and unlooked-for announcement that proceeded from
one of the lookouts, a boy ten or twelve years old, however, put a momentary check to the whole proceedings. As
this interruption has a close connection with the dénouement
of our story, it shall be given in a separate chapter.

Chapter XXX

So deem'st thou—so each mortal deems
Of that which is from that which seems;
But other harvest here
Than that which peasant's scythe demands,
Was gathered in by sterner hands,
With bayonet, blade, and spear.

SCOTT

IT EXCEEDED DEERSLAYER'S power to ascertain what had produced the sudden pause in the movements of his enemies, until the fact was revealed in the due course of events. He perceived that much agitation prevailed among the women in particular, while the warriors rested on their arms in a sort of dignified expectation. It was plain no alarm was excited, though it was not equally apparent that a friendly occurrence produced the delay. Rivenoak was evidently apprised of all, and by a gesture of his arm he appeared to direct the circle to remain unbroken, and for each person to await the issue in the situation he or she then occupied. It required but a minute or two to bring an explanation of this singular and mysterious pause, which was soon terminated by the appearance of Judith on the exterior of the line of bodies, and her ready admission within its circle.

If Deerslayer was startled by this unexpected arrival, well knowing that the quick-witted girl could claim none of that exemption from the penalties of captivity that was so cheerfully accorded to her feeble-minded sister, he was equally astonished at the guise in which she came. All her ordinary forest attire, neat and becoming as this usually was, had been laid aside for the brocade that has been already mentioned, and which had once before wrought so great and magical an effect in her appearance. Nor was this all. Accus-

494

tomed to see the ladies of the garrison in the formal gala attire of the day, and familiar with the more critical niceties
of these matters, the girl had managed to complete her dress
in a way to leave nothing strikingly defective in its details,
or even to betray an incongruity that would have been detected by one practiced in the mysteries of the toilet. Head,
feet, arms, hands, bust, and drapery were all in harmony,
as female attire was then deemed attractive and harmonious,
and the end she aimed at, that of imposing on the uninstructed senses of the savages by causing them to believe their
guest was a woman of rank and importance, might well have
succeeded with those whose habits had taught them to discriminate between persons. Judith, in addition to her rare
native beauty, had a singular grace of person, and her
mother had imparted enough of her own deportment to prevent any striking or offensive vulgarity of manner, so that,
sooth to say, the gorgeous dress might have been worse bestowed in nearly every particular. Had it been displayed in a
capital, a thousand might have worn it before one could
have been found to do more credit to its gay colors, glossy
satins, and rich laces than the beautiful creature whose person it now aided to adorn.

The effect of such an apparition had not been miscalculated. The instant Judith found herself within the circle, she
was, in a degree, compensated for the fearful personal risk
she ran by the unequivocal sensation of surprise and admiration produced by her appearance. The grim old warriors uttered their favorite exclamation, "Hugh!" The younger men
were still more sensibly overcome, and even the women
were not backward in letting open manifestations of pleasure
escape them. It was seldom that these untutored children of
the forest had ever seen any white female above the commonest sort, and as to dress, never before had so much splendor shone before their eyes. The gayest uniforms of both
French and English seemed dull compared with the luster of
the brocade, and while the rare personal beauty of the wearer
added to the effect produced by its hues, the attire did not
fail to adorn that beauty in a way which surpassed even the
hopes of its wearer. Deerslayer himself was astounded, and
this quite as much by the brilliant picture the girl presented as at the indifference to consequences with which she
had braved the danger of the step she had taken. Under such

circumstances, all waited for the visitor to explain her object, which to most of the spectators seemed as inexplicable as her appearance.

"Which of these warriors is the principal chief?" demanded Judith of Deerslayer, as soon as she found it was expected that she should open the communication; "my errand is too important to be delivered to any of inferior rank. First explain to the Hurons what I say; then give an answer to the question I have put."

Deerslayer quietly complied, his auditors greedily listening to the interpretation of the first words that fell from so extraordinary a vision. The demand seemed perfectly in character for one who had every appearance of an exalted rank herself. Rivenoak gave an appropriate reply by presenting himself before his fair visitor in a way to leave no doubt that he was entitled to all the consideration he claimed.

"I can believe this, Huron," resumed Judith, enacting her assumed part with a steadiness and dignity that did credit to her powers of imitation, for she strove to impart to her manner the condescending courtesy she had once observed in the wife of a general officer, at a similar though a more amicable scene. "I can believe you to be the principal person of this party; I see in your countenance the marks of thought and reflection. To you, then, I must make my communication."

"Let the Flower of the Woods speak," returned the old chief courteously, as soon as her address had been translated so that all might understand it. "If her words are as pleasant as her looks, they will never quit my ears; I shall hear them long after the winter in Canada has killed the flowers and frozen all the speeches of summer."

This admiration was grateful to one constituted like Judith, and contributed to aid her self-possession quite as much as it fed her vanity. Smiling involuntarily, or in spite of her wish to seem reserved, she proceeded in her plot.

"Now, Huron," she continued, "listen to my words. Your eyes tell you that I am no common woman. I will not say I am queen of this country; *she* is afar off, in a distant land; but under our gracious monarchs there are many degrees of rank; one of these I fill. What that rank is precisely it is unnecessary for me to say, since you would not understand it. For that information you must trust your eyes. You *see* what I am; you must *feel* that in listening to my words, you listen to one who can be your friend or your enemy, as you treat her."

This was well uttered, with a due attention to manner and a steadiness of tone that was really surprising, considering all the circumstances of the case. It was well, though simply rendered into the Indian dialect, too, and it was received with a respect and gravity that augured favorably for the girl's success. But Indian thought is not easily traced to its sources. Judith waited with anxiety to hear the answer, filled with hope even while she doubted. Rivenoak was a ready speaker, and he answered as promptly as comported with the notions of Indian decorum, that peculiar people seeming to think a short delay respectful, inasmuch as it manifests that the words already heard have been duly weighed.

"My daughter is handsomer than the wild roses of Ontario; her voice is pleasant to the ear as the song of the wren," answered the cautious and wily chief, who of all the band stood alone in not being fully imposed on by the magnificent and unusual appearance of Judith, but who distrusted even while he wondered. "The hummingbird is not much larger than the bee, yet its feathers are as gay as the tail of the peacock. The Great Spirit sometimes puts very bright clothes on very little animals. Still, He covers the moose with coarse hair. These things are beyond the understanding of poor Indians, who can only comprehend what they see and hear. No doubt my daughter has a very large wigwam somewhere about the lake that the Hurons have not found on account of their ignorance?"

"I have told you, Chief, that it would be useless to state my rank and residence, inasmuch as you would not comprehend them. You must trust to your eyes for this knowledge; what red man is there that cannot see? This blanket that I wear is not the blanket of a common squaw; these ornaments are such as the wives and daughters of chiefs only appear in. Now listen and hear why I have come alone among your people, and hearken to the errand that has brought me here. The Yengeese have young men as well as the Hurons—and plenty of them, too—this you well know."

"The Yengeese are as plenty as the leaves on the trees! This every Huron knows and feels."

"I understand you, Chief. Had I brought a party with me, it might have caused trouble. My young men and your young men would have looked angrily at each other, especially had my young men seen that paleface bound for the tortures. He is a great hunter and is much loved by all the garrisons, far and near. There would have been blows about him, and the trail of the Iroquois back to the Canadas would have been marked with blood."

"There is so much blood on it now," returned the chief, gloomily, "that it blinds our eyes. My young men see that it is all Huron."

"No doubt; and more Huron blood would be spilled, had I come surrounded with palefaces. I have heard of Rivenoak and have thought it would be better to send him back in peace to his village, that he might leave his women and children behind him; if he then wished to come for our scalps, we would meet him. He loves animals made of ivory and little rifles. See; I have brought some with me to show him. I am his friend. When he has packed up these things among his goods, he will start for his village before any of my young men can overtake him, and then he will show his people in Canada what riches they can come to seek, now that our great fathers across the salt lake have sent each other the war hatchet. I will lead back with me this great hunter, of whom I have need to keep my house in venison."

Judith, who was sufficiently familiar with Indian phraseology, endeavored to express her ideas in the sententious manner common to those people, and she succeeded even beyond her own expectations. Deerslayer did her full justice in the translation, and this so much the more readily since the girl carefully abstained from uttering any direct untruth, a homage she paid to the young man's known aversion to falsehood, which he deemed a meanness altogether unworthy of a white man's gifts. The offering of the two remaining elephants and of the pistols already mentioned, one of which was all the worse for the recent accident, produced a lively sensation among the Hurons generally, though Rivenoak received it coldly, notwithstanding the delight with which he had first discovered the probable existence of a creature with two tails. In a word, this cool and sagacious savage was not so easily imposed on as his followers, and with a sentiment of honor that half the civilized world would have deemed supererogatory, he declined the acceptance of a bribe that he felt no disposition to earn by a compliance with the donor's wishes.

"Let my daughter keep her two-tailed hog, to eat when venison is scarce," he dryly answered; "and the little gun, which has two muzzles. The Hurons will kill deer when they are hungry, and they have long rifles to fight with. This hunter cannot quit my young men now; they wish to know if he is as stouthearted as he boasts himself to be."

"That I deny, Huron," interrupted Deerslayer, with warmth; "yes, that I downright deny as ag'in truth and reason. No man has heard me *boast*, and no man shall, though ye flay me alive, and then roast the quivering flesh, with your own infarnal devices and cruelties! I may be humble, and misfortunate, and your prisoner, but I'm no boaster, by my very gifts."

"My young paleface *boasts* he is *no* boaster," returned the crafty chief; "he *must* be right. I hear a strange bird singing. It has very rich feathers. No Huron ever before saw such feathers. They will be ashamed to go back to their village and tell their people that they let their prisoner go on account of the song of this strange bird, and not be able to give the *name* of the bird. They do not know how to say whether it is a wren or a catbird. This would be a great disgrace; my young men would not be allowed to travel in the woods without taking their mothers with them to tell them the names of the birds."

"You can ask my name of your prisoner," returned the girl. "It is Judith; and there is a great deal of the history of Judith in the palefaces' best book, the Bible. If I am a bird of fine feathers, I have also my name."

"No," answered the wily Huron, betraying the artifice he had so long practiced by speaking in English, with tolerable accuracy; "I not ask prisoner. He tired; he want rest. I ask my daughter with feeble mind. She speak truth. Come here, daughter; you answer. *Your* name, Hetty?"

"Yes, that's what they call me," returned the girl; "though it's written Esther, in the Bible."

"He write *him* in Bible, too? All write in Bible. No matter —what *her* name?"

"That's Judith, and it's so written in the Bible, though father sometimes called her Jude. That's my sister Judith, Thomas Hutter's daughter—Thomas Hutter, whom you called the Muskrat; though he was *no* muskrat, but a man, like yourselves—he lived in a house on the water, and that was enough for *you*."

A smile of triumph gleamed on the hard, wrinkled countenance of the chief when he found how completely his appeal to the truth-loving Hetty had succeeded. As for Judith herself, the moment her sister was questioned, she saw that all was lost, for no sign or even entreaty could have induced the right-feeling girl to utter a falsehood. To attempt to impose a daughter of the Muskrat on the savages as a princess or a great lady she knew would be idle, and she saw her bold and ingenious expedient for liberating the captive fail, through one of the simplest and most natural causes that could be imagined. She turned her eye on Deerslayer, therefore, as if imploring him to interfere, to save them both.

"It will not do, Judith," said the young man, in answer to this appeal, which he understood, though he saw its uselessness; "it will not do. 'Twas a bold idee, and fit for a general's lady; but yonder Mingo"—Rivenoak had withdrawn to a little distance, and was out of earshot—"but yonder Mingo is an oncommon man, and not to be deceived by any unnat'ral sarcumventions. Things must come afore him in their right order to draw a cloud afore *his* eyes! 'Twas too much to attempt making him fancy that a queen or a great lady lived in these mountains, and no doubt he thinks the fine clothes you wear are some of the plunder of your own father—or, at least, of him who once passed for your father—as quite likely it was, if all they say is true."

"At all events, Deerslayer, my presence here will save you for a time. They will hardly attempt torturing you before my face!"

"Why not, Judith? Do you think they will treat a woman of the palefaces more tenderly than they treat their own? It's true that your sex will most likely save you from the torments, but it will not save your liberty, and may not save your scalp. I wish you hadn't come, my good Judith; it can do no good to me, while it may do great harm to yourself."

"I can share your fate," the girl answered, with generous

enthusiasm. "They shall not injure you while I stand by, if in my power to prevent it—besides——"

"Besides what, Judith? What means have you to stop Injin cruelties, or to avart Injin deviltries?"

"None, perhaps, Deerslayer," answered the girl, with firmness, "but I can suffer with my friends—die with them if necessary."

"Ah, Judith—suffer you may, but die you will not until the Lord's time shall come. It's little likely that one of your sex and beauty will meet with a harder fate than to become the wife of a chief, if indeed your white inclinations can stoop to match with an Injin. 'Twould have been better had you stayed in the ark or the castle; but what has been done is done. You was about to say something when you stopped at 'besides'?"

"It might not be safe to mention it here, Deerslayer," the girl hurriedly answered, moving past him carelessly, that she might speak in a low tone; "half an hour is all in all to us. None of your friends are idle."

The hunter replied merely by a grateful look. Then he turned toward his enemies, as if ready again to face the torments. A short consultation had passed among the elders of the band, and by this time they also were prepared with their decision. The merciful purpose of Rivenoak had been much weakened by the artifice of Judith, which, failing of its real object, was likely to produce results the very opposite of those she had anticipated. This was natural, the feeling being aided by the resentment of an Indian, who found how near he had been to becoming the dupe of an inexperienced girl. By this time Judith's real character was fully understood— the widespread reputation of her beauty contributed to the exposure. As for the unusual attire, it was confounded with the profound mystery of the animals with two tails and, for the moment, lost its influence.

When Rivenoak, therefore, faced the captive again, it was with an altered countenance. He had abandoned the wish of saving him, and was no longer disposed to retard the more serious part of the torture. This change of sentiment was, in effect, communicated to the young men, who were already eagerly engaged in making their preparations for the contemplated scene. Fragments of dried wood were rapidly collected near the sapling, the splinters which it was intended to thrust into the flesh of the victim, previous to lighting, were all collected, and the thongs were already produced that were again to bind him to the tree. All this was done in profound silence, Judith watching every movement with breathless expectation, while Deerslayer himself stood seemingly as unmoved as one of the pines of the hills. When the warriors advanced to bind him, however, the young man glanced at Judith, as if to inquire whether resistance or submission were most advisable. By a significant gesture she counseled the last, and in a minute he was once more fastened to the tree, a helpless object of any insult or wrong that might be offered. So eagerly did everyone now act that nothing was said. The fire was immediately lighted in the pile, and the end of all was anxiously expected.

It was not the intention of the Hurons absolutely to destroy the life of their victim by means of fire. They designed merely to put his physical fortitude to the severest proofs it could endure, short of that extremity. In the end, they fully intended to carry his scalp with them into their village, but it was their wish first to break down his resolution and to reduce him to the level of a complaining sufferer. With this view, the pile of brush and branches had been placed at a proper distance, or one at which it was thought the heat would soon become intolerable, though it might not be immediately dangerous. As often happened, however, on these occasions, this distance had been miscalculated, and the flames began to wave their forked tongues in a proximity to the face of the victim that would have proved fatal in another instant, had not Hetty rushed through the crowd, armed with a stick, and scattered the blazing pile in a dozen directions. More than one hand was raised to strike the presumptuous intruder to the earth, but the chiefs prevented the blows by reminding their irritated followers of the state of her mind. Hetty, herself, was insensible to the risk she ran; as soon as she had performed this bold act, she stood looking about her in frowning resentment, as if to rebuke the crowd of attentive savages for their cruelty.

"God bless you, dearest sister, for that brave and ready act," murmured Judith, herself unnerved so much as to be incapable of exertion. "Heaven itself has sent you on its holy errand."

" 'Twas well meant, Judith," rejoined the victim; " 'twas

excellently meant, and 'twas timely, though it may prove ontimely in the ind! What is to come to pass must come to pass soon, or 'twill quickly be too late. Had I drawn in one mouthful of that flame in breathing, the power of man couldn't save my life, and you see that this time they've so bound my forehead as not to leave my head the smallest chance. 'Twas well meant, but it might have been more marciful to let the flames act their part."

"Cruel, heartless Hurons!" exclaimed the still indignant Hetty. "Would you burn a man and a Christian as you would burn a log of wood! Do you never read your Bibles? Or do you think God will forget such things?"

A gesture from Rivenoak caused the scattered brands to be collected; fresh wood was brought, even the women and children busying themselves eagerly in the gathering of dried sticks. The flame was just kindling a second time when an *Indian* female pushed through the circle, advanced to the heap, and with her foot dashed aside the lighted twigs in time to prevent the conflagration. A yell followed this second disappointment, but when the offender turned toward the circle and presented the countenance of Hist, it was succeeded by a common exclamation of pleasure and surprise. For a minute, all thought of pursuing the business in hand was forgotten, and young and old crowded around the girl, in haste to demand an explanation of her sudden and unlooked-for return. It was at this critical instant that Hist spoke to Judith in a low voice, placed some small object, unseen, in her hand, and then turned to meet the salutations of the Huron girls, with whom she was personally a great favorite. Judith recovered her self-possession and acted promptly. The small, keen-edged knife that Hist had given to the other was passed by the latter into the hands of Hetty, as the safest and least-suspected medium of transferring it to Deerslayer. But the feeble intellect of the last defeated the well-grounded hopes of all three. Instead of first cutting loose the hands of the victim and then concealing the knife in his clothes, in readiness for action at the most available instant, she went to work herself, with earnestness and simplicity, to cut the thongs that bound his head, that he might not again be in danger of inhaling flames. Of course this deliberate procedure was seen, and the hands of Hetty were arrested ere she had more than liberated the upper portion of the captive's body, not including his arms, below the elbows. This discovery at once pointed distrust toward Hist, and to Judith's surprise, when questioned on the subject, that spirited girl was not disposed to deny her agency in what had passed.

"Why should I not help the Deerslayer?" the girl demanded, in the tones of a firm-minded woman. "He is the brother of a Delaware chief; my heart is all Delaware. Come forth, miserable Briarthorn, and wash the Iroquois paint from your face; stand before the Hurons, the crow that you are; you would eat the carrion of your own dead rather than starve. Put him face to face with Deerslayer, chiefs and warriors; I will show you how great a knave you have been keeping in your tribe."

This bold language, uttered in their own dialect and with a manner full of confidence, produced a deep sensation among the Hurons. Treachery is always liable to distrust, and though the recreant Briarthorn had endeavored to serve the enemy well, his exertions and assiduities had gained for him little more than toleration. His wish to obtain Hist for a wife had first induced him to betray her and his own people, but serious rivals to his first project had risen up among his new friends, weakening still more their sympathies with treason. In a word, Briarthorn had been barely permitted to remain in the Huron encampment, where he was as closely and as jealously watched as Hist herself, seldom appearing before the chiefs and sedulously keeping out of view of Deerslayer, who until this moment was ignorant even of his presence. Thus summoned, however, it was impossible to remain in the background. "Wash the Iroquois paint from his face," he did not, for when he stood in the center of the circle, he was so disguised in these new colors that at first the hunter did not recognize him. He assumed an air of defiance, notwithstanding, and haughtily demanded what any could say against "Briarthorn."

"Ask yourself that," continued Hist, with spirit, though her manner grew less concentrated, and there was a slight air of abstraction that became observable to Deerslayer and Judith, if to no others. "Ask that of your own heart, sneaking woodchuck of the Delawares; come not here with the face of an innocent man. Go look in the spring; see the colors of your enemies on your lying skin; and then come back and boast how you ran from your tribe and took the blanket of the French for your covering. Paint yourself as bright as the hummingbird, you will still be black as the crow."

Hist had been so uniformly gentle while living with the Hurons that they now listened to her language with surprise. As for the delinquent, his blood boiled in his veins, and it was well for the pretty speaker that it was not in his power to execute the revenge he burned to inflict on her, in spite of his pretended love.

"Who wishes Briarthorn?" he sternly asked. "If this pale-face is tired of life: if afraid of Indian torments, speak, Rivenoak; I will send him after the warriors we have lost."

"No, Chief, no, Rivenoak," eagerly interrupted Hist. "The Deerslayer fears nothing; least of all a crow! Unbind him— cut his withes—place him face to face with this cawing bird; then let us see which is tired of life."

Hist made a forward movement, as if to take a knife from a young man and perform the office she had mentioned in person, but an aged warrior interposed at a sign from Rivenoak. This chief watched all the girl did with distrust, for, even while speaking in her most boastful language and in the steadiest manner, there was an air of uncertainty and expectation about her that could not escape so close an observer. She acted well, but two or three of the old men were equally satisfied that it was merely acting. Her proposal to release Deerslayer, therefore, was rejected, and the disappointed Hist found herself driven back from the sapling at the very moment she fancied herself about to be successful. At the same time the circle, which had got to be crowded and confused, was enlarged and brought once more into order. Rivenoak now announced the intention of the old men again to proceed, the delay having been continued long enough, and leading to no result.

"Stop, Huron; stay, Chiefs!" exclaimed Judith, scarce knowing what she said, or why she interposed, unless to obtain time; "for God's sake, a single minute longer——"

The words were cut short by another and a still more extraordinary interruption. A young Indian came bounding through the Huron ranks, leaping into the very center of the circle, in a way to denote the utmost confidence, or a temerity bordering on foolhardiness. Five or six sentinels were still watching the lake at different and distant points, and it was the first impression of Rivenoak that one of these had come in with tidings of import. Still, the movements of the stranger were so rapid, and his war dress, which scarcely left him more drapery than an antique statue, had so little distinguishing about it that at the first moment it was impossible to ascertain whether he were friend or foe. Three leaps carried this warrior to the side of Deerslayer, whose withes were cut in the twinkling of an eye, with a quickness and precision that left the prisoner perfect master of his limbs. Not till this was effected did the stranger bestow a glance on any other object; then he turned and showed the astonished Hurons the noble brow, fine person, and eagle eye of a young warrior in the paint and panoply of a Delaware. He held a rifle in each hand, the butts of both resting on the earth, while from one dangled its proper pouch and horn. This was Killdeer, which, even as he looked boldly and in defiance on the crowd around him, he suffered to fall back into the hands of its proper owner. The presence of two armed men, though it was in their midst, startled the Hurons. Their rifles were scattered about against the different trees, and their only weapons were their knives and tomahawks. Still, they had too much self-possession to betray fear. It was little likely that so small a force would assail so strong a band, and each man expected some extraordinary proposition to succeed so decisive a step. The stranger did not seem disposed to disappoint them; he prepared to speak.

"Hurons," he said, "this earth is very big. The great lakes are big, too; there is room beyond them for the Iroquois; there is room for the Delawares on this side. I am Chingachgook, the son of Uncas; the kinsman of Tamenund. This is my betrothed; that paleface is my friend. My heart was heavy when I missed him; I followed him to your camp to see that no harm happened to him. All the Delaware girls are waiting for Wah; they wonder that she stays away so long. Come, let us say farewell, and go on our path."

"Hurons, this is your mortal enemy, the Great Serpent of them you hate!" cried Briarthorn. "If he escape, blood will be in your moccasin prints from this spot to the Canadas. *I* am *all* Huron."

As the last words were uttered, the traitor cast his knife at the naked breast of the Delaware. A quick movement of the arm on the part of Hist, who stood near, turned aside the blow, the dangerous weapon burying its point in a pine.

At the next instant, a similar weapon glanced from the hand of the Serpent, and quivered in the recreant's heart. A minute had scarcely elapsed from the moment in which Chingachgook bounded into the circle and that in which Briarthorn fell, like a log, dead in his tracks. The rapidity of events prevented the Hurons from acting, but this catastrophe permitted no further delay. A common exclamation followed, and the whole party was in motion. At this instant, a sound unusual to the woods was heard, and every Huron, male and female, paused to listen, with ears erect and faces filled with expectation. The sound was regular and heavy, as if the earth were struck with beetles. Objects became visible among the trees of the background, and a body of troops was seen advancing with measured tread. They came upon the charge, the scarlet of the king's livery shining among the bright green foliage of the forest.

The scene that followed is not easily described. It was one in which wild confusion, despair, and frenzied efforts were so blended as to destroy the unity and distinctness of the action. A general yell burst from the enclosed Hurons; it was succeeded by the hearty cheers of England. Still, not a musket or rifle was fired, though that steady, measured tramp continued, and the bayonet was seen gleaming in advance of a line that counted nearly sixty men. The Hurons were taken at a fearful disadvantage. On three sides was the water, while their formidable and trained foes cut them off from flight on the fourth. Each warrior rushed for his arms, and then all on the point, man, woman, and child, eagerly sought the covers. In this scene of confusion and dismay, however, nothing could surpass the discretion and coolness of Deerslayer. His first care was to place Judith and Hist behind trees; he looked for Hetty, but she had been hurried away in the crowd of Huron women. This effected, he threw himself on a flank of the retiring Hurons, who were inclining off toward the southern margin of the point, in the hope of escaping through the water. Deerslayer watched his opportunity, and finding two of his recent tormenters in a range, his rifle first broke the silence of the terrific scene. The bullet brought down both at one discharge. This drew a general fire from the Hurons, and the rifle and war cry of the Serpent were heard in the clamor. Still the trained men returned no answering volley, the whoop and piece of Hurry alone being heard on their side, if we except the short, prompt word of authority and that heavy, measured, and menacing tread. Presently, however, the shrieks, groans, and denunciations that usually accompany the use of the bayonet followed. That terrible and deadly weapon was glutted in vengeance. The scene that succeeded was one of those, of which so many have occurred in our own times, in which neither age nor sex forms an exemption to the lot of a savage warfare.

CHAPTER XXXI

*The flower that smiles to-day
    To-morrow dies;
All that we wish to stay,
    Tempts and then flies:
What is this world's delight?—
Lightning that mocks the night,
Brief even as bright.*

SHELLEY

THE PICTURE NEXT presented by the point of land that the unfortunate Hurons had selected for their last place of encampment need scarcely be laid before the eyes of the reader. Happily for the more tender-minded and the more timid, the trunks of the trees, the leaves, and the smoke had concealed much of that which passed, and night shortly after drew its veil over the lake and the whole of that seemingly interminable wilderness, which may be said to have then stretched, with far and immaterial interruptions, from the banks of the Hudson to the shores of the Pacific Ocean. Our business carries us into the following day, when light returned upon the earth, as sunny and as smiling as if nothing extraordinary had occurred.

When the sun rose on the following morning, every sign of hostility and alarm had vanished from the basin of the Glimmerglass. The frightful event of the preceding evening had left no impression on the placid sheet, and the untiring hours pursued their course in the placid order prescribed by the powerful hand that set them in motion. The birds were again skimming the water, or were seen poised on the wing high above the tops of the tallest pines of the mountains, ready to make their swoops in obedience to the irresistible laws of their nature. In a word, nothing was changed but the air of movement and life that prevailed in and around the castle. Here, indeed, was an alteration that must have struck the least observant eye. A sentinel, who wore the light infantry uniform of a royal regiment, paced the platform with measured tread, and some twenty men of the same corps lounged about the place, or were seated in the ark. Their arms were stacked under the eye of their comrade on post. Two officers stood examining the shore with the ship's glass so often mentioned. Their looks were directed to that fatal point, where scarlet coats were still to be seen gliding among the trees, and where the magnifying power of the instrument also showed spades at work and the sad duty of interment going on. Several of the common men bore proofs on their persons that their enemies had not been overcome entirely without resistance, and the youngest of the two officers on the platform, wore an arm in a sling. His companion, who commanded the party, had been more fortunate. He it was that used the glass in making the reconnaissances in which the two were engaged.

A sergeant approached to make a report. He addressed the senior of these officers as Captain Warley, while the other was alluded to as Mr. ——, which was equivalent to Ensign —— Thornton. The former, it will at once be seen, was the officer who had been named with so much feeling in the parting dialogue between Judith and Hurry. He was, in truth, the very individual with whom the scandal of the garrisons had most freely connected the name of this beautiful but indiscreet girl. He was a hard-featured, red-faced man of about five-and-thirty, but of a military carriage and with an air of fashion that might easily impose on the imagination of one as ignorant of the world as Judith.

"Craig is covering us with benedictions," observed this person to his young ensign, with an air of indifference, as he shut the glass and handed it to his servant; "to say the truth, not without reason; it is certainly more agreeable to be here in attendance on Miss Judith Hutter than to be burying Indians on a point of the lake, however romantic the position or brilliant the victory. By the way, Wright, is Davis still living?"

"He died about ten minutes since, your Honor," returned the sergeant to whom this question was addressed. "I knew how it would be as soon as I found the bullet had touched the stomach. I never knew a man who could hold out long, if he had a hole in his stomach."

"No; it is rather inconvenient for carrying away anything very nourishing," observed Warley, gaping. "This being up two nights *de suite*, Arthur, plays the devil with a man's faculties! I'm as stupid as one of those Dutch parsons on the Mohawk—I hope your arm is not painful, my dear boy?"

"It draws a few grimaces from me, sir, as I suppose you see," answered the youth, laughing at the very moment his countenance was a little awry with pain. "But it may be borne. I suppose Graham can spare a few minutes, soon, to look at my hurt."

"She is a lovely creature, this Judith Hutter, after all, Thornton, and it shall not be my fault, if she is not seen and admired in the parks!" resumed Warley, who thought little of his companion's wound. "Your arm, eh! Quite true. Go into the ark, Sergeant, and tell Dr. Graham I desire he would look at Mr. Thornton's injury as soon as he has done with the poor fellow with the broken leg. A lovely creature! And she looked like a queen in that brocade dress in which we met her. I find all changed here; father and mother both gone, the sister dying, if not dead, and none of the family left but the beauty! This has been a lucky expedition all around, and promises to terminate better than Indian skirmishes in general."

"Am I to suppose, sir, that you are about to desert your colors in the great corps of bachelors and close the campaign with matrimony?"

"I, Tom Warley, turn Benedict! Faith, my dear boy, you little know the corps you speak of, if you fancy any such thing. I do suppose there *are* women in the colonies that a captain of light infantry need not disdain, but they are not to be found up here on a mountain lake, or even down on the Dutch river where we are posted. It is true my uncle, the general, once did me the favor to choose a wife for me, in Yorkshire, but she had no beauty—and I would not marry a princess unless she were handsome."

"If handsome, you would marry a beggar?"

"Aye, these are the notions of an ensign! Love in a cottage—doors—and windows—the old story, for the hundredth time. The twenty——th don't *marry*. We are not a marrying corps, my dear boy. There's the colonel, old Sir Edwin ——, now; though a full general, he has never thought of a wife; and when a man gets as high as a lieutenant general without matrimony, he is pretty safe. Then the lieutenant colonel is *confirmed*, as I tell my cousin, the bishop. The major is a widower, having tried matrimony for twelve months in his youth, and we look upon him now as one of our most certain men. Out of ten captains, but one is in the dilemma, and he, poor devil, is always kept at regimental headquarters, as a sort of *memento mori* to the young men as they join. As for the subalterns, not one has ever yet had the audacity to speak of introducing a wife into the regiment. But your arm is troublesome, and we'll go ourselves and see what has become of Graham."

The surgeon who had accompanied the party was employed very differently from what the captain supposed. When the assault was over, and the dead and wounded were collected, poor Hetty had been found among the latter. A rifle bullet had passed through her body, inflicting an injury that was known at a glance to be mortal. How this wound was received no one knew; it was probably one of those casualties that ever accompany scenes like that related in the previous chapter. The Sumac, all the elderly women, and some of the Huron girls had fallen by the bayonet, either in the confusion of the melee, or from the difficulty of distinguishing the sexes where the dress was so simple. Much the greater portion of the warriors suffered on the spot. A few had escaped, however, and two or three had been taken unharmed. As for the wounded, the bayonet saved the surgeon much trouble. Rivenoak had escaped with life and limb, but was injured and a prisoner. As Captain Warley and his ensign went into the ark, they passed him, seated in dignified silence, in one end of the scow, his head and leg bound, but betraying no visible signs of despondency or despair. That he mourned the loss of his tribe is certain; still, he did it in a manner that best became a warrior and a chief.

The two soldiers found their surgeon in the principal room of the ark. He was just quitting the pallet of Hetty with an expression of sorrowful regret on his hard, pockmarked, Scottish features that it was not usual to see there. All his assiduity had been useless, and he was compelled reluctantly to abandon the expectation of seeing the girl survive many hours. Dr. Graham was accustomed to deathbed scenes, and ordinarily they produced but little impression on him. In all that relates to religion, his was one of those minds which, in consequence of reasoning much on material things, logically and consecutively, and overlooking the total want of premises which such a theory must ever possess, through its want of a primary agent, had become skeptical; leaving a vague opinion concerning the origin of things, that with high pretensions to philosophy, failed in the first of all philosophical principles, a cause. To him religious dependence appeared a weakness, but when he found one gentle and young like Hetty, with a mind beneath the level of her race, sustained at such a moment by these pious sentiments, and that, too, in a way that many a sturdy warrior and reputed hero might have looked upon with envy, he found himself affected by the sight to a degree that he would have been ashamed to confess. Edinburgh and Aberdeen, then as now, supplied no small portion of the medical men of the British service, and Dr. Graham, as indeed his name and countenance equally indicated, was by birth a North Briton.

"Here is an extraordinary exhibition for a forest, and one but half gifted with reason," he observed, with a decided Scotch accent, as Warley and the ensign entered; "I just hope, gentlemen, that when we three shall be called on to quit the twenty——th, we may be found as resigned to go on the half pay of another existence as this poor demented chiel!"

"Is there no hope that she can survive the hurt?" demanded Warley, turning his eyes toward the pallid Judith, on whose cheeks, however, two large spots of red had settled as soon as he came into the cabin.

"No more than there is for Chairlie Stuart. Approach and judge for yourselves, gentlemen; ye'll see faith exemplified in an exceeding and wonderful manner. There is a sort of *arbitrium* between life and death in actual conflict in the poor girl's mind that renders her an interesting study to a philosopher. Mr. Thornton, I'm at your service now; we can just look at the arm in the next room, while we speculate as much as we please on the operations and sinuosities of the human mind."

The surgeon and ensign retired, and Warley had an opportunity of looking about him more at leisure and with a better understanding of the nature and feelings of the group collected in the cabin. Poor Hetty had been placed on her own simple bed, and was reclining in a half-seated attitude, with the approaches of death on her countenance, though they were singularly dimmed by the luster of an expression in which all the intelligence of her entire being appeared to be concentrated. Judith and Hist were near her, the former seated in deep grief, the latter standing in readiness to offer any of the gentle attentions of feminine care. Deerslayer stood at the end of the pallet, leaning on Killdeer, unharmed in person; all the fine, martial ardor that had so lately glowed in his countenance having given place to the usual look of honesty and benevolence, qualities of which the expression was now softened by manly regret and pity. The Serpent was in the background of the picture, erect and motionless as a statue, but so observant that not a look of the eye escaped his own keen glance. Hurry completed the group, being seated on a stool near the door, like one who felt himself out of place in such a scene, but who was ashamed to quit it unbidden.

"Who is that in scarlet?" asked Hetty, as soon as the captain's uniform caught her eye. "Tell me, Judith, is it the friend of Hurry?"

" 'Tis the officer who commands the troops that have rescued us all from the hands of the Hurons," was the low answer of the sister.

"Am I rescued, too? I thought they said I was shot, and about to die. Mother is dead, and so is Father; but you are living, Judith, and so is Hurry. I was afraid Hurry would be killed, when I heard him shouting among the soldiers."

"Never mind—never mind, dear Hetty," interrupted Judith, sensitively alive to the preservation of her sister's secret, more, perhaps, at such a moment than at any other. "Hurry is well, and Deerslayer is well, and the Delaware is well, too."

"How came they to shoot a poor girl like me and let so many men go unharmed? I didn't know that the Hurons were so wicked, Judith!"

" 'Twas an accident, poor Hetty; a sad accident it has been! No one would willingly have injured *you*."

"I'm glad of that—I thought it strange: I am feebleminded, and the red men have never harmed me before. I should be sorry to think that they had changed their minds. I am glad, too, Judith, that they haven't hurt Hurry. Deerslayer, I don't think God will suffer anyone to harm. It was very fortunate the soldiers came as they did though, for fire *will* burn!"

"It was, indeed, fortunate, my sister; God's holy name be forever blessed for the mercy."

"I daresay, Judith, you know some of the officers; you used to know so many."

Judith made no reply; she hid her face in her hands and groaned. Hetty gazed at her in wonder, but naturally supposing her own situation was the cause of this grief, she kindly offered to console her sister.

"Don't mind me, dear Judith," said the affectionate and pure-hearted creature. "I don't suffer, if I do die; why, Father and Mother are both dead, and what happens to *them* may well happen to *me*. You know I am of less account than any of the family; therefore, few will think of me after I'm in the lake."

"No, no, no—poor, dear, dear Hetty!" exclaimed Judith in an uncontrollable burst of sorrow. "I, at least, will ever think of you, and gladly—oh, how gladly—would I exchange places with you, to be the pure, excellent, sinless creature you are!"

Until now, Captain Warley had stood leaning against the door of the cabin; when this outbreak of feeling, and perchance of penitence, escaped the beautiful girl, he walked slowly and thoughtfully away, even passing the ensign, then suffering under the surgeon's care, without noticing him.

"I have got my Bible here, Judith!" returned her sister in a voice of triumph. "It's true, I can't read any longer; there's something the matter with my eyes—*you* look dim and distant—and so does Hurry, now I look at him; well, I never could have believed that Henry March would have so dull a look. What can be the reason, Judith, that I see so badly today? I, who Mother always said had the best eyes in the whole family. Yes, that was it; my mind was feeble—what people call half-witted—but my eyes were *so* good."

Again Judith groaned; this time no feeling of self, no retrospect of the past, caused the pain. It was the pure, heartfelt sorrow of sisterly love, heightened by a sense of the meek humility and perfect truth of the being before her.

At that moment, she would gladly have given up her own life to save that of Hetty. As the last, however, was beyond the reach of human power, she felt there was nothing left her but sorrow. At this moment Warley returned to the cabin, drawn by a secret impulse he could not withstand, though he felt, just then, as if he would gladly abandon the American continent forever, were it practicable. Instead of pausing at the door, he now advanced so near the pallet of the sufferer as to come more plainly within her gaze. Hetty could still distinguish large objects, and her look soon fastened on him.

"Are you the officer that came with Hurry?" she asked. "If you are, we ought all to thank you, for though I am hurt, the rest have saved their lives. Did Harry March tell you where to find us and how much need there was for your services?"

"The news of the party reached us by means of a friendly runner," returned the captain, glad to relieve his feelings by this appearance of a friendly communication, "and I was immediately sent out to cut it off. It was fortunate, certainly, that we met Hurry Harry, as you call him, for he acted as a guide, and it was not less fortunate that we heard a firing, which I now understand was merely a shooting at the mark, for it not only quickened our march but called us to the right side of the lake. The Delaware saw us on the shore, with the glass, it would seem, and he and Hist, as I find his squaw is named, did us excellent service. It was, really, altogether a fortunate concurrence of circumstances, Judith."

"Talk not to me of anything fortunate, sir," returned the girl huskily, again concealing her face. "To me the world is full of misery. I wish never to hear of marks, or rifles, or soldiers, or *men* again."

"Do you know my sister?" asked Hetty, ere the rebuked soldier had time to rally for an answer. "How came you to know that her name is Judith? You are right, for that *is* her name; and I am Hetty; Thomas Hutter's daughters."

"For Heaven's sake, dearest sister; for *my* sake, beloved Hetty," interposed Judith imploringly, "say no more of this."

Hetty looked surprised, but accustomed to comply, she ceased her awkward and painful interrogatories of Warley, bending her eyes toward the Bible, which she still held between her hands, as one would cling to a casket of precious stones in a shipwreck or a conflagration. Her mind now reverted to the future, losing sight, in a great measure, of the scenes of the past.

"We shall not long be parted, Judith," she said; "when *you* die, you must be brought and buried in the lake, by the side of Mother, too."

"Would to God, Hetty, that I lay there at this moment!"

"No, that cannot be, Judith; people must die before they have any right to be buried. 'Twould be wicked to bury you, or for you to bury yourself while living. Once I thought of burying myself; God kept me from that sin."

"You! You, Hetty Hutter, think of such an act?" exclaimed Judith, looking up in uncontrollable surprise, for she well knew nothing passed the lips of her conscientious sister that was not religiously true.

"Yes, I did, Judith, but God has forgotten—no, he *forgets* nothing—but he has *forgiven* it," returned the dying girl, with the subdued manner of a repentant child. " 'Twas after Mother's death; I felt I had lost the best friend I had on earth, if not the *only* friend. 'Tis true, you and Father were kind to me, Judith, but I was so feeble-minded I knew I should only give you trouble; and then you were so often ashamed of such a sister and daughter; and 'tis hard to live in a world where all look upon you as below them. I thought then if I could bury myself by the side of Mother, I should be happier in the lake than in the hut."

"Forgive me—pardon me, dearest Hetty; on my bended knees, I beg you to pardon me, sweet sister, if any word or act of mine drove you to so maddening and cruel a thought."

"Get up, Judith; kneel to God—don't kneel to me. Just so I felt when mother was dying. I remembered everything I had said and done to vex her, and could have kissed her feet for forgiveness. I think it must be so with all dying people, though now I think of it, I don't remember to have had such feelings on account of Father."

Judith arose, hid her face in her apron, and wept. A long pause—one of more than two hours—succeeded, during which Warley entered and left the cabin several times, apparently uneasy when absent and yet unable to remain. He issued various orders, which his men proceeded to execute, and there was an air of movement in the party, more especially as Mr. Craig, the lieutenant, had got through the unpleasant duty of burying the dead and had sent for instructions from the shore, desiring to know what he was to do with his detachment. During this interval, Hetty slept a little, and Deerslayer and Chingachgook left the ark to confer together. But at the end of the time mentioned, the surgeon passed upon the platform, and with a degree of feeling his comrades had never before observed in one of his habits, he announced that the patient was rapidly drawing near her end. On receiving this intelligence, the group collected again, curiosity to witness such a death—or a better feeling— drawing to the spot men who had so lately been actors in a scene seemingly of so much greater interest and moment. By this time Judith had got to be inactive, through grief, and Hist alone was performing the little offices of feminine attention that are so appropriate to the sickbed. Hetty herself had undergone no other apparent change than the general failing that indicated the near approach of dissolution. All that she possessed of mind was as clear as ever, and in some respects, her intellect was perhaps more than usually active.

"Don't grieve for me so much, Judith," said the gentle sufferer, after a pause in her remarks; "I shall soon see Mother; I think I see her *now;* her face is just as sweet and smiling as it used to be! Perhaps when I'm dead, God will give me all my mind, and I shall become a more fitting companion for Mother than I ever was before."

"You will be an angel in heaven, Hetty," sobbed the sister; "no spirit there will be more worthy of its holy residence!"

"I don't understand it quite; still, I know it must be all true; I've read it in the Bible. How dark it's becoming! Can it be night so soon? I can hardly see you at all; where is Hist?"

"I here, poor girl; why you no see me?"

"I do see you, but I couldn't tell whether 'twas you or Judith. I believe I shan't see you much longer, Hist."

"Sorry for that, poor Hetty. Never mind; paleface got a heaven for girl as well as for warrior."

"Where's the Serpent? Let me speak to him; give me his hand; so; I feel it. Delaware, you will love and cherish this young Indian woman; I know how fond she is of *you,* and you must be fond of *her.* Don't treat her as some of your people treat their wives; be a real husband to her. Now bring Deerslayer near me; give me *his* hand."

This request was complied with, and the hunter stood by the side of the pallet, submitting to the wishes of the girl with the docility of a child.

"I feel, Deerslayer," she resumed, "though I couldn't tell why—but I feel that you and I are not going to part forever. 'Tis a strange feeling! I never had it before; I wonder what it comes from!"

" 'Tis God encouraging you in extremity, Hetty; as such, it ought to be harbored and respected. Yes, we *shall* meet ag'in, though it may be a long time first, and in a far distant land."

"Do you mean to be buried in the lake, too? If so, that may account for the feeling."

" 'Tis little likely, gal, 'tis little likely; but there's a region for Christian souls where there's no lakes nor woods, they say, though why there should be none of the *last* is more than I can account for, seeing that pleasantness and peace is the object in view. My grave will be found in the forest, most likely, but I hope my spirit will not be far from your'n."

"So it must be, then. I am too weak-minded to understand these things, but I *feel* that you and I will meet again. Sister, where are you? I can't see now anything but darkness. It must be night, surely!"

"Oh, Hetty, I am here at your side; these are my arms that are around you," sobbed Judith. "Speak, dearest; is there anything you wish to say, or have done, in this awful moment!"

By this time Hetty's sight had entirely failed her. Nevertheless, death approached with less than usual of its horrors, as if in tenderness to one of her half-endowed faculties. She was pale as a corpse, but her breathing was easy and unbroken, while her voice, though lowered almost to a whisper, remained clear and distinct. When her sister put this question, however, a blush diffused itself over the features of the dying girl, so faint, however, as to be nearly imperceptible, resembling that hue of the rose which is thought to portray the tint of modesty, rather than the dye of the flower in its richer bloom. No one but Judith detected this expression of feeling, one of the gentle expressions of womanly sensibility, even in death. On her, however, it was not lost, nor did she conceal from herself the cause.

"Hurry is here, dearest Hetty," whispered the sister, with her face so near the sufferer as to keep the words from other ears. "Shall I tell him to come and receive your good wishes?"

A gentle pressure of the hand answered in the affirmative, and then Hurry was brought to the side of the pallet. It is probable that this handsome but rude woodsman had never before found himself so awkwardly placed, though the inclination which Hetty felt for him (a sort of secret yielding to the instincts of nature, rather than any unbecoming impulse of an ill-regulated imagination) was too pure and unobtrusive to have created the slightest suspicion of the circumstance in his mind. He allowed Judith to put his hard, colossal hand between those of Hetty, and stood waiting the result in awkward silence.

"This is Hurry, dearest," whispered Judith, bending over her sister, ashamed to utter the words so as to be audible to herself; "speak to him and let him go."

"What shall I say, Judith?"

"Nay, whatever your own pure spirit teaches, my love. Trust to that, and you need fear nothing."

"Goodbye, Hurry," murmured the girl, with a gentle pressure of his hand. "I wish you would try and be more like Deerslayer."

These words were uttered with difficulty; a faint flush succeeded them for a single instant, then the hand was relinquished, and Hetty turned her face aside as if done with the world. The mysterious feeling that bound her to the young man, a sentiment so gentle as to be almost imperceptible to herself, and which could never have existed at all had her reason possessed more command over her senses, was forever lost in thoughts of a more elevated, though scarcely of a purer character.

"Of what are you thinking, my sweet sister?" whispered Judith; "tell me, that I may aid you at this moment."

"Mother—I see Mother, now, and bright beings around her in the lake. Why isn't Father there? It's odd that I can see Mother when I can't see *you!* Farewell, Judith."

The last words were uttered after a pause, and her sister had hung over her some time in anxious watchfulness before she perceived that the gentle spirit had departed. Thus died

Hetty Hutter, one of those mysterious links between the material and immaterial world, which, while they appear to be deprived of so much that is esteemed and necessary for this state of being, drawn so near to, and offer so beautiful an illustration of, the truth, purity, and simplicity of another.

CHAPTER XXXII

A baron's chylde to be begylde! it were a cursed dede:
To be felawe with an outlawe! Almighty God forbede!
Yea, better were, the poor squyère, alone to forest yede,
Than ye sholde say, another day, that by my cursed dede
Ye were betrayed: wherefore, good mayde, the best rede that I can
Is, that I to the grene wode go, alone, a banyshed man.

NOTBROWNE MAYDE

THE DAY THAT followed proved to be melancholy, though one of much activity. The soldiers, who had so lately been employed in interring their victims, were now called on to bury their own dead. The scene of the morning had left a saddened feeling on all the gentlemen of the party, and the rest felt the influence of a similar sensation, in a variety of ways and from many causes. Hour dragged on after hour until evening arrived, and then came the last melancholy offices in honor of poor Hetty Hutter. Her body was laid in the lake by the side of that of the mother she had so loved and reverenced; the surgeon, though actually an unbeliever, so far complied with the received decencies of life as to read the funeral service over her grave, as he had previously done over those of the other *Christian* slain. It mattered not; that all-seeing eye which reads the heart could not fail to discriminate between the living and the dead, and the gentle soul of the unfortunate girl was already far removed beyond the errors or deceptions of any human ritual. These simple rites, however, were not wholly wanting in suitable accompaniments. The tears of Judith and Hist were shed freely, and Deerslayer gazed upon the limpid water that now flowed over one whose spirit was even purer than its own mountain springs with glistening eyes. Even the Delaware turned aside to conceal his weakness, while the common men gazed on the ceremony with wondering eyes and chastened feelings.

The business of the day closed with this pious office. By order of the commanding officer, all retired early to rest, for it was intended to begin the march homeward with the return of light. One party, indeed, bearing the wounded, the prisoners, and the trophies, had left the castle in the middle of the day under the guidance of Hurry, intending to reach the fort by shorter marches. It had been landed on the point so often mentioned, or that described in our opening pages, and when the sun set, was already encamped on the brow of the long, broken, and ridgy hills that fell away toward the valley of the Mohawk. The departure of this detachment had greatly simplified the duty of the succeeding day, disencumbering its march of its baggage and wounded and otherwise leaving him who had issued the order greater liberty of action.

Judith held no communication with any but Hist, after the death of her sister, until she retired for the night. Her sorrow had been respected, and both the females had been left with the body, unintruded on to the last moment. The rattling of the drum broke the silence of that tranquil water, and the echoes of the tattoo were heard among the mountains so soon after the ceremony was over as to preclude the danger of interruption. That star which had been the guide of Hist rose on a scene as silent as if the quiet of nature had never yet been disturbed by the labors or passions of man. One solitary sentinel, with his relief, paced the platform throughout the night; and morning was ushered in, as usual, by the martial beat of the reveille.

Military precision succeeded to the desultory proceedings of bordermen, and when a hasty and frugal breakfast was taken, the party began its movement toward the shore with a regularity and order that prevented noise or confusion. Of all the officers, Warley alone remained. Craig headed the detachment in advance, Thornton was with the wounded, and Graham accompanied his patients, as a matter of course. Even the chest of Hutter with all the more valuable of his effects, was borne away, leaving nothing behind that was worth the labor of a removal. Judith was not sorry to see that the captain respected her feelings and that he occupied himself entirely with the duty of his command, leaving her to her own discretion and feelings. It was understood by all that the place was to be totally abandoned, but beyond this, no explanations were asked or given.

The soldiers embarked in the ark, with the captain at their head. He had inquired of Judith in what way she chose to proceed, and understanding her wish to remain with Hist to the last moment, he neither molested her with requests nor offended her with advice. There was but one safe and familiar trail to the Mohawk, and on that, at the proper hour, he doubted not that they should meet in amity, if not in renewed intercourse.

When all were on board, the sweeps were manned, and the ark moved in its sluggish manner toward the distant point. Deerslayer and Chingachgook now lifted two of the canoes from the water and placed them in the castle. The windows and door were then barred, and the house was left, by means of the trap, in the manner already described. On quitting the palisades, Hist was seen in the remaining canoe, where the Delaware immediately joined her, and paddled away, leaving Judith standing alone on the platform. Owing to this prompt proceeding Deerslayer found himself alone with the beautiful and still weeping mourner. Too simple to suspect anything, the young man swept the light boat around and received its mistress in it, when he followed the course already taken by his friend.

The direction to the point led diagonally past, and at no great distance from, the graves of the dead. As the canoe glided by, Judith, for the first time that morning, spoke to her companion. She said but little, merely uttering a simple request to stop for a minute or two, ere she left the place.

"I may never see this spot again, Deerslayer," she said, "and it contains the bodies of my mother and sister! Is it not possible, think you, that the innocence of one of these beings may answer in the eyes of God for the salvation of both?"

"I don't understand it so, Judith, though I'm no missionary and am but poorly taught. Each spirit answers for its own backslidings, though a hearty repentance will satisfy God's laws."

"Then *must* my poor, poor mother, be in heaven!—bitterly —bitterly—has she repented of her sins. Surely her sufferings in this life ought to count as something against her sufferings in the next!"

"All this goes beyond me, Judith. I strive to do right, here, as the surest means of keeping all right, hereafter. Hetty was oncommon, as all that know'd her must allow, and her soul was as fit to consort with angels the hour it left its body as that of any saint in the Bible!"

"I do believe you only do her justice! Alas! Alas! That there should be so great differences between those who were nursed at the same breast, slept in the same bed, and dwelt under the same roof! But, no matter—move the canoe a little further east, Deerslayer—the sun so dazzles my eyes that I cannot see the graves. This is Hetty's, on the right of Mother's?"

"Sartain—you asked that of us; and all are glad to do as you wish, Judith, when you do that which is right."

The girl gazed at him near a minute in silent attention; then she turned her eyes backward, at the castle.

"This lake will soon be entirely deserted," she said, "and this, too, at a moment when it will be a more secure dwelling place than ever. What has so lately happened will prevent the Iroquois from venturing again to visit it for a long time to come."

"That it will! Yes, that may be set down as settled. I do not mean to pass thisaway ag'in so long as the war lasts, for to my mind, no Huron moccasin will leave its print on the leaves of this forest until their traditions have forgotten to tell their young men of their disgrace and rout."

"And do you so delight in violence and bloodshed? I had thought better of *you*, Deerslayer—believed you one who could find his happiness in a quiet domestic home, with an attached and loving wife ready to study your wishes, and healthy and dutiful children anxious to follow in your footsteps and to become as honest and just as yourself."

"Lord, Judith, what a tongue you're mistress of! Speech and looks go hand in hand, like, and what one can't do, the other is pretty sartain to perform! Such a gal, in a month, might spoil the stoutest warrior in the Colony."

"And am I then so mistaken? Do you really love war, Deerslayer, better than the hearth and the affections?"

"I understand your meaning, gal; yes, I do understand what you mean, I believe, though I don't think you altogether understand *me*. Warrior I may now call myself, I suppose, for I've both fou't and conquered, which is sufficient for the name; neither will I deny that I've feelin's for the callin', which is both manful and honorable, when carried on accordin' to nat'ral gifts—but I've no relish for blood. Youth is youth, howsever, and a Mingo is a Mingo. If the young men of this region stood by and suffered the vagabonds to overrun the land, why, we might as well all turn Frenchers at once and give up country and kin. I'm no fire-eater, Judith, or one that likes fightin' for fightin's sake, but I can see no great difference atween *givin' up territory afore a war, out of a dread of war, and givin' it up a'ter a war because we can't help it—onless it be that the last is the most manful and honorable.*"

"No woman would ever wish to see her husband or brother stand by and submit to insult and wrong, Deerslayer, however she might mourn the necessity of his running into the dangers of battle. But you've done enough already in clearing this region of the Hurons, since to you is principally owing the credit of our late victory. Now, listen to me patiently, and answer me with that native honesty which it is as pleasant to regard in one of your sex as it is unusual to meet with."

Judith paused, for now that she was on the very point of explaining herself, native modesty asserted its power, notwithstanding the encouragement and confidence she derived from the great simplicity of her companion's character. Her cheeks, which had so lately been pale, flushed, and her eyes lighted with some of their former brilliancy. Feeling gave expression to her countenance and softness to her voice, rendering her who was always beautiful trebly seductive and winning.

"Deerslayer," she said after a considerable pause, "this is not a moment for affectation, deception, or a want of frankness of any sort. Here, over my mother's grave, and over the grave of truth-loving, truth-telling Hetty, everything like unfair dealing seems to be out of place. I will therefore speak to you without any reserve and without any dread of being misunderstood. You are not an acquaintance of a week, but it appears to me as if I had known you for years. So much, and so much that is important, has taken place within that short time that the sorrows, and dangers, and escapes of a whole life have been crowded into a few days; they who have suffered and acted together in such scenes ought not to feel like strangers. I know that what I am about to say might be misunderstood by most men, but I hope for a generous construction of my course from you. We are not here dwelling among the arts and deceptions of the settlements, but young people who have no occasion to deceive each other, in any manner or form. I hope I make myself understood?"

"Sartain, Judith; few converse better than yourself, and none more agreeable, like. Your words are as pleasant as your looks."

"It is the manner in which you have so often praised those looks that gives me courage to proceed. Still, Deerslayer, it is not easy for one of my sex and years to forget all her lessons of infancy, all her habits, and her natural diffidence, and say openly what her heart feels!"

"Why not, Judith? Why shouldn't women as well as men deal fairly and honestly by their fellow creatur's? I see no reason why you should not speak as plainly as myself, when there is anything ra'ally important to be said."

This indomitable diffidence, which still prevented the young man from suspecting the truth, would have completely discouraged the girl had not her whole soul, as well as her whole heart, been set upon making a desperate effort to rescue herself from a future that she dreaded with a horror as vivid as the distinctness with which she fancied she foresaw it. This motive, however, raised her above all common considerations, and she persevered even to her own surprise, if not to her great confusion.

"I will—I *must* deal as plainly with you as I would with poor, dear Hetty, were that sweet child living!" she continued, turning pale, instead of blushing, the high resolution by which she was prompted reversing the effect that such a procedure would ordinarily produce on one of her sex; "yes, I will smother all other feelings in the one that is now uppermost! You love the woods and the life that we pass here, in the wilderness, away from the dwellings and towns of the whites."

"As I loved my parents, Judith, when they was living! This very spot would be all creation to me, could this war be fairly over once, and the settlers kept at a distance."

"Why quit it, then? It has no owner—at least none who can claim a better right than mine, and *that* I freely give to you. Were it a kingdom, Deerslayer, I think I should delight to say the same. Let us then return to it, after we have seen the priest at the fort, and never quit it again, until God calls us away to that world where we shall find the spirits of my poor mother and sister."

A long, thoughtful pause succeeded, Judith having covered her face with both her hands after forcing herself to utter so plain a proposal, and Deerslayer musing equally in sorrow and surprise on the meaning of the language he had just heard. At length the hunter broke the silence, speaking in a tone that was softened to gentleness by his desire not to offend.

"You haven't thought well of this, Judith," he said; "no, your feelin's are awakened by all that has lately happened, and believin' yourself to be without kindred in the world, you are in too great haste to find some to fill the places of them that's lost."

"Were I living in a crowd of friends, Deerslayer, I should still think as I now think, say as I now say," returned Judith, speaking with her hands still shading her lovely face.

"Thank you, gal—thank you, from the bottom of my heart. Howsever, I am not one to take advantage of a weak moment, when you're forgetful of your own great advantages, and fancy 'arth and all it holds is in this little canoe. No—no—Judith, 'twould be onginerous in me; what you've offered can never come to pass!"

"It all may be, and that without leaving cause of repentance to any," answered Judith, with an impetuosity of feeling and manner that at once unveiled her eyes. "We can cause the soldiers to leave our goods on the road till we return, when they can easily be brought back to the house; the lake will be no more visited by the enemy, this war at least; all your skins may be readily sold at the garrison; there *you* can buy the few necessaries we shall want, for I wish never to see the spot again; and Deerslayer," added the girl, smiling with a sweetness and nature that the young man found it hard to resist, "as a proof how wholly I am and wish to be yours—how completely I desire to be nothing but your wife—the very first fire that we kindle after our return shall be lighted with the brocade dress and fed by every article I have that you may think unfit for the woman you wish to live with!"

"Ah's me! You're a winning and a lovely creatur', Judith; yes, you *are* all that, and no one can deny it and speak truth. These pictur's are pleasant to the thoughts, but they mightn't prove so happy as you now think 'em. Forget it all, therefore, and let us paddle after the Sarpent and Hist, as if nothing had been said on the subject."

Judith was deeply mortified, and what is more, she was profoundly grieved. Still, there was a steadiness and quiet in the manner of Deerslayer, that completely smothered her hopes, and told her that for once, her exceeding beauty had failed to excite the admiration and homage it was wont to receive. Women are said seldom to forgive those who slight their advances, but this high-spirited and impetuous girl entertained no shadow of resentment, then or ever, against the fair-dealing and ingenuous hunter. At the moment, the prevailing feeling was the wish to be certain that there was no misunderstanding. After another painful pause, therefore, she brought the matter to an issue by a question too direct to admit of equivocation.

"God forbid that we lay up regrets in afterlife through any want of sincerity now," she said. "I hope we understand each other at least. You will not accept me for a wife, Deerslayer?"

" 'Tis better for both that I shouldn't take advantage of your own forgetfulness, Judith. We can never marry."

"You do not love me—cannot find it in your heart, perhaps, to esteem me, Deerslayer!"

"Everything in the way of fri'ndship, Judith—everything, even to sarvices and life itself. Yes, I'd risk as much for you, at this moment, as I would risk in behalf of Hist, and that is sayin' as much as I can say of any darter of woman. I do not think I feel toward either—mind I say *either*, Judith—as if I wished to quit Father and Mother—if Father and Mother was livin'; which, however, neither is—but if both was livin', I do not feel toward any woman as if I wish'd to quit 'em in order to cleave unto *her*."

"This is enough!" answered Judith in a rebuked and smothered voice; "I understand all that you mean. Marry you cannot, without loving, and that love you do not feel for me. Make no answer if I am right, for I shall understand your silence. *That* will be painful enough of itself."

Deerslayer obeyed her, and he made no reply. For more than a minute the girl riveted her bright eyes on him as if to read his soul, while he sat playing with the water, like a corrected schoolboy. Then Judith herself dropped the end of her paddle and urged the canoe away from the spot with a movement as reluctant as the feelings which controlled it. Deerslayer quietly aided the effort, however, and they were soon on the trackless line taken by the Delaware.

In their way to the point, not another syllable was exchanged between Deerslayer and his fair companion. As Judith sat in the bow of the canoe, her back was turned toward him, else it is probable the expression of her countenance might have induced him to venture some soothing terms of friendship and regard. Contrary to what would have been expected, resentment was still absent, though the color frequently changed from the deep flush of mortification to the paleness of disappointment. Sorrow, deep, heartfelt sorrow, however, was the predominant emotion, and this was betrayed in a manner not to be mistaken.

As neither labored hard at the paddle, the ark had already arrived, and the soldiers had disembarked before the canoe of the two loiterers reached the point. Chingachgook had preceded it, and was already some distance in the wood, at a spot where the two trails, that to the garrison and that to the villages of the Delawares, separated. The soldiers, too, had taken up their line of march, first setting the ark adrift again, with a reckless disregard of its fate. All this Judith saw, but she heeded it not. The Glimmerglass had no longer any charms for her, and when she put her foot on the strand, she immediately proceeded on the trail of the soldiers without casting a single glance behind her. Even Hist was passed unnoticed, that modest young creature shrinking from the averted face of Judith, as if guilty herself of some wrongdoing.

"Wait you here, Sarpent," said Deerslayer as he followed in the footsteps of the dejected beauty, while passing his friend. "I will just see Judith among her party and come and j'ine you."

A hundred yards had hid the couple from those in front, as well as those in the rear, when Judith turned and spoke.

"This will do, Deerslayer," she said sadly. "I understand

your kindness, but shall not need it. In a few minutes I shall reach the soldiers. As you cannot go with me on the journey of life, I do not wish you to go further on this. But stop; before we part, I would ask you a single question. And I require of you as you fear God and reverence the truth not to deceive me in your answer. I know you do not love another, and I can see but one reason why you cannot, *will* not love me. Tell me, then, Deerslayer"—the girl paused, the words she was about to utter seeming to choke her; then, rallying all her resolution, with a face that flushed and paled at every breath she drew, she continued—"tell me, then, Deerslayer, if anything light of me that Henry March has said may not have influenced your feelings?"

Truth was the Deerslayer's polar star. He ever kept it in view, and it was nearly impossible for him to avoid uttering it, even when prudence demanded silence. Judith read his answer in his countenance, and with a heart nearly broken by the consciousness of undeserving, she signed to him an adieu and buried herself in the woods. For some time Deerslayer was irresolute as to his course, but in the end he retraced his steps and joined the Delaware. That night the three "camped" on the headwaters of their own river, and the succeeding evening they entered the village of the tribe, Chingachgook and his betrothed in triumph, their companion honored and admired but in a sorrow that it required months of activity to remove.

The war that then had its rise was stirring and bloody. The Delaware chief rose among his people until his name was never mentioned without eulogiums, while another Uncas, the last of his race, was added to the long line of warriors who bore that distinguished appellation. As for the Deerslayer, under the sobriquet of Hawkeye, he made his fame spread far and near, until the crack of his rifle became as terrible to the ears of the Mingos as the thunders of the Manitou. His services were soon required by the officers of the crown, and he especially attached himself in the field to one in particular, with whose afterlife he had a close and important connection.

Fifteen years had passed away, ere it was in the power of the Deerslayer to revisit the Glimmerglass. A peace had intervened, and it was on the eve of another, and still more important war, when he and his constant friend, Chingachgook, were hastening to the forts to join their allies. A stripling accompanied them, for Hist already slumbered beneath the pines of the Delawares, and the three survivors had now become inseparable. They reached the lake just as the sun was setting. Here all was unchanged; the river still rushed through its bower of trees; the little rock was wasting away by the slow action of the waves in the course of centuries; the mountains stood in their native dress, dark, rich, and mysterious; while the sheet glistened in its solitude, a beautiful gem of the forest.

The following morning the youth discovered one of the canoes drifted on the shore in a state of decay. A little labor put it in a state for service, and they all embarked with a desire to examine the place. All the points were passed, and Chingachgook pointed out to his son the spot where the Hurons had first encamped and the point whence he had succeeded in stealing his bride. Here they even landed, but all traces of the former visit had disappeared. Next they proceeded to the scene of the battle, and there they found a few of the signs that linger around such localities. Wild beasts had disinterred many of the bodies, and human bones were bleaching in the rains of summer. Uncas regarded all with reverence and pity, though traditions were already rousing his young mind to the ambition and sternness of a warrior.

From the point, the canoe took its way toward the shoal, where the remains of the castle were still visible, a picturesque ruin. The storms of winter had long since unroofed the house, and decay had eaten into the logs. All the fastenings were untouched, but the seasons rioted in the place, as if in mockery at the attempt to exclude them. The palisades were rotting, as were the piles, and it was evident that a few more recurrences of winter, a few more gales and tempests, would sweep all into the lake and blot the building from the face of that magnificent solitude. The graves could not be found. Either the elements had obliterated their traces, or time had caused those who looked for them to forget their position.

The ark was discovered stranded on the eastern shore, where it had long before been driven, with the prevalent northwest winds. It lay on the sandy extremity of a long, low point that is situated about two miles from the outlet, and which is itself fast disappearing before the action of the elements. The scow was filled with water, the cabin unroofed, and the logs were decaying. Some of its coarser furniture still remained, and the heart of Deerslayer beat quick as he found a ribbon of Judith's fluttering from a log. It recalled all her beauty and, we may add, all her failings. Although the girl had never touched his heart, the Hawkeye, for so we ought now to call him, still retained a kind and sincere interest in her welfare. He tore away the ribbon and knotted it to the stock of Killdeer, which had been the gift of the girl herself.

A few miles farther up the lake another of the canoes was discovered, and on the point where the party finally landed were found those which had been left there upon the shore. That in which the present navigation was made, and the one discovered on the eastern shore, had dropped through the decayed floor of the castle, drifted past the falling palisades, and had been thrown as waifs upon the beach.

From all these signs, it was probable the lake had not been visited since the occurrence of the final scene of our tale. Accident or tradition had rendered it again a spot sacred to nature, the frequent wars and the feeble population of the colonies still confining the settlements within narrow boundaries. Chingachgook and his friend left the spot with melancholy feelings. It had been the region of their first warpath, and it carried back the minds of both to scenes of tenderness as well as to hours of triumph. They held their way toward the Mohawk in silence, however, to rush into new adventures as stirring and as remarkable as those which had attended their opening career on this lovely lake. At a later day they returned to the place, where the Indian found a grave.

Time and circumstances have drawn an impenetrable mystery around all else connected with the Hutters. They lived, erred, died, and are forgotten. None connected had felt sufficent interest in the disgraced and disgracing to withdraw the veil, and a century is about to erase even the recollection of their names. The history of crime is ever revolting, and it is fortunate that few love to dwell on its incidents. The sins of the family have long since been arraigned at the judgment seat of God, or are registered for the terrible settlement of the last great day.

The same fate attended Judith. When Hawkeye reached the garrison on the Mohawk, he inquired anxiously after that lovely but misguided creature. None knew her—even her person was no longer remembered. Other officers had again and again succeeded the Warleys and Craigs and Grahams, though an old sergeant of the garrison, who had lately come from England, was enabled to tell our hero that Sir Robert Warley lived on his paternal estates and that there was a lady of rare beauty in the lodge who had great influence over him, though she did not bear his name. Whether this was Judith, relapsed into her early failing, or some other victim of the soldier's, Hawkeye never knew, nor would it be pleasant or profitable to inquire. We live in a world of transgressions and selfishness, and no pictures that represent us otherwise can be true, though, happily for human nature, gleamings of that pure spirit in whose likeness man has been fashioned are to be seen, relieving its deformities and mitigating if not excusing its crimes.

AFTERWORD

Every eminent novelist has the power of varying his themes and of producing masterworks in a variety of moods. James Fenimore Cooper is no exception. Critics sometimes speak carelessly of his famous quintet of Leatherstocking Tales as if each book were part of a unitary whole. The fact is that although the five novels are bound together by the personality of Leatherstocking (alias Deerslayer, Hawkeye, and Natty Bumppo), and although in four of the five the conflict of red man with white furnishes most of the action, the books differ widely in scene, spirit, and incident.

The Deerslayer is as much the most romantic of Cooper's narratives of the American frontier as *Rob Roy* is the most romantic of Walter Scott's tales of the Scottish border; in Leatherstocking, Chingachgook, the former pirate Tom Hutter, the Indian Rivenoak, and the spirited Judith Hutter, Cooper offers a group of characters as memorable as the captivating girl Di Vernon, the dashing outlaw Rob Roy, and the delightfully canny Baillie Nicol Jarvie in Scott's immortal work. Both books are linked with history: *The Deerslayer* with events in the province of New York 1740-1745, *Rob Roy* more directly with the Jacobite insurrection of 1715 and the ensuing repressions. In both we have sharp contrasts between human groups; Cooper painted the warfare of savages and settlers, Scott the collisions of Highlanders and Lowlanders. In both, nature plays a central role, and Cooper did nearly as well by Lake Otsego and its wild surroundings as Scott did by Loch Lomond and the craggy Highlands.

It is easy to understand why *The Deerslayer* was Cooper's own favorite among the Leatherstocking Tales. It is distinguished not only by its romantic (at times melodramatic) quality and its range of character studies, but by other merits: its success in catching the freshness of youth in Leatherstocking and Chingachgook, here shown at the beginning of their careers; the quaint passages of philosophic musing that Cooper puts into Leatherstocking's mouth; the vivid painting of scenes on and about the lake where he had spent so much of his boyhood; and the masterly handling of suspense, so that interest never flags. The book is not so poetic as *The Prairie,* which deals with Leatherstocking's old age; it offers no such realistic study of life and manners in a frontier setting, as does *The Pioneers;* it is less closely woven into the texture of colonial history than *The Last of the Mohicans;* but it enacts the most rapid drama of all Cooper's tales.

Unquestionably Cooper was still near the height of his powers when he published *The Deerslayer.* As early as 1821, when he wrote *The Spy,* the first American novel with qualities of real greatness, he had proved his ability to create a striking character and to tell a stirring story. In the next half dozen years he had executed his best work in *The Pilot*—the first true sea novel ever written—*The Pioneers, The Last of the Mohicans,* and *The Prairie.* Then, his first three Leatherstocking books done, he turned to other themes than the forest, the Indian, and the ambush. He went abroad; he became interested in social controversy; he involved himself in suits over lands and libels; he even made foolish forays into satire. His best work in this period lay in such naval stories as *The Two Admirals.* Then with renewed inspiration he unexpectedly brought out *The Pathfinder* and *The Deerslayer* in 1840-41.

It was remarkable that after so long an interval Cooper should return with unabated gusto to the fortunes of Leatherstocking and Chingachgook. In so doing he proved that the true home of his romantic instincts was not the ocean and not such semihistorical episodes as those of *Mercedes of Castile,* but the forest. It is a little hard for readers of *The Deerslayer* to follow such critics as Carl Van Doren when they speak of the woods as a romantic sanctuary, a temple breathing holy calm, and a teacher of peace, virtue, and order. In these pages the wilderness seems to us full of treachery, peril, and battle. Its recesses attract outlaws like Tom Hutter and brute adventurers like the scalp-hunter Hurry Harry; its thickets afford lurking places for vindictive, bloody-minded savages. But Cooper loved the beauty and sublimity of the scenes he describes in his opening paragraphs, when a bird's-eye view of the whole region east of the Mississippi presented one vast expanse of greenery, dotted in its "solemn solitude" by glittering lakes and intersected by wandering river lines. He puts his feeling into a speech that Leatherstocking directs at Judith Hutter.

As for farms, they have their uses, and there's them that like to pass their lives on 'em; but what comfort can a man look for in a clearin' that he can't find in double quantities in the forest? If air, and room, and light are a little craved, the windrows and the streams will furnish 'em, or here are the lakes for such as have bigger longings in that way; but where are you to find your shades, and laughing springs, and leaping brooks, and vinerable trees, a thousand years old, in a clearin'? Then as to churches, they are good, I suppose . . . but Judith, the whole arth is a temple of the Lord to such as have the right mind.

It was remarkable also that Cooper, in the enterprise of recreating Leatherstocking in youth after already having depicted him in prime manhood and in old age, should succeed so well in harmonizing the early and the later appearances of his hero. At practically every point the young man is consistent with the central figure of the later tales; as consistent, at least, as any man of twenty-three can be with himself at forty and at seventy. We see here the same true-minded, openhearted, generous personage that we meet later—a good deal more naïve and more candidly talkative, as he ought to be. Though this prologue to the other four books has a freshness and liveliness all its own, it blends harmoniously with them. The youthful Leatherstocking who so hotly denounces the red followers of Rivenoak ("a venomous set of riptyles") for their cunning ferocity is the same man who in *The Last of the Mohicans* fiercely denounces Montcalm for permitting the massacre of helpless British prisoners at Fort William Henry.

At the same time Cooper here enlarges our conception of Leatherstocking. The young man is fresh from the influence of the Moravian missionaries; they have confirmed his natural piety, humanity, and sense of justice; and in his lament over the first foe he has had to kill we feel a genuine grief. It is a true idealist who utters a sad soliloquy as he straightens the limbs of the Indian who had attempted to put a bullet in his back.

"I didn't wish your life, redskin," he said, "but you left me no choice between killing or being killed. Each party acted according to his gifts, I suppose, and blame can light on neither. You were treacherous, according to your natur' in war, and I was a little oversightful, as I'm apt to be in trusting others. Well, this is my first battle with a human mortal . . . . I have fou't most of the creatur's of the forest, such as bears, wolves, painters, and catamounts, but this is the beginning with the redskins . . . . And why should I wish to boast of it a'ter all? It's slaying a human, although he was a savage; and how do I know that he was a just Injin, and that he has not been taken away suddenly to anything but happy hunting grounds?"

An equal impression of idealism and moral depth springs from Leatherstocking's short disquisitions on a future life, in which he devoutly believes; on the relativity of ethics—"A white man's gifts are Christianized, while a redskin's are more for the wilderness"; and on the superiority of God's law to that of King and Parliament: whenever they come into conflict, then man-made laws "get to be onlawful, and ought not to be obeyed." Leatherstocking has worked out his own philosophy, too, on the relations of man and woman, as he shows in his heart-to-heart talk with Judith when he rejects her virtual proposal of marriage; they are unsuited to each other, he declares, and that ends the matter. He is a little in love with Wah-ta!-Wah, the lovely girl pledged to Chingachgook, but he puts all thought of her aside in justice to his friend and to his ideas of racial purity.

One pre-eminent merit of *The Deerslayer* lies in the originality and skill of Cooper's plot. It is essentially simple, never confusing the reader, but it suffices to furnish a tightly woven narrative full of variety, color, and unexpected turns. Never do we meet a violation of probability like several that mar *The Last of the Mohicans*. It is true that Mark Twain carped at one initial scene in *The Deerslayer*, the escape of Hutter's ark from the Indian-beset tributary of Lake Otsego in which it had been moored. But Clemens forgot that Cooper described the stream as one with a swift current, and the Indians had but an uncertain means of dropping aboard. Taken in all its major parts, the story claims our faith.

And what a story it is! Certainly Cooper had one of his best inspirations when he invented in Hutter a refugee from law and order, a miscreant with a terrible past to conceal, who has immured himself and his two motherless daughters in a castle built on a shoal in the deep waters of Lake Otsego, with an attendant ark to communicate at need with the almost trackless shores. It was a logical second step to bring Leatherstocking upon the scene just as hostile Indians, the Mingoes, made an encampment upon the lake's shore. And it was a triumph of romantic imagination to make the purpose of Leatherstocking's visit a rendezvous with Chingachgook, a Delaware chieftain and his closest friend, who was in hot pursuit of the Mingoes who had kidnapped his sweetheart.

The plot provides a well-varied conflict of whites and Indians in a natural setting of exceptional picturesqueness. It provides also, in its dramatis personae, a wealth of contrasts. They include the contrast between Hutter's beautiful and strong-minded but reputedly wanton daughter, Judith, and her pure but half-witted sister, Hetty; the contrast between the Christian rectitude and pacifism of Leatherstocking and the pagan ruthlessness of Hurry, anxious only to take Mingo scalps while keeping his own; the contrast between the two Indians who throw their strong energies into the action—Chingachgook, fearless, determined, and sleeplessly alert, but reluctant to kill, and Rivenoak, an embodiment of Indian fiendishness at its worst. In the background we dimly discern two still larger contrasts: that between the untouched wilderness and the onset of civilization represented by settlers, hunters, and a garrison of troops, and the contrast between British and French civilizations as the rival powers struggle for mastery of the continent.

In no other book does Cooper so dexterously maintain suspense as in *The Deerslayer*, nor is all the suspense warlike. Interest is never keener than when Judith, Leatherstocking, and Chingachgook open Thomas Hutter's mysterious chest and find not only his treasures but further proofs of his former life on the far side of the law. The two love stories, Judith's ill-omened attachment for Leatherstocking and Chingachgook's ultimately successful passion for Wah-ta!-Wah, add a somewhat tame suspense of a special sort; love was never Cooper's forte. But the final events carry interest to a breathless point. Our only regret is that it should be broken, and the tale ended, by a rather disappointing *deus ex machina*, the arrival of a powerful body of redcoats just as knives have been sharpened and wood lighted for the final phase of Leatherstocking's torture.

The Deerslayer throws special light on two charges often brought against Cooper's handling of his materials and does much to strengthen his position against them. Both require notice, but both may be summarily dismissed.

One charge is that Cooper's presentation of the Indians and Indian life is at once superficial and excessively favorable; that he popularized that romantic view of the noble red man violently denounced by Theodore Roosevelt in *The Winning of the West*. The fact is that Cooper never pretended to give a realistic, and still less a scientific, depiction of the aborigines. He knew that some of them *were* men of noble character—as noble as Massasoit or Logan or Chief Joseph; he knew that others, and especially those corrupted or embittered by white men, had the devilish traits depicted in some of the Mingoes. Cooper had never lived with the Indians, nor studied the lore accumulated by men who knew them well, nor explored the rudiments of the science of ethnology. As a writer of romance, he naturally made his good Indians all too good and his bad Indians all too bad. His real weakness was that he rendered them figures of melodrama, not of the real world. He never even studied the subject historically, so that he gives a highly distorted view of the respective roles played by the Algonquin (Delaware) and the Iroquois (Mingo) tribes in our colonial history.

His view was that which he put into the words of Wah-ta!-Wah: "Mingo is cruel and loves scalp for blood—Delaware love him for honor." On one side he presents the honest, chivalrous, humane Chingachgook and Uncas, and on the other Satanic types whose sadistic cruelties freeze the blood. Their clash sometimes give birth to melodrama that almost equals the wild stories by Charles Brockden Brown, and surpasses the extravagance of Richard Montgomery Bird's *Nick o' the Woods*—to cite only our early novels.

The Indian has been so generally maligned that Cooper performed a real service in his presentation of Chingachgook and Uncas, who had their counterparts in many tribes. He must also be credited with a just appreciation of two great Indian superiorities, to which he was the first widely-read author to do justice. He comprehended the remarkable gift of eloquence possessed by some red leaders, and in *The Deerslayer* and several other novels he gives us memorable examples. He understood also that while the Indian was inferior to the white frontiersman in markmanship and in the use of most of the white man's other tools, he was far superior in woodcraft. He could read the clouds, he could spell the meaning of a bent twig, he could understand the nature of wild bird and beast, with a precision impossible to any civilized rival.

The other charge most frequently brought against Cooper, that he was unable to depict a true woman and gave his readers colorless, namby-pamby heroines instead of the resourceful, intrepid women and daughters of our real frontier, gains credence from his weaker novels. It is forcefully refuted by *The Deerslayer,* however, and a single reading of that book throws it out of court. Cooper's gentlefolk were likely to be insipid. Judith Hutter, however, no more belonged to the gentlefolk than Leatherstocking himself, and in every critical situation she shows force of character and decision. She is mistress of the castle and the ark; she hesitates not a second when an Indian raider has to be pushed off the boat to drown; she loses neither nerve nor hope when pursued across Lake Otsego by another canoe sped by lusty savages. We may well believe that the hints of loose conduct given currency by Hurry were slanders born of his chagrin when she refuses him. Her protection of her weak-minded sister, her influence over her father, her true womanliness in her conversations with Leatherstocking—all these instances and more do her credit. She has her faults, but lack of strength, enterprise, and vigor were not among them.

Yet even Judith is surpassed, in courage, steadfastness, and above all in energy of speech, by the true heroine of the novel, Wah-ta!-Wah, or Hist. The two most impassioned pieces of eloquence in the volume are Hist's excoriation of Hurry Harry for his needless slaying of a Huron girl and her spirited repudiation of any idea that she might leave her own people for a union with a Mingo brave. Of this latter speech Leatherstocking justly observed: "That's worth all the wampum in the woods."

It is a rich, an intensely exciting, and, despite its patches of theatricality, an elevating romance that Cooper has given us in *The Deerslayer;* the story of an America now so far lost in time and change that it is hard to believe it ever existed. But it did exist, and some memory of it, in our all too artificial day, ought to be cherished by the nation.

Allan Nevins

The Huntington Library

SELECTED BIBLIOGRAPHY

OTHER WORKS BY JAMES FENIMORE COOPER

The Spy, 1821   Novel
The Pioneers, 1823   Novel (Signet Classic CT480)
The Pilot, 1824   Novel
The Last of the Mohicans, 1826   Novel (Signet Classic CT521)
The Prairie, 1827   Novel (Signet Classic CT519)
The Red Rover, 1827   Novel
Notions of the Americans, 1828   Social Criticism
The Bravo, 1831   Novel
The Monikins, 1835   Satire
Sketches of Switzerland, Parts I and II, 1836   Travel
Gleanings in Europe (England, France, Italy), 1837-38   Travel
The American Democrat, 1838   Social Criticism
Homeward Bound, 1838   Novel
Home as Found, 1838   Novel
The History of the Navy of the United States of America, 1839
The Pathfinder, 1840   Novel (Signet Classic CT357)
The Wing-and-Wing, 1842   Novel
Wyandotte, 1843   Novel
Afloat and Ashore, 1844   Novel
Satanstoe, 1845   Novel
The Chainbearer, 1845   Novel
The Redskins, 1846   Novel
The Crater, 1847   Novel
The Oak Openings, 1848   Novel
The Sea Lions, 1849   Novel
The Ways of the Hour, 1850   Novel

SELECTED BIOGRAPHY AND CRITICISM

Beard, James Franklin (ed.). *The Letters and Journals of James Fenimore Cooper*. 2 vols. Cambridge, Mass.: Harvard University Press; London: Oxford University Press, 1960.

Boynton, Henry W. *James Fenimore Cooper*. New York and London: D. Appleton-Century Co., 1931.

Cooper, James Fenimore (grandson of the novelist) (ed.). *Correspondence of James Fenimore Cooper*. New Haven, Conn.: Yale University Press, 1922.

Cunningham, Mary E. (ed.). *James Fenimore Cooper: A Reappraisal*. Cooperstown, N. Y.: New York State Historical Association, 1954.

Dondore, Dorothy Anne. *The Prairie and the Making of Middle America: Four Centuries of Description*. Cedar Rapids, Iowa: The Torch Press, 1926.

Grossman, James. *James Fenimore Cooper*. New York: William Sloane Associates, Inc.; London: Methuen & Co., Ltd., 1949.

Hazard, Lucy Lockwood. *The Frontier in American Literature*. New York: Thomas Y. Crowell Co., 1927; New York: Barnes & Noble, Inc., 1941.

Leisy, Ernest E. *The American Historical Novel*. Norman, Okla.: University of Oklahoma Press, 1950.

Lounsbury, Thomas R. *James Fenimore Cooper* (American Men of Letters Series). Boston: Houghton Mifflin & Co., 1882.

Outland, Ethel R. *The Effingham Libels on Cooper*. Madison, Wisc.: University of Wisconsin Press, 1929.

Parrington, Vernon L. *Main Currents in American Thought*. 3 vols. New York: Harcourt, Brace & Co., 1927.

Ross, John F. *The Social Criticism of Fenimore Cooper*. Berkeley, Calif.: University of California Press, 1933.

Rourke, Constance. *American Humor*. New York: Harcourt, Brace & Co., 1931.

Spiller, Robert E., and others. *Literary History of the United States*. 3 vols. New York and London: The Macmillan Company, 1948.

————, *Fenimore Cooper: Critic of His Time*. New York: Minton, Balch & Co.; London: G. P. Putnam's Sons, 1931.

Van Doren, Carl. *The American Novel*. New York: The Macmillan Company, 1921.

Waples, Dorothy. *The Whig Myth of James Fenimore Cooper*. New Haven: Yale University Press; London: Oxford University Press, 1938.

Winters, Yvor. *Maule's Curse: Seven Studies in the History of American Obscurantism*. New York: New Directions, 1938.

A NOTE ON THE TEXT

The text of this edition is based on the W. A. Townsend and Company edition published in 1859 and reprinted by the Riverside Press in their collected edition of Cooper's works in 1872. The spelling and punctuation have been brought into conformity with modern American usage.